You Are My Love

You Are My Love

By
Dann Butler

© 2021 by Dann Butler

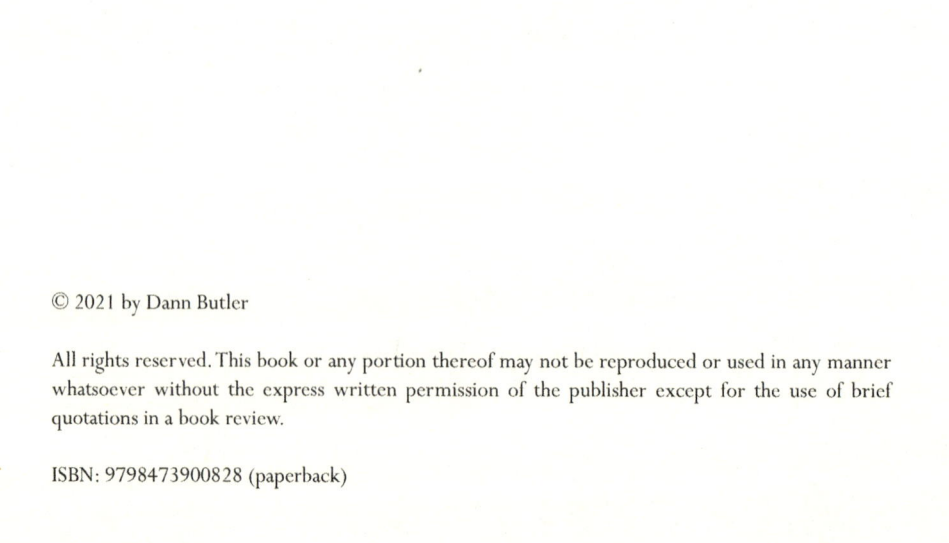

All rights reserved. This book or any portion thereof may not be reproduced or used in any manner whatsoever without the express written permission of the publisher except for the use of brief quotations in a book review.

ISBN: 9798473900828 (paperback)

For Gretchen

Since day one I've wanted you to understand my love for you, but have always struggled to find the words. Hopefully the characters in this story display a small glimpse into those emotions…

Always and forever, you are my love.

D.

Author's Note

Has someone said they love you today? You understood the words, but did you understand all the emotions behind them? I tried for thirty something years to find a way to share those emotions with my wife. As music is one of my great passions, I've written her numerous songs even a musical or two and still somehow I was never able to convey the feelings and emotions this woman brings to me day after day. After a neck and shoulder injury left me with time to contemplate life, I began writing a story in hopes each character would mirror the feelings, emotions and possibly paint a more distinct picture of my love for her. It wasn't until I was diagnosed with a terminal disease I finished her story ... but even now I can't say it's finished, because each day she fills my heart with a new way to love her.

CHAPTER ONE

For Jim Brooks, three things were guaranteed on Christmas Eve: the weather would be cold and wet, he would have enough wrapping paper and/or tape to wrap all but one gift, and there would be a trip to the mall with his wife, Ann, to exchange her birthday present. That's right, birthday present. She was a Christmas baby, and though she made a wonderful present for her parents, it meant forever sharing her special day with the hustle and bustle of the season. School and church pageants, parades, decorating, shopping, dinner parties, a drive through Christmas Tree Lane, visiting Santa—all delightful experiences that weave a patchwork of treasured childhood memories, but they made it difficult at best to create or enjoy birthday memories. So Jim made sure through the years to separate Christmas from her birthday as best anyone could when surrounded by tangled balls of colored lights intertwined with old strands of garland and tinsel, while listening to the musical contributions from the animal kingdom such as chipmunks, dogs, cats, pigs, roosters, and any other animals with vocal capabilities lending their talents to versions of "Jingle Bells," "Silent Night," and most other popular refrains in a twenty-four-hours-a-day, nonstop, commercial-free, special edition of your favorite Christmas carols. Not to mention all the trappings of the holiday retail media blitz: Ho, ho, ho! Buy! Buy! Buy, Spend! Spend! Spend!

In so doing, it was essential he focus his attention on the smallest of details, such as birthday presents could never be placed under the tree and never under any circumstance be wrapped in paper depicting Santa, snowflakes, the nativity, or cozy paintings by Thomas Kinkaid, Norman Rockwell, or even Charles Shultz. No! He must try his very best to make her birthday completely separate, something special. And yes—this meant he needed helpers. His number-one go-to choice had been and would forever be his daughter Amy. Like private detectives with note pads in hand, they shadowed Ann's every move through malls, street fairs, and vacation spots, even using nameless informants at crystal, candle, and Pampered Chef parties in their attempt to acquire that one gift she truly wanted but would never buy for herself. Yet even with all this help, Jim managed to surprise her with the wrong size, shape or color gift every year. And this year was no different.

Oh, how simple it should have been. Amy suggested it with absolute confidence, claiming, "Mom loves 'em. She even bought one for Grandma and Aunt Tru. Besides, if she had one of her own, maybe she'd stay off yours."

The thought of regaining complete ownership of anything made his pulse rate jump. "Let's do it!" he whispered almost sinisterly. And then it even became simpler—his wonderful daughter volunteered to pick it up and have it wrapped and ready in plenty of time for the big day. Overjoyed, he felt his happy dance coming on.

So off to Barnes & Noble Amy went to buy a Nook. One size, one shape, one color—it was as simple as that. And if for some reason his wife didn't like it, he could always point the blame in Amy's direction. Oh yes, this would be the wife's best birthday he'd ever had.

The hour had come for her to open her present, but on the table sat not one but two identically wrapped boxes; the paper showed an array of fireworks shooting out bright-yellow letters that proclaimed "Happy Birthday," and each had been adorned with multicolored ribbons and a small silk flower, with a card meticulously placed against each box.

Quickly he looked at Amy. Had something changed? Had Barnes & Noble sold out of Nook tablets?

Immediately he used their secret father-daughter facial code system for "What's going on here?"

Just as quickly, Amy smiled, wrinkled her nose, and winked, assuring him all was well. His eyes flashed with concern, moving from Amy to the presents and then back again. This time she smiled, tilting her head slightly to the left and indiscernibly nodding three times. He now understood completely. Codename "Don't worry, Dad; it'll be just fine" was complete. Jim felt the muscles in his shoulders begin to relax.

At first Ann looked puzzled, just as she did every year, as though she expected no one to remember her birthday, much less present her with presents. Then, looking at them both, she pursed her lips, rolled her eyes, and said, "I can't believe you guys did this. Today's just another day; I don't have birthdays anymore."

Her heels clicked across the hardwood floor as she moved in to examine her presents.

"Oh, you're going to like this one, Mom. But first…"

Now Jim remembered his wife sending away for the Capt. Zoom's personalized birthday CD, way back when Amy was just a little girl, and over the past thirty-some years, this annoying little ditty had worked its way into becoming (albeit one he would love to forget) a family birthday tradition. Only the names had changed.

Amy hit a small remote, and the room filled with the low rumble of a rocket ship taking off followed by the familiar musical fanfare, and Amy began to sing along with Capt. Zoom. "Hey, Mommy…It's your birthday…" As the song progressed, Jim could tell Amy had put in long seconds of practice, and it was truly paying off. There were smiles on the faces of her and her mom as together they danced around the room laughing and twirling, singing and giggling until their eyes began to leak, ending in hugs of pure joy and love. Wiping the tears away and slightly out of breath, Amy handed her mom one of the colorful boxes.

"We thought this was the perfect gift for you, so we went in together on it," she said, smiling at her dad. Jim knew this was her way of telling him, we're in this together if mom doesn't like it. He smiled, tilting his head slightly to the left, and nodded three times indiscernibly.

The card matched the wrapping paper and was given a respectful affirmation of surprise and approval. Then the silk flower was set on the table and the ribbon gently slid around the corners and off the end of the box. In what appeared to be one continuous movement, the paper was torn down the middle, removed, crumpled, and set aside for the recycling bin. There was an ever-so-slight tremble in Ann's hands as she recognized the Nook emblem embossed on the top of the box.

"How did you two know I wanted one of these?"

"Oh, Just a wild guess!" Jim shrugged. "Let me see it. I'll get it charged up for you."

Amy handed her the other box, and the gift opening ritual began once again. "I don't know if you'll like this or not, Mom. I just kind of grabbed it. I couldn't believe how many they had. There were so many to choose from. But I have the receipt, so if you don't like it, you can always return it."

What! Jim thought. *What did she say? Re…return it! But, but what happened to one size, one shape, one color!* He could hear them talking, laughing, but it all sounded distorted, muffled, as if his ears were now refusing to hear anything at all. Small beads of sweat were building on his forehead. Was it becoming harder to breathe? Was he having a heart attack? *No! No*, he thought. *My breathing is just fine; no pain in my chest…water—that's what I need. Just a nice, cool glass of water.*

The ritual had now progressed to the opening of the lid, where glaring up from the box for all to admire was a bright plastic Nook cover that looked as if it had spent the last three months sliding around in the back of a painter's truck. Ann recoiled, startled by the appearance. Even Amy seemed surprised, but shrugging, she tittered, "I must've grabbed the wrong box. That's not the one I picked out; that thing's hideous. Like I said, I have the receipt. You'll be able to return it with no problem."

"No, no, no, no, no!" Jim jumped in quickly, a small trickle of sweat rolling down his jawline. His heart instantly began racing, but he knew he had to play this cool. Inhaling deeply, and much like a seasoned ballroom dancer, he effortlessly glided across the floor.

"That's one of those new avant-garde designs everybody's talking about," he blurted. "Yeah, by that famous artist…umm, what's his name?"

Snatching the cover from Ann and holding it in both hands so as to hide its true ugliness, he continued. "Oh, you know who I'm talking about—that guy…he's a big to-do New York artist. His work sells for millions; everybody wants his stuff. You don't want to return this! I bet it'll be a collectable someday. Who knows how much it could end up being worth!"

Ann stared at him in utter disbelief. Then, looking at Amy, she gave one of her patented sighs and shook her head. "Don't worry, honey. Your dad and I can run it back to the store; it'll give me a chance to pick out one that, if nothing else, will keep your dad from ever looking like a fool on *The Antiques Road Show*."

Their laughter echoed through the room, so in submission Jim put his hands up and said, "The guy's famous; you just never know about this kind of stuff."

Ann only glanced at him to watch his words fall deafly to the floor. Then, without missing a beat, she gave him a hug and continued talking to Amy.

"Besides, there's a book I want to pick up for one of the girls at work. Oh, and they always have such cute calendars; maybe I can find something for Mrs. Marley while I'm there. She loves those books by…"

For a short time, Jim listened, hoping one of them would magically fall in love with the ugly case. But after only a few minutes, his ears went silent in protest, and he could feel the muscles tightening in his shoulders.

❁

Typically Jim loved going to Barnes & Noble; for him it was always a wonderful place, almost a serene experience. The selection of material, the many places to sit and read, the no-pressure-to-buy atmosphere, an informed staff, the cozy little coffee area, and of course that wonderful smell of a real bookstore. It was true—he loved his Nook, but for him there was something magical about the smell of paper and leather, hardcover and soft, rows and rows and walls and walls of wooden bookshelves, filled with stories that captured the imagination while lulling him into that unique realm of emotional conveyance. Yes, typically, he loved going to Barnes & Noble, but Christmas Eve was not typical. The serenity was replaced by hordes of grumpy shoppers moving quickly up and down aisles, hovering over tables of discounted merchandise, confusing Tolstoy with *Toy Story*, and asking the staff questions like "I think my great-grandma Maggie likes to read, so what should I buy her?" Hmm, *A book maybe?*

And that magical smell now temporarily replaced by…well, hordes of grumpy shoppers. Yes, Christmas Eve was not typical. *But wait*, he told himself. *Maybe I shouldn't say that. After all, typically it is the day we exchange my wife's birthday present, and this year by no real fault of my own, I find myself flung once again into a maelstrom of last-minute Christmas chaos. Feels pretty typical to me.* He grinned.

Oh yes. He smiled, almost forgetting. *How's the weather, Jimbo?* WET? Of course it was. It was always wet in Seattle! The rain began just before September, turning to light snow flurries a few days after Halloween, increasing to heavier snow flurries from November through winter, with light to moderate rain showers from midwinter through mid-August. Add a few scattered sun breaks each month to give everyone a small window of opportunity in which to mow their yard without the need of an umbrella, and there you had it. And today's forecast? Thirty-something, windy, and wet! See...cold and wet, as predicted.

❈

The warmth of the heater felt almost too good to leave, but with unexpected vigor Ann dashed from the car before he could remove the keys from the ignition. Stepping out, Jim was thankful the wind had died down since they'd left the house; however, the rain continued to come down in icy-cold sheets. Glancing ahead, he could see it would be a hundred-yard dash to the storefront, dodging the many water-filled potholes disguised as little shallow puddles and sidestepping two young couples with strollers running wildly to keep junior and princess from melting in the rain.

Jim, for the most part, was a gentleman and was prepared to drop Ann at the store entrance and then drive around until a stall became available. But as traffic caused them to crawl through the parking lot, she suddenly shouted, "Hurry—turn here; that guy's pulling out."

As he made the sharp turn onto a long, narrow lane, she again yelled, "Hurry up; go, go, go. Don't let that little Volkswagen take our spot; hurry!"

The Volkswagen in question was much closer to the now-vacant spot but was momentarily detained by a pedestrian at the other end of the drive, giving Jim an easy, if not a somewhat unethical, victory.

As he made a dash for the front door, it was impossible for him to make out what the driver of the Volkswagen was yelling, what with the sound of the rain and her incessant honking. He could barely hear himself reply, "Yeah, yeah, and a Merry Christmas to you too."

Ducking into the building, just as the heavy glass door was abruptly covered by a drenching cascade of water and slush, he could hear even more honking and shouting. Standing in front of him was a young, wide-eyed couple preparing to venture outside. Shaking his head with all the disgust he could muster, he said, "Can you believe that woman? She almost soaked us all. It's the naughty list for her." Laughing, he then quickly blended into the crowd, nonchalantly making his way to Ann's side.

"Amy wasn't kidding. There has to be over a hundred covers to choose from." she said, staring at a large kiosk filled with shelf after shelf of Nook accessories. "Looks like I'm going to be here awhile. You might want to look around or find something to read. Maybe have a cup of coffee. Just make sure it's decaf, and watch the whipped cream. We have Hawaii coming up soon." She nodded, lifting her eyebrows and directing her gaze to his waist.

"Yes, dear," he mocked under his breath.

"Did you bring your phone?"

The look on his face said it all. He knew, and was sure she knew, his phone was lying on the kitchen counter, or the desk in his office, or next to his favorite chair, or maybe in his jacket pocket. Quickly he stuffed his hands into his pockets and just as quickly shrugged. "Nope; not there."

He knew it was lying somewhere, eagerly awaiting his return when it could alert him with its annoying beeps and buzzes that he had missed calls. This, of course, providing it survived on what trickle of charge would be left, as he consistently forgot to plug the thing in.

Now the look on Ann's face truly said it all, although she would insist he pay attention and heed what she was telling him, and it was something he thought about many times over the next half hour or so: "Don't be roaming all over the place. I'll come find you when I'm done." And with that she began searching for her new cover.

Free time is a precious commodity, even if it's spent wandering through section after section of a bookstore, and for Jim, it was always difficult to find a good starting point—Westerns, mysteries, biography, history, perhaps fiction, or maybe just a periodical to sit and enjoy with that cup of coffee his wife suggested. Yes, a good magazine is always a safe bet to help kill some time. Now, where would they be…

Soon he was standing in front of a magazine rack that ran the entire length of the store's back wall and held hundreds of titles, most of which he had never heard of, many with topics he would never have guessed could necessitate any measurable profit from what he could only assume would have a modest readership; titles such as *The Designer Guide to Antique Spinning Tops*; *Yo-Yos and Wooden Blocks*; *Ball Bearing Monthly*, and *Flannel Shirts of the Northwest*.

He scratched his head in amazement as he moved along in search of something relatable but couldn't recall a single subject that truly interest him, and only one or two titles caught his eye at all. But then, like a long-lost friend, it came into view. "Here we go," he said aloud.

He knew Ann would not be pleased to find her husband sitting in the coffee area, sipping on a double-chocolate candy-cane, grande with extra whip, grinning ear to ear, thumbing through the latest edition of *Mad* magazine. So, without hesitation, he decided the coffee would have to wait while he rapidly flipped through the pages until he found the latest installment of *Spy vs. Spy*. Just then from behind, he heard the voice of a small child excitedly asking a teenage girl how much was the large book he held in his hands.

"Do I look like I work here, kid?" she snapped, pushing the boy out of her way.

His features softened, his smile faded, his shoulders sagged as he watched her storm off down a long aisle disappearing into the crowd. He stood motionless for a moment looking at the book in his hand, and then he looked up toward the slender man. Their eyes met only briefly before Jim averted his attention back to his magazine. Moving farther away, the boy began looking from one side to another in hopes of finding a kind-looking person he would feel safe approaching for assistance, so it surprised Jim when the boy turned around, walked back, and looked up at him once more. Drops of water clung to his pullover. His hair was damp and mussed, curled in short strawberry-blond wisps over his ears and across his forehead. Bright-green eyes looked to the man in search of compassion. Slowly raising the book with both hands, he asked, "Mister, I know you don't work here, but could you help me, please. I need to know if this book is more than fifty cents."

You Are My Love

People, especially children, seldom asked Jim for assistance, although he wasn't big or rough or scary looking, but apparently he did come across as unapproachable when out in public. And now, as this boy inched a little closer and held the book a little higher, Jim felt an awkward moment of panic. The child had caught him off guard. Quickly Jim looked around, verifying it was him the boy was asking for help. Or perhaps he was searching for his own rescue party.

"Yes! Yes it's more than fifty cents," he replied, hardly acknowledging his presences.

The child lowered the book but not his gaze. "How do you know? You didn't even look at the price tag." His voice was soft, gentle, and quiet. The melodic notes of excitement gone, he turned to leave moving only a few yards.

"Wait!" Jim called, rushing toward him. "You're right. I'm sorry; here, let me take a look."

The glint in the boy's eyes rapidly spread to his cheeks, pulling forward a smile that would wiggle its way down to his toes. His excitement and joy were contagious; Jim too smiled and felt an involuntary wiggle in his shoes. There was a sudden wonder the man had not experienced since his own child was that age. An invisible bond of trust and innocence only a small child can give, a twinkle of time as fragile as crystal and soft as rain.

Examining the book, he found no price. It was then that Jim noticed the beautifully illustrated cover depicting a great wooden ship caught in the boiling rush of crashing waves, its bow moments away from being destroyed on large jagged rocks stretching out like bony fingers from a dark island. The title was scrawled across the bottom in a style of calligraphy he couldn't quite make out. It took him a moment of careful study before realizing it was written in Spanish, a language he had failed to learn in middle school and repeated in high school to no avail. Though not 100 percent sure, he didn't believe the boy could speak Spanish any better than he could, leaving him in a true dilemma. It was obvious the book cost more than fifty cents; it was also obvious this small boy of four or five couldn't read very well if at all—Spanish or English, it wouldn't have mattered. So Jim thought he would just make up a price, hand him back his book, and he'd be on his way.

But he made the mistake of looking into the child's face before telling him his lie, and he felt the muscles in his shoulders begin to tighten.

Jim didn't want to be the one to rob the boy of his excitement, so with a half-hearted laugh followed by a big smile and a happy-go-lucky tone to his voice, he said, "Well, this one doesn't seem to have a price. Let's go find a clerk; they'll be able to help you out."

Jim heard his inner voice yelling loudly, "You coward; you big old coward; be honest with the boy and tell him it's written in Spanish; reach out and help this kid."

"I am," he silently replied in his thinking voice. "Just shut up and watch."

Walking toward the information desk, his inner voice interrupted once again, this time whispering, "Where's the kid's mother?"

Hmm…he thought with a wide grin. There's my way out; my open door, my ticket back to free-time bliss. Stopping suddenly, causing the boy to nearly run into him, he bent down to the child's level. "Where's your mom?" he asked, almost a little too gleefully. "I'll bet she could help you find a good book."

"Oh, the book isn't for me. It's for my mom," he said, looking surprised. "My Aunt Peg's keeping her busy so I can look around for a book to give her for Christmas. She loves to read, and she loves to read stories to me."

Again the boy's excitement touched Jim, and for a flash he longed to join in the quest for the book his mother would unwrap on Christmas morning, tucking the memory in the archives of her heart to be called up in those melancholy moments every parent experiences once their child is grown. And then, suddenly, the boy's expression changed. Eyes wide, he jumped around the end of the bookshelf and pressed his back flat against the wooden surface.

Jim poked his head around. "What's wrong? Are you okay?"

"That's my mom and Aunt Peg!" he said, pointing his index finger from his waist as not to attract attention before scooting around the corner to disappear down the next aisle.

The two ladies, both in their late twenties, were obscured by a large display, their laughter subdued as one read aloud while the other listened over her shoulder. Though they were a considerable distance away and immersed completely in their literary experience, Jim knew the boy had never been off their radar. He considered approaching them, but if this was Aunt Peg's way of distracting Mom, he didn't want to blow the kid's cover. Besides, he wasn't clear which one was Mom and which was Aunt Peg.

Stepping around the corner, he saw the boy scurry farther down the aisle, vanishing behind the backside of a rather large woman he now used as a shield while waving for him to join him. Jim didn't hesitate, and soon both were moving through the store at a pace that can only be described as two boys on a mission. Jim would later remember saying excuse me and other apologies at least half a dozen times as they maneuvered through the hordes of people up and down the aisles, around tables, and over a long cushioned bench; however, in his haste, he would be unable to describe or identify any of those people he had so inconsiderately bumped into. Truth be known, he was enjoying the adventure and only felt a slight twinge of remorse for his childish behavior.

Surprisingly, the information counter was the only spot in the store that wasn't crowded. This, Jim supposed, was because everyone was standing in the aisles. So he and the boy walked boldly to the front of the counter, where they took just a second to catch their breath. He glanced at the sales girl's name tag as she finished typing at the computer. "Be right with you," she said without looking up.

"Not a problem. Take your time…Debbie," he replied cheerily.

Her fingers paused; her lips parted slightly as she looked up briefly. The tapping of nails on a keyboard resumed for a few more seconds, and then she asked, "How can I help you?"

Jim suddenly realized his next sentence would end his leg of this wonderful quest, and the young boy, who had so bravely summoned his assistance, would disappear down the aisles to, in all likelihood, never cross his path again. He also became aware his smile was beginning to diminish, and he couldn't seem to bring it back. Even as he looked down at the boy's face, glowing with delight, he felt pangs of sadness move over him. Five minutes ago he didn't even know the kid's name, didn't even know he existed, and now he was feeling as though he was about to say farewell to an old friend. *But wait*, he thought. *I still don't know his name.* Without hesitation he asked, "What's your name, kid?"

"I'm Michael, sir."

Jim's smile made its way back across his face into his cheeks, brightening his eyes, and once again there was a wiggle in his shoes. Taking the boy's hand, he introduced himself and then added, "Michael, this is Debbie. She'll be able to help you." He turned to the young lady. "We were unable to find a price on this book," Jim said loud enough to ensure Michael would hear.

"I can check that for you." She smiled, taking the book. Her slender fingers moved over the keys. "What! Aah, biscuits; my terminal went down again."

Her voice salted with irritation, she pressed the intercom. "Manager assistance at the information desk." She rocked back on her heels, flipped her hands upward in the universal sign for "I don't know what to tell you," frowned, looked straight at Jim, and sighed heavily. "I don't know what to tell you."

Minutes passed. Their eyes scanned the aisles for approaching assistance, and then Jim noticed Michael had drifted to a small display of Christmas books, the old-fashioned covers capturing his attention. He walked over to join Michael, who was closely examining a large sticker on the back of one of the books.

"I can't read it! I think the price is smudged or something," he said, looking up at Jim. "Here, see if you can read it, and I'll look for another one."

He was right. The ink on the sticker was smudged, and the price unreadable. Not that it would matter, as Jim believed young Michael would not be able to read the price anyway, and he was sure it was still more than fifty cents.

"I think I found one," he called out. "No, this one's different. But maybe it's okay; my mom loves books about Christmas and the Baby Jesus. This one has a picture of a…what's it called…manger? That's where the Baby Jesus was born. But you knew that, huh?"

What a wonderful kid, Jim thought. *I hope his mother knows just how much he loves her.* He then looked in the direction they had seen the boy's mom and Aunt Peg and noticed they hadn't made any forward progress, still laughing and reading exactly where they had been earlier. The woman reading over the other's shoulder looked toward where he and Michael now stood. She quickly took account of Michael's presence, studying carefully his surroundings. And as if by some family gift of telepathy, Michael almost immediately looked at her, forming his small fingers into an OK sign. He then held up the book with his other hand, his excitement clearly noted by the woman's wave.

So that's Aunt Peg, Jim thought. And for a moment there was something familiar about her, but as she disappeared behind a tall gentleman, the feeling vanished with her.

Michael ran to the counter and set the book down softly as he looked up at the young woman. He spoke in short bursts, restraining himself to a loud whisper. "Debbie! Debbie! I think I found one my mom will love! Look. It's about Baby Jesus and Christmas, and the picture is so pretty; I know she'll love it. I know she will."

He was having trouble containing himself, his voice becoming louder, less restrained. "Can you see how much this one is, please? Please, Debbie?"

Debbie's assistance had arrived—a tall, picturesque woman with long brown hair and designer horn-rimmed glasses, wearing a beige blouse and a soft plaid skirt. Diligently she worked at the keyboard to resolve the issue and restore the terminal to life. Behind her stood a man of some years, his moderately long white hair curled softly over his collar, his beard meticulously groomed, a pair of small glasses set forward on his nose, and he seemed to have a perpetual smile. Though he carried a little extra weight, he was of average height and soft-spoken. Jim would later describe the man in a short Christmas story he was writing, adding, "I suppose to some I've painted a picture of Santa Claus; this is not my intent but purely the gentleman's description."

And it was. The man appeared to be there only as an observer, not offering direction nor receiving any, yet unlike Debbie, who was standing at the far end of the counter, arms crossed looking disconcerted, he stood closely watching the tall woman's actions as the blank monitor flickered once, twice, and then glowed to life, ready for her to begin the login procedure.

"Debbie?" Michael called once more, still without a response. "Debbie? I need your help."

"Everything's still down. You'll have to wait a minute," she responded with a sharp glance.

Michael held the book as high as he could, even standing on his tiptoes to bring it closer to her line of vision. "But I just need to know how much this is. I know my numbers, but…"

"I'm busy right now, so you'll just have to wait," she snapped, cutting him off abruptly. "They'll have the problem fixed in a minute."

Her voice, sharp and impatient, brought the old man to look at her, his brow furrowed. But she didn't notice him, her attention focused on her peeling neon blue nail polish.

"I just need to know," Michael said, slowly bringing the book to lie flat on a counter.

Her voice came sudden and harsh. "I said you'll just have to wait. Where's your mother anyway?"

Jim started to move toward the boy but heard him say, "I'm sorry, but I just needed to know if it's more than fifty cents."

Debbie laughed. "Fifty cents? Of course it is! This isn't Goodwill; you can't buy anything for fifty cents in here! Go find your mom; maybe she can afford to buy it for you."

"It's for my mom…for Christmas!"

Again Debbie said something under her breath no one could make out, causing the old man to straighten up and move rapidly to her end of the counter. "Young lady," he said, standing before her, his voice now gruff with concern. "Have you no manners at all, or even just some common decency! There's no excuse for such rudeness. If you were my…I would…"

His look of disgust said more to his point than any speech he could've given. He turned from her and slowly walked toward Michael.

"Little boy, wait there. We'll find something for your mother," he said softly.

"For fifty cents, I doubt it," Debbie huffed.

Her impudence garnered looks from the few now standing in line behind Michael, but the man gave her no satisfaction of a reply or even an acknowledging glance. He simply walked to Michael, placed his hand on the boy's shoulder, and with a warm smile and soft tone, said, "Walk with me, son; we have much to choose from. I heard you say your mother likes Christmas and the Baby Jesus…well, so do I."

You Are My Love

A slight click was heard from the intercom speaker. "Any available associate, please report to the information counter." Then another click followed again by soft Christmas music. The tall woman leaning over the keyboard released the button on the intercom, turned to Debbie, and said, "My office; Now!"

From those few gathered around came an inaudible sound as loud and powerful as any jet engine. It roared up silently through their smiles and nodding of heads, an ovation of the heart for this tall woman of integrity. From a distance Jim watched as Michael walked with the old man. In his hand he still held the Christmas book the boy only moments ago had handed him. Without taking his eyes off the boy, he returned the book to its display.

As though stung by a bee, Michael spun around. His gaze finding, Jim he ran to him. "Thank you, mister! Thank you for your help. It was fun." Not waiting for a response, he ran back to the old man.

Jim said to himself, "Yes, yes, it was…thank you, Michael."

He continued to watch as the old man and Michael sat on one of the cushioned benches. Soon there were introductions, handshakes, and laughter—a lot of laughter. Jim looked around to find his mom and Aunt Peg and discovered they had moved on to the little coffee area. Mom was sitting at a small table by the front window. Aunt Peg ordered from the barista while leaning back in an effort to locate Michael. Before moving to the register, she stepped back even farther, her eyes darting down the aisles in what was becoming a desperate search. She bumped into a short, well-dressed man and stepped to his side, never dropping her gaze.

Waving his arms and quickly moving to a wider spot in the center of the aisle, Jim hoped she would see him pointing toward the bench where Michael and the old man now sat. She did! She leaned one way and then the other, gestured to him the okay sign, and mouthed the words *thank you*.

He heard the old man's laughter and longed to be a part of their conversation. Though Jim would never intrude, he was not above eavesdropping. He casually moved to a strategic spot just at the end of a long bookcase, a large display camouflaging his presence. So as to not look too conspicuous, he pulled a book from the shelf, opened it to the middle, and placed his finger on the open page.

"She reads to me every night," he heard Michael say.

The old man nodded and replied, "She's a pretty wonderful mom to do that."

Michael responded instantly, "Yeah, she is!"

"Well then, we'll have to find her something special, something you can enjoy together. What kind of stories does she read to you?"

Michael thought for a moment but didn't answer.

"You did say she likes Christmas stories, and stories about Jesus? Does she read stories from the Bible?" the old man asked.

Attempting to hear Michael's small voice better, Jim stepped closer. The boy continued to think, biting his lower lip and shifting his head from one side to the other. The old man sat patiently, intent on giving Michael all the time he needed. And then finally he began to speak, slowly at first, then more natural as his thoughts came together.

"Sometimes the stories are long, but most of the time they're short. The Jesus stories are my favorite. And the angels—we like them too. Once she read a story about pirates, but I didn't like it." He paused, gazing off once again in thought. "Pirates are scary, aren't they?" he asked with some hesitation.

"Oh yes, they are. They even scare me!" the old man said, sitting back with a shiver.

"Me too, so we don't read those stories anymore. We don't read about dragons either. Or witches! Or bears, or mean people." Then, speaking discreetly as though revealing one of his deepest secrets, he said, "There's one other thing we never read about, never ever."

Not wanting to miss the frontrunner on Michael's we-don't-read list, Jim leaned in closer, placing his cheek against the end of the thick wooden bookshelf to better steady himself. Holding his breath, he listened intently, waiting to hear what this young boy found more frightening than pirates, dragons, witches, and bears. Stretching to draw closer, Jim's heart pounded.

"Excuse me," someone whispered, tapping his shoulder.

Startled, a small noise rushed from his lungs. Dropping the book to the floor, Jim whirled around quickly, expecting to see pirates or witches or mean people, because even in his state of near panic, he knew there were few talking bears and almost no dragons left in the world.

Standing before him, hand to her mouth giggling softly, was Aunt Peg, her soft red hair falling gently over her shoulders. Her bright-green eyes sparkled like those of Michael.

"Shhh," she said, attempting to stifle her giggles. "They'll hear you." Quickly she bent down and retrieved his book. "I'm sorry; I didn't mean to startle you."

"Oh! No you...you didn't..." he stammered, breathlessly.

Taking the book from her hand, he turned to avoid any further eye contact, then placed the book on the end of the bookcase, straightened his coat, and brushed back an errant lock of hair. He wanted to say something, anything, but his vocabulary had escaped him. His legs felt like Jell-O, making it impossible to walk away. With options being what they were, he was left to turn and face the pretty young woman. It was her gentle smile that softened the moment.

"Okay, I may have been a little startled," he admitted, reluctantly returning her smile.

She peeked over his shoulder and through the display to Michael and the old man. "Come here," she whispered, gently tugging on the sleeve of his coat, moving them a few yards farther back down the aisle. "I saw you with Michael, and I just had to come over and say hello. It's been so long."

"So long," he replied, not really meaning for the words to slip out. Should he know who this was? he wondered. But as he studied her features, they became vaguely familiar—the hair, the eyes, the smile, even the tone of her voice set upon the edge of his memory like a sculpture shadowed by clouds of age and ambiguity.

Her smile broadened. "It has to have been eight years or more."

Thinking *Are you kidding me? I can't even remember where I laid my cell phone this afternoon, and you expect me to remember you from eight years ago. Please.* But as he studied her features, the clouds began to part, emitting the glorious light of recognition glistening with rays of treasured memories from long ago. *Yes! Yes, I do know this young lady!* He smiled.

But even before his face could register the happiness he felt at this chance reunion, she said, "I'm Peggy. Peggy Callahan. At least that's what it was back then. Now I'm—"

"Aunt Peg," he said hurriedly, with slightly more enthusiasm than expected. He couldn't tell if her look of surprise was because he knew who she was or the astuteness of his tone, so in a more subdued voice, he continued. "Michael pointed you and your sister out on our way to the information counter. But I had no idea it was you two. I'm sorry I didn't recognize you. I..."

Peg's laughter was filled with warmth as she took his hands in hers, holding them tight with compassion. "Like I said, Mr. B. it's been a while. Rachel and I have changed a lot since you saw us last."

The years had only slightly matured her youthful appearance, and before he could speak, the young woman lunged forward and hugged his neck with impulsive fluidity. "I'm so glad to see you, Mr. B." she said, giving him a little squeeze before letting go. "I couldn't believe it when I saw Michael talking to you. I thought, no way, that can't be...and the next thing I knew, you both disappeared down the aisle."

"He asked for my help, so I took him to the information counter."

Her look told him she must have watched a good portion of their journey. "We...took the long way."

"Obviously," she said, tilting her head in a successful effort at being sarcastically coy. "I couldn't figure out what you two were doing running all over the store, but I have to tell you, it was fun to watch, especially when you bumped into that lady and knocked her books all over the floor."

"What!" he gasped, quickly scanning the store for an irate woman.

Peg's burst of laughter was more than relieving, an instant reminder of the great sense of humor she had had as a young girl, and apparently it, too, had not changed much over the years.

"You're bad." He laughed. "You haven't changed a bit. I suppose your sister hasn't either?"

"We weren't that bad, were we?"

"Just bad enough to be memorable, and believe me, I'm thankful there were only the two of you girls. I don't think I could have survived a third."

"I don't think our dad could have either," she said, rolling her eyes.

The Callahan girls had always been attractive and talented young ladies. Peg, outgoing and slightly rebellious, had a flair for getting into mischief, whereas her sister, Rachel, was shy and reserved, preferring to blend into the background, though it seldom worked out that way. And now, all these years later, he wondered if either had changed much. He wanted to ask if her sister was still singing, but before he could, from the other side of the bookshelf they heard the old man's laughter, followed closely by that of Michael's. They were too far away to make out their conversation, but it was obvious they were enjoying themselves.

"What a great kid."

"Thanks, Mr. B. He is a great kid. A handful at times, as you found out, but overall, he really is a pretty good kid. God only knows he's been a true blessing for my sister."

Peg glanced in the direction of the coffee area, where Rachel now sat staring out the window. It was apparent even from this distance she was more lost in thought than watching the rain. Again laughter rolled over the bookshelf, causing Peg to turn back around quickly.

"I should probably go get him. I don't want him to be wasting that gentleman's time—or even worse, just being a bother."

"No it's okay," Jim said, putting his hand up. "He's helping Michael find a book to give to his mom for Christmas."

"A book? What kind of book?" She looked confused, adding, "Never mind. It's not important. He knows I already bought something for him to give his mom. He helped me wrap it this morning. Besides, he can't buy a book; he doesn't have any money."

"Oh, but he does. He has fifty cents, and this gift seems pretty important to him."

"Fifty cents. That won't buy—"

"The old man's aware. I heard him say they have a lot to choose from. Must be a sale on children's books or something."

Interrupted by Michael's jubilant laughter, Peg rushed to look through the display, Jim following close behind. They watched as the old man pretended to fly the bench like an airplane, straddling the padded frame, extending his arms outward, leaning gently, dipping down as though banking first to his left, then to his right, then swooping back to the center, where his voice roared like an engine and sputtered to a halt before he leaned over and crashed to the floor, filling the air with more of his boisterous laughter.

"I believe I've missed the runway," he resounded over the child's laughter.

Peg continued to watch the two of them for another moment, assuring and reassuring that Michael was not only in good hands but was perhaps an entertaining break for the old man as well. In a very soft voice not meant for anyone to hear, she sighed. "I love it when he laughs like that. It's been…" Her look was distant and soft, lost somewhere in another place, another time, yet as clear as here and now. This was not a look of sorrow but one of empathy. A memory that tugged at her heart yet filled it with joy. A moment in which her heart spoke to her, and she could not hide or disguise the emotion it brought.

"Peggy!" Jim said softly.

Her eyes blinked away the memory, rapidly returning her smile. "Don't you just love his laugh?" she said, her voice still softer than normal. "He's such a blessing."

Once more her eyes sparkled. And again they heard Michael and the old man laughing, now quieter and with no accompanying sound effects.

They stood listening, watching; and after a few minutes, without saying a word, she moved around the end of the display to where Michael and the old man sat. Bending down, quietly saying something to the two of them, the old man stood to shake her hand and Michael hugged her tightly. There were a few moments of conversation before she walked back to the display and turned to look at them again. Michael flashed an okay sign, and she responded in turn before disappearing behind the display to meet Jim midway down the aisle.

"I just feel better now. Motherly instincts, I guess."

"Oh, so you have kids too?"

"Well sort of…I have a husband." She chuckled. "I got away this afternoon only because it's the dog's turn to watch him."

She winked and smiled. "You have to join us for a cup of coffee, Mr. B. My sister would love to see you again…please! I know she's always wanted to thank you."

"Thank me?" he replied, deepening the wrinkles of his brow.

Peggy looked toward her sister, who was still sitting at the table watching the rain and sipping her coffee, and then turned to Mr. B. "Well, yes. After all if it weren't for you…there'd be no…Michael."

CHAPTER TWO

*J*im believed God was in total control, guiding the planets, the moon, and all the stars in perfect order to His will. No chaos; no accidents; no surprises. He sat in total complete control of all things and everyone. So that made him wonder why it was, every time he was left speechless, in an awkward situation, or somehow looking like a complete buffoon, God saw fit at that very moment, that instant, that nanosecond, to have his wife move as silent as a vapor to suddenly occupy the same three square feet he inhabited in God's vast universe. It seemed God didn't want her to miss even the slightest opportunity to stand next to him shaking her head in wonder and disbelief as Jim struggled to find his footing, the right words, or, on occasion, just allow time for the wheels and cogs to line up and click into place his ability to comprehend and understand a given situation. He believed that at some point in their relationship, Ann had told God that those moments amused her heart and thanked Him for all the many occasions He provided. Jim also believed there were times when, if he were to listen very, very closely, he would actually hear God chuckling right along with her. And Jim believed, oh how easily this could turn into one of those times.

There'd be no Michael? he repeated twice to himself, though never speaking out loud. Was he supposed to know what she meant; was it a joke; should he smile or be afraid; and would he look stupid asking her to explain? He felt the pressure beginning to build. In his mind a cartoon image of himself flushed red like a rising thermometer ready to burst caused him to gather enough words to form a question. His attempt to seek an explanation was cut short by a cool chill up his spine, freezing the words deep in his throat. In a blink, the young woman shot past him with the swiftness of a deer, and before he could react, he heard a familiar twitter of surprise coming from his wife.

The blend of greetings and laughter, giggles and chatter were harmonious as both women held each other at arm's length, hugged briefly, and then stepped back to view each other once more.

"Peggy! Peggy Callahan! Look at you all grown up," Ann gushed, implying that perhaps miraculously after all these years, Peggy might not have noticed she was no longer the lanky teenage girl she had been when they last spoke.

This was one of the many things Jim didn't understand about his wife. Her memory was only slightly better than his, and if you asked her what she had for dinner last night, she'd shrug and say the first thing that came to mind; yet when it came to names and faces, she connected the dots rather quickly. This was handy for him, as she never hesitated to stay close to his side, keeping him informed as to who was who at parties and social events he would have probably forgotten to attend in the first place.

The women's conversation turned to the prattle he could only smile and nod at, leaving him to again wonder why Peggy's sister would want to thank him and how he fit into Michael's existence. And though he was pretty sure his wife hadn't caught his latest awkward moment, he would have sworn, standing there in the middle of Barnes & Noble on Christmas Eve with hordes of shoppers, their hustle and bustle and the giggles and squeaks coming from his wife and Aunt Peg…somehow he heard the quiet chuckling of God.

❧

"Is Rachel here?"

"Yes," Peggy said, pointing toward the coffee area. "But I didn't tell her I saw Mr. B. She has no idea; and now with you…" There was no need to finish her sentence; Ann understood exactly what Peggy was up to and couldn't wait to surprise Rachel.

"Oh, it's been so long," Ann said, smiling at Jim. "The Callahan girls all grown up…I'm so excited, aren't you?"

Before he could answer, Peggy once again gripped his sleeve. "Of course he is. I was just telling him how thrilled Rache will be to finally be able to thank him…and you, Mrs. B., for introducing her to Michael's dad."

From somewhere in Jim's head he heard a hissing sound as a valve opened to relieve the pressure.

"What! Who's Michael?" Ann exclaimed. "Rachel has a family? Oh, my…I can't believe it. Where's the time gone? Wait—do you have a family?"

Peggy, placing a finger on her lips, began quietly ushering Ann down the aisle, stopping just short of the end to peer unseen once again through the display. There was much pointing and whispering, adjusting for a better view, and soon they were tiptoeing back to where Jim waited. All smiles and giggles, their prattle continuing, leaving Jim to once again smile and nod on cue. Even so he noticed Michael and the old man making their way to the opposite end of the store.

"Let's go. I'm dying to see Rachel." Ann said, placing her hand in the crook of her husband's elbow.

"I'll be right there, I'm going to check on Michael," he told her. "Him and the old man are headed to the other end of the store."

"You're so nice, Mr. B. Thank you."

"It's my pleasure. And let Rachel know I'll be there," he said, quickly walking away.

"Oh, Mr. B., don't forget your book." She grinned, picking it from the shelf where he had laid it.

Ann took it. "I'll just put it with my stuff. I still have to…" Her voice trailed off as she examined the cover. Peggy glanced at it also, and both women stared at him blankly.

"I'm sorry; I was just holding it while I was hiding. I didn't want anyone to see me."

The women looked at each other and then back in disbelief.

"I wasn't planning on buying it. It goes right over there. Give me it; I'll put it back."

Reaching, he felt some resistance from his wife. Following her eyes to the book's cover, he saw in his haste he had blindly grabbed *The Ins and Outs of The Karma Sutra*. He didn't need to look at Ann to realize that at the first opportune moment, she would be waiting to hear a better explanation.

Peggy attempted to cover the moment with a smile, saying, "Don't be too long, Mr. B. Rachel will…"

"Oh, he won't be," Ann interjected with dead certainty. "I'll have a cup of decaf waiting for you, so don't let it get cold," she insisted, shooting him a look.

And he didn't have to listen very closely to know, God was on the floor of heaven, rolling with laughter.

❦

Michael and the old man were not hard to locate, and without much surprise, Jim found them under a sign that read Religion. Michael held the two children's books the old man had alluded to earlier. Running to a nearby couch, he placed the books on one of the cushions and then quickly ran back. The old man stood at the far end of the bookshelf glancing over the selection and speaking softly to the boy. Without looking down, he asked, "Michael, do you know what Christmas is about?"

"I think so! It's about..."The boy shifted his weight from one foot to the other and then shoved his hands in his pockets as he thought about what the correct answer could be.

The old man continued to move slowly through the books on the top shelf, not hurrying Michael for an answer nor offering a safe direction.

"I know it's Jesus's birthday, and Santa brings us presents, but only if we're good. That's what my mom told me, and she knows a lot about Jesus. And she took me to see Santa, and he said I've been good this year, and he's coming to my house on Christmas Eve." The boy stopped and thought a moment. "Well, not my house. We're visiting my aunt and uncle right now, 'til we get a place. Aunt Peg said we'd set out some cookies for Santa and carrots for his reindeer. I hope they like carrots!"

"I know for a fact they love carrots." The old man chuckled. "Now, it sounds like you have a pretty good handle on things, Michael. And your mom sounds like a very wise woman. Ah, yes, here's the one I'm looking for."

Pulling down a rather large book, he showed the boy the cover. "Do you know what this is, Michael?"

Jim was unable to hear the boy's answer, as he was surrounded by five young people in their early to midtwenties, two boys wearing leather jackets with silver spikes across the shoulders and spiked bracelets to accent their spiked hairdo. A third boy appeared to have fallen face first into his father's tackle box, and Jim found himself counting a dozen or so piercings in his eyebrows, nose, cheeks, and lips, not to mention the ones along the tops of his ears and the large disks in his earlobes. He wore a camouflage jacket over camouflage pants tucked into camouflage army surplus boots, looking as though he expected war to break out at any moment on aisle three. The two girls were soaked to the bone, their hair lying in wet strings covering large parts of their face where multicolored streaks of makeup ran in small streams to drip from their chin.

Gathering next to a small table, the group blocked Jim's sight of Michael and the old man. Attempting to look around the group, he overheard one of the girls say angrily to tackle box boy, "We would've been here half an hour ago, but some guy cut me off and took my parking spot. I drove around for twenty minutes hoping another would open up and finally gave up and parked across the street. We had to run all the way back in the rain. You've seen how far that is, and it's coming down in buckets!"

The other girl, just as unhappy, remarked, "I wish I knew what that guy looked like. I'd flatten his tires, but I don't remember which car was his. I'm so—"

"Where's the bathroom in this damn place anyway? I need to dry my hair," the first girl demanded. "I thought you said it was back here. You guys don't know crap."

Quickly, Jim grabbed a book off the shelf, glanced at its title for peace of mind, and then held it just high enough to give him some cover. "Excuse me, miss. I couldn't help but overhear. The bathrooms are at the other end of the store. Just turn left at the big coffee sign. It's down a little hallway; you can't miss it."

"Thank you," she said sweetly, without even giving him a second look.

"Yeah, thanks," said the other girl as they stormed off with not so much as a glance back at the three boys, who now stood dumbfounded watching the girls walk away. The boys looked at each other vacantly and then moved through the aisle like a single organic entity lumbering after its prey.

The old man walked toward a huge couch in the center of an open reading area. Michael carried the large book, his eyes not leaving the cover. Jim wasn't sure, but he thought the old man glanced at him and half smiled as they sat down. He watched him turn slightly to face Michael, allowing his bent leg to dangle over the edge. The boy placed the book between them and then assumed the same position, facing the old man. He was so focused on the book he didn't notice Jim move behind yet another display. Though not as close as before, Jim hoped he would be able to hear at least pieces of their conversation.

At this point Jim was beginning to feel a little like a stalker and was sure a review of the security tape would only reinforce his feelings. The only other time he had ever followed anyone undercover was with his wife as they shadowed their daughter and her girlfriends through the mall one afternoon. Oddly enough, they were very good at it, on more than a few occasions standing within five feet of Amy's little group, and not once were they spotted.

It was in a little shop they watched their daughter fall in love with a porcelain mask that she couldn't afford to buy, so after the girls left the store to continue their boyfriend shopping, Mom and Dad bought it and resumed their stalking adventure right up until the appointed time they were to pick Amy up at the main entrance. They snuck out a side door, jumped in the car, and picked her up just as planned. On the drive to dinner, Ann began to play her usual game of twenty questions, never letting on that Amy had hardly been out of their sight all day. Over dinner they presented her the mask. The look on her face was incredible, but they knew it was the feeling in her heart that was priceless.

❦

Jim felt justified looking after Michael. After all, he had Aunt Peg's blessing. So there he stood, lurking at the corner of a bookshelf, looking through yet another large display, attempting to hear a conversation between an old man and a little boy; neither of whom he would have given a second look thirty minutes ago, though he was now held spellbound by the young boy's mission and the old man's kindness.

It was at that moment he felt a change come over the room. An odd presence seemed to capsulate the area with a peacefulness that settled in around them much like an invisible dome, dampening the noise as though isolating the three of them from the rest of the store. Jim knew they felt it also, as it was the only time their gaze drifted away from the book or each other, peering first toward the long expanse of the store, then in unison to the ceiling, and back to each other. It was not clear to him at the time, but as he thought about it over the next few days, Jim came to believe it could have been the Holy Spirit giving them a moment of privacy to bond with each other and the Lord.

Michael adjusted himself as a young child will do to bolster their attention in anticipation of something marvelous to come. And as the old man opened the book, it was obvious the boy was not disappointed.

"That's Adam and Eve; they lived in a garden," Michael said, pointing to the picture.

"It's the story of creation," the old man began. "It explains how God created everything—the earth, the sun, the moon and the stars, all the plants and all the animals, and then God created Adam and Eve to live, work, and walk with Him through a beautiful garden called Eden."

The old man's voice was soft, songlike, filled with certainty and knowledge that was more felt than heard. The boy gazed into the old man's eyes as though searching for a defining sign between reality and fairytale. But the old man's soft gray eyes didn't blink, and soon Michael was satisfied with whatever he found stirring in the old man's soul. He then contemplated the pictures in the book. The old man smiled, turning the page.

Michael burst forth with excitement. "Oh look! That's Noah. He put all the animals on a big boat because it rained for a long time and they didn't know how to swim."

"Oh yes, the Flood. God saved Noah and chose Noah to be a savior of sorts."

Michael didn't look up. Again the old man smiled and continued turning pages.

Michael gasped. "That's beautiful! Who is it? Is that God?"

The old man shook his head. "No! That's Moses. He; he was chosen by God to lead His people to the Promised Land."

"What's the Promised Land?"

"Well…that would be one of the long stories your mother could read to you sometime," the old man said through a smile, flipping more pages.

"Wait, stop!" Michael shifted his position to get a closer look, his voice filled with excitement. "Turn back. Were those lions?"

The old man quickly turned back.

"There. It is lions, great big lions. Are they going to eat that guy?"

"No!" The old man laughed. "That's Daniel. Daniel in the lion's den."

"Why is he in the lion's den? Doesn't he know lions eat people? Isn't he afraid?"

Again there came that wonderful laugh, "You see, Michael, there were people that didn't like Daniel, so they persuaded the king to make a law that for thirty days, everyone had to pray to the king, not to God. If anyone disobeyed, they'd be put to death. But Daniel loved God and continued to pray to Him. So the king, even though he liked Daniel, had no other choice but to order him thrown to the lions."

Michael was transfixed on the old man's face, listening intently. His small fist clinched and unclenched, his mouth fell agape, and his eyes widened, lifting his brow. "Did they…eat him?" he asked, taking a shallow breath.

The old man glanced down at the picture. Michael's eyes followed swiftly to the page and then back to the old man's face. There was a long pause, allowing the tension to hang in the air like a thick invisible fog.

Slowly he turned to meet Michael's stare. "The next morning the king called out to see if Daniel's God had saved him, and after a moment or two, Daniel replied, 'God sent an angel to shut the mouths of the lions.'"

"An angel? A real angel?" The boy gasped. "I know lions can't eat angels, but how could he hold all their mouths shut at the same time? Look," Michael said, placing his finger on the open page. "There's a bunch of lions around Daniel."

There was no hesitation in the old man's voice, no pondering a way to elude the question or even an attempt to explain the supernatural power of angels. The old man simply said, "He's an angel, one of God's mighty warriors, and God sent him to protect Daniel."

The explanation was simple, amazingly simple, so simple perhaps only a child would understand it. It captured, matter-of-factly and without question, that an angel is an angel, his relationship with God as a mighty warrior, and the task God had entrusted to him—to protect Daniel. There are some who would say it didn't truly answer Michael's question, but for a child living in a world of superheroes, it painted a very clear picture. After all, to a child, a superhero is a superhero, a mighty warrior who will always find a way to protect those in danger. Now, throw in he was sent by God, and what do you have? An angel, God's mighty warrior there to protect Daniel. Pure and to the point.

But Michael seemed to understand there was more to the story. Sinking slowly into a sitting position, he bit his bottom lip and stared blankly into the space of the room, giving himself a place to form a clear vision of the old man's words. After a moment, his voice reserved, he began. "The angel did what God told him to…but it was God that saved Daniel…right?"

"Yes! It was God that saved Daniel."

Pleased with himself, Michael sat up a little taller. "I like this book. It has great stories, and the pictures are so real looking. Not like the cartoons in my books."

It was Michael who began to flip the pages as the old man replied, "Yes, this book has a lot of great stories. You told me your mother reads to you about Jesus. Well, there are a lot of stories about him in this book. Why, there are even stories with an angel named Michael and a fisherman named Peter, and sometimes I like to pretend that I'm that fisherman."

"Can I pretend to be that angel, the one named Michael?"

"Of course. But you know, he's not just any angel. He's the chief prince, God's greatest warrior, and the mightiest angel of all! But I have to tell you…" The old man paused, letting his words fall around the boy in a tone of secrecy. "You know how you don't like dragons…"

Michael sat perfectly still, his eyes wide with fear, his face drawn tight with anxiety. He swallowed hard and then breathlessly replied, "Uh huh."

Again a hush dangled between them. The old man surveyed the room and abruptly returned to hold a long, penetrating gaze into the eyes of a rather apprehensive young boy. The corners of the old man's mouth began to twitch, and ever so slowly, a slight grin appeared.

"Michael doesn't like them either. As a matter of fact…he hates dragons."

The old man allowed a slight chuckle to escape as the boy breathed his relief. "And he's not afraid of them either. A long, long time ago he threw the biggest dragon ever out of heaven. And I believe he's looking forward to casting that same dragon into a fiery pit someday."

The boy didn't wait to hear any more. He leaped from the couch and, taking a stance directly in front of the old man, loudly proclaimed, "I love Michael. I'm gonna pretend I'm the mighty warrior, the angel Michael, and I'll never be afraid of dragons again, ever. Because I know the real Michael will protect me, just like the angel that protected Daniel."

Walking in a large circle, cutting the air with an imaginary sword, the boy roared, "I'm Michael, the greatest angel ever. Take that, you stupid dragon."

The old man's song of laughter filled the air once more as he watched his little friend battle an imaginary dragon. And Jim once again felt a joyous smile all the way to his toes.

"There is another angel you might like. His name is Gabriel," said the old man, motioning for Michael to join him.

"Is he a mighty warrior too?" Michael responded, taking his place back on the couch.

The old man was now turning large clusters of pages. "Oh, Gabriel is just as special as Michael. He is the angel that visited the shepherds the night Jesus was born."

"Why did he do that? Were they mean shepherds? Was something trying to hurt them?"

The old man smiled and then turned the book slightly, saying, "Here's a picture of Gabriel and the shepherds. And if we turn to the next page…"

"It's the Baby Jesus, in the staple."

"Stable," the old man gently corrected.

"Stable, yeah. And I think that's his mom, and the tall guy must be his dad. Why do they live with all those animals? And look, there's an angel up above the house. Is that…umm…"

"Gabriel. But it could also be Michael standing watch over Baby Jesus. Or maybe even another angel. We don't know for sure; the Bible doesn't say."

The boy shook his head in agreement and then asked, "Could you read this story to me."

"I would love to, but I think your mother may be looking for you, and we don't want her to worry."

"Oh please, please read it to me. My Aunt Peg's with my mom, and

You Are My Love

if I know my Aunt Peg, she knows exactly where I am. She always knows. Please, please read it."

Without realizing, as though being led, Jim found himself stepping from behind the display, walking toward Michael and the old man. *What am I doing?* he thought.

But something inside told him this was the right time to leave. Deeply saddened by the thought of missing out on the old man's telling of the night Jesus was born, he knew if he didn't step forward with information regarding Michael's mom and Aunt Peg, the old man would close the book, bringing an end to what he believed was not just an extraordinary moment for himself, but truly a blessed moment for a young boy and an old man.

As he approached, they both looked at him and smiled with no apparent surprise at all. "Hi, Michael. Your mom and Aunt Peg are having coffee with my wife. Seems we're all old friends that haven't seen each other in a while. I'll let them know you're listening to a story, and when you're finished, just come up to the coffee area."

Michael's eyes sparkled even more than Jim remembered. He didn't question how he knew his mom or Aunt Peg, although Jim would find out later, he and Aunt Peg had not concealed themselves as well as they thought.

Hurrying to leave, he heard the old man say, "You're welcome to stay and join us here on the couch. Or we could even wait for you to return, couldn't we, Michael?"

Jim didn't know if he was afraid he'd be too much of an interruption or if he was just fearful to hear the boy's response. "No, I need to join them, but thank you. Thank you both," he said before turning to leave.

Moving away, he felt an urge to turn back, to take a place on the couch and maybe contribute to the conversation. But he knew it was not his place to stay. His mind and heart, though terribly saddened, were in agreement. This was a moment to be shared exclusively by the storyteller, his young audience, and, perhaps, as he had thought a moment ago, the Holy Spirit.

❦

Hearing their soft conversation fade behind him, Jim was gripped with a sense of loneliness. Yet a moment later he felt as though he had awakened from a daydream, instantly surrounded by hordes of shoppers, a cacophony of sounds, and a sudden craving for a double-chocolate candy-cane grande with extra whip. It could even be decaf; he didn't care any longer.

Approaching the small wooden gate leading into the coffee area, his mouth began to water. Sitting at a table next to the front window were his wife and Peg. Quietly he mouthed, "I'm going to grab a cup of coffee. Where's Rachel?"

Ann motioned for him to turn around, and as he did, the slender redhead rushed to greet him with a hug.

"Oh, Mr. B., I can't believe this."

"It's been way too long, young lady."

Laughing, she shifted her attention to the table. "That's exactly what Mrs. B. said." Her laughter faded into a smile. "You two always did say the same things, but it's true—it has been way too long."

Putting her arms down and taking his hand, she exclaimed warily, "I know it may not seem like it, but I think about you and Mrs. B. all the time. I've missed you two so much."

"We've missed you too, Rachel."

She gave him another quick embrace and stepped back. He could see that like her sister, she had grown into a beautiful young woman. Her hair lay just above her shoulders in soft ginger waves, partially covered by a black wool cap still holding tiny beads of moisture that glistened in the light. And just like her son, her eyes shimmered and sparkled, her smile a warm welcome to those she chose to share it with, and Jim imagined that would be most everyone. Clearly the boy's enthusiasm came as a direct inheritance from his mother.

As though knowing what he was thinking, she glanced toward the back of the store. "You've met Michael?"

"I did. And let me tell you, he's a great kid. As a matter of fact...well, tell you what. Let's go sit down, and we can get all caught up. Oh, wait a second; I'll be right there. I just want to grab a cup of coffee. Would you like anything?"

Stepping toward the counter and rubbing his hands together with unbridled anticipation, he began to imagine the rich chocolate delight that would soon tickle his spirit.

"Oh, Mrs. B. already has a cup waiting for you." Rachel pointed.

His body jerked to a stop in midstride, and his head snapped around to see Ann holding a cup, smiling as if to say, cheers, honey!

"Oh yes, that's my wife, always looking out for me," he muttered.

So there he sat, sipping on a decaf, nonfat, chocolate substitute with soy milk froth and a sugarless candy cane for a stir stick. But he had to hand it to his loving wife—she did remember…he wanted a grande.

They began sharing memories of school, music, choir, and the drama team. At one time or another, both Callahan girls had been actively involved in each of these groups, and each girl came with her own set of challenges. Peggy was always bubbly, outgoing, high spirited, and a little wild and crazy—more of a let's-just-roll-with-it-and-see-what-happens kind of girl. For her, rehearsals were social events, fraught with short detours of singing and acting, both of which she performed only slightly above average and with much-needed supervision, only taking it as serious as necessary to get through a scene and back to her friends.

Rachel, on the other hand, loved rehearsals. Her ability to memorize lines and melodies was nothing short of phenomenal. But when it came to following simple stage direction, she struggled terribly, many times entering or exiting a scene from the wrong direction or moving about the stage lost in search of her mark. Many times she would start speaking from the shadows or begin a song just on the fringe of the spotlight; these actions were usually met with subdued laughter from the cast and crew and on a few occasions shared with a live audience. But once she no longer needed to focus on where she was to be in a scene, she would become the brightest light onstage. When she sang, her vocals were strong and pure, garnering the attention of everyone in the room. Every performance was from the heart, delivering a measure of authenticity instantly recognized by all. Yes, Rachel Callahan had a gift, the ability to speak to an audience with incredible precision, conveying not just a lyric or the lines of a character, but the emotion within both. And now, as Jim listened to her stories of the past that seemed so distant to him only moments ago, he began to remember each one as if he had just left rehearsal hours before.

As he began one of his own humorous anecdotes, Ann piped in, playfully tapping Rachel on the leg. "I saw you have a son. Well, I saw him from a distance anyway."

"I do!" Rachel said, leaning forward, placing her forearms on her knees, and clasping her hands in front of her. "A five-year old little boy named Michael—or maybe I should say he's every bit a five-year-old little boy. This kid's a high-energy, dirt-encrusted, frog-carrying, full-of-snot bundle of perpetual motion. But he's also the most loving, caring, sensitive little guy ever. Not that I'm prejudiced, you understand."

Her eyes swept the aisles, where perhaps she hoped to see him running to join her. Then, looking at Jim, she continued. "Peg told me he had you running all over the store with him."

"Oh, you should've seen it, Mrs. B.," Peg blurted. "They were like two little boys running all around the place."

"Yes, I'm sure they were, and the only difference is one's just a little taller than the other." Ann scoffed, leading Rachel and Peg in a round of laughter.

Their giggles covered anything he was about to say anyway, so Jim fell back on his training as a good husband and just nodded and smiled, content to be the moment's entertainment.

"I hope he wasn't too much of a bother," Rachel said contritely. "And I don't want to imply that he's shy, but he must've really felt comfortable to approach you for help, Mr. B."

Jim thought, *Not exactly the term I would have used, but* comfortable *is good. Yeah, we'll go with* comfortable.

Ann shook her head. "Desperate would've been my guess," she said, reaching for her coffee. "Seriously desperate."

Again Jim nodded as another short burst of laughter settled around him.

Peggy turned her attention to the far end of the store. "The man he's with right now is such a wonderful guy. When I lived downtown, I'd stop by Rainier Chapel every once in a while and see him and his wife there almost every time. And then last week I stopped in here looking for this book, and there he was. He even remembered me. He looked up the book and found their shipment would arrive the next day. I told him I couldn't get back in until, well, today, so he said he'd put one aside for me. He's such a sweet man!"

Rachel produced the book from a bag next to her chair. "It's hysterical. If you'd like, I'll send it along when we finish. Which will probably be tonight," she said, handing it to Ann. "It's called *Camping with Iris: Do You Have Gas or Was That a Bear*."

Peg leaned in. "I just love him. He always writes about his wife, Iris, and she sounds like a real crackup. To let him tell stories about her like that, she must really love this guy. Have you read any of his stuff?"

"Oh yeah, Linc and..." Jim spoke up, uncrossing his legs and adjusting the sleeves of his jacket, giving time to adequately gather the full attention of both young ladies. He knew the question had been focused more toward Ann, but he believed he would have a more interesting answer. He was wrong.

Stopped by his wife's familiar glare, which, if left uncontrolled, could freeze water at the equator, Jim chose to simply say, "Lincoln Trudeau is one of Ann's favorite authors. I myself find his work just mindless drivel—bathroom reading, really."

Readjusting his sleeves to prevent frostbite, Jim noticed the glare fading as Ann began to use the secret wife facial code system that she had developed and perfected through years of dedication and countless reiterations several times a week over the entire span of their marriage. It was much like the secret father-daughter facial code system, just simpler and quicker. First, she sent a telepathic signal triggering him to look her way. This could even be effective from across a room and on rare occasions even from one room to another. Then, as their eyes locked, her eyebrows would go flat; her lips become a thin, straight line; and her head tilted upward ever so slightly. At that very moment, with the signal discreetly passed on, he would scratch his chin to acknowledge verification. It all would take place in an instant, and no one had ever caught on, not even their daughter. So it then became his job to simply sit back and look attentive, allowing his wife to lead the conversation. Codename "Don't say a word; I'll handle this" was then complete and ready to be executed.

Smiling broadly, Ann chuckled. "Just yesterday, we were talking about another Trudeau book; maybe you've read it, *Come Quick, the Toilet's on Fire*? I thought I was gonna pull something, I was laughing so hard."

"Yes!" both girls squealed.

Excitedly, Rachel added, "I love the part where she hot glues cat hair to those old furry ear muffs and gives them to her mother-in-law, who's deathly allergic to cats."

"Gesundheit!" Peggy sneezed, acting out the part. "You must be coming down with a...oh, wait a minute; you have a little fur ball on your nose."

As the laugh train pulled out of the station, all three women jumped on board. Jim sat back, a happy observer.

"I think my daughter bought that for me for Christmas," Ann said, stretching the truth like hot taffy in July. "It was on my list anyway; if she didn't, I'll be making her some earmuffs." And the train rolled on.

In that moment at the other end of the store, the young boy sat in silent wonder as the old man, finishing the story, gently closed the book. The boy slowly opened his eyes and moistened his lips, preparing to speak, but his thoughts were fleeting, like smoke carried on the wind, unable to take on form. He turned to stare into the face of the old man, his voice soft and quiet.

"It was like..." His eyes blinked rapidly as though clearing a path for his thoughts to travel. Again he moistened his lips; his breath was shallow, hesitant to carry the weight of his words. Unable to speak, he yet again sat silent, eyes falling to the dark leather cover of the book. It wasn't fear that gripped him so tightly, nor did he feel confused. But even at his age, he knew the difference between reality and make-believe, yet slowly his eyes again lifted to the face of the old man, and again he spoke with uncertainty.

"It was like...I was..." But his voice trailed off and then ever so deftly returned in a single, quiet gust. "There." He waited for the old man's response, but none came. "Like I was..." But his voice again fell silent.

As much with his eyes as his lips, the old man smiled tenderly. "Like you were...the shepherd boy?"

CHAPTER THREE

*T*here was little movement from the old man or the boy, each adjusting slightly just for comfort, and then the old man began to speak in a tone that wrapped around the boy with the coziness and security of a soft warm blanket.

"You see, Michael, sometimes when we read or hear stories out of this book, we can close our eyes, and it truly does feel like we're there. That's because this book is special. Not magical, but very, very special. It's the Bible, God's written word. It opens our minds and our hearts like no other book can. God gave it to us so we may know and understand not just the stories and the pictures on the pages, but the people themselves, their emotions, how they felt, how they lived, and even how they died. He wants us to know they were real people just like you and me. They laughed and they cried. Some were fearless standing up to giants, and some hid in fear. There were those who succeeded and those who failed. Some turned away from God and chose a different path altogether, and some chose to follow God's way.

"Jesus said, 'I am the way.' From the pages of this book, he calls to us, 'Follow Me,' and for those of us who hear his voice and follow in faith, he writes vividly on our heart that we are His. He walks with us and speaks to us and leads us through these stories to the hearts and feelings of the people in this book. And from that, we sometimes learn a little about who we are and a lot about who God is."

The old man watched the boy's face, and to his amazement, he didn't see a blank stare, bewilderment, or the slightest inclination of confusion. Instead, in the eyes of this small child he saw a light, a light the old man seemed to know and understand well. A light he had seen many times in many places, in the eyes of the young as well as the old, in those of the wealthy and those of the poor, hungry, cold, and afraid. On the battlefield it would sometimes appear as a shooting star in the eyes of many a dying soldier, a visible acceptance of Christ, a response to His call to walk with Him, know His love, to be with Him for eternity. In that instant, through faith alone, the light of Christ begins to shine within us.

The old man smiled, realizing he had painted a complex picture that demanded simplification for this young child. So with that same comforting tone, he said, "Today when you closed your eyes, you opened your heart and listened in faith. In other words, you knew the story was true, that it really happened, that there really was an angel that spoke to a shepherd, and for a moment you understood exactly how that shepherd felt. You in a way became that little shepherd boy."

The two sat quietly. The boy, running his small hand across the leathery cover, took a deep breath and sighed. "So I wasn't really there?"

"Physically you were sitting right here with me. But…" The old man studied the boy's face. "Where you and Jesus wandered off to…I couldn't say."

The boy's face became aglow with exhilaration. "I was with Jesus?"

The old man smiled. "Always."

A young couple now stood by the bookshelf containing Bibles. "I'm sure this is the one she wants," the girl said, pulling one from the shelf. "And besides, the lady up front said all the Bibles are half price. It's a great study Bible. It's the same one my mom has."

"Wow!" the young man said, looking at the price.

The girl held his arm. "Yeah, it's still expensive, but she'll love it. You know she'll love it."

"Yeah but…" he countered.

"We'll never find it again for half price."

Rolling his eyes and clutching her hand, he sighed. "I guess I can handle sack lunches for another week or two…or three."

There was a squeeze and "Thank you," and then quickly they headed toward the front of the store.

The boy, overhearing the couple's conversation, turned to the old man. "Is half price a good thing? Like when mom buys things on sale or something?"

With joy in his voice, the old man rocked forward, wide eyed, and his wonderful laugh danced through the air. "Why, yes, half price is a wonderful thing." He then cocked his head slightly and with a nod and a wink, added, "If I were lucky enough to find something for half price, I'd snatch it up before they were all sold out. Providing I had enough money, that is."

The boy jumped to his feet and reached into his pockets, producing a small red dinosaur, two rubber bands, a stub of yellow pencil, a toy Jeep with only three wheels, four pieces of bubblegum, two still in slightly tattered wrappings, and what appeared to be an old stuffed gray mouse. Scattered among the cache was an array of coins totaling fifty cents. The boy was hardly able to contain himself, his hands and voice trembling in frenzied rhythms.

"The book—the 'special book.' I have fifty cents; is that enough? Look, is this enough for the Bible?"

He rambled until the old man, suppressing his laughter, pretended to clear his throat and spoke in a mockingly stern voice of somber authority, saying, "Well, let me see! First we need to understand what they mean when they say something is half price."

The old man held the book up giving it a scrutinizing once over. Stroking his whiskers, he furled his brow and muttered something to himself. The boy did not look away, his gaze fixed firmly on the man's face. Clearing his throat and still speaking soberly, he said, "The way I understand it—and keep in mind I work here, so I guess I would know better than most—is that half price for this particular item…ah Bible…means half the price you were prepared to pay in the first place. And if I remember correctly, you were prepared to pay fifty cents. Is that correct?"

The boy just stood there unable to think of anything to say, so he simply nodded his head.

"Well then, that would make the price…I need a moment to figure this out. Five take away three, carry the two, and it's after four o'clock, so there's no Bible tax…okay, your total comes to…" The old man turned away and coughed twice into his clenched fist. "I seem to have a tickle in my throat. I don't suppose you have a cough drop hidden somewhere in those pockets, do you?"

Frantically Michael studied the treasure in his hands, knowing there wasn't but hoping there would be something even slightly resembling the remains of a cough drop. The old man had to swallow hard to keep a laugh from bubbling up.

"Well, that's okay. It seems to be getting better; I think I'll be just fine. Now, where were we? Oh, yes. Your total comes to…twenty-five cents."

The boy looked puzzled. The old man covered another bubble of soft laughter with yet another cough. "Let me see what you have there. Here you go. Give me those two dimes and these five pennies."

After a moment of intense concentration and a slight mishap resulting in most of the pocket booty falling to the floor, the transaction was complete.

"And here's your book, sir," the old man said graciously. "Now, let's take it up front, and I'll ring it up for you. Oh, and look—you even have enough left over for the gumball machine. I like the bright-red ones best, don't you?"

The boy took possession of the book and immediately turned to set it on the cushion next to the old man.

"Is something wrong?" asked the old man.

The boy stood motionless, his eyes catching the light. "No!" he said quietly, shaking his head. Then, moving quickly, he put his arms around the old man's neck and hugged him tightly. The old man heard the boy's small muffled voice say, "Thank you. Thank you so much."

❦

"Are you still writing, Mr. B.?" Rachel asked, attempting to draw Jim back into the conversation.

"Once in a while, but nothing like I used to."

Ann rolled her eyes. "Don't let him fool you. He writes all the time. He just finished an Easter program for Chris Peterson's church down in Olympia."

Both sisters snapped to attention. "Chris Peterson?" they cried gleefully in unison.

Peggy, taking the lead, asked skeptically, "You mean Chris Peterson from school? No way. Our Chris Peterson?"

Jim nodded. "That would be the guy. Now he's Pastor Chris Peterson."

Peg reached over and playfully pushed her sister. "Oh, he had such a crush on you, Rache."

Shaking her head in make-believe disgust, Rachel pushed back. "No he didn't! We hung out once in a while. He was always teasing me because I was so shy. Unlike you and Kathy Taylor, I didn't constantly try to get his attention or follow him around like a lovesick puppy dog."

Peggy blushed and shook back her hair. "It's true. Kathy and I—Kathy mostly—we thought he was so gorgeous."

Hastily Ann added, "He still is a very handsome man."

Even Jim had to agree. When Chris Peterson walked into a room, every female head turned. At six four and built like a strapping young lumberjack, you'd expect him to grace the cover of *GQ*, not be preaching the grace of God.

The girls' attention didn't drift from Ann's face. They leaned forward as though transfixed in anticipation of her next words, and she would hold their anticipation for a moment longer as she took a slow, satisfying sip from her cup.

"I just love him!" she finally said. "He's an amazing pastor, a truly gifted teacher, and one of the most…" Her nose wrinkled, realizing she'd picked up Jim's cup by mistake. Perplexed, she gagged. "This is awful! How do you drink this?" Before he could remind her it wasn't what he wanted, her attention shifted back to the girls, and blindly she dug through her purse for the little tin of breath mints she always carried. Peg impatiently squirmed on the edge of her seat. Opening the tin, Ann made an offer to everyone before taking one of the mints herself, then carefully replaced the tin back in its special compartment in her purse. Pleased with being neat and tidy, assured her precious mints were tucked safely away until the need came around again for clean fresh, minty breath, she leaned back in her chair, folded her hands in her lap, and smiled.

Everyone sat quietly waiting for her to resume the conversation, but it was clear the mints had not only erased the foul taste from her mouth, but also any memory of what she had been in the middle of saying. As the seconds passed, Jim found himself oddly amused with the surrealism of the moment. Rachel became fidgety, straightening her blouse, clearing her throat, and gently rocking to and fro in what he believed was a subtle attempt at attracting his wife's attention. Peggy, on the other hand, sat on the edge of her seat like a tightly wound spring. He could see a physical tension taking place in the young woman, much like a nervous tic. It began as a minor vibration, or would perhaps be better described as a rhythmic bounce beginning in her feet, moving with intensity through her legs and after a few more seconds, quivering violently through her body, bursting forth in a sudden release of verbal beseeching.

"Chris? Amazing pastor, gifted teacher, one of the most what, Mrs. B.?"

"Oh, it's me! I'm sorry; I thought you were getting ready to say something," Ann sniggered, staring at her husband, though her attention soon diverted back to the girls.

"Yes, Chris Peterson is all that." She giggled. "Amazing pastor, gifted teacher, and one of the most…"

Her gaze shifted beyond the girls to the large windows at the front of the store. "Oh, look. It's starting to snow."

Rachel hesitantly looked to the large window; Peggy's stare didn't follow. Her eyes, widening slightly, remained locked on Ann. Her body tightened, and her feet began to bounce.

"I love the snow, don't you Rache?" Ann asked, taking another sip. "Well, just as long as it doesn't get too bad anyway."

Peggy was wound tight, and as her mouth began to quiver, Ann continued watching the snow, taking another sip of her coffee. "Remember the year…"

Unable to articulate, Peggy gripped the sides of her chair, her words coming out in small, squeaky noises. And with that, Ann leaned forward, taking the woman's hand and began to laugh. "I forgot how fun it is to mess with you; you'll forgive me, won't you. I've missed you…I've missed you both so much."

The three of them had a girls' moment, and then Peggy put her hands on her hips and with total exasperation said, "Okay, now you have to tell me: Chris is one of the most what?"

"He's one of the most loving fathers I've ever known," Ann said sincerely.

"He's married?" Peg shrieked. As if stunned by hearing the overwhelming disappointment in her own voice, she blushed even deeper than before. "I'm sorry! Of course he is." She giggled nervously. "I'm sure there were plenty of women who would've jumped at that opportunity. After all, who wouldn't be overjoyed to have Chris Peterson fall in love with them? Oh, wait…I know who!"

Rachel glared at her sister, and then they gave each other a push and a smile. Though Ann smiled, it came with a long pause, causing her smile to fade slowly as her eyes wandered in search not of what to say next, but how. Rachel noticed it first and with only an expression conveyed to her sister the sudden change in Ann's demeanor.

"It was so sad," Ann began softly, and then she abruptly gasped, staring at Jim with concern. "We need to call Chris this evening."

Instinctively she took his hand as she continued to talk to the girls. "It was Christmas Eve a year ago. He and his wife and their daughter, Beth, were driving home from church when a seventeen-year-old girl ran a stop light. It was terrible. The police found marijuana in her car and said she had been drinking with friends just before the accident. They believe she was doing about fifty when she hit the side of Chris's car."

Pausing just long enough to squeeze her husband's hand and get a better grasp on her emotions, she took a breath. "I don't know how any of them survived. Only by the grace of God, I imagine. Chris fared the best. He only broke his arm and was pretty bruised up for a while, but poor little Beth fractured her hip and was in a coma for two weeks due to a head injury. There for a time they didn't know if that baby was going to make it or not. And for that whole two weeks, Chris never left her bedside—well, except for his wife…Linda's…"

She took another deep breath to help support the invisible dam in her tear-filled eyes. A poster on the far wall became her focal point, but this was noticed only by Jim.

"He went to the funeral, but I don't think he remembers much about it. And who knows; maybe that's a blessing. Isn't that what they always say?"

Jim produced a tissue from the side pocket of his wife's purse and handed it to her as a tear ran gently over her cheek.

Rachel's gaze fell to the floor. "And his daughter? How is she now?"

Again the woman took a deep breath, this time as if cleansing her mind before continuing. "She's fine. She still walks with a slight limp sometimes, and there will be some lasting effects due to what the doctors call a mild brain injury. It's nothing you would even notice if you weren't looking for something. They believe because of her age, she may even develop normally, maybe just a little slower in some things."

Ann paused to stuff the tissue in her jacket pocket. "She works with a speech therapist almost every day, but I think that's more precautionary than it is necessary. She even sang in the preschool choir as part of the Christmas program. She had a one-verse solo, thanks to someone I know."

She took her husband's hand and with a gentle squeeze deferred her latent anguish, allowing his warm, loving touch to soothe her heart. "And I have to say she's just adorable. A true blessing for Chris and all of us."

Jim felt her unconsciously squeeze his hand once more just before letting go, and he knew her heart was so overflowing with emotion she would need to quietly share it with him later.

"And Chris?" Rachel inquired affectionately.

"His recovery's been a little slower," Jim said. "But understandably. After all, a part of him died along with his wife that night, leaving Chris with not only physical and emotional scars, but some deep spiritual wounds as well. And sometimes those are more painful and take longer to heal. And for some people, they...well, they never heal."

Peggy slumped back in her chair as though momentarily exhausted by the tragic news. Her eyes, reflecting the pain she felt in her heart, moved from Ann, coming to rest on her sister.

Softly, Rachel asked, "Does he have a support group?"

Ann grinned half-heartedly. "There's actually one at his church, but of course he didn't feel comfortable going there. So a friend of his gave him the name of a place in Olympia. He drove there and sat in the parking lot for an hour. He never went in, and he never went back. After that he refused to even discuss it. I think he felt like...I don't know. I just don't know."

Rachel's concern deepened as her voice rose. "But he has someone he talks to. Someone he opens up to—a counselor, psychologist, friend, someone, right?"

Ann shook her head. "Chris doesn't open up. He's locked the accident inside and refuses to let it out." And with a glance, she passed the conversation back to Jim, who shrugged, unsure what to say next.

"I guess I'm as close to Chris as anyone." he began. "And at this point, Chris refuses to discuss it with me. I know he hurts, and I know he's angry—angry with God; he's told me that. But I don't know how to reach him, I've never lost a spouse, and I can't possibly know what he's going through or what he's feeling. But I do know when someone's been a faithful servant and suddenly their loved one is taken, their life turned upside down, it leaves some enormous questions. And in a time of such horrific grief, only God can answer those questions. But most times our sorrow, our loneliness, our confusion, and our anger become so loud we can't hear God speak to us. But when and if we allow Him, He quiets our soul and holds us up with the scarred hands of his Son.

"Chris knows this! And even through his pain, his anger, I've heard him teach it, preach it, and shout it from the mountaintops—literally! His heart may be broken, but his soul remains on fire for the Lord. And like Ann said, he's not just an amazing pastor, he's a loving, caring man who truly ministers to his congregation...no, to his whole community. He doesn't think twice about lifting their needs up in prayer, yet I know he hasn't approached God with his own needs, his anguish, his sorrow, and the feelings only he and God know lay heavy on his heart. Honestly, I believe the best thing anyone can do for Chris and for Beth is to just keep them covered in prayer and believe God has a plan to heal them both."

The four sat quietly for a moment, Ann thankful for the man she married, the two women still admiring the man they had most respected growing up.

"We don't see the same joy Chris used to have for life," said Ann. "he's always pursued it with open arms, fire in his eyes, longing to embrace whatever God put before him. Chris was fearless that way, loving a challenge, thriving on it. Just look at his ministry. It's already one of the largest in the Northwest and growing every month. Thirty-some outreach programs. Everything from low-income medical clinics to a biker poker ride on Veterans Day. His church is alive and extends deep into the community. And it's all because Chris has shown his congregation by example how to serve and lead others to Christ. He brings the Bible to life, showing everyone he touches that God is alive and in control. One of his favorite sayings is, 'There's no obstacle…'"

Rachel joined in softly. "'…greater than our God. Just lay it at his feet, step back, and watch His awesomeness take over.'"

She didn't lift her head. A single tear fell to the floor, her voice soft, filled with broken breath. "He used to say that a long time ago when we were kids. I've never forgot it."

Rachel's breath shuddered, smoothing out as she inhaled deeply. "I'm one of the people he led to Christ. I was in eighth grade. During a school assembly, I became captivated by his telling of Jesus calming the storm. It was like his words touched my heart. He painted this beautiful picture of Jesus's love. I gave myself to Christ right there, right in the auditorium."

Jim handed her a tissue, and she took it without looking up and without breaking the rhythm of her thought. "You'd see him in the hallway or out on the campus talking to someone, and all of a sudden you'd hear him say, 'Let's take a second and pray about that.' Or 'Let's lift it up to God. He'll get you through this.' And now, he won't even ask God to minister to his own heart. What's wrong with him? What's he thinking? Has he…"

Jim didn't know quite what to make of Rachel's reaction. It seemed logical his wife would feel a tug at her heart as she remembered the events that had unfolded in their dear friend's life this past year, but Rachel seemed lost in memories of her own, evoking emotions rooted far more deeply than mere childhood friendships would kindle. And thinking back, as kids, teenagers, they weren't exceptionally close—not in a romantic, puppy-love sense anyway. But of course, thinking back, there had been many times over the years when he had heard Chris speak fondly of his 'dear friend Rachel,' even using some of their escapades as illustrations in his teachings. So maybe their bond went deeper than he had ever imagined. Maybe…

Nudging him out of his fog, Ann's voice, like a distant echo called, "Honey! Honey! Get her some water."

"No! Please; I'm fine," he heard Rachel say as the fog lifted.

He watched as Peg rubbed her sister's back. Almost instantly Rachel looked up, her eyes moist and red, their sparkle only slightly dimmed. And then to everyone's surprise, a broad smile parted her lips, bringing a warm glow to her face. "He just needs to go camping. That's all."

Taking a moment to catch her tears in a tissue before they could begin their run, she again smiled, even looking somewhat amused as she took a short sip of Peg's coffee. After clearing her throat, she began telling her story to an audience of three very perplexed listeners.

"We were at a youth rally, and they put us in these small groups of maybe ten or fifteen people. And since Chris and I were the only two from our church in that group, we naturally gravitated toward each other."

"Naturally. Uh huh, sure," mocked Peg, taking another opportunity to playfully push her sister.

Rachel shrugged it off with a sigh of sisterly disgust, bringing Ann to smile.

"Anyway, they asked if any of us had ever had a life-changing experience. Of course, we all just sat looking at one another, hoping they'd give us an illustration and move on to whatever lesson we were supposed to learn from it, because none of us even knew what a life-changing experience was. We were fourteen, fifteen years old. We went through life-changing experiences every day, although we didn't know it at the time. It was just called…going to school."

School, Jim thought. That was so true! For most of us, our first experiences with "life" begins at school. It's where we learn to develop our social skills; to understand our capabilities or lack thereof; to spread our wings and fly high above all expectations or crash to the resounding applause, hoots and hollers, catcalls, and laughter of an entire classroom, or even on occasion the entire student body. It's where hallways become the arteries of gossip and life can change while walking from one class to the next. Quickly you learn to observe your surroundings. Listening closely, you discover whose table you're invited or not invited to sit at for lunch. Who likes who and if you're invited to the dance, the party, or the game and who wanted or didn't want to invite you.

Did you hear about this and what about that, she told me and he told you, I heard they broke up, I heard they're steady, he said, she said, they said, oh and by the way, have you heard about Hugo and Kim…Aah, yes, school.

Rachel was right; it is a place where life-changing experiences occur every day, leaving most victorious and few defeated, some unblemished while others carry the scars of childhood into and on through their adult life.

"The man and woman leading the class didn't say a word," he caught Rachel saying and turned his attention back to her. "And neither did any of us. We could hear the kids in the next classroom laughing and having fun, and when they'd get quiet, we could hear the big clock at the back of the room ticking off the seconds. Finally, one girl said her parents got a divorce, and not having her dad around changed her life immensely. She didn't bother to elaborate or offer any explanation, so again everyone just sat around quietly looking at each other, listening to the clock tick."

There was the slightest hint of excitement rising in her voice, a sense of happiness, of joy in the sharing of a long-ago memory about a long-ago friend that even today occupied a special place in her heart. "Then all of a sudden, Chris starts telling us about a time he and his family went on a camping trip to the desert. They were far away from any big cities, so it was dark, really, really dark, and there wasn't much of a moon either. He couldn't sleep and decided to leave the tent and lie under the stars. He said he'd never seen so many stars. From horizon to horizon, the night sky was aglow, stretching out forever, making him feel so small and insignificant by its enormity.

"He began to feel uneasy, yet he didn't want to go back into the tent. He felt drawn to just lie there and stare at the stars. As he did he began thinking about creation—why God would create the heavens in the first place, with its infinite worlds, never to be seen by human eyes, and distant landscapes never to be explored. What was the point?

"Chris had everyone's attention, even the teachers. Of course, we were all thinking the same thing. What was the point? And he answered it so profoundly, even now when I look up at the stars, I think about it."

Rachel smiled, stopping to look at each of them, their interest clearly visible. "It was under a desert sky Chris said he came to know God as more than just a literary figure in the Bible. It was like God placed the answer on his heart by letting him see just how small he really was—an infinitesimal speck of dust in the vastness of God's creation. And it was at that moment he realized just how great God is. Lying there beneath the stars, he came to understand that God, the creator of all that he could see, for as far as he could see, knew him and loved him personally. Above all else in His creation, God loved him, Chris Peterson. And if God would attend to the minutest detail on the most distant, darkest landscapes, how magnificent must we all be for Him to proclaim His love for us above all else, to sacrifice his own Son that we may live forever with Him in heaven. He went on to say, if any one of us were the only person to have fallen into sin, God would've still sent his son to die for us and rise as our Savior, because that's how much God loves us, every one of us. Then he said, 'Jesus didn't die for everyone.'"

Rachel studied their faces and was not disappointed to see the lines of confusion move quickly and deeply across their brows. "You can imagine everyone's reaction. It was like the whole room just stopped. No one moved. I don't think anyone even took a breath or blinked an eye. Even the clock seemed to stop ticking. But then, Chris looked at all of us and said, 'He died for every, one—each of us—individually.'"

Rachel sat quietly.

Drifting down around them from an overhead speaker was the sound of a single guitar, masterfully rendering a beautifully crafted version of "Silent Night." In a moment of reflection, best described as serene, each of them was spiritually transported to lie beneath their own starry view of creation, to hear God's voice speak to them personally as he touched their heart.

Rachel took a sip of coffee and began moving the cup in small circles, watching the swirling dark liquid like a whirlpool draw her deeper into her memory.

"I remember later that night, Chris and I were sitting on the lawn in front of the church waiting for his mom to pick us up. He saw me looking up at the stars and said, 'Pretty amazing, aren't they! It's like they go on forever and ever. The Bible says He holds the universe in the width of his hand. But God's love says He holds us in His heart. Now, that's something truly amazing. And it too will go on forever and ever.'"

Ann leaned forward. "I've heard him say that before. I guess I never realized he shared such insight with people way back in junior high school. But Chris has always been pretty special. I love listening to him talk about the Lord. His sermons are always so...personal. Like God gives him just the right thing to say at just the right time, and just for you personally. You know what I mean?"

But before anyone could answer she continued, setting a more jovial tone. "I guess that's why he has one of the largest congregations in the Northwest. Oh, and his sister Bailey—she put together an incredible worship team. I have to give her credit too."

Rachel laughed, her eyes sparkling with life once again, her voice light and airy. "Well, that doesn't surprise me at all. She has a beautiful voice and probably understands worship better than anyone I've even known. She's been a leader since...what? Junior high school, Mr. B.?"

He nodded. "From birth. I think she came out singing 'Go Tell It on the Mountain.'"

They all laughed. Ann looked at him for some kind of confirmation, saying, "It was just a few weeks ago, Bailey announced she'd be moving to Tampa in February. Her husband, Ted, is taking a senior pastor position, and boy, has it caused some real concerns for the music department, as you can well imagine."

Rachel looked at Jim. "Why don't you step in, Mr. B.?"

"I'm old! Besides, they need a singer, not just a music director. Don't get me wrong; they have some good voices up there. None like Bailey, of course, but it's like you said: she's not just a great singer, she's a great leader as well. It doesn't matter if it's a small youth rally or the whole church. She has the ability and the heart to lead people to God through worship."

Peg's face lit up. "Rachel does that. She led worship down in Irvine, and it was incredible. I can't even tell you. She even..."

Jim's attention went to Rachel, who fumed with irritation. "I worked with a great pastor and a fabulous worship team, but I've never been as gifted as Bailey Peterson. That much I can assure you. Remember youth choir? She was born to be a worship leader. And it all came natural for her. No, I'm not in her league at all."

"Overall, you were a far better musician than Bailey, even vocally," Jim interjected. "You weren't as outgoing, but once you relaxed you could hold your own."

"I have videos of Rache' leading worship," Peg said, staring firmly at her sister. "Not to mention a DVD of you and Mike performing that duet together."

Peggy was so excited she bumped the table, almost toppling over Jim's still-full cup, but even that didn't slow her down. Jim couldn't help but smile as she went on. "Rachel arranged all the music—the orchestra, the singers, everything. It was so beautiful. She was awesome, and the—"

"Enough, Peg!" Rachel said, surprisingly harsh. Diverting her attention from her sister, she picked the book up off the table and placed it back in the bag, making it quite obvious she was uncomfortable with where Peggy was taking the conversation. "That was a long time ago!" she continued. "Besides, I had very little to do with it. God knew it would be a special moment, so He made the whole night exceptionally beautiful…okay, Peg? That's it! Done!"

There was a shared look between the sisters, and with unspoken words they reached out to clinch the others hand for reassurance. Then, with a deep breath, Peg leaned toward Jim and whispered in quiet defiance, "She really is awesome."

Ann, having spent a long career identifying the illusory expressions on the angelic faces of her students, found no challenge in picking up the implicit dialogue between the two sisters, who as schoolgirls were never very competent at such behavior and obviously had not improved with age. Of course, Ann, being Ann, would not let a distraction this blatant slip by, and somewhere within a case of mental giggles, she heard a familiar little voice say, "There is strange behavior afoot."

And so would begin the Ann Brooks Extraction of Concealed Information process, a term Jim never spoke aloud but thought frequently, as he had witnessed her method firsthand hundreds, maybe thousands, of times over the years. Believing it was a natural talent and not a practiced skill, he knew it always began with that disarming smile and innocent rise of interest in her voice. And then, the questions rested on her lips only momentarily before jumping off in a slow succession of casual inquiries delivered with such smooth precision it would make a CIA interrogator envious. Jim also believed there was a second stage to the process, although he had never experienced it personally, mainly because she was so darn good at the first.

So with a faint grin resting at the corners of his mouth, he mentally began the countdown. *Here it comes, ladies, in three…two…one.*

"So, Rachel"—Ann smiled disarmingly—"you performed with your little boy?"

"No," she exclaimed sternly, glaring at her sister.

With an inquisitive nod and a rising inflection in her voice, Ann shrugged. "It's just…well, I thought Michael was your son's name."

Proving to be an easy mark, Rachel took a deep breath and exhaled loudly. "It is my son's name. He's named after his father, Mike Donahue."

Ann's jaw slacked into a mischievous grin that helped to encourage a reserved, albeit somewhat discreet tone. "Oh yes…my little lovebirds."

CHAPTER FOUR

"Damn!" Peggy gasped. "Michael's by the front door. Psst…psst… Michael…" Peggy moved swiftly through the coffee area, making her way closer to the boy, who stood next to a giant gumball machine. Hearing her call, he quickly turned. A large red gumball rolled across the floor.

Looking at Ann, Rachel shook her head and grinned. "The old guy pointed us out to Michael and then headed toward the back. He's been feeding that gumball machine for the last couple of minutes."

Turning to look back at Peggy, who was moving people out of her way, Rachel remarked, "I love to watch my sister get all rattled like that. She'll make a great mom someday; at least I hope so anyway, as long as it's a little girl. One boy in the family is plenty. Matter of fact, he's too much sometimes."

Jim noticed Peggy stooping down to talk with Michael, holding a large bag she had taken from him. It was apparent something was amiss. The woman saw him watching her and pointed to the bag, lifting her shoulders and shaking her head with noticeable animation, conveying visibly her confusion as to where Michael had acquired the bag and its contents. With great urgency they headed toward the rear of the store.

"Is something wrong?" Ann inquired of her husband.

"I'm not sure," he said, slowly rising out of his chair to track their progress. "Maybe I should go check."

"No, no! Sit down, they're fine." Rachel said, leaning across the table to touch his hand with a reassuring gesture. "I'm sure it's nothing. But whatever it is, I promise you my sister will come back with every little detail. Honest! Trust me on this one."

Sitting down, Jim scanned the large glass windows making up the front of the store, their reflections resembling a living Leroy Neiman canvas. Over the next minute he found himself periodically glancing up in hopes of scouting Michael and Aunt Peg's progress. But the two soon became mere streaks of color immersed in the obscure shapes reflected in the mirror-like windows.

Wondering how his wife would resume her prying, he heard her begin simply with an easy natural flow—just three little words, and she was off and running.

"My…little…lovebirds."

Rachel looked at him and shook her head in disbelief. He made a feeble attempt to redirect the examination. "I'd love to hear how you learned to arrange orchestration. Sure, you play piano; but…"

Even before he could finish the statement, his wife shot him a look. Quickly backpedaling, he corrected. "Lovebirds…I think the topic is now lovebirds."

Rachel gave them both a glance. "So now you're going to gang up on me? Peg walks away, and I find myself in a tag team match with the two of you. You haven't changed a bit. I love it."

From a purse draped over the back of Peggy's chair came the unmistakable sound of ZZ Top, "Gimme all your lovin', all your hugs and kisses too."

"I need to get this. It's Peg's husband."

As Rachel attempted to locate the phone somewhere in the bottom of the oversized purse, it continued to sing. "Gimme all your lovin', don't let up until we're…"

"Hey, Kevin, Peg's chasing after Michael. Where are you?"

She stood looking out the window. "Come on in. You can meet the two minds that molded us into the women we are today. We're having coffee. Just turn…there you are. Do you see me?"

Sheepishly she looked at Ann. "I'm sorry. I hope you guys don't mind, but honestly, I don't think you know what an influence you were on us."

Leaning forward using his best eighteenth-century eloquence, Jim took Rachel's hand as though to dance the minuet. "Oh, but of course we understand, don't we, darling?" he said to his wife. "After all, we're the two minds that molded you and your sister into the women you are today."

It was hard to contain their laughter to just the little table, so to the delight of those around, Rachel quickly reeled it in by pointing out Kevin as he walked through the parking lot. The snow was beginning to stick to the trees and shrubs along the walkway, triggering a memory Jim didn't want to share at that moment. Excusing himself, he walked to the window to watch the snow, and once there he thought of Amy. Stuck in a box, buried in the back of his closet, was each and every letter his daughter had ever written to Santa. From crayon scribbles to printing with pencils, high school loops and heart-dotted *i*'s, to the beautiful, intricate script of the mature young woman she was today. And every year, her Santa letter ended with the same eight words, which were the same eight words he lift up in prayer, that his little girl wouldn't be disappointed. "Please bring us a white Christmas. Thank you."

Staring out the window, he thought, *It looks like God placed an open bag of snow on the back of Santa's sleigh. We'll have a white Christmas by morning. Thank you, God. You are truly awesome.*

"He's daydreaming. Just poke him," he heard Ann say.

Spinning around, he came face-to-face with Kevin, whose rugged looks and gentle smile made him impressive by anyone's standards, especially the women. And like Chris Peterson, his broad shoulders, deep voice, and strong handshake made him very much a man's man.

"It's really warm in here. Must be all these people," he said, removing his overcoat to reveal a red and white lanyard with a large tag identifying him as Medical Staff.

"Do you work at St. Joe's?" Ann asked, with excited interest.

"Yes. Sometimes a little more than I'd like."

"Are you in nursing? I have a friend that works there, and her schedule gets pretty crazy."

"They're what keep the place running, that's for sure," he responded.

"Kevin's an OB/GYN," Rachel said proudly.

"And that's why I'm so late getting here to pick up Michael," he said, folding his coat over his arm. "If you'll excuse me, I better go find Peggy. Michael and I still need to go home and get dressed for the party. Do you and Peg have everything you need, Rache?"

"We got it all, Kev," she said, giving him a hug.

"You're the greatest, Rache. I owe you. And incidentally, Mr. B., Mrs. B., it's been a pleasure to finally meet you, and I apologize for my late arrival. Sorry, no pun intended. Well, maybe just a baby one." Everyone jauntily groaned in unison. The young doctor grinned apologetically. "Nevertheless, I'm sure we'll get together soon."

Again he shook Jim's hand and then reached for Ann's. Casually she pushed it aside. "Are you kidding? We're like family now." She gave him a hug and sent him on his way.

"He seems like a nice man, and handsome as all get-out—and a doctor to boot. Your sister's one lucky girl."

"Yeah, he is pretty wonderful."

A few moments of silence managed to creep in before Ann inquired, "Are you expecting anyone else?"

Rachel looked confused and a little surprised. "No! Not that I'm aware of."

"No more kids to be rescued, phones to be answered?"

"No!" Rachel replied slowly, cautiously. "Why?"

"Good," Ann said, guiding the woman to her seat. "My lovebirds—where did they fly off to?"

Taking Ann's hands lovingly in her own, Rachel's body seemed to shrink down, her face pleaded for understanding, and her voice echoed the sentiments. "Mrs. B., I'd love to tell you the whole story. I've even had dreams of sitting with you and you Mr. B. sharing what's happened over the last ten years, but maybe now, here in this place…I'm just not sure it's the right time. At least…"

Ann, sensing the woman's distress, leaned across the table. "It's all right, sweetheart. I shouldn't have been so pushy. I'm sorry. It's just seeing you, I want to hear all about what you've been up to; what you're doing, where you've been. My word, Rachel, you're a mother now!"

Jim again glanced out the window to the gently falling snow, then over to the colorful abstract reflections, ever changing along the immense wall of glass. He watched as one of the shapes began taking on a recognizable form, then another and another. Moving quickly to the lower edge of the glass, soon he could see three human forms seemingly leap from the window to stand next to the front door. Kevin scooped up Michael. The two kissed Peggy goodbye, glanced toward him and waved, then hurriedly left through the large glass entryway. Peggy still carried the mysterious bag and was quickly making her way to rejoin the group. Ann and Rachel were continuing their subdued conversation with smiles of affection and the occasional compassionate hand stroke. Jim again watched the snow gently fall.

Peggy plopped down next to Rachel, shoving the bag under her chair. Tersely she stared at her sister. "Don't ask what's in the sack."

Taking a deep breath, she continued on what could only be perceived as a mild rant. "Today was Peter's last day—you know, the nice old man that works here; the guy that was reading to Michael. Turns out, he's a seasonal worker that donates his earnings to provide books for children. I informed the store manager, we are not some charity case and demanded to see Peter myself. But of course he's already gone home, slipped out the back door, got on a bus, and disappeared into the night. And nobody here will give me any information on him. They just smile and say, 'It was given from the heart. That's what he does. It's a wonderful gift from a wonderful man. Enjoy it, and have a wonderful holiday.'"

"I'm confused." Rachel frowned.

"So am I! But for now, it's a wonderful gift, and Michael has a wonderful tale for you later, and…" She laughed, shaking her head. "It was on sale for half price. Michael bought it for you with his own money. Well, in a manner of speaking. Seems fifty cents goes a long way here today. Coffee, anyone?"

"Gee, I understand perfectly now," sniped Rachel.

"Glad I could clear it up for you."

"As clear as mud…sissy dear, clear as mud."

Both ladies burst into giggles before Peggy, half blushing, said, "I may have overreacted a bit, it was a nice thing for the old man to do, and like I said, I don't know." She paused. "Never mind. Forget I said anything. We'll talk about it tomorrow. Everything's fine. Oh, wait. I mean everything is wonderful, simply wonderful."

Peggy got up and began to walk to the counter.

"Are you really getting more coffee?" Rachel asked.

"Why? Are we done?" Peggy said, her momentum slowing. "I was hoping we could have one more cup, if no one has anything pressing to get to. We still have an hour or so to kill before meeting up with the boys, so if you could hang out for just one more cup, it would be, well…wonderful, just wonderful."

Leaping from his chair and rushing past Peggy toward the counter, Jim exclaimed, "We'd love to stay for another cup. Coffee's on me. You can help carry it."

As he and Peggy walked to the counter, she turned to Rachel. "You've always wanted to tell the Bs thank you. Well, now's as good a time as any. They need to hear it."

Quizzically, Ann glanced at Rachel, who sat motionless in a state of absolute defeat. Jim, on the other hand, could smell Ann's victory in the form of a double-chocolate candy-cane grande with extra whip.

Mike Donahue was an exceptional student, talented pianist, and aspiring theatrical director who had a heart for the Lord and a desire to learn. As the young man's mentor, Jim considered himself fortunate, having watched him blossom over the years to become not only one of the most proficient musicians he knew, but a true leader who never hesitated to assist, acknowledge, and praise those less talented members of the team, cast, or crew. He also excelled academically and would graduate midterm of his senior year.

That August, Mike came to Jim's office with news he'd been accepted into the University of California Irvine, Masters of Fine Arts program, providing he passed the audition. Neither had any doubts, leaving Jim elated but also selfishly troubled. In less than a week, rehearsals for a new Christmas program would begin, and the production was large. Jim knew without Mike to assist, it would be tough going. A few days later, he was back in Jim's office with what his parents insisted would be "the best thing." He would stay in Seattle, attend the University of Washington, live at home, and they would pay his tuition. After all, as they explained it, they didn't want their son living in the crime-ravaged neighborhoods of Southern California. But this wasn't Mike's desire. He'd come to see Jim for one reason—not to solicit advice or an opinion, but simply to ask Mr. B. to pray with him. And there in Jim's office, they laid his dreams and aspirations at the feet of Christ. Mike didn't pray for a solution or miracle, but simply for guidance to be in God's will.

As he started to leave, he turned to Jim. "Thanks for always being there, Mr. B. I knew you'd understand. So if we can…let's just keep this between us for now, okay? I'm not gonna make any rash decisions. I remember you once saying, 'When you pray for an answer, you must then listen for God's response.' So for now, I'll wait and listen. One more thing: you know I love my parents and never want to hurt them. But this is my dream. Shouldn't it be my decision?"

Jim knew by the young man's tone he didn't expect an answer, so he just looked at him. "Keep praying about it, Mike, and I'll do the same. Remember, God has a plan."

Mike would leave a few weeks after the last performance of the Christmas program in hopes of finding a job playing music somewhere in the greater Southern California area before the spring flood of musicians hit the pavement, snatching up all the good-paying gigs; that way he'd have an income and be established in an apartment before school started in September. But of course everything hinged on the audition and his eligibility for a student loan. His parents withdrew their offer to assist financially and their membership in the church that same week.

The day he left, he stopped by Jim's office, where they spent time sharing stories mixed with laughter and a little sadness, and eventually they ended in prayer. As he was leaving, Jim handed him a long, narrow walnut case. Inside was a white birch Mollard conductor's baton, and engraved on the side was "Ex. 15:1 The Lord is my strength and song."

Jim didn't go with him out to his car, but as he walked through the halls, he picked up three or four other faculty members and ten or so friends eager to see him off. Everyone gathered around his car saying their goodbyes; then he made a large U-turn in the parking lot and came to a stop at the driveway exit. He stepped out of the car, placed two fingers to his lips, and then pointed to those gathered in the lot, then to the chapel, and lastly heavenward. Even from inside his office, Jim heard him yell, "God bless. I love you all."

Over the next year, Jim received a few short notes from him, mainly talking about school, waiting tables, and how he couldn't find a church he liked. He'd always end by saying, "I know you're praying for me…just please, pray a little louder."

There was never a return address on the envelope, and sometime during the following year, the letters stopped altogether. That is, all except one, which arrived a few years later. He didn't say much, but he enclosed an invitation to the Seattle Showcase Theater, for the Northwest premier of an original musical—his. Dates were to follow. They never did, and the manager of the theater could only tell Jim the production had been canceled for unspecified reasons. But now, he was about to learn why.

❦

"It was you, Mr. B., who threw us together. Oh, Mike had worked with me before, but only in groups. This was different. This was one-on-one." She blushed. "Like always I was struggling with my character, my cues, and finding which mark was mine onstage. I would just be up there wandering around in circles, as you always liked to point out. It was awful. I was terrible. Looking back, I'm surprised you used me at all."

"You know that's not true," Jim said. "You may not have been a natural when it came to musical theater, but you had a great voice, and your musicianship was—"

Ann gently tapped his hand. "Let her finish."

"Thanks, Mr. B., but still, I don't know why you had any faith in me. And then, convincing me that with a little extra help, I could play a lead role…" She paused just long enough to roll her eyes. "But you arranged for Mike to be my coach and direct this one scene. That was really frightening because it was a transitional scene, and if it wasn't done perfect, the whole ending of the play would just fall apart. You placed a lot of trust in him, and he never forgot that. A few years later, he wrote you a letter, but he…well, there was a lot going on back then. I'm sorry to say it was never mailed. I still have it packed in a box. I'd love to give it to you, and I know he'd want you to have it. It just got misplaced for a while."

Jim gave a little shrug. "So how did you two end up married? I know he went to Irvine to study."

"I guess that's where Mrs. B. comes in," Rachel said, focusing her attention toward Ann.

"From that September, when rehearsals started until the first week in January, when Mike left for college, we spent a lot of time together. I mean a *lot* of time together. But it was mostly innocent, I swear. Mike was nineteen, and I was seventeen—not to mention my dad didn't like him at all because, well, he was a musician, and you know how my dad was. 'If a man comes home from work not reeking of oil, sweat, and whiskey, then he be not man enough to marry any daughter of mine.'" Rachel laughed, mimicking her father's stern Irish brogue. "Okay, maybe I'm exaggerating a little bit, but you remember how my dad was, right?"

Setting her cup down, Ann laughed. "Do I ever! Oh yeah, I remember very well. He wouldn't stand for any boys chasing after you girls."

Peggy nodded her head as Rachel continued. "One day after rehearsal, we were taking some props back down to the basement. I slammed my hand in one of the cupboards, and it hurt so bad it brought tears to my eyes. Mike had me sit on the stairs while he wiped away my tears, and then, gently kissing my hand, he said, 'Replace the hurt with a kiss from the heart.'"

Looking at her husband, Ann shook her head. "Why can't you say things like that? Go ahead, sweetie," she said turning her attention back to the young woman. "I didn't mean to interrupt."

Rachel smiled at Jim and continued. "I wanted so bad to throw my arms around him and kiss him right then and there, but in walked you, Mrs. B. Even though we hadn't done anything wrong, we felt so guilty we couldn't even look at you. And you just walked by us as if we weren't even there. Without so much as a glance, you said, 'I think you two lovebirds better get back upstairs.'

"We were so embarrassed. I couldn't look you in the eye for days. It was maybe a week or so later, we were standing in the foyer just holding hands, you walked through the front door, and as you passed, you said, 'So how are my lovebirds today?' And again, I was so incredibly embarrassed. I swore I'd never kiss another boy at school ever again." Her eyes twinkled. "It was a promise I didn't keep, of course."

Rachel stopped to take a sip of her coffee, giving Peggy just enough time to tap the table in front of Ann. "You used to catch me kissing boys all the time. It never stopped me."

Rachel laughed. "Boy, is that the truth. It didn't even slow you down, Peg."

"Ha, ha, ha very funny. At least I had boys that wanted to kiss me."

Adjusting herself in the chair, Rachel smirked and went on. "Where was I? Oh yeah! About a week later, I kissed him out in the parking lot and then ran back into the choir room to grab my script. And there you were, Mrs. B., staring out the window. You didn't even turn to face me. You just said, 'Rachel, you two lovebirds need to be careful. If your dad were to see that…well, just be a little more discreet sweetie; that's all.'

"I could've died on the spot. I called Mike that night and told him what you'd said, and he agreed. We knew if my dad ever caught us, he'd pull me and Peggy both out of the play, and he wouldn't have been too nice to Mike either. I can't begin to tell you how careful we were after that.

"But then on opening night, I was so nervous anyway, my whole body was literally shaking. All of a sudden, Mrs. B. walked up to me with Mike and said, 'I need the two of you in my office.'

"I thought I was gonna throw up right there. Without a word we walked upstairs to the office. You unlocked the door and ushered us in. You looked at Mike and said, 'One minute; no longer!' And then you stepped out and closed the door. I stood there speechless. I didn't have a clue what was going on. Then he pulled a little present out of his jacket pocket and handed it to me. My hands were shaking so bad I didn't think I could open it. I just stood there looking at it, at him. I knew for sure I was going to throw up, and at that moment, from the other side of the door, we heard, 'Thirty seconds.'"

Ann stifled a giggle, leaving only a slender grin in the wake of a pleasurable memory.

Rachel too was reliving the moment. "I tore the paper off, and there was a small red velvet box. My hands were shaking so bad…did I say that already? Well, I don't care. They were. I quickly opened it, and inside was this necklace—a beautiful gold chain, and dangling from it, two little gold lovebirds.

"'Fifteen seconds!'

"Mike put it on me, saying, 'Lovebirds forever, Rachel Callahan.' And then he lightly kissed my lips. It was ever so brief, and yet it was the most memorable kiss he ever gave me."

A single tear began to make its silent journey down her cheek. Ann reached for a tissue, but Peg, whose eyes were also teary, had already produced a handful.

"August sixteenth, the day of my eighteenth birthday, I packed up my little Volkswagen and was determined to drive eleven hundred miles down the coast to Irvine. Honestly…I hadn't thought it through. The longest trip I'd ever made alone was a couple hours to Portland, and on the contrary to what everyone believed, my decision to go to Irvine was pretty much spur of the moment. Mike didn't even know. We had only spoken a few times since he'd left, so I thought I would just surprise him.

"As I got ready to leave, my sister freaked out, and my dad disowned me, calling me every name he could think of, and for my dad, that was quite the list. I was crying and shaking so bad I drove four blocks and pulled into the school parking lot, where I just sat on the lawn and tried to figure out what I was doing. Scott Cuzio drove by and waved. Ten seconds later Chris roared by on a motorcycle he'd just bought from Bobby Timmons that morning. He turned around right in the middle of the street, pulled into the parking lot, and joined me on the lawn. I was still pretty upset, but I laid out my game plan, plus all of my what-ifs—you know, what if I go, what if I stay, what if I break down, what if I hate it when I get there, what if, what if, what if? Honestly, I was driving myself crazy with all the what-ifs, so it was nice to have somebody I could talk to about all of it. And after listening to me ramble on, in typical Chris fashion, he said he didn't think I should go. He didn't believe I was doing the right thing, but if my mind was made up, God wouldn't abandon me, and neither would he if I needed him. Mike was a good man, and if that was my decision, he'd keep us in his prayers.

"We only talked for a couple minutes, and then, even surprising myself, I walked over and sat on the bike. I'd never been on a motorcycle in my life, but I said, 'Take me for a ride.' He didn't say a word, just climbed on, and we were off—no helmets, no leather jackets, nothing.

We were rebels without a cause. The wind blowing through my hair…I loved it."

"Who wouldn't love holding on to Chris Peterson for dear life?" Peggy said.

"Would you stop?" Rachel chided. "So then we got back to the school. He just dropped me off, didn't even turn off the bike, and said, 'Don't go anywhere. I'll be back in ten minutes.' He made me swear to it on Peggy's life…I was so tempted to drive away and never look back."

Peggy leaned over and hugged her sister. "But you love me."

With little acknowledgment, Rachel continued. "He got back and parked the bike—but didn't shut it off, mind you. He handed me this little bamboo plant in a gravel-filled vase, quickly explaining he'd read somewhere it was for good luck, and then he stuck a little card in the pocket of my windbreaker, gave me a hug, kissed me on the forehead, quickly asked God to keep me safe, and then took off.

"I think that was when it all hit me. I was suddenly alone and scared to death. I walked up to the practice rooms and was surprised to find Mrs. Bevans making preparations for her summer classes. We waved, and I walked on down to room G. I loved that old piano. It's still there, isn't it?"

Jim nodded his head. "Oh yeah! I'm like you. I love the sound of that old Wurlitzer upright. The trustees put electric keyboards in all the practice rooms, but I wouldn't let them touch that one. It's probably my favorite piano in the place—other than the Steinway, of course. I'm taking it with me when I retire, and they can do what they want with the room after that."

"Well, then I need to get over there one more time before you retire," she blurted.

Obviously annoyed, Ann grumbled, "Yeah, yeah, yeah; old piano. You got in the car and drove to Irvine…I take it Mike was surprised to see you?"

"Oh yeah, he was very surprised. But that lasted less than a minute, and then he was angry, really, really angry." Her lips twisted with disgust. "It all took place on his front porch. He didn't even invite me in the house. He told me this was a prime example of what an inconsiderate, irresponsible, immature little girl I was. That I had no concept of reality and that I should concentrate on my own future, not his."

Her eyes recalled her rage. "I was furious and responded by saying a few things I'm not proud of..."

"Dad would've been proud of you, though," Peggy whispered loudly.

There was no apology in Rachel's tone as she spoke over her sister. "I got back in my car and drove off. I was too mad to cry, but I beat hell out of my steering wheel."

Knowing that same anger, Jim, not wanting to interrupt Rachel's flow or gain his wife's attention, silently chuckled.

The woman's expression softened. "I sat at the end of the block wondering what I was gonna do. A few minutes later, he reached through my window and took the keys. We had an argument right in the street, and he somehow got me in the passenger seat and drove us down to the beach, where we sat watching the sunset."

To avoid speaking as memories dampened her cheeks with a trickle of tears, she brought her hand to lie upon her lips. Tenderly a smile signaled her words it was time to proceed. "We watched the sun set and watched it rise, and somewhere between the two, we became lovebirds again. Five thirty in the morning at the end of Balboa pier, he got down on his knee and proposed in front of five or six fishermen. All I could think of was how Chris would use this as some great biblical illustration. So right there, chuckling to myself, Mike and I started our life together."

Jim knew his wife would have something to say like, oh how sweet, how wonderful, how romantic...but Rachel didn't allow that to happen. She placed her focus directly on him.

"The following year I also was accepted at UC Irvine, as a music theater major." The statement made her laugh, and as she wiped away the remaining tears, her warm, soft laughter seemed to bring the stream to an end. "I know it must be hard for you to believe Mr. B., me a trained stage actress. But still, every once in a while I miss my cue or wander around in circles looking for my mark, so really, I guess not much has changed." She giggled.

"I'm sure a lot has changed..." He laughed, nodding his head. "UC Irvine—that's quite the accomplishment."

"You laid the foundation, Mr. B. All those music interpretation and performance classes—that's what got me in the front door, so thank you, more than I can ever express. Thank you."

He watched Ann roll her eyes. "Yes, yes, he's so wonderful. Now tell me more about you and Mike and the wedding."

Rachel blushed slightly. "Blue jeans and a blouse at a little chapel on the side of Mount Baldy, not long after I arrived."

Peggy giggled. "How long after you arrived?"

Rachel took another quick sip of coffee. "So we lived together, studied together, waited tables together, and once in a great while, we even found jobs acting that paid. We always seemed to make just enough money to get us through the month, but even that didn't seem to matter. We were doing what we loved, with the person we loved. And there were those wonderful times we were able to work onstage together—not just at school, but doing community theater and a couple of dinner playhouse productions. We even did summer stock in Austin one year. And then one summer Mike found this church down by Newport. Without meaning to, he pretty much took over their worship team, which soon included a drama department. I tried to help, but I didn't have much spare time. I wasn't like him; I had to study my butt off to keep my scholarship, whereas with him it just came so easy.

"It was his senior year. The church offered him a full-time salaried position. But he turned it down, saying he didn't feel it would be fair to the church or to God if he couldn't give one hundred percent. I reluctantly agreed with him, even though the money would've been nice, and we sure could have used it. He continued volunteering and studying, and somehow he even found time to do some writing. I mean, I lived with the guy, and I still don't know how he found time to do everything."

At some point Peggy had slipped away and now returned with a variety of cookies. Dunking one in her coffee, Rachel watched it break in half and sink to the bottom. She made no comment, though Ann smiled and Peggy laughed out loud. Again Rachel pressed on.

"The last school play Mike directed was a musical he'd written the year before. No one could believe all four performances sold out, especially with the first scheduled for Valentine's Day—a surprise for me. And it was quite a surprise. Even in the playbill, he'd written this beautiful dedication."

Her eyes betrayed her smile as they again filled with tears. When she spoke, her voice was soft, almost musical. "The play was called *Lovebirds*," she said, smiling at Ann while wiping away another trickle.

But before Ann could react, Jim asked a question he was afraid to hear the answer to. "If you don't mind me asking, where's Mike now? Did he... just up and..."

His voice dropped off, leaving Rachel looking briefly puzzled, and after a moment, she said, "Leave us? No! No he...well, not..."

There was something in her tone, her pause, that lifted Ann's attention and made Jim regret asking the question. Something maybe not meant to be detected, but it brought silence about the four of them; hanging like a thick fog shrouding the conversation. Finally, her eyes filling with tears, her voice just above a whisper, she began to speak.

"I'm sorry Mr. B., Mrs. B. I didn't mean for you to learn this way. I wanted to contact you. I thought about it; honest I did. Over and over I picked up the phone, I started letters, but the next thing I knew, I was surrounded by all this responsibility and fear. I was so numb inside, I couldn't function. I couldn't think, I didn't know what to do. Mike was gone. God had taken him, and I couldn't..."

Jim's heart sank. He watched as Peg put an arm around her sister. Ann grabbed his hand tightly, but oddly, his eyes were drawn to the snowfall. Rachel quickly composed herself but did not rush to begin her story, choosing to allow Jim and Ann time to absorb what they had heard.

Time, Jim thought. *This will take time to digest.*

After a minute, slowly, watchfully, Rachel began. "I swear to you, I didn't know what to do. I felt lost, alone. Even though I had my son, my church, my worship team, I..." Her voice dropped off to nothing.

"It's okay, sweetie. We understand. We're here for you now," Ann said, moving close to hug her.

"But I should've contacted you. Especially you, Mr. B. You did so much for Mike; he loved you. He talked about you all the time to his friends, the worship team, his professors...you were his inspiration. He wanted to come see you. He thought you'd be so proud of him. I'm just sorry he didn't. Forgive me, Mr. B., please."

Unable to speak, Jim simply shook his head and mouthed in a very weak and breathy whisper, "There's nothing to forgive."

Leaning forward and kissing her index finger, she placed it on the back of his hand. "Replace the hurt with a kiss from the heart."

He squeezed her hand and then wiped a tear from her cheek. She smiled, leaned back in her chair, and with a nod assured her sister she was okay.

"Even with all these loving friends around me, I couldn't manage to function. I couldn't stop crying. I felt alone all the time, suffocating emotionally. And I—like a lot of people, like Chris, I'm sure—became angry with God. I screamed at God, shook my fist at him, and finally, one day I just turned my back on him and walked away.

"I was broken, feeling beyond repair. Even when Peg came down to stay with me, I was empty, dead inside. I worried about my son—how he would get along without his dad. The kid loved him so much. Always wanting to be next to him, always underfoot. I can't tell you how they both loved spending time together. He still wears one of his dad's T-shirts to bed sometimes."

Focusing on Ann, she confessed. "Okay, I wear one too." And she immediately raised her hand to stop any possible comments. "You don't have to say anything. I know it's not a good idea. I've read all the books, but the authors of those books are all sleeping with someone they love tonight, and you know what? So am I."

Brushing the hair back from her face, she took a moment to reflect. With emotions intact, she spoke softly. "After an exceptionally lonely day faded into an equally lonely night, I went to bed and broke down. I don't know how long I cried. An hour, two hours, I don't know. But the next thing I knew, my son came in, crawled in next to me, and snuggled close. He told me he had a dream about his daddy, and it woke him up. I held him tighter and told him not to worry; it was just a nightmare. But he insisted it wasn't and began to wipe away my tears. Then he said, 'Everything will be okay, Mommy. Daddy knows we love him and miss him, and he loves us too. But now he's in heaven. Isn't that why we go to church? So we can be with Jesus someday like Daddy?'

"I laid there all night, my son in my arms, my husband in my heart, and my Lord in my life once again."

CHAPTER FIVE

*O*ver the next ten minutes, a number of topics were discussed; however, Jim didn't speak at all. The weight of grief upon him numbed his senses as a continuous reel of long-ago memories paraded through his mind, images of the talented young man he had once so adored. At sixteen Mike had been one the most promising students Jim had ever worked with, and over the next few years under Jim's guidance, he flourished as a musician, becoming one of the most sought-after players in the Seattle area, pursued not only by the Christian community but in secular venues as well. With a natural prowess to blend words and music into a soul-awakening experience, he quickly became a prolific songwriter. It wasn't long before he became interested in the theater, both as an assistant to Jim and a production coach. Within a few months, he had written his first skit, after that came a one-act musical. And like always, Jim was there to assist. They'd work closely through every aspect of the creative processes, spending countless hours developing and fine-tuning Mike's idea, his melodies, or whatever it was until achieving what he recognized as his vision of the project. True, it wasn't always to Jim's liking or taste, but it was Mike's project, and Jim was there only to bring out what the student already saw and heard as an artist. It was through these long, sometimes tedious sessions they built a bond, a friendship that even to this day touched Jim's heart.

With talent comes popularity, something Mike relished though never abused. He was well liked and admired by all, but he had few close friends. He was never pretentious, although his audacious attitude on occasion didn't set well with others, mainly teachers, a pastor or two, most of the elders, three visiting choir directors, and four out of six members of the school board. As for Jim, he loved it, encouraged it, and told Mike many times, "Always stand boldly for what you believe, and let your talent speak loudly for itself." Pearls of wisdom that came back to haunt him more times than he cared to remember. In reality, most of those listed above disagreed with Jim's actions, citing that Mr. Donahue had become disrespectful, even confrontational toward authority. Jim, however, knew Mike's heart, and he knew also the same had been said about him back in the day...and, well, he had turned out all right.

So he continued to encourage the young man, advising him to never be afraid to voice an opinion. Just be willing to listen openly to the opinions of others and graciously accept the final outcome. Jim knew it was that assertive attitude coupled with incredible talent that allowed Mike's artistic vision to soar, develop, and capture perfectly the mood of a scene, lyric, or melody. Of course, not all his concepts were met favorably by the powers in charge. Even Jim winced a time or two.

They had treasured their time working together, and Jim admitted he pushed him pretty hard. This was evident one late afternoon when Mike came to his office angry, confused, and upset, wanting to quit because he felt Jim expected more out of him than anyone else on the team. He was right. Jim did expect more out of him than the rest; his talent demanded that from them both.

"If you expect to achieve the goals you believe yourself capable of," Jim explained, "you'll need to take advantage of every opportunity and set your personal standards well above the rest. And then, someday you might make it beyond the local stage."

Mike never again complained, but instead continually set the bar higher each step of the way, developing his skills and musicianship as a performer, writer, and arranger well beyond anyone's expectations, including his own.

After Mike left for college, Jim believed, half-heartedly anyway, that he would drop by his office someday just to say hello, but that was not to be. Rachel did mention a letter, and Jim wanted desperately to read it, if for no other reason than to feel Mike's presence leap from the page. But for now, in this setting, he would be content to enjoy his memories of a wonderful young man and give thanks to God for briefly allowing their paths to cross.

By this time Ann and the girls had moved on to much lighter fare. There was not the laughter that had earlier segregated them from the studious types scattered about the tables of this caffeinated reading den, and thankfully, nor were there tears. Jim picked up his cup and, without making eye contact, moved stealthily to a small raised table next to the front window, where he stood and continued watching the snow fall gently, silently to the ground. Seconds later he heard Ann say, "He'll be fine. Just needs some alone time." And with that he let his mind frolic through memories like a child through freshly fallen snow. Some made him smile; others left him melancholy, wishing he had somehow found a way to stay in contact with this brilliant student and friend.

After a while he felt a hand on his shoulder. "Mr. B.," he heard Rachel say softly, "I'm sorry..."

But even before his mouth could form the words, his throat tightened in rejection. She took his hand, and a gentle transference of warmth and compassion extended beyond her words, her smile, and her tender eyes, as though her touch alone carried the sentiment of her heart in its appeal. Though she didn't repeat the words, he heard them again, as soft as the wisps of snow drifting to the ground. Once again he felt her lips touch the back of his hand, and it was there he found the strength to speak once more.

"Kisses really do replace the hurt with a heart," he said.

They spent the next few minutes in quiet conversation, embracing memories and sharing smiles.

"Gimme all your lovin', all your hugs and kisses too."

Peg fumbled for her phone, answering in a smoky, seductive voice. "Naughty girl's hotline...umm, is this Santa?"

Her mouth dropped open, and her eyes widened dramatically. Blushing deeply, she bit her lip to stifle a giggle that managed to escape anyway.

"Michael! Put Uncle Kevin on the phone." She blushed, rolling her eyes. "No, you must've heard me wrong. I said 'hottie girl hotline.' Hottie girl— that would be me, Michael—the Hottie Girl...quit laughing and hand the phone to your uncle."

With a serious case of giggles that spread rapidly to the others, she snapped, "Kevin, what were you thinking? Yeah, we'll meet you there in about twenty minutes or so. Yes, yes, yes, we're on our way. Yes, sweetheart…okay! Now… blow me a kiss, and call me your hottie girl. I know he's sitting there; just do it…blow me kisses. Now say it…say it…ooh, I like that; and I wuv you, too, my little shnookums." Impishly, she smiled. "Thanks, babe. Love you too. Gotta go…" With her next breath, her voice sultry, she cooed into the phone, "See you soon…Santa…"

Plans were made for the girls to get together a few days after Christmas for a lunch date. Jim was invited but bowed out due to a previous commitment. All pertinent information was exchanged, Ann providing the girls her and Jim's cell numbers, since he couldn't remember his; loudly proclaiming, "If I can't remember what I did with my phone, how can I be expected to remember the stupid number?"

There were hugs, Christmas wishes, a round of "we'll see you soons," and one last wave goodbye. Ann staked out a position in line, and Jim found himself once again alone, staring through the large front window watching the snow come to rest on the fresh white landscape.

❦

The old man stepped cautiously from the bus into the cold, snow-filled air of his lower downtown neighborhood. "Merry Christmas, young man!" he boomed to the bus driver as he stepped to the curb.

"And to you, old-timer." The door squeaked closed, then opened again swiftly with a jerk. "Say, you need a transfer?"

The old man didn't look back, just raised his hand and waved, making his way down the block. "No, thanks. You drive safe, and have a Merry Christmas," he called back.

Walking steadily the half block, his small apartment on the second floor of a run-down brownstone, sat directly across the street from his destination— the Garden Street Café, a small diner where he had taken supper nearly every evening for the past year and a half. The neighborhood, once a thriving part of the business district, now smelled of big-city blight, decayed buildings, and abandoned storefronts. Cold and colorless, its streetlights, like its future and the future of those living within its impoverished tenements, flickered dimly, their shadows waning; and darkness came, and with it death brought by neglect and abandonment.

With the short walk behind him, the old man, as he did every evening before entering, looked above the door to the gold block lettering across the dingy glass transom. Though it was cracked and peeling, he could clearly make out the words: "Ruth Brother's: EST 1936." He shook his head and smiled as a warm sensation of comfort chased away the persistent chill, one not related to the winter air but to the dour loneliness the day's end relentlessly brought him. Even so, this was always a treasured moment for the old man, and he paused only briefly before walking through the doorway. It was time enough to whisper, "Thank you. Now right this way, my darling."

Swinging open the thick glass door with its iron security bars, he would be greeted by the surprisingly pleasant aromas of the daily special wafting through the air, filling his nostrils with homemade goodness and warmth. Never rushing, he sauntered with poise and took his usual place at the first stool along the age-worn hardwood counter. A few odds and ends and a wall of old photographs were all that remained of the original restaurant. Slowly, methodically, and by doing most of the work themselves, the current owners had reestablished the room's original charm. A welcome change from his first dining experience there, for sure.

At that time, the walls were painted with grease and nicotine from years gone by. The lights hung from the ceiling by long black cords, their bulbs dressed in soiled scalloped shades, circa 1940. But the tile floors, though discolored, chipped, and cracked, were for the most part clean. He had never imagined himself dining in such an establishment, much less becoming its most regular customer. How many times that first year after moving in across the street had he stood looking in through the dirt-streaked front window only to retreat back to his apartment still hungry? In addition to the hunger, there were nights his heart would not allow restful sleep, painting his dreams with visions of his beloved wife, bringing him to flee his bed soaked in sweat and misery to walk the deserted streets for hours in search of nothing more than complete and total exhaustion.

It was at the end of one of these late-night wanderings that he found himself standing in front of the diner, cold and damp from the evening's unremitting drizzle. As he stepped from the curb to walk the short distance to his apartment, there came a sudden downpour, forcing him to turn and seek shelter in the doorway of the diner. There he stood trembling, not so much from the cold as from the years of suppressed emotion that now unexpectedly heightened with such intensity and swiftness he'd never known before. Clinching his hands around the iron bars of the door, he bowed his head and sobbed, "I know you can hear me Lord; I miss her. I miss her so much."

As he stepped backward over the cracked pavement into the darkened street, large drops of rain pelted his upturned face. Stretching his arms out to his side, he wailed. "Lord, if you're not going to call me home, lay your hand on my heart. Minister to its restless cries, Lord. Please. Please. She was my li…" his voice breaking, he sobbed profoundly. The rain became even more intense, yet the old man stood his ground, praying, lifting his hands to the heavens. Lightning flashed in the distance. "Lord, hear my prayer. Please, Lord." He sighed breathlessly into the night.

Slowly blinking away the water, he opened his eyes, and though strained with age and fatigue, the world somehow miraculously snapped into focus a sight he'd never noticed before. A warm, comforting glow beckoned his attention to the lettering on the transom above the doorway. Shaking the rain from his face, he stepped closer, and then rushed closer still. Clearing the rain and tears from his eyes with a brush of his sleeve, he anxiously stood reading it once again, then again, and still again. His laughter filled the street, even drowning out the sound of the rain and the approaching roll of thunder.

"Thank you, Lord," he cried out. "Your humor is only surpassed by your mercy and love." Then, for the first of what would become his evening custom, he pushed the door open and stepped inside. It was not the run-down interior or the stale coffee offered in an old, darkly stained mug that made him feel welcome. Yet he did. For the first time in years, he felt elated, filled with a sense of being whole again, complete, as though recovering a part of himself that had been absent for so many years. It was then the old man realized that with God, there is nothing left to chance. This had been God's plan all along. After all, that could be the only explanation for the sign above the door. It was God's hand that painted it all those many years ago. To be an answer to prayer, a comfort for one broken-down old man filled with despair, his optimism as vacant as the streets he roamed. God knew his prayer even back then, knew how he would agonize for the wife he loved so desperately, so preciously. Yes, his wife—born Ruth Anne Brothers, August 28, 1936.

From that night on, he would push the door open, giving thanks to the Lord and tenderly inviting his wife to join him.

"I was gettin' a little troubled over you, Peter," said the waitress, pouring him a cup of coffee. Her gentle smile, always there to greet no matter the time of day or how many hours she'd been on her feet, was now twisted, demonstrating her agitation. The woman's light-blond hair, pulled into a short ponytail, was streaked with silver strands that had begun to appear five years ago, just after her twenty-fifth birthday. And though her name tag read Noreen, Rennie was what she had gone by since running away with her boyfriend, Dutch Harmon, at age fifteen.

She placed the pot back on the warmer, crossed her arms, and tapped her foot. "I thought you might of forgot we're closin' up early today—Christmas Eve and all."

"Rennie, I'm so sorry. I was afraid you'd already be gone, so I was thrilled when I stepped off the bus to see the lights still on," the old man said apologetically.

A large, rough-looking man in his midthirties peered around the metal wheel hanging in the center of the pass-through. "Aah, she's been frettin' about you for hours. Hell, she's run outside a dozen times looking up and down that street for ya. I'm surprised her feet didn't get frostbit. I told her you were probably getting' drunk and chasing women at some Christmas party somewhere." He laughed and took a short sip from a black Harley-Davidson mug. "You know, Pete, you put on one of them Santa outfits, and man, you'd have all the ladies from miles around lining up to sit on your lap. Girls got a thing for you, that's for sure. It's them whiskers, if you ask me."

"Nobody asked you." Rennie barked, moving quickly to the pass-through. "Dutch, it's Christmas Eve. Don't be an ass."

"Aah..." he waved her off, winking at the old man.

Dutch and Rennie had taken the place over two years prior, only three days after arriving in Tacoma from Landers Creek, Georgia. Amara Stevens, the owner at the time, had just ended her third marriage and buried her father all in the same month. Her ex left her with a rat-infested double-wide she promptly abandoned, a box of bills, a piece-of-junk Chevy pickup, and a rash she needed to have looked at soon. Her father, on the other hand, left her $12,000 and the keys to a long-outdated family business, which in her opinion and that of almost everyone else she had talked to, was worthless. Even the salvage companies weren't interested.

She started working with her father at age ten and at some point in her late teens dreamed of someday getting a job as a cocktail waitress in one of the quaint little bars along the Oregon coast, or maybe even at that big casino in Lincoln City. Lately she'd fantasize about hitting a mega jackpot and hooking up with some good-looking guy who didn't live in a trailer and actually had a paying job. A guy who wouldn't beat her up or cheat on her or just up and leave, like most of the men she'd encountered. With it being only a six-hour drive to the Oregon coast, she would escape everything that had always chained her down to this godforsaken place. Simply drive off and never look back—it should be easy; her father was dead, the business was dead, her marriage was dead, there were no excuses left, and no reason to stay. But could a change of scenery really change her life? Of course it could. It would; it had to. At twenty-seven, all she had in life was $12,000 and her good looks. If she stayed here any longer, both would be spent soon.

That morning she sat at the counter, memories washing over her in waves, never expecting it to be so hard to walk away. But she refused to cry over this slum hole. The faces of long-past relatives stared down at her from the many photographs that hung on the walls—images captured through the decades, depicting her family history and the history of the very room where she sat. From the time she was a little girl, she imagined the photos were there watching over her, her guardian angels, but today she felt as though they were glaring, their eyes cold with anger and hurt, their smiles a frozen mockery of laughter at what a miserable failure she had become, someone who would always just up and walk away from hard times instead of spending time working hard to make things better.

From her pocket she produced a small leather pouch. Dumping its contents onto the counter, her hands moved with the skill only countless repetitions bring. Soon she held the thick glass pipe to her lips, and then came a snap followed by an orange glow. As she inhaled deeply, her eyes scanned the faces on the wall.

"Isn't this why you all came—to watch me fail once again? Six and a half weeks of sobriety up in smoke, as they say. Well, I don't care. Today I'm leaving you all, and you'll never have to see me again. You can just hang around this place until it rots out from under you."

Again she placed the pipe to her lips, but her laughter snatched it away. "None of you even got my joke...you can just...hang around—get it? Hang around." Her laughter disappeared in a wash of disgust. "Aah, forget it. None of you were ever bright enough to get my humor anyway. You never understood me, any of you."

Grabbing a beer from the cooler and walking into the kitchen, she turned on her father's grease-laden boom box. Sharing his taste in classic rock and country, she began swaying back and forth as Garth Brooks filled the small kitchen area and a little part of her heart.

"I'm gonna miss you, Daddy!" she whispered to his apron still hanging from the peg next to the doorway. She increased the volume, made her way out to the counter, and stuffed the leather pouch and its contents back into her pocket. There weren't many things she wanted from the old place, but she managed to fill a small box with a few possessions that at one time or another had meant something to her. At the bottom of her third beer, she walked to the middle of the room and looked around for what she knew would be the very last time. She removed only two pictures from the walls, their outlines left to glare nakedly back into the room like eyes in a giant mask. And for the first time in her life, Amara felt eerily unwanted in the building where she had spent most of her life.

She'd already gone through her father's upstairs apartment the day before, removing personal items from the closet, a stack of old papers in a drawer, and two cartons of cigarettes from the top of the fridge. The cupboards were filled with a mish mosh of dented pots and pans; an assortment of chipped dishes and cups, no two alike; and drawer upon drawer of tarnished utensils and flatware all collected through the years from the diner. But it was in the bedroom she found an unexpected surprise: sitting on his dresser in a frame with broken glass, an old picture he'd taken of her mother some twenty-four years ago, just a week before she'd left them both to run off with a guy from Brooklyn, never to be heard from again.

Setting the clothes in a box next to the alley, she knew someone would come along and get some use out of them. Everything else went into the dumpster. Now, it was time to leave…perhaps another beer or two and a couple more songs, she thought, moving toward the cooler. "No, I have beer and music out in the truck. Why do I want to hang out in this old dump?" But as luck would have it, Dutch and Rennie walked in hoping to find a cheap breakfast. After all, that was what the sign out front advertised.

It was just after noon when they returned to their rust-eaten camper parked in the vacant lot directly behind the building. Even with his stomach still empty and grumbling, Dutch returned satisfied. In his hand was a manila envelope, its contents a signed contract of ownership to the name Garden Street Café; all the contents, including appliances and furnishings (every piece in desperate need of repair); two sets of keys; the combination to the safe; and the phone numbers to the building's management company. Dutch had definitely returned satisfied, not to mention $2,500 lighter.

Sitting in the tight confines of their camper, where everything they owned was stuffed into large green trash bags and old tattered suitcases, or loosely crammed, jammed, or wedged into cracks, crevices, and holes, Dutch was bursting with excitement.

"This is a great day, baby. Who'd of thought we'd own our own business? And for just twenty-five hundred bucks. Oh man, Rennie, I feel good about this, baby. Really, really good. This move is gonna change our luck. Damn, it's gonna change our whole life."

He thought for a moment, cracking open a fresh Budweiser. His cheeks flushed, and his eyes widened. "Damn, baby. It's already changing…we've only been here three days, and we're already business owners, Rennie. Yeah, man, our luck's changin', baby. I can't ever remember being this happy… 'cept for maybe the day I married you."

He drained the bottle with one continuous tip. "Isn't this great, Rennie? Isn't it great? Hell, let's go upstairs and check out that apartment she was talkin' about comes with the place. She said it has furniture and everything. Damn, Rennie, we can move in right now," he yelled, grabbing another Bud. "Baby, I'm so excited. Ain't ya excited, Rennie? Ain't ya excited?" Careful not to spill his beer, Dutch leaped to his feet and began to dance.

Rennie watched for a few seconds and then looked down to the small table before her. There lay the remainder of their life savings—forty-three dollars and change. Rennie was far less excited.

❖

Sitting at his usual spot at the counter, a hot cup of coffee waited.

"How was your last day at the bookstore?" she asked.

"Oh, Rennie, I met the most wonderful little boy today!" the old man beamed. Then a pall of confusion washed over him as Rennie disappeared through the swinging door leading into the kitchen and quickly returned without her apron and without a word. Quickly she headed toward the front door. "We're locking up. You need to do something with that coffee."

Holding the warm cup tightly in his hand, the old man sat stunned. There was a loud click as the lights at the far end of the room went out, followed by a second click that darkened the kitchen except for a small light from somewhere in the back.

Dutch appeared from the darkness, hastily moving to the end of the counter. "Don't worry; I grabbed ya a to-go cup, 'cause me and Rennie need to be gettin' a move on. We're gonna have us a real special Christmas Eve dinner. Slow cooked prime rib with all the fixins."

The old man was embarrassed. More unsure than unstable, he gathered himself slowly. "I'm sorry…" he said, standing up and placing a dollar bill on the counter. "I guess time just got away from me this afternoon. Please, both of you, accept my apology. I didn't mean to detain you. Go, enjoy that wonderful dinner. It sounds magnificent."

Though his voice remained cheerful, his eyes held glints of sadness. The wooden floorboards creaked a sharp echo through the large, empty room as he walked slowly for the door. Putting a hand in his overcoat pocket, he felt the shallow rectangular box he'd wrapped the night before. Thinking that he'd almost forgotten to give it to them brought a new flush of embarrassment, instantly cooled by a sigh of relief. Retrieving the box proved difficult, causing him to stop midway to the door and try more diligently. But even then it would not lift out easily. The narrow box had slipped through a long slit worn in the bottom of his pocket and lay trapped in the lining of the jacket.

Dutch snatched up the dollar bill, folded it with one hand, and then walked up to the old man. "Hey, coffee's on me tonight. Merry Christmas." He laughed.

The old man continued in his attempt to retrieve the box. Placing one hand under his jacket, he held it in place using the lining. Then, working the other hand through his pocket, he maneuvered the slit deep enough over the box to tightly grasp it.

"You know, Pete, I don't want to be late for this dinner it means a lot to us."

"Yes! Yes, Dutch, I'm hurrying. It's just I have a little something in my pocket I'd like to…"

"It really is important to us Peter…" Rennie added.

With great frustration the old man huffed, "I can't seem to get this blasted thing out of my pocket, and I know I won't see you two tomorrow. So if you'll just give me a minute…"

Dutch didn't acknowledge the old man's struggle but took him by the shoulders. "Hold on a second, Pete. Do you know what makes a Christmas Eve dinner so damn special?" he asked, stuffing the dollar bill in the old man's shirt pocket. "It's when ya can spend it with family. And, well, tonight for the first time in…hell, I don't know how long, me and Rennie are gonna be able to do just that—to have Christmas Eve dinner with family."

"Oh, you have guests coming. I'm so excited for you, Dutch. I don't want to hold you up any longer, but I have this…"

"Pete, look at me. I don't think you understand."

The old man looked into the man's steel blue eyes, but it was unclear what they held. The box slowly moved into his hand and rested on the lip of the pocket.

"Well..." Dutch began, "you been coming in here every night since we bought the place, and I know it's not because of my gor-may cookin', and you're too much of a godly man to be chasing after my Rennie. So for the life of me, I don't know why the hell you keep showing up."

The old man's head tilted in bewilderment. Had he done something to anger Dutch? In his search to understand, he looked to Rennie, but she quickly glanced away, busying herself by turning the sign in the window to read Closed. His mouth suddenly felt dry, and his hands began to quiver. There was a need to take a deep breath, yet even that eluded him. His throat was tight, his face flush; he felt the sudden sting of despondency cloud his eyes. And for a moment the box slid easily back into his pocket, but he couldn't let it go. After all, he had brought it to give to them.

"But I'm sure glad you do," Dutch shouted with a smile.

The old man had no time to react as Dutch continued.

"Pete, I want to thank you for being the man you are. I feel like you're more than a friend. Damn, Pete, you're one of the best guys I've ever known. And...well..." Dutch looked at the floor and shook his head. He didn't like this; he'd been raised to believe real men didn't bare their feelings to anyone other than their mother, and maybe their wife on occasion, but never ever toward another man. There were just certain things you didn't do, didn't say, and having never spoken to another man in this manner, he was feeling uneasy, self-conscious, as though he was stripped naked, exposed for the whole world to see.

It was now his turn to look to Rennie for assistance, but she remained silent, standing by the door, arms folded, conveying her Mona Lisa smile Dutch recognized as telling him, "You're doing great, baby. Just keep right on going."

So he did. His words felt like rocks and were hard to roll off his tongue. He had never spoken of such things or expressed such feelings with anyone other than Rennie, and even then it would be due to her mulish insistence.

"Well, I guess what I'm trying to say is..." Again Dutch paused, his words getting heavier, rolling slower each time he opened his mouth. "Is...just that...well...Rennie...well, she thinks of you as family, and well, dammit, Pete, so do I."

Suddenly the words began to come easier. "But I gotta tell ya, you're a far better man than any in my family. Rennie's too, for that matter. You're always kind and caring and giving. You've never had anything bad to say about anybody I know of."

Dutch seemed to have found his voice and didn't want to slow down in fear he would miss saying something he felt important for the old man to hear.

"And yeah, my language sometimes gets away from me, but not once have you ever said a word, or rolled your eyes, or any of that. You just let me go on and on and on. And over the years, you and me and Rennie, we've all sat and talked football and hunting, beer and marriage, and everything else under the sun. You even showed us some business stuff that if you hadn't... well, damn, I'm just glad you did. And I don't know how, but you always seem to roll everything around to being like something in the Bible. Not preaching! No, you've never preached at me. And I can't explain it, but over the years, me and Rennie have listened to ya, and I like to think we've learned a little something and become better people for it. And on more than one occasion, something you said would come back to us in the middle of a big ol' fight, and next thing you know...well, let's just say I enjoy the making up part, if you know what I mean."

Rennie tapped her foot, raised her eyebrows, and once again, Dutch was in line and focused.

"Oh...dang it, Pete. I'm not any good at this kind of talk," he ruffled. "So I'm just gonna get right to it. You see, we were talkin', and...well...she thinks of you kinda like a...a dad."

Dutch didn't have to look at Rennie to feel her eyes piercing through him like needles pushing through a voodoo doll. Backpedaling, he quickly added, "And so do I. Hell, you've taught me more and spent more time talking to me than my own dad ever did."

Looking to Rennie, her smile of approval encouraging, he continued. "So here's the thing: you're coming up to our place for dinner. Christmas

Eve dinner. That's what families do—they have a big old Christmas Eve feast. Now, we've been fixing up stuff all day. Wait 'til you try some a Rennie's cornbread and honey butter. I know most people don't think of cornbread with prime rib, but you just wait, I'm telling ya. And you know what, Pete—I mean Peter—I know you prefer to be called Peter; I just forget… anyway, Peter, you can say one of them blessings people say on holidays and such. I'd like that. I'd like that a whole lot. Wouldn't we, Rennie?"

The old man was stunned, speechless. The last Christmas Eve dinner—or any meal, for that matter—he had shared with another human being was with his beloved Ruth Anne, five years ago. It was not the food, standard hospital fare, that remained locked in his memory, but how her beautiful sapphire blue eyes shone clear and bright that evening for the first time in months. So lustrous, like pools of moonlit water filled with tenderness and a deep peacefulness so soothing, so calming, and so inviting the thought of leaving her side never approached him.

He sat on her bed making up stories of people and places they'd known; a familiar task he had performed for her amusement countless times over countless years. He watched as she began to drift. Her eyes fluttered, opening once momentarily to search for him. Softly she smiled, her forefinger gliding leisurely over the top of his hand, coming to rest with a gentle tap and then gliding back again. Her smile did not fade but simply relaxed, and he knew he would never again gaze into the eyes that had loved him for nearly sixty years. There he remained, holding her hand, stroking her forehead, continuing to speak to her lovingly.

❦

"Peter?" Rennie asked, concerned by his distant stare.

His eyes were moist, and in contrast to his snow-white beard, his cheeks, a rich deep red, seemed to almost glow. "Rennie, Dutch, I…I don't know quite what to say. I'm afraid you've left me speechless."

Dutch smiled at the old man's delight, but even more so in knowing he could safely tuck away all that sentimental sissy stuff that made him feel so uncomfortable, so downright weird inside. Surely Rennie wouldn't expect him to get all gushy gooey, sweetie pie, lovey-dovey for a long, long time after this. After all, Dutch would be the first to tell you, it's a proven fact, a man can only hold so many feelings in him at a time, and right this minute, Dutch felt pretty much drained and wanted to keep it that way for some time to come.

It was a great feast, just as promised. Their modest apartment, redecorated with paintings and furniture from a local thrift store, had little room for the small Christmas tree next to the window overlooking Garden Street. Just off the kitchen was the dining area. A table that had nicely sat the three of them, now cleared from dinner, held three empty cups of coffee. The clock in the living room began to chime, but no one noticed the time—only that it was getting late.

"Rennie; would you be so kind as to bring my overcoat," the old man asked.

She returned with the coat, and the old man draped it across his lap. With ease he retrieved the gift-wrapped box and held it in his hands for a long moment before placing it between Dutch and Rennie. Dutch began to protest, but the old man stopped him with the slightest raise of his hand.

"Merry Christmas to the only kids I've ever had. I know my Ruth Anne would've loved you both. Especially you, my dear. She always wanted a little girl."

Rennie smiled. The old man took her hand. "I need to be going," he said quietly. "It was a wonderful dinner, and I'll never be able to thank you enough for this most beautiful evening." Pausing a moment, he looked at the gift, and then a faint smile moved over his face. "I would love for you to attend church with me tomorrow morning, Dutch. And, of course, you too, Rennie. But if you already have plans, I understand."

Responding hastily, Rennie laughed. "I can't remember the last time we had plans for anything, so I think it's a great idea. I haven't been to a Christmas service since I was a kid. Thank you, Peter. This'll be great. We'll all go together, say seven thirty in front of the restaurant."

Dutch looked as if someone hit him in the forehead with a bat. "Seven thirty! Are you two nuts? It's Christmas, for Pete's sake. " Quickly he looked at the old man. "Sorry, Peter. That's just one of them expressions. I didn't mean to offend you."

"No offense taken," the old man said with a grin. He could sense Rennie had inadvertently pushed her husband's buttons, and that always made for interesting entertainment, providing the young lady didn't squelch the fire before it could flame, and the old man was not about to let that happen… not tonight anyway. So stroking the whiskers on his chin, pretending to think out loud, he added, "Yes, seven thirty. Hmm…that would certainly ruin the whole morning…" And then he let his pocket watch tick twice before saying, "But then again, Reverend Parker is having a six o'clock service if you'd prefer. That would leave us plenty of time to stop by the mission. They always need help with breakfast, you know, especially so on Christmas." And that, Peter thought, should provide a sufficient spark.

Rennie fought back the urge to giggle, aware of the old man's intentions. "That's a wonderful idea, Peter," the woman said cheerily. "Shall we say five thirty then?"

The small room fell quiet. Dutch, unable to find his voice, quivered wide-eyed with disbelief. When he finally did speak, it came as a gush of blathering syllables, none actually forming words. He paused to regroup; this took less than another tick of the old man's watch, and then, bringing both hands down hard on his lap, Dutch roared, "Five thirty? Have you two lost your mind? I don't plan on even getting dressed until noon; matter a fact, I may not get dressed it all. It's a holiday. Don't church folk get holidays? I mean, everything's closed on Christmas. What makes the church so damn special they need to stay open? Especially that bleeping early. Don't they know people are opening gifts, making memories, drinking Mimosas… come on, what the hell…it's Christmas, for Pete's sake."

Dutch threw his hands up, shaking his head, continuing to rant. "Nah, I can't do it. Maybe sometime when it's not a holiday. Then we'll go if they have something around ten or eleven. Check and see. Maybe they got something in the afternoon. I like to sleep in on Sundays. But no, we can't do tomorrow. Not on Christmas, no way! That's just stupid crazy."

Folding his arms across his chest, he leaned back in the chair, looking around the room as though surveying his kingdom. With an air of self-satisfaction, Lord Dutch had spoken, and there would be no further discussion on the subject.

The old man was beaming. "Yes indeed, a most wonderful evening." He laughed loudly. "An incredible feast," he added. "Most enjoyable indeed." Shaking the younger man's hand, he stood to leave. Cupping Rennie's outstretched hands in his, he winked. "And the entertainment, my dear, was delightful."

The cold air met him at the top of the steep stairwell. He was stiff from sitting so long and knew it would take time to navigate the uneven stairs down to the street. He had declined Dutch's offer for assistance, assuring his friend he could walk just fine by himself, a luxury age had not yet stolen from him.

※

Rennie stood at the window watching the old man make his way along the sidewalk. Picking up the box, she gave it a gentle shake. "What do you think it is?"

"Hell, I don't know. Probably some little thing he picked up at that bookstore, I imagine. And what'd he mean by entertainment? Did you catch that?"

She hadn't heard anything Dutch said. Her attention focused on the bottom of the box, where a neatly folded note had been securely taped. It was apparent the hand that had written it had done so with a slight tremble. They looked at each other as Rennie carefully unfolded it and began to read:

My dear Rennie and Dutch,

I'm afraid my penmanship has surrendered to the infirmities of age, so I will try to keep this short and legible. For a long time you two have been a tremendous blessing to me. I've felt a great love for you both, much the way a father feels for his children, and I believe now is the time for me to pass something on…to my children.

Open the box.

I'm not going to ask that you accept these, because I believe, as happened with me and my Ruth Anne, when you slip them on, you will feel the love of those who have worn them before, and you will never want to remove them. So it is with love that I now pass them to you. As a symbol of your love, wear them. Allow each one to represent the heart your partner has placed in your hands and in your care for the remainder of your life. May they also serve as a reminder of God's love—endless, precious, and free. You are in my prayers, God's grace, and blessings. Merry Christmas.

PS.

And if you value our friendship, my patronage, there will never be a discussion on this matter. (I hope I make myself clear, Dutch.) Not a word. No discussion; no returns; no problem.

Merry Christmas,
I love you both,
P.

Rennie held the rings for a moment in the palm of her hand and then placed them on the table as if unbelieving. Dutch could not take his eyes off them. He lowered himself into his chair, continuing to stare at their brilliance.

"Put it on me!" Rennie said, looking at Dutch. "Oh, I know we can't keep 'em; just put it on me. I want to feel you put it on my hand. I've never had a ring, and you know that's been just fine with me, but I want the opportunity to feel what it's like when your husband slides a ring onto your finger…"

Dutch didn't see the tears in her eyes, but he moved almost mechanically to fulfill her wish. His thoughts were elsewhere.

"Oh my God, Dutch. They're beautiful. The diamonds are so…sparkly. And look on the side. There's a little cross. There's one on yours too. These are so…so beautiful. Try it on. It can't hurt to just try it on. I know we can't keep 'em, but look how beautiful. Even the man's is so beautiful…I can't believe this ring belonged to his wife. She wore it for, I think he once said, sixty years. It has to mean more to him than anything in the world. For him to part with these… well, I just can't believe…"

Dutch rushed to the window and saw the old man only a few feet from the entry to his building. He dashed from the apartment, taking the dark, narrow stairway in three long leaps. He didn't feel the cold on his bare arms as he ran down the street. Peter, startled by the clatter of the door, turned to be tightly embraced. It was not the run that left Dutch gasping, but the tears that stole his breath. He held the old man tightly, sobbing, and the old man held him in his arms.

Dutch somehow forced himself to speak. "My dad up and left when I was two, and my mom, she cared more about partyin' than she ever did about me. Except for Rennie, there ain't never been anyone love me."

"There is now," the old man softly assured Dutch, feeling him sob again and again.

After a few minutes, Dutch whispered into the scarf around the old man's neck, "So, Dad, what time did you say church starts?" And without letting go, Dutch glanced at the ring he would continue to wear for the remainder of his life.

Across the street, the curtain in the second-floor window did not relax until the old man looked up and saw Rennie smile and blow him a kiss. She walked into the bedroom and lay across the bed reading the note once more before moving to the closet and placing the note in her secret box that held memories from her childhood through to the last birthday card Dutch had given her. And even though he had given it to her a month early…she never said a word.

❦

"As I lay me down to sleep,
"I pray the Lord my soul to keep.
"If I should die before I wake,
"I pray my soul the Lord to take.
"God bless Patches and Kiki, and Grandma, and Grandpa, and…"

An hour earlier, a continuous medley of Christmas songs accompanied the smells of fresh-baked cookies up the stairway, where the buttery aroma even now lingered in the air. There was a hug and a kiss, a soft touch to the cheek, and a gentle click from the princess lamp on the nightstand. The sound of footfalls stopped, turned, and paused in the frame of the doorway.

"Close those pretty blue eyes. You have a big day tomorrow."

"Daddy?"

"Yes, sweetheart?"

"Sometimes I miss Mommy."

"I know you do, Beth. So do I."

From the chimney, smoke rose and drifted slowly through the branches of the snow-covered evergreens, the air motionless, disturbed only by the gentle sound of small waves lapping at the black rocks that shone through the snow, etching a faint outline of the water's edge around Brennan's Cove. A soft warm glow poured from the front window of the home, falling across the large wooden porch to stretch over the white drifts before gradually fading into the darkness of the forest beyond. There was a rustling deep within the distant brush, a muted cry, and then…only darkness.

CHAPTER SIX

The air was crisp in the morning light. Mount Rainier stood majestically, watching over the Brooks backyard. On a clear day, this fourteen-thousand-foot volcano can be seen from as far away as Portland, Oregon, to the south and Vancouver, British Columbia, to the north, but it's rare that the mountain makes a full appearance at all. It's shy, slumbering under a year-round blanket of snow and an almost ever-present bank of clouds, only peeking out occasionally as if to glimpse the presumptuous people erecting cities and neighborhoods throughout its narrow valleys, carved remnants of an earlier destructive path that undoubtedly will someday carry its molten flow to the banks of Puget Sound once again. Yet still we encroach upon its slopes, undaunted, drawing ever closer to its deadly beauty.

But it was mornings like this Jim loved standing on the deck, a warm cup of coffee in his hand, taking in the grandeur of the mountain, silence filling the air as he listened to it sleep. The snow had continued to fall well into the afternoon on Christmas Day, but now, after a day of filtered sun, the distant countryside stretched out like a Bev Doolittle canvas. Patches of brown and white fashioned a hidden Pinto landscape along the edge of the foothills while the mountain pulled her snowy blanket tight around her peak. Jim watched as an eagle launched into flight from the evergreens atop the bluff overlooking Ohop Lake. Soon it was joined by a second, and together they soared, circling, disappearing over a rise of trees, reappearing minutes later to his almost silent encore of approval. Yes, he loved mornings like this.

"Good morning," Ann stated, sliding open the patio door to peek her head out. "Do you need that warmed up?"

"Yeah, sure. Thanks."

Taking his cup, she disappeared and then returned to the deck with hot coffee for two. "Looks like a beautiful morning."

"I watched the eagles head out for breakfast this morning."

Mid-sip, over the rim of her cup, Ann looked at him. "If that's your way of asking me to the Eagles Nest for breakfast, it won't work. You know I hate that place."

Scanning the empty sky, he pointed to the bluff. "There were two circling the lake a bit ago." Steam rose from his cup. "But now that you mentioned it, I could go for some breakfast. What do you say I treat you to Flo's?"

Averting her eyes from her search of the sky, she again lifted her cup. "I can't this morning. I have some things to do, but I'll take a rain check."

"Yeah, I should head out pretty soon myself. I'd like to get to the cabin around noon. I still have that half a cord of wood Jim Mare's son delivered back in November. It'll need to be split and stacked."

Watching Ann's reaction, Jim wanted to believe she was again searching the sky for the eagles and not just rolling her eyes, although her cynical smile indicated otherwise. Shaking her head in mild disbelief, she smiled smugly. "I thought you were going to pay him to do that?"

"No! I'm more than capable of doing it myself. Besides, it'll be good exercise."

"Yeah it'll be great—if you don't have a heart attack or bury the ax in your foot."

"I know how to split wood, thank you, and my heart's just fine," he assured her, raising his cup in tribute to his good health.

"Just keep your cell phone handy," she said seriously. "You do have your cell phone, right? No, let me rephrase that! You *will* have your cell phone…right." Her smile had completely disappeared, replaced by the infamous ice stare.

"I do. It's right here in my shirt pocket, and I won't let it out of my sight until you get there. And look," he boasted, holding it close for her to see, "fully charged, turned on, and ready to go. So, what do you think of that!"

Hoisting his sails of pride and arrogance, Jim watched them billow with an air of self-satisfaction. But without so much as a glance, a glimpse, a nod, a peek, or a visual acknowledgment of any sort, Ann noted, "It'll be dead by morning. Did you pack the charger?"

There was a moment of silence as his once-proud sails quickly deflated around him. Fortunately, a familiar pawing sound at the patio door drew Ann's attention. It was Jass, the five-year-old yellow Lab, eagerly wanting to join them for a little fresh air. The dog liked to be out in the cold and even enjoyed playing in the snow, and he insisted on taking Jim for a walk once a day, rain or shine, whether Jim needed it or not. Staying close by Jim's side, he led the man to the long row of mailboxes at the end of the lane, sniffing out information on who or what had been on his road recently. But once they reached the mailbox, the game began. Jass would rush back toward the house, getting fifty or sixty yards ahead before running back to nuzzle the contents in his master's hand. Once satisfied no one had mailed him a cheeseburger, he again rushed off to patrol his road.

As a rambunctious pup, Jass became an avid participant in the sport of deer chasing, an event that only lasted mere seconds yet left him feeling daring and courageous right up to naptime, when he would dream of the chase all over again. But he held a healthy respect for the elk that were sometimes seen grazing in the open fields around the house. Watching from a safe distance, his piercing barks and low vicious growls alerted the herd of his ferocity, frightening them into a frenzied stampede, resulting in more of a nonchalant stroll before stopping to graze once again. Even so, you would never see him charge them like he did the deer, because they, as it turned out, were avid participants in the sport of dog chasing. And that was a game Jass didn't care for at all.

Along with the deer and elk, Jim would sometimes get a reprieve from the games during wintertime. In the Northwest there is no such thing as late afternoon during the winter months, because it gets dark early, around four thirty or so. And once the sun went down, Jass never ventured out beyond his own backyard. Even when nature called, the yard must be lit up by dual floodlights, and he would still wait for someone to walk out the door first before cautiously moving to the lawn. It wasn't that he was afraid of the dark; he did just fine in the house with the lights out. Even riding in the car at night was not a problem. But to be outside, under the stars, exposed to the elements, where wild animals roamed and something might get his tail…no! Not the dark, not by himself. Not ever!

He loved a campfire as long as there were people to sit next to, or to play with in the glowing light. Of course, when it burned down to just embers, playtime was over, and it was time to find someone to lie next to or seek suitable shelter. So it was true—he might not be the bravest pooch on the block, but in his defense, he was an irrefutable protector, standing ready and willing to defend home and family against any and all unwelcome intruders. This had been proven on two occasions. The first was when Jim wanted to surprise his wife with the fulfillment of his boyhood dream to own a motorcycle. And not just any motorcycle, a Harley—a great, big, loud, look-at-me-ain't-I-bad Harley-Davidson.

Jim asked Chris Peterson if he and his wife, Linda, would mind picking it up at the dealership for him. They could bring it out to the house and hide it in the barn along with all his new riding gear, and when he and Ann got home, they'd all have a little barbecue, and they'd share in the big surprise. But halfway through the barbecue, Jim quietly sneaked off to the barn, where he donned his new black leather boots, pants, chaps, jacket, gloves, and shiny black helmet with a dark-tinted visor. He thought he looked and felt ominous, almost interplanetary. Without a doubt his wife would ooh and ahh over her modern-day black knight riding up on his powerful chrome steed.

Believing the noise would somehow lessen the surprise, he decided not to ride it into the backyard. This was an easy and wise decision, considering he'd never ridden a motorcycle before and was not completely clear on how to start the thing or what to do once it was running. Because of where the barn sat, it was easy for him to push it unnoticed along the back fence, where he adjusted his helmet, pulled down the visor, and rushed quickly through the gate into the yard. Big mistake. Big, big mistake! Before he could say a word, coming at him full force, all teeth and claws, bristled fur and eyes of fire, looking like a possessed hound from hell…was Jass.

As he attempted to escape, his muffled cries filling the helmet remained largely unheard. He ran back through the gate and directly into and over his brand-new Harley, breaking his right arm just below the elbow. As he lay helplessly sprawled across the bike, Jass immediately found the only part of his body not protected by leather, and…well, Jim still had a scar where Dr. Campbell stitched up his…left cheek. Needless to say, right there in the doctor's office, Ann nixed the motorcycle idea, citing that if he could have a motorcycle accident without ever getting on it, he should take that as a sign from God. Jim believed it was sometime between the fifth and sixth stitch that he begrudgingly agreed.

The second time, when told by Ann, who could've written *War and Peace* in less than a page, went like this:

"It was a simple burglary attempt. Jass held the man at bay while I emptied an entire can of pepper spray on him and then doused him with a can of Raid from under the sink. The police came and took him away. End of story."

Jim told her repeatedly, "That's not a story. It's not even a statement. It barely qualifies as a blurb, especially considering the man told the court he was glad the police came when they did, because he was afraid this crazy woman and her savage dog were going to permanently blind or devour him one hand and foot at a time. And truth be known, I believe the first 911 call may have been made by the intruder himself."

All this just proved Jass was a great dog, even sharing the interests of the family, whether it be strolling through the garden with Ann, spending a week or two at Amy's, or lying under the piano as Jim wrote. He loved being with family. And he loved going to the cabin at Brennan's Cove, on Hood Canal.

"Do you have anything you want me to take to the cabin?" Jim asked.

Jass snapped his head around to stare at him, his ears perked, his head tilted from one side to the other.

"I do," Ann answered quickly. "I set it by the front door. Oh, and that new bed I picked up for Jass is in the garage. The one at the cabin has a big tear, and it smells like wet dog."

Jass looked at Ann, dropping his ears before looking back at Jim. "She's talking about you? Saying your bed stinks like a wet dog. What does she know, huh?" Jim huffed.

Jass wagged his tail and nuzzled his master's hand in agreement.

Ann ignored them both. "What time are you boys leaving?" she asked, scouting the sky once again.

Jim snapped his head around to stare at her. "I thought you'd bring him up tomorrow with you."

"Don't be thinking!" she shot back, winking at Jass. "It's day after tomorrow, and I'm bringing supplies for the week and stuff for the dinner party. I won't have room for him too."

Before Jim could say a word, her tone changed to that of someone speaking to a small child. "Isn't that right, Jass? You want to go to the cabin with Daddy, don't you, good boy?"

"I am not that dog's daddy!" Jim scowled.

"Tell him, Jass, you are my daddy, and I wuv you, and I want to ride with you, Daddy. We'll have so much fun…and if you don't take me, Mommy will make you go with her today, and you would much rather take me than go shopping, isn't that right, Daddy?"

Excitedly, Jass began to prance in a small circle, speaking in a growly bark as Ann cheered him on. "You tell Daddy, let's go. Come on, I'm ready to go…don't forget my new bed!"

It was all Jim could do to keep from smiling, more at his wife's antics than those of the dog. And besides, Jass was a great travel companion. Never once had he complained about stopping for a snack or the radio being too loud or Jim singing along and drumming on the steering wheel when that perfect road song came on. And once at the cabin, Jass would be pretty self-sufficient, needing very little supervision. Of course, the same could not be said for Jim, something Ann knew all too well.

"I left a list on the table of things I need you to do for the parties, so don't blow them off like you usually do. You know the mood that'll put me in!"

Jim knew all too well the mood she was referring to, and he made a mental note to get things done before she arrived. "No worries, my sweet." He shrugged. Your wish is my command. I'll take care of your list before I do anything else. Everything will be shipshape, spick and span, clean as a whistle by the time…"

"Just worry about the list," Ann said, rolling her eyes. "Change the bedding, clean the fireplace, vacuum the floors, and sweep the porch. That shouldn't be too hard. You have two days to do it in, so I'm pretty sure you can handle it. And don't forget the extra table leaf. It's under the bed in the guest room, and the extra chairs are in the shed. They'll need to be cleaned up."

"That'll be easy to remember. I'll add it to my own list." He smirked, pointing to his head. A small grin left its mark on Ann's cheek, a clear indication she didn't believe for a second he had a list, mental or otherwise. Without admitting she was right, he returned her smile, quickly hedging his statement. "You know, just in case, you might want to add it to that list of yours."

Her grin broadened. "You just reminded me, there's a couple other things I need you to do, so I'll just make a whole new list before I forget. And remember, I'm counting on you," she implored, her eyes narrowing slightly.

Being counted on always left Jim feeling a little uncomfortable, and this time was no different. He knew when it came to domestic responsibilities he wasn't all that trustworthy, often forgetting little things like setting out the trash on Tuesday, picking up this or that from the market on his way home, removing his wet shoes at the door, and so on. However, when she needed his assistance for the important stuff like her annual New Year's parties, he had never once let her down.

The festivities began on the evening of the thirtieth with Ann's family-style dinner, a traditional sit-down affair much like an old-fashioned after-church supper with platters of Grandma's southern fried chicken and all the fixins to go with it, not to mention a culinary surprise or two mixed in just for fun. But more important were the invited guests themselves—a handful of folks Ann treasured as the people who had blessed her life, some family, some extended family, but each one sharing a special bond with their host. The following evening would be the Ball at Brennan's Cove, an event for a hundred or so local residents, catered by Life of the Party Catering, suppling a wide variety of gourmet hors d'oeuvres, smoked meats, pastries, drinks, hats, noisemakers, and a midnight fireworks display over the waters of the cove. Music was always provided by D. B. Cooper and the Loot, a fifteen-piece ensemble guaranteed to fill any dance floor, specializing in everything from big bands to country, disco to jazz, and most everything in between.

"I put my stuff together a few days ago. It's in the den," she said. "I'll just leave it by the door for you."

Jim nodded and disappeared upstairs, where he packed a few pairs of jeans, two pairs of slacks, tennis shoes, dress shoes, seven shirts, and enough necessities to last the week into a small suitcase with plenty of room to spare. Walking down the stairs, he found the sight hard to believe but not surprising. Sitting next to the front door was one oversized suitcase, a large duffel bag, an overnight bag and an extremely heavy garment bag, five plastic shopping bags filled with who knows what, and one very large note that read, "Dog bed in garage…don't forget it."

"I can tie the sofa and love seat on top, but you'll have to bring the kitchen sink with you." He laughed, staring at Ann.

She kissed him on the cheek and started upstairs. "I'm meeting Rachel and Peg around eleven thirty at Darby's for lunch. There's that little shop around the corner; I want to see if I can find a new tablecloth. While I'm in the area, I thought I'd stop in that popcorn shop and get one of the assorted buckets. I know you like the cheese flavor, but is there another one you want to try?"

Before Jim had time to think, much less answer, she continued. "You know what? I'll go ahead and pick up two party buckets. That's six flavors, and I'll make sure yours is in one of them. Hey, don't forget his bed; I love you; drive safe."

She disappeared from the top of the stairs, and it was only a matter of seconds before she reappeared at the banister. "Make sure you call me later, I want to know you got there okay."

"Yeah, I'll give you a call this evening…"

"And take Jass for a walk. He'll need it after the long ride."

"I love you, sweetheart. And just so you can rest easy, I'll call you this evening during our walk. How's that?" Jim called to her, opening the front door.

"That's wonderful, honey, but if that's the case, I think you may need these," Ann quipped, holding up his cell phone and stepping aside so Jass could peer down through the wooden balusters.

It was an honest mistake; he had set the phone on the bed while packing and just got busy, but as for the dog, he was convinced Jass had hidden somewhere upstairs just to get him in trouble with Ann. And though he couldn't hear them, he knew there were dog snickers behind that innocent puppy-eyed look peering down on him. Ann tucked Jim's phone under Jass's collar, saying in that same annoying tone as before, "Are you ready to go to the cabin with Daddy, Jass?" The dog covered her with kisses, and Ann scruffed his fur. "You're a good boy, Jass. Now take it to Daddy!" In obedience to her instructions, Jass rushed to Jim's side.

From the top of the stairs, she said, "Make sure you call me when you take him for a walk. Love you!" Ann giggled sarcastically.

You Are My Love

"Love you too…and I'm not that dog's daddy!"

❧

Fog drifted in wisps over the water; sunlight and shadows interspersed with shades of gray painted ever-changing beauty to the cool morning. The smells were of saltwater and evergreen, bacon sizzling on the stove, and a fireplace emitting that distinct campfire scent of burning wood. Faint sounds of hurried footsteps came from the short wooden pier, moving across snow-covered sand and rock to climb the stairway to a large deck on the home's main floor.

Though a private residence today, its beginnings were as the Sportsman's Lodge, catering to Seattle's ultra-wealthy. The informal retreat built sometime in the early nineteen thirties was forced to close shortly after the bombing of Pearl Harbor, never to regain its short but celebrated popularity again. By the summer of sixty-seven, after numerous owners, bankruptcies, foreclosures, and neglect, the property was abandoned, left to the brutal elements of Puget Sound, before being purchased in the mid-eighties for little more than the value of the land. However, it would take a small army of architects, engineers, and contractors eighteen months to convert the weathered property to the magnificent home it was today.

Originally the lodge was comprised of three two-and-a-half-story structures stretching out ninety feet like spokes from a central hub. This hub, with a high domed ceiling and curved walls of red cedar and stone, framed by thick posts and beam supports, created a beautiful array of geometric patterns, colors, and shapes along the interior of the main lobby before continuing through two wide stilted archways on opposing sides of the room. At the rear and offset slightly to the left was a third archway entirely of stone, leading to the largest of the three structures. Though the floor sat ten feet lower than the other two, its roof towered an extra fifteen feet above them both, bringing the steep cathedral ceiling to rise majestically above the hardwood dance floor of the onetime Grand Olympic Ballroom.

The other two wings housed guestrooms and suites, a sauna, the formal dining room, a gentleman's club, and, next to the reception hall, a guest lounge. At the end of each building a wide bank of thick French doors flanked by soaring glass windows provided each wing its own unique view, and it was for the distinctive view that each would be named.

The Forest: Perhaps the simplest of the three wings, at one time provided guestrooms on both the upper and lower floors. At the far end was a small glassed-in sitting area and near the central hub, a stairway leading to a subterranean wine cellar and tasting room. Now, just off this central hub, was a large yet crowded office; ten feet to the right, two elegant staircases sat within the spacious foyer. The first swept downward in a flowing half circle to the well-stocked wine cellar below; the second began on the right and rose in a half circle to the master suite and indoor balconies. This foyer also offered entry to a state-of-the-art home theater and three two-bedroom suites located at the far end of the wing, all of which opened onto an interior garden where picturesque windows and thick glass doors led to an area of natural terrain extending twenty yards to the steep banks of Spirit Creek and the dense forest beyond.

The Grand Olympic Ballroom: It offered the snowcapped Olympic Mountain range in the distance and a long swath of Puget Sound in the foreground. The glass doors opened onto the Grand Terrance, a series of slate patios that followed down the tiered landscape to a second and third patio encompassing a creek-fed pond, ending near the knolls that lifted ten feet before plunging to the shore of Twana Bay.

The Cove: Its upper floor had once been the home to LeRoy's, an elegant dining experience in the culinary styling of New York's popular Delmonico's. Club members could also visit Zella's, offering the best in liquor, cigars, and cardrooms, where high-stakes games with expensive buy-ins would sometimes last into the wee hours of the morning. Down on the first floor was the main dining room; as with LeRoy's, the tree-lined banks of Brennan's Cove could be viewed by guests from every table in the room. A closer view could be obtained from the massive step-down deck. But with the remodel, only a few of the rooms remained, most being removed to expose the magnificent A-frame ceiling.

The man's footsteps continued across the wide deck, where eagerly he pushed open one of the glass doors with a sharp bang, the sound ringing harshly through the vast open room. Gone was the formal dining room and the whole second floor, in their place a living area designed for casual entertainment as well as quiet, intimate moments by the fire or simply losing track of time staring onto the dark waters of the cove. The floor and upper two-thirds of the ceiling had been finished in wide hickory plank, a beautiful backdrop for the original post-and-beam supports that ran throughout each of the structures. The bearing walls were a combination of textured Sheetrock and locally harvested logs. Toward the opposite end of the room, stones outlined the fireplace before melding into the colorful used brick of the hub's curved walls. This area was now the kitchen, its old world charm enhanced by La Cornue's colorfully styled appliances and a wide granite island that followed the curvature of the room. The domed ceiling had been reconstructed using various shades of gray oak, casting a more laid-back atmosphere over the entire expanse. In the center of the room, an incredibly large, well-worn table welcomed guests. Never referred to as a dining area, it was simply known as the Gathering Place.

"He's back. He hasn't been around for months, and all of a sudden, he's back."

Softly she called out, "Who? Who's back?"

"Great. Where'd I leave my camera?"

"Next to the window. Now, who's back? And shut that door!"

Rushing to the spotting scope that stood at the base of the large center window, the man spoke fervently. "Hurry; come here. I almost have him dialed in…there; there he is…"

She stepped into position and looked through the angled eyepiece. Just shy of 150 yards, sitting on the bow of the old weathered rowboat that remained permanently anchored to the large and frequently submerged rock, sat a familiar face. Sensing her watching, his head turned slowly, his dark eyes fixing upon hers, piercing a primeval fear somewhere deep within, and for a moment, her breath left.

But it was his splendor that captured her heart and softened her qualms, bringing the slightest of smiles to ride within her returning air.

"Look close—his leg. Is there a…"

"Oh yes, it's there. It's definitely him," she said slowly, stepping back away. "Take a look…"

And the man did.

But it was the little boy inside the man that joyfully exclaimed, "It is him. I knew it was him; I knew it."

The woman felt her unwelcome smile widen and quickly hid it by saying, "I don't like seeing his face that close up, but I'm glad to see he's still alive." Before turning back to the kitchen, she asked, "How do you want your eggs this morning?"

"Does it matter? They always come out scrambled anyway. Besides, I'll eat later. I'm going to grab my fishing pole—"

"Lincoln Trudeau!" the woman barked hoarsely. "You and that Old Fisherman can spend all day out on the water if you want, but not before you sit down and have some breakfast. So hang up your jacket. It'll be ready in just a few minutes."

Her weak voice managed to carry well through the open room. "And by the way…scrambled eggs it is," she added, disappearing around the corner.

"But Trudy…"

Music suddenly filled the room, and with the discussion unquestionably over, he hung up his jacket and walked back to the front window. The boat was empty. His heart sank. But before he could turn to run outside, he saw his old friend lift a large salmon from the waters just outside the cove. Its talons held the big fish tight, its strong wings easily lifting its prey into the air. Flying low, circling the rim of the cove, he then disappeared down the tree-lined banks of Hood Canal.

It was five years ago they first saw the eagle his wife nicknamed the Old Fisherman. Lincoln sat in his kayak watching the sunrise cast a silver glimmer over the water. His line taut, he paddled steadily, almost soundlessly, into the wide channel of the canal. Always loving the outdoors, he'd never considered himself an outdoorsman. In earlier days, he and Trudy had spent much of their time on the water, exploring the coastline of Northern California, occasionally taking a trip to Sonoma County, hiking, camping and fishing along the Russian River or a little farther north to the redwood forest or Mount Shasta.

It had never bothered him that he wasn't much of a fisherman; he always believed he was just where the fish were not. If he were on this side of the boat, they'd be on the other. If the line sank to the bottom, they'd jump on the surface. And when craving a nice fish dinner, it meant a trip to the market, or better yet, to one of his favorite haunts, the Crispy Clam. But that didn't detour him from the sport, because it wasn't about catching fish. It was about everything else. The peace, the quiet, the sky, the wind, the feel and the sound of the paddles cutting through and pushing against the water, the motion of the boat and the soothing stillness it brought to his mind—a time of meditation, of inward exploration, and more often than not, a time of prayer, though that was not something he did often.

He watched the eagle circle twice as he paddled into the morning sun, stopping only once when the bird lit on a fallen tree that extended many yards out over the water. The long kayak moved silently with the current to within twenty feet of the glorious bird. They held each other's gaze for a time, even after he'd drifted quite some ways away. The small anchor made little noise going into the calm dark water. How quiet. How peaceful. How beautiful this magnificent bird. He watched as it soared into the air, carrying itself high above the water, gliding leisurely amid the drafts of the morning thermals. Uninterested in the small prey that scurried along the banks or the dark outlines of fish just under the surface, his attention remained on the man.

The pole bent with a slight tap, and then again. Suddenly it whipped down, almost taking it from the rod holder. Lincoln grabbed for the pole and nearly lost his paddle in the effort. Soon he was reeling in something larger than anything he'd ever felt on his line before, not that he had many things to compare it to. Adrenaline shook him, heightening his senses, but he remained calm, not allowing the excitement to trigger a mistake that would cost his victory over whatever monster fought him from below the waters dark surface. As he held the pole high, it bent sharply over his shoulder as twice the fish circled the boat in an effort to escape. His arms, burning under the strain, shook with pain and determination. Over time his clenched teeth delivered a nagging ache along both jawbones, causing the muscles in the back of his head and neck to tighten fiercely. With eyes held closed in a contorted mask of agony and fatigue, feeling as though his jaw would break at any moment, he released the pressure with a loud roar.

It was then, as if answering him, encouraging him, the eagle screamed, swooping low to glide smoothly over the water. His first thought was that eagle was going to take his fish. And it easily could have. But the great bird chose to move back to its perch on the fallen tree, continuing to watch this battle between man and fish.

Eventually both began to tire, each sensing, knowing the end would come soon, yet neither was willing to forfeit the battle. More time passed with only an occasional tug on the line, and many times neither the fish nor the man knew for sure who caused it.

Looking to the shore, the man noticed the shadows had not moved. *Impossible*, he thought. This fight had been going on for an hour at least, the shadows lied. Or perhaps this battle had gained the attention of God himself, and He was holding the sun still in the sky just as he had for Joshua as he battled…who? "Who did he battle?" There came another small tug on the line.

Maybe I never knew, he thought. "No! I think it was the Amalekites. Yeah, I'm pretty sure that's who it was," he said to the fish. "The Amalekites." A small drop of sweat rolled down the bridge of his nose and onto his cheek, coming to rest just under his left eye. It was only a slight distraction.

"But then again, it could've been the Midianites." He groaned. "That's right, fish. It could've been the Midianites." Another small drop ran to meet the first. "Oh, wait a second. It was the Amorites. Of course it was the Amori…"

A slightly larger tug. Instinctively he tightened his grip. At almost the same instant, he realized the two small drops were becoming more than a little distraction. They were now a full-blown irritation, and he could see another running down the slope of his nose to join them. Slightly increasing his grip, he shook his head sharply to remove these three small annoyances, only to dislodge the many beads perched on his brow, causing them to run like tiny rivulets, stinging, burning into his eyes. A burst of pain pushed him backward into the thinly padded seat, his head thrashing one way, then the other. Unable to dry them on his sleeve without moving the pole caused him to immediately abandon that option. Fluttering his eyes only increased the pain, as did closing them tightly. Relaxing the lids brought some relief, and he knew if he just waited, his own tears would wash and soothe the burning eventually. So he sat quietly.

It was in this brief instant of blindness he found a humorous ray of light. He snickered weakly. "The Amorites. Who am I kidding. I don't know who it was, and neither do you, fish. For all either of us know, it could've been the electric lights, the parasites, or the fly a kites. We'll have to ask the bird; I bet he knows."

I can't let my mind wander, he thought. *I have to focus on you, fish.* But his strength was depleted. Using all he had left to hold the tip of the rod above the water, the moments passed, until the only movement he felt was the rocking motion of the kayak. He cranked the reel slowly at first—one click, two, and then he waited. There was no answer from the fish. Again he cranked it slowly—three clicks, then five. But again, there was no response from the fish. Once more he began cranking in the thin line. It came easier, quicker, onto the reel. But his aching muscles would not rush to triumph, moving slowly, steady, first in yards, and then in feet. Every muscle, every fiber in his neck, arms and back, burned like hot coals, slowing his progress to mere inches.

And then…it was over.

CHAPTER SEVEN

By late morning the sun had arrived fully, warming the normally cool forest air to just above comfortable, and like a sentinel, the woman stood at the end of the dock anticipating her husband's approach. Long, smooth ripples floated slowly over the surface as the kayak made its way into the deep, still waters of Brennan's Cove. Each stroke of the paddle brought audible sighs of determination, exhaustion, and relief from the weary man…and, too, his wife.

Hood Canal was a vast natural waterway and like any body of water, it had its dangers, some charted or clearly visible, others remaining hidden mysteries capable of providing unthinkable outcomes. When he traveled the waterway alone, she worried. This was the longest he'd been on the canal alone. Over the last hour, she had agonized, and she would spend the next hour just holding him.

From the pier she waved and blew him a kiss, then watched as an eagle flew low over his head and came to rest on the bow of the old boat tied to the submerged rock in the middle of the cove. The man passed within a few feet of the bird as it spread its enormous wings, its cry echoing off the water into the forest, in tribute to the man's hard-fought accomplishment.

Carrying the fish up the stairway, he heard the eagle once more. He turned and watched as it soared high above the canal and then swooped with grace down to touch the water's surface, removing its own meal with ease before returning to the small boat. Again, gripping the fish in its talons, it climbed into the air, where it cried a last goodbye. The man raised a painful arm and bid the bird farewell.

Over the next few weeks, Lincoln rose early to sit on the deck waiting for the bird to return. Trudy awoke alone for the first time in memory;

however, she would neither encourage nor discourage what she considered her husband's odd behavior, but simply hug him, stroke his hair, kiss his cheek, touch the end of his nose with her finger, say, "I love you, Lincoln Trudeau," and then retreat to the kitchen to prepare their breakfast.

Two weeks passed, and it was evident the bird was not going to return; it had all been some kind of misinterpreted coincidence. But then, while trying to ease a long-delinquent hot flash in the cool moist air of morning, Trudy watched the bird land on the bow of the old weathered boat. It was early, her voice weak as she ran quickly through the house searching for Lincoln. Within minutes she was guiding him to the front room window, where she lay back, not accompanying him onto the deck. His smile touched her heart. Curious, he made his way down to the short dock. He walked cautiously to the end and leaned against a tall piling and watched in awe. The great bird began to chatter quietly. After a few minutes, Lincoln spoke in return. Their conversation was brief, ending with the eagle taking flight high above the cove, its cry echoing through the air.

Lincoln glanced up to see Trudy leaning against the deck rail, in her hand the camera. "What would I do without you, Tru…" he whispered to himself and then called out loudly, "I love you."

Over the next few months the eagle would show up two or three times a week, and he would spend the morning with Lincoln on the waters of Hood Canal; almost always returning with dinner. He would then become scarce for a month or two, occasionally returning to fish with his human friend.

※

"You'd better get in here; your eggs are getting cold."

Lincoln smiled as he walked to the kitchen.

"What are you smiling about?" she asked, somewhat annoyed.

"I'm smiling because I have the privilege of enjoying breakfast with the woman I love," he said, putting his arms around her, holding her tight. "And besides you make the best scrambled eggs I've ever had, sweetheart." He held her even tighter. "Of course, they're the only kind of eggs you ever make, but they are the best."

His teasing laughter filled the room. Trudy, not one to forgive quickly, spun around to playfully beat her fist into his chest. Their duet of laughter brought about a loving embrace that was interrupted by the sound of large tubular door chimes. Both looked surprised, but it was Trudy who moved across the room to open the thick wooden door.

"Hi, Miss Trudy. Is Mr. Trudy home? I saw the Old Fisherman...you know the one—Mr. Trudy's bird. It was on the boat, the old boat right out there. Is he home, Miss Trudy? Is he home?"

Opening the door wide and stepping aside, Trudy looked to her husband. The little girl's face lit up with joy hearing the strong, familiar voice of the man she insisted on calling Mr. Trudy.

"Hey, sweetheart. So you saw my bird this morning. That's pretty exciting, huh!"

"I did, I did, Mr. Trudy! Right out there sitting on the boat, not more than five minutes ago. My daddy saw him too. It has to be your bird; it has to be! I even heard it yell for you. You know..." She made a high, piercing squeal that made Lincoln's eyes widen.

"Beth..." a masculine voice called from the front steps.

Trudy, still holding the heavy wooden door, turned to see her neighbor and dear friend Chris Peterson standing in the doorway.

"Sorry, Tru. I was fixing us a bowl of cereal when she spotted that silly bird, and she was off like a rocket...oh, sorry, Linc," Chris said, chuckling, stepping into the room. "I meant to say...she spotted Mr. Trudy's most glorious, magnificent, incredibly beautiful bird."

Beth turned on her heel to face her daddy. "It is Mr. Trudy's bird, but his name is the Old Fisherman, isn't it, Mr. Trudy?"

"Yes it is, sweetheart." Linc smiled. "Come on in, Chris. Can we interest you and Beth in some breakfast? A little bacon, toast, and scrambled eggs. Oh, but these aren't just any ol' scrambled eggs. These are the best scrambled eggs on all of Hood Canal. Now, I don't know this for a fact"—he spoke softly, focusing his attention on Beth—"but I think that's probably the reason the Old Fisherman dropped by this morning—to have some of Miss Trudy's scrambled eggs."

He and Chris laughed, and Beth join in. Trudy did not, instead choosing to ignore the comment, and not waiting for Chris to answer, she quickly set two more places at the table.

"Can I help, Miss Trudy?"

"Sure you can. Why don't you sit up on the counter and keep me company. Tell me how those new verses are coming along."

Beth ran into her arms. Trudy picked her up, squeezed her tight, twirled her around, and set her on the counter. "I know three of them by heart already," Beth said proudly. "Do you want to hear them?"

Trudy gasped. "Three? You know three of them already? I can hardly believe that. Let's hear."

Beth rocked her bottom, shimmied her shoulders, and took a deep breath.

"The first one's easy." She smiled. "Prodwords thirty, dots five: 'Every word of God proves true.' Tru—that's what people call you sometimes, huh, Miss Trudy?"

"Yes, they do." She giggled, with everyone clapping their hands to acknowledge Beth's success. "You know the verse, but that first word is Proverbs thirty—verse five. No dots."

Beth bit her lip as she thought hard, and then, looking at Trudy for approval, she repeated, "Proverbs thirty…verse five…Got it!"

Trudy couldn't help but smile. "You're doing great, Beth. We'll work on it a little more next week. Now, show me the others."

Beth sat at attention, her teeth and hands tightly clenched, her eyebrows raised, her knees moving in and out with elation. "I know this one good, don't I, Daddy?"

Chris gave a thumbs-up, Mr. Trudy winked, and Miss Trudy was there with her gentle smile if she ever needed help. After clearing her throat and swallowing hard, Beth said, "Psalm nineteen…one, no dots, 'The heavens declare the gory of God.'"

No one moved; no one spoke; they just looked at each other in a moment of silence. "Oops…I mean the glory of God." Beth giggled. "Not gory; God's not…gory." Her sweet laughter moved around the room, touching her daddy, Mr. Trudy, and most of all, Miss Trudy.

"That was wonderful," the woman exclaimed, clapping her hands. "You really do know that one…good."

"That was wonderful, sweetheart!" Mr. Trudy chimed in.

"I have one more, and I know it good too. And I drew a color page for you, Mr. Trudy. You're gonna like this one, I promise. Daddy, can I go get it, please? It's on the kitchen table. Please, Daddy?"

"I thought you were helping Miss Trudy fix breakfast. It wouldn't be nice to run out after promising to help, now, would it?"

Her disappointment was thick and heavy, resting on the shoulders and hearts of everyone in the room. "No sir!" she said softly, without looking at anyone directly.

Before Chris could say any more, Lincoln rushed to her aid. "You know, Chris, it's scrambled eggs, and Lord knows Tru doesn't need help breaking a few more eggs. Besides, Beth colored it for me, and I'd love to be able to look at it while she recites that verse. I think if she ran real fast, she could probably be back before any of us realize she's even gone; at least that's what I think." Winking at Beth, he shrugged and asked, "Don't you think so, sweetheart?"

Beth nodded her head quick and fast.

"I guess I'll help you fix those eggs, Tru," Chris joked.

It wasn't long before Beth returned with her color page. "See, Mr. Trudy? He's my guarding angel, and this time I stayed in some of the lines too. And look—he has red hair. I love red hair, don't you, Mr. Trudy? Don't you wish you had red hair?"

Lincoln shook his head as though fluffing his mane and then laughed. "I kind of like my hair just the way it is."

Beth stood looking confused. "But Mr. Trudy, you don't have any hair."

Lincoln ran his hand over his head and then, openmouthed, sat straight up. "Where did it go? I know it was there yesterday; I brushed it and curled it, and I think I saw it this morning when I was brushing my teeth."

Beth began to giggle as Mr. Trudy continued. "Let's see...then I took a shower, and..." With great shock he put both hands on his cheeks and muttered, "Oh, no. I must have done it again."

Beth's eyes were wide. Her little smile quickly formed a perfect O. Holding both fists tightly under her chin, she panted, "What? What? What have you done again?"

Slowly his hands moved toward his head. "Instead of shampoo, I must've accidentally used…" Looking pitiful, he leaned closer to her. Then, grasping his head tightly, his voice troubled and forlorn, he sniveled, "Hair remover!"

They all laughed.

"Mr. Trudy, you must use that every day, 'cause you never have any hair," Beth piped, causing everyone's laughter to rise to the top of the dome.

Finally Trudy said, "Okay, let's hear this verse, and then we'll get everyone fed."

Beth moved to Trudy's side, partially out of habit, but mostly for the woman's encouraging hand. "This is my favorite," she told the woman. "Are you ready, Mr. Trudy?"

"I'm ready whenever you are, sweetie."

Swallowing hard, she began. "Sams, thirty-four seven, dot…oops, let me start over."

"Psalms," her dad corrected with a heartening smile.

"Yeah, Psalms, thirty-four seven. 'The angel of the Lord camps around those who love him.'"

Clapping his hands, thinking *Close enough*, her father's smile broadened. Miss Trudy gave her a hug, and Mr. Trudy asked if he could hang her color page on the refrigerator. And then he did.

Chris led the blessing, and this, like always, left Beth feeling proud of her daddy. Everyone loved to hear her daddy talk to God. Sometimes the whole church would say the same things with him, and other times he would talk by himself. People often raised their hands and closed their eyes, and sometimes people even cried because his words were so beautiful. She knew everyone loved to hear her daddy talk to God, but no one loved it more than her.

Sometimes she would talk to God when no one was listening, like after her daddy tucked her in and turned out the light. She would lie perfectly still, being as quiet as a church mouse, a phrase she'd heard Mr. Trudy use, and then, in a whisper as soft as angel's breath, she would ask God to let her grow up to be just like her daddy. She would list all the ways she wanted to be like him, and she always ended with two things, one of which she heard her daddy say many times: "So, God, in all that I do, let it please you."

The other was her own, and she perhaps felt it and understood it more than anything else she ever said to God. "And God, the next time you see my mommy up in heaven, tell her me and Daddy misses her."

❦

Breakfast with the Trudeaus, though rare, was always a special treat for Chris—a time with friends to whom he owed so very much yet who would bristle even at the thought that he could ever feel that he owed them a thing. How blessed he was to have them as neighbors. But it wasn't rare that Beth came to visit. For this little girl walked across the compound connecting the properties quite often. She made the trip every morning, Tuesday through Friday, for ninety minutes of reading, singing, and memorization as part of her ongoing rehabilitation and speech therapy. A program designed especially for her by retired therapist, Teresa Belle Trudeau, better known as...Miss Trudy.

CHAPTER EIGHT

*I*n 1976, as a young resident at San Francisco's Moffat Hospital, Andrew Lincoln Trudeau was on the fast track to becoming a surgeon like his father. That is, until he and a friend rode their bikes through the Botanical Gardens of Golden Gate Park one afternoon. There he happened to see the most beautiful girl he'd ever laid eyes on, sitting alone, reading a book on the cool sloping lawn just beyond Alvord Lake. Unable to look away, he slowed the bike to a crawl, circling back twice before coming to a complete stop some thirty yards from where she sat. Bob Stewart, a second-year resident and weekly biking partner, pulled alongside. Lincoln nodded toward the girl. "There she is! I'll be right back."

Laying the bike down, he walked away with no further explanation. Kneeling beside her on the soft grass, extending his hand he said, "Hi. My name's Lincoln Trudeau; I believe I am the man you're gonna spend the rest of your life with."

That didn't come out quite right, he thought. "What I mean is, do you believe in love at first sight? Me either—that is, until just a minute ago when I saw you sitting here. I knew right then we were meant to be."

She looked at his friend, who simply shrugged, then back to the annoying person kneeling beside her.

"Look, I know you probably think I'm nuts or just another guy trying to pick up on you, but come on. Think about it for a second. Don't you think I could come up with better lines than these?" he said, half smiling in an attempt to present himself as that intelligent, cool guy he saw every morning in the mirror.

"I honestly believe I'm in love with you. And if you'd just…maybe give me a chance to explain…"

Not only is he annoying, he's crazy, she thought. Or worse yet, he was setting her up for some cruel practical joke. Slowly, guardedly, she closed her book and stood up. He moved with her. Quickly, she started to walk away. But as nonaggressively as possible and keeping distance between them, he stepped in front of her again. Immediately she turned in a different direction; he again moved to block her way.

"Please, just hear me out," he pleaded.

Remaining motionless, she took a deep breath and still said nothing.

"To be honest, I don't know what's going on here either." He grinned. "I saw you, and I had to meet you. No, that's not true…" He unconsciously scratched his head, confusion cluttered his thoughts.

As he paced in frustration, she took advantage of the extended distance he created and began to walk away.

"Wait," he begged, moving close to her. "Bear with me for a second, please," he again pleaded, attempting to collect his thoughts. But it was useless. This close, the light scent of her perfume only clouded his thoughts further, leaving him unable to concentrate on anything other than how incredibly beautiful she was and how at any minute she could flee from his life forever.

He tried to speak but only stumbled over his words again. Out of pure desperation, he began talking and prayed it would come out right.

"I can't explain it, but I just want you to believe me, please. I really didn't give any thought to meeting you when I ran over here. I didn't know what I was going to say; I just saw you sitting there, and I knew you're the woman I'm supposed to be with forever. Oh, I know how that sounds, but I swear to you, it's true."

Without expression, tilting her head slightly, she stared into his eyes. Holding her book close against her breast, she didn't move, nor did she take her eyes from his.

"I'm sorry I frightened you." he said calmly, attempting to repress his anxiety. "Listening to myself, even I think I sound like some kind of lunatic. But please, if you would let me just start all over, my name's Linc. Lincoln Trudeau."

He extended his hand; she didn't respond. "I'm doing my residency up at Moffat. I know that sounds like a pickup line as well, but it's true. I really am, and I'd be honored if you'd let me buy you lunch. Or better yet, dinner tonight."

Her eyes fell away as she stepped around him. But again he moved to face her. Now her eyes narrowed with anger, this time continuing to stare at him as she moved yet again, snapping her head forward to walk away once more.

This time he did not step in front of her, but simply moved to her side, continuing to talk as they walked across the grassy meadow toward the pond.

"Okay, what am I thinking. Of course you can't go out tonight. You probably already have a date. You may even have a boyfriend, for all I know. No, I bet you have a different guy for every night of the week."

She suddenly stopped. Her face, red with anger, conveyed a message he clearly understood.

"Oh, wait, no. That's not what I meant at all."

Her walk resumed, hurried. She was annoyed by his unrelenting pursuit yet captivated and even slightly pleased by the attention. Sure, she thought his approach was unorthodox, to say the least, but he was tall, handsome, and had eyes that were captivating. Even his voice was intriguing, almost seductive. Her stride slowed as a sudden feeling of comfort attempted to bring a smile to her face. But it was her sensible conscience that sounded the alarm, awaking her from his charismatic spell. That face was probably on a wanted poster somewhere, she suddenly thought, and resumed her hurried pace.

"What I meant was I'm sure you have all kinds of guys that ask you out. Look at you! You're the most beautiful woman I've ever seen. I just want an opportunity to meet you, have a conversation. At this point, an afternoon here in the park would be great. I'd settle for an hour. A half hour. Okay, fine. Just give me ten minutes. I just want to talk to you. I just want to hear your voice."

She stopped and looked at him, and for a moment he thought she was going to speak, but she only stared at him through a wall of silence.

Sighing heavily, he said, "Even if you have a boyfriend, saying hello to me isn't like you're cheating on him. I mean…I don't know; maybe you're living with somebody. Not that it makes a difference to me. As far as I'm concerned, you're just living with the wrong guy. I'm the one you're supposed to be living with…well, I mean…marry."

Although displeased and somewhat angry with his incessant dialogue and insinuating accusations, she didn't turn away.

"Hey, Linc, we're gonna be late. I still need lunch and a shower before afternoon rounds," Bob Stewart called out.

"Go on ahead. I'll see you there," Linc said without taking his eyes from her face.

Speaking to her, the soft tones of his voice returned. "I'm not leaving until you tell me your name."

Though a small fiber of anger continued to twist within, she remained where she stood, noticing for the first time the color of his eyes: light brown, nothing extraordinary, nothing special, yet warm and tender and somewhat intriguing. Ruggedly handsome, with the slightest hint of a beard, his lips parting faintly to display a boyish grin. She felt herself embrace her book. And it was with that that her inner alarm sounded once again and was quelled instantly with a tap to her inner snooze button, which brought about her slender smile. A small flame incinerated the twisted fiber, leaving her anger like smoke and ash to be carried away on the gentle breeze.

"Excuse me, miss," called his friend from the walkway. "He may be big and ugly, but he's harmless. Just make sure he gets to rounds by one o'clock, or Dr. Richter will have his—"

"I'll be there. Go eat or shower or something," Lincoln shouted to his friend before turning back to face the young lady. "The guy's a real worrywart. It's only eleven thirty or so. Plenty of time for that lunch I was talking about?"

Broadening only slightly, her smile was enough to nudge his heart, and once again she began to walk, slower, as if casually strolling with a friend, taking in the sights and sounds of a sunny day in Golden Gate Park. The cool grass on her bare feet felt refreshing, uplifting—or maybe it was... church bells chimed the hour from somewhere beyond the trees. Stopping to silently count—ten, eleven, twelve—she looked at him questioningly.

His smile now broadened as he glanced through the trees, following the sound. "Seems their bell's a little fast."

Unable to contain her smile, it left a slight blush to her cheeks. For a moment he was speechless, captivated, fulfilled simply by her presence.

"I know!" he exclaimed suddenly, "There's this little place just over on Fredericks Street. It's a ten-minute walk, and I guarantee it's the best pizza in the city..."

The smile that only moments ago captivated quickly vanished. Shaking

You Are My Love

her head no, she walked toward a small path that split a long line of trees, exposing the busy street just outside the park. After quickly she slipped back into her shoes, her stride was not hurried; neither was it the casual stroll as before, but it seemed to now move with purpose. Taken back by her action, he stood speechless, this time unable to comprehend her sudden change.

Jogging the few steps to catch her, he said, "I'm sorry. Whatever I said, whatever I did to offend you, I'm sorry."

As they passed through an opening in the trees, the street noise escalated around them. Her pace remained steady, yet he persisted. "As I've already proven to you, I'm not the smartest boy on the block. If by inviting you to have lunch…"And then it came to him.

"I've got it—you detest pizza!" He waited for a response. None came. "You're allergic to cheese?" Again he left room for a response, and again none came.

Her stride was persistent, as were his queries. "You only eat Chicago style? New York style? You hate Italian food altogether? You never eat food that's round? Triangular? Tossed in the air? Work with me here, okay? You were once kidnapped by a Norwegian chef named Giuseppe, who fed you nothing but lutefisk pizza for sixteen days straight?"

She came to an abrupt halt, shaking her head, rolling her eyes, and secretly biting the inside of her cheek to thwart her laughter. Nonetheless, Lincoln believed he saw another smile. She remained silent for the next four blocks; he did not. "If you're not gonna tell me anything about you, well then, you'll just have to hear all about me."

And as they walked, he talked about his childhood, his parents' divorce, his mother's adoration for her only child, and his father's lofty expectations for the doctor he expected his son to become. From summer camp to college, paperboy to physician; his passion for painting, sailing, astronomy, penny stocks, and all things rustic became topics to share. How he'd once dreamed of becoming a magician. His plans of volunteering as a doctor assisting the underprivileged, spending a year with no agenda whatsoever, and his great desire to someday have a home on the water—or maybe in the forest; either way, it would be fine. But for now he'd have to remain focused on completing his training and going into practice with his dad in San Diego, a duty he was adversely against but realized it would benefit him in the long term.

Only occasionally did she acknowledge his presence, managing to accomplish some light window-shopping and the purchase of a newspaper, even at one point entering Tuscano's Italian Market and picking up a loaf of freshly baked sourdough bread.

"So, you do like Italian?" he spouted. "We could share that over a bowl of Cioppino, maybe a bottle of Chianti," he quipped.

She smiled and kept walking.

They continued to move up the street, he occasionally coaxing a soft giggle or two, making it difficult in her persistence to ignore. From the tower of the large church now only a few blocks away, an immense bell signaled the half hour. Immediately she came to a stop, giving him the same questioning look as before, and then, impudently, she grinned and held her head with a slight tilt as if to say, now what are you going to do, smart guy? Time's up.

Emphatically he began shaking his head. "Oh, no you don't. No! Not even! You're not getting rid of me that easy. Don't think you can lead me around like a little puppy until I have to run off to work. No, that's not gonna happen. I'll miss rounds altogether. I don't care, because I'm not leaving until you talk to me, tell me your name, tell me to get lost, tell me to go—"

She placed her finger across his lips. They were as warm and soft as she'd imagined. Her scent again faint filled his senses. From her purse she pulled a pen and small pad of paper, quickly writing: "No questions!!! My name is Trudy. Lunch tomorrow, same time, same place. Now get to work."

No questions? No questions, he thought repeatedly. But the lines of puzzlement quickly softened as he read the note once more, the words almost jumping off the page. Trudy. Lunch tomorrow. His heart was pounding so hard he felt flush. "Trudy..." he whispered to himself. "Your name's Trudy?" he heard himself ask. "What I mean is, your name's Trudy."

Indicating it was with a simple nod, she pointed for him to go.

"Tomorrow..." he said, slowly backing away.

Emphasizing his need to hurry, she repeated the gesture again, firmly.

"Tomorrow..." he said a second time, backing faster, and then, more instinctive than deliberate, he rushed to stand close to her one last time.

Smiling as though tickled by the caressing breeze gently brushing her long hair, his image filled her vision. Close enough to feel his breath, she didn't move. Smelling her soft fragrance, he didn't move, and the sound of the city became silent around them.

"Thank you," she heard him whisper.

He knew he had to walk away this very instant, or he would stay. Turning from her, he pushed the thought away with every step. Hurriedly she grabbed his arm, turning him back to face her. On the small pad, her hand scribbled feverishly a second note.

"Oh no…" he groaned, turning to run back down the street in the direction they'd come. But again he stopped. Returning, he lightly embraced her, speaking softly into her ear. "Trudy…please be there tomorrow… please." He released her and stood studying her face, memorizing each feature. A moment later, with great reluctance, he was gone. She watched him race down the street, his husky stature, once easily visible, growing faint, distant, as he wove through and around objects and shapes that obstructed and sometimes concealed him from view. Silhouettes of storefront awnings painted dark holes in the otherwise sundrenched sidewalk, and it was there in one of these shadows she watched him disappear; lost, absorbed by the city.

It was only then that she noticed the city around her come alive with sound once again, and she too felt alive, a tingling all over.

"Trudy…" echoed his voice, through the narrow street. "Trudy…"

At the corner of the next block, waving wildly from atop a bus stop bench, he called her name once more. Some passersby turned to follow his gaze, searching the street for the focus of his efforts. Blushing and laughing, embarrassed by the attention, one hand covering her mouth, she timidly, intuitively waved back.

"Tomorrow…" his voice echoed joyfully through the street. "Tomorrow…"

This time, watching him disappear, her emotions were somewhat mixed. But it was the smile that remained long after that made her stop and wonder—maybe he wasn't as crazy as she first thought. Her eyebrows rose slightly, and her lips came together to form her impish grin. Oh, but wouldn't it be fun if he were?

Glancing down at the pavement, she noticed the small pad lying a few feet away where he'd dropped it. Picking it up, the last note she had written him became clearly visible.

"Didn't you have a bike?"

Chuckling, she tossed it back into her purse, crossed the street, and walked another three blocks to her apartment, her smile never fading.

❧

The next day Lincoln arrived at the grassy meadow shortly after eleven a.m. By noon she still hadn't arrived, and around a quarter after, he began to worry. In his mind he replayed their last moments. Could it be possible he misunderstood? No! He recited the note word for word not once, but many times over. "No questions!!! My name's Trudy. Lunch tomorrow at the same place…"

"Seems simple enough!" he said aloud. "So, where the heck is she?"

It's hard to pass the time when it moves by so slowly, and it never moves slower than when you're waiting. And when the wait is accompanied by uncertainty, well, it almost doesn't move at all. Seconds stall in their march to become minutes, leaving hours too swollen for patience to endure.

Children played not far from where he sat. The heavy wrought-iron bench with wood slat seats, being only marginally comfortable, caused him to stand or walk along the pathway. Anxiety eventually turned the walk into a long pace. Twenty yards or so to the east, returning to the bench, and then twenty yards to the west. From beyond the tree line came the twelve-thirty announcement. How funny, he thought. On his rides through the park, he'd hardly noticed the bells, but yesterday, because of her, they filled the air with song, with beauty, even becoming…oddly romantic. Now, however, they rang with tension and anxiety. As hard as he fought to keep his thoughts positive, they began to collapse, allowing one question to rise to the surface: Had she lied just to get him to leave her alone? It was twelve thirty; he believed he had the answer.

Oh, what a fool you are, Linc Trudeau, he thought. *How could you ever expect someone like her to be interested in a big ol' dork like you?* The laughter from old insecurities ridiculed him mercilessly as he wrestled with his thoughts. *Here I am sitting in the hot sun in the middle of a field waiting for some girl named Trudy. And that's probably not even her real name. It's probably something stupid like…*

And then he saw her. Standing stationary at the edge of the walkway, fifty feet separating them, he could still see she was every bit as beautiful as he'd remembered. Moving toward her, he saw she was holding a small cardboard sign. In black marker she'd written "I'm sorry."

Sadness touched her eyes and mouth, stealing away the smile and life he had seen so vivid the day before. She flipped the sign over, and he read, "I was afraid you'd be gone. Are you mad?"

He shook his head, "No, I'm not mad. But I was only going to wait another hour or two before drowning myself in that fish pond over there."

He smiled. She didn't wait for him to see her grin before she rushed to hug him.

❦

Constructed over sixty years ago, the building of brick, wood, glass, and tile captured the very essence of Italy, but it was the aromas that captured the hearts of its patrons. Home to Rock n Wood Pizzeria, "traditional pizza, cooked the traditional way." That had been their motto from day one. The room was large yet intimate, seating parties of two to sixty-two, opening to an adjoining wine room with racks of all shapes and sizes along two of the walls. Though beautiful, it was not meant to depict classic Italian elegance but merely to be a comfortable place for neighborhood families to gather, enjoy each other's company, and partake of a meal steeped in tradition.

The wall behind the front counter was red high-gloss tiles. In front stood the eye-catching bright-yellow domes of the twin wood-burning brick ovens, coals glowing along their back walls. Suspended above the counter was a menu written in Italian, with English subtitles.

"So pizza's okay?" he asked, staring at the choices he'd memorized years ago.

She glanced at him as if to say, of course—we're here, aren't we?

Still attempting to look cool by studying the menu, he didn't look at her when he spoke. "I asked, only because I'm aware of your aversion to tossed food; or was it round food…triangles?" And without taking her eyes from the menu, she playfully nudged him in the side with her elbow.

"Okay, then. What kind of pizza would you like?"

She held up a finger, walked to an empty table nearby, and began to write. He quickly moved to sit with her, but before he could get comfortable, she handed him the small piece of paper from her ever-present tablet.

"Well, apparently you know Italian."

Using her index finger and thumb, Trudy indicated "a little."

"I don't know what this says…"

With the simplest of gestures, she had him walk it to the counter, without her.

The staff seemed to know him; a tall woman in her late twenties coming out of the back greeted him by name. Trudy was quick to notice the wedding ring on her finger.

"I take it she's the reason you were late yesterday?" the woman asked discreetly. "I heard Richter was fuming. Had you on the carpet for half an hour…man, Linc, that's a lot of butt chewin'. Are you able to sit today?" Then she stole another glance over his shoulder. "She must be something special if you're still with her after that."

"Yeah," Lincoln replied. "She is."

Holding the paper in front of him, his attempt to pronounce the words could only be described as pathetic, leaving the woman to read it herself.

"She speaks Italian?" The woman's face lit up.

"No…she doesn't spea…" Lincoln froze.

Trudy watched with curiosity.

"Yeah, I mean she speaks a little I guess, but…"

"I'd love to meet her. Let me get this started, and I'll be right out…"

"No!" Lincoln said, abruptly. "I mean, now's not a good time, Mia. This is our first date, and I'd love to…"

A softness came over the woman. "It's your first date, and you brought her to my family's restaurant. My mama's going to love you even more than she already does when I tell her this."

Looking to Trudy, she said, "Parli italiano?"

Using her index finger and thumb, Trudy indicated "a little."

"This was my papa's favorite. Mine too. And usually we have to wait until July and August, but the season started early this year. I do my fichi in little chunks instead of slices. Is that okay?"

Trudy nodded her head to confirm.

Lincoln pulled out his wallet, asking, "What's fichi? I don't recall ever seeing anything like that on the menu."

"It's not. We bring it out for private parties, wine dinners, things like that. Special occasions."

"So what is it?"

The young lady began to slowly walk toward the kitchen, "È favoloso."

"Which means what?"

"Fabulous," Mia said, returning to the counter to smile at Trudy.

Lincoln also smiled, though somewhat wearily. "What makes it so fabulous? Some special sauce or something?"

"Figs."

It took a split second to register, and then he snapped his head toward Trudy. "Figs?" Getting only a smile as a reply, he again faced Mia. "Figs?"

The woman pointed to an archway. "There's a table in the corner of the wine room where nobody will bother you two, including me. I'll get this right out, and then I'm back to the hospital to peek in on that little girl that came in yesterday, and after that I'm headed home to spend some time with my hubby before he forgets who I am."

Hurriedly she walked away, then quickly turned to say to Trudy, "You'll have to come back again so we can sit and talk. I have a feeling your Italian's better than you're letting on. Have fun and keep an open mind with this one. He's a little brighter then he comes across."

❖

The pizza was amazing, with highlights of pancetta, arugula, goat cheese, and dollops of fresh fig drizzled with a balsamic reduction. "Who would've guessed?" Linc said, all but done with his first slice. "Figs. Guess I'll have to learn some Italian—or bring you along more often."

They sat for over two hours laughing and enjoying a conversation of written and spoken words, with Lincoln never once asking the obvious question. Her laughter was satisfying to his ears, her ability to express herself through gestures, expressions, and, of course, her writing, satisfied his mind. She was incredibly articulate, detailing her point quickly. He found her remarkably witty, with a sense of humor that at times had him laughing uncontrollably. How simply she conveyed her thoughts and emotions, and how simple it had been for him to fall in love with her.

It was her idea for the short bus ride to Ocean Beach, where they sat in the sand, walked the dunes, and shared their interests, goals, and dreams. By four thirty the wind brought a cool chill to the air just ahead of the fog. It was time to retreat into the city, and she decided Lincoln should pick the destination. "You may regret this!" he told her.

"Are you going to be there?" she had written.

"Of course."

"No regrets then!"

"We have one stop to make first."

She looked at him curiously.

"You'll see...and remember; no regrets."

The bus was crowded, leaving them to stand for most of the twenty-minute trip, though neither seemed to mind. Lincoln pointed out two of his favorite hangouts. First, a small record shop called Ear Wax, explaining it wasn't your typical record store. This place had a catalog of new and used records dating from the nineteen twenties, right up to today. The second, a café simply named the Breakfast Place. They were open from 4:00 a.m. to 2:00 p.m., and just like the sign said, they only served breakfast. Sure, they were a little pricey, but well worth it once a month or so.

"Their eggs Benedict are the absolute best. I'd bet money on that."

Trudy scribbled a note: "Shall we say...five bucks?"

As he started to read, she shook her head, holding up ten fingers.

He laughed. "Ten bucks? Are you kidding me? I think we better stick to five. That way, when I take your money, I won't feel so bad. I'm telling you, this place is the absolute best."

"The bet stands at ten...Bozo."

He shook his head. "So the old adage is true: a fool and her money are soon parted." (The following Sunday morning, Trudy giggled as Lincoln stuffed ten one-dollar bills into her purse.)

Their bus stopped at Parnassus Avenue and Belvidere Street, a beautiful old neighborhood a half a mile or so from the UCSF Medical Center campus. Trudy stepped off the bus staring at the well-maintained vintage homes that lined the streets. Lincoln moved around her, turned the corner, and then over his shoulder said, "You better hurry. We're going to be late. Not to mention it's getting cold out here. Come on."

The temperature was dropping. Her shorts and thin summer blouse, comfortable that afternoon, had become no match for the onslaught of damp ocean air that had already begun to cool the city. She hurried to catch him, looking into his face as she did. Even after glancing away, his smile continued to wrap her with feelings of comfort. And as they walked, her hand found his. All day he'd wanted to hold her hand, but with great discipline had refrained, not wanting to do anything that might frighten or offend or give her cause to disappear from his life forever. And though he didn't look at her, she could see a small grin push back the side of his face. From then on, the ocean chill went completely unnoticed.

Leading her along a narrow walkway passing between two houses to a small guesthouse in the rear caused her to stop. Her suspicious look made him laugh. "Yes, it's my place, but don't worry. You don't have to come in, but you're going to need some warm clothes, and I think I have just the thing for you."

He walked to the front door, with her reluctantly following a short distance behind. A turn of the key, and the door opened. Warm air rushed to greet them. Waiting outside crossed her mind, but only momentarily, as she realized it would be nice to step inside and warm up a bit. So with some caution, she followed him into the small front room.

"You can leave the door open if you'd like. I'll just be a minute," he said, disappearing around a corner.

Stepping farther into the room and closing the door behind her, she was taken aback by its miniature size. There was not much to it—a couple of overstuffed chairs with a TV tray between them, a small wooden desk and a folding chair, a shelf that held a portable TV and stereo, and large speaker cabinets at each end of the room. Against two of the walls were homemade bookshelves filled with what she believed to be mostly medical books. She did notice a few on painting, astronomy, art, magic, and numerous copies of *National Geographic*. At the very top, prominently displayed, was a large book with the painted face of a circus clown on the cover. The title read *The World of Clowns*, by George Bishop.

The desk was cluttered but still had a sense of organization. An old Underwood typewriter held a single piece of blank paper. Just to the right, an open notebook showed sketches of what she recognized as the Japanese Tea Garden back at the park. A large scheduling calendar hung from the wall; handwritten in the dates were times and places and a smattering of small notes. Most were written in blue pen, although two stood out clearly as they were written in red. The largest covered an entire weekend still three weeks away. It read, "Sonoma, Mom's b-day." The other, written yesterday, read simply, "Lost my bike and my heart. Her name's Trudy."

This made her smile.

In the small kitchen sat a table for two, and just off to the right the tiniest bathroom she'd ever seen—so small she had to step inside to believe her own eyes. It would be impossible to use; even she would have difficulty maneuvering in such a cramped space. The thought of his big frame attempting to squeeze into the narrow shower stall at first made her giggle, and then it made her laugh.

"I see you've taken the tour of the castle. I'd show you the dungeon, but we need to get going. Here, try these on. I bought them for my mom so she'd have something warm to wear when she came to visit, but she hasn't been by lately to need them. They've been hanging in my closet now for a couple months."

Moving to the kitchen, he called back, "I'll go ahead and step outside while you change. Just yell at me when you're done. Oh yeah, there's a little more room in the bedroom, but wherever you feel comfortable... I'll just be outside."

She grabbed his arm and shook her head as if to say, don't be ridiculous, and then sat him at the kitchen table. Minutes later she emerged from the bedroom wearing a fashionable San Francisco Giants jogging suit. It was soft and warm and made her want to curl up in front of a fireplace instead of battle the cold San Francisco evening.

"You're so beautiful." he said.

She blushed, pushing him back with a gentle shove. "I'm serious; you'll be the most beautiful woman in the park."

Confused, she placed a finger in his palm, printing, "The park?"

"I love the park. It's where I found you." He smiled, removing a tag from her sleeve. A few minutes later, he emerged from the bedroom wearing a pair of jeans and a sweatshirt. From the small refrigerator he took two bottles of water, and they were out the door. He held her hand as they walked to the street, where he stopped at a slightly battered VW Bug.

Opening her door, he answered her question even before she could give him one of her looks. "It's mine. It's ugly, but it's paid for. Besides that, my dad hates it." Once inside, he turned to her. "I didn't think to ask. Do you like baseball?"

She shrugged, grabbed her pad, and wrote, "I've never been to a game. Do they sell hot dogs?"

"Yeah, they do. Best dogs in the city."

"Then why are we just sitting here? Let's go!"

Hot dogs and a cold beer chilled her enough to snuggle into his side during the top of the first inning. By the bottom of the inning, with his arm around her, she was toasty warm, staying that way for the remainder of the game. And it was the quickest game he could remember, or at least it seemed that way. By eleven thirty, they were parked in front of her apartment. At eleven forty, she closed the front door behind her and for a moment leaned against it, smiling. She hadn't wanted the evening to end, even entertaining his suggestion to stop at the all-night diner on Fulton Street for coffee. But tonight, that would be out of the question. Her brother Eric would be knocking on the door at three thirty ready for a day of fishing, the fulfillment of a promise she now regretted making.

She ran to the window and pulled back the curtain just in time to see the little car's taillights fade into the dark misty night. Though more thought than word, a soft, breath-filled whisper escaped her, forming its own fog on the cold glass, only to quickly disappear like the sound that had created it.

She set the alarm clock, fed the goldfish, and went to bed. There she lay thinking what a wonderful day it had been, remembering their conversations, the warmth of his hand, the sound of his laugh, the love in his eyes. Oh, how she had wanted him to kiss her good night, but he hadn't. *He's a true gentleman*, she thought as sleep came to carry her away. *A big old, wonder… fully cra…zy…sweet…gen…tle…man…*

Instinctively she tucked the covers under her chin and nestled deeper into her pillow. The room was still, the sights and sounds of the city at rest, her breath slow and even. Drifting, she pictured his face, his smile, and then, dreamily she thought, *I must be crazy too…I think I'm fall…*

She gasped sharply, sitting straight up in bed. Sleep was elusive after that, making the night long and restless, the sound of the alarm almost welcoming. She didn't shower or put on makeup, choosing only to wash her face, brush her teeth, and place her hair in a ponytail pulling it through her new SF Giants cap he'd bought for her after the game.

Like always, her brother was right on time, arriving with a partially eaten breakfast burrito and large coffee he'd picked up for her along the way. Driving through the dark streets, he asked twice if there was something wrong, and twice she shook her head no. He knew better but would let it go, at least for now.

She loved their boat, dedicating much of her free time to helping repair, remodel, and most of the time reconstruct the old nineteen thirties tug Eric had found six years ago rotting away in a salvage yard down in Palo Alto. Fresh out of the Marine Corps and only finding part-time work on the docks, he'd made the decision to go ahead and invest all his savings into the old relic, some used engine parts, and six months of mooring fees at the end of a tumbledown pier. He named the boat *Changes*, telling his friends it was after the popular David Bowie song; but the truth was, he wanted it to represent and help bring about some desperately needed changes to his future. And it did. Within a week he became a card-carrying longshoreman. And on his first day off, he made a quick trip to his aunt and uncle's house in Lodi to reclaim everything he'd left when he joined the corps.

Like most restorations, it doubled in budget and took twice as long to complete; but in the end it was beautiful, seaworthy, and more than capable of someday making the voyage of his dreams up the coast and through the inside passage to Alaska. It was Trudy's plan to accompany him on what she knew would be her own wonderful journey. Once there she'd look around, check out what opportunities were available, and then eventually make the decision to stay close to her brother or return alone to San Francisco. But that was still a year or two away.

Pulling out of the marina, the great boat moved effortlessly over the water. Setting the course for the open sea, Eric relaxed on the long padded bench behind the ship's mahogany wheel. Trudy stood to his right staring out the window, and again he detected something odd in her behavior. Normally this would be the time she'd slide onto the bench and take over the controls. But instead she stood silent, her gaze straight and distant. Eric, too, sat motionless watching her, wondering what thoughts must be entertaining her, mesmerizing her. He knew eventually she'd let him know, but in the meantime, they'd have a great day on the water, rippin' holes in the ocean, playing some Jimmy Buffett, killing a few fish, and maybe she'd even join him in a beer or two which always made her a little giddy and helped her to relax and open up.

Minutes passed. She remained still, her gaze never changing. Unnoticed, Eric slowly reached above her head. He pulled a large red handle, and a deep, low tone blasted through the air, staggering her with surprise.

"Wake up, little sister. It's a quarter past six. We're on the water, and it's time for you to wake up the city," he exclaimed, coming to his feet.

Eagerly she stared at him, her smile an open gateway of pending laughter.

"Tell me, young lady…how exactly are you planning on accomplishing this spectacular feat?"

The sudden excitement caused her to blush. *There's my sister*, he thought, hearing her soft laughter and watching her hand tremble faintly as it moved slowly over the wide console of buttons, lights, switches, and dials. She was no stranger to the wheelhouse. Truth was, she could pilot the vessel every bit as well as her brother. But to wake the city—now, that was something special.

Adjusting his cap, Eric leaned against the frame of the open doorway. Trudy glanced at the early-morning skyline. A large black dial covered by her grasp, turned smoothly to the right, stopping only once as she examined the setting. Smiling, she bumped it up another few notches…four…five…and a couple extra for good measure. She removed her hand, and the word *Volume* became clearly visible. There were two switches just above the black dial; she pushed one that read All Speakers. Her hand paused over the second, labeled

CD. As she looked at Eric, her smile grew. He winked his approval. Taking a deep breath she paused, exhaled completely, and flipped the switch.

The air erupted with the rhythmic sounds of drums, percussion, and piano, followed by the unmistakable voice of Joe Cocker singing "Feelin' Alright?"

Eric grabbed her by the hand, and they danced out onto the narrow walk of the wheelhouse and down the stairwell to the main deck. When Joe belted out the chorus, she watched as dockworkers waved, whooped, hollered, and danced along the wharf. In the marina, some early-rising boaters boogied on their decks while a number of passengers on an inbound ferry could be seen singing and dancing to the impromptu wake-up call for the good citizens of the City by the Bay.

Soon enough the song ended. The volume turned down, her brother again sat at the controls, she by his side. "What do you say we forget about fishing this morning and head over to the Tail for a decent breakfast."

Breakfast sounded great, especially at the Whale's Tail, one of her favorite places along the bay. She smiled and nodded her head.

"Oh yeah, and because you did such a great job rousing the city, I'll even let you pay."

She sneered in response.

"No! No! Don't try to argue about it. I insist," he protested. "I'm so hungry I just might order the whole right side of the menu..." He looked at her comically and then added, "Nah; I'll take it easy on your pocketbook. Three or four lobster cake breakfast specials ought to do just fine."

She pushed him, and he laughed. "We better hurry before all the tourists get there. You know how they love those lobster specials."

Throttling up the engine only partially drowned out his laughter, but that was okay with her. She didn't mind his teasing—most of the time, anyway, and she never grew tired of hearing him laugh. Leaning against the door frame, she inhaled deeply the cool air, watching a lone seagull circle above and disappear into a bank of high fog. In the large window, an opaque reflection caught her eye. It was her new cap. Adjusting the brim, she thought of Lincoln—his face, his voice, the touch of his...

"No!" She groaned, chasing the thoughts away before they could once again consume her.

You Are My Love

Eric looked at her enquiringly. A gentle wave of her hand dismissed any need for conversation, leaving her to casually step out and stand against the deck rail. Perhaps not truly wanting the memories to leave, her fingers stroked the brim once more.

As the boat moved across the bay, the cool spray of salt air blowing over her face brought not only energy, but gently awoke her to reality. It's always easier to think realistically, logically, in the light of day, and she couldn't think of a better place to do that than on the water with her big brother. She looked back at him, pulled her notepad from her pocket, and began to write.

Moments later she entered the wheelhouse and handed him the note, which he took with only a casual glance before setting it on the console and leaning down to open a small cupboard off to his side.

"Hey, that reminded me—Jennifer and I killed this the other night over dinner," he said, handing her an empty wine bottle. "I thought you might want to launch a note this morning."

She smiled. How many times had she placed a message in a bottle, sometimes releasing it in the bay, other times waiting until they were beyond the harbor entrance, watching the tide carry it far out to sea. The messages varied in content depending on her mood at the time; ranging from one word to one page. Sometimes simple but almost always thought provoking. Whether comical, philosophical, emotional, or occasionally even poetic, to her they were simply inscriptions from the heart, secret thoughts given to ride the waves and currents until delivered to the one person the sea chose to share its gift with.

Launch a bottle—that's perfect, she thought. Quickly snatching the note from the console, she rushed down the stairwell to the deck below. Eric called out, "Bring that back. I haven't read it yet…"

But she ignored him, quickly rolling up the note and placing it in the bottle.

Eric's voice blared from the PA speaker. "At least tell me what it says…"

She pushed the note tightly into the glass neck and watched it fall to the bottom. "Trudy, tell me what it says," he yelled, sticking his head out the window. "Don't make me come down there…"

She sealed the bottle with the cork and threw it as far as she could, observing it disappear under the waves to emerge some distance away, bobbing on the cold, dark surface of the sea. Typically she would stand on the deck watching the bottle drift away; not so today. She raced back up to the wheelhouse. Leaning on the railing just outside the doorway, Eric pointed it out. It took a moment for her eyes to focus, but then she watched it vanish into the distance, its dark-green color blending seamlessly into the waves continuing to pull farther away. For the next ten minutes, he bugged her to tell him the message, tickling her, threatening to throw her overboard to recover the bottle, and finally, getting her in a headlock and applying knuckle bumps to the top of her noggin. She laughed so hard she had to give in before wetting her pants, but he wouldn't stop until she'd crossed her heart twice, promising to tell him over breakfast what the note had said. Once the excitement died down, she began to wonder what exactly she'd say. This would take some thought.

Returning to the main deck, she sat on the curved bench outside the captain's stateroom, possibly her favorite spot in the entire world—at least of the few places she had been so far. A place where she found solace merely watching the world drift by, where she could peacefully, safely reflect on events of the past, matters of the day, or hopes for the future. Sometimes at night, miles out to sea, with the darkness of the sky and water defined only by the stars above, she envisioned the how-comes, what-ifs, and the whys of her life. She never sought answers in this special place but allowed them to drift to her on currents of wind or sea, shifting clouds or in the creak of the boat as it rocked her to sleep. Twice they were clearly announced by passing seagulls and once by the foghorn at South Tower Pier.

Far-fetched? Just a vivid imagination? Maybe! But it was what she believed. This place was her magic eight ball, where innermost questions might be asked and answers miraculously appear. And this morning she had questions—many, many questions, intimate questions. Questions in and of her heart, her thoughts, her emotions. So many how-comes, what-ifs, and whys. Everything began running together, making it impossible to decipher which answers went with what questions. With frantic desperation, she whispered, "What do I do?"

The answer came quickly, miraculously. Yes, it was true. It could've been just her imagination; after all, they were still some distance from land, and the engine still roared to hold their speed. But it was what she believed that mattered to her, and she believes the answer had come drifting ever so softly through the air. Beautiful, consoling was the peaceful sound of distant church bells. As she bowed her head, the words coming loudly from her heart remained unspoken. "I'm so afraid. This man…these feelings…is it possible to…and what about my…oh…I'm so confused. I need your help, Lord. Take my hand…speak to me. You know my thoughts; you know my…Lord is this truly? Am I?"

Leaning back, she closed her eyes, allowing her feelings not only to comfort her mind but her heart as well. Had she ever felt this wonderful, so at peace? She was sure she had. She must have, but for now she didn't want to think about such things. Instead she'd simply lie back and enjoy this beautiful morning in what was her favorite spot in the whole world.

Small patches of fog clung to the orange spans of the great old bridge and then rolled along the cliffs to the shoreline and into the sea. As the boat approached the small village of Sausalito, with its colony of musicians, artists, and poets, all seem to beckon her, to speak to her in melodies and sonnets of ardent love. From a hillside loft, the soundless voice of a muse rode the soft gray breeze. A moment of secrets and whispers was shared, forming fingers of mist and fog, drifting, curling, lying upon the water, a final caress before bidding a vaporous farewell.

A mighty blast of the boat's horn vibrated her eyes open. She smiled and held herself tightly, whispering, "Lincoln…his name is Lincoln."

Her voice, engulfed in the roar of the engine and crash of waves on the bow, was rescued by a swirling wind to be carried high above the boat and beyond the now thin layer of fog. She looked to the sky as if to watch it leave. She removed the pad of paper from her jacket pocket and jotted down a single word, folded it in half, and then folded it again. The drone of the engine changed, and the large boat began slowing steadily as Eric prepared to enter the no-wake zone leading to the small waterfront mooring area. Then came a second short blast. Tucking the piece of paper into her shirt pocket, she got busy preparing the lines for docking.

At breakfast Eric patiently waited for her to bring up the note. He sat quietly, indicating it was she who needed to implement the topic of conversation, and she did. But she wasn't ready to discuss the note, so she wrote, "How's Jennifer?" And then: "Tell me about the concert last weekend.

Sorry I couldn't go. Did you get the contract to remodel that houseboat? Are you really getting a dog?"

Hoping to stay off what she knew was inevitable, her topics came rapid-fire, allowing for little pause between subjects. But Eric knew how to play that game and began answering every question with just one word. Soon they sat quietly eating their breakfast. At first she didn't mind. It gave her a chance to savor what she had long considered the ultimate breakfast at the best breakfast place on the bay. However, halfway through her eggs Benedict, she gave up and wrote, "It said, 'Do you believe it's possible to fall in love after one date?'"

He studied it for a minute. "Hmm…" Not the strangest question she'd ever launched in a bottle, but definitely something to chew on. He laughed to himself, taking a bite of toast.

"I don't know, Tru," he said, pondering the question further. "Love is different things to different people, I guess. You know there's puppy love, true love, and, of course, everlasting love, like Mom and Dad had."

Taking another bite of toast, he looked out the window. "Too much work," he said as three large sailboats headed for the open bay. Noticing her annoyed look, he quickly added, "I meant sailing, not falling in love." He thought for a split second. "Well, I guess that's a lot of work too." Neither her gaze nor her expression had changed since she'd revealed what the note said.

"You're wanting an answer, aren't you?" he asked, somewhat surprised. "Well, I don't know, Tru. I mean, this is a hard one—complicated, you know? Especially if you really think about it." Again he took a bite, giving himself time to process his thoughts. "I guess I believe a lot of people are easily fooled by infatuation, thinking they've fallen in love. But after a while it turns out to be just lust. At least that's what I've seen…

"A lasting relationship is the last thing on anyone's mind nowadays. It's strictly about their needs—you know, the one-night stand, and then move on." Feeling more than a little uncomfortable, he took a chug of orange juice. "And that's not love or lust. It's just plain selfishness."

Stopping to gather his thoughts, he again looked out the window. She remained attentively focused until his attention resumed. "Man, Tru, this really is a tough one when you think about it. I'd love to be a mouse in the corner when somebody opens that bottle. I just hope they give it some thought, not just shrug it off and toss it away. Do you ever think about that? The people who find these notes, I mean. If it ended up on the right beach at the right time, and the right person picked it up, man...it could change someone's life profoundly. You ever think about that?"

She pointed to the note and then at him.

"You mean how I feel personally?" he asked, his smile almost becoming a laugh. "You know I've dated a few ladies, but dating is not being in love. I mean, really, you and Ma are the only two women I've ever loved—maybe ever will love. Who knows? Honestly, take Jennifer. We've been dating for almost a year, and sure, we have some fun, but love? No! And I think we've both known that right from the start. On our first date it was just lust, plain and simple. And over the last year, yeah, we've grown close, but are we in love? No. We have a hard time understanding each other; it's like we're from different worlds. You know what she asked me just last month? When I was going to grow up and sell my boat and buy a real home."

Grunting loudly, he ripped another bite from his toast. "Yeah, can you believe it? So, as for me, I'd have to say no, it's not possible. It just doesn't happen; couldn't happen. Not love anyway. Not after one date. Hell, maybe never." He shoveled in a big lump of crab cake. "This is really good. How about yours?"

She didn't comment.

He set his fork down, picked up his napkin, brushed it over his mouth, and glanced out the window in thought once again but quickly brought his attention back to his sister. "Now, if I use you as an example, I'd definitely have to say it's totally, completely, absolutely, and entirely impossible. You just don't enjoy interacting socially. You never have, and...well, I just don't know that you ever will. And that's not a bad thing. But I can count on one hand the number of dates you've been on."

Lifting up two fingers, he shook his head and continued. "Now, that'll definitely put a crimp in your chances of falling in love after a first date. But it doesn't matter, since you're really not a member of the dating scene anyway..."

He reached across the table and took a piece of toast from her plate. "Besides, those guys were jerks to begin with. They didn't even try to communicate with you. They just wanted...well..."

He tore at the toast, finishing it in two bites. "But you know what, Tru?

I think someday, out of the blue, some lucky guy will come along and fall madly in love with you for you—you know what I mean. The person you are. He'll see you the way I see you. You'll laugh and have conversations like we do. His interest will be in your mind, not just your..."

Again he helped himself to another piece of her toast. "Yeah, this guy's going to treat you so great...you're not gonna know what..."

He stopped. There was something behind his sister's beautiful eyes, something he hadn't seen since she was a child but definitely still recognized. That mischievous little grin she got when holding back a secret. Intrigued, he wondered: Could this be why she'd been so quiet all morning? Had she met someone, someone she didn't run away from, someone she actually... The cap! How could he not have noticed it before? To think she'd allow someone to get close enough to her to trigger an emotional response was almost inconceivable. Yet here she sat with a brand-new cap she would have never bought, the start of that silly little grin and this odd question on the table. He knew in some bizarre way it all added up to one thing...and he hated it. He had to be wrong about this; silently he prayed he was wrong. There's no way she...no way would he allow some guy...

"More coffee?" the waitress asked.

Trudy held Eric's cup for her to fill, smiled, nodded a thank-you, and resumed her previous position holding the attention of her big brother, her smile becoming all the more prominent. This time it was Eric's stare that had not drifted. He couldn't pinpoint his emotion: anger, hurt, betrayed... protective? Protective, of course. The thought of anyone hurting his sister...

He stopped just short of opening his mouth as an old reality came to him. It seemed he and God had spoken many times about this very matter over the years, and wasn't it he who had prayed for someone to come into her life? Someone who would love her just the way she was?

Turning away, he gazed out the window to three distant sails, one leading the way, the other two in pursuit. Way too much work, he thought. And then it dawned on him—*Wait a second; maybe I'm wrong. Of course I'm wrong. My little sister runs away if a guy even so much as says good morning.* Looking back around, he leaned across the booth, saying happily, "I love you, Tru. Are you going to finish that plate?"

Questioningly and somewhat regretfully, she looked at her meal and slid it in front of him. He took a bite of hobo potatoes and started on what was left of the eggs Benedict, sopping up the sauce with another bite or two of potato. His conversation retreated back to finding the bottle and his relationship with Jennifer, both topics dying quickly.

"Let me ask you, Tru: Do you think it's possible to fall in love with someone after one date?"

Her grin slowly began to twist into that cute little smirk he'd always loved. Pulling a note from her shirt pocket, she laid it on the table in front of him. He didn't pick it up; his eyes moving between the note and the plate, he finished the potatoes, washing them down with her orange juice. Finally, he reached for the note.

He wasn't sure why he didn't want to open it; he just knew he didn't. As he flipped open the first fold, his eyes remained focused on her, watching the smirk slowly turn into a thin smile. Hearing the paper rustle as he finished the second fold, his eyes remained fixed on her. Only after taking a deep breath, and even then with some hesitation, he read the single word: "Yes."

They spent the next hour and a half talking, he as a concerned brother and she as a woman in love, each of them revisiting the question many, many times, he perhaps hoping her answer would change and she hoping perhaps to change his answer. But in the end, he had to admit, he'd never seen her so happy, so excited. He would meet this Lincoln Trudeau for himself, take him out to Sully's for a beer, and they'd get acquainted. Very acquainted! He'd simply explain to Mr....Dr. Trudeau, if he truly was a doctor, that if his beautiful sister got hurt in any way, there'd be consequences. And as a former marine, this was not a threat—it was a promise.

That day came soon enough. Eric and Lincoln spent the afternoon at Sully's drinking and talking about their love for this wonderful woman and then drank some more. Around midnight, Trudy became a smidge concerned, deciding to walk from the boat to the bar just a few blocks from the marina. What she encountered when she arrived was not very pretty but was awfully amusing. The owner was glad to see her, as were many of the patrons. And after effortlessly herding them from the building, Trudy would become a leaning post for these two overgrown, extremely inebriated boys, buddies, friends, pals. And at one point, she heard Eric say, brothers.

At five o'clock the next morning, the diesel engine roared to life, Trudy at the helm for an unscheduled day of fishing on the bay with the two men she loved. And yes, there was music. That evening Lincoln drove her home, where he kissed her good night at the door. And again, there was music. They spent time together at least once a day over the next few weeks. Sometimes for hours on end, other times for just a quick kiss or an I love you; see you tomorrow. But through their time together, Lincoln never once asked why she didn't speak.

Eric had started to bring it up that night at the bar, but Lincoln would have nothing to do with it, quickly informing him that her speech, or lack of, was not an issue. When and if she ever chose to share an explanation, that would be fine. But it would be her choice, her doing, her conditions, in her time. As far as he was concerned, they conversed quite nicely as it was. With new respect, Eric bought another round.

❖

Lincoln invited her to accompany him to Sonoma for his mother's birthday weekend. She immediately declined, citing reason after reason. Lincoln replied with only one of his own: "I want the woman I love to meet the woman I love."

Over the next week, Trudy finally, at least half-heartedly, agreed to go. The night before they were to leave, over a plate of barbecued mac and cheese, she wrote, "You know she'll ask why I don't speak."

With shock in his eyes, Lincoln raised his hand to his mouth. "You don't? Are you sure?" he exclaimed with a smile. "When did this happen? Because it sure feels like I can't shut you up half the time."

Through Trudy's smile Lincoln sensed her trepidation. His smile faded, and she watched his eyes sadden and felt her heart breaking. She began to write, but laying his hand atop hers, he stopped the pen, interrupting her words with spoken ones of his own.

"Trudy, I love you more than anything, and I'd never ask you to do something you felt you couldn't. I'd love for you to go. I'd love for you to meet my mom, and believe me, I know how hard it would be for you and how hard this decision must be. But I think you and Mom would hit it off great. They say she and I are a lot alike—one more thing that drives my dad up the wall. So believe me, Tru, she'll take one look at you, and...no, she'll take one look at me—at us—and she'll know just like I did, you and I are meant to be. And just like me, she'll fall in love with you right on the spot."

His eyes were no longer sad but were filled with the love she had grown accustomed to over the past few weeks. And like always, it quickly moved from his face straight to her heart. She slid her hand from under his and wrote: "I've never been to Sonoma before...do they sell hot dogs?"

After helping with the dishes, Lincoln adjourned to the living room. Trudy walked to the bedroom and returned minutes later with a large comforter, a pillow, and a dusty old scrapbook. She made Lincoln sit quietly as she penned another note:

No questions.
    Here are a couple of things you need to know.
    Number one: You can't go home tonight. I'm afraid if you did, I might change my mind and not go tomorrow, and that would make me very sad. The couch is pretty comfortable.
    Number two: This is the scrapbook of my accident and why I seldom speak. I can't be here when you read it, so I'm going to walk down to Tuscano's and buy your mom a nice bottle of wine for her birthday. I should be back in an hour or so.
    PS: I promise I won't change my mind in the next hour. And I can only pray...you don't either.

She grabbed her sweater and purse. As she leaned down to kiss his cheek, he thought he noticed tears in her eyes. And then she was gone. He opened the scrapbook to the first page, and there was one of her notes, yellowed with age, the handwriting not as practiced as now. It read:

Other than my brother Eric, no one else has ever seen this book. And in all honesty, not in my wildest imagination did I dream anyone ever would. You are the first, and you will be the only. So, whoever you are, all I ask is that you continue looking at me the way you always have. Never love me less than you did yesterday, and know that I will love you the same. Did I say love? It's hard for me to even imagine that right now. But if you're reading this, you need to know you own my heart, and I will love you forever.

Lincoln read the headlines: "Three-Year-Old Sole Survivor in Fatal Crash."

"Baby girl escapes with minor injuries."

"Mother and father perish; baby has scrapes and bruises."

The pictures were horrific. Lincoln wondered how anyone could have survived. There was a news photo of a young child, tears on her cheeks, arm in a cast, her head wrapped in wide strips of white bandages. The copy was simple and to the point: after being released from the hospital with only minor injuries, the girl and her seven-year-old brother would stay with their aunt and uncle in Lodi, California.

There were fourteen pages in the scrapbook, with only a few pictures of Trudy and her brother. In most of those, they were together but rarely the main subject. There was a large professional picture of Eric in his marine uniform. Underneath Trudy had written, "My big brother."

The next two pictures were also the last. A mature Eric, brooding and explosive, dressed in blue jeans and a white T-shirt, leaning against the front fender of a faded red '51 Ford pickup, his arm around a scrawny fifteen-year-old Trudy, her arms around his waist, a large smile on her face. Underneath she had written, "RESCUED. I told you he'd come back for me. Go to hell, Lodi. We're off to The City."

Directly below was a picture of a dilapidated old tugboat listing to one side, tied to what appeared to be an abandoned dock. Written in Trudy's hand: "My new home. It's beautiful. I love you Eric."

There were copies of medical recommendations stating her physical injuries were minor, though she suffered great emotional and psychological trauma as a result of witnessing the death of her parents. It was believed the child would need to be evaluated by a psychologist and that her speech should most likely return over time with the help of a speech pathologist.

Trudy's note: "I only remember ever seeing Dr. Stoddard. He's my aunt's family doc. He told her I'll talk when I'm ready, and headaches like these are common in all kids; not to worry; I'd grow out of it. I haven't yet, and it's been ten years. I suppose that's not entirely true. I can talk; I just can't speak above a whisper, which makes it hard to be heard over all the laughter."

At the top of the following page she had written, "I shall tell you the story of Ella: It was in the forest of her imagination as she hid from a world that knew little kindness for a child who could not roar. She loved to dance and sing in whispers, sheltered from scorn, under the bear's umbrella."

The next two pages were blank, as if waiting to be filled with Ella's story. After that, the pages were filled with notes, scraps of paper kept much like a diary, with dates and events giving some insight into her childhood but mainly addressing the physical and emotional agony of a young girl ridiculed by peers, shunned by society, and forced to become shy, introverted, and eventually reclusive in order to survive. Page after page she detailed her struggles with pain, emotion, fear, and the separation of human contact, leaving her confused and unable to concentrate and having bouts of anger, guilt, and shame, many times feeling disconnected from the world, with Eric being her only savior. Well, him and the kindly old bear holding an umbrella Eric had given her on her sixth birthday.

Something Lincoln noticed right away was the way in which the notes were written. Even the ones written when she was obviously very young—seven, eight years old—were not penned by a girl feeling sorry for herself, or, for that matter, designed to be read by anyone at all, especially her aunt and uncle. They were simply written as so she wouldn't forget the journey she had been through. On the very last page was a note written recently, within the last year, by the sound of it:

> Life has been wonderful. I have a job working with handicapped children, and someday I hope to become a certified therapist. The staff no longer acts or treats me like I'm one of the patients (although Rosalie insists on calling me handicapped, which I'm not). Now they just tend to avoid me. But on many occasions, they've come to me seeking my opinion and my assistance with some of the more challenging kids we have. Even I'm amazed at the connection these

children make with me. It's almost like they sense a bond between us. I think I might have found my niche in life, and I've been looking into returning to college. God, I hate the thought of classrooms again.

On my eighteenth birthday, I moved off the boat and into my own apartment. Eric was really pissed. He was afraid something would happen and I wouldn't be able to yell for help. He bought me a big gun and taught me how to shoot. And sometimes when he drops by to visit, he'll check the nightstand to make sure it's there, loaded and ready to go. I love my big brother.

That's the good news.

The bad news is, the headaches are back.

Lincoln didn't wait for her to return but ran to Tuscano's, where she was still gazing at the many bottles of wine. He didn't say a word. He simply took her in his strong arms. Gently, he held her close. For a moment she could feel his arms tremble. He didn't notice, nor would he have cared, that there were tears on his cheeks. "I love you more than I did yesterday, and I'll love you even more tomorrow."

She pulled him close, rising to her tiptoes, her mouth lying close to his ear, where for the first time he heard her breath a whisper of broken words: "I...I love you...Lin con...Tru...deau."

❦

Trudy was barely out of the car before Lincoln's mother Carolyn rushed out of the house all smiles and waving arms, welcoming them both with hugs and kisses. Overwhelmed, Trudy could only blush and giggle. Lincoln quickly moved to put his arm around her, saying, "Mom, I'd like you to meet Trudy." There was the slightest pause, and then he added, "Here, she brought you something."

Trudy handed her the bottle of wine from Toscano's and a note, written on stationery she'd been saving for a special occasion. At first Carolyn thought it was something for her birthday and started to give Trudy a hug. Lincoln quickly interjected, "You need to read the note now, Mom."

She was taken aback, confused, not knowing what to make of her son's odd request. A quick glance at Trudy provided her no further insight, so she began to read:

I know you'll have questions, so please feel free to ask whatever you'd like. I don't speak due to an accident that happened when I was three.

Your son accosted me in the park three weeks ago, and I haven't been able to get rid of him since—which is okay, because I have fallen hopelessly in love with him. I hope I'm not intruding or being out of line when I say (okay, when I write) I'm truly honored he invited me to meet you and celebrate your birthday. And just a side note: thanks for raising such an incredibly loving man.

She looked into the eyes of her son and began to tear up. Then she looked into those of Trudy and began to sob, throwing her arms around the young woman. "You're going to be my daughter-in-law, aren't you?"

August 27, 1977, 3:00 p.m. It was a simple affair held at the end of an immense west-side pier supplied by friends of the bride. In attendance were fourteen dockworkers, three foremen, and all their wives; one child-services worker and guest; numerous doctors, nurses, interns, and students; two teachers; and assorted family members of the groom. The event was catered by Rock n Wood Pizza.

The groom was handsome, the bride stunningly beautiful, and when it was time for Eric to give his sister away, he embraced her tightly, placing her hand in that of Lincoln's and then pausing for a needed moment. His voice was shaky, his eyes damp, and after two failed attempts, he finally said, "This is the toughest thing I've ever done, but it's also the best." He cleared his throat one more time, looked at his sister, and took a second deep breath.

"Trudy, I know how much you love this guy, and Linc, I know you love her every bit as much as I do." Pausing, he looked at them both and then focused his attention solely on Lincoln. "So it is my honor to present you my little sister."

After the ceremony, there was dining, music and dancing, champagne, and toasts. His mother cried with joy, lovingly hugging her new daughter-in-law. Later in the evening, she and Lincoln danced.

"I'm sorry your father didn't show up."

"I'm not!" Lincoln smiled, twirling her. "He made it clear he doesn't approve, will never approve."

His mother huffed, "He's such a..."

Again her son twirled her. "Said he doesn't want to hear from me until I've come to my senses. Even called me an ingrate."

"Oh, I can only imagine what he called Trudy. She wasn't there, was she? He has no sense of decency..."

"She heard. So then she spent a couple of days working on a letter—you know, trying to get it just right—and dropped it in with the invitation. He mailed them back unopened. Well, at least that's what he wanted us to believe. Tru found part of a parking stub stuck to the back of the invitation."

"What an idiot..."

Again her dress fanned, catching a slight breeze from another quick twirl, then one more and she was back in the arms of her son. As evening settled onto the bay, Lincoln and Trudy walked to the decorated gangplank at the end of the pier. Someone had even decorated the boat and hung a large sign on the back that read Just Married. At seven fifteen, to the applause and cheers of all in attendance, Trudy sounded the horn and blew an extra kiss goodbye to her brother, and the newlyweds began sailing off into the sunset. Five hundred yards out, a large black dial turned to the right, two switches were flipped, and the air erupted with the rhythmic sounds of drums, percussion, and piano; and then the unmistakable voice of Joe Cocker singing "Feeling Alright?"

❦

The headaches did return, gradually at first, starting with a small, dull ache in the back of her head, annoying for a day, sometimes two, and then disappearing for as long as a week. They were different than before. The throbbing remained mild—tolerable, in fact—nothing like the intense pain that used to debilitate her for days on end. She thought, *I can live with this*, and she never bothered to mention it to Lincoln.

That December he became concerned when he came home early to find her lying on the bed in a lethargic state. On the back of her head was a melted ice pack, indicating she'd been there for a number of hours. Trudy explained it away by saying that sometimes the medication made her drowsy. Lincoln knew she had a prescription for Darvocet, which he also knew made some patients tired, so he didn't feel the need to pursue the matter any further at the time. He jotted down a note to himself, neurology appointment ASAP, and taped it to the top of his folder. By the next morning, she was back to her old self, making plans to stop by the hospital and have dinner with him in the cafeteria. At five thirty-five, he met her at the main entrance. Almost the instant she kissed him hello, the headache returned. The cafeteria was noisy and crowded, the food line congested, but she didn't care. She loved being there with him. Moving through the line, he touched her hand, softly kissing the back of her neck twice, making her blush. He whispered in her ear, "I love you, Mrs. Trudeau."

On her tray was a small salad, a bowl of Jell-O, and a soft drink. Nurse Pedley later said she'd seen the tray shake just before it fell to the floor. Kathy Thompson and Mitch Braden from radiology thought the girl winced and gasped for air just before collapsing in a heap, and one of the servers behind the counter screamed, "Oh my God. Someone call an ambulance."

❀

Lincoln wasn't used to being on this side of the waiting room door. But he had a large support group of fellow colleagues that would stay with him for as long as it took to receive word on Trudy's condition. He attempted to contact Eric a number of times, but no one picked up the phone at the marina office or the one on the dock just twenty feet from the boat. Dr. Kellie Morgan volunteered to drive to the marina, saying, "I know which boat it is. I take the ferry every morning. It's not like you can miss him; he's beautiful…I mean his boat is beautiful."

Lincoln feebly smiled. "Thanks, Kellie. I can't tell you how much I…" But she was out the door before he could finish.

Over the next hour, nurses brought or relayed reports to him: she still hasn't fully regained consciousness; the lab reports aren't back yet; they want to do a spinal tap. And then came the word Dr. Moylan had arrived.

Dr. David Moylan was codirector of the Center for Neurological Disorders and was considered one of the top neurotrauma surgeons in the state. Lincoln had met him once briefly while working in the ER and was amused to hear the nursing staff referred to him as "the magic man," a name that Lincoln now prayed would hold true. Whatever the cause for Trudy's collapse, the summons of Dr. Moyer brought into light the seriousness of her condition. Lincoln was no longer worried and concerned. Now he was afraid.

As the minutes ticked by, the members of his support group grew. Most remained seated; all remained hushed. Unlike the other clocks throughout the building, this one made no sound as the hands moved incessantly slow over the face, leaving him time to ponder the memories of the last four months and silence to consider if they'd be all he would leave the hospital with. The hollowness of life without her and the thought of returning to the apartment alone tore at his heart. He'd need someone else to pack things up; he'd be unable to stand not seeing her at the table, on the couch, or waiting for him to come to bed. And the rooms—they would still be fresh with her smell, her presence. Her life. No, he couldn't return home. And how would he tell Eric?

It was quiet in this room, he thought, a harbor from the sounds of life and death that so often filled these hallways. A space of innocuous design specifically intended for privacy, meditation, and inner prayer while tempering the sound of sobbing loved ones in the throes of loss. Yes, this was a quiet room where all you could do…was wait.

❧

Dr. Moylan entered with no introduction, nor did he require one of Lincoln, walking directly to him extending one hand while placing the other on Lincoln's shoulder as though speaking with an old friend.

"It's a pleasure to see you again, Lincoln. I'm sorry it's under these circumstances. Walk with me; I want to show you something."

Headed to radiology, Dr. Moylan explained his concerns and inquired of Trudy's background. Lincoln immediately told him everything he could remember, including the incident of the night before and how just this morning he'd filled out financial statement papers in hopes of having her seen here at the hospital.

"How long has she had Dysarthria?"

"Her whole life, I guess. Well, since she was three…since the accident. I've only heard her speak maybe two or three times, and then only slightly above a whisper. Her speech is not so much slurred but sluggish and disjointed…"

"It's unlikely the accident initiated the tumor. I mean, twenty years is a long time for it to grow unnoticed. But it's also not unheard of. But if that's the case, it would sure explain a lot."

The two discussed the options, the possibilities, and probable prognosis. Lincoln knew they were exploring a hypothetical scenario that had the potential to change rapidly, the outcome teetering on the edge of a scalpel and the steady hand of the surgeon, where the difference between success and failure might be measured in millimeters and prayers.

Dr. Moylan stood to shake Lincoln's hand, saying, "I'll see you tomorrow morning before the surgery."

"Oh, I'll be here." Lincoln smiled.

"I know you will." The doctor smiled back. "I'm having a cot put in her room right now."

Back in the waiting area, Lincoln explained the situation and thanked everyone for being there, declining the offers of those volunteering to stay, all insisting they'd check in first thing in the morning. Minutes later he found himself alone. The future, hidden by uncertainty, left him numb, anxious, and afraid, and though it was his memories of her smile, her giggle, her tender love that filled his heart, it was knowing her strength, her determination, and strong will that gave him hope and allowed him a smile.

Eric arrived ten minutes later, Kellie by his side. Lincoln filled him in, explaining all the details, leaving nothing out. The big man was trembling. His eyes filled with tears, and there in the quiet room, he fell to his knees and prayed.

Eight weeks after surgery, the petite young woman walked the pier to the boat, her husband on one side, her brother on the other, and Kellie following close behind. In the wheelhouse she took her spot at the controls and began to move the boat forward. It moved smoothly out into the bay. She smiled and took the hands of the two men, who continued to stand by her side, and then, though somewhat slow and slightly muddled, but well above a whisper, she said, "I...love you guys." And with a turn of the dial and the click of two switches, the air erupted with the unmistakable rhythmic sounds of drums, percussion, and voice of Joe Cocker.

❦

"Mr. Trudy, can I go see if he's back?"

"That's fine with me, Beth, but you'd better run it past your daddy first."

"Go ahead, baby girl. Just stay on the deck, and don't be tracking snow and mud across the floor."

Beth ran over and hugged Miss Trudy. "Thank you for the breakfast." Then she disappeared outside.

"Jim should be pulling in sometime late this morning to get the place aired out before Ann shows up tomorrow or whenever," Lincoln said.

Chris's eyes widened. "I sure hope she makes her Rice Krispies things this year."

Lincoln's eyes also lit up. "Those things are sinful. They're addicting. Tru got mad at me last year because I only saved her two or three. I'd have sat there and eaten the rest of 'em, watching football, if she hadn't walked in when she did."

Trudy walked over to the table. "He left me one. The man ate a dozen or more in an afternoon and left me one. And I don't think it was a whole one either. I'm pretty sure he cut the end of it off."

The three of them laughed and enjoyed coffee together. It wasn't long before Beth returned, bored and ready to be entertained. Mr. Trudy was more than happy to oblige, recently mastering three new magic tricks. Trudy silently adjourned to her cozy secluded office in the upper loft of the Olympics View section of the home. There, taking in the rugged beauty of the mountains, pausing to read her notes recounting her last thoughts, she quietly, secretly, began to work her own magic.

CHAPTER NINE

"Do we need to put our snowshoes on?"

"Not yet, but I'll strap them to my backpack just in case we need 'em later to get back to the car. While I do that, look in the back seat and get the lantern, the flashlights, and there's a thermos of hot chocolate back there too. Oh, and Michael, look underneath that blanket. I think there's a Christmas present you forgot to open."

Michael rushed to the back seat of the car and quickly lifted the blanket to find a large package. Ripping the paper revealed a red helmet with a large spotlight on the front. Snapping the light on, he placed the helmet on his head and yelled, "It's just like yours, Uncle Kevin. I'll be able to see in the dark and everything. And look—it fits good. Can you help me buckle it?"

Kevin checked the fit, adjusted the strap, and took Michael's picture. "You'll be the best-dressed guy in the cave today. Grab your flashlight. I'll carry the lantern, and hand me that thermos. You better turn off your headlight to save the batteries. It gets pretty dark in there."

Michael stared at Kevin without moving. "Real dark?"

Kevin placed the palm of his hand at the very end of Michael's nose. "Can you see my hand?"

"Yeah…"

"Once inside, you won't be able to without that light."

Michael quickly snapped the light off.

"You need to tell me if you get cold or tired, and once we're inside, if you feel uncomfortable, you have to let me know. Got it? We don't have to go all the way to the end if you don't want to. It can be a little spooky your first time."

"Got it!" The boy walked another five steps in silence before asking,

"Just how spooky can it get, Uncle Kevin? I mean, not that I'm afraid or nothin'. Just curious, that's all."

❧

The air held a brisk chill, the sky was clear and blue, and there were fresh footprints in the snow leading well beyond the Road Closed sign at the top of the hill. Only two other cars were parked in the lot, leaving Kevin to believe that at least for the most part, Michael would be able to experience undisturbed silence, rare during the summer months, when the cave became a bustling hive of families, scout troops, and tourists wandering its passageways more enthralled with reaching the end than in its beauty.

The Forest Service didn't maintain the upper road during the winter months, but it provided a Sno Park at Trail of Two Forest a little less than a mile from the cave entrance. The visitor center would be closed, but the cave remained open year round. Kevin planned on the hike up taking half an hour to forty-five minutes, a little more if they needed to use their snowshoes, which, as it turned out, they did not.

Reaching the upper parking lot in a little under an hour, they made their way to the entrance. At first Michael thought it didn't look like a cave at all, but just a big hole in the ground. Standing at the top of the steep walkway, he saw its wide metal steps leading down into the belly of a cavernous chamber. The large opening around him allowed snow to pile at the bottom of the steps, leaving a white circle on the dark, sandy floor. He attempted to look into the long black tunnel leading deep into the side of the mountain, but the morning light died quickly after reaching only twenty yards or so. This reminded him to turn on his headlamp.

Kevin began the descent first, once again noticing the snow had been disturbed recently by others. At the first landing, he paused, looking up at Michael. "Are you coming?"

Rubbing his hands on his pants, Michael took a minute to muster the courage to take the first step. His foot nestled into the snow with a crunch; his eyes scanned the gaping mouth and peripheral darkness of the Great Room below. There was a flow of air he hadn't noticed before. Even through his gloves, the metal handrail felt cold. He adjusted his helmet, checked the strap under his chin, and slowly, cautiously took another step. Continuing to watch the dark tunnel to the right of the Great Room, he suddenly came to an abrupt stop. Was that a noise?

Kevin was looking up at him and didn't appear to have heard it. For a few seconds, Michael listened intently and then shrugged it off as imagination. Gradually he took another step, then another, quickly moving down the steep stairway and stopping to stand next to Kevin on a large stone landing, part of the stairway leading to the floor.

"This next part doesn't have a railing, so you'll want to be extra careful and step where I step," Kevin told him.

Michael's eyes again focused on the yawning mouth of the tunnel. The opening was high, the walls wide. Large rocks and a few giant boulders littered the sandy floor. It was all mysteriously enticing and enchantingly beautiful yet cold and foreboding at the same time, enhanced by its alien appearance and heavy damp air. Broken shards of frozen shadows stretched their way beyond the vast ingress to rest at the base of the steps. A chill ran through him. Almost rhythmically he began moving down the last twelve steps, not hurrying, not exerting his small frame, and not taking his eyes off the gaping tunnel but to occasionally assure his next step before quickly directing his attention back to the blackness at the end of the cavern. Three steps from the bottom, his rhythm broke when he paused briefly to question his bravery.

Their descent had been slow and wary, yet quick shallow whiffs of breath escaped into the large open grotto where they now stood. His small gloved hand pointed toward the dark tunnel. "Are the apes in there?"

At first Kevin wasn't sure he'd heard the question correctly, but then, realizing what Michael must be thinking and what must be going on in the young boy's mind, it was difficult not to laugh. He knelt down, acting as if adjusting the boy's jacket and helmet, and looked Michael in the eyes. "There are no apes in this place. It's just named after the people who discovered it. They belonged to a club called the Mount Saint Helens Apes. So from that day on, this place has been known as the Ape Caves."

Michael's relief was not obvious at first, but cautiously he made his way off the snow mound onto the dry sandy floor. Once there, he stared apprehensively into the long, dark tunnel.

"Are there any bears...or lions...or anything else that might eat us?"

Now Kevin laughed, and a slight echo returned. "Nope. It's just a big empty hole in the ground. Absolutely nothing to be afraid of. But let me know if you start to feel uncomfortable, and we'll turn around and come back out. No big deal!"

"So there's nothing hiding in the dark that'll jump out at me?"

"Not a thing, except me if you wander off too far."

Michael looked around and noticed an additional tunnel at the opposite end of the cavern. "Which way do we go, Uncle Kevin?"

Kevin turned on his headlamp and pointed to the one going slightly downhill. "There are two sections, an upper and a lower. I thought since it was quite a hike up here to begin with, and this being your first time spelunking..."

Michael's face contorted, expressing his question.

"It means to explore a cave!" Kevin smiled. "I thought we'd go ahead and do the easy one. And then if you like it, next time we'll do the harder one."

Michael's confidence was riding high now that he knew there were no apes to carry him off and no bears to gobble him up. Even so, he stayed within touching distance of his uncle as they made their way closer to the tunnel's darkness. Maybe to bolster his courage, he looked at Kevin and said smugly, "I'm not afraid of the dark at all, so maybe after we get in there a ways, we can stop and have some hot chocolate? Oh, I'm not cold—I just thought it sounded good. I like hot chocolate. It sure looks dark in there...I wonder if anyone ever got lost...you've been here a lot of times, haven't you, Uncle Kevin? I bet my mom would like it here. She likes stuff like this. You're gonna turn that lantern on pretty soon...aren't you, Uncle Kevin?"

Before he could respond, there was an unearthly howling from the black depths of the tunnel, causing the hair on Michael's neck to bristle. He dropped the flashlight, his mouth opened wide, his eyes even wider; he could not look away from the dark opening. As if suddenly frozen to the sandy floor, he was unable to move his feet, unable to move at all. A chorus of wails, shrieks, and howls charged toward him through the darkness. His throat closed, his scream continuing to build, unable to escape. He shook violently, releasing his feet from the grasp of the sand to spin around quickly, feet moving, arms outstretched, the steep stairway in view, he stumbled, regained his balance, and continued forward. With a large gasp of air, his pent-up scream released to fill the Great Room. "A…a…apes…" he cried.

Kevin rushed to his side. "Michael…Michael, it's just people. There's no apes. It's just people having fun howling in the dark. Listen to me!" And gently he forced Michael to focus on him.

Michael's eyes clouded with tears but never spilled over. The corners of his pursed lips drooped, his chin quivered slightly.

"There's nothing to be afraid of. Honest," Kevin said calmly. Even through the layers of clothing and heavy jacket, he could feel the boy's shoulders trembling in his hands, his chest heaving with every breath. "Look. They're coming out. See the lights?" He smiled, releasing his hold. "They're just people laughing and talking. Fooling around. Nothing to be afraid of. There's nothing in here that'll hurt you. I promise; you have my word. I'd never let anything happen to you."

Michael lunged forward and hugged Kevin tightly.

"Besides…" he laughed. "Your Aunt Peg would hang me by the thumbs if anything happened to you. And wouldn't that be a sight? How would I operate on people with my thumbs stretched all the way down past my knees? No, that wouldn't be a good thing at all. I sure don't want to get your Aunt Peg upset…"

"No, you sure don't. She's a lot like my mom that way!" Michael said, catching his breath through a half smile.

The man stood up still, keeping a hand around Michael's shoulder. "I could tell you stories, my little friend. Oh, could I tell you stories." Kevin chuckled.

They watched as distant beams danced over the walls and ceiling along the mouth of the tunnel. Moments later three young couples came into view, flashlights in hand. No one noticed Michael's quiet sigh of relief. The group stopped for a moment to share conversation. One of the girls handed Michael a long multicolored glow rope from around her neck.

"I think you're gonna like this. It's really cool. When you get way back in there, turn off your lights and spin it around on your arm like this. It looks really cool. Anyway, here you go. Have fun. By the way; I like your helmet. That's awesome, and it matches your dad's. How cool is that?"

"He's my uncle..."

"You've got a pretty cool uncle, kid. Hope you have fun. Remember to spin that thing."

Michael waved thank-you, then placed it around his neck. "Wow! I think this is gonna look cool in there, don't you?"

Kevin nodded his head and smiled. "So she said!"

Cautious at first, Michael soon became comfortable exploring in the darkness, even finding Kevin's explanations of some of the sights interesting. On the walls were something called cave slime. It was alive, and you shouldn't touch it, Kevin said. And this, of course, deepened the interest for Michael. In the beams of his flashlight he examined it closely. In spots the ceiling sparkled, and large boulders were held suspended between long rock fingers hanging from the ceiling and walls. The floor was littered with boulders and rock formations along the pathway.

After about forty minutes, the passage noticeably began narrowing to no more than a few feet high. Then it came to an abrupt end.

"Can I touch the end, Uncle Kevin? I don't see any cave slime on it."

"You've earned it."

"Can we see how dark it is? Can we turn off our lights?"

"Hang on," Kevin said, removing the fluorescent necklace from around Michael's neck and tucking it deep inside one of the pockets of the backpack.

"Okay, the lantern will be the last thing we turn off. Ready, Michael?"

"Yeah!"

"Flashlights off." Kevin watched the boy closely. "Headlamps...off."

Michael's eyes were wide with excitement.

"How you doing?" Kevin asked.

The boy nodded his head, okay.

Even with the darkness held at bay by the broad light of the lantern, Michael felt the darkness had moved toward them—ominous, as if alive. This was not the darkness that shrouded his bedroom when his mother turned out the lights or the darkness of night as he walked the streets with her on

Halloween. *Halloween?* He clenched his teeth. *Why did I think of Halloween?* he silently asked himself. A shiver ran through him, and he looked up at Uncle Kevin. Shadows cast by the lantern sitting on the floor made his uncle's face look distorted, monstrous. His own large shadow loomed on the low ceiling above, bringing animation to the ever-so-cramped encasement.

At that moment everything about Michael froze, as if the boy was paralyzed. He was unable to look away, nor could he run. A scream became frozen to the pit of his stomach. Even the breath in his lungs felt solid, unmoving, refusing to allow the slightest gasp to enter…or exit.

Kevin knelt down next to him, the shadows melting into a warm orange glow over his face. "Are you okay? Are you ready?" he asked, mistaking Michael's noticeable fear for the normal anxiety of a young boy.

Unable to murmur a word, Michael slid his arm through the crook of his uncle's elbow, clinching him tightly. There came a loud click from the lantern.

Later Michael would attempt to describe the darkness to his mother and Aunt Peg, but even he knew his description, no matter how hard he tried, would be insufficient. After all, a six-year-old doesn't understand it's not just the darkness, the absence of light, or the pitch black that envelops you while encapsulated within a hundred billion tons of earth. It's the uncertainty pressing in around your consciousness, crushing you with the weight of self-doubt and fear. When your own heartbeat breaks the silence of your confines and you must remind yourself to breathe. How that first breath is filled with faith, the second with hope, and soon you're choking on the acrid air of panic, exhaled into a reality of complete and total isolation. Yes, that's when the absence of vision becomes but a mere aspect of the experience. And yet, to this courageous young boy, his explanation of really dark—really, really dark, darker than when I close my eyes and put my hands over them—would convey perfectly the self-doubt, the fear, the faith, hope and panic that accompanies the darkness when you're only six years old. As the seconds ticked by, Kevin continued talking, eventually engaging Michael in one-syllable conversations. Michael thought their voices seemed muffled by the darkness, or maybe it was because Uncle Kevin was just speaking softly. Ten seconds had passed, and still he could see nothing. He tried to see his hand in front of his face, just like Kevin encouraged him to do; and as his hand touch the end of his nose, it surprised him, causing him the slightest flinch before the darkness became filled with his contagious laughter. Soon they found themselves laughing almost uncontrollably as Kevin asked, "How many fingers am I holding up?"

"Three!" Michael said excitedly.

"Hmm..." Kevin's voice sounded puzzled. "It could be three...or it might be four. I don't really know because I can't see them either..."

And they both laughed again. But through the games and laughter, Michael never once let go of Kevin's arm.

The games and laughter continued, and Kevin couldn't remember a time he'd ever sat this long in the darkness of the Ape Caves. As a teenager with his church youth group, or the time with his weekend explores club, even the countless times with buddies and friends, none were able to last more than thirty seconds before someone required the lanterns be lit. And on more than one occasion, he too breathed a sigh of relief when multiple lanterns and flashlights would almost instantly light up the room after someone started the succession.

It must be coming up on a minute, he thought, yet their laughter continued lighting up the moment. *Is this what it's like to be a father? To share something so incredible that time doesn't stop but merely escapes the moment? When a child's laughter possesses the ability to abate one's most primitive fear? When love and trust shine through even the blackest depths, coming to rest on the heart with glowing warmth? Is that what it's like to be a father?*

Michael's laughter stopped, breaking Kevin's thought. "I want to draw something in the sand, and you guess what it is, okay?"

"Sounds like fun," Kevin replied.

"But you have to promise you won't let go of me..."

"I've got you, and I'm not about to let go...promise!"

Michael attempted to draw carefully in the sand, all the time reminding Kevin, "Don't let go..."

Another ten seconds lumbered by. "Okay, done! Now you draw something, and I'll hold on to you. Then we each get three guesses..."

The guesses turned into another fun game, and the pictures in the sand were quickly forgotten about. There was a rumble from Michael's stomach that brought on a case of the giggles, and when Kevin made the motion for a hot chocolate break, Michael wasted no time voicing his opinion with a resounding "Oh yeah...hot chocolate! I forgot all about that."

Kevin's hand found the lantern. There was a faint click followed directly by a louder click, and the darkness fled as a warm, steady glow illuminated the narrow walls and ceiling, stretching into the darkness of the long tunnel. Michael turned on both flashlights and was reaching to turn on his headlamp when he noticed Kevin pulling the round metallic thermos from his backpack. He shined his flashlight once again to the dead end and said, "I wonder why it just stops here..."

"Well, the lava had to stop somewhere, and I guess this was as good a place as any," Kevin said, not wanting to be technical.

"What lava?" Michael asked, staring up at him.

"From the volcano. Remember I showed you Mount Saint Helens this morning as we drove down? This is just below that, but on the other side of the mountain."

"We're under a volcano?"

Kevin smiled, turning his headlamp on. "Not really under it. More on its side. But we are under one of the old lava flows. That's how this tube was formed—hot lava moves under cold lava, kind of like an underground river, leaving what they call a lava tube. This one's about two thousand years old, but I have photos of some in Hawaii where you can still see the hot lava inside of them."

Michael sat digesting the information while Kevin removed two cups and began unscrewing the lid from the thermos. "Uncle Kevin, you said if I felt afraid or uncomfortable, I should let you know. I think I'm letting you know now."

They began the trek back immediately. Michael's breath became short and labored with nervousness, eagerness, and fatigue, but once he set the pace, there was no slowing him down. It only took twenty minutes to make their way back to the base of the stairway. Exhausted, Michael was still exuberant about reaching the outside, doing a short victory dance before brushing the snow from a wooden bench. He removed his backpack and sat waiting as Kevin poured their somewhat delayed cup of hot chocolate. He took a deep breath of fresh, cool air and viewed the snow-covered scenery.

"I like it here. It's quiet and pretty. I didn't know this was a volcano; it looks like just a big mountain with lots of trees. I always thought volcanoes had smoke and lava coming out of them."

Kevin pulled out two energy bars. "Not when they're sleeping..."

Michael nodded his head, took a bite of his bar and a sip of chocolate, and whispered, "Maybe we should be quiet. We don't want to wake it up."

They talked about their adventure as they finished their snack, and then Michael walked to the large opening and looked down into the Great Room. He stood silently by himself. Watching him from the bench, Kevin wondered if it was possible that he and Peg would someday have a son, or even a daughter, he could love as much as he did this little boy.

Michael came back and stood beside the bench. "Uncle Kevin, can we pray?"

Kevin smiled slightly. "But we're out of there now, and the mountain is still asleep..."

"Oh, no. Believe me, I prayed while we were in there. Matter of fact, I prayed a lot on our way out. But look at this place, Uncle Kevin—the trees, the sky, and even the cave. I mean, the tunnel...the lava tube—it's all really beautiful, and even though I got a little scared, I knew you were there to protect me."

And then, without the slightest pause, Michael stepped closer to his uncle. "And I knew if we needed it, God would send an angel to protect us both. So can we just pray and tell Him thank you."

They bowed their heads. Michael thanked God for His protection, for all the beautiful things around them, and most of all for a wonderful day exploring in the darkness. Kevin thanked God for Michael.

They were getting ready to leave when the boy ran back one last time to look down into the deep hole. Kevin joined him, placing his hand on the boy's shoulder.

"Uncle Kevin? Can we come back someday and go through the upper one?"

He pulled the boy close to his side. "Whenever you want, Michael. I think that'd be a lot of fun, although it gets just as scary in places."

"Angels, Uncle Kevin. They'll watch over us."

❖

Trudy looked at the clock. It was hard to believe she'd been sitting at the screen for well over an hour. "Save...print," she whispered, and with a sigh of elation began her celebration routine.

She took a small remote from the desk drawer, snuggled deep into her chair, and pressed the Play button. Her hand moved slowly, almost tenderly, over the edge of a gold frame housing a picture of a slightly younger Lincoln Trudeau accepting his first award from the Writers Guild. His nervous look made her smile, filling her heart just as the warm voice of Van Morrison began to fill the room.

"Have I told you lately...that I love you?" she whispered along with the soft tones of the troubadour.

Originally written as a prayer, Trudy always held a special regard for the song, playing it only on two types of occasion, the first being those times she needed to sit reclusively and open her heart to God. The beautiful words expressing her thoughts precisely always seemed to lead her into prayer and a simple moment of thanks. The other occasion, like today, also led her, evoking a heartfelt mood, a state of mind, loving and compassionate, joyously thankful for the very special man she married so long ago. And yes, Lincoln Trudeau was a very special man. For not only had he kept her secret and even shared in it, he had lived it with her, for her—some might even say as her. And it was that which always tickled her heart and made her giggle.

"Oh, how this man must love me," she sometimes whispered to the objects in this room, and of course this was one of those times. Her eyes again scanned the picture. "And how I love this man," she softly said aloud, permitting the music to flow over her like the comfort of a warm blanket.

She inhaled deeply. Her voice filled with tender emotion, she continued to accompany Mr. Morrison...

Fill my heart with gladness

Take away my sadness

Ease my troubles that's what you do…

But she would not sit for long. She took the sweater from the back of her chair and wrapped it over her shoulders, preparing a warm cup of tea from the copper kettle that sat atop a simple hot pad. Her work complete, she stepped out onto the balcony. The smell of salt air and evergreens refreshed her. The view of the Olympics, blissful, and the warm tea clutched in her hands brought a sense of peace and comfort to her soul. This was her spot of serenity, set aside for her only and respected as so by her loving husband. A place where the world was not invited, intrusions not permitted, and interruptions were dealt with quickly and severely. A place reserved solely for times of contemplation, reflection, and gratification, usually in that order.

The morning air was cool as it pierced her thin sweater, and within minutes she recoiled from its touch to move quickly back inside. Hurrying to the fireplace, she sat on the warm hearth stirring the embers of a dying fire. And as the small flames brought warmth to her body, the soft music continued on an endless loop, bringing warmth to her heart. She readjusted the volume and then began to speak. The words were not important to anyone but her, so Trudy spoke them very softly, as she often did in moments such as this. Moments of profound peace in a forbidden room filled with treasured objects overhearing quiet secrets, the whispers of her heart, her soul, her life. Moments lovingly shared with God…to the music of Van Morrison.

Brought on by design, Trudy's mood was tranquil, allowing her creativity a rest, a time to say goodbye to the characters that had walked from her imagination into the stories of her heart. A time that also brought a slight feeling of loss, as though saying farewell to old friends, and it was a time of movement, a journey of distance immeasurable by any standards yet one every storyteller must take. Be it a blink, a turn, a step back from the imaginative into the doorway of reality, there must come that moment of closure when the final chapter closes with The End.

"Farewell, my friends…" she whispered into the fading glow of embers. "Thank you for sharing your stories with me."

Saying goodbye to friends, fictional or not, had always been hard. Her eyes filled with tears, clouded with sadness as she searched her thoughts for an adequate distraction. Standing, turning her head to regard the photos along the mantle, her eyes rested on one long cherished. Like a bookmark placed in volumes of memories, the photo returned her to a captured moment of life. A warm smile that perhaps had merely been veiled now brightened her eyes with its presence, unlocking a long-ago scene, filling her thoughts, her heart, and then wistfully transporting her into a cocoon of nostalgia even the soft music could not penetrate. The photo was of her and Lincoln beside Jim and Ann Brooks, the four of them leaning against a ship's railing, the lights of the Seattle skyline fashioning a backdrop of festive color shimmering on the dark waters of Puget Sound. Hours earlier they had met for the first time while waiting to board the *Royal Argosy*'s dinner cruise. Trudy's quick reaction to Ann's slight wardrobe malfunction saved what could have been a most embarrassing moment.

"Don't worry. I have safety pins, and if need be, even a sewing kit," Trudy said discreetly, assisting Ann.

"They're not letting anyone on board for another fifteen minutes." Jim said, looking around the pier. "Hey, there you go! The Sea Grill—they'll have a ladies' room."

"Don't let 'em sail without us!" Ann called over her shoulder as she and Trudy rushed for the door. "I can't thank you enough…" she said, glancing at Trudy. "But a sewing kit? Who carries a sewing kit?"

Trudy just smiled.

The Sea Grill was crowded, loud, and most definitely specialized in seafood, as evident by the nautical decor and lingering aromas from decades of prepared fish. The hostess, dressed in a medieval wench's costume, was young and perky, having a well-practiced smile and slight tilt to her head. She happily greeted patrons with a melody of pubescent cheerfulness.

"Welcome to the Sea Grill. How many in your party? There's a forty-five-minute wait. Serving, Butler, party of four…Butler!" All while standing behind a tall wooden desk with a large ship's wheel secured to its front.

As Ann and Trudy hurriedly approached, the young girl went into action. "Welcome to…"

"Where's your restroom?" Ann interrupted abruptly, at that same moment spotting a sign at the end of the long bar: Heads This Way. Not waiting for an answer and with Trudy in tow, she began to make her way down the crowded aisle.

Her routine broken, the young hostess stood befuddled, unconsciously waving a menu in the air while hoping to regain the women's attention. No one in the place was more surprised than she was when she quickly collected herself and shouted, "The restrooms are for customers only…"

Without a glance or the slightest hesitation in their progress, Ann yelled back, "Fine. Bring us two glasses of Merlot."

Once inside, Trudy began making repairs to the dress. Their conversation, though not completely one sided, continued to be led by Ann, with Trudy commenting occasionally in quiet tones, only answering direct questions. So it wasn't long before Ann giggled. "It's okay to speak up. They know we're in here."

Trudy's hands didn't pause, but an extra moment passed before she replied. "This is how I talk…sorry, my voice isn't very loud."

Trudy was unprepared for the response. Ann quickly spun around to face her straight on. "Promise me you'll bang pots and pans together if you ever need to warn me the building's on fire. Promise? Cross your heart?"

Ann's giggling was met sternly by Trudy's simmering anger, causing Ann's smile to fade quickly. Their stare held solid. Ann hadn't meant to offend and wished she could somehow take back the insensitive remark, apologize, and beg this nice woman's forgiveness. But for now she couldn't even form the words "I'm sorry."

Trudy's gaze, cold and unfaltering, continued to hold Ann captive. And then, reaching into her jacket pocket, Trudy's fingers wrapped around a cold steel object lying at the bottom. Slowly she removed it, her stare continuing to entrance. Bringing the object close to Ann's face, she spoke firmly. "If I can't find any pans to bang, would you like me to use this instead?" She smirked, dangling a shiny metal whistle from her forefinger.

Ann's heart sank. "I…I'm so…"

Trudy's smile widened. "Oh, don't worry about it. I used to carry pans around for just such an emergency, but they were bulky and made my clothes look lumpy."

Ann chuckled. "So now you bang whistles together? We're all going to die, aren't we?"

Unquestionably, it was at that moment their friendship truly began.

❀

As the captain greeted each guest, both men hesitantly boarded the ship, glancing twice toward the door of the Sea Grill. Yet neither made mention of their wives' delay to the staff but continued, enthralled in conversation while making their way to the spacious dining room. When the ladies did arrive, to their delight, Jim and Lincoln were sitting at the table Ann had reserved months earlier at her brother Teddy's request. But in typical Teddy fashion, he had called that afternoon saying he and his girlfriend were running late but would try to meet them on the boat. Ann knew odds were pretty good she and Jim would be dining alone. Now that seemed to be a blessing, as Lincoln and Trudy had accepted the invitation to join them at the quaint little table for four next to the vast window.

Across the room at a table for eight sat two empty chairs; a somewhat rude mom and dad with four teenagers, all of whom were in varied stages of irritation, filled the remaining six seats. Trudy took Ann's hand. "Thank you. I owe you big," she said with an affectionate squeeze.

Lincoln ordered a bottle of wine and toasted a safe voyage and a memorable evening. And as the evening progressed, details were shared. The Brooks' had recently purchased their home in Eatonville, had a little girl who just graduated kindergarten, and had spent most of last summer repairing the large five-bedroom log cabin Jim's father had built in the early sixties out on Brennan's Cove. Ann planned on spending most of this summer enjoying the fruits of their labor. Jim would spend it putting the finishing touches on a new musical for his high school performing arts class.

The Trudeaus lived in Sausalito, worked in San Francisco, and dreamed of someday relocating to the Northwest. Lincoln enjoyed all aspects of the outdoors, as did Trudy—to a point, anyway. Content to lock herself away, reading, writing or relaxing with a glass of wine, good music, and the smells and joy of trying new recipes, she openly and proudly admitted to being somewhat of a recluse.

Lincoln was a pediatric surgeon at San Francisco General, and Trudy, a consultant for the Wilshire Pediatric Speech and Language Center. However, both played down their vocations and seemed genuinely curious and enthusiastic to hear more about the Brooks'.

"We're just teachers." Ann laughed, shaking her head. "You two are out there saving kids' lives and—"

"Pardon me—just teachers?" Lincoln quickly interjected. "You're giving them the knowledge to get through life, Ann. The gift of teaching is as powerful and precious as any gift there is, including healing."

Trudy took Jim's hand in hers. "And you, Jim. Music, drama, the arts? You're teaching them perhaps the most important lessons needed in life—how to behold, believe, and dream. That's what makes all things possible."

Then she included Ann with a simple touch to the back of her hand. "You two save kids every day by reaching an inner part of them few physicians can—their mind. You provide them with the abilities to triumph in a world of endless opportunity by opening the door to their future through education. You deserve and have all my respect."

"And mine," Lincoln added.

With a slight smile that couldn't hide her moment of satisfied recognition, Ann stumbled over her thoughts, quickly responding sincerely, "That's very kind and wonderful…thank you both. But it doesn't change the fact that you're doctors. You affect children's lives even when mothers and fathers and teachers can't. You are the heroes."

Topping everyone's glass, Lincoln said, "To all of us whose gifts touch the lives of the future."

"To us!" they cheered.

Ann enjoyed listening to the soft-spoken Trudy and her humorous anecdotes, most of which involved her good-natured husband who didn't hesitate to share stories of his own, some of which Trudy would rather he'd not, but it allowed her the sheer pleasure of shrugging him off with the same nonchalant elegance she had demonstrated the day they met in the park.

Jim too shared stories; no surprise to Ann. But yet…there was a surprise. It came in how close the four had grown in such a short time, a fact that each one at some point in the evening pondered silently to themselves before eagerly being swept up in the moment once again by the other three. Nothing was ever said, and nothing needed to be. Sometime after dinner Trudy removed a small tablet from her purse and placed it in front of Ann along with a pen. "If you only had time to write one thing to change the course of someone's life, what would it be?"

Though it took a minute, the expression on Ann's face slowly became one of wonderment at the scope of the question. Trudy sat quietly watching as Ann pondered her response, then further added, "You may or may not know the person that'll read your note. And don't show anyone what you've written. Make it as short as possible but long enough to get your point across."

Then she motioned for the waiter, who leaned down close enough to hear her over the soft strains of the band and mingled conversations of the other guests. She spoke quietly in his ear. He didn't speak, simply nodded and smiled before hurrying away from the table. "I ordered another. I hope that's okay," she said, pointing to the empty bottle. "It just feels like a special occasion."

No one objected, and everyone agreed. It did feel like a special occasion.

Ann began to write. After completing the first sentence, she looked up. "It's kind of heavy, but it changed the course of my life once upon a time."

Trudy's eyes sparkled, coy and mischievous. "Don't tell us what it says. Just roll it up to about the size of your finger. That way, no one can peek."

A small chuckle came from Lincoln. Ann looked at him, tore the page off, and began to roll. "Didn't you say you like magic? Are you going to guess what I wrote?"

"No, it's not a trick," said Trudy, shaking her head. "I promise none of us will ever know what you've written." She then slid the tablet in front of Jim. "Okay, do you have any words of wisdom you'd like to pass on?"

Hastily he picked up the pen. "As a matter of fact, I do. It's a quote from—"

"Jim!" Ann cried in disbelief. "You're not supposed to tell us! Just write and roll…short and sweet…you kidding me? Is the conversation moving too quickly for you, honey?"

"Oh no." Lincoln laughed, looking at the two women. "Are you long-lost sisters or something? I thought Tru was the only wife who said things like that. Oh, man...I feel your pain, Jim. I really do!"

Lincoln tipped his glass, finishing the last mouthful. "Oh, look. Just in time." The waiter appeared with another bottle, placed the cork next to Trudy, and began to pour.

"You have a quote you wish to write?" she asked Jim.

Before saying anything, Jim leaned over and kissed Ann on the cheek. "I do!" he said, setting the pen on the table. "But before I do, I have a toast."

Hoisting a glass, Lincoln and Trudy smiled eagerly. Ann managed a cautious grin, raising her glass with a slight measure of reluctance. Had he ever made a toast before? Not that she remembered. And though she would never admit to it, a small prayer escaped her.

With the flair of a gentleman and the confidence of a rogue, Jim began to speak. "Here's to safety pins and sewing kits, broken straps and nimble fingers, to threads of circumstance and happenstance, and a swatch or two of fate and perfect timing. Tonight I believe we've witnessed the fabric of friendship brought together by a stitch of kindness. So join me if you will...a toast to friendship."

"To friendship..." they chimed.

Elated, Lincoln and Trudy thanked Jim. Ann rolled her eyes and shook her head mainly for show, all the while breathing a silent *Thank you, God.*

A minute later Jim got around to scribbling down the quote he'd thought of earlier. He tore the paper from the tablet. "Write and roll," he said, winking at Ann. "And you thought I never listen to you. See, baby, I hang on your every word."

Lincoln chuckled; Trudy playfully punched him in the shoulder.

Ann looked to Jim with a half smile. "You're the one she should've punched."

So Trudy did.

The banter and laughter continued for some time, and then, all of a sudden, Trudy sat up at full attention, both hands flat on the table. "Look at that chocolate cake. And what the heck are those she's bringing out? Oh, look. He has a tray of chocolate-covered strawberries."

You Are My Love

Trudy was slipping into a dessert trance. A quick glance across the table revealed Ann had also fallen under the aromatic spell of chocolate. Lincoln and Jim looked at each other and lifted their glasses in a gesture of brotherhood.

"Dessert trumps notes. You better put it in your pocket for now," Lincoln said.

Curls, swirls, chunks, and squares; chewy, crunchy, smooth, and creamy; light, dark, white, and even red; cookies, candies, wafers, and rolls; frostings, custards, pudding, and mousse; and, of course, cake upon cake, layer upon layer of decadent chocolate bliss presented for approval by the chefs themselves. So it was to no one's surprise that it didn't take long for the girls to satisfy their chocolate imbalance, break the spell, and leave them needing a walk around the deck in the cool night air.

The sea, the boat's vibration, the distant lights of a city skyline. Trudy closed her eyes, allowing her own heartstrings to serenade from within. She hugged Lincoln snugly around the waist. He held her tightly, her essence causing his heart to dance. Placing soft kisses on the crown of her head, he whispered, "I love you, Tru…"

Ann, too, stood staring at the skyline. "It's so beautiful." She sighed.

As Jim stepped around to face her, his lips lightly brushed hers. "Yes, you are, my love."

"You're so silly." She blushed.

"Hey, sailor, get your hands off of my friend," cried Trudy—as loud as she could manage, anyway. And then, with the proficiency of a sleight-of-hand magician and a little help from Lincoln, she produced two empty wine bottles. "Did you bring your notes?" she asked, her eyes sparkling with the same coy, mischievous look they had held earlier.

❖

Splash.

Ann was beside herself with excitement. "If I would've known that's what you were going to do, I probably would've written something else. But how fun! You do this all the time?"

Trudy smiled. "Once or twice."

Lincoln shook his head, silently mouthing *All the time.*

Ann continued. "Wouldn't you like to be there when someone finds it? I can just imagine…"

"Hey, would you like me to take your picture? That's a gorgeous backdrop," asked a young woman identifying herself as the ship's photographer. "If you like it, it'll be available for purchase at the end of the cruise. And I think you're gonna love this one. Sharing a beautiful background like this with best friends—how could you not love it?"

After a little shuffling and laughter came "Smile…" Click. "Okay, it'll be in the main lobby waiting for you. It should be easy to spot; it'll be the prettiest one there. Oh yeah, and just so you know, it's illegal to throw anything from the ship…except maybe you, sailor boy, if you don't get your hands off her friend." The young girl giggled and turned to walk away. "I can have your waiter bring more wine; just kidding. Enjoy your stroll."

After docking and not wanting the evening to end, the foursome moved on to Chambers on the Fifth; a small, intimate coffee house located just off the downtown promenade near the hotel where the Trudeaus were staying. The quiet atmosphere was ideal for Trudy. Her voice, tired and somewhat strained, carried effortlessly in the blend of conversation. And with conversation came more laughter and more stories, and it was in these stories that shared hobbies and interests were revealed. Music and arts, the love for rich coffee on rainy days, and fog as it rolls over the water, campfires, Times Square, Mayberry, traveling, staying home, reading, creating, and writing.

Sometime just before midnight it was decided, mainly by Ann, who refused to take no for an answer, that the Trudeaus would join her and Jim at their cabin on Brennan's Cove for a few days of rest and relaxation before returning home to San Francisco. And so it was the next day that the Trudeaus laid eyes on the old run-down lodge that eighteen months later would become their dream home.

Less than twenty-four hours after they met, it was obvious to all that their friendship was indeed uniquely special. Over the next few years, they'd spend most weekends, holidays, trips, and vacations together.

But mostly, times were spent simply enjoying nights under the stars at Brennan's Cove, where soon a sense of family emerged. The Brooks' daughter, Amy, almost immediately asked if she could call them aunt and uncle, and with their blessing it is to this day how she introduces them. Lincoln always made her laugh, letting her tag along when he and her dad went fishing, hiking, Christmas tree chopping, stargazing, snipe hunting, or just making a run to the market. Over the years, being somewhat of a tomboy, she'd garnished more than her share of bumps, bruises, scrapes, blisters, cuts, slivers, hundreds of insect bites, a black eye worth fifty cents, twelve stitches, and one cast on her right arm, all while under the watchful supervision of her dad and Uncle Linc—a sore subject with Ann and Trudy to this day, and still, Amy sometimes says tongue-in-cheek, "I was a pretty lucky girl to always have a doctor right there when I got hurt. Yep, pretty lucky, don't you think?"

She also loved spending time with Trudy. Working in the garden, baking bread and cookies, going on long walks through the forest, taking pictures of animals, collecting rocks, and most of all, listening to Trudy's beautiful stories. Stories about talking bears, ballerinas, boats, and a host of other subjects that somehow seemed to intertwine from story to story. Trudy made story time a special time, reserved for the two of them. Although Ann did join on a couple of occasions, she could see her daughter felt distracted by her presence. And then there were those very special times when Trudy told the stories by the warmth of the fireplace. Afterward, music would fill the air as if by magic, and they'd close their eyes pretending to dance like ballerinas, twirled by kindly old bears around the Grand Ballroom.

Trudy and Lincoln loved this little girl as if she were their own. The child they never had. Ann treasured the many things they brought to Amy, but none was greater than the sense of love and security only family can bring. Of course, there was Uncle Teddy, who'd pop in once or twice a year bearing gifts and after half an hour leave on some made-up pretense to meet with a new girlfriend. And though Amy loved him, she found herself feeling sorry for him in so many ways.

Jim, having no family to speak of, looked upon Trudy as a sister-in-law, often shaking his head at the similarities she and Ann shared. Five years his senior, Lincoln was like a big brother; someone he looked up to, leaned on, and trusted in. Lincoln's occasional practical joke completed their brotherly relationship. Together they made up a pretty wonderful family, sharing an incredible bond of love, dependability, and trust almost immediately. It was because of this bond that one rainy evening only eighteen months into what they knew had become a lifelong friendship, Trudy invited them to her office for "a little...confession."

CHAPTER TEN

"What do you mean a confession?" Ann teased. "What could you possibly have to confess that you haven't told me already?"

Lincoln knew what was coming. He and Trudy had discussed it numerous times, and now, with the last of the renovation complete, they agreed it would be the best thing for the friendship and for the peace of mind it would afford in the long run. After all, it would be nice to share their secret with the only two people they knew they could trust with such information, and at that point Trudy had not even shared it with her brother—nor did she expect to anytime soon.

So it was not the confession that brought the surprised look to Lincoln's face. It was where it was to take place. Lincoln knew Trudy's office was her sanctuary, as was that entire wing of the house. From floor to ceiling, the renovation of the Grand Ballroom had been her vision, her canvas, where she became the muse that guided the artisan's hand. The craftsman's skill and painter's brush fashioned with whimsical sophistication the architecture and artistry lifted entirely from the pages of her imagination.

From the rear edge of the hub, a series of steps and terraces led to an enormous stone archway housing two immense wooden doors with long bars of twisted wrought iron encased within thick panes of beveled glass, giving the entry a gated yet elegant appearance onto the indoor courtyard. An array of potted plants, ferns, shrubs, and trees dispersed throughout, provide the room a landscape of living art. Bold as well as subtle touches of art abounded at every turn. But perhaps the most striking piece was an eight-by-twelve-foot canvas, abstract in its depiction of a young ballerina dancing upon wet pavement in the glow of an old-fashioned street lamp. Not an original concept and not meant to be, it was simply the artist's vision. But the reflections on the puddles, if one were to study them closely, showed a significantly different scene, one invisible to most of the world but clearly seen and captured by the painter's brush. Within the distorted ripples, standing beside the beautiful young dancer, holding an open umbrella, was the figure of a great bear.

Other paintings using the same dramatic palette and abstract style dotted the room, though none celebrated ballerinas, street lamps, puddles, or bears. There was, however, tucked back just to the left of the entry, two permanent guests, exquisitely hand carved and ready for the ball: Theophilus Bear and his cousin Kodiak.

Both the ceiling and rosewood floor curved gracefully, shaping the distinctive room into a slightly augmented horseshoe. The inner wall, with a broad center section of river rock framed between two colossal timbers, presented a beautiful contrast to the burled walnut panels extending another ten feet on either side before sharply curving at both ends to become the main entry to the Grand Ballroom. Once inside, the sheer size and scope of the room become breathtaking—cathedral ceilings towered three stories above a unique hardwood floor of imported woods from many parts of the world, producing a collage of natural colors and textures, angles and curves depicting fluidity as if standing atop the brushstrokes of a colossal painting. And in a very real sense, it was a true piece of art. The walls were adorned with millwork from the nineteen thirties, and the beautiful curved wall no longer a wall at all from this side, but a rock chimney of a castle-size fireplace one could easily stand inside. Within the firebox, reaching out toward the hearth, was an iron grate in the shape of giant bear claws, measuring four feet across to easily accommodate four-to-eight-foot logs, depending on the evening's festivities. The rock chimney and thick timbers rose impressively through the high ceiling. Many of the stones were sculptured into faces of bears, eagles, cougars, owls, and frogs, to name but a few. Carved into the massive center stone slightly above the rest was the outline of an open umbrella.

At the opposite end of the ballroom, gigantic windows framed picturesque views of Puget Sound, with the Olympic Mountains in the distance. It was a view where the summer skies were often brilliant sunsets and lingering hues of twilight seemed to fade with defiance into the darkness of night—the perfect backdrop for the small white lights that twinkled from the trees of the grand courtyard. The winter skies were bleak with ever-changing shades of gray, sometimes heavy with rain and wind. Other times a dense mist rolled through the forest-covered hills, quickly spreading over the surface of the various waterways of the sound. But on this night, like most, the rain came as a constant drizzle.

Trudy's excitement showed as she hurriedly led the way into the ballroom. Looking somewhat confused, Ann rushed to stay beside her. "In case you've forgotten, Tru, this isn't the way to your office. Where are you taking us?"

Trudy grinned what Ann often referred to as "the trouble grin." "Up," she said in a whispered voice. And with that she moved to a well-concealed door adjacent to and set back from the left main entry. Trudy pulled the door open to reveal an original stairwell leading to one of two identical balconies that ran along both sides of the deep room. In each corner a large circular veranda overlooked the room below. From the floor to the steep ceiling, twenty pane windows provided an elegant touch and during the day allowed additional lighting not only to the sitting areas themselves but the Great Room in general.

Trudy again led the way. Dumbfounded, Ann called to her, but she continued to move farther up the stairwell. "Really, Tru—hidden stairways, confessions. What's next? Are you going to tell me you're bank robbers?" Ann looked seriously at Lincoln. "You're not, are you?"

"No!" He smiled.

Jim laughed. "They're not bank robbers. They're murderers, criminally insane, escaped from an asylum back east somewhere."

Lincoln's smile quickly became laughter as Jim began a perfect impersonation of Detective Colombo. "It all makes sense. He murdered Professor Plum in the ballroom with a disco ball. Then, with his wife leading the way, he made his escape through a secret passage...and just one more thing: What did you pay for those shoes?"

Lincoln's laughter filled the stairwell.

Once at the top, Trudy quickly moved along the outstretched balcony. She didn't need to look back to know the others had stopped far behind her.

"Hang on, Tru," Lincoln called out. Ann and Jim were at the first veranda looking out over the newly finished floor below.

Jim was stunned, but it was Ann who spoke up. "That's my painting."

"*The Guardian...*" Lincoln added.

Every detail of the beautiful watercolor that hung above the fireplace at the Brooks cabin was captured perfectly. Every color, every nuance exactly the same, just thousands of times greater in size. Ann studied the incredible floor. Again the same dramatic palette and abstract style as the paintings in the foyer, but this time a much different subject. So massive the piece, that when standing on the floor, the features were unrecognizable. Only from above could the partial face of a bear with sympathetic eyes come into focus. The floor was framed by a wide border, two-foot-square blocks, three-dimensional in appearance, each topped in onyx black, the sides sloping grains of gold and brown complete the breathtaking illusion. Centered in front of the fireplace were two squares with wood inlays of ballet slippers and an umbrella.

"I knew the floor was unusual, beautiful, but I had no idea...I mean, it's amazing," Ann said, astonished. And then, speaking more to herself than anyone, "A bear...the damn floor's a bear face!"

Lincoln chuckled. "It's designed so it doesn't come into perspective until you're standing above it. Otherwise, it just looks like a very colorful floor."

Ann slowly shook her head in disbelief. "I knew she loved her bears, but..." And then she called out to Trudy, "I think this is a sign of obsessive behavior, missy. You might want to speak to your doctor."

Though no one could hear, Trudy chuckled to herself as she continued to walk. Ann glanced to the sitting area behind her. Antiques from the nineteen thirties and forties were tastefully placed about. A stylish lamp table flanked by two leather barrel chairs sat in front of a highboy bookshelf. Sitting atop the rear corner was a life-size hand-carved wooden bear, his legs draped over the side, his mouth slightly agape with a look of joy as he read a large book. Directly in front of the window sat a long credenza, and just in front of that an antique desk. Resting in the center was an old Underwood typewriter that beckoned to transport a willing operator back in time, if only for a paragraph or two. On top of the credenza were two stunning wood sculptures, both approximately twenty inches tall, each incredibly detailed. To the left, a tugboat. Waves breaking over the bow gave it a sense of motion, of urgency. To the right, a young girl sat cross-legged peering out the window, in her arms a small button-eyed teddy bear with a striped patch on one knee. But Ann couldn't take her eyes off the delicate intricacies of the bear and without shifting her gaze said, "I know Tru tells Amy stories about friendly bears, but I thought Theophilus and Kodiak were—"

"We'd better catch up with her," Lincoln interrupted, giving Ann a slight grin.

Hesitantly she turned to join the two men as they made their way along the balcony to the other sitting area, where Trudy waited. It too held a number of antiques from the thirties and forties along with an assortment of odd-shaped vases, bookends, trinkets, treasures, and, to Ann's amusement, another life-size bear; sitting before him a beautiful little girl. The bear sat cross-legged, a closed umbrella resting in his lap. He stared intently at something held in his giant paw. Ann moved closer, fascinated by the detail and skill, amazed at how the artist had truly given the figure life, but more so, capturing in the bear's enormous face, emotion, a sense of awe and wonder, softness and love. Even the immense paw with its four-inch claws appeared gentle, held open at an angle that expressed tenderness, and there on the wrinkled folds of his paw lay a small pair of ballet slippers and a single rose.

Just as astonishing was the little girl, her head tilted looking upward to the bear, her features smooth and distinct, capturing midsentence her frozen words in time. So delicate, so intricate that even the grain of the wood perfectly illustrated the subtle waves of her long, flowing hair. Beside her sat the same button-eyed teddy bear as before. The piece captivated Ann to touch the roughness of the bear's arm. Her hand moved ever so gently to the smoothness of the paw, and then the back of her finger skated over the girl's cheek and contoured neck to finally follow down the curve of her long hair.

Ann knew she'd never seen it before, yet there was an overwhelming feeling of recognition. Again she looked at the bear's incredible face, and again she felt his tenderness. *He's not just a piece of wood*, she thought. *I know him...I know her...but...* Ann turned to see Trudy with an odd smile, motioning her to join them, and again hesitantly, reluctantly she left her fascination. But as she did, she saw something she hadn't noticed before. Quickly her eyes returned to the wooden sculpture, and there, barely visible, sticking out from under the folds of the girl's dress, was the corner of what could've only been a writing tablet, the shaft of a number-two pencil appeared to lie across it. Ann immediately looked at her friend. Trudy's attention was elsewhere, as was Jim's, but Lincoln saw the questions forming behind Ann's stare, and he smiled.

Just to the left of Trudy was an antique phonograph. Around it, etched into the logs of the wall, dragonflies hid within the shadowy limbs of broadleaf trees rising up the sloped ceiling, its branches becoming smaller as it climbed, eventually blending into the natural grain of the wood giving the impression of disappearing high above them. On her right stood a wardrobe, an antique armoire pushed snugly against the wall, a three-dimensional circular carving in its center.

"I know that picture..." Ann gasp, looking closer, slightly amused. "*The Lion, the Witch and the Wardrobe*—that's the original book cover. I remember it from when I was a kid."

Trudy's smile broadened, and her voice was soft, weak. "I like how the children step into the wardrobe and pass from one reality into another. I wanted so badly to be able to do that as a child. And now...well, I can."

She placed her hand on one of the large brass knobs. Jim noticed a small sign next to the wardrobe; it read "Secrets and whispers fill this place." Quickly he covered her hand with his own, feeling the cold brass knob between her fingers. "Is this where you keep the bodies?" He grinned.

"Only the fresh ones." She grinned back, raising an eyebrow. She turned the knob slowly, and with a gentle push, the entire facade swung open. A muffled click, and soft, warm light chased away the shadows, exposing a chamber both relaxing and inviting, its charm instantly offering the mind serenity.

The room was an immense loft with the perception of boundless space, an illusion enhanced primarily by a towering triangular window framing the same picturesque views as the ones below, but still with the feeling of a cozy log cabin. Numerous ferns, shrubs, and potted trees brought their own tranquil touch to the space. Resting on some of the branches were silk butterflies, dragonflies, and even small hand-painted tree frogs, ladybugs, and a miniature treehouse with a tiny light inside.

On the same wall, more out of the way than hidden, was an inconspicuous doorway opening onto an exterior terrace, its run stopping just short of the window so as not to mar the view from inside. But that night, like most winter nights in Brennan's Cove, the view was of a sky heavy with clouds, the balcony cold, damp, uninviting. And though the room was not chilled, the fireplace sparked to life with the arrival of guests, bringing yet more beauty and comfort to the already peaceful atmosphere.

Trudy made her way to stand by the fireplace, where, along the mantle, a collection of picture frames housed memories of Lincoln and his mother, Trudy and her brother, the boat, the bridge, the city, and two wedding photos. At the very end was the picture of the four of them the night they first met on the dinner cruise. Above the photos hung an elegantly framed oil reproduction of William H. Beard's *The Bear Dance*.

Trudy retrieved something from her desk before moving to sit on the sprawling slate hearth covering a large area of floor in front of the fireplace. Pillows of all shapes and sizes lay close by offering a measure of comfort once the slabs become too hard and uncomfortable to enjoy. Facing the fireplace was a short leather couch she knew would be taken up by Lincoln and Jim. Ann, like Trudy, would prefer to lounge on the hearth, enjoying the warmth of the fire, eventually cuddling with a pillow or two as the night progressed. As Trudy made herself comfortable, she watched the two men quickly move to the front of the loft to peer over a slightly rounded banister, discussing the floor below. Her attention turned to Ann, who moved about the room in uncharacteristic silence.

The room was filled with memories of Trudy's past, some good, some bad, some that needed explanation, and some that defied explanation altogether. There were many oddities scattered about that only she and Lincoln would know and appreciate, objects representing a collection of life's moments and events that continued to hold a unique meaning. A gearshift knob from an old Volkswagen, a small vial filled with water from San Francisco Bay, a well-used steamer trunk, her mother's pocketbook, her father's glasses, shells and rocks and pieces of driftwood alongside an empty wine bottle from Toscanos with a note protruding from its neck. There was a wide collection of antique figurines, many lead-cast reproductions of artistic eccentricities; a mouse paddling on a leaf with a bucket full of cheese on its back; a rabbit peeking out of a top hat; a squirrel examining a nutcracker, birds of all kinds and dragonflies of all sizes, butterflies on flowers and frogs with umbrellas. A variety of chestnut folk art from the eighteen hundreds also added to the whimsical nature of the room.

On a table directly across from Trudy's desk sat yet another figurine of a young girl and a bear, this one made of porcelain with lines so precise and graceful it stole Ann's breath as it captured her imagination. The girl, dressed as a ballerina, practiced a pirouette, her arm stretched high above her head assisted ever so delicately by a single claw from the bear's paw.

Continuing to wander about the room, Ann examined each piece with wild fascination as Jim and Trudy sat by the fire while Lincoln poured everyone a glass of wine.

"Ann…" he called, holding a glass out toward her. "Please, come join us. I believe Trudy has a confession she'd like to share."

Ann was standing next to a tall but narrow bookcase that contained only three shelves, all gathered near the center. The bottom shelf held three military metals housed in a glass display case. On the top shelf were two framed letters. One in the script of a child, written in crayon, simply read, "I have a voice. I love you Ella…" It was signed Kathy P. The second was a two-paragraph letter handwritten on White House stationery, signed Nancy and Ronald Reagan. And on the center shelf lay two books. Between them was a small pewter umbrella.

At first she wasn't sure what she was staring at. And then, suddenly, it all became very clear, making perfect sense. The figurines; the carvings; the many bears, ballerinas, and umbrellas throughout the house. The stories Trudy shared with Amy all lived in this room, danced in the grand ballroom. Her eyes focused on Trudy. *No!* she told herself, repressing any notion her friend, her sister could ever possibly be…

Dazed with disbelief, Ann picked up one of the books. Her voice slow and measured, she looked at Trudy. "You're…Belle?"

When she heard her thoughts out loud, the words flowed easier, though remained filled with astonishment. "Belle Trudeau? I can't believe this… you're Belle Trudeau."

"Who's Belle Trudeau?" Jim asked, but no one responded.

Slowly Ann walked across the room. "How could I not have known? Amy's always talking about the stories you tell her—the bear, the little girl, the umbrella, for Pete's sake. I've read your books. How could I not have known? I don't know what to say, Tru—I mean…Belle."

"Don't say anything…" Trudy replied, reaching up and taking Ann's hand to sit beside her on the hearth.

She looked at Ann and then to Jim. His expression of complete bewilderment allowed her smile to return. "Yes, I wrote the books. But understand, Belle Trudeau was just as much a character as those she wrote about. So one day she and the bear just walked into the forest never to be heard from again." Trudy's voice became a whisper. "Personally…I think the damn bear ate her."

"Don't you dare tell Amy that," Ann jokingly scolded.

"Look, I'm sorry I didn't tell you both sooner, but honestly I didn't think much about it. But what I'm about to tell you, I've thought about a lot."

"We both have." Lincoln said, handing Ann a glass of Merlot. "We've discussed it off and on for quite some time now, and as close as the four of us are…well, it's like you said Ann. What could we possibly have to confess that we haven't told each other already? We've all shared some pretty intimate facts; that's for sure. But I hope once you've heard it you'll understand why we've been so hesitant."

Mystified, Ann held up the book, her eyes dashing quickly between Lincoln and Trudy. "Wait! This isn't it?"

Shrugging, Lincoln looked at his wife. "This is your confession, my love."

There was no sound. It was as if the whole room held its breath. Figurines, carvings, statuettes—all seemed to be waiting for Trudy to speak. She took a sip of wine, a deep breath, and then reached behind her.

"We want you to have a special copy of Lincoln's latest novel," she said, her soft voice filling the quiet space. The book was covered with the infamous pink-and-orange striped borders, characteristic of the Iris collection that continued to elevate Lincoln's celebrity status with each new release.

"Yours is the only copy that has a dedication; hand written by the author." Lincoln added.

To Ann and Jim

Beyond friendship, with you I share "secrets and whispers"

Love, Tru

❦

The alarm on the printer woke her from the memories. The room, no longer filled with the vocals of Van Morrison, seemed equally warm with Tony Bennett and k. d. lang's "Dream a Dream of Me" drifting in the background. Her thoughts, of course, rushed to Lincoln, but she could no longer spend time standing around daydreaming. She had much to do, so she would just have to daydream on the move.

The manuscript finished, there was now a precise ritual to be followed. Nothing complicated, nothing dramatic, and nothing eccentric. Just her way of creating a wonderful moment of celebration with the man she loved so very much. She'd print it off, set it on the Gathering Place, open a bottle of champagne, and present her husband with Lincoln Trudeaus latest novel.

He'd stay up late into the night reading the humorous story his brilliant wife had written. It always made him laugh to think people could believe he possessed such a talent, and it also made him sad that she chose never to be recognized for it. Some thirty years earlier, Trudy had written her first book, a children's story entitled *When the Lamb Roared*, about a shy young girl named Ella who, with the help of a kindly old bear, found her voice. It quickly became a bestseller, and soon after, a second book followed, *Under the Bear's Umbrella*. Its theme was based on love and protection. It, too, became a bestseller, and along with it the demands for personal appearances, book signings, and even an offer from late-night TV shows came pouring in. None were accepted.

Though the surgery to remove her tumor had been successful, and with hard work she learned to speak very well, her voice remained uncommonly soft, quiet, and easily strained, many times leaving her to reluctantly fall back to pen and paper. But it was what the surgery couldn't repair that kept her from making public appearances. The childhood years of ridicule, relentless teasing, and the baseless hatred and disgust from so many had left permanent scars of fear and shyness, the mortar and stone of which she'd construct a great wall of protection and isolation where life could be reclusive and safe. No, she refused to speak publicly then, now, or anytime in the future. Sadly, the award-winning children's author Belle Trudeau would never write another book.

However, three years later, at the encouragement of her husband, she wrote *Hello, Mary? There's a Cow in Your Pool*, a humorous account centered around the escapades of Iris, a woman who, in her efforts to embrace life fully, perpetually throws caution to the wind, leads even when she herself is lost, and believes most rules and road signs are only meant as vague suggestions. This while enjoying with her girlfriends an unending array of adult beverages, garage sales, bunco parties, power walks to the corner mailbox, and occasional impromptu pool aerobics in her backyard. She's the wife of the author, her story told through his eyes.

Lincoln had barely finished reading the first chapter when he realized he was falling in love with Iris and the characters of Sunny Hill Estates. "This is a chick book," he said when Trudy passed through the room. "But I like it. It's funnier than all get-out, and her husband's great. I kind of feel sorry for the poor guy. But it does make it funnier that he's the one telling the story."

Trudy was unsure if he honestly enjoyed it or not, but over the next few weeks, he spoke of it often, quoting Iris on more than a few occasions, even pointing out a woman at the mall he thought could be Iris's nemesis, her snooty next-door neighbor, Mary Gunderson.

The experience of writing again was fulfilling, and knowing Lincoln enjoyed it made it all the better. But it was when he asked, "What are Iris and the girls up to next?" that her adrenaline soared in a rush of excitement she hadn't experienced in years. Immediately she began putting a first draft together.

One evening not long afterward, Lincoln found a new manuscript sitting on the kitchen table of their small apartment. A few minutes later, Trudy arrived with a bottle of champagne, undoubtedly picked out by Francesco, down the street at Toscano's. A congratulatory toast was given. Trudy retired to the bedroom to listen to music; Lincoln spent the rest of the evening enjoying every page.

"Are you going to write another?" he asked, lying across the bed.

"I'm sending them to Carol Lane," Trudy answered. "If she likes 'em, they'll do a small run just to see how it sells. She insisted on four local book signings right up front. That's in the publishers contracts nowadays."

"How's that going to work, Tru? I mean, last time and all…"

Trudy scooted out of bed and made her way toward the bathroom. "Oh, it'll be fine." As the door closed, Lincoln heard the click of the lock, and then in the quiet of the night, Trudy's soft voice carried easily from behind the door. "I put the copyright in your name."

At first Lincoln adamantly objected, but then in a way only Trudy could manage, he finally agreed to play along, believing this type of book stood little chance of being published and even less chance of ever selling.

He was wrong. Soon copies were being distributed nationally and then internationally, remaining on the Times Best Sellers list for twenty two months, during which time Trudy had written two more, *Gardening with Iris: Fake Flowers Need Less Water* and *Is That a Booger in Your Oatmeal?* Both outsold the previous, and like before, numerous offers for personal appearances came pouring in.

It was only after Trudy pleaded with him that Lincoln reluctantly agreed to carry on the facade. But even now, he rarely appeared at book signings or interviews, and he insisted Trudy be by his side at every award and honors presentation that came along. "It may be my voice telling them thank you, but it's your talent they're honoring," he told her. "So I'll be damned if you're not gonna be there to experience it." And to this day the subject remained nonnegotiable.

Everyone loved to hear Lincoln speak. After all, he was entertaining, possessing the uncanny ability to capture the wit, humor, and style in which Trudy wrote while blending his own mixture of sophistication and small-town country-boy charm into his narration. At these functions he would always tell a short story and make reference to his lovely wife, whom, he was quick to point out, in no way bore similarities to Iris, and he would openly give thanks to God. He would then walk offstage, find a place of solitude, and privately, quietly, give thanks to God for the love he and Trudy shared and the blessings He had given them.

Yes, not only was it love at first sight, or love after one date. It was true love right from the very beginning, the kind of love that binds with every breath, every word, every laugh, and every tear. A love harder than diamonds yet as soft as the morning sunlight falling through the trees, a love that flourishes with hopes and dreams, dances without reason or melody, and measures time in kisses of good morning and good night. When hello and goodbye need always be accompanied by "I love you" and promises are honored and everlasting. Love, enduring and beautiful, treasured above all else. This... is their love. And the Trudeaus not only continued to love each other after their many years of marriage, but they had been able to do something few couples did anymore—remain in love. Recognizing the difference between loving someone and being "in love" had given strength to their relationship, responsibility, and duty to each other and themselves. So as never to become complacent in this beautiful emotion, they shared the enjoyment of the other's company and delight in the simplest gesture of compassion. "You are my love," he often told her. "And you mine," she would reply.

❈

A few years ago, there was an addition to her office, one that perhaps meant more to Trudy than any other. It wasn't a figurine or a painting but simply another book proudly displayed alongside the first two she had written so long ago. But inasmuch as she created the fanciful characters that drifted in and out of all three books, she did not pen this last collection of tales. In the opening sentence, the storyteller explained, they came to her on delicate whispers while visiting a secret place hidden deep within the forest.

Trudy knew a truer statement there never could be. And she also knew, like the two previous books, this would bring love, courage, and hope to children around the globe, and it was all due to the fascination of one small child who never tired of hearing about a great bear and a little ballerina name Ella.

The small child had grown into a young woman, and on a quiet night around an outdoor fire, she asked permission to write down the whispered tales from her childhood. The following year, with tears and hugs, it was her honor to present Trudy with a copy of her first book.

Secrets and Whisperers from a Quiet Belle
By Amy Brooks

❈

Perched once again on the bow of the boat permanently anchored in Brennan's Cove, the Old Fisherman had returned. Hearing sounds carried on the midday breeze, his head rotated from right to left, then sharply cocked at an odd angle to catch intently sounds from beyond the small waves lapping against the shoreline. There was much in the air this chilly morning he sensed: the laughter of the child and that of his friend. The woman standing on her high perch while voices and sounds signaled her presence—how quickly she moved back inside. Again he tilted his head and listened closely. It was the sound of a pickup moving through the long wind of gravel road leading to the three homes on Brennan's Cove. But this was not the sound demanding his attention. No, that sound came only twice—short, quick, and from deep within the dense underbrush of the forest. It stirred the great bird's soul, alerting him with an icy prod. Outwardly he showed no response, yet his heart pounded with a beat of caution, fear. His eyes moved watchfully to the forest beyond the small waves lapping against the shoreline.

❈

"That was a long drive, wasn't it, boy?" Jim said, turning off the truck. Jass impatiently pawed at the door, as if to say, *Come on—I need out; hurry up.*

Reaching across the seat, Jim opened the door, and Jass took off like a shot toward the Trudeaus' front door. Lincoln swung it open, and there beside him stood Beth.

"Jass!" she squealed as the big yellow dog rushed up the porch steps. "I've missed you so much," she cried gleefully, throwing her arms around his neck. "Do you want to play in the snow before it melts? Come on, let's go."

Lincoln gave a wave to Jim and then walked over to help him unload. "Did you leave anything at the house?"

"Just Ann!"

Lincoln spotted the suitcases. "Yeah, but did you leave her anything to wear?"

They both laughed and made their first trip into the house. Lincoln, dropping the new dog bed on the front porch, said, "Tru sent me over yesterday to air the place out a little bit. She put fresh sheets on the beds, and I suppose she knew you were bringing a new bed for Jass because she had me throw the old one in the burn pile. And man, it really smelled bad, like a pack of wet dogs."

"Well, she knew about the bed before I did, then. This morning was the first I'd heard—"

From outside came the high-pitched sound of an eagle, vicious barking, and Beth screaming, followed by the sound of Jass running down the snow-covered hill at breakneck speed. Jim hurried out the door. "Jass! Jass! Get up here!"

The eagle cried once again, opening its wings but never leaving its perch. "Jass," Jim called out as the dog hit the short wooden pier.

It was at that very instant, poor ol' Jass realized this was a bad idea. And the look on his face, which only the eagle could enjoy, must've been priceless when he hit that slippery wooden pier. Feet splayed out in all directions, attempting to stop before reaching the end. He made a grand effort, but a futile one.

As Jass began his swim to shore, the eagle squealed its laughter, spread its mighty wings, and passed but mere feet above the dog's head before disappearing out over Hood Canal. Lincoln and Jim ran to the water's edge,

Beth not far behind. In trouble and embarrassed, the dog, shivering, pulled himself from the cold water. Not pausing to shake off, he hurried to scamper up the hill. Jim called, "Stop. Sit," but Jass chose to take his scolding away from the crowd and ran to the porch, where he found comfort on his brand-new bed.

CHAPTER ELEVEN

Beneath chandeliers of crystal accenting the tin ceiling tiles original to the ninety-year-old building were dining tables draped in gray and white linen with porcelain settings awaiting guests. The walls were dressed with Linenfold paneling, darkly stained in rich shades of reddish-brown, yet lighter than the deep cherry furnishings, railings, and backbar of the small lounge directly to the left of the entrance. With style and sophistication, Celtic crosses and cultural art adorned the large dining room, enhancing its elegance. The staff members were gracious, and the menu was filled with rich, flavorful food that brought comfort to the soul, making it easy to see why Darby's had long been a favorite spot of area diners.

"Sorry we're late, Mrs. B. We had to park almost three blocks away, and then, just as we got to the door, Peg remembered she'd left her phone sitting on the console. She'll be here in a few minutes."

Both ladies hugged. Rachel then took a seat directly across the table from Ann. "None of my friends call me Mrs. B. except Trudy once in a while, when she's playing around. So please, from now on I'm Ann."

"That'll be hard, Mrs. . . . Ann." Rachel giggled. "I mean, I've never thought of you as anyone other than Mrs. B."

"And I've never thought of you as anyone other than a student. But you're not anymore. You're a grown woman, a mom, and someone I can now think of as a friend."

"Thank you, Msss . . ." Both women laughed and then quickly regained their composure. "Thank you, Ann," Rachel amended. "You know, even back in school—and I know this is gonna sound stupid to you, but I always thought of you more as a friend than a counselor or teacher. Well, unless I was in trouble. Then I'd try to avoid you at all costs."

Again they giggled, and Rachel continued. "But you were there when I didn't have anyone to talk to, not even Peggy. Come to think of it, especially Peggy." She smiled, rolling her eyes. "But really, you always made time for me."

Ann grinned, and Rachel quickly leaned forward. "And don't tell me it was your job! I know better!"

Though she was flattered, Ann was caught a little off guard and didn't know how to respond. Fortunately, Rachel didn't leave time for a response. Picking up her water glass, she held it up to make a toast. Ann responded in turn. "Here's to an old friend and a new friendship."

"Mornin', ladies. Can I get you something to make a real toast with, or maybe knock the chill off, perhaps?" inquired the handsome young waiter, his stare coming to rest on Rachel.

Caught for a moment by his warm, thick accent and inviting smile, she looked to Ann, who said cordially, "Yes, thank you. I think I'll have your Irish chocolate breve."

"Mmm, that sounds good. I'll have one too," the charming redhead added.

"So we have two Irish chocolate breves?"

Shaking her head, Rachel smiled. "No, three. My sister will be here in a few minutes. Sooner if she knew hot chocolate was coming."

"I have a sister like that meself. Would you like me to wait until she gets here to bring hers out?"

"No, she'll be here any minute. Also, I've a question, if you don't mind."

"By all means."

"Your name's Kirian..." Rachel inquired, reading the tag on his vest.

"Yes, It's Irish. I'm Irish, born and raised on the Emerald Isle. Fresh off the boat, as they say." He smiled proudly. "And listen to you, pronouncing me name like it was your own..."

"It was my dad's name. He was from Killarney."

"So you're Irish, then? Well, of course you are. Anyone as lovely as yourself would have to be. I have family in Killarney. Who knows—you and I could be cousins...or something."

"Or something!" The doubt reflecting in her tone brought a roguish grin to the young man's face.

"True, it's unlikely, I suppose," he replied, his grin beginning to fade. And just as quick, it was back. "But I do come from a long line of chocolate lovers, you know. Coincidence? I'm not so sure."

Ann smiled at his charm; Rachel blushed at his wit. "Okay, so getting back to my question."

"That wasn't your question? My apologies…I thought you wanted to know if I was Irish."

"I'm afraid the accent kind of gives it away. Well, that and your pin."

The waiter's rosy cheeks turned a deeper red as he looked to the front of his vest, where a small metal lapel pin claimed 100 percent Irish.

"That's my girlfriend's doing. She…" The young man paused, noticing Rachel's widening smile. "You know, let's move on to your question."

"Celtic?" Rachel asked, pointing to a sign that read Live Music.

"It is. It's just next door at our pub, Friday and Saturday nights, eight to whenever and Sunday afternoons, twelve to four. As you can imagine, it gets pretty lively. The fiddle player is a young lady from Killarney. I think the rest of the band is from Ennis and Dublin. They're pretty good. It's like a bit a home."

Rachel nodded. "My parents moved here when I was five. My dad loved his music. A good jig and reel could really get him going, but it made him homesick too. I don't believe he ever got used to being over here."

An air of compassion and understanding came over the young man, his eyes lamenting his own feelings for home. "Yes, I can understand that. I too miss it." He pointed to a painting hanging on the opposite wall. "That's the Ha'penny Bridge, in Dublin. I used to walk across it twice a day to get to work. I hated it at the time, but I sure miss it now."

And with all the quickness of a finger snap, his rosy cheeks rose to accommodate that same roguish grin he'd flashed earlier. Nodding toward the entrance, he smiled warmly. "The vision coming through the door could only be kin to you. I'll be right back with that chocolate."

Rushing to the table, Peggy whined, "Oh, Mrs. B. I'm so sorry. I couldn't—"

Rachel candidly winked at Ann before interrupting. "Peg, you act like you're still in high school. Grow up, for, heaven's sake. Her name's Ann. It's okay to be an adult now. You can call her Ann."

Not knowing what to think, Peggy stood a little stunned. Ann moved out of the circular booth and gave the woman a hug. Peg sneered at her big sister, whose laughter was only tolerable because the hot chocolate had arrived.

The drink was delicious, as was lunch. Rapidly the hour turned into two, followed by an interlude of shopping where each lady found must-have treasures—Ann, a tablecloth, placemats with matching napkin rings, and three buckets of assorted popcorn; Peggy also found a new tablecloth, two crocheted doilies, a heart-shaped picture frame, and, like Ann, three buckets of assorted popcorn. Rachel, however bought only one item—a long sterling silver bookmark in the shape of a shepherd's hook. Dangling from its end was a chain with an oval emblem of an angel wielding a sword. Across the top in raised lettering was the word "Michael."

"Dessert, anyone? Tell me you love cake," Ann coaxed, looking down the street. "Jim brought me here a couple of months ago. It's so wonderful; please tell me you love cake."

"Of course. Who doesn't love cake?" Peggy answered.

"This isn't just any cake; it's like tasting the history of cake. They use all different kinds of stone-ground flour and meal from a local gristmill, all-natural sweeteners, honey, fruit, and even different kinds of salts. It's simply incredible. Come on, dessert's on me."

Ann moved quickly down the block. "I'm parked right up here on the corner. We'll just throw everything in the trunk and get it when we're done."

A quick visit to the car, and the three women walked to the other side of the street. A large signpost read Welcome to Poet's Corner. Upon entering the immense semicircular vestibule of the old brick building, they paused just long enough to allow a whiff of baked goodness to titillate their senses. The smells came to them through folding glass doors at the far right of the entrance. Standing wide open, the doors themselves were somehow as intriguing and inviting as the layered fragrance that invisibly beckoned visitors to enter and enjoy; the ladies would do both.

There was no debate as to what would be ordered, all agreeing the logical decision was the large sample plate, which offered each guest six pieces of cake designed to be enjoyed much like a wine tasting. Selections were brought out individually and served with tasting notes and a brief history, as well as a place at the bottom to write remarks. For an extra charge, you could have a pairing of a beverage to complement each tasting. Peggy couldn't pass it up. "That sounds great. We'll take it."

They spent as much time eating and talking as they had earlier over lunch, later referring to this as their six-course dessert dinner, though oddly enough, they never felt uncomfortably full. Finishing the last piece of cake, with the oohs and aahhs beginning to die down, Ann asked, "I don't recall seeing you with a bag, Rachel. Didn't you find anything fun, something you just couldn't live without?"

"I did. A bookmark," she stated, retrieving it from her purse. "Remember the other day Michael bought me a book for Christmas?"

Peggy sat back and folded her arms in a huff. "That's not exactly what happened."

Ann smiled, remembering the incident and Peggy's displeasure at the time. Apparently it had not dissipated much over the last few days. She continued to grumble. "That old man should've had Michael come get me. If nothing else, he should've at least asked our permission before giving Michael that expensive Bible. And believe me, I know where he goes to church, and I'm gonna show up one of these Sundays and talk to him about it. It's not right. It's just not right."

Rachel set her fork down. "And what are you going to say? Your kindness was atrocious? How dare you make little kids laugh and giggle!" She paused methodically, knowing it would only further emphasize her next statement. "Oh, and openly sharing Jesus with innocent little children. Why, that's just plain hateful. He should be ashamed, utterly ashamed. You go get him, Peg."

With the slightest chuckle, Ann picked at the few remaining bites on her plate. For a moment, fond memories clutched at her. She'd always enjoyed the banter between these two; and if memory served her correctly, Peggy almost always had the last word. Taking a sip of coffee, she waited. But it was not to be. Though clearly Peggy had a lot to say, she refrained, allowing Rachel to continue uninterrupted.

"I wish I could thank him for the kindness he showed Michael and let him know how much I appreciate what he did. Not just for my son, but for the other kids as well, their moms and dads, family and friends. It makes me wonder, how many lives has he touched? How many has he changed? I just find people like him so amazing. They do these wonderful things for all the right reasons, never seeking admiration or compensation, a pat on the back, or even a simple thank you. They're just amazing."

The large room was not only quiet, but silent, suddenly devoid even of the filtered sounds from outside that only moments ago droned like aleatory music, composed and staged by the very streets of the neighborhood.

Rachel's gaze fell to the table; "Quietly leading people to Christ through love and kindness." she remarked softly, before looking up. "Can you imagine? What a concept!"

Neither woman was quick to respond. They sat quietly as little by little the instrumentation of the neighborhood gathered about the room performing its uniquely familiar melodious drone. "And of course I want to pay him for the Bible, but I don't want to make him feel uncomfortable about it."

Her cold stare caused Peggy to flush warmly with embarrassment, and with a slight nod of her head, she added, "Maybe he'll allow me to make a donation to his church, or volunteer—"

Peggy delicately interrupted. "Have I mentioned his church isn't far from here? If he still goes to that one. I haven't been there for…well, it's been a while. But if it'll make you feel better, we'll stop by on the way home. There's almost always someone there."

"That's fine! But I don't want to go if you're gonna have an attitude. I mean really, Peg. You just need to let it go."

Peggy said nothing, holding up both hands as if to fend off any further scolding.

"Okay!" Rachel uttered, shoveling in one of the few remaining bites of an interesting cake called Gâteau Basque. Ann thought, *Maybe Peggy doesn't always get the last word after all.*

It was Ann who pushed the conversation back to the bookmark. Rachel shared its beauty, sharing too Michael's eagerness for her to read the story of Daniel and the Lion's Den and how, upon seeing the picture of the angel above the den, he began acting out and reciting the story on his own, his focus, of course, resting more on the angel and the lions than on Daniel himself.

But it was his odd description of the angel—"a Mighty Warrior of God" and "the General of the Angel Army"—that caught her somewhat by surprise. Obviously he hadn't read it from the text, and the angel was never described as such in any children's Bible she was aware of, which made her realize the old man's storytelling had left an indelible impression on her son, kindling his desire to learn more about angels and the wonderful, loving God they served. But this brought with it an onslaught of questions from the boy.

"What about Jesus? Does he have His own angels? Is my daddy an angel? A warrior? Does he have wings?" These along with ten others were questions he asked that night after saying his prayers.

"Angels!" Ann said softly, almost to herself. "My grandma talked about angels all the time. Claimed it was an angel that led her to Christ."

Shocked, Peggy leaned across the table. "Your grandma saw an angel?"

Ann laughed. "No!" But then her expression changed. Her soft grin faded, leaving a thin line where it had once been. She thought for a moment and, after taking a deep breath, added, "Well...yes. But not when it all first started, although she swore an angel sat with her the night my grandpa died. And I have to believe it's true, because she wasn't the same after that."

Confused, Rachel asked, "What do you mean she wasn't the same?"

Peggy, too, was confused. "She saw angels, but she just couldn't see this one particular angel? And if she didn't see it, how'd she know it was even there? I mean, she must've heard or seen something?"

Ann shook her head. "No! Not really."

Regretting mentioning angels at all, she sighed deeply and thought, *Why? Why would I bring this up? I don't like talking about it, and it's not a story I'm good at telling.* She exhaled silently, asking the question, *Really, God?* and then took another deep breath, looked at the two women staring at her for answers, and calmly said, "How about if you give me the opportunity to completely change the subject?"

"Not a chance!" Peggy cried without consulting her sister. "Angels fascinate me. Always have! And if your grandma sees angels, I want to hear about 'em."

Rachel made it obvious she too had questions, although if it made Ann uncomfortable, the subject could be changed no matter what her sister wanted. But Ann decided reluctantly to continue, after first jotting down a mental note: *Never speak of angels again! Ever!!!*

Before starting, she took a sip of coffee and looked at the girls. "I want you two to remember I gave you an out," Ann stated, dangling the comment like a worm on a hook…hmmm. No bites. "Okay then. There were no bright lights, no unearthly voices. It was simply something she sensed. According to her, it wasn't something she felt emotionally, but a physical presence just as real as if someone had walked into that hospital room and sat on the bed beside her."

Peggy rubbed the sudden goose bumps on her arms. "But how did she know it was an angel? I mean, it could've been—"

Without truly meaning to, Rachel cut her off. "You said she changed after that. Was it because of what she believed she'd experienced or the loss of her husband? How did she change exactly?"

Once again, Ann smiled broadly. "According to my mom, it may or may not have been an angel, but it was definitely an act of God that caused such a drastic change in my grandma. She wasn't a believer at all—not in God or Jesus, or heaven or hell, and definitely not in demons and angels. But even so, she never stopped my grandpa from going to church. He'd always been strong in his faith, active in his church, and even taught Sunday school on occasion. But not once did she go with him. Not even on Christmas or Easter. She just didn't want any part of it.

"When my mom came along and Grandpa insisted on taking her to church with him, Grandma began to resent the bond that formed between them, and it showed. She treated both of them terribly. Then, when my mom moved to Washington State to attend Bible college, Grandma became even worse. Of course, when my parents got married and Grandma found out her new son-in-law was a preacher…well, you can only imagine. All hell broke loose." She chuckled, watching the girls' reaction. "I guess what I'm trying to say without really saying it is, she was not a very pleasant person to anyone."

Pausing to examine the scant remains of the Gâteau Basque, Ann felt questions again forming on the lips of the sisters. She held up one finger, hoping to maintain momentary silence as she warmed her coffee from the elegant carafe left on the table. As she poured, Peggy, true to form, started to speak, but she was quickly muzzled by the raising of Ann's finger once again.

Peggy watched as coffee filled Ann's cup. She even waited to speak until after a splash of cream had been added and Ann had finished her first sip.

"You know that finger thing used to work when we were kids…"

"I know!" Ann smiled, examining her finger as though it were a magic wand. "Seems I haven't lost my touch."

All three women giggled, with Peggy and Rachel relaying how they too use the power of the finger to quiet the men in their lives. Peggy, making it clear she wished to get back to the conversation, huffed, "So, back to the angel!"

"Yes, back to the angel," Ann said, sneaking in one more quick sip.

"It was early evening. My grandparents had just finished supper and were sitting on the porch enjoying the sound and smells of a late summer rain. In the distance an occasional flash of lightning and roll of thunder filled the sky. This was the gentle beginnings of what was to be the worst thunderstorm to move through Bitterroot Valley, Montana, in recent memory.

"After about ten minutes, and without any warning at all, Grandpa slumped over and fell to the floor, clutching his chest. Grandma knew right away it was his heart and ran into the house to call an ambulance. But the storm had already knocked out the phone service, leaving her with only one option. Amazingly, within minutes she had this big ol' rancher loaded into the cab of their Ford pickup, heading to the hospital up in Missoula. She had to drive directly into the storm they'd been watching, and she feared there'd be flash flooding on the old county road leading to the highway. And honestly, I've been on US 93. It's not much more than a two-lane road itself. But that didn't matter. She knew she had to get him to the hospital right away.

"Just before they reached the highway on ramp, lightning hit a tree about fifty yards off the road, and she began to cry. She was afraid…not for herself; she was a tough ol' farm girl. But a storm this size could bring things to a dead stop in nothing flat."

"She began to pray, didn't she?" Rachel asked abruptly.

"That's when the angel appeared, isn't it?" Peggy added.

Ann shook her head and smiled. "No, she didn't pray, and no, the angel didn't appear. Mmm, not exactly, anyway."

Ann swirled her coffee. Peggy reached across the table and held Ann's cup with both hands. "I don't want to seem rude, but drink the damn coffee already and get to the angel part. I'm about to pee my pants because of all this anticipation!"

Ann was hardly surprised by Peggy's outburst, and with a gentle chuckle, she finished the last sip before setting the cup on the table. Rachel, hiding a wink from her sister, asked, "Would you like a refill, Ann? I'll just get us a refill. It'll only take me minute or two."

Peggy's eyes darted quickly between Rachel and Ann, at one point even glancing at the empty cup. Her mouth fell open in an attempt to speak, but her words, suppressed by the weight of disbelief, stalled in utter confusion. It was Rachel's full-on laughter that finally pulled the slack from Peggy's jaw, allowing her to relax and even join in with a small snigger of her own. Though none was needed, she made an apology to Ann.

"Okay, my grandma was afraid. This was one of the worst storms she had ever driven through, and it seemed like she was right in the heart of it, taking her almost twenty minutes just to reach the highway and another forty-five or more to the hospital in Missoula.

"She'd laid my grandpa across the seat, resting his head on a pillow placed over her legs. And like I said, he was a big man, but she attempted to make him as comfortable as she could. But there was a time just before turning onto the highway she thought for sure he'd died right there in her lap. She once told me that was the loneliest moment of her life. It was then she whispered a prayer…well, sort of, anyway.

"She said, 'God, I know you and I have shared him for all these many years, but I'm not ready to totally give him up to you just yet. There's things I want to tell him, and I'm going to tell him, dead or alive. Things he needs to know. Things I've hardly ever said, unless of course he says 'em first—you know. Are you listening to me, God?

"'He loves You, and I've treated him terribly because of that sometimes.

But please, he deserves to know before he goes to his grave, he was loved by me more than anything in the whole world…he deserves to know that. And to know that he was the greatest husband a woman could ever ask for. I'm not asking this for me. I don't deserve your help or understanding, but he sure does. He deserves to hear how much I truly love him, have always loved him. So if you've already taken him…well, just work one of your miracles and somehow let him hear my voice. Please, God, please! Let him hear my voice.'

"My grandpa didn't open his eyes. He didn't try to talk, but very gently he moved his finger on the side of her leg. She looked into the storm clouds and whispered, "Thank you, God," and began sobbing uncontrollably. Even through her tears, she started talking about the day they met at the town picnic, their first date, their first kiss, their wedding day. Years of pent-up feelings poured out of her. Apology after apology for failing to show him every day how much she loved him, and every once in a while, she'd feel his finger lightly stroke her leg.

"It must've been around seven, seven thirty, my dad and my brother Teddy were in watching TV. Mom and I were dishing up ice cream in the kitchen when the phone rang. I started to make my usual dash to answer it, but she stopped me, pointing out I had chocolate all the way up to my elbows. She answered it. Their conversation lasted less than a minute, and the only words I heard her say were 'I'm leaving right now.'

"From where I stood, I could see her trembling. She looked so pale, so weak, it scared me. I'd never seen my mom like that before. She'd always been strong; she was Mom. I rushed to her, yelling into the living room, 'Something's wrong. Mom needs you.' Two seconds later my dad paused in the doorway just long enough for her to look at him and say, 'It's my dad.'

"A quick prayer was said, and Dad was on the phone to the airlines while Mom packed. Within minutes, she was rushing back down the hallway. Dad called out, 'The earliest flight is tomorrow morning at ten forty-five.'

"'I'll drive! I can be there in eight hours. Call the hospital and let Mom know I'm on my way.'

"She only slowed down for hugs and to grab some cash out of the cookie jar atop the refrigerator. I don't believe she was to the end of the block before my dad sat us down and said the first of many prayers that night." The final pieces of cake were delivered to the table, along with a fresh carafe containing a new exotic coffee. Each woman sampled the fare before her, giving thumbs-up to both confection and drink. Peggy was quick to bring the conversation back around to Ann's story. "You lived in Seattle at the time?"

"Olympia."

"Wow, that's quite a drive." Rachel frowned. "Especially under the circumstances. I'm surprised your dad agreed to…"

Ann looked at her with a slight scowl and tilt of the head. "My mom and I are a lot alike! Do you honestly believe…"

"Enough said!" Rachel exclaimed, holding up one finger.

For an instant Ann was confused. And then, blushing at the mockery, she led the laughter that ensued.

"No, I can't picture Mr. B. ever trying to stop you," Rachel said.

Peggy felt she needed to say something. "Oh, neither can I. Mr. B. just wouldn't—"

"Stop!" Ann snapped, and with a tepid smile she sipped at the delicate concoction steaming in her cup. "Okay, ladies, from now on you have my permission to call him Jim. Got it? I don't want to hear any more Mr. B., or Mrs. B., or even watch out for the bumblebee. Comprende?"

Immediately recognizing the tone from their days in Ann's office, both ladies nodded their understanding, with Peggy unconsciously adding, "Yes, ma'am." Her eyes widened. "Ann. Ann is what I meant to say…yes, Ann…"

Rachel interrupted by sliding what was left of her cake over to her sister. "I doubt it, but this might help keep your foot out of your mouth." Not allowing Peggy to respond, she then quickly summarized. "Now, Ann, the family's in prayer, Mom's driving to Montana, and your grandma's at the hospital."

"Yes!" Ann jumped in, ready to move on. "It was around nine o'clock that evening. They moved him to a private room that was still part of the cardiac care unit. The cardiologist told grandma, 'The damage to his heart was massive. All anyone can do now is try to make him comfortable.'

"But even a doctor's voice can't penetrate the overpowering numbness that sets in at a moment like that, her mind protesting what her heart already knew. God was calling him home, and nothing could change that. Not the greatest surgeon, the newest miracle drug, or that array of monitors and machines that continued to softly whir, drip, blink, and beep at his bedside. No! This was a time between him and God. A moment set aside for earthly goodbyes before heavenly greetings. Grandma only hoped. No prayed my mom would arrive in time.

"The doctors and nurses were gentle, their actions compassionate.

"'We've done everything we can for now,' she heard one of the doctors say, and then everyone filed solemnly out of the room. It was quiet. A dim yellow glow of light hidden behind the headboard brought to her a moment of serenity. It was in that moment the room just felt different all of a sudden. There were no unusual lights, no detached voices, or anything like that. She just knew something or someone was there with her as she sat on the edge of the bed.

"Within minutes of feeling this presence, she experienced an unyielding compulsion causing her to rush from the room to the nurse's station, where breathlessly she asked directions to the chapel and if there was a Bible there she could borrow. But even before getting a response, there was a tap on her shoulder.

"Beside her stood an elderly gentleman, tall yet slight in appearance, weathered, tired, and weak, unmistakably a patient.

"His voice, gentle and soft, quivered with age. 'Please, take mine.' He smiled, extending a frail hand. In it lay a slightly worn black leather Bible.

"Thanking him, she rushed back, returning to her place on the edge of the bed, where she began flipping pages, mostly reading out of context, sometimes starting mid-chapter or even mid-verse. She became frustrated, yet she continued to read. Time after time, she turned to another section and read a little more before flipping through pages yet again. She felt lost, not knowing where to turn or what to read next. After a while she almost couldn't read at all, her vision so terribly blurred with tears.

"The presence never left, but only seemed to intensify. It wasn't long before she found herself at the beginning of Psalms, which she read for the next hour, this followed by the book of John, all the while remaining acutely aware of the presence around her.

"Many times she held the Bible tight against her chest, quietly mumbling words of affection to this man who had cared for her, showered her with love, and shared his desire for her to join him in the worship and service of what he'd always assured her was a loving, understanding, and merciful god. These were the things that now flooded her memory. The image of him sitting in that old recliner reading his Bible, sharing with her what God placed on his heart, even though he knew very well she didn't care and wasn't truly listening anyway.

"And there were the times he'd stand on their creaky old porch looking out over the meadows, admiring a simple rainbow, or bask in the orange glow of an Indian summer sunset, and then suddenly call to her as if in dire emergency, and she would drop whatever task at hand to run to his side. And it was there he would greet her with arms open and declare, 'Behold the hand of God, my sweet Carrie, for He is truly the Author of Creation in all its majesty.'

"She'd return in a huff to her chores, allowing the screen door to slam behind her. Not a moment would pass before he'd laugh and call out after her. 'Oh, but just wait, my sweet Carrie, until you see the sunrise He has for us tomorrow.' She honestly believed early morning was his favorite time of day.

"And then, there was that silly song he'd taught their daughter when she was about three or four years old. They'd sing it together every morning while he was shaving, right up until the day she left for college. And even then he continued to sing it, just with slightly less enthusiasm.

"Grandma envisioned the two of them standing at the sink, his face covered in lather, his little girl sharing a hairbrush for their microphone. And then for a moment she had to think, 'How did that song go? This is just plain stupid that I can't remember…I've listened to it every morning for… oh, oh yes…This is the day; this is the day that the Lord has made, that the Lord has made. Their voices rang loud enough to spook the livestock down at the McMurtry's barn just under a mile away.'

"Now it was that memory in particular that made her smile and then made her weep. Throughout the night she never pleaded for God to take him or let him live, but simply to make him comfortable. She knew this was the very moment her husband had prepared for all his life. What was it he used to say? 'Someday death will lay its hand on me, and in that very instant, I'll close my eyes to this old world. Oh, but in the next moment, my eyes will open to be greeted by the loving face of grace, our Savior Jesus Christ. Rejoice with me, sweet Carrie. Rejoice that we have been chosen by God.'

"Outside, the rain began to ease, leaving the clouds to break apart in great sections, revealing the vast stars to twinkle and the moon to shine. But she never saw them, choosing instead to remain at his side, where occasionally, resting her head on his chest, she prayed aloud. It was there she came to understand this warm, loving presence had not come to usher her husband into heaven like she first believed, but to sit beside her, comfort her, give her the assurance she wasn't alone. Once she understood that, a more subtle realization opened to her. She believed and accepted with no reservations and no comprehension of how her husband wasn't simply lying there waiting for death to arrive. He was in prayer, speaking to God not with his mouth or his mind, but with the voice of his spirit, his soul.

"Her heart melted. Tears flowed silently onto the blanket that covered his chest. She kissed his lips and whispered 'I love you' over and over again. To the day she died, she believed—no, she knew—the last act her husband would do in this life was to pray for her. As she sat on the edge of his bed, a warm breeze ruffled her hair and settled around her. In an instant she came to understand she was being held by an angel sent from God, in answer to prayer.

"Sometime around four thirty in the morning, a nurse showed my mom into the room. She stood stunned, not so much at the site of her father, but at that of her mother sitting on the bedside reading the Bible aloud. They embraced only momentarily before Mom took her place on the other side of the bed. She stroked her father's cheek, ran her hand over his thick gray hair, and put her hand to her lips as she began to sob. 'I'm here, Daddy' was all she could manage. When Grandma started to get up to comfort her, my mom shook her head. 'No! No please keep reading. That's his favorite passage.' So as my grandma continued to read, my mom whispered softly about meaningful moments she and her father had shared.

"Sometime later his breathing began to weaken. A nurse appeared briefly at the door and quickly left without completely entering. Both women leaned down, each placing her head next to his. The room, beginning to fill with muted shades of orange and red from a slightly obstructed sunrise, became ever so quiet. And then my mom laid her head on her father's shoulder. Her voice strained with grief, she began to quietly sing. 'This is the day… This is the day that the Lord has made… that… the Lord…'"

"Really!" Peggy sniveled, wiping away a face full of tears. "This is how it's gonna be every time we get together?"

Rachel's eyes were also tear filled, but they didn't dampen her devilish smile. "Would you like a tissue instead of that dirty napkin?" she asked her sister.

"No, I'm fine!" Peggy snapped before turning her attention toward Ann, who was about to take a bite of cake in an effort to hide her amusement.

"It probably wasn't even a true story, was it?" Peggy said curtly. "I remember you and Mr. B. both would make up these stories that would have everybody in tears, and then—"

"Psst… you have a little cake on the side of your nose," Rachel said, pointing in an effort to be helpful.

Peggy ran the napkin along the side of her nose.

"Mr. B.? Oh, you must mean Jim?" Ann exclaimed with a grin.

Flustered, Peggy blushed. "Yes, Jim! Okay, I got it."

Rachel pointed to her sister's cheek. "Now you have a little frosting…"

Peggy crumpled the napkin, wiped it gently back and forth over her cheek, and again she looked to her sister for approval.

"No, no, no! The other side… no, not your face. The other side of the napkin. Now you have stuff on both cheeks."

Frustrated and irritable, Peggy tossed the napkin on the table. "You're messing with me, aren't you?"

Rachel didn't hold back her laughter, letting it carry through the now empty shop, and after a moment Ann, too, was laughing. Peggy held out as long as she could, which turned out to be no time at all, and she joined in cheerfully to complete their euphonious harmony.

As normalcy returned, Ann took it upon herself to revisit Peggy's question about the story's authenticity. "Yes, sweetheart, the story is true, every last word of it. As a matter of fact, what I didn't tell you is what first convinced my mom grandma's angel was real."

"Oh no, no more. I...I just can't take it," Peggy protested, shaking her head.

Ann wanted to giggle but saw something in her friend's demeanor that made her take pause.

"It's nothing like that, Peg," she said gently. "If anything, it's more along the line of what I think you were expecting in the first place. Something that...you know...makes you just kind of go...ooooh."

Peggy barely got a sound out before Rachel spoke up. "If there's really more to the story, of course I want to hear it."

"I do too!" Peggy responded quickly, triggering a brief exchange of sisterly tension, capped with patronizing shrugs, followed by small bursts of suppressed giggles.

Rachel pulled a small packet of tissues from her purse. Placing them in front of Peggy, she turned and impishly winked at Ann. Clearly this was Rachel's way of guiding a sense of composure back into the moment. Brushing a strand of hair from her face, Peggy straightened in the chair, asking Rachel, "How do I look? Is my makeup okay?"

With hardly a glance, Rachel replied, "You're a mess. Now, can we hear the rest of the story, Ann?"

"Peggy, you look beautiful," Ann affirmed warmly.

"In the eye of the beholder..." Rachel goaded, with the sibling disdain of a twelve-year-old.

Quickly Peggy jeered, "Don't think you're so—"

"May I?" Ann said, allowing only the slightest pause to restore order and capture the full attention of both ladies. There would be no further tussle between the sisters, their volley of banter ending simply with the faint familiarity of Ann's authoritative tone that once upon a time would, and apparently still could, freeze them in midsentence, leaving Ann to continue.

"A little later that morning, Mom and Grandma were getting ready to leave when they passed by the nurses' station. 'Oh, wait a second,' Grandma said, quickly returning to the room. There on the windowsill was the Bible.

She returned to the nurses' station and asked about the elderly gentleman, saying she would like very much to return his Bible and thank him personally."

"He was the angel, wasn't he?" Peggy cried out.

Ann thought about taking a moment to enjoy a bite of cake while allowing Peggy to twist in the wind but quickly decided against it. Even so, there'd be no urgency in revealing the answer. And though Peggy's slight squirm and bouncing knees hadn't become visible as of yet, the clenched fist pressing tightly against her lips in an effort to stifle any further commentary outburst seemed to suffice nicely as a visual penance for the interruption.

"No, he was not," Ann replied, sampling a bite of cake more out of impulse than reconsideration.

As if deflated, Peggy's shoulders slumped slightly, and Rachel quietly refilled everyone's cup. Dabbing the corners of her mouth, Ann folded her napkin and set it on the table. She beamed. "Don't you just love this place?"

Rachel smiled in agreement. Peggy set silent, though her right knee had begun to quiver slightly, detected only by a minute ripple on the surface of her still-full water glass.

Placing her arms on the table, Ann began once more. "Now, as I was saying, Grandma wanted to return the Bible personally, so she stopped at the nurses' station to inquire about the elderly patient who had offered its use. One of the nurses flippantly, albeit politely, told her, 'This is ICU. None of our patients stroll the hallways handing out Bibles.'

"'But I do!' came a pleasant voice, commanding the attention of everyone around. His six-foot-two-inch frame moved confidently down the corridor, extending a hand first to my grandma and then my mom, introducing himself simply as Dr. Weldon."

CHAPTER TWELVE

"Grandma often described doctor Weldon as stunningly handsome, with a smile that melted butter, but was quick to add, 'He wore his hair all shaggy, like some kind of hippie, and I didn't care for that at all.'

"After expressing his condolences, he reached for the Bible, saying, 'It was just coincidence I had this with me last night…'

"'This isn't your Bible!' Grandma snapped, turning away slightly. 'At least, you're not the person that handed it to me.'

"'I'm sorry?' he replied, somewhat stunned.

"'It's not yours. There was an elderly man. Frail. He's a patient; I'm sure of that.'

"The doctor looked at my mom with disbelief and then with heartfelt sympathy and concern, saying, 'You were under an incredible strain last night, Mrs. Evans, so when I heard you ask for a Bible…I…'

"'Doctor, with all respect, I would've remembered you. The person I saw, the person that handed me this Bible, was old and sick. His hair quite gray and thin. He spoke softly, very soft. Oh yes, and he had a tattoo on his forearm. I can't recall exactly what it was, but…'

"Tenderly, the young doctor smiled, pushing the open sleeve of his lab coat up to reveal two small wings resembling those of an angel tattooed on his right forearm. 'Like this?'

"Grandma stared, taking in the detail. This was definitely what she'd seen. An uncomfortable silence made it difficult to glance at his warm face, but she did. Though it came on slowly, for the first time in many years she began to blush. However, the slight glow to her complexion was short lived."

"'May I see that again?'

"The doctor again smiled. 'Of course…' And again he displayed his forearm.

"Cautiously moving closer to view the illustration from a new perspective, she shook her head timidly. 'No! That's not it.' And then, about to look away, she stopped abruptly, her deep set eyes riveted on the young doctor's forearm. 'Would you mind raising your sleeve a little higher?'

"And without comment, he complied.

"Grandma shook her head confidently. 'No! Definitely not what I saw last night. The wings are the same, but there was something above them. Something like…well, I don't know. I didn't stop to read it at the time.'

"'So you're saying there was a word written above the wings?'

"'Could've been a word. The gentleman's arm was thin and wrinkled, and he had a number of those red bruises—you know the kind—but I'm positive what I saw wasn't a bruise.'

"Dr. Weldon took a moment to process Grandma's recall of the incident, I'm sure looking for signs of psychological and emotional disorders people sometimes experience immediately following the death of a long-term mate. But then, out of the blue and more to himself than to her, Grandma hears him say, 'With God, all things are possible!' And then his stare, almost pleadingly, returned to her. "'Mrs. Evans, would you and your daughter be kind enough to accompany me to my office? There's something I'd like to show you. It won't take long.'

"The office was small, sparsely decorated with two casual chairs, a mahogany book shelf, credenza and matching desk, and an executive chair. Dr. Weldon insisted Grandma sit there and offered my mom one of the chairs in front of the desk, while he chose to stand.

"Taking off the white lab coat and casually draping it over the back of the remaining chair, he began to speak softly, unhurried, as if visiting with old friends.

"'I came home with this the day I graduated high school,' he said, turning his arm to better expose the tattoo. 'My stepfather wasn't happy about it, and neither was my mom at first. But having grown up seeing them on her father's forearm every day of her life, she understood the significance and knew I hadn't done it as a rebellious act, but simply as my flawed attempt at honoring my grandpa. I had idolized the man all my life, and the story behind the wings had always…well, I won't bother you with all that, Mrs. Evans. I brought you here to…'

"But Grandma felt strangely compelled to hear about the wings, imploring the doctor to please tell the story behind them. Now, my grandma never cared about anyone's story before, no matter how interesting the person might have been, at times rudely showing her disinterest by simply walking away without a word or staring into space while mentally going over a grocery list or the owner's manual of her old Waring blender. So when she insisted on hearing the story, my mom couldn't believe it. She was just as surprised as when she saw her reading the Bible. Maybe even more so, because there was no logic behind this at all. She didn't know these people or owe this doctor anything, so why was she being so polite? She had to have been up to something. But of course the good doctor didn't know any of that, so without much hesitation and feeling somewhat obligated at that point, he launched into his story."

❦

Right around 1900, while still in his teens, John Morris had become a roughneck on the oil rigs of northeast Texas. But then, on the morning of July 11, 1905, a series of events began to unfold that changed his life forever. At 11:37 he sounded the alarm to evacuate the rig's platform. Men jumped from the drilling floor and began to run, only making it ten yards before hearing a loud hissing sound coming from the borehole. At thirty yards, they turned to see a plume of vaporous gas jetting forty feet into the air. They also saw John lying unconscious at the base of the steps. Before anyone could react, there was a loud rumble. Mud, gas, and oil buckled the platform and then rose from the borehole sixty feet in the air. A casing shot upward through the skeleton of the wooden tower breaking supports as it did and came to rest just yards from where John lay. In that instant the derrick disappeared behind a ball of flame. So intense was the heat, it drove the men back another twenty yards, leaving everyone to assume he was dead, incinerated by the blast. A few minutes later, seemingly from out of nowhere, a man using a heavy wool blanket as a shield ran to his side and carried him to safety. As they loaded him onto a wagon for the two-mile trip to the infirmary, he began to come around. His eyes fluttered open, attempting to focus on a familiar face. Wincing in pain, he waited a moment and tried opening them again. To everyone's surprise, he smiled and asked for a cold beer. A loud cheer went up from the men, and cold beer was immediately located and administered.

It was a miracle he was alive, but more so was the lack of serious injury—a mild concussion, a sprained ankle, and a few scrapes and bruises. Nevertheless, the doctor there in Humble kept him overnight for observation. Early the next morning, his crew dropped by with hot biscuits and gravy from the little place where they gathered every morning before heading into the fields. No one gave a speech but simply shook John's hand and thanked him for saving their lives. But there was one question on everyone's mind: This blowout hadn't seemed to give any warning, so what made him sound the alarm to clear the derrick?

He didn't have an answer. It must have just been a feeling. Intuition, maybe. But that didn't ring true for him or anyone else in the room. Nevertheless, no one thought it mattered, and they were just thankful to be alive. It wasn't long after they all left, and a man John had known only as Deke entered the room. They'd spoken once or twice, but nothing more than a social greeting. Deke was known as a hard worker who kept to himself, requiring only two things—respect or a wide berth. And at six five, not many men argued, and when someone did, it was settled quickly, decisively, and always in Deke's favor. That morning when his big frame filled the doorway, there wasn't another man in the world John wanted to see more. He knew it had been Deke under that blanket.

So as not to be overcome by emotion, John spoke up quickly, saying, "You know, you save a man's life in the fields, he's obligated to buy you a new set of work clothes and a big ol' steak at the Rice Hotel. I don't expect that to cover what I owe you, but—"

"You don't owe me anything," Deke said. "Except maybe an explanation."

John didn't know what he was talking about, and apparently it showed. So Deke cut right to it, explaining how he'd heard the blast and witnessed

You Are My Love

the fireball from a quarter mile away. He and his crew, expecting to find dead and injured all over the yard, grabbed two long wooden boxes filled with emergency supplies and ran to help. By the time they arrived, the whole structure was engulfed in flames, smoke so thick and black Deke could only catch glimpses of the burning platform—and, of course, John still lying on the ground only a few feet in front of it. He never spoke a word, just grabbed a wool blanket from one of the boxes, draped it over his head and shoulders, and made his way across the yard to the base of the steps. Even as he approached, he felt something was wrong, unnatural. Though John lay only feet from the intense gas flames that held everyone at bay, the air immediately around him felt cool. His clothes weren't scorched, not even hot to the touch. His face and arms, streaked with oil, were also unburned. Even his hair hadn't been singed.

Then Deke stood quietly and waited for an explanation, but of course John didn't have one and maybe for a split second even thought that Deke had just imagined the whole thing. But no; John had been around the fields long enough to know anyone caught that close to a blowout of that nature typically died where they stood. Even those lucky enough to be blown from the inferno usually suffered internal injuries, broken bones, or a cracked skull, but none escaped without serious burns, and most would succumb to their injuries before ever reaching a doctor.

Deke allowed him a moment of reflection before saying anything more, and then in a tone surprisingly gentle yet filled with assurance, said, "You've got some guardian angel there, my friend. I thought for sure I'd be dragging a dead man out of those flames—that is, if I didn't die in the process. She put you under her wings. Hell, I could feel her with me, too, every step of the way. You may not believe in such things, and that's fine by me, but I was fully conscious, wide awake, and very much aware of the whole situation. I lived every second of it firsthand, and I'll believe it was an angel what saved us both to the day I die."

"Now, the thing was, John knew Deke was right. He'd spent most of the night lying awake struggling to recall the sequence of events leading up to the blast, though few memories existed, and those what did were cloudy and distorted. Some, as if pulled from an obscure place in his imagination, made no sense at all. Now, listening to Deke, he began to wonder just how cloudy and distorted those memories really were.

"Deke made it clear he had never seen the angel, but he had heard her voice—soft, comforting, like someone singing a hymn while praying all at the same time, a voice moving on the wind, not coming from any one place, but as if it were simply in the air surrounding him. It was the damnedest thing he'd ever heard. And that was the other thing—when had he actually heard it? There was a part of him that believed it was while still working across the road, even before the explosion occurred. But why, and how could he have heard something that soft, that beautiful, and that delicate over all the noise on the drilling floor? Yet he had; he now believed that was why he'd told his crew to hold up drilling for almost a full minute before the distant blast shook the ground and pierced the air with its tremendous roar and fiery plume. He remembered as he ran toward the destruction, first his heart and then his mind being calmed by the presence of the voice...the hymn, the prayer.

"I'm no hero," he told John. "I just followed the voice of an angel and did what I was led to do. If there's a hero in this mess, it's you. You saved the life of every man on that platform. I'm sure you'll get your fill of steak dinners and have quite the wardrobe once you get out this place. And by the way, I stopped by your rooming house this morning on my way over. A Mrs. Cubbins sent you some clean clothes. Pretty sweet landlady you got. I guess as soon as she heard you'd been hurt, she made the ride to see for herself you were still alive. She said the doc had you pretty well sedated, so she just peeked in from the door."

Setting the clothes in a chair, Deke stared again at John. "You know, to have a guardian angel look after you is one thing, but to be cared for by a beautiful little angel with Mrs. in front of her name...well, let's just say if I were her husband—"

"You can stop there," John told him. "It's not like that at all. Me and Laura grew up out in Cane Island. I guess now they're calling it Katy, after Charlie Mare's wife. He has that saloon next to the train station. Anyway, last year Laura married Bart Cubbins, a really great guy from Fulshear. He built that house for her as a wedding present. A week after she moved in, he was still working up at Spindletop. There was a blowout...he didn't make it. Damn bankers all claimed they were sorry, and Beaumont Oil made their token gift and paid the undertaker, but of course, no one really offered to help her out. To make matters worse, it wasn't long before she found out she was carrying Bart's baby. That's when she decided to rent out some of the rooms to help make ends meet. I took the first one and rented the others to guys I knew could be trusted. They look out for her same as I do. You know how the town's getting."

Deke thought about it and grinned. "So in reality...you're her angel?"

"I'm her friend. That's all."

By six forty-five, the two men considered the doc a no-show, so John got dressed while Deke found him a cane. The two walked out the front door into a glorious Texas sunrise, both feeling it was good to be alive.

They rode back to Moonshine Hill. The town had started as a tent encampment and quickly grew into a boomtown of about ten thousand rowdy oil workers. It didn't take long before houses, shacks, and shanties started popping up, and pretty soon the place had two or three grocery stores, a dance hall, a two-room schoolhouse, and a church. But it was the six or seven saloons everyone flocked to most often. So after stopping by to see Mrs. Cubbins, the saloon was, of course, where Deke and John spent all that day drinking and talking about a wide variety of subjects—their different backgrounds and how they were raised, John by his mother, Deke by his father. Pretty soon they felt a strong bond developing unlike anything either had felt before, and according to both men, it made for a great beginning to their friendship. As evening came, so did John's friends and crew, and not long after, Deke's crew also arrived. Everyone wanted to buy the two heroes a drink, pat them on the back, and shake their hands. But Deke, being a loner, had other things on his mind. So he raised one last whiskey before slipping out the back door unnoticed.

Early the next morning, Deke paid twenty-five cents for a hot bath, with ten cents extra to have his clothes pressed, and gave Mrs. Rhodes fifteen cents for a large bouquet of flowers from her garden. He then rode to the northern edge of town, where standing on the wraparound porch gliding a watering can over an array of brightly colored flowers was Mrs.

Cubbins. Her appearance was considered common—bib apron, pouter pigeon blouse, and trumpet skirt. But to Deke there was nothing common about her. On the contrary, he perceived her as the epitome of elegance, playful with an air of confidence and strength and yet, within her eyes an enticing gentleness shone brightly, leaving him spellbound atop his saddle. It was for this reason she was the first to speak.

"What's wrong, cowboy? You need help getting down?"

Acknowledging her with a thin smile and a tip of his hat, he still refused to hurry, savoring her vision another second or two. His dismount came smooth, as did his gait to the base of the steps, where he stood staring up at her, his thin smile appearing once again. Politely she responded by yielding a smile of her own. This in turn, for a second time, caused him to pause a moment too long, giving her yet another opportunity to speak before him.

"John never came home last night, so if those flowers are for him, you're out a luck, cowboy."

※

At the other end of town, John woke in the back of a wagon parked outside a crowed dining room and was not surprised to find hangover added to his list of aches and pains. Everyone shouted greetings as he hobbled through the front door, but it was Otto, the big German, who asked, "How about them wings? Your angel, she like 'em…yes?"

Some lighthearted laughter came from most of the men, and it wasn't until someone showed him the fresh tattoo that he even knew it existed. Otto shouted in more broken English, "They good, my friend? All night we hear you want never forget angel saves you under wing; you pass out, I carry next door my shop; make sure you never forget. Look good, yes?"

This time the raucous laughter filtered beyond the walls to the street outside and quieted only after Reverend Taylor stood to speak. Years of delivering fire-and-brimstone sermons to hungover roughnecks had left his voice strong, powerful, and authoritative, though that morning he needed only raise a hand to silence the room.

"I've heard a lot of talk about you and Deke this morning, most elevating you both to what is sure to become Moonshine Hill legend, myth, and folklore—that is, if it hasn't already. Even so, we all agree it's a miracle either one of you made it out alive, especially you, John, considering you should've been dead from the blast before Deke ever arrived on-site. I'd have to call you pretty damn lucky, which is what we've all decided to call you from now on: Lucky! So if I was you, I'd try to get used to it. I don't think it's going away anytime soon."

Laughter erupted, filling the room. The reverend paused for a moment and then shook the man's hand as if pumping for water from a dry well. "We all want to thank you for saving your crew and thank Deke for saving you. So this Sunday, right after church, there'll be a potluck at Celebration Park to honor you both." Pointing to the tattoo, the preacher smiled. "I guess we should include that angel of yours too. What ya say, Lucky?"

Peggy by this time had finished most of her cake and her sister's as well. Ann picked at hers and continued. "Doctor Weldon then walked to the credenza and brought back a small wooden picture frame, which he handed Grandma, saying, 'That was taken last Christmas, three weeks before his eighty-fifth birthday. If you look closely, you can see the bottom part of the wings.'

"But Grandma didn't need a closer look. She recognized the man's face instantly, and without taking her eyes from the photo, she asked if he was still alive."

Peggy bit the inside of her cheek to keep from blurting out, "He was a ghost, wasn't he?" Her rapidly bouncing knee vibrated the table, signaling Ann to take a moment and enjoy a long sip of coffee, but she didn't.

"'Oddly enough, Mrs. Evans, he's in the room directly above your husband. He slipped into a coma little over twenty-four hours ago. My family's with him now.'

"Grandma handed him the Bible and stood to leave. Her voice filled with concern, she said, 'I won't take up any more of your time, Doctor. You should be there with them.'

"As she made her way toward the door, her movements became slow, somewhat erratic, and then suddenly she stopped. 'It was a name,' she said. 'There above the wings. It was a name!'

"The room went silent. Grandma and the doctor stared at each other until finally he asked, 'Mrs. Evans, do you have a few more minutes?'

"Grandma didn't answer but returned to her chair. Doctor Weldon made his way to a water cooler in the far corner of the room and returned with three plastic cups of chilled water. Grandma was thankful and took a refreshing sip almost immediately. My mom, however, shook her head and declined in silence."

Rachel sipped from Peggy's water glass and wondered if it was just the power of suggestion or perhaps the abundant sweetness from too many desserts that made it taste so incredibly refreshing. Either way, it didn't matter. Her attention, not wandering far, had already refocused on Ann. Peggy's knee bounced in anticipation of hearing the rest of the story.

❖

Wanting to talk to the reverend privately, John rode in the buggy with him to the church, where they spent over an hour discussing what Deke had told him and the bits and pieces he'd remembered for himself before praying together. Under his breath John asked God to show him a sign that it truly was an angel, or if angels even existed in these modern times of 1905, and why did God choose to save him? He knew of two Christian men who had perished in the fields, and he was sure there had to have been others. So he asked again, this time not meaning to, he spoke aloud, "Why me, Lord? Why did I live?"

The reverend had a standard list of answers for such questions, but he knew John and knew he was a good man who for some time had been working on becoming a better Christian, barring the festivities of last evening. He also knew it was not the time to paint God's love and grace with a broad brush. This man was searching for and needed precise detailed answers. But the reverend was also aware, when it comes to angels, like religion in general, even a little brush needs a liberal coat of faith to bring the detail to light. He then began to pray.

"God, if you sent an angel to save this man's life, surely you have a path for him to walk. Show him that path, and let his journey begin. Let him know he's not alone and guide him on his way. Write your word upon his heart that he may serve you boldly. Strengthen him, show him your ways, and bless him, Father, for he is yours."

John didn't totally understand the prayer but was amazed he could recall every word. Even thirty minutes later, after visiting with the reverend's wife and five-year-old twin boys, the words were perfectly preserved. But the line he continued to repeat in his mind was "Let his journey begin." It just felt good saying it. He wondered if the journey would be real or hypothetical, but he didn't ask, thinking he had taken up enough of the preacher's time as it was. Then it dawned on him: having ridden with the reverend, how would he get home? The swelling in his ankle had gone down some; he supposed he could try walking. The reverend insisted he take the church buckboard, saying he'd stop by later to pick it up. After all, it was a beautiful day for a walk.

When he returned to the rooming house, there was a young lady waiting to see him, introducing herself as Emily Graham, a nursing graduate from Houston. Making no time for pleasantries, she informed him that his mother had fallen ill with fever and been admitted to the hospital three days earlier. As there was no family when the woman was admitted, Emily had received permission to stay by her side until the family could be notified. She'd kept a detailed log of her observations, noting the times of every event throughout the night. If the woman moved, Emily wrote it down; if she spoke, though incoherent at times, notes were taken and deciphered later. It was through these notes she realized the woman was asking for her son, pleading that he come home, and on one occasion she broke down in great sobs, which caused her temperature to rise, racking her body with chills still again. But it was the woman's episodes of delirium that caused Emily herself to sob. The pleading, the prayers, and the words "my son, my son," spoken through cries of torment and sorrow, were heartbreaking to the young nurse. Nevertheless, she stayed vigilant, never straying far from the woman's bedside.

As the fever lessened on the second day, the woman slept, though not soundly, waking often with muffled sobs and prayers, and Emily would soothe her back to sleep in a voice filled with heartfelt compassion. Twice the woman opened her eyes to look at Emily, once asking in a clear voice, "Where's my son? Where's John?"

But Emily's answer went unheard, as the woman quickly drifted back to sleep. The girl wondered if anyone had tried contacting the son. An inquiry to admissions came back that the woman had collapsed in Foley's Department Store, which provided the hospital and authorities her name and address from a delivery slip. But no further information had been obtained. Emily knew this because nothing further had been done. Maybe a note left on a door, but clearly if contact had been made, a relative or someone would've shown up by now. Though feeling somewhat guilty, a quick search of the woman's purse provided the full name and address of her son, apparently living in a rooming house out in Moonshine Hill.

Emily had been to this tough little town once before as part of a medical team sent to investigate the yellow fever scare earlier that year. Thankfully, a scare was all it amounted to, allowing her to leave after only three days. But three days had been more than enough time to learn that Moonshine Hill, like Humble and the boomtowns of Spindletop, was rapidly becoming a dangerous place for any woman. After her brief stay, she swore never to return. But now she would return, and the following day, just after sunrise, she set off in her uncle's buggy expecting to arrive midday. Surely someone at the rooming house could tell her where to find John H. Morris. Maybe too, he wouldn't be as dirty, foul, and obnoxious as the rowdy oil workers she'd dealt with before, but, of course, she wasn't counting on it. That thought alone almost caused her to turn the buggy around and pray for God's understanding, but instead she pushed forward, praying for courage all the way to Moonshine Hill.

Only minutes after their introduction, John began preparing for the trip back. He quickly watered Emily's horse before securing it to the rear of the buggy. He then supplied a fresh horse of his own. Mrs. Cubbins handed him a small basket, saying it was lunch for the two of them, adding, "Your friend Deke called on me this morning, insisting the baby and I go for a stroll with him down to the river park about noon. I was just making up a little picnic, so the biscuits and chicken are still warm. You'll find a big jar of that black water tea you like and a smaller jar of Mr. Perkins's home brew, but don't be getting that girl drunk. It took a lot for her to come out here to fetch you. And don't think I didn't see a bit of a look when I mentioned your friend Deke. Stop worrying about me, John Morris. You and he seem to be cut from the same cloth, maybe the only two real gentlemen left in this whole dang town. And when he come riding up this morning on that big chestnut Morgan of his, armful of fresh-cut flowers, he really thought he was something. And just between me, you, and the noonday sun…I intend to find out if he's right."

John was dumbfounded. For the past fourteen months, she'd deeply mourned the death of her husband, not allowing even the wealthy landowners to call on her. Suddenly Deke showed up, and her heart began to beat again. It just didn't sit well. And why hadn't Deke discussed his intentions with him beforehand?

"There's that bit of a look again," she teased.

Though it bothered him to admit it, he told her he didn't know Deke very well, but he seemed like a straight-up guy. She needed to just be mindful.

Hoping to be back in a day or two, he didn't feel the need to speak with Deke before then, but they would definitely talk on his return. After helping Emily into the carriage, he turned back to Mrs. Cubbins to thank her again.

"Mindful, Laura Cubbins," he said. "You don't know anything about that man."

"I know he risked his life to save you."

"Mindful," he again cautioned.

As she hugged him, she remembered something Deke had said, something not bothersome, just odd. "Maybe you can tell me what Deke meant by when you found your angel, he found his. What are these angels he's talking about? You know anything about that?"

"I do, but I have to get to Houston. Sounds like a good discussion for the two of you to have over that picnic."

Hoisting himself onto the seat of the carriage proved more difficult than the buckboard, causing a bolt of pain to shoot across his ankle, stirring inappropriate words that fortunately didn't make it past his clenched teeth. A few deep breaths and a smile from Mrs. Cubbins signaled it was time to leave, but not before she called to him, "Tell her I love her, and she's in my prayers."

Along the way, Emily further filled him in on his mother's condition, and after saying everything that could be said, it was John who changed the subject, wanting to know where Emily was from. Why nursing, and why Houston?

He learned she had three older brothers, but they weren't close. Two had joined the navy, and the other left on a cattle drive, never to return. She preferred the ocean over the desert and mountains over the ocean, hated the city, loved the country, and would eventually settle down where there were grassy meadows up against tree-filled mountains. From a canvas bag under the seat, she produced a large thick book.

"Right there," she said, pointing to the beautifully illustrated cover. "That's where I want my house—right at the edge of that meadow so I can look at it every day."

Glancing at the cover, John tugged on the reins, bringing the carriage to an abrupt stop, his eyes never leaving the book.

"Everything okay?" she gasped.

But his eyes remained locked on the book.

Puzzled, she asked, "What is it? You don't like my book, my house, the mountain...what?"

But he again said nothing.

After a moment, meeting her stare, he answered, "No, I love all of it. It looks like a beautiful place. It's the title that caught me a little off guard, that's all."

Even more puzzled than before, she read it aloud, hoping to understand what he meant. "*Your Journey Begins with Me.*"

His stare remained on the book and then fell easily back to the soft features of Emily Graham. She waited for him to speak, but when he didn't, she inquired, "Have you read it?"

Chuckling more inward than out, he shook his head, confirming his disinterest.

"Well I love it; I've read it twice now," the woman said. "It's about a man and woman who set out in search of a new start and find each other along the way. It's not only a journey about them traveling through the countryside, but through life, their love for each other, and for the God they come to know along the way. It's just such a beautiful story. Here, take it. It's probably not the kind of book you like to read, if you like to read at all. I don't know, and I don't know if you believe in God. I know your mom does; ninety percent of what she was mumbling were prayers and hymns, and..."

"What did you say?" he blurted out, looking more concerned than surprised.

Emily couldn't tell if he was upset or shocked and immediately began asking herself questions. *Didn't he know his own mother was a Christian? Well, of course he did. What a ridiculous thought. Obviously they're close. Maybe he doesn't approve. Doesn't believe. Thinks all Christians are touched in the head. But wait a minute—he came home from the church...*

"Emily?"

In the reverend's buckboard, Mrs. Cubbins had said something about...

"Emily?"

Prayer...

"Miss Graham; are you all right?" he asked after not getting a response.

She focused her attention on his eyes and just nodded her head.

With a sense of urgency, he asked, "When...when did it start—the prayers, the hymns? When did she start that?"

"I'm not sure. A couple of days ago. Night before last, mostly, but they seemed to ramp up yesterday morning. I have it written down, the times... the prayers...even the hymns, the ones I knew, anyway."

Deke's voice came to him clearly. "I never saw the angel, but I heard her voice—soft, comforting, like someone singing a hymn while praying all at the same time..."

"I have my note pad, but they're not organized. I just scribbled them down. I'm not even sure why."

But she knew why. They had touched her heart deeper than anything she had ever heard before—the prayers of a woman so ill she wasn't even aware of the world around her. "If you want, I can read them while you..."

But then suddenly she remembered the personal entries she had jotted down next to the prayers. What if he saw those? And surely at some point he would ask to see the notes, to read his mother's words for himself.

"I'm a little embarrassed, but I have to tell you, John, your mom's prayers were so loving, so beautiful…" She paused to collect her thoughts. Her stare, led her attention to focus on a lone white cloud drifting on a sky of blue. "Her prayers were somehow more than words, even more than just emotions. I began to fall in love with you… well the man of her prayers anyway. Honestly, John, it was like she was speaking right to my heart."

Her nervous laughter made him smile, and then he said, "Sorry to be such a disappointment. Mom always gave me more credit than I deserve."

Returning his smile, she nodded. "Yea, you know, now that I've met you, maybe she did!"

Her giggle was pleasant, beautiful he thought, looking into her soft brown eyes before releasing the brake. The carriage lurched forward. Instinctively Emily locked her arm with his. A smile came to them both, hers accompanied by a slight blush. "Let the journey begin," he said aloud, staring up at that same little white cloud.

As the attractive young nurse continued to read, he recognized his mother's voice in the words, the prayers, the hymns, and how each expressed her deep love for him and reliance on God. After only a short time, he turned to ask Emily to stop and saw tears in the woman's eyes. Wiping them away, he touched her hand in a reassuringly manner, not knowing he was touching her heart. Both smiled, but neither spoke for the next mile.

"If you don't mind, I'd love to read that book sometime. Nothing better than a good story. I have one I think you might find pretty interesting. It starts like this: a couple of days ago, my crew and I were working on this rig…"

He was right. Emily loved the story but hated the tattoo and hated the name Lucky even more, saying, "That's what people name their dog. Don't expect me to call you that unless you're fetching a stick. Besides, you being alive had nothing to do with luck. You're alive because of a loving, prayerful mother, a very brave friend, and a compassionate God. But luck? No, John! Luck had nothing to do with it."

She thought for a second. "I suppose I can go along with the protective wings of an angel, though. And now that I really look at that tattoo and know the story behind it, those wings are really beautiful. Hey, that reminds me. Ready for a piece of chicken?"

※

Over the next few days, he watched his mother slip in and out of consciousness. At one point, clearly realizing he was sitting by her side, she began to softly weep. Unable to speak, her face shone more love than all the words in the world could ever express, and soon her eyes found Emily. Was it her eyes or her smile that beckoned the young lady to sit beside her son? John would always say it was something in her smile, but Emily saw something in her eyes.

With her son safe by her side, she passed peacefully in her sleep the following morning. He held her hand for what seemed a long time, but not nearly long enough, and then laid it against his cheek, already moist with tears. Nothing in that moment seemed real. In the past she would have wiped away the tears, held him with understanding arms, and lovingly said, "It'll all work out." *But what now?* he thought. *What now?*

From behind him came a discreet whimper. It was Emily. Continuing to hold his mother's hand, he stood motioning for the girl to again sit where she had spent so much of her time. *How beautiful*, he thought, *to care that much for someone she never knew.* And it made him sad that this woman would never know how alive his mother had been, had never heard her laughter, her poetry, or her music. Had never seen the way she loved to sing and dance, how easily she brought cheer to a rainy day with just a song and a laugh or a game. Her wit so sharp, her humor somewhat quirky and cute, occasionally getting her into trouble at church, but eventually she'd say to the pastor, "I would think if the Almighty has seen fit to forgive me from the cross, surely you can from the pulpit?"

But what he treasured most, would miss the most, was her incredibly oversimplistic logic of things. An approach to life filled with playfulness, childlike curiosity, and innocence, where every decision, no matter how great or small, would be based solely on her perception of right or wrong.

Often she would tell him, "Most decisions are based on intellect or emotion—your brain or your heart. Almost everyone says never follow your heart because it's always changing how it feels. But they're wrong! Why? Because your brain thinks too much. It's always searching for an easier way, looking for something better or finding an excuse to put things off and do nothing at all. But your heart—that's where your dreams are stored, your appetite for life and the desire to pursue your passions. So I say go ahead follow your heart. If it turns out to be wrong, so what? Pick yourself up, dust yourself off, and let your heart lead the way again. Just remember, work hard at what the heart wants, because if you truly put in the effort, there's nothing better in the whole wide world than to live in your dreams, your passion, and your desires. And that, my boy, is as right as rain."

Funny he would think of that now, standing by her bed feeling so alone in the world. He made no attempt to hide his sorrow. Tears fell openly as he kissed her forehead. Emily stood, eyes swollen, cheeks stained from rivers of tears. She offered his mother's hand, and he cradled it in his own, touching her fingertips to his cheeks, softly wiping away his tears, and still they returned quickly. Emily's hand moved over his to rest against his mother's palm. Gently he cupped the hands of both women in his own, placing his lips on the back of his mother's and then on Emily's. The room was still, quiet, filled with a remarkable peace that seemed to physically caress the young couple like the softness of a gentle breeze on a summer's day, filling the room with the scent of honeysuckle and lavender.

It was midmorning before they left the room, Emily asking twice if he preferred to be alone to say his goodbyes. Each time he declined and each time squeezed her hand, acknowledging a solemn thank-you for being there. Once outside they walked to the garden, Emily's favorite spot in all of Houston. He said it would have been his mother's favorite also, having a great love for flower gardens. They talked for only a short time, making their way to the horse stable, and then hugged farewell.

By late in the afternoon, he was in Katy, making arrangements with the pastor of his mother's church, which stood directly across the road from the ranch where she'd grown up and not far from the small house he had spent most of his life calling home. Because of her sporadic attendance over the past year and recent withdrawal of membership, the pastor thought a gravesite service would accommodate the small number of mourners he anticipated. Also because she was no longer a member, a donation for his time would be required. How many years had she faithfully attended this church? he thought before flipping a five-dollar gold piece in the pastor's direction. Too many to be treated like the outcast this man of God portrayed her as, membership or not. But he held his tongue, only speaking to confirm the funeral would be day after tomorrow at half past eight.

After his meeting with the pastor, he went straight to his mother's house. As he opened the front door, the familiar smells of home embraced him with the lingering presence of thousands of meals, fresh-baked breads, and batches upon batches of made-with-love cookies, all triggering memories that flooded his eyes with tears, but also made him smile. There was nothing unusual about finding her bedroom window slightly raised, an old wooden dowel holding it open, giving the honeysuckle and lavender planted outside a reason for their beautiful fragrance. Birds sang and clouds rolled by; the tall grass in the adjoining fields bowed to the wind; a dust devil spun its way down the dry dirt road. Holding her robe next to his chest, he inhaled deeply the scent of his mother. It wasn't long before he walked each room of the house, feeling as if she would be right around the corner. Even as he walked out the back door, he half expected to see her gathering clothes off the line or watering her garden. But as his mind worked through the realities of loss, his heart felt numbing disappointment. That is, until he turned to go back inside. Standing in the doorway was Emily.

Quickly running down the steps, she was in his arms before the screen door slammed closed. In a voice laden with sentiment, she said, "I couldn't let you do this by yourself. I was the only one left at home when my mother passed, and I just didn't want you to feel alone like that."

Six thirty the following morning, Emily awoke to the alluring smell of fresh coffee. A minute later, John knocked lightly on the door of his old bedroom, calling for her to join him in the garden when she was ready. With an allure more for coffee than vanity, it wasn't long before she hurried out the back door to join him. Halfway through her first cup, he laid out the morning itinerary: breakfast in Katy and then a five-minute ride out to

Ina's place, his mother's oldest and closest friend, and sometimes…her only friend.

While they were preparing to leave for breakfast, a lovely young girl in her early teens appeared at the back door. John recognized her as Gabriela Diego, a neighbor from just down the road. Her father, Alejandro, hurried across the yard, surprised to see John come to the door, but he was even more surprised when Emily joined him. When the girl asked about Ms. Morris, her father saw something in the faces of John and Emily that drove him to cautiously place his arm around his daughter with loving protection. But as John broke the news, Alejandro felt the words pierce his daughter's heart, taking her breath, returning it in short quick sobs. She hugged her father tightly, rushed to hug John, and glanced empathetically at Emily before running home to tell her mother. It was only then Alejandro allowed his own emotions to surface. Minutes later, his wife hurried across the yard, out of breath, shaking, needing no other validation than a simple nod of her husband's head.

Placing a hand over her mouth, tears streaming from partially closed eyes, she turned and slowly began to walk through the garden, allowing the lavender and honeysuckle to soothe her with sweet memories. It was there among the wildflowers she prayed.

※

When he and Emily arrived in Katy, breakfast no longer seemed that important, so they continued to Ina's. From the moment she opened the door and saw his face, Ina knew. She just knew. "It's Pearl, isn't it?" she asked.

His embrace was exactly the answer she expected. After all, he'd been taught that some particulars didn't need spoken words to be communicated efficiently. Silent emotion expressed them just fine, and death was right up there with love, hate, and pregnancies when it came to elaborating silently— Pearl 101. But damn, even without words, this hurt like hell. Even so, she only allowed herself a brief cry. There'd be plenty more tears every time she thought of Pearl; she also knew that would come multiple times a day for the rest of her life.

Ina instantly fell in love with Emily and spent the better part of the morning sharing stories of John and his beloved mother, from the night he was born in a barn (literally) to him accidentally shooting his mother in the leg with an arrow and then telling the doctor there must have been an Indian raid. But there was something John did from the time he was eight years old until as recently as a few months ago that meant more to her and Pearl than anything else. "He'd write a note," she told Emily, smiling warmly, "and then cut it right up the middle, leaving one half for his mother to find. And the other half he'd place on my door so we'd have to get together to read the whole thing."

"Your ma kept every one of them. They're probably in her Angel Box."

John knew nothing of an Angel Box but would begin looking for it that afternoon. In the meantime, he was reminded to roll up his sleeve and show Ina his tattoo and even shared Deke's story with her. After listening quietly, Ina asked, "Do you believe in angels, John?"

But before he could respond, she asked Emily the same question, again not waiting for an answer but quickly adding, "Pearl believed. Ever since we were kids, she claimed angels were guiding her, watching over her. Of course, there were times I was convinced it was more likely the devil himself than an angel." She laughed. "The girl was always at the center of some kind of uproar." Again she smiled, her eyes watching distant memories. "But that was just Pearl, wasn't it?"

Her smile never faded as her memories continued to lend visions of her lovely friend, a friend whose eccentric behavior had always brought a swirl of gossip and rumors from classmates and townsfolk alike, not that Pearl ever paid much attention to any of it. She loved animals, not so much people, although concessions were made from time to time. And one of those concessions had been Ina. They met at church shortly after Ina and her family moved to Cane Island, from Galveston. There was an instant connection between the girls, though neither knew exactly why, as they were opposites in almost every way. Yet they fit together like two lost pieces of a puzzle. So well, in fact, that Pearl began to tell people they were sisters, twin sisters. It was just that Ina preferred blond hair to auburn, blue eyes to gray, and never wanted to be more than five foot tall. That was why she was born to a different family. And just like everything else Pearl came up with, Ina agreed wholeheartedly.

Pearl was a born philosopher and by age twelve an avid student of the Bible, even learning a little Greek from the late Reverend Nikolas. But three years later she was a restless teen who could outride, outrope, and outswear the toughest boy around, a secret she pledged to keep after soundly defeating nineteen-year-old Gareth Nash in an impromptu contest as the two rounded up strays on her father's ranch. Six months later, when Gareth married Marilyn Heisetter, a debutante from Houston, Pearl told Ina the whole story.

Book learning came easy for Pearl, though she was a horrible student and hated school. Her mother taught her to cook, play the piano, and work in the garden, but it was her father who taught her to ride, ranch, and explore the back trails, telling her, "You need to find your way in this old world, whatever and wherever it may lead."

And Pearl did, often going for long rides by herself through the countryside, chasing her thoughts and coming across secret places she later would share with Ina. And it was one of these places she called The Pond, where her life would change forever.

Nestled deep within a large thicket of old-growth pecans, five miles northeast of Fulshear and less than an hour's ride from her families ranch, The Pond lay undisturbed, hidden from the eyes of the world, a special place meant for only her and Ina, their dreams of romance, husbands, marriage, and family, all of which made them swoon on the long hot days of summer. But it was not just a spot for dreams. It was Ina's escape from an abusive father and Pearl's escape from everything else, a sanctuary protected from the many cruel winds that sometimes blew across the coastal prairies of Cane Island. The girls agreed never to divulge the location or even speak of it to anyone—a pact made and sealed with the blood from a cut to the palm of their right hands along with Ina's insistence they swear an oath on Pearl's Bible, by then something that Pearl had secretly all but discarded from her life.

Two years later, barely seventeen, on a warm afternoon in May, as the pecan trees were beginning to blossom, Pearl would glance up at the faded scar, closing her fist tightly, shielding it from the betrayal she now committed.

By July, the need to hide the scar along with the promise it represented had no more place in her life than her Bible, yet she thought about both often. But this was a time for dreams to come true, and how many times had she dreamed The Pond would be the place? A rendezvous where forbidden love could be expressed openly, freely with the man she adored even if it meant they remain, like the place itself, hidden from the world.

And so it was their love would remain secret, buried in her heart, where only she and this wonderful man knew it existed. How many times that summer had she wished she could share with Ina, her secret, her feelings, the fulfillment of her dreams. But it was not to be. Her friend was spending the summer in Galveston with family, which was why she felt comfortable bringing him to The Pond in the first place. But even when Ina returned in early September, Pearl said nothing.

It was the first week of October, when the trees were heavy with pecans and the air still warm on her skin, when she would meet him for what she knew would be the last time. Blaming her tears on other things, she held him tighter than ever before. After that there was nothing pleasant about their exchange. Repressing her emotions, she watched him ride off through the trees and then made her way to the gently sloping bank and down to the water's edge, immersing herself in its cool freshness. A strong breeze suddenly rippled over the water and rustled the leaves, but it lasted only a second or two, causing her to gaze first to the top of the tree under which they had lain just a short time ago. Her eyes slowly fell to its broad trunk, and there, sitting within its shade, was a solitary figure. Had he returned?

As she studied the image, her heart began to race. Cautiously she called his name, but there was no response. For only a moment, she thought perhaps it was a shadow. But no, it had to be him, and again she called out, but her words were cut short. From the figure came a comforting glow. Not as light, but subtle hues she somehow understood to be the very aura of love. Without fear she stood, her naked body caressed by the warmth of the late afternoon sun glistened, forming streams that ran over her skin in a silent return to the pond. Something stirred within her, and something spoke to her heart. The glow around the figure became bright, too bright for her gaze. Covering her eyes, she turned away. Instantly it was gone.

The voice, the light, the figure—everything gone. Again she felt no fear. Stepping from the pond, she fell to the ground and began to sob, and again without understanding how exactly, she knew even though she had walked away from God, He had not walked away from her but sent an angel to watch over her and the child she now carried.

The next morning at church, Ina commented on how different Pearl looked—happier than she'd seen her in a while. "There's something different about you," she said suspiciously. "What's changed? What have you done?"

Pearl smiled and simply embraced her friend…and Ina knew; she simply knew.

Pearl never revealed the father's identity, bringing wrath, ridicule and rejection from the community and her own family. Though it wasn't easy being alone and on her own, she embraced the joy of pregnancy. It was during this time she turned back to her music, her Bible, and God, never to abandon any of them again.

"Did she ever take you to The Pond? Probably not, I imagine," Ina asked, shaking her head.

The quizzical look on John's face told the woman, not only had Pearl never taken him, but she'd never mentioned it at all. So Ina spent the rest of the morning telling John and Emily stories of her and Pearl and the occasional visit angels made to his mom, that lovely five-foot-ten, gray-eyed, auburn-haired twin sister of hers, born five hundred miles and six months apart.

As they were leaving, Ina excused herself from the room and returned with a large envelope. On the front, written in Pearl's distinctive hand, were the words *John: Love, Mother*.

Ina handed it to him. "She gave me this before you were born, and every so often, she'd come over and add something new to it. She never told me what it was, and I never asked or looked inside. Open it tonight when you're back at the house. Maybe in the garden. I think she'd like that."

"Come join us."

Her embrace was exactly the answer he expected. Ina turned and smiled at Emily, hugging her tightly. The girl whispered softly in Ina's ear, "Pearl taught me to believe in angels too."

You Are My Love

Ina felt a tear roll over her cheek. "I know," she whispered. "I believe her angels brought you and John together."

❈

On the morning of the funeral, John and Emily arrived at the cemetery to find over a hundred people gathered to pay their respects. Humbled and embarrassed, the pastor stood silent as many of the mourners stepped forward to share memories and stories, laughter and tears, songs of all sorts, praise and love for the woman who had somehow managed to touch each person's heart directly with her kindness, gifts, and talents. As one gentleman put it, "It was the sharing of her childlike vision and wonderment that stirred those of us who couldn't be sufficiently silent long enough to hear our prayers being answered or behold God's glorious treasures around us. I believe I speak for many gathered here this morning when I say, Pearl Morris was one of the most glorious treasures God ever placed in our great state of Texas. You take care of her now, Lord. We'll all miss her."

All the kind words made John proud of his mother, and many made Emily and Ina weep. It was Pearl's wish to be laid next to her parents, though all had not been forgiven over the years, she felt that was where she belonged. Within weeks a fourth grave would be filled in the small plot of land, and a large marble tombstone connecting the final two graves would read "Pearl and Ina—Twin Sisters Eternally."

Nine days after his mother's funeral, John returned to the rooming house only minutes before it started to rain. As if expecting his arrival, Mrs. Cubbins ran to greet him before he could make it up the front steps. Sitting at a small table on the porch watching the gentle rain move in, she cried again over his mother's passing, explaining she had received his courier only the day before the funeral, and besides, "Your mom knew I loved her, and she knew I'm not up to another funeral, not yet. We did hold a little memorial here at the house for her, and that nice young preacher, Brother Taylor, dropped by to say a few words."

Again her tears flowed, and again John was her comfort. He knew it would be easy to shed more tears, share more stories, and relive memories of a time the three of them were as close as family, times as recent as two months ago when his mother came to visit and spent most of her time doting on the baby. But for now there were things that needed to be shared, changes in his life that would affect her profoundly. He thought he would start by explaining his relationship with Emily but changed his mind at the last second.

"How was your picnic?" he asked, gently squeezing her hand.

A light breeze brushed her hair out of its way and filled the air with the smell of dampened earth and wildflowers. Thunder rolled in the distance. In the stable an anxious horse neighed, and from inside the house, the momentary fussing of a sleeping baby was heard. Her answer was as soft as the rain. "He's a beautiful man." She smiled, but deep frown lines quickly overcame her. "Just last night I told him I was having feelings for him, but I refuse to let the fields have another piece of my heart. So as long as he's working the rigs, I prefer he stay his distance from me and the baby, and I haven't seen him since."

Her eyes filled with tears as another round of sorrow flooded her thoughts. Quickly she took a deep breath. "For as long as I can remember, you've been there for me, but when that nurse showed up, I prayed you wouldn't come back. Dammit, John, I'm afraid one of these days the fields will claim you just like they did..."

Kneeling, he took her hand with the tenderness she'd known from him all her life; his voice deep, calming, his stare loving. "You can stop worrying; I'm not going back. And as for you and the baby, things are going to be okay. There's a man in Houston willing to pay substantially more for this place than it's worth. Take it, Laura! You've hated this place since day one. Damn oil is on everything. Take the money, and get the hell out of here before it makes you and the baby sick. It's no place to be raising her up. I'm meeting with him around one tomorrow. I'd like you to be there; but we'll get to that later."

The rain picked up, but hadn't dampened the porch. "Now tell me, what's this about feelings for Deke? How'd all that come about? I know he was pretty smitten with you..." Cocking his head, pretending to be in thought, he added, "But now that I think about it, a change might be good for you both. I mean, if he feels the same as you and all."

"Are you trying to rush me into something, John Morris?" she scolded. "Because it sounds to me like you've lost your mind. I expected you to be all blustered up, stomping around, cussing and swearing, telling me to stay away from that man, like you did with Lucas back when we was school age. Or even when Bart started comin' round, you weren't none too happy about him either."

The screen door swung open, and the sound of boots shuffling across the porch grabbed her attention. It was Harland Mays, one of the boarders. Seeing John, he removed his hat and held it close to his chest. "Sorry to hear about your ma, Lucky. Terrible thing to lose a ma. And she was so young. And damn handsome woman too; I hope you know I mean that with all respect," he added with a nod.

John had almost forgotten about the nickname but didn't care much, since in a few days he'd never see this town or its inhabitants again. Lightning danced across the sky, bringing a clap of thunder that seemed to roll all the way to Houston. Harland looked up at the darkening sky and put his hat back on. "Sure don't like being out in these storms, but I guess a job's a job, and I better get to mine while I can. Sorry again about your ma, Lucky… Mrs. Cubbins…" Tipping his hat, he turned to walk away.

"Harland," Laura, called, "if you see Deke, let him know I need to talk to him as soon as possible."

He nodded. "I saw him in the office this morning, but I don't know I'll see him again. Picked up his pay, and out the door he went. I think he's changing location or companies or something. If I were you, I'd ride by his place, or check the cantina. If he's not having supper with you, Mrs. Cubbins, and he hasn't left town, that's where he'll be, over at the cantina. He eats there every night. Of course, if I run into him, I'll let him know y'all want to see him."

Tipping his hat once again, Harland went through the house to the stable. Mrs. Cubbins watched John rock back in his chair flashing a devilish smile she knew all too well. Folding her arms across her chest, she asked suspiciously, "What are you up to, John Morris?"

From his pocket he removed a small silver key and slid it in front of her. Then he retrieved a wide envelope from the saddlebag he'd placed next to the table when they first sat down; this he positioned next to the key. On the front of the envelope, faded and without much detail remaining, was a sketch of two angels peacefully watching over a young boy and girl playing in a flower garden. Flashing the same smile as before, he asked, "You believe in angels?"

"Of course. Your mother pert' near raised me. How could I not?"

And again John grinned. "That key's your future. The documents in the envelope will help shine some light on the past. You'll also find three letters in there. I encourage you to read the one from my mother first. It's somewhat faded but legible; appears she wrote it a long time ago. Then read the one I wrote just last night, and finally the third. I know you're going to have a million and one questions, but honestly I don't have any more answers than what is here. So read 'em over...all of 'em. And then we'll talk. I'll go check on the baby and be right back."

As she had been instructed, the first letter she read was from Pearl, and it brought confusion, disbelief, and tears. Yet it filled her heart with a kind of love she knew had always been there. John's letter brought much of the same, but it was the third that stirred old feelings of hurt, abandonment, distrust, and many more tears. She had just finished when John returned to the porch with a rare bottle of Kentucky bourbon.

"I thought you could use one," he said, pouring them both a glass.

Her hand was shaky, her voice weak. "Swear to me, John, you know for sure this is true. Swear?"

His look, tender and sweet, expressed his affection. In his eyes, for maybe the first time as an adult, Laura saw the same joy that had been permanently captured in those of his mother—a sparkle celebrating some childlike happiness. How had Pearl described it? What was it she used to say? "I'm just making the love in my heart easier for you to see."

Touching his glass to hers, he grinned. "It's true. You, Laura Nash Cubbins...are my half-sister."

❦

"Dos cerveza, senor Deke?"

"What do you think? Have we given him enough time?"

Emily thought for a second and then shrugged. "Dos cerveza…"

Deke laughed, loudly confirming, "Dos cerveza, Felina. Gracias."

The elderly barmaid, whose soft brown features had begun to fail her years earlier, whirled from the table just as she had a million times before, though perhaps not as fluid as she once had.

Deke stared at the young lady next to him. "You said you have no doubts. So when did you know?"

"I'm not sure." Emily shrugged. "Maybe on the road to Houston that first day. Or at his mother's bedside. Honestly, I don't know. But I knew when he left for Katy I never wanted to be without him. Of course, I didn't know if he felt the same or not, or what he'd do when I showed up at his mother's place, but I had to find out. Part of me half expected him to want to be alone and send me packing, but when he saw me at the back door, the look on his face wasn't all surprise. There was a lot of love in those eyes, that smile. So I can tell you for certain at that moment we both knew we shared something very special, and it's just grown from there.

"You know, Deke, when John saw you sitting here and asked you to stay with me until he met with Laura, I felt pretty uncomfortable. I mean…" Glancing around as if checking her safety, her eyes came back to rest on the rugged man. "You're an oil worker, a roughneck," she whispered. He looked surprised and heard her add, "I didn't know how sweet you were. No wonder she's falling in love with you."

Deke glanced around. "Shhh. I have a reputation…" He grinned.

Felina set the beer on the table and quickly returned to the bar. Distant thunder rolled through the room. "Looks like that storm's gonna miss us," Deke surmised, reaching for a beer. The room lit up, thunder crashed with a powerful blow, and there was an audible gasp from every person in the cantina.

"Looks like I was wrong." He smiled, taking a long drink. "What if you and John are wrong, and a year, two years from now, you can't stand to be around each other?"

There was no hesitation in Emily's voice. "See that tree in the courtyard? It's young, just a few years old. It's been scorched by the sun, pelted by rain, beaten by hail, and some of its leaves stripped by the wind. And yet it survives.

Now, imagine its roots as the heart of a relationship, a marriage. They become stronger and thicker with every storm. And with each passing season, the tree continues to grow. Look at its limbs. Some are large, some small. Some are twisting out in all directions, leaving each one different from the rest. Now think of the limbs as representing ideas, opinions, dreams, and goals of each individual, branching out, growing and yet remaining connected to the heart. As the years pass, the tree stands as one of a kind in its own beauty. Its many branches have grown in strength while each remains different, yet all bloom the same blossom and bear the same fruit because they share the same heart. The tree as a whole survives, and it's the same way with marriage. Stay connected at the heart, and you can weather whatever comes."

The softness of Deke's expression caught her somewhat off guard, but more than that was the softness in his voice. "You paint a beautiful picture, Nurse Emily. I see why he's falling in love with you."

She blushed, and one corner of her mouth pulled tight in a thin smile, accentuating the small dimple in her chin. As before, there was no hesitation in her response. "The credit goes to John's aunt Ina, his mother's best friend since forever. You'll meet her tomorrow. I just love her. Her stories are beautiful, funny, and romantic all at the same time. After the funeral she took me and John to this place her and Pearl used to go…hidden away, nothing around except a huge pecan grove surrounding this beautiful pond. We weren't there two minutes before she asked us if we knew we were in love and then told us the story about the tree and marriage and finally about John's mom seeing an angel. But I'll leave that for him to share with you."

She sipped at the cool beer. "And then, all the way back to Katy, she pointed out places and trails she and Pearl use to ride…sometimes sneaking off to meet in the middle of the night. It sounds like those two were really something together. But I get the impression his mother instigated ninety-nine percent of it. I've never had anyone I was that close to—as a friend, I mean. Anyhow, John took me back there yesterday. It's where he proposed… where I said yes, and where we want to have the ceremony."

As Deke watched, Emily's eyes began to brighten and dance. Her shoulders rose upward, following the lines of her growing smile. "Maybe we could have a double ceremony," she cried.

It was Deke's turn to reply without hesitation. "Three…" was all he said.

Confusion quickly twisted Emily's face into a mockery of its former elation. "Three?" she asked, not knowing what to make of his comment.

"Three." He grinned. "That's how many beers it takes for you to start talking crazy."

And for the next fifteen minutes, they talked about how crazy the last two weeks had been for both of them. She had fallen in love, lost her job, and was about to marry a man she hardly knew. Crazy!

Deke confessed to falling in love with Laura and the baby. He had quit his job and that very morning had purchased a beautiful ring, which he pulled from his vest pocket and set before Emily. Opening the small metal case, she was stunned by the finely crafted filigree setting and its magnificent center stone. Looking at Deke, she muttered, "Now, that's crazy!" Glancing at her ringless left hand, she laughed. "My guy's had a lot going on!"

Again she looked at the ring. "Deke, she's going to love this—that is, if you ever get the courage to ask her." Then Emily thought for a second. Her eyes twinkled as she smiled. "Felina," she called. "Dos tequila, por favor."

Deke looked at her, his grin questioning. "Ma'am, trust me. The tequila here is not for a dainty young lady such as yourself…"

Picking up her beer, she smiled. "Oh, it's not for me. Cheers Deke!"

❦

Fifteen minutes later, to Laura's surprise, they joined her and John on the front porch. Comments were made regarding Deke and Emily's intoxicated state, and it was decided the newly discovered siblings needed another shot or two of Kentucky bourbon to catch up. Laura declined, saying one was her limit because of the baby.

Emily said, "That reminds me. I have something for you and the baby."

"And I have something else to show you too," John said.

"And I have something to ask you, Laura," Deke said, stepping forward.

Emily pulled John back away from the table to stand with her, allowing Deke a comfortable space. The man, timid and shy by nature, began to tremble, struggling to remove his hand from his pocket. He glanced back at Emily, and she gave him a smile and a nod of confidence. John just looked puzzled, and Laura seemed confused. Though the storm had moved farther north, distant thunder softly rumbled continuously. Deke took in a deep breath and knelt down on one knee in front of the still-seated Laura. The open box looked small and delicate in his large palm. Her eyes quickly filled with tears as she heard him say, "We've spent a lot of time getting to know each other these last few weeks, and I don't have much to offer you and the baby other than my heart and my love. But I know I can make you a good husband, if you'd consider being my wife."

The sound of twelve men on horseback raced past the front of the house. "Lightning hit the storage tanks. The whole place is on fire," one man called out, slowing to make sure they heard. "There's a hundred men working that yard; they're probably trapped if they're alive at all."

John ran to the other end of the porch and looked out toward Humble. He could see black smoke filling the sky above a massive orange glow. He and Deke ran to the barn and saddled their horses. Emily and Laura rushed in moments later. "You be careful, John," Emily said, with both a smile and fear on her face. "We have our wedding Saturday, and it won't be as much fun if you're not there."

Holding her tight, he whispered promises in her ear.

Deke could see the sheer terror in Laura's face, even though she stood ten feet away. He moved quickly to her. "I quit this morning. I swear to you I did, but men's lives…"

"Put this on me," she cried, holding the box with a trembling hand. "You're not going anyplace until I get a chance to say I'll marry you, Deke…" Her smile turned to a chuckle as tears of dread and fear flowed down her face. "I don't even know your last name. It doesn't matter; I love you, and yes, yes I'll marry you."

She leaped into the big man's arms, never wanting him to let her go. He slipped the ring on her finger and once more held her tightly. Kissing him again, she whispered, "I love you."

He returned the words.

She wiped her tears and took his hand. "I have a message for that angel of yours. I expect you back. And that goes for you, too, John Morris. I'm not burying any more damn heroes. Now go do what you have to, and keep that angel close by. You hear me?"

John smiled. "She can't get much closer than this." And with that he raised his sleeve to expose the wings on his arm. But then he pushed it slightly higher, and the name Pearl appeared.

With no further goodbyes, the two men mounted their horses and joined the many others now making the ride to the burning fields. Soon Laura arranged for Mrs. Rhodes to watch the baby while she and Emily volunteered at the makeshift hospital set up just outside Humble. They would remain there until late the following afternoon before returning to the house, exhausted. By then, news had already spread—fifty, sixty, maybe even seventy men and almost as many mules had perished in the flames, and there was no sign of Deke and John. Around seven thirty that evening, as a warm westerly wind picked up, the two men returned covered in smoke, mud, and oil. But that didn't matter to the girls, who immediately ran into their arms, ecstatic to see they were alive, safe, and unharmed.

By the time the men cleaned up, Laura and Emily had food on the table. John decided since they'd missed the appointment in Houston, he'd go ahead and take this time to tell everyone his plan.

"It took me a few days to find it," he began. "And even then, it was just by chance I discovered this old piano bench mother had cut the legs off, and hidden beneath some loose floorboards under her bed. The Angel Box. Looking through the contents, I had to laugh. When it came to me and you, Laura, she saved everything. Pictures we drew as kids, notes, songs, stories. It's all there; she kept everything. And then I found a book—more like a diary, with things about the two of us and you and the baby, and things about our father, good and bad. You know, I never cared for Nash, and now I care even less. He never liked me and barely wanted anything to do with you. That's why Mom took you in like she did. But enough of that. That's not what she would have wanted us to take away from this.

"That old bench is filled with wonderful memories, and we'll go through it together in a few days. It'll be fun. In the meantime, seems she was quite the businesswoman. My grandparents died when I was three—the fever,

I think. I'm not sure why she didn't take over the ranch, but she chose to lease out the land, taking the money and investing it in other things. Funny I never questioned where she got money for us to live on. Guess kids don't think about that stuff.

"But that brings me to why we need to talk. She loved you so much, Laura. You were the daughter she never had, and even before Ina gave me all this paperwork, I told Emily whatever mother left, if anything, a chunk of it was going to you and the baby. Well, I didn't need to follow through with those provisions. She already had, setting aside a little something for you and a little something else for the baby, but we'll get to that later. She asked that I continue to look after Ina, and of course I will. Now, here's the part I never would have guessed."

He studied the look on Laura's face, knowing she imagined his mother's china and the painting at the end of the hall would be going to her, along with a few other mementos she and Pearl had shared interest in over the years. John shook his head, giving a slight smile to Emily. "No, I never would have guessed her estate to be much more than the house and its possessions."

Pausing, he noticed Laura nodding her head in agreement. "But I was wrong!" he said, broadening his smile. "Seems she had a knack for business. Along with a good sum of money in the bank, she had numerous railroad and petroleum stocks, properties in Katy, downtown Houston, and all along the coast—Galveston, Port Aransas, Corpus, and a half dozen other places. And you remember the uncle she used to talk about up in Montana? Well, he passed on last December. Since he never married, he left his place to her. Only catch is, it doesn't have much of a view because of the all the mountains, and it's surrounded by cows—at present, about three hundred head on twenty six hundred acres."

Laura sat stunned. Was he pulling her leg like he sometimes did? But a glance to Emily assured her it was true. Unable to find her voice or words to fill it, Laura remained silent, listening as John continued.

"I know all this is a lot to take in, and there's a lot for us to go over, but here's my plan. Deke, you told me you and your pa ran a small cattle ranch up in Ogallala. Is this something you think we can pull off? Can we do this?"

Like always, Deke didn't speak quick enough, allowing Laura time to locate her voice and fill it with words enough to spend the next hour asking the million and one questions John predicted she would. And as predicted, he also didn't have all the answers. But over the next few days, most were responded to by attorneys and bankers eager to assist. The meeting with their father was not as pleasant as John had hoped, yet it went exactly as Laura knew it would. The only light shed was that Laura's mother knew nothing of the affair with Pearl, but had simply become fed-up with ranch life, motherhood and the Nash clan, abandoning it all to be with a wealthy businessman in New York less than a year after Laura's birth. Pearl immediately took the baby in, but Gareth, knowing old rumors would return and certainly cripple his social standing, claimed Pearl was being well paid to care for the child—a claim as untrue as most everything else the man had ever said about Pearl Morris. That afternoon, after walking out his front door, Laura never spoke to or answered her father's letters again.

The pecan grove seemed to be the perfect setting for the double ceremony Emily suggested, and as it turned out, The Pond was one of the first pieces of real estate Pearl Morris had ever purchased. Before John left for Montana, he carried out all his mother's wishes. The Pond became a public park. Seventeen families, like the Diego family, were given the deeds to their homes—homes built by PM Industries out of Houston, each one sitting on a five-acre plot. And the little church? Turned out she owned it as well, and soon after the funeral, it got a new piano—and a new pastor.

At Ina's funeral, Deke was the first to hear the singing, followed by Emily, who also heard girlish laughter. When Laura heard it as well, she began to weep, becoming so shaky she had to sit on the ground. And when John heard the voice, he rubbed his tattoo and whispered to the wind, "Thank you for teaching us to follow our hearts. We love you, Mom. We love you both."

❦

Peggy took a moment to blot a solitary tear; Rachel gently squeezed her sister's hand and smiled at Ann as if to say, please continue.

"Doctor Weldon again brought everyone fresh water, and my mom, for a second time, declined without saying a word. The doctor, being gracious, placed it on a small end table next to her, turned to my grandma, and said, 'So you see, Mrs. Evans, the belief in angels has been a part of my lineage for some time, passing down stories from one generation to the next, not only as bedtime tales and Sunday school lessons but conversation around the dinner table as well. And believe me, it doesn't need to be a holiday for the subject to arise. My great uncle Deke still hears the angel sing. Grandma Em swears she wakes on occasion to the smell of lavender and honeysuckle even in December. And my grandpa—well, if angels are real, he's the man they gather round.'"

Ann looked at the ladies. "Grandma sipped the cool water and then studied the photo once more. Without taking her eyes from it, in a voice almost distant, she pondered openly, 'On Pearl's deathbed she prays for her son to be safe, and an angel protects him and changes his life. On my husband's deathbed, he prays for me, and an angel comforts me and changes my life. Now your grandfather...'

"'Is lying upstairs praying for me?' the doctor interrupted. 'I can tell you he's been praying for me all my life, because unlike the rest of the family, I...well...'

"His voice trailed off but quickly returned, calm and soothing, a practiced tone used with his patients many times over the years. 'Mrs. Evans, I don't have an explanation for what happened last night in front of the nurse's station. I know I'm the one who physically handed you that Bible, but...'

"'Doctor, please.' Grandma stopped him. 'Before last night I never believed in much of anything. Not miracles or any of that walk-on-water stuff people get excited about. But this morning...this morning, I believe. I believe in all of it—God, Jesus, the Bible, the whole big bunch. I believe it all. And I know my husband went to his grave praying for a miracle that somehow I would see the light—have a come to Jesus moment, as they say. So to answer his prayer, God sent not one but two angels to lead me to the Lord. Yes Doctor, an angel joined me at my husband's bedside last night, and it was that angel that sent me into the hallway in search of a Bible. And yes, I believe your grandfather may have been praying just as my husband was, that someone close to him is shown the way to Christ. I also believe the angel by your grandfather's bedside placed that Bible in your hand and sent you to me. Did the angel somehow bring your grandpa along? I don't know! But I can tell by the look on your face and the tremble in your lip, you know I'm not making this up. He was there, tattoo and all.'

"My mom, who moments earlier declined any water at all, picked up the cup and finished it in one gulp, then raced across the room on rubbery legs to refill it again…twice, all while grandma continued speaking with complete confidence.

"'I don't know how all this angel stuff works, Doctor. If they sometimes show up through other people, for other people, or with other people. But this is what I do know. In the midst of my sorrow, your family's sorrow, there were angels. Gifts from God, wonderful, beautiful gifts that appeared when I…we…needed one the most, and I'm ever so thankful to have been comforted and led by one. The other thing I know is this: you and I, Doctor—we shared an amazing experience orchestrated by God himself. Isn't that what your daddy would've said, Karen?'

"Grandma didn't wait for an answer, mainly because I think my mom was in total shock and couldn't have spoken a word even if the room had been on fire. Instead, Grandma continued with heartfelt emotion. 'My husband and daughter have faithfully served the Lord every day of their lives, and now, through the love of Christ, I'll serve Him for the rest of mine. So you see, Doctor, I believe I've found my explanation concerning that bible. And I pray you find yours.'

"Standing silent for a moment. He picked up his grandfather's picture and studied it for a brief second. 'I believe I have, Mrs. Evans. You see, I never believed either. I always told my grandpa I was a man of science, not science fiction. It's only been recently my wife and I started going to church with him and Grandma. It was just last week my wife was baptized. Grandpa didn't ask me why I hadn't made that same commitment. He simply said, when God calls you to be His, you'll know it, and you'll follow. I just pray you're listening and I'm still around to see it happen.'

"Again the room fell silent, and again it was Dr. Weldon who spoke. 'Mrs. Evans, if you don't mind, I'm going to head upstairs to tell Grandpa thank you for continuing to pray for me…that it was through his prayers and God's love that angels led me to the Lord this morning.'

"They embraced, holding each other not as strangers, not as friends, but as members of a family neither quite understood at that moment yet somehow knew they'd share for eternity. My mom couldn't remember ever seeing Grandma show any true emotion toward anyone, not even to her or my grandpa, so this just added to her state of shock. At some point she heard Grandma ask if she was okay, but she couldn't even nod her head, much less speak. It wasn't that she didn't want to. Oh no, she wanted to yell as loud as she could. Who is this woman talking about God and angels, and what has she done with my mom? I heard her tell my dad once that she half expected Rod Sterling to suddenly appear in the middle of the room and begin a *Twilight Zone* monologue.

"Doctor Weldon insisted my grandma take the Bible, assuring her when the offer was made, 'Please take mine,' that was exactly what his grandfather meant.

"As they entered the lobby, Grandma suddenly stopped, her eyes exploring the large, cavernous room with its tinted-glass front and three-story ceiling. As she moved slowly toward the center, her eyes not resting in one particular place, she began turning in all directions, continuing to scan the lobby, hallways, gift shop, and even the empty space above. Clutching the Bible to her chest, her face little by little began to glow with childlike amazement.

"'There are many angels in this place, doctor,' she marveled, continuing to turn her gaze about the room. 'Yes; the Lord has sent many, many gifts.'"

❦

Ann's smile was slight, but it overflowed with an abundance of love reserved only for the warmest of memories.

"I think that's what I miss most about my grandma—that beautiful glow. It never left her."

For the next few moments, Ann sat undisturbed, quietly taking in the sweetness of the past. Rachel knew the importance of such moments. Moments when the mind races to capture the heart and burst forth a personal treasury of memories precious and dear, bound with their own twinkling threads of time.

Peggy had only vague notions of such things, but she too sat quietly contented, eyes closed, envisioning the modern atrium at Saint Joe's hospital filled with angels. How wonderful it would be to see such a sight, she thought. Smiling to herself, she made a mental note to pause and say hello the next time she passed through the lobby to meet with Kevin.

Ann's heart let go of the moment with a sigh. "She was so wonderful... my grandma."

"Did she move in with your parents after that?"

"No. The farm held too many memories for her to give the place up, but too many for her to stay too. So she leased out the land and made the move to Missoula, returning to the farm every summer. From May through August, every weekend she opened the place to churches, Christian organizations, artists, and painters, even holding small, intimate concerts for Maranatha groups like those down in Southern California at the time. Some of the local residents didn't like it. It didn't fit their image of God-fearing Christians, so they nicknamed the place the Jesus Freak Farm. Now, I don't know if my grandma was just being cantankerous or if she actually fell in love with the name, but she had it painted on the barn and put up a big sign at the end of the drive: Welcome to Jesus Freak Farm."

"The barn was bright yellow. I remember a big picture...or poster or something in your office." Peggy laughed. "Not that I spent a lot of time in your office."

Ann grinned along with Rachel and then said, "Let's just say you were there somewhat less than often but more than once in a while."

"So she became the woman of God she promised?" Rachel asked.

"Oh yeah..." Ann chuckled. "On fire, Spirit filled, Bible thumping, praise God, the Lord is in the house, evangelical Christian. And I have to say, over time she began seeing a lot of her neighbors at the concerts and events being held at The Farm, as it got to be known."

Speaking up quickly, Peggy asked, "Did she continue seeing angels?"

"She did, but she always referred to them as Gifts."

"What a beautiful thought." Peggy moaned. "Gifts—like gifts from God. And she could see them? I mean, like they were real?"

Ann sipped the last drops of her coffee. "Absolutely! But still, the best authority we have is not Grandma, but God's word. And it speaks abundantly of angels."

She paused for a moment, and her eyes moved to Peggy, not looking for her reaction but simply to answer her question more directly.

"But according to Grandma, they're as real and alive as me and you. Sometimes we hear stories of an angel protecting people from a storm, a fire, a flood, or whatever disaster befalls us. But they don't always come as glorious winged creatures. Sometimes they're just faces in the crowd, blending in, moving about unnoticed by the world. On any given day, we may say good morning to one in the market or divert our gaze from one seeking our kindness, compassion, or generosity."

Ann thought for a second, measuring how much further she should go with this. It was so unlike her to open up about anything. That was typically left for Jim, and Amy when she was around; they were the storytellers. She smiled, picturing her grandmother leaning over her shoulder whispering, "Sometimes angels guide us on paths we never intended to walk, my darling."

"Shortly before Grandma died, she spent a few months at our cabin out at Brennan's Cove," Ann continued. "During which, she and my neighbor Trudy would disappear into the forest for hours or walk along the shoreline or sometimes just sit by the fire up in Tru's office. I asked them once what they found to talk about day after day. My grandma laughed and said, 'We have much in common; we both see things the world does not.'"

Peggy's attention perked up. "Does your neighbor see angels too?"

"Not that I'm aware of, but it sure wouldn't surprise me. Tru has a very...let's say complex imagination and does see things in a way the rest of us never would. But what I was going to tell you is a few months after Grandma went back to Montana, she passed away. Trudy was kind enough to give me a little private mourning time—about six months, actually, before showing me what she and Grandma had done together. Adding, before she met Grandma, she thought people claiming to see angels were kooks, looking for the *National Enquirer* to knock at their door with fame and fortune.

"Up in her office, she presented me with four cassette tapes filled with grandma talking about Gifts...Angels. Then Trudy handed me a journal filled with some of the stories Grandma had told her. They were written like bedtime stories for children, or maybe I should say bedtime stories for me from my grandma. Amy was five or six at the time, and I'd tuck her in bed and read her one of the stories. It was a very special time for us both.

"Shortly before Grandma left, Trudy showed her the blank journal and asked permission to fill the pages with the stories she had shared, as a present for me. On the inside cover, before a single word had been written, my grandma wrote, 'To Ann and Tru. Believe: for they walk among us as God's precious Gifts.'

"'Love, G ma.'"

❀

"Pardon me, ladies," a voice as southern and sweet as Tupelo honey interrupted. "I know you're up to your eyebrows full of cake, but I have an extra galette des rois …Unfortunately I only have the one," she continued, setting a square eighteen-inch cakebox in the center of the table. Opening the lid displayed a thick braided cake with white glazed icing dripping down the sides. Tinted sugar crystals of purple, green, and gold lay in broad sections across the top. "Lagniappe…"

The quizzical frown and slight tilt of Peggy's head broadened the young lady's smile. "It's what we say in N'awlinz."

Peggy giggled. "I've always wanted to go to Louisiana. It's so beautiful. The food, the music, Mardi Gras…but now, I'm sorry, what is…lan-yap?"

"Lagniappe. It means a little extra…a gift."

A glint of surprise and disbelief moved swiftly around the table, accompanied by a touch of apprehensive laughter. Ann quickly and cheerfully explained, "When you walked up, we were just finishing a rather deep discussion about…gifts. So you caught us a little by surprise."

"Forgive me. I didn't mean to intrude…"

"No, no, no, you didn't," Ann assured her. "Please, tell us about this ga le…"

"Galette des rois …king cake," said the young lady shyly. "Its history is a little odd, and because I don't start serving it publicly until January sixth, the beginning of Mardi Gras season, I haven't received the tasting notes from the printer quite yet, or you could read the official story. But traditionally it's a cake commemorating the visit of the Magi to the Christ child. And when you serve it, make sure you tell your guests there's a tiny plastic Baby Jesus hidden in it. Tradition says whoever gets it has to buy the next cake."

Ann continued to examine the beautiful dessert. "I can't believe how much work must've gone into this. Not to mention the ingredients themselves. Please let me pay you for this; it's not right that—"

"No, please. It's a gift—lagniappe. I made three for my husband's New Year's Eve party, and because of the recipe, it's easier to make four. So you ladies take this home and enjoy."

She turned to walk away, but the women insisted she join them at the table, and as they were the only ones there and she was tired and needed a break anyway, she accepted the invitation.

"I'm Ann. This is Rachel and Peggy."

"Dix. Thanks for coming in."

"Is that short for Dixie?" Peggy asked.

"No. I'm Creole and come from a large family, Dix is sort of French for the number ten."

Peggy's eyes widened. "Ten? Like in ten kids! Your poor mom!"

"Eleven!" Dix added. "I have a twin sister named Fini. That's French for *finished*. I'm pretty sure my dad was drunk when he named us."

With introductions made, Dix ran behind the counter and returned a few minutes later with a large carafe of specially brewed coffee. As she filled their cups, she explained, "This is my favorite. My husband calls it 'after-dinner afterglow.' It's Oldtown White Coffee from Malaysia." Her eyes locked on Ann. "Lagniappe!" She grinned, slightly raising her cup.

Ann smiled graciously. "Thank you, Dix, for everything."

The aroma was exceptionally pleasing, the taste deep, rich—the perfect drink to enjoy on a cool, starry night, Ann quietly reflected. But not this night; this night she'd do something she'd not done in some time—spend an evening with her emotions, enjoying fond memories of her grandma.

For Peggy, the transition from angels to cake would normally be a bumpy juncture, but throw in her fascination with Mardi Gras, and the road became easier to travel. "Are these cakes pretty popular during Mardi Gras?"

Dix nodded. "There's thousands, probably tens of thousands served up during Mardi Gras. I should tell you, though, mine ain't exactly traditional. My dough is a touch bit moist, and my almond cream filling is made with an Amaretto reduction. So if you have issues with nuts or alcohol, even though the alcohol is cooked off, this wouldn't be the cake for you."

From the bottom of Peggy's purse, her cell phone burst into song: "Gimme all your lovin', all your hugs and kisses too." Hurrying to answer it, she giggled. "It's my husband."

The conversation was short. "If it was lying on the bed, then I packed it. Let your mom know they don't have to pick us up at the airport. I've rented a car; I'm not going through that again! Okay, we'll be home soon. Dinner? No, you and Michael go ahead and grab something. What do you mean? Okay, bye…no, no, no…tell me…you know…louder! Sweeter! Thank you. Love you too."

"Everything okay?" Rachel asked.

"Everything's fine. He's just excited to see his family, especially his sister Kara. She was pregnant last year and couldn't make the flight from Paris. We have a little niece we haven't even seen yet."

"Paris," Ann cooed.

"Yeah, I know. I can't wait to go to their place one of these times."

Dix probed gently, "Where y'all meeting for New Year's? I take it, it's like a family reunion, tradition kind a thing?"

"It is, and it's a really big deal in his family, something you don't miss unless you're pregnant and living halfway around world away. Everyone meets at his parents' house on Maui…"

"Maui…" Ann said, grinning.

"Yeah it's beautiful. Their house sits right there at White Rock. You can watch the sunset from their garden, lie on the beach, do a little snorkeling."

Again Dix probed. "Big family?"

"Kevin has two older brothers. One's married and has two adorable little girls. The other's sworn to bachelorhood, but that doesn't stop him from bringing someone new every year to the party. And then, of course, Kara, his baby sister, and her family."

Ann's attention moved to Rachel. "Are you and Michael going?"

"No, we're house sitting and planning on watching the ball drop in Times Square—that is, if we don't fall asleep on the couch first."

Always trying to be helpful, Peggy said, "You can see the Space Needle from the park at the top of the hill. It's only about a twenty-minute walk. You could put some hot chocolate in a backpack. Put on some warm clothes and a thick jacket under your raincoat. Don't forget the umbrella. Just think how pretty it would be looking across the bay. All the city lights…and the fireworks from the Space Needle. Michael would love it. Or better yet, take him to the Needle. You wouldn't even need a jacket. You'd have fifty thousand of your closest friends huddled together to keep you warm. Again, don't forget the umbrella."

Her giggle brought grins to the faces of Ann and Dix.

"No," Rachel replied, unamused. "Popcorn, blankets, couch, TV. Dry, safe, warm, and cozy—and most likely sound asleep by ten."

They talked for another thirty minutes before preparing to leave. It was decided that Ann's party guests would get to enjoy the king cake, and they all would meet back at the shop before Fat Tuesday to enjoy a sampling of their own. Dix got up from the table, hurried to the counter, and returned a moment later.

"Here's my card. I wrote my cell number on the back. Call me a day or two before y'all are coming in. I have something else that's not on the menu I'd love for you to try. It's a Corsican dessert. It's one of my favorites."

Neither Ann nor Rachel remembered to ask about the coffee.

❧

That evening Ann poured a glass of Chardonnay and sat on the deck under a tall mushroom-shaped propane heater allowing thoughts and emotions to wander their way around and through her melancholy night. By nine thirty, she had made three phone calls—the first to her mother in Olympia, the second to Rachel, and the third was to Jim.

"Honey, I miss you…Yes, I've had a glass of wine. I called to say good night and let you know I'm coming up tomorrow instead of…Because I miss you!…Just one…No, glass, not bottle…Oh yeah, and I'm bringing a surprise for dinner."

CHAPTER THIRTEEN

A small bell rang above the door, and the aroma of breakfast hung in the air—sausage, maple syrup, toast, and coffee. The counter was lined with the usual morning patrons, Mr. and Mrs. Briggs sat in one booth, their four kids in another, and a small array of businessmen and women filled the remaining six. Rennie poured coffee at a large table in the far back of the room where five police officers were seated, two with menus still in hand.

"Peter, come in out of the cold and join us. Breakfast is on the lieutenant here," one of the officers shouted. Laughter pierced the heavy aromas, filling the room.

"Seriously, Peter, come join us," the lieutenant said, standing up to get another chair.

The old man made his way to the back of the room, where Rennie gave him a hug and whispered quietly in his ear, "Are you okay? You look tired." She whispered.

One of the officers chided, "Hey, Pete, Dutch gets a glimpse of her smooching on your ear, he'll be out here with a cleaver."

The laughter was broken up by the old man himself. Not with a quick-witted remark like everyone expected, but with silence and forced smile. "Just coffee, Rennie. I have someplace to be this morning, and my bus should be here in about ten minutes," he said softly.

Not all the officers at the table knew him, but to the ones who did, clearly something was wrong. He looked disheveled and tired. His face was saggy, his eyes red and puffy. Perhaps he'd been ill, one officer thought, and the same thought crossed the mind of Lieutenant Robert Redding.

Bob Redding had known the old man for the better part of a year, after responding to a shots-fired call at a local convenience store. Arriving on scene, Redding saw the old man sitting in the doorway, rocking back and forth with the lifeless body of a young boy in his lap. The night clerk, clearly shaken, explained hysterically, "They just drove through the parking lot and shot him…shot him right there…right there in the doorway. This old man tried to save him, but clearly he was dead. He was dead right there in the doorway. Shot dead right there."

Officer Redding remembered hearing the old man softly singing a hymn over the young boy. It was an image that would stay with him for the rest of his life. After that, or maybe because of it, he noticed the old man walking the streets at odd hours of the night, a cane in one hand, Bible in the other. He would stop the car and roll down the window, and they'd visit briefly, ensuring the old man was okay and not seeking or needing assistance. There were times the officer would see him sitting on one of the old iron benches by the fountain at Colony Park. He'd walk over and explain to him it wasn't safe to be there at that time of night. The old man would look at him and smile, saying somewhat jokingly, "Have you seen where I live? They tell me it's not safe there at night either."

And then one morning about five thirty, he saw him standing at the curb in front of the Garden Street Café.

"Are you okay?"

"I've forgotten my Bible," he said, nodding his head toward the old brownstone across the street. "I'm debating. Do I get it now or after breakfast? I'll tell you what. I'm going to have you make the decision for me. If you'll have breakfast with me, I'll fetch it after. And if you decline, well, I'll get it after anyway, but breakfast won't be as nice without you. I know the place doesn't look like much, but I promise you it's the best breakfast in town. Everything is homemade except the plates."

Redding never understood what possessed him to join the old man that morning, but now, once a week at the end of his shift, he and some fellow officers come in for the best breakfast in town, and sometimes they get to share it with their friend Peter.

"Must be something pretty important for you to miss breakfast. They have something going on at the church?" asked Redding.

"No. I'm going to visit an old friend this morning. Catch up on the latest, discuss aches and pains and the procedures that accompany them—all the stuff old men talk about."

Rennie reached across to grab his cup, and there on her finger was the ring. He touched her hand. "I'm sorry, dear. I'd better get that to go. I guess today I'll be like one of those yuppies that bring their Starbucks on the bus. Of course, mine will cost less and taste better. Isn't that right, Ruthie?"

Rennie's smile faded momentarily, returning as a faint grin. Busy laughing and joking about other things, the boys in blue ignored the slip, or let it go by unnoticed. All except Bob Redding, who watched Rennie's faint grin disappear completely before she made her way quickly along the counter and through the doors leading into the kitchen. A minute later she returned with his coffee and leaned down, saying quietly, "Dutch wants to see you before you leave." And then she quickly headed to the register, where customers waited patiently.

"Well, you'll have to excuse me, gentlemen. Seems the proprietor would like a word. I'll just bet that new dishwasher didn't show, and he wants me to stand in."

His humor has returned, Redding thought, *but not his step*. Moving away from the table, Peter seemed stiff, cautious, and slow, nothing like the fluid figure Redding had grown to recognize even at a distance in the dark. After making his way to the far end of the counter, a young man burst through the swinging doors carrying a tray of clean cups. The old man turned to face the officers and gave a shrug before sauntering into the kitchen.

Dutch set two plates on the pass-through, hit the small bell, and turned to the oven to remove a batch of fresh biscuits. "Let me grab these real quick. You can take a couple with you."

Dutch set the tray on the stainless steel counter before placing them on a large holding rack. He gave Peter a quick handshake and hug and then began. "Did you have a rough night? Looks like you could use some sleep."

"Why is everyone so worried about how I look this morning? And to answer your question, I slept very well, thank you. Well, until about three o'clock, when Layla came home with that new boyfriend of hers. They were so drunk they had a hard time getting up the stairs, and when they finally made it into her apartment, they got into an argument, and…I guess now that I think about it, I didn't sleep very well."

"You should mention it to the boys out there. Maybe they can do something. Talk to Layla or beef up patrol for a while. You know—something."

"She's usually pretty quiet. Nice young lady; she won't keep this guy around. Now, what was it you wanted to see me about? I got a bus to catch."

Dutch flipped the biscuits onto the cooling rack and then placed three into a small white bag, adding a napkin, a plastic knife, and a small bottle of homemade jam. "Here you go. You get some rest today. As far as dinner, if you're tired, I'll bring you something. And maybe we can open our Bibles."

※

The old man's bus arrived as scheduled. The twenty-five-minute ride gave him time to close his eyes and drift through thoughts, much like dreams, of his beautiful Ruth. And though each day brought a greater level of loneliness, separation, and longing, he found an odd comfort around Rennie and Dutch and was overjoyed that they, too, now shared a connection with Ruth Anne. Rennie had always enjoyed hearing him speak of her, but now, these last few days, Dutch, too, had a desire to see photos and grow to know her through the old man's memories and love. Perhaps tonight, after dinner, he would take over one of the photo albums he kept stored in a box under his bed. He was sure they'd get a kick out of seeing him as a scrawny twenty-year-old kid in blue jeans and leather jacket, straddling his uncle's new 1954 Harley-Davidson while giving his best impersonation of Marlon Brando in *The Wild One*. But then they'd turn the page. A five-by-seven color photograph, rare for 1954, would show Ruth playfully annoyed, gazing into the camera lens. Her dazzling sapphire eyes would captivate them just as they had him when he snapped the picture. Her flirtatious smile would light up a room and her laughter. Oh, if they could hear her laughter…if he could hear it just one more time…

The bus came to a stop. His mind temporarily put the memories away, allowing his racing heart to rest. But what a wonderful idea to share those early photos with Dutch and Rennie tonight. Of course, Rennie would insist on hearing the stories behind each one—and that wouldn't be such a bad thing either. Yes, it would be a wonderful evening.

The complex was large, with walkways spreading in many directions from the circular bus stop. The grass, though damp, had been trimmed earlier that morning, leaving the smell of fresh-cut grass to linger in the still morning air. Slowly he made his way down the familiar path to the large blue building. Automatic doors opened into an immense lobby. At the end of a short hallway sat the receptionist he remembered as Helen.

"Good morning, Helen," he said sprightly, taking a seat in one of the chairs along the wall.

Recognizing his voice, she looked up cheerfully. But seeing the small bag in his hand, she sternly barked, "You know you can't have anything to eat or drink. Nothing on your stomach—"

"I haven't had so much as a sip of water. But when I'm done, I brought homemade biscuits and jam for the two us." He smiled.

High above Brennan's Cove, the morning sky was layered with various degrees of cool temperatures, capturing mist in small ghostlike patches of fog as the great eagle soared on invisible ribbons of air to survey his kingdom. He would not disturb the man today, nor fish the cove's dark waters. Instead, his eyes searched the forest floor. There was not the abundance of small prey there had been on the last full moon, and this bothered the great bird, so he continued to circle, inspecting his domain.

"Chris and Beth are eating breakfast at their house, but Jim will be over shortly," Lincoln said, moving up behind Trudy to give her a hug.

"Can't you see I've got my hands full? Now get out of the kitchen, or I'll put you to work."

"I don't suppose you're gonna make some of that sausage we got from Nels, are you? That guy makes the best dang sausage ever. Oh, is that pancake batter? You making pancakes?" Again he hugged her around the waist, and again she wiggled away.

"Okay, I said I'd put you to work. Get the syrup out of the downstairs pantry, and set the table. Maybe that'll keep you——"

Her voice broke sharply. Clearing her throat with a small cough and a sip of honey-lemon tea, she faced him and whispered, "Just get the table ready." Another quick cough, and she could speak a little louder. "And set a place for Beth. It doesn't matter if that kid was stuffed to the gills. She'll want a panca..." Again the words caught in her throat.

Filled with concern, Lincoln didn't move. "You doing okay, sweetheart?"

"Fine. I've just been talking a lot lately, and I didn't sleep very well last night. So I'm tired and cranky, and I don't want to be loved on when I'm trying to do things."

She stood still, staring at him for a long moment. Even before the glint in her eye could be seen, she moved swiftly, putting her arms around his waist, her head against his chest. "But I'm not doing anything after breakfast."

Lincoln held her softly, kissing the top of her head. "I think we could both use a little quiet time after breakfast, my love."

❦

From inside the house, her father called, "Beth; we're leaving pretty soon. Don't get anything on your dress."

The girl quickly looked down at her dress just to assure she hadn't gotten anything on it while jumping off the porch or running across the damp yard to pick up Jass's very soggy chew toy lying in the mud. Satisfied, she called back, "Okay, Daddy, I won't."

The screen door of the Brooks' cabin swung open with a creak. "Jass!" Beth squealed in delight. From the porch the dog sniffed the crisp morning air. "Jass, come here! Come here boy...Jass...Jass...Jasper...come!" Her demand was loud and gruff, but it softened immediately with the sound of muddy little hands playfully patting the front of her pretty red dress in an attempt to coax the dog to her.

Lincoln giggled. "Oh, no. She used his full name...he's in big trouble now. Maybe I should go to his rescue."

Trudy squeezed him hard. "I don't think it's Jass that will need to be rescued."

"Elizabeth Anne Peterson," her father's voice boomed. "What are you doing?"

Looking up but continuing to hold on to her husband, Trudy whispered, "Oh, no. He used her full name…"

Lincoln quietly chuckled. "I'm pretty sure I won't need to set a place for her this morning."

Again he kissed Trudy on the forehead. "You know what that means, don't you? I have time for another hug and kiss before I have to set the table."

"You're incorrigible, Lincoln Trudeau," she whispered.

Taking her in his arms, he kissed her passionately, taking her breath and leaving her weak in the knees. Clutching the back of his shirt with both hands, she held him tight, feeling his warm breath against her face. "You are my love…Trudy Fruity," he said softly.

"Hey Linc, I found that guy's number," Jim called out, making his way up the front steps and across the porch to tap a short courtesy knock on the half-opened door. "I don't smell breakfast. Am I too early. Lincoln? Trudy? Anyone in there?"

Lincoln sneaked in a parting squeeze. Trudy wiggled free and moved swiftly toward the stove, glancing back at him over her shoulder, the look in her eyes and smile on her face conveying perfectly her affection. *How beautiful she is*, he thought, making his way to the stairwell. Trudy had thoughts of her own, which brought a glint of guilt to her face, causing Lincoln to pause.

"Come on in, Jim. Tru's just been horsing around all morning." He grinned, not taking his eyes off her. "Say, if you don't mind setting the table, I'm just gonna grab some more syrup from the pantry downstairs—that is, if I can get her to leave me alone long enough." But this time the look that came over her shoulder caused him to scurry down the stairway.

"Good morning, Jim. Sit. I've got the table." she said, quietly pointing to the Gathering Place. "Apparently Linc can't multitask today. You want coffee?"

The strain in her voice was apparent and surprising. He hadn't noticed it yesterday or even last night over dinner. She looked well—radiant, as a matter of fact, smiling, moving about the kitchen with a flow almost dancelike. But still, he'd inquire just the same.

She pulled a mug from the cupboard and cream from the fringe and then made her way to the end of the counter, where a fresh pot of coffee had just finished brewing. She filled the mug and walked to the table. "My voice is just a little tired this morning." She grinned, speaking softly before taking a seat next to his. "I'm sure if I go easy today, it'll be fine by tonight. Now, enjoy your coffee, and no more questions about it."

Immediately he poked fun. "Wow. I didn't know you could read minds, Tru."

"You and Linc are like reading a book." She snickered, taking a sip of tea.

Even considering the state of her voice, he waited, suspecting there'd be a follow-up remark. Warmly she smiled and took a second sip. An awkward silence fell between them until finally, exasperated, he spoke up. "Are you kidding me? That's it? I thought for sure you'd have some snide remark about how we're like reading a comic book or books filled with blank pages, or somethig."

Posing as if giving his comment thought, she took another sip and said rather offhandedly, "It was a test."

A deep frown drew lines of confusion on his brow. "What are you talking about, a test?"

Standing to return to the stove, she paused just long enough to say, "I wanted to see if I was the only mind reader in the room. And apparently I'm not. Seems you knew exactly what I was thinking, almost word for word."

Her soft laughter faded quickly as she walked away, and he, knowing she'd be too far away to respond, tried using it to his advantage by shooting a verbal jab across the room. But the words were cut off sharply by Trudy forming a hand puppet, its mouth snapping shut tightly. This was clear evidence that distance played no part when it came to Trudy conveying a point, yet another fact he had come to know and understand many times over through their long friendship. And then he watched as she moved to a small chalkboard at the end of the counter. In large letters she wrote, "To be continued…tonight."

Acting as if surprised, Jim responded, "Is that a challenge? Are you honestly challenging me, not to a mere conversation, a bit of chitchat, or a measure of small talk, but to a true repartee? You are aware it will take more than a strong voice and a naked hand puppet to defeat the master of twaddle. You must first possess rapid-fire, nonstop, no-holds-barred wit, guile, and wisdom." He paused a moment, as if contemplating a profound thought. "But, of course," he continued, pointing a finger in her direction, "putting a dress on that puppet might help a little…"

Trudy's hand puppet rose up slowly from beneath the counter wearing a loosely draped floral dishtowel. Taking a moment to give Jim a quick look-over, it turned its nose in the air and with a loud snap disappeared, leaving both Jim and Trudy laughing. She walked to the stove.

Jim reached for his coffee but stopped, saying loudly, "Tonight! I almost forgot. Ann called. She's driving out this afternoon instead of tomorrow. Said she's swinging by the Smokehouse to pick up stuff to munch on later. That way, no one has to cook. We can get together over at our place or maybe even around the fire pit…"

Trudy pointed to the old spinet piano sitting directly across from the rock fireplace in the Great Room overlooking the cove. This of course was always Trudy's first choice of where to gather, mainly because with some gentle coaxing, Jim or other guests would fill the home with song.

"Are you telling me, Lady Trudeau, you wish to sing tonight?" Jim asked, eagerly standing at attention. "It will be an honor to be your accompanist this evening. Now, Madam, will you be performing top forty, classic standards, country, or Broadway musicals? I'm afraid I'm not very proficient in punk, grunge, or heavy metal, so if that's your gig…"

Her face brightened in amusement. Using the chalkboard she scribbled, "Opera?"

"Opera. But of course. I assume madam wishes to perform Mozart's 'Queen of the Night'?"

Looking delighted, she gave him two thumbs-up.

Lincoln's heavy footsteps up the stairs were drowned out by his less-than-pitch-perfect singing voice. "Close your eyes and I'll kiss you… Tomorrow I'll miss you…"

Jim suddenly rushed to Trudy and began speaking in an extremely poor nondescript European accent. "I am so terribly sorry, Madame Trudeau, but your recital this evening has been cut, canceled, axed, kaput, pfft pfft. I have just learned Sir Paul McCartney has arrived and will be performing in your place."

Unable to hold back her laughter, it came out in small squeaks and titterings, which always made Jim laugh even harder. And from the stairway they heard, "La, la, while I'm away...I'll write home...You know I can hear you two. What's so funny?" Lincoln asked, making his way up the last few steps. "It better not be my singin'. After all, I think I'm in pretty good voice this morning. Got any requests?"

Trudy's hand puppet made one last-appearance.

❦

"Hey, little man, time to wake up. We have a lot to do this morning."

"We do?" He groaned with a stretch.

"We have to take Aunt Peg and Uncle Kevin to the airport. After that, I thought we'd drive through my old neighborhood. I'll show you the school where me and your daddy met."

"It must be pretty old. They've probably torn it down by now."

"They haven't condemned it yet, smarty-pants. The principal is meeting us there. She said she had something of Daddy's you might like."

"She knew Daddy?"

"Your daddy, Aunt Peg—we all went to school there."

"What is it?" Michael said, sitting up in bed.

"I don't know. She didn't say. But get out of bed, get dressed...clean clothes. I want you to look nice when you meet her. She's someone very special to me."

"Then that makes her special to me too, Mommy," he said, giving her a hug.

I'm sure this sweetness will wear off with age, she thought, closing her eyes, squeezing him tightly while taking full advantage of the moment. Michael also treasured these times. Being held by his mom was still one of the greatest joys he knew.

"What's her name?"

"You call her Mrs. B."

"Is that what you call her?"

"That's what all the cool kids call her."

"That must be what Daddy and Aunt Peg used to call her then?" Michael giggled.

"Hmm...yeah, they were so cool..."

The short ride to the airport was filled with a hypercaffeinated Peg sitting in the back seat telling Michael stories about her school days with Mrs. B. As Rachel drove, she listened closely to her sister's tales, interrupting twice by calmly using the single word "No!" and directing the story in a more appropriate direction. Kevin, who sat in the front passenger seat, said over his shoulder, "I met her last week only for a minute. You're gonna like her. You're gonna like her a lot. And you've already met her husband, Mr. B."

"I have?"

"You met him last week at the bookstore," Rachel said.

He smiled excitedly. "Is he the guy that read to me about Michael the angel? What's his name...uh, Peter. Like Jesus's friend."

In the rearview mirror, Rachel caught a glimpse of a still albeit somewhat less perturbed Peggy as she prepared to again criticize the elderly gentleman. Quickly Rachel exclaimed, "Nope, the other guy! The one you asked for help." She then smiled into the mirror for her sister to see. Peggy made a face and stuck out her tongue and puckered her lips as though blowing a kiss to Rachel.

Michael's excitement didn't falter. "I liked him a lot. He made me laugh."

"He always made me laugh too," Peggy said. "I used to have so much fun on the drama team. It was such a blast. Of course, your mom was more into it than me, mainly because she has such a beautiful voice." It was now Rachel's turn to send kisses via the mirror. Replying to Rachel with a wink, Peggy continued talking. "The first time he heard your mom sing...how old were you, Rache? Like twelve...thirteen?"

"Fourteen."

"It doesn't matter. He put her in the choir, then on the drama team. And wasn't it your junior year he had you lead the worship team?"

"Bailey led worship. I was just part of the team."

"Yeah, whatever. I really couldn't tell you because I was usually hanging out with Kathy and them, so I never knew who was up there singing. But I can tell you, Mr. B. always had your mom right up front. Not to mention he gave her all the good parts on the drama team."

"Bailey always got the lead."

"Hmph! He had your mom do almost all the school assemblies and morning chapel—or, as we all called it, Little Chapel on the Prairie."

Michael scrunched his face. "Why?"

Once again using her rearview mirror, Rachel locked her sister in her sights. "Peg!"

"Your mom played the piano and sang these Christian folk songs. What were they called, Rache?"

"They weren't folk songs. They were Hillsongs."

"Yeah! Whatever."

"I know Hillsongs. They rock," Michael shouted.

"Whatever!" Peggy pretended to glare. "They didn't rock when your mom played 'em."

"I bet they did! She rocks good." Michael defended.

Though she didn't like to, Peggy had to agree. "Okay, I'll give you that. She could rock when she wanted to. Like at church and youth group. But for some reason, it never happened in chapel."

The sisters' eyes met once again in the mirror, and Rachel said, "I played what Mr. B. wanted, and he loved it."

"Uh huh. Teacher's pet."

"Far from it! But he did like the way I led chapel. And besides, I know for a fact he wasn't the only guy who liked it..." Rachel murmured teasingly.

Peggy bristled. "If you're talking about Chris, the only reason he liked it is because he had a cru—"

"Peg!" Rachel called out.

"You know it's true," Peg snapped back.

"No more."

"I just think—"

"Enough," Rachel said sharply, cutting her off.

There was no retort from the back seat, the younger sister casting her eyes to the floorboard. For the next few seconds, the mirror remained only half full, and the blended sounds of engine, tires on pavement, and the twiddling thumbs of a small boy were all that could be heard as the SUV moved down the road. Reaching into her purse for lipstick, Peggy also found two sweet lemon drops she shared with Michael. His, though sweet, was also bitterly sour and made his face wrinkle. Hers, too, was sweet, but it held just enough tart sarcasm demanding to be heard, she couldn't contain it.

"I was just saying," she smiled sweetly into the mirror. "Chris always gave the little sermonette afterward, and then he'd have everybody stand up and hold hands while you played your little piano in the background. It was like being in an episode of *Little House on the Prairie*. I kept expecting Nellie Olson to walk in."

"We didn't need Nellie. We had you."

Rachel and Peg both looked into the mirror. One smiled, and one winked, and kisses were exchanged by both.

"Hey, Rache, do you remember that time—I think it was right before Christmas—when Mike and Mr. B. did the music for chapel?" The memory caused Peggy's excitement to build rapidly, making it impossible for Rachel to answer. "It was awesome." Peggy's voice rose. "Everybody thought Mr. B. was on the platform just to introduce whoever would be leading chapel that morning. But then he walked over to the piano and just started playing. No words, just all this beautiful music. After a couple of minutes, he said into the microphone, 'My friend, Mike Donahue,' and the place just went crazy. Mike played an electric keyboard and Mr. B. the piano. And just as you'd expect, these two were incredible together. To this day I haven't heard anything that compares."

"I agree," Rachel said. "There was just something about what those two did on that little stage. Their performance was blessed, anointed, God inspired, or whatever else you want to call it, but it brought people to their knees. Mike used to tell me he should've stayed here and just studied under Mr. B."

"Did he teach my daddy how to play piano?"

Peggy giggled. "Are you kidding? He taught your daddy how to do everything—music, theater, worship, everything. Your daddy was always good. But Mr. B. just made him better. And did you know if it wasn't for Mr. B., you wouldn't even be here?"

"Is that true, Mommy?" Michael asked, looking to his mom curiously.

Again Peggy spoke before her sister could answer. "He had your mommy and daddy work together on a play. That's where they fell in love." Peggy smiled warmly into the mirror. "But it was Mrs. B. that always caught them—

"Okay, Hawaiian Airlines," Rachel shouted, stopping sharply along the curb. "Peg, you have everything? Purse, tickets, muzzle?"

There were plenty of hugs and kisses. Kevin picked Michael up in his arms. "I bet I could stuff you in one of these bags, and no one would even know you were there."

Michael chuckled hard. "I don't think so, Uncle Kevin. Aunt Peg put a bunch of stuff in there. Besides, I have to stay with Mom. There's nobody to take care of her, and I think we're gonna make popcorn and watch fireworks on TV."

There was another series of rushed hugs, goodbyes, and we'll miss yous, and then everyone was off. A few blocks from the airport, Rachel stopped at a doughnut shop, where she bought a cup of coffee, hot chocolate, and a doughnut with blue and white sprinkles for Michael to enjoy on the thirty-minute drive to the school. Michael was somewhat disappointed to learn Mr. B. wouldn't be joining them but ask to hear another story about his mom and dad when they were young.

Entering the school parking lot, he was amazed with the size of the old two-story brick buildings. The grounds were mostly grassy fields with wide cement paths that carved outlines through the tree-lined campus, which covered an entire square block. Even with his mother by his side, the neoclassic entrance of the main building loomed formidable in the eyes of the young boy, causing a brief chill to grip his small body.

"You okay, little man?" his mother asked, feeling him shiver.

"Fine. This place is big. Did you ever get lost?"

"No. But there were times I felt lost."

Michael was instantly taken with Mrs. B. and her with him. Twice within the first ten minutes, Ann found herself teary eyed but hid it well, just below the surface of her laughter. It wasn't so much he was like his father. On the contrary, he was the image of his mother, not only in appearance but sharing that same inquisitive nature tempered with the quirky shyness Rachel had possessed all through school. Ann loved him.

"How would you like to see some pictures of your mom and dad when they were…ah…" She mentally cited a short list of possible adjectives—shy, confused, ambitious, sneaky, determined, lovebirds. She smiled graciously settling on, "When they were students here."

"I'd like that a lot, Mrs. B.," he gushed.

Rachel was much more apprehensive, watching Ann produce three photo albums, the front covers designed to resemble theatrical posters. Though the titles were the same, *A Labor of Love*, the artwork, clearly original illustrations done in colored pencil, intricately depicted three separate stage productions.

"Oh my g—" Rachel gasped. "That's me. Seriously, that's me!"

"That is you, Mommy! Look, that's your birds!"

The artist had captured a thin gold chain draped around the soft contours of Rachel's neck, the lighting drawing focus not only to her face but emphasizing dramatically the lovebirds resting gently on her skin.

As if returning to Ann's office had magically transported her back in time, Rachel spoke shyly, her voice like that of the timid seventeen-year-old in the drawing. "Mrs. B.…I…don't understand."

Ann smiled warmly, turning all three albums to face Rachel. "Every year I sit down with Jim." She paused, looking at Michael. "Mr. B.…" The boy returned her smiled and nodded, and Ann continued. "Every year we put together an album of the drama department, using photos taken by Mr. Jason's photography class, myself, or, as is in this case, a very good friend of yours—Chris Peterson."

Immediately opening the album to the first page, there was the original photo taken by Chris. Though not as dramatic as the cover, it was nonetheless captivating. The stage, only semi-lit, darkened the scenery to mere silhouettes, allowing the focus to remain entirely on the close-up of Rachel.

"Wow, Mommy. You were pretty when you were young!"

"What's this 'when you were young' stuff? It wasn't that long ago, mister."

Ann chuckled softly, and Rachel smirked. "I don't think I look all that different. My hair's the same. Maybe one or two little wrinkles, but I still wear the same dress si...Okay, maybe I'm a little more mommy-ish now, but just a skosh. And if I really wanted to, I could fit into that dress."

Michael looked at the cover once again, running his finger over the beautiful artwork. "You're still pretty. You're just not young pretty, that's all."

It was everything Ann could do not to laugh, and Rachel ignored the comment altogether, focusing on the album. "Okay, why am I on the cover? I wasn't the lead; Bailey was. I had a small solo toward the end, and look at me. I was scared to death."

Michael looked closely at the photograph and then at the drawing. "You don't look a-scared, Mommy. You look beautiful, like a real singer or a movie star or something."

"Oh don't you kiss up now..." She giggled, putting her arm around him. "I was shaking, I was so scared. You just can't see it because of all the makeup and lights. They hid my fear pretty well back then." Glancing at the photo, she laughed. "You know, I sure don't remember Chris taking that picture. If I would've seen him standing there with a camera, that would've put me right over the edge..."

"You were probably just so a-scared you knocked it out of your memory."

Smiling with artificial pride like only a mother can, she boasted, "Well, Dr. Donahue; that must be the reason. I was just so a-scared I knocked it right out of my memory. I'm glad you're so smart."

There was a brief moment filled with mommy tickles and little boy giggles, and then Michael said, "Turn the page. I want to see more pictures of you...and Daddy."

"No, wait a second. Ann, you have to know why I'm on the cover. I mean really, I was always a lot more labor than love, so I'd think Mr....Jim would want to forget my performances not commemorate them."

Ann looked slightly amused. "Oh, I don't think so, Rache. Mr. B....see, now you've got me doing it." Both women shared a short laugh, then Ann's timbre changed slightly, signaling the gravity of what she was about to say.

"To this day Jim says you were one of the most talented kids he's ever taught, even referring to you as the brightest diamond in the rough he ever found. So you may not have always found your mark, but your talent showed through no matter where you stood, making you someone very special in that man's eyes."

"Oh, believe me, I never felt very special." And then a smile began to form. "You know, thinking back, he always did make me feel pretty darn wonderful. I just couldn't figure out why."

"Mom," Michael whispered, not wanting to interrupt, "I need to use?"

"Right outside the door and down the hall to your left." She pointed, indicating which way was left. The boy ran to the doorway and down the hall. "Thanks, Mom." His voice, along with his quick footsteps, echoed back through the office door.

Ann didn't wait for Rachel's attention to continue. "Jim has what he privately—and I mean very privately—refers to as The One Club."

The sincerity in her voice caused Rachel to remain silent for a moment before she asked, "The One Club?"

Ann's smile was vague, her eyes maintaining the gravity of the moment. "Even though you hold the distinct honor of being one of its members, you probably didn't even know it existed."

Rachel looked perplexed. "I don't recall ever hearing about it, but clubs were never my thing anyway, unless you consider youth group or drama teams a club, which I guess in some ways they are. But that's not what you're referring to, is it?"

The room was left with a second moment of silence, just long enough for Rachel to again look at the drawing and ponder Ann's mysterious lead-in and its purpose. Obviously Mr. B. and his secret club were behind it, but why had she been singled out to be on the cover? Was it something good? Something bad? Was it an honor or a joke? She'd always believed Mr. B. was one of the few people who understood her, tried to help her, and even encouraged her to sing, act, and play the piano. But wait—had he secretly thought what a foolish girl she was, thinking she had talent? But no; he was always proud of her achievements. Always standing by her, always raising her up, even offering her the lead on occasion, insisting she was ready, saying, "You can do it. Just leave your shyness in the dressing room. It'll be waiting for you when you get back."

And if Mr. B. were to have a secret club, she thought, it would have to be wonderful, imaginative, and overflowing with artistic magic. And if she was a member, well, it was like Mrs. B. said: it would be a distinct honor. But she knew of no such club, and even if there were, to believe she could be a member was absolutely ludicrous. But then again, Mr. B. always did take a special interest in her…

"Tell me about this One Club. It sounds intriguing, a little mysterious, and for some reason not very surprising, other than you did say I'm a member."

"I did, but I think maybe Jim should be the one to explain," she said in an attempt to backpedal out of the conversation.

"Maybe he should, but since he's not here and you brought it up, it kind of falls on your plate."

Rachel's answer came filled with a piercing directness that pulled at the corners of Ann's mouth ever so faintly, letting go only an instant before rising into a smile. Twice in as many days Ann regretted her choice of topics, this being the greater of the two. The One Club belonged solely to Jim, and he had one simple rule: never discuss it with anyone. Only a trusted handful of people knew of this enigmatic, ethically debatable, society of key-holding honorees. Its members, such as Rachel, were never told, at least not outright, anyway, of its existence. But this was different, Ann justified silently to herself. Rachel would expect and deserve full disclosure as to why it was her portrait on the cover, and if Jim were here, he'd tell her, and then they'd all sit around and enjoy recounting old times for the rest of the day. That was how Jim would've handled the situation. But of course, there was the fact that he'd never have brought up it up to begin with. Ann found herself wishing one of Grandma's angels would somehow come to her rescue, a wish that might not be too far-fetched when and if she ever confessed her blunder to her loving husband.

"Rache, if Jim ever brings this up, which I can't imagine that happening… but if he does…please…"

"Act surprised?" She smiled understandingly. "I'll make him believe I couldn't be more surprised if my butt fell off."

With each conversation, Ann loved the woman Rachel had become more and more. "All right." She sighed, clasping her hands together in nervous preparation.

"Every once in a while there's one of you students that Jim says, 'Watch this one. This one's got it; this one's going to be great; this one's going to do amazing things. Watch this one. Just watch this one.' And he'll work with that student to hone their craft, be it music, drama, worship—even sports once or twice. If he sees talent, true talent, he'll do everything in his power to bring it out, development it, and give the student a chance to perform and pursue their dreams.

"Now, all of that said, it's a pretty small club—twelve, fourteen members over the span of his career. But that's because they're not just talented people willing to work hard. They're truly exceptional people to begin with. People like your husband Mike, Bailey Peterson, and you.

"From early on, everyone knew you and Bailey could sing, but Jim recognized it as more than that. He'd talk about how gifted the two of you were, your friendship, always being there to support each other and constantly pushing each other to the next level. He had real admiration for you girls, so I never doubted you'd make the club. The only surprise for me was the timing. Jim presented you with yours at the end of your junior year instead of the first week of senior year like he typically had with the others."

"What are you talking about?"

"The key."

"Key?" Rachel asked.

"You don't remember?"

Rachel was beginning to feel a little embarrassed. "A key?" She brooded, tapping a single finger to her lips as she thought. "Now I'm really confused. I sure don't remember any key. Oh, wait—are you talking about the key to the practice rooms? That key?"

Ann giggled heartily. "That's the one."

"He gave me that so I could teach after school and Saturday mornings as part of the Reach the Youth summer program. It was my first job. I was so excited I didn't have to work at McDonald's."

Ann subconsciously played with a pencil on her desk, giving Rachel an extra moment to recall the memory. Slowly, Rachel's eyes began to sparkle, her cheeks flushed, and a broad smile came to her lips. "I can't believe this. I do remember. We were here in your office. Mr. B. handed me my own key...and..."

Tickled, Ann exclaimed, "Raised his glass of Coke and said something to the effect of, Rachel Callahan, welcome to the one club you have to earn your membership."

"He did," Rachel squealed. "I thought he was talking about a teacher's club or something. I didn't know, and I was too embarrassed to ask. You know—I didn't want to seem totally stupid. But I guess that didn't pan out, now, did it?"

Ann set the pencil down. "Did you ever look at it? The key? Did you ever check it out?"

"Well sure...I mean, no not really. It's a key! Okay, it's a really bright-red key, but still, it's a key."

"Not exactly. There is an insignia engraved on it."

Rachel attempted to visualize the key, but since she had never committed the details to memory, her effort was hopeless. But then, with a slight squeal, she reached into her jacket pocket and produced a large key ring, and there, among a numerous collection of keys, was a bright, shiny red one, easily separating itself from the rest. She held it up. "I've never taken it off. It's kind of my good luck charm, and I could never get rid of it. Especially me being Irish, what with a clover on the side."

Ann began laughing. "A clover? And what's on the other side?"

Rachel turned the key over and examined both sides repeatedly, eventually understanding for the first time, the engraving: 1 ♣.

Tightly holding it between her forefinger and thumb, shaking her head in disbelief, she confessed, "I never would've guessed."

"It's a Jim thing," Ann said, shrugging. "Every member's been given a red key with that logo. The reason it's bright red is so it stands out in a crowd, just like its owner. Like I said, it's a Jim thing. Nobody gets it; nobody understands it; but it keeps him entertained. You know how he is—very talented and just a little weird…or vice versa. To him it's a hidden Easter egg, left for the world to find."

Rachel smiled. "It's a really good one."

"Don't encourage him. He's weird enough as it is."

Ann focused her attention back to the album. "As far as all the covers, when he makes that final decision as to what goes on it, for him it has to sum up the year at a glance. Why did he choose you? I don't know exactly. You'd have to ask him. But let me say this: you made the cover of one of his most treasured possessions. And I might add, after thirty blah, blah years of *Labor of Love* albums, yours is one of only three that features a single individual on the cover. The first was our daughter, Amy, when she was about four or five years old. He made the mistake of casting her in one of his first stage productions here at the school."

"I only met Amy a few times when she'd come home from college to visit you guys, but even so, I can't imagine the daughter of Mr. B. messing up onstage."

"Oh, Amy wasn't the problem. Jim was! He was a nervous wreck. It was Amy's big scene, and he became so wrapped up in watching his little princess perform, he forgot to cue the orchestra. She finally put her hands on her hips and yelled, 'Daddy! My music!' At that moment somebody snapped her picture."

The women chuckled, and Ann continued. "Another moment caught on film that made the cover was Mr. B. himself, falling off the stage."

"What!" Rachel shouted, putting her hand to her mouth.

Ann grinned and rolled her eyes heavenward. "Oh, yeah. Four years ago, first rehearsal of the season, he's acting like the cool Mr. B., and he borrows one of the boys' skateboards. The details after that get a bit fuzzy. It seems every year his drama team has at least one episode where something happens and suddenly everyone present develops a case of pubescent short-term memory loss. Now, of course, having been a member of that team, you probably can't recall any of those episodes, correct?"

There was an awkward grin from Rachel, making it clear she'd neither confirm nor deny being privy to, or having knowledge of, such activities during her years with the team. "Did he roll right off the end of the stage?"

"No." Ann shook her head, trying her best not to laugh. "The photo shows him, the skateboard, and a large beach umbrella soaring into the air just left of center stage."

The urge to laugh got the better of her. "It's a great picture—skateboard flying past his head, the umbrella is underneath him, and he has this look on his face of, 'Lord, please let me die, because if this doesn't kill me, my wife will...' And I wanted to, believe me. I can't begin to tell you how mad I was. I mean, to do something that stupid in front of...what, fifty, sixty kids. I couldn't believe how irresponsible. As you can tell, it still irritates me. The album's in his office. I'll grab it before we leave."

Rachel somehow found it easy to imagine the scene. After all, Mr. B. had always been quite the character, the teacher everyone wanted to hang out with, a man who genuinely cared about his students, took pride in his department, and loved the Lord—all in all, not a bad role model. However, there was a mischievous side to the man also, playful, a little crazy, and he often considered himself just one of the boys. So yes, it was very easy for Rachel to imagine the scene, and it made her giggle out loud.

"I don't mean to laugh. It's just I can see it happening. Obviously God didn't let him die, and you didn't kill him...well, yet anyway, so I assume he was okay?"

"Oh, he would've been if he'd landed on his head, but apparently he landed on his feet, breaking two bones in his left ankle. The doctors patched him up with metal plates and a couple of screws and told him to stay off it. Yeah, you can imagine how well that worked out. He returned to class three days after surgery and for the next six months hobbled around on crutches, walking casts, and eventually a cane. When the doctor and physical therapists finally released him, he was so thrilled he took me dancing that night. I made him promise never to get on a skateboard again. By the way, you know who just happened to drop by the day of the accident and take that picture?"

A slow-moving grin appeared on Rachel's face. "Chris?"

"Chris Peterson!"

"Chris must like to take a lot of pictures," Michael remarked, walking back into the room.

"He loves taking pictures. My neighbor Trudy calls him the memory maker because he's always running around taking pictures of everything. If you turn the page, you'll see another picture Chris took."

Michael turned the page, and even from where Ann sat, she could feel Rachel's heart drop.

"That's you and daddy at a piano? Ooooh, he's kissing your cheek. K-I-S-S-I-N-G," Michael crooned teasingly.

Rachel collected herself enough to calmly say, "He was playing a song for me and singing in my ear because of all the noise around us."

Glancing at the picture again, Michael shook his head. "Nope! That's a kiss. K-I-S-S-I-N...Oh, and look, look there, way in the back. That's Aunt Peg running toward you guys."

"That explains all the noise," Ann joked.

Michael was caught between surprise and amusement by the woman's remark until his first small chuckle allowed a cascade of laughter to follow, and a second look at the photo only increased his laughter more.

Rachel had taken a moment to stare out the window in hopes of steadying herself. Breathing deeply, she whispered to Ann, "Not as ready as I thought for this…" And without further pause, she focused her attention back on Michael. "That's your Aunt Peg, all right. And that girl running next to her is Kathy Taylor. You can bet they're not running to see me, but Chris, the guy they both had a huge crush on."

"They both liked the same guy?"

"All the girls had a crush on Chris," Ann said.

Michael thought for a moment. "I bet Daddy was glad you weren't like all the girls, huh?"

Rachel smiled. Her gaze moved to Ann and then to the window once again. A light breeze caused small evergreens along the drive to wave softly. A young boy and girl rode new bicycles across the dormant winter grass, followed closely by Mom and Dad, who struggled to keep pace. Rachel wiped away the small pools of tears that momentarily blurred her vision, and though it was hard, pointed to the photo and said, "That was taken just a week before Daddy left for Irvine. See that sweater he's wearing? I gave it to him for Christmas."

For a moment Ann thought looking through the album might be a mistake. But then again, last night on the phone, Rachel had asked if she had any old pictures of Mike. Ann remained quiet, remembering the details of their late-night conversation.

"I know we do, and Jim probably knows right where they are," Ann had told her. "Tell you what. After New Year's, we'll have you out for dinner. It'll be fun to sit and go through them together."

A minute later she remembered the albums in Jim's office but chose not to say anything, instead quietly listening as Rachel spoke of school memories, the old crowd, and whatever happened to…It was during that part of their conversation, gently opening the glass doors to the tiered patio, Peggy twice checked on her big sister, bringing a hot cup of tea and then returning a short time later to drape her with a large quilt from the den. A whispered good night, and Peg retired to the warm comfort of her bedroom.

Rachel and Ann continued talking for another thirty minutes, neither wanting their evening to end but knowing that inevitably, goodbyes were drawing near. Finishing her last sip of wine, Ann's voice softened with the breath of clandestine mischief.

"I have this great idea…" It only took one sentence for Rachel to silently disagree with its greatness, yet as the conversation went on, she felt a twinge of excitement, which she quickly buried under layer upon layer of flimsy excuses, which Ann was equally quick to point out was okay so long as you didn't hide under them forever.

Pulling the heavy quilt tight around her body, leaving only her eyes exposed, Rachel struggled for a definitive yes or no. Finally, the conversation at a standstill, Ann declared flatly, "Okay, then, I'll see you in the morning?"

Anxious seconds passed with uneasy silence. Tensely, Rachel's body constricted in the big wicker chair. Her knees folded to her chest, her frame becoming small. The quilt covered her entire head, and from her cocoon came a short burst of nervous giggles followed by a long, soft groan, "Ah… I'm not so sure it's a great idea, Ann."

The young woman heard no response, so again she pulled the quilt tighter. "But…" She sighed heavily. "Oh, what the hell. We'll see you tomorrow at nine."

Now, Ann sat watching her friend digest memories and emotions of long-ago love, transforming them into stories of once upon a time her five-year-old could understand. But soon she noticed something else, something wonderfully beautiful: Michael's amazement with the photos and stories had dried his mother's eyes, placed laughter on her lips, and filled her heart with joy. Each new page, regardless of its content, brought questions from the boy. But there were two photos in particular that perked his interest far more than the rest. The first was of sixteen-year-old Bailey Peterson sitting atop a grand piano as part of what his mother remembered was a dress rehearsal. *She's the most beautiful girl I've ever seen*, the boy thought, enthralled by her thespian mystique. But then he remembered the photo of his mom, and without hesitation, forgoing the need to return to the front of the album for comparison, he decided Bailey would have to settle for being the second-most beautiful girl he'd ever seen. And like all proper young gentlemen, he was instinctively aware there'd be no need to speak of the matter to anyone, especially his mother. No, he was content to merely sit, be silent, and turn the page. And it would have worked but for one last glance to the nearly angelic Miss Peterson smiling up at him from atop that piano. Drained was his mental fortitude. Instantly his hands became damp and clammy, and his mouth felt as if he'd just chewed all the stuffing out of Pooh Bear. Without a word he ran to the water fountain down the hall, taking six big swallows before running back.

"Are you okay?" His mother said, laughing.

"I'm better than okay. You know why?" He beamed, a little out of breath.

Rachel's mouth twisted into an odd little smirk. These were the exact words his father would use to misdirect an unwanted inquiry.

"Because you're my mom. And you're so beautiful. Really! Really, Mom, you are."

"Uh huh…" she said suspiciously. "You either want something, or something's up."

"Nope, nope, nope. Nothing's up here." He smiled, looking more toward Ann than his mom. Then, acting as if he were pushing up his sleeves, he boomed, "See? Nothin' up my sleeve."

His antics caused Ann to laugh openly. Rachel, on the other hand, just smiled and shook her head. Could such nonsense be hereditary? she wondered. Surely he couldn't remember his father doing such things, even though he had done them all the time. But still, to repeat it word for word like that.

Knowing she was reading too much into it, she simply pointed to the album. "Continue."

Michael felt confident she would never know how taken he was by the photo of Bailey, and just to be sure, he wouldn't even look at it again. Smugly he turned the page with a grin of personal satisfaction. The laminated pages made slight squeaking noises, as if to offer up their own haughty laughter, because there on the next page, two photographs smiled up at him, both of Bailey Peterson. Instantly he coughed and swallowed hard in an attempt to clear the imaginary Pooh stuffing from his mouth.

Four pages later he came across the second photo. The image was not of Bailey or his mom and dad or any of the people Mrs. B. referred to as "the old crowd." For that matter, there were no people in it at all, but merely a deserted stretch of sandy beach with two vacant lounge chairs. Lying in the sand between them were two empty bottles, one Orange Crush, the other Dr. Pepper. Pressed into the wet sand were two sets of footprints disappearing into the white foam of the surf. Superimposed at the bottom of the photo were the words "California Dreamin'."

Rachel's phone rang. Recognizing the number, she stood and excused herself to the hallway. Michael's gaze followed her only briefly, then fell back to the intriguing scene. There were two things in the photograph he recognized immediately: first the bottle of Orange Crush, his and his mother's favorite soft drink. The other was the two words at the very bottom. They were exactly like the words on the cover of one of his mom's special CDs.

"Mrs. B., what's that say?"

"It says, 'California Dreamin'…"

"Yeah, that's right. I kind of knew it, but sort of not. But I know the song.

Mom sings it around the house sometimes, and you know what? Sometimes I don't think she even knows she's singing it. She does that a lot. Guess it's 'cause she's always singing something. But when she sings that song, it's really pretty. You should have her sing it for you."

"She did back when she was a student here. And she caused quite a stir."

Ann turned the page to show a series of ten photos covering two pages, taken during Rachel's performance. "Wow…" Michael said, pointing to one of the shots on the second page. "See there, Mrs. B. . . . now there she looks a-scared."

After answering two or three questions regarding the chaos that erupted onstage during Rachel's performance, Ann decided any further discussion or explanation should come from his mom. And as timing is everything, she was just walking back into the room.

"Hey, kid, Mark and Cassie said hi, JJ got a dog for Christmas, and CeCe wants to know where her postcards are. I told 'em you'd call next week."

She peered at Ann. "I'll miss Cass a lot. She's been a great friend, the best assistant ever, and what with me moving back here, I thought it would be an easy transition for her take over as the new worship leader. That's been her desire for a long time, and she's ready musically and spiritually. She loves the Lord and the team, and the congregation loves her to pieces. And yet she has all these fears. Really, she calls me a couple times a week to get a little reassurance."

"I think we all need that at times." Ann smiled.

Rachel only half grinned, saying, "Just remember that when I call you crying, I don't know if I'm doing the right thing, made the right move, or maybe I should've just stayed in SoCal?"

Her grin disappeared completely, leaving in its wake the apprehensive gape of a woman staring up a mountain of tentative possibilities from a pit of alarming certainties, and it was frightening. Rachel felt it, Ann saw it, and Michael turned another page. But again she caught herself staring out the window. The small evergreens along the drive continued to wave. There were no signs of the boy and girl on their new bikes, but on the far side of the big open field, resting on a wrought-iron bench, bicycles lying in the dormant winter grass, sat the mom and dad holding hands in the warmth of the morning sunlight. Ann touched Rachel's hand, not as if to ask, are you all right? but to say, I'm here.

Reassurance, Rachel thought, lightly squeezing Ann's hand in return. Tender comfort spread from this touch, traveling rapidly to the heart and mind of both women, leaving a notion of security one needed to give, one needed to receive. But in an instant, the lines of giving and receiving were blurred by the circular bonds of friendship. Ann felt it; Rachel saw it, and Michael turned yet another page.

"Hey, you were supposed to wait for me. Turn back to where we were. I'd like to see these too, you know."

"Oh yeah!" Michael said, quickly turning back a few pages. "You can tell me about when you sang 'California Dreamin' and what you did to cause all this."

She looked at the pages containing the photographs. "And just what makes you think I caused that?"

Without taking his eyes from her gaze, he said, "Mrs. B. said you caused a stir…isn't that a stir?"

※

With each new page there still came emotions, deep-rooted memories, and fresh heartaches for Rachel. Of course there were hidden tears, but they only made the laughter richer, the hugs warmer, and her son's smiles even more precious. And like so many times in the past, there to support her was Mrs. B.

Rachel thought about that for a moment and imagined every former student visiting this campus. This office would undoubtedly address her by the moniker she'd always carried—Mrs. B. A quick look around told you that was whose office you were in. It was on the door, the nameplate on the desk, and even in bold print in the school yearbook. And more than likely, it would continue to inadvertently stumble from Rachel's lips a few more times before they left the building and she had the opportunity of getting to know her as Ann Brooks her friend.

Somewhere in the second album, she realized she'd begun to enjoy this time with her son, her friend, and the place where it all began. It was midway through the third album she asked if they would mind if she went for a walk alone, assuring them she'd be back in just a bit. Oddly enough, the assurance wasn't needed. Michael felt very content hanging out with Mrs. B., and the feeling was definitely mutual.

"Here's my passcode. It's the master for all the locks. Just double-check 'em when you leave. And your little red key—it still opens the practice rooms from the outside, but you can no longer enter the hallway without the passcode."

Ann walked around and hugged Rachel before taking a seat next to Michael. "Go, take your time, enjoy the memories. We'll be here when you get back."

Rachel hugged her friend and kissed her son, then began walking the empty hallways, replaying scenes and faces, sights and sounds of times distant yet so incredibly present. The hallways led into classrooms and eventually to the lunchroom down through the east wing, ending at the double doors of the auditorium. Hesitantly she punched the code into the keypad. As she pushed against the doors, they opened more easily than she remembered. The lobby remained decorated from this year's Christmas production, but for a brief instant, the room transformed, filling with images of long-ago posters featuring Bailey Peterson and Steve Nelson in the original production of…

Her eye caught the cast photo mounted on a small easel sitting atop a long table in the center of the room, garnished with programs fanned into small stacks on a red-and-white tablecloth. How well she remembered Bailey and Steve insisting she be included in the photo of featured performers, Steve then pulling her into the frame beside him, whispering something in her ear that made her blush.

She turned, and in an instant it was gone. The new posters hung about the room. New cast members filled the frame, and the warm breath of Steve Nelson's soft whisper lingered as a sweet memory, bringing her to blush even now. "You were a naughty boy, Mr. Nelson, a naughty, naughty boy."

Hoping her levity would help lighten the next step of her journey, she swung open the inner doors and stepped inside the great auditorium. Stopping momentarily at the top of the aisle, she wondered if she really wanted to take this walk. But first she needed to muster the courage to face why she needed to take it. Frozen in place, her focus was drawn to the stage. As in the past, and in keeping with theater superstition the world over, "never leave a stage dark," a "ghost light" declared its presence. This single bulb housed in a sturdy iron cage atop what resembled an ornately decorated mic stand broadcast little illumination beyond its center-stage position. And now, as back then, a second ghost light adorned the entire stage in a soft evening-blue hue, cast from a single lamp high in the overhead grid. Emitting the same enticing beauty that made her fall in love with this stage as a fearful young girl, it almost seemed as though nothing had changed. Nothing at all. So it came as no surprise to feel a cool draft, perhaps the past, greeting, embracing, stroking her arms with chilled hands that moved up her back, caressing, moving her hair and releasing a momentary shudder she barely noticed.

Her focus remained unbroken. But it was not the ghost light, nor the beautiful hue it bathed in that summoned her to come close. No! The stage remained silent, motionless. It was her own inner voice whispering all the reasons why she must once again be in this room, on this stage, drenched not only in its beautiful light but in all of her treasured memories. She began to walk. One step, then a second and a third. With every few steps, her pace slightly quickened. Rows of empty seats began to gradually stream past. The short, muted echo of footfalls on carpet grew louder, quicker, unwavering. And then…silence.

Motionless, she stood at the end of the aisle looking up at the dimly lit stage. Her heart was racing, not due to the long expanse she'd just run, but because of the short distance that now lay before her. There, in the breadth of a few yards, the vast separation between past and present narrowed quickly, suffocating today with yesterdays. This was something she'd experienced many times since Michael's death. Places they had shared, walked through together, stood as a couple, united as one, lovebirds forever, a husband, a wife, a father and a mother, a family in Christ…a widow, a son, a memory. Had she stood here before? Only every morning as she opened her eyes to see his empty pillow. Only in every room of the house, every corner of the yard, at church, the school, the grocery store, the park—yes, she had stood here many, many times before, but she knew it was because of that that she took this walk this morning.

Slowly moving with no resounding footfalls at all, she ascended the stairs at the side of the stage, taking even slower the last four steps. On the stage, scenery frozen in place seemed to beckon for lights, action, and applause. But still there was only empty silence broken by occasional footsteps as she moved over the old hardwood floor and about the props.

There's an eerie feeling wandering through a darkened set. The imagination attempts to fill the space with expected realities, and when none are found, the mind allows the unwelcome formation of visions, apparitions, or, at the very least, a sortie of questions as to what lingers deep within the shadows. But she'd walked this empty stage too many times to be swayed by its fictionalized places and make-believe worlds. The only thing lingering in these shadows were the memories of a young girl's first love. *Oh, but wait*, she thought, pausing to take in the area once again. *That's not altogether true now is it. Memories of love? Yes! Beautiful memories every one…but wait, that's not exactly true either*, she thought sadly.

"So why have I come?" she asked in her best stage voice of the seats at the back of the house. She smiled to think how proud Mr. B. would be if he could hear her project like that. But her smile faded swiftly, replaced by an air of sadness. But that, too, didn't remain. Quietly she spoke, not allowing even the front row the pleasure of her voice. This conversation was not for the house, nor was it for the phantom actors halting their performance in the softness of the ghost light to give their attention. No, this conversation was intentionally private.

"I've come to talk," she announced, her voice modulating slightly as though taking command of the stage. "Right here! Right on this exact spot is where we were introduced. It's also the first place you held my hand, made me laugh, asked me out, and told me to grow up. Yep, a lot of firsts on this spot."

She took long strides, half expecting the spotlight to follow her across the stage, talking as she went. "Oh, but wait a second. Let me show you this other spot. After all, it's where you got us in so much trouble with Mr. B., I wanted to drop out of the play." She stopped, and her voice mellowed. "I wonder if he ever told Ann…I'll have to ask her."

Her intensity resumed as if unbroken. "I'll just bet I've mentioned this before, but just in case I haven't, that was the first time I ever had detention. Notice I said first time, Mike Donahue! But I can assure you it wasn't my last. Oh, I never mentioned that before. Hmmm," she sneered, shrugging. "And that brings us over here."

She pivoted sharply on her heel and made her way to one of the narrow side curtains. "Our first argument," she snapped. "Okay, that's not fair. You kissed me behind it a lot more than we argued. Oh, and your kisses," she purred. "They always made me feel…"

For the next few minutes, she walked quietly around the set, speaking softly to herself about love, kisses, and the times they'd shared, occasionally pausing to look out over the empty seats of the auditorium. "I don't know why, but after you left, I wanted to believe I'd look up and see you sitting out there during a performance." Her body turned slowly to the left, even taking a few steps before her eyes let go of the vacant seats. But she knew it was not the emptiness that kept her head from turning. It was where she was to go next that stalled her gaze. Hiding behind closed lids, peeking out only after her head bowed and refused to raise, her eyes moved across the heavily worn floor to rest on the glossy black Steinway before her. Her knees felt weak, but surprisingly, she found herself smiling, rushing to touch the keys, to sit on the bench and place a foot on the gold pedals. With great force she struck a single chord. Thunderously it rang from the stage, filling every corner of the massive room. She didn't remove her hands from the keys or lift the pressure from the pedal. She sat motionless, virtually breathless, listening as the deep, rich tones gradually, almost leisurely began to diminish, fleeing through the faint light into the darkened shadows of the building itself. After a number of minutes, when the notes could no longer be heard, the vibration of each string undetected, she gently released her touch.

"And this piano?" she softly murmured into the stillness of the room. Lifting her foot from the pedal, she slammed the heavy wooden cover over the keys with a loud clap that splintered the silence, filling the shadows with a sharp, resounding pulse that dissipated quickly in their darkness.

"Well, I can't even talk about this piano," she huffed, spinning around to turn her back to it. Standing she paused for almost a full minute before storming halfway across the stage, only to turn back abruptly. "No, wait. Yes, I can."

As she took a few steps toward the great instrument, her voice began to modulate not in volume, but strength.

"Damn you, Michael Donahue!" she cried out. "You sang to me, wrote songs for me, and you see this bench," she snarled, pushing it with her foot. "This beautiful bench? This bench is where you made love to me with words and melodies about dreams and dreamers that didn't just arouse my naïve adolescent sentimentalities. They truly melted my heart."

Suddenly aware of tears stinging her eyes, she inhaled a stuttered breath of denial. There would be no sobbing, no breakdown, no tantrum, and no anger—okay, maybe just a little anger, she decided. And a small tantrum wouldn't be out of line either. But definitely no…

Quickly making her way backstage, she paused, noticing the backdrop was the same one it had been back then, just much nicer than she remembered. Or then again, maybe it wasn't the same at all, now that she looked at it. Stepping behind a dividing curtain, she walked past a large electrical panel with long wooden levers that controlled the overhead stage lighting.

"There," she said, pointing to an area draped in thick black shadows. "And there…over there, up there, and right down there, in that little hidden stairwell nobody ever uses. Yeah! There. How many times did you hold me, express to me so affectionately your feelings…your love. Yes, you were the first to say the word, to call it love, remember? Oh, how incredibly happy I was, and how incredibly frightened. I was so afraid you'd leave me, that I'd just come to school one day and you'd be gone and I'd never see you again. And when I told you that, you held me, you held me so tight I thought I'd just melt into you. You spoke to my heart in whispers that for me would last forever. You kissed my lips and wiped the tears from my cheeks. And then…and then you made me fall in love with you. You kissed the tip of your finger and carefully placed it over my heart, saying 'Replace the hurt with kisses form the heart.'

"Okay, let's not talk…about…th…"The words struggled to find breath, dissolving on her lips as they waited to be spoken. A few minutes marched by, returning her composure as they passed. "That was a tough one. Oh, but wait. I have an even better one for you, Mike Donahue."

Hurriedly she continued her walk backstage, passing the cueing desk, rigging, numerous dollies, trolleys, tables, and crates, until finally reaching the back wall, where, resting in small heaps, were numerous sets of productions past and future. Recognizing odds and ends, lamps, tables, and chairs that had been painted and repainted and painted again with each passing class brought a welcome wave of pleasant nostalgia. At the end of this long, cluttered wall, a single doorway opened to a descending flight of stairs leading to a number of rooms ranging greatly in size on either side of the narrow hallway. To the left, girls' dressing rooms; to the right, boys', and then another seven rooms began about three-quarters of the way down the hall. Most were small, ten by ten; two, however, measured twenty by twenty. Both inner and outer walls were fabricated sections of alternating glass and metal, permanently set at slight angles with forest-green baffles, allowing for slightly more privacy. Each room had a solid wood door from the hallway, but three also had outer doors that opened to a grassy area known as The Slope. Stenciled above each door were the words Practice Room, followed by a letter from A to G. At the end of the hallway were two metal doors with tall rectangular windows; above them a large brass sign: Band Room.

Walking steadily past the dressing rooms, she continued down the hall, never rushing, never slowing, her shoes echoing softly the measured steps of the long, empty passageway. Keeping tempo with her stride, she'd convey a story in one or two sentences regarding each room, accompanied by a rush of laughter, sarcasm, disdain, or love. How easy it would be to dwell on the love; after all, these were the rooms where their relationship developed from high school crush to grown-up passions in almost no time at all. Not as overzealous teenagers exploring half-baked ideas of sexuality, though the discussion and opportunity presented itself on more than a few occasions; but these rooms, and one in particular, heard the details of their dreams, their plans, their desires and their love. It was where she, in a moment of recklessness, first whispered, "I love you too."

Entering the last practice room, she brushed her hand over the worn keys of a familiar friend. "Did you miss me?" she asked affectionately. It was on this very piano, an old Wurlitzer upright, she'd taken her first lesson.

Hour after hour, week after week, practice after practice, listening to the strings sing her progress, her triumphs, her struggles, and her many, many failures. From "Twinkle, Twinkle, Little Star" to Beethoven's "Für Elise," she grew to understand that practice does not always make perfect, that talent must be nurtured through desire for it to flourish.

Reading music came easy; some even said she was gifted. But taking the notes from paper to fingers had remained challenging, making her piano teacher, Irene Thompson, almost give up sometimes, insisting she stick to singing and playing the guitar for the worship team. But her love for the instrument continued, and soon she was sneaking into the practice rooms whenever she could. But then, one afternoon, her sophomore year, Mr. B. heard her struggling. And after listening for only a few minutes, he walked in the room and took her music book away, saying she could have it back as soon as she wrote him a song. Chords and a melody only—no words. He would give the book back when she was done. And without saying much else, he walked out with the book in hand. She went to his office nine days later and nervously played the simple song she'd written. But he didn't return her book, instead handing her a small textbook entitled *Coloring Music with Theory*.

"It's a good song, but it's not finished. Read the first chapter, and have your rewrite on my desk in a week," he told her. So she did. Moving through four chapters in eight weeks and continuing to enrich her simple song was beyond amazing to her. Frustrating was that her dexterity had improved only slightly, leaving the mechanics of the piece awkward in her hands, a trait that would not improve for many months. Yet she continued. On the twelfth week, with the fifth and final chapter complete, she nervously entered Mr. B.'s office prepared to perform the final rewrite. Speaking from his desk, he told her, "Leave your music on the piano and take a seat outside. I'll come get you when I've finished."

Out in the hallway she watched the second hand sweep the face of the big clock at the end of the hall. The first four minutes produced no sound from the other side of the door. Silence also prevailed through minutes five, six, and seven. Then suddenly there it was, spilling out to drift through the hallway. No longer just her piece of music, but a piece of her soul, painted with shades of melodic tones that maybe didn't dance exactly through chordal hues and overtones as the book described, but it was a fair interpretation of how she heard her simple little song. Two boys she recognized as seniors walked by. Stopping to listen, one asked, "Is that yours?"

She was so nervous she could only nod her head confirming it was.

The boy smiled. "Nice!"

The other added, "You're in!"

She smiled back, having no idea what he was talking about, and it would be another fourteen minutes and fifty-five seconds before she found out.

An advanced placement course, Mr. B.'s composition and theory class was by audition only before a panel consisting of Miss DeLaria, who taught music interpretation and performance dance; Mr. Mercer, orchestra and advanced choir; and Mr. B. himself. The auditions were held in mid-August, which gave her seven months to continue studying, he explained, handing her another book, *Vocal Essentials, Methods, and Scales*. Its weight alone was intimidating. But like always, Mr. B. knew the best way for her to beat intimidation was by adding sheer panic.

"This'll take you a while to get through," he said. "At the end of each chapter are scales and exercises. They're not to be performed until you fully comprehend the methods and techniques described in the chapter. Anyone can sing the notes. It's how the notes are sung that separates one singer from another. I've arranged for Maddie Doyle to be your vocal coach. Maddie's my student aid this year, so track her down and work out a schedule—today if possible. I'll get together with Mrs. B. this afternoon and take care of all the red tape. I'll have you transferred from Fundamentals of Worship to Performance Arts. That way this becomes extra credit, and you won't have to pretend you're awake in Filbert's class anymore. Meet me back here two weeks from today. Be warmed up and prepared to perform the first exercises a cappella, and write an original melody for piano based on the chapter."

He could tell by her face that sheer panic, trumped intimidation every time. Yet there was a smile, a clear indication his challenge had been accepted. As she stood to leave, he opened the desk drawer. "I promised I'd return this when the song was done," he said, handing back her old songbook. "And it was done very well, Miss Callahan."

That was a defining moment for the young girl. Her voice would become her main instrument, the piano a tool for writing, arranging, and accompaniment. Due to Maddie's diligence, Rachel completed the book in a little less than five months, allowing her ample time to prepare her audition. She was first choice across the board, even being selected one of three featured vocalist for next year's advanced choir. The following year brought another talented girl to Mr. B.'s attention, but unlike Rachel, she struggled to read music and had difficulty utilizing the methods she was being taught. She failed her audition miserably, keeping her out of Mr. B.'s composition and theory class, but she was allowed in the advanced choir with the provision that she show continuous improvement in reading skills and vocal methods. It was Rachel who came to Bailey's rescue. Understanding that Bailey, like a lot of singers, had learned music by listening, Rachel decided that would be the best way for her to learn how to read it also. Placing the music in front of her, she'd say, "Bailey, I want to hear what this sounds like."

It still took a lot of work from both girls. But at midterm assembly, Bailey received an excellence award, and to Rachel's surprise and utter embarrassment, she, too, was called onstage and presented with an achievement award. A very proud Mr. B. posed with Bailey and Rachel for Chris Peterson to snap a photo.

❧

The old Wurlitzer spoke the same chord Rachel had asked of the Steinway earlier; its voice softer, its richness petite. Still, it filled the small room with magical beauty that filled Rachel's heart and lifted her soul. Her touch was no longer distressed but incredibly gentle and surprisingly tender, for this old piano had been her first true love. Its gorgeous tones now embraced her as if to ask, Where've you been? I've missed you too. Like old friends, the two spent a moment getting reacquainted, her hands caressing the keys more than actually playing the notes.

"Hey, listen to this." she said aloud. And from the soundboard, notes resonated with perfect structure and technique.

"Surprised? I know. Chopin—bet you didn't see that comin', did ya?"

Suddenly the song changed to a little Scott Joplin ragtime. "Now I'm just playing with ya—tickling your ivories, as they say." Rachel laughed. "Okay, you'll like this one, I promise." And once again, delicate was her touch on the old keys; the notes carried softly in the air.

"Remember? He told me this would be our song. You heard him; you heard everything. Even when we didn't speak at all...you heard." She closed her eyes and continued to play.

Not wishing to sing the words, she began humming along with the melody, stopping just after the chorus. "He wrote that for me—an expression of his love, he said. And then..." The beautiful arpeggios crashed into silence.

"He dumped me."

Minor chords formed a melodramatic dirge, her hands playing what her heart felt, the sad tones falling heavy around her.

"He thought some time away would be good for both of us. That maybe we were allowing things to move along too quickly. School would be too intense and demanding for him. And then he said I still needed to figure out what my passion was and how I planned to pursue it. I was under the impression I had, and that's what I was doing. When I reminded him I wanted to be a singer, maybe do theater work, he said, 'It's great for a high school girl to have dreams, but what happens after you graduate?' He acted like this was the first time we'd talked about any of this, and he didn't want to talk about it any further. His mind was made up. I needed to 'set obtainable goals' for myself. Those were his exact words. But in the very next sentence, he said he also believed we were in love and that maybe someday, once school was behind us, our careers on track and our lives calmed down, we'd get married, start a family, and live happily ever after. And then he left... oh, I don't mean he left me; he just walked out to the parking lot and drove home. He called me later that night—not to apologize, of course, but to let me know that I was acting like an immature little high school girl who... okay now, say it with me: 'needed to grow up and set obtainable goals.'

"I just remember crying and telling him we needed to talk before he left for Irvine. I knew the chapel would be empty the following morning. We could meet there around nine o'clock. To be honest, I don't know if he agreed or not, but when I saw his car in the parking lot, I made sure I was there long before nine. Not that it mattered, because from the doorway of the chapel, I watched him tell everybody goodbye. He saw me. He even blew me a kiss, and then he left. And this time…I mean he left me."

The piano gasped an inharmonious response. Rachel picked up the tempo slightly, her hands rapidly interpreting the change in mood.

"I was furious, crushed. I cried for a week, not talking to anyone. I just wanted to curl up under the covers and die. But before I knew it, a week had gone by, and then two, and three, then four. Eventually the pain began to lessen, but I knew I still…" She lifted her hands in silence. "You know what? That's not true!"

Sound swept through the room as her fingers moved blindly across the keys. "I didn't still love him. I made up my mind I didn't want to ever see him again. I kept asking myself how he could leave without even saying goodbye. And that just made the hurt even worse. His mom wouldn't give me his address or anything. She told me to quit chasing after her son and slammed the door in my face. There're no words to describe the pain. I know that's cliché, but it's so true. And I think the less you understand something, the more it hurts. And there was nothing about our breakup I understood. And yet I felt the whole thing was somehow my fault."

The music slowed to a soft jazz, giving her old friend time to comfort her with tones of resounding love that danced upon her skin. And after almost a full minute, she asked, "And you know who came to my rescue? Who pulled me out of my stupor?" The tempo picked up again, leading into a syncopated riff before coming to a stop. "Mrs. B., that's who!"

The soft jazz resumed, continuing a somewhat up-tempo mode. "Yep. Out of the blue, she showed up at my house one Saturday morning about eight o'clock. No phone call, no nothing. All she said was that she had an errand to run and would like for me to join her. No more explanation than that. And come on—you know Mrs. B.; she can be pretty damn intimidating. I mean really sweet, but, well, you know.

"The woman takes me for a pedicure. Yeah, a pedicure! I thought that was only for movie stars and the like. And that was exactly how she made me feel—like a movie star. She didn't build me up with a bunch of accolades or force me to listen to what she thought I should be doing. She just showed me the sun was still shining and life was filled with fun new adventures if I wanted them. Next, she took me to Anthony's Homeport for lunch… swank-eey," Rachel embellished.

"For our appetizer she ordered a half dozen oysters on the half shell. Thought I was going to puke just looking at those slimy little snot balls. But after a pep talk, I downed my first raw oyster. Neither of us said much for the next minute or so. I think we were waiting to see if that little sucker was going to try and make an escape, if you know what I mean. I just sat staring at that big ol' plate between us, and then I picked up another and said, 'Let the adventure begin, Mrs. B.'

"But it really didn't. Oh, maybe a little, but mainly I concentrated on my senior performance programs. I'm sure you remember that. But that was when I also realized I needed a social life, which was somewhat surprising, since I'd never had much of one before. Oh sure, I'd hang out with friends and even had a crush on one, but nothing serious. I was too shy for that kind of stuff. But I needed to be around people, friends. It really helped to put things behind me.

"I started getting out of the house more. I got back into youth group, even went to a few school basketball games. It was fun. Sometimes maybe even too much fun, I think. I felt my life was coming together in ways I'd prayed for since I was thirteen. I was at the top of the performance arts class, the district chose me to sing the national anthem at a Mariners game, Bailey and I performed three songs at the national Youth for Christ concert down in Portland, and suddenly I'd developed an insatiable appetite for raw oysters. And then one night…"

The music stopped abruptly, "The phone rang."

A familiar melody embraced her memory. "You know the first thing he said to me?" And then her words rose to meet the music in perfect synchronicity as she sang, "I love you…for sentimental reasons…"

Slow, sweet chords immersed under the melody of the old Nat King Cole standard. "That's right. He tells me, 'I love you and I miss you so much.'"

Continuing to play, she laughed and giggled as though having a light conversation with an old friend, which was exactly what she was doing.

"I honestly believed I was over him. And just between you and me…I was. Maybe I was still angry; I don't know. But it took a lot more phone calls before I realized this was an answer to prayer. For the next three weeks, every other night, right at ten o'clock, he'd call. We'd only talk for ten minutes because he couldn't afford extra minutes on his plan. But those ten minutes would get me through the next forty-seven hours and fifty minutes.

"We never made plans. Nothing specific, anyway. No dates were ever set, no timelines discussed. Just that we missed each other, and maybe someday we'd get together again. Once, he talked about marriage. Where we'd live, the house, the furniture, the pets, the kids—lots of kids. And when he insisted we had to have a pool, I looked out my kitchen window and watched yet another Seattle rainstorm pour off the patio awning. From that point on, I imagined our house would be in Southern California. But again, no plans were made.

"That night I went to bed thinking about living in California, which wasn't such a bad idea at all, since that was where a lot of people from school were headed. Chris Peterson had been accepted at Biola, the navy wanted Bobby Timmons to report to San Diego, and Jeff Bryant received an athletic scholarship at Stanford. And what about my best friend, Bailey Peterson? you ask. The following year, she was headed to Westmont, in Santa Barbara. It was our own little California invasion."

For just a moment, two melodies intertwined, and she began to sing, slowly, softly, "I'd be safe and warm…If I was in LA…California dreamin'…"

The gentle melody continued as she spoke. "By that time, the senior class had already made 'California Dreamin' their rally song. So Mr. B. asked if I wanted to sing it with the stage band at the end-of-year assembly. He also talked Mr. Jason into letting his class put together a slide show of beach scenes to play on the screen behind us. As we started singing, the coolest thing happened. Nobody planned it…it just happened. The seniors in the audience began standing up and singing right along with us. Pretty soon they were walking onto the stage, singing and hugging. Some of us…well, some of them…were even crying. It was really an emotional moment. And a little scary, too, I found out."

She resolved the melody, anxiously glanced at her watch, and stood up.

"I need to get going." And with a touch of sadness in her voice, she leaned over the bench and began to play 'I'm so glad we've had this time together…' Yeah, yeah, yeah, I know. I don't sound anything like Carol Burnett. I'll stop back by soon. I still have a lot to tell you, and besides, I've missed you. But right now I need to get back to Mrs. B. and my son. Oh yeah…" She laughed. "I have a little boy."

She pulled open the door, stepped partway into the hall, and then turned back around. "Yeah, I made it to California. And yes, I married Mike. That's my son's name—Michael."

She gazed lovingly at the old piano and thought, *You're the oldest friend I have; you've always been here for me.* "Thank you, dear friend. I promise I'll be back soon."

The room went dark. The door closed but quickly reopened, and light bathed the piano once again. Moving the bench out of her way, she grabbed the side of the piano and with great effort moved it out from the wall a little less than a foot before taking a moment to rest. Running her hand down the open-backed frame of the instrument, she realized it would need to be moved out a bit farther. It seemed harder this time, moving only a few inches with each lift and push. Catching her breath, she panted, "Have you gained weight?" But that brought her to think maybe someone had done work on her old friend. The thought carried with it an uncomfortable feeling that made her question out loud, "Did someone find it?" This seemed to give her the strength she needed to move the heavy upright in one burst of energy.

There was easily a decade of dust on the back and in the small open trough along the bottom. Still unable to get behind it, she could explore most of the narrow channel by sitting on the floor and extending her arm. A rush of anxiety made her flush when at first she didn't feel it.

"Someone did find it," she heard herself gasp softly.

Again her hand searched the dusty trough, but still it was not there. Repositioning, she ran her fingers along the inside of the channel, feeling nothing but layers of dust. Her anxiety rising, she stretched as far as she could…and then, her fingers touched something. *Yes*, she thought, *there's something there.* As she pressed her fingers deeper into the wooden channel, a small cloud of dust rose and settled. Instinctively she did it again, this time blowing the fine dust away. And there it was.

Sitting on the floor, her back against the wall, she began to laugh. There was no name on the envelope, just traces of dust and age, smudged with her fingerprints. But the note inside seemed not to have aged at all, the heartfelt words, triggering the same emotion they had long ago, once again made her cry…

A few minutes later, entering the hallway, she walked to the double doors of the band room but didn't enter, choosing instead to walk across the commons to the gymnasium. Inside, everything seemed smaller than she remembered, but she guessed most things do when you've been away so long. Standing at center court felt surreal, almost dreamlike. Looking along the bleachers made the hair on her arms stand up. Swallowing hard, rolling her shoulders to relax, she took one step forward, positioning herself directly on the wooden inlay of the school emblem.

"Oh say can you see, by the dawn's…"

Giggling, she scurried off to her seat, climbing the center aisle of the hardwood bleachers. "Row three…four…" Gradually the game began to fill the air behind her. The sound of a ball resonated as it bounced off the hardwood floor. "Five…six." Teams rushing down court, the squeak of rubber on wood as a player pivots sharply. "Seven." The smell of popcorn, people and play swirled about her. The stomping of feet vibrated the wooden structure. "Excuse me…pardon me," she said, moving cautiously to her seat. But no one was sitting. The crowd, on their feet, cheered loudly. On the floor, the varsity team was playing their rivals, Seattle Christian. It was their free throw. Number thirteen missed; Bobby Timmons stole the rebound and drove it past midcourt, passing to Scott Cuzio, to Chris Peterson, to Doug Huffman, who was going to take it in for the game-winning layup. But wait…the shot was nearly blocked…and right there in midair, Huffman tossed the ball to Peterson, who made the game-winning shot from the top of the key.

She heard herself cheer and didn't feel a bit silly swooning her way back down onto the court. "Hey, Doug. Good game!"

The empty room echoed her footfalls as she walked slowly past the front of the bleachers and then paused, closing her eyes for a moment, trying hard to remember Doug's smile. Gentle and warm, even alluring at times. His husky laugh always the loudest, his stories the funniest, and he was the only person Chris Peterson ever turned the pulpit over to. He loved motorcycles, rock 'n roll, playing drums, and witnessing for Christ. But there were two things she believed he loved even more: Armando's pizza and Bailey Peterson.

Keeping her eyes closed for another moment allowed his smile to spread to her. "Doug, you could always make me smile," she said, opening her eyes. "That's why Mike didn't like you."

Her smile broadened, her eyes twinkled. "But you didn't care. You just kept right on. I think you did it more to spite him than anything." And that too brought a smile to her face. "Whatever happened to you, Mr. Huffman? Last I heard, you left for Canada, started a church, a band, a family, and a wood-fired pizza parlor. I hope things went well, big guy."

Approaching the end of the bleachers, she turned and looked back across the floor. "Hey, Doug…I know you could've made that layup," she said, softly looking up at the basket. "You made her brother the hero on purpose. I want someone to love me like that someday—give up everything just to see me smile. Good game, Doug. Maybe I'll see you at Armando's later?"

Turning the corner, she could see the exit, but just like that night long ago, she stood at the end of the bleachers until she felt it was safe. Only then, ducking behind the lower-level seats, did she make her way through the narrow conduit to the opposite end of the old wooden structure. At one time Mike had called her a bleacher rat for scampering underneath them, but that was a while ago, and she didn't care anyway.

Slow-to-leave stragglers made their way to the exits, their mixed conversations passing her in a blend of revelry and gibberish. Peeking around a thick column, she could see him talking with Mr. B., Steve Nelson, and Dave Harris, the leader of the pep band. And for a brief second, she thought Mr. B. had spotted her. Stepping back farther behind the bleachers, she held her breath, as if perhaps that would help conceal her. Waiting to be confronted, her heart beat faster, and faster still when she found the courage to take a second peek just in time to see them disappear through the wide double doors at the far side of the court to the boys locker-room. Backing up against a hardwood brace, she waited. The room emptied out quickly, and at one point she, too, thought about walking out into the cold misty night and just driving home. But she wouldn't. If she were to be completely honest with herself…she'd wait however long it took.

"I thought you forgot about me."

"And I thought I saw you leave with everyone else."

"I promised I'd wait for you." She grinned.

Smiling, he replied sheepishly, "Do you always keep your promises?"

Her grin lingered, and her eyes sparkled. "You don't have to say anything. I made the bet; SC lost, and I'm where I said I'd be."

Helpless in her gaze, he stared deep into her sparkling green eyes. Softly he moved his hand over her cheek, brushing a lock of red hair from where it caressed. He smiled. Her lips parted slightly, and he thought for a second she would return his smile, but she did not. Instead, motionless, it was now she who stood helpless. His hand slid once more across her cheek until finding the nape of her neck, where tenderly he held her. At first his lips merely lay beside hers, as gentle as a whisper. Her fragrance soft, as if she'd run straight into his arms from a garden in bloom, carrying the many scents of summer with her. Pressing his lips against hers, holding her close, it was only then he realized she was trembling. Leaning back, resting again on the thick wooden brace, the rhythm of her heart beginning to slow; her lips now parted fully to reveal the once-timorous smile the boy had expected so many years ago. With it came a stillness; a hush. Ever so empty was the space around her; and ever so quite. Alone…opening her eyes, she was surprised to find they were filled with tears, but she quickly accepted it as the price of a return journey, if only in memory…to a most enchanted evening.

❦

"Mrs. B.? When my dad went to school here, did he write songs?"

"Your daddy was always writing songs."

"Did he write songs for my mommy?"

"I think he did. Yes."

"And for Jesus?"

"Yes, he wrote a lot of those."

"What about…for Bailey? Did he write songs for her?"

"I know she sang some of his songs…"

He sighed. "I bet they were pretty. Pretty girls sing really pretty, you know."

Rachel burst into the room. "So, Bailey, is it? Your first crush is gonna be on my best friend from high school? You know she's old, right? Same age as Aunt Peg. And she's married. And I can only imagine this guy must really be something. Bailey's never been won over easily; just ask Doug Huffman."

All Michael had heard was "Bailey…your first crush…" Everything after that had been muted by the heat of embarrassment. But wait! His mom wasn't even looking at him. Neither was Mrs. B. Quickly he surmised his mother had just been joking around. After all, there was no way she could possibly know it was true…or could she? he wondered.

"Oh yes—Darling Doug," Ann recalled. "Or what was the other name you girls used?"

Gasping, Rachel countered, "He was always just Doug to me."

Looking at Michael, Ann nodded. "That's true. Your mom wasn't like her…" She stopped just short of saying "sister," instead emphasizing the word. "*Friends*. And while all the girls were chasing after the boys, the boys just wanted to hang out with your mom."

Rachel shook her head, stating in a flat monotone voice, "Not true."

"Your mom was the cute little singer everyone thought was cool and mysterious."

"I was shy and dorky."

"The voice of the school…"

"That was Bailey. Is there a point to this?" Rachel exclaimed.

"Nope!" Ann replied, turning to wink at Michael. "It's just, before your mom and dad met, she was the girl everybody wanted to date."

"Again, not true. And again, Bailey!"

Mrs. B. wrinkled her nose and shook her head, making Michael laugh.

Then she brought her attention fully to Rachel. "As far as I know, Bailey only went out with Doug Huffman."

Her eyes widened. "That's it! I remember now. Buff-man; Darling Doug Buff-man. That's what they called him." Ann laughed.

Rachel shook her head. "I thought for sure they'd end up married. They were exclusive from ninth grade on."

"I thought they would too. They were such a cute couple," Ann said.

Looking at her son, Rachel nodded. "Those two were so cute and sweet, you could get a sugar rush just sitting next to 'em. The king and queen of everything there was—homecoming, prom, even the Halloween ball…oh, sorry—Harvest Dance." She leered at Ann and winked at her son. "They were the hot couple on campus, no doubt about it. And then Doug followed her off to college, and what did she do? Kicked him to the curb! Broke his little heart in a million pieces. He was so upset he jumped on his motorcycle and rode off into the snowy north country to live out the rest of his lonely life in an igloo."

Michael sat for a long moment staring at his mom. "You're lying, huh?"

"Yep!" Rachel teased. "Hey, what do ya say I treat everyone to pizza. I know this great place."

As they were leaving the office, Michael ran to the water fountain just as Rachel recognized a large photo on a table by the door. She picked it up and laughed. Ann, looking over her shoulder, also laughed. "I forgot all about that one, and it's one of my favorites of you."

The photo was cropped to show the heads of the three people. All wore heavy clown makeup, with Rachel in the center facing the lens, the camera captured her look of surprise and delight beautifully as the other two, one on each side with just their profiles showing, leaned in to kiss her on the cheeks.

Holding the frame with a sense of affection, Rachel asked, "Can you believe they put that in the year book?"

"It's a great picture," Ann said, picking up a small plastic tote. "Besides, I've never seen the three of you look more natural."

"Those two were the clowns. I was just an innocent dupe in the Chris and Mike show," Rachel said. It took a moment for her grin to show up completely, and with almost a purr in her voice, cheeks flushing slightly, she recalled, "Maybe innocent is not exactly the right word."

As the three of them walked down the long corridor to the parking lot, Ann thought she heard Rachel humming "Some Enchanted Evening…"

CHAPTER FOURTEEN

"Here you go Mr....," the driver called over his shoulder. "Garden Street."

The bus came to a stop with a series of lurches and squeaks, and the doors snapped open with a soft hiss. But his single passenger remained seated and with one hand waved the driver to continue on his route.

"Ah, mister, this is your stop. Garden Street," the driver urged with true concern. "Are you okay, man? I mean, you are right?"

Without making eye contact, the old man nodded and continued to stare out the side window. The young driver closed the doors, the engine revved, the wheels turned, and the chimes from the Old Clock Tower informed the city it was noon.

❖

Chris pulled his truck to the rear entrance of the sanctuary, where he, Lincoln, and Jim would attempt to move the heavy old walnut desk from his office onto the bed of the truck. Beth would assist from a safe distance by waving her princess wand.

"Can I go play now?" she asked, full of energy once the task was complete and boredom set in.

"Aunt Bailey will be here any minute, and she'll be really mad if you're all dirty. And you know, just maybe, after you get your picture taken, she'll take you for ice cream."

"I'll bring one back for you, too, Daddy."

"I'm afraid it'd melt all over your pretty dress before you got back here, sweetheart."

"No it won't. If it starts melting, I'll lick it. It won't get on my dress. Promise…"

❧

"I didn't think we'd be so busy this mornin', what with the holidays."

"I'm just glad you have some help. She working out?"

Rennie attached another order to the metal wheel. "I'd say so. She runs circles around me, and people seem to like her. Why?"

"Comin' up on thirty days, that's all."

"Your point?"

"I told her we'd talk about a raise after thirty days…"

"Dutch, honey, I gave her a raise and made her full-time weeks ago. She's happy, I'm happy, and you just need to stay back there and look pretty for mama."

"I thought I was the boss!"

Rennie's ponytail danced behind her head as she walked away. "Stop thinking, baby. It just gets in my way."

The boys at the counter laughed, as did a handful of people at a table. Dutch smiled and returned to the kitchen, where he continued looking pretty.

❧

The eagle had disappeared from the sky, as had the wisps of fog. All that remained were layers of cold air, which seemed to deny passage of the sun's warmth to the cold hard ground. The air was crisp, but it felt good as she and the dog walked the narrow trail to the falls. Just under a mile from the three homes at Brennan's Cove, the trailhead immediately split. A weathered sign indicating an upper and lower path illustrated routes and distances to the Jupiter Falls. Both were abandoned fire trails built and maintained by the US Forest Service. These were not roads but merely narrow swaths cut through the dense forest and could be easily reclaimed once left unused for even a short period of time. The sign indicated the lower trail as being straight, flat, and having no views until opening onto the three boulder-laden pools at the base of the falls. The upper trail, a nine-mile loop with vistas overlooking the Sound and the Cascades, quickly became a grueling trek even for the conditioned hiker. Conquering it once many years ago and preserving the memory on film, she vowed to never do it again.

Attached to a lanyard worn around her wrist was a small metal clicker to which the dog obediently responded when running too far ahead, exploring bushes off the trail, or being seduced by the scent of something lingering just beyond the trees. Sniffing the ground, he knew where humans strayed from the path, but more frequent was the scent of unseen creatures who roamed through the thick underbrush. This, most times, would unnerve the dog, and he would quickly take in the air, checking if anyone or anything remained close by. Content that no imminent threat of confrontation existed, he'd prance along the trail, stopping every so often to simply admire the surroundings and check the air again. This was the dog's way of strolling along the boulevard, whistling a tune with his head in the clouds, not a care in the world. Another scent, another sniff, another all clear…yes, life is good in Brennan's Cove. Life is very good indeed.

Pausing, he looked back at his quiet companion. Once satisfied with the woman's proximity, he thought of dashing a short distance ahead but remembered her gentle affections when he patiently waited for her. Pats and pets and quiet whispers in his ear always left him nuzzling for more. He loved her soft bubbly laughter, one of the many things that separated her from those of her kind. She was never loud, yet he knew when she was upset, angry, happy, or sad. More than any person he had been around, she was the easiest to understand, and he loved leading their walks through the forest. Life was good, and he was a good boy, he thought. Prance, prance, prance, another scent, another sniff, another…prance, pra—

Stopping suddenly, he returned to the scent, scanning the edge of the trail with his eyes, sniffing the air again and again. He sensed something hidden within the dense thicket of underbrush some distance ahead, but he saw nothing. As he moved his snout over the ground, an odor raised the hair from the nape of his neck to the end of his tail. He looked back to find the woman thirty steps away. His eyes scanned the area around her. Testing the air, he determined she was safe and again focused on the intimidating odor. It was close, twenty, thirty steps farther up the trail. A gentle breeze lifted his head, filling his nostrils with more unusual aromas. But one, one held a note of familiarity. Home, he thought. Home! Run! Chase...no! Bad! With great caution he moved forward, inspecting the ground and the air with every step. But it was not of home. Not entirely; there was something else. Pausing, he released an audible whimper, which came in one short breath. He shuddered.

The smell became stronger, frightening yet captivating. With nose to the ground, eyes focused many yards ahead, he cautiously moved closer. The odor grew to a stench heavy and thick in the air, and on the ground it became visible. Speckles at first, and then droplets, finally appearing as long, dark streaks giving way to a large area saturated with shallow pools of warm, fresh blood. Quickly he backed away. The woman's footsteps were approaching rapidly. He growled a warning at the scene. In the same moment, there came a rustling in the brush that drew his attention to a small bird taking flight. Nervously he backed up and again heard the woman's footsteps behind him. Close, closer...his low growl made it evident to whatever the threat might be that he would stand and protect the Quiet One.

His head turned to find her, to warn her. From within the thick brush, a large twig snapped. Baring teeth, his muscles tightened, his nails dug into the ever-moist soil of the trail. Ten feet away, the underbrush suddenly parted forcefully as the massive beast's head and upper body jutted from the foliage, its black winter mane profusely stained and dripping with blood. Its bulging black eyes stared without blinking. Gigantic nostrils flared rapidly, repeatedly, while its soft mouth moved faintly with each labored breath. But no cries were heard, only the wheeze of spent air coming from the deep gash in its throat.

The woman gasped. The dog growled viciously, standing his ground. He sensed the woman moving away and knew he must stay close to protect her. Running to her side, he again took a fierce defensive stance, allowing her to continue back down the trail. Twice she snapped the metal clicker, signaling him come, and he'd run to her side, quickly resuming his stance.

The beast struggled at the brush in desperation. The dog stood and watched. Click-click. But was unable to turn or avert his gaze. Click-click… click-click. The animal heard the dog whimper and watched him back away, still protecting the woman. These were the final moments of the dying elk.

The entire journey back to the house, he never once ran in front of the woman but continued to protect her retreat. Entering the large compound, she began to slow and soon sat on the wide steps of the porch overlooking Brennan's Cove. They were both trembling, but as she sat catching her breath, the dog nuzzled, gently showing his love.

"You are a good boy," she whispered. "My big protector…" After a while she added, "We better swing by and let the state park boys know something's killing their elk. And afterward, what do you say I treat you to lunch up at Nel's place?"

Rhythmically his tail began to hit the corner of the steps. "You're a good boy, Jass," she whispered. He again nuzzled her gently before walking into the yard. And as the eagle appeared high above the trees, the dog began to prance.

※

"Pepperoni, black olive, and pineapple. It's what she gets every time. Sometimes with extra pepperoni, but she always gets black olive and pineapple no matter what. Do you like pepperoni, Mrs. B.?"

"I do. Is that your favorite?"

Thinking, Michael frowned for a second. "Yeah, I guess so. We never get anything else. My friend JJ doesn't like pizza, any kind of pizza. Now, his sister Cee Cee, she loves it. But she doesn't like squash. Do you like squash, Mrs. B.? Oh look, here she comes."

Rachel sat down, giggling. "This place hasn't changed all that much over the years, and the sink still has the chip in it from when Bailey climbed out the window."

Ann closed her eyes and smiled. Michael scratched his head, and Rachel added, "A story for another time. Do we know what we want?"

Waiting for the order to arrive, Ann set a small white box on the table. "Mr. B. asked me to give you this. It's an award your daddy worked very hard to earn, and it's been sitting in the school trophy case for ages waiting to be returned to its rightful owner."

Opening the box revealed a large gold medallion on a red, white, and blue ribbon. An envelope stating National High School Music Theater Awards had been tucked under the black satin lining.

Michael's expression was nothing short of astonishment. "That's so awesome. Can I wear it?"

"Just for a minute. We'll get a frame and hang it up in your room."

"But I don't have a room. We don't even have a house."

Ann couldn't help but giggle. Rachel pushed her son playfully, saying, "We're moving. We're not homeless; you'll have a room soon enough."

The boy sat and admired the heavy medallion around his neck while his mom read the letter to him. The waitress brought their pizza and commented to Michael about the award, and the boy spoke proudly of his father. Rachel said grace, and they all enjoyed the pepperoni, black olive, and pineapple pizza. It was just as good as she remembered, and for a passing moment, she was transported back to senior year, the old crowd cheering their latest victory.

"Jim also has something for the both of you, but that'll have to come right from him."

Rachel shook her head and started to speak, but Ann held up one finger. Michael laughed. "She does the same thing you do, Mommy."

Rachel stuffed her mouth with pizza to keep from commenting.

Shortly after one o'clock, the old man stepped from the bus a world apart from Garden Street. The ride had made him tired, but not being far from the waters of the sound, the salt air was invigorating, something he had loved as a boy growing up in this neighborhood and something now as he inhaled deeply stirred a lifetime of memories. He began to walk, not allowing himself to think about the past, nor the future, choosing only the present to occupy his mind. But he wouldn't kid himself either. He knew where this walk was about to take him, and he was smart enough to know that once he arrived, the past would greet him with open arms, while the future waited on the corner farther up the block. And that was fine with him. He'd known for a very long time that each passing day brought him closer to the end of that block, and soon…the future would have nowhere to run.

In reality the old neighborhood hadn't changed much. Sure, the trees had grown; new shrubberies had been planted; and the old houses, built sometime in the nineteen thirties, now wore modern coats of paint in an effort to restore them back to the past. But it all remained so recognizable, he could remember the names of the residents on each side of the block, though most, if not all, were long dead by now. *But maybe not*, he thought. "After all, I'm still here," he said aloud.

He wasn't sure the year his parents bought the house. Even now he had memories of being six or seven, playing outside all day long, rain or shine, and in the summertime, he and the rest of the kids would gather around the street lamps until well after dark. *You couldn't do that now*, he thought, shaking his head in disgust. "Why are we so obsessed nowadays with hurting the children?" he asked the wind. But if the wind answered, he didn't hear it, focusing instead on the house in front of him. It was a simple two-story wood frame home with a wide wraparound porch, two long windows flanking each side of the front door, although now it was a very modern double-door entry.

"Something I can help you with?" the thirtysomething man called, walking down the driveway.

"No, no. I was just thinking what a beautiful home you have."

"Thank you. The company we bought it from restores these old places. I think they spend two or three months researching photos and blueprints before even picking up a hammer. They say you could take pictures from then and now, set 'em side by side, and you'd never be able to tell old form new."

The old man began to notice other changes. The front steps were no longer brick, and the upstairs gables had smaller windowpanes. Granted, they were slight changes, but they were obvious ones to him. Without taking his eyes from the home, he said, "It sounds like you love the place."

"It was my wife that found it, but yeah, I think I love it more than she does. You know, it just feels like home. And no, we're not interested in selling, if that's why you stopped."

"Oh, no. It's just I used to have one…not exactly like this, but very similar." The old man smiled.

"I'll bet yours didn't have six French doors running all along the back."

The old man looked startled and then chuckled. "No, mine didn't have anything like that."

"They're great when you're having a party or just need some fresh air. And during the summertime, man, it's nice. I'm telling you, the ingenuity that went into these old places was remarkable. They knew how to build houses back then."

He and the proud young homeowner spoke for another few minutes before the old man bid him farewell. Preparing to cross the street, he looked down at the curb. There, etched in the old cement, was the reason he had come. The names Ruth and Peter were still clearly visible. The date, however, was almost worn smooth.

"She told me not to put a date." He chuckled to himself. "I should have just written 'forever,' like she wanted."

The old man made two more stops on his trek through the old neighborhood, neither taking much time, as he knew exactly what he needed before entering the establishments. The Northwest evening would be approaching soon, carrying with it clear skies and plummeting temperatures. It was now perhaps time to catch the bus back to Garden Street.

❀

A sign in the window of the empty ranger station read, "Office Closed. For overnight camping see instructions on payment box." Trudy left a note in the box and drove back out of the park. Five miles north on Highway 101 brought her to an unpaved parking area in front of a small storefront with a greater structure connected at the rear.

"Hey, Trudy, is that Jass in the truck with you, or did Linc forget to shave this mornin'?" Nels joked, walking into the market from an attached shop.

She laughed, pointed to her throat, and shook her head with a scowl.

"Try these," he said, removing two long wax straws from a wide-mouth jar. "Honey and herb extract I harvest myself. Squeeze some on your tongue and let it melt until the straw is empty. In an hour or two, if you need, do it again with the second. But I doubt you'll need to. Don't drink anything right away; let the herbs and honey do their magic. My mother believes the high mountain herbs not only soothe but heal." He shook his head and grinned. "We're only a few hundred feet above sea level. Superstitious old woman; she only likes them because they taste like whiskey. You like whiskey, Tru?"

"I enjoy a nice scotch once in a while," she answered softly.

"You'll enjoy these, then. They're healthy. No alcohol; I used to make 'em for the kids all the time for sore throats. They seem to like 'em." Opening the top of the straw, Trudy found the golden contents almost instantly soothing, and it did have a hint of well-aged scotch.

Nel's place was not a convenience store. There were no metal racks holding canned goods, potato chips, or toilet bowl cleaners. Although some stopped by, it wasn't designed for the yuppie tourists who came to rent cabins, stay in RVs, swim, boat, or fish the sound—and definitely not for those who happened to be looking for a restroom while on a scenic drive. From creaky wooden floorboards to mismatched tables, bins, cabinets, and barrels used as makeshift displays for homemade foods and products, most prepared or handcrafted nearby, it was simply a local market for local patrons. There were always fresh-baked breads, homemade butter and cheese, and a wide variety of meats, fish, game, and poultry in the two refrigerated display cases. On the wall behind the counter, a series of whiteboards listed the cuts available and their prices. Above that, a large sign outlined in red, "Wild Game Sold Here. Processing available with tags. Price is nonnegotiable and must be paid on pickup. Once the order is ready, storage fees apply and accumulate daily, so leave it as long as you like but know after seven days it belongs to me, and you may purchase it back at a much higher price." The brush-painted signature simply read "Nels."

At six five, 290 pounds, he was a big man. High cheekbones, dark-brown complexion, red at times, with long black hair usually pulled through the back of a cap into a ponytail, which loosely hung just below his shoulders. His wife was of the Quileute tribe, native to western Washington, and had lived all forty-one years of her life on the peninsula. Though clearly Nels was Native American and knew the peninsula, its rivers and streams, backwoods, and forests as well as anyone, the waters were somewhat murky as to where he was from originally, which didn't matter much since he never spoke about it, even when asked.

With the straws still between her lips, Trudy walked to the far end of the shop, where in the corner, a large basket sitting atop a wooden wine barrel held rawhide chews of all shapes and sizes. Picking one from the assortment, she looked out the window where Jass waited patiently in the front seat for her return. Quickly she exchanged the chew for one much larger before making her way to the center of the first display case, where she studied the eight varieties of bacon and ten kinds of sausage, all smoked on-site by Nels himself. In the very last row were links considerably larger than the others and visibly rich with smoke and spices. The sign at the bottom read Not Jimmy Dean's. Even after years of seeing it every time she came in, it made her smile.

For the next few minutes, she pointed, Nels wrapped, and conversations were answered with a nod. Lastly she had him retrieve a doggie bag from a refrigerator back in his shop—a healthy meal for the dog, as certified by the local vet, made from Nels' special formula. It even came with a dessert treat.

Meeting her at the counter, he totaled the purchase, indicating the straws were a gift. Almost to the door, she stopped and returned to the register. Nels didn't have a chance to ask the reason before she spoke in a voice quiet, smooth, and less strained than when she had arrived.

"Something killed an elk up by Jupiter Falls. Ripped its throat out. Jass and I came up on it not more than an hour ago. I went to report it, but the rangers weren't around, so I left a note. I'm just afraid kids or campers might hike back in there and...anyway, I was just thankful I had Jass with me. And I was surprised he was so protective. Kept turning around making sure nothing came after us..."

"I'll start making phone calls. My boy can post warning signs at the bottom of the trailhead and on the bulletin board up at the campground."

His voice held little expression as he walked to the back of the store.

"Wintertime, not too many people venture back in there. And Trudy, you should never go in there by yourself, not even with the dog…even a brave dog!"

He took another large rawhide from the basket and handed it to her. "Tell the dog I said thanks. And Trudy, Jupiter's a beautiful spot, but it's true wilderness, even at the falls. Not a safe place to go alone."

She giggled nervously. "I never thought about coming across a bear, especially this time of year."

His dark eyes became intense. "It was no bear did that."

❄

Chris pulled into the large common driveway at Brennan's Cove just after four thirty. Jass was the first to greet everyone, including Beth, who had changed into play clothes at Aunt Bailey's. Lincoln helped Chris slide the old desk onto the tailgate as Ann came running off Trudy's porch, quickly making her way across the commons into the arms of her husband.

"I missed you." she whispered into his ear before joining the two other men. "I remember that desk. Thing weighs a ton," she cried. "How did you three get it in there?"

Lincoln pointed to Beth. "Princess power. How else?"

"I think getting it down is gonna take a bigger princess. What do you think, Chris?" Ann smiled at the young man before looking back toward the porch.

Normally he would've laughed and focused on the project at hand, but there was something in her voice, in her actions, that drew him to follow her gaze. At first his mind tried to clear his eyes of their apparent fatigue the long drive sometimes brought on. But his vision was crystal clear. Still, he continued to blink for another second and then inhaled sharply. The cold air caught deep in his lungs, his scalp tingled, and an expression of disbelief raised his eyebrows to stretch a growing smile. There, beside the front door, stood Rachel.

He moved slowly at first across the compound, his eyes never left her, nor did hers from him. She watched his pace increase, as did the joy on his face. Quickly she moved from the door to the top of the steps. He saw clearly the smile that had always lifted him, but it was his smile, filled with jubilant laughter, that caused her to unconsciously release a muted squeal of her own. The log handrail was smooth to the touch. Later she would have no memory of gliding her hand over it or moving down the wide steps to the cold damp ground. He would have no memory of pausing reflectively before their embrace. Taking her hands, helpless in her gaze, he stared deep into her sparkling green eyes.

"I thought you forgot about me," he said, as much from his heart as his lips.

To anyone else the words would have meant little. But Rachel understood the deep sincerity behind them. Even delivered with gentleness, their message proved powerful. Helpless in her gaze, he stared deep into her sparkling green eyes. Softly he moved his hand over her cheek, brushing a lock of red hair from where it caressed. He smiled. Her lips parted slightly, and he thought for a second she would return his smile, but she did not. Instead, motionless, it was now she who stood helpless. His hand slid once more across her cheek until finding the nape of her neck. They embraced with tenderness neither tried to hide; whispered words brought a wonderful magic each had long missed. Laughter and gaiety followed as they were joined by all—all except Ann, who was busy wiping tears on Jim's sweatshirt as they walked. It was Trudy who ushered everyone inside, leaving Chris and Rachel alone on the steps to take a moment just outside the door, where they again looked into each other's eyes. He couldn't help but embrace her one more time, and it was only then he realized...she was trembling.

"Jim told me about Mike. I'm so sorry, Rache. He was—"

Gently pulling away, she interrupted. "And I'm sorry for you and your daughter. We'll talk. Just not tonight. I need tonight."

Laying her head against his chest, she held him tightly. For a few moments she couldn't let go, and when she did, he smiled and took her hand, then softly kissed her forehead. Frozen by his steely blue eyes, she was afraid he would know her thoughts, sense her emotion.

"Are you okay?" he asked.

Her heart leaped into her throat. She took a deep breath, but it continued to pound. All she could think to do was smile and try not to laugh.

"I'm better than okay. You know why?" She giggled cheerily. But try as she might, Rachel couldn't contain her laughter.

And with fond memories of his old friend Mike, Chris joined in. Trudy, standing closest to the door, heard their laughter and thought it sounded musical. Ann put her arm around Jim, who was talking to Lincoln, who was playing with Beth, who suddenly noticed the boy standing by the fireplace. Taking her small hand and carefully turning Lincoln's chin toward the Great Room, she whispered, "Who's that boy, Mr. Trudy?"

"I'm not sure, sweetheart. Why don't we go ask him."

Chris and Rachel walked through the door, both still giggling but somewhat more composed. She quickly made her way over to Michael only moments before Lincoln and Beth.

"He must be yours," Lincoln inquired, his baritone voice soft and comforting.

Rachel smiled as Michael moved shyly to hug her legs. "He is. This is Michael; I'm Rachel. We're friends of—"

"Yes, I know, and you're pretty as a picture. Allow me to introduce my little friend. This is Beth. And as much as I would like to take credit for her, she belongs to the gentleman standing…oh wait, that's right. You two already met in the front yard."

From across the room, a smile from Chris lit on her gaze, bringing Rachel to blush, but only slightly. Lincoln extended a hand. "And my name is Lincoln, but my friends, and Chris, just call me Linc." He chuckled.

Before accepting his hand, she asked, "Well then, may I call you Linc?"

He beamed with delight. "By all means," he said.

"Thank you, Linc, but I don't shake hands with friends." She grinned, leaning close for a hug.

Chris whispered in Trudy's ear, "I think I've noticed that about her."

The adults set around the Gathering Place. Michael was fascinated with the fireplace, and Beth was fascinated with Michael. "I've never seen a fireplace this big before," he admitted. "My Aunt Peg has one, but it's small and different, not all rocky like this. This one's huge!"

"This one's little." The girl laughed blissfully. "Want me to show you the big one? It's ginormous—like big, big! Miss Trudy thinks maybe a giant built it; that's why it's so ginormous. Come on. It's in Miss Trudy's dancing room. But we have to ask before we go in."

Permission was given with a reminder not to touch anything and to stay off the big stairways. However, before leading her new friend to the dancing room, Beth stopped and whispered to Ann in secret, "Is his mom a real princess? She looks like a real princess."

Ann smiled, casting her stare to the little girl's father. "I'm pretty sure some people think so."

Beth studied her father. His smile brought her warmth, his laughter tickled her with love, and the way he gazed at the beautiful woman beside him left her to believe she must be a real princess.

❦

At first Michael didn't notice the two carved bears standing in the formal entry of the indoor courtyard. His eyes instead attempted to take in the full scope of the room—the plants, the artwork, the high ceilings, and finally resting on the magnificent rock wall. It wasn't until he heard Beth say, "Look, these are my friends," that he turned to see the nine-foot, wood carved bears standing behind him. He was speechless. Never had he seen bears with top hats, tuxedos, and smiles. And though he was only five, he recognized their elegance. One carried a book under his arm, while the other, Beth's favorite, leaned casually on a closed umbrella.

The little girl quickly ran down the curved entry into the ballroom, with Michael following close behind. There was an odd moment when he first entered the room in which he felt a bit frightened by its sheer size. The girl was right. The fireplace was ginormous, almost as big as his entire bedroom back in Irvine. And the towering rock chimney with its carved animal faces was most impressive, but again somewhat frightening. Beth quickly changed all that by pulling him with her to the center of the curiously colored floor, where she gleefully announced, "Hello, room. It's me, Beth."

Colored light began to paint the room, as if by magic since there were no visible lamps. Her giggles twittered through the air as if revealing to the boy a secret. And he stood in wonder.

"Will you play my song, please?" she asked.

Soft notes rose from the far end of the room, where Michael noticed a red high-gloss grand piano, but no one was there to play it. A female's voice filled the room with lyrics all too familiar to the boy, and he watched as Beth pretended to dance and sing along. Subtle violins came from what seemed to be everywhere, as if the room itself were set within an invisible orchestra pit. Never had he heard anything as pure and beautiful. Each section, each instrument's tone and timbre so easily heard and distinguished it became breathtaking, and this thrilled the boy. He listened. She danced, and the chorus began.

> Let it go
> Let it go
> Can't hold it back anymore…

The young girl twirled twice and then abruptly and most unexpectedly held perfectly still…as if…frozen. There, dancing across the floor with princes like grace was the boy's mother. Trudy watched from the entry as the song played on.

> Let it go
> Let it go…

Rachel joined Beth, something Michael was thankful for, as this was not a song he would ever dance to anyway. It was a girl song…although it sure never sounded like this before.

Looking around, Michael thought, *What's that over there?*

Trudy sighed and thought, *Enjoy this special moment, my little Beth.*

Twirling the girl, Rachel thought, *You're so beautiful.*

And Beth believed she was dancing with a princess.

Soon Michael was wandering about the room finding touches of whimsy that would go unnoticed until stumbled upon, and sometimes, even then he had to look very, very close. Approaching the red piano, he noted the top was not smooth like the one at church but had a series of three very thin wooden sections stacked one atop the other, diminishing in size to form a double-beveled frame over the entire center of the lid. There, finely engraved into the wood, was the basic outline of a large open umbrella.

As the song ended, Trudy made her way to where Beth and Rachel were finishing their dance. The room, sensing her presence, smoothly adjusted the lighting and music to her most recent mood preference. Softly in the background, the iconic voice of Steve Perry floated through the air while the room awaited her request.

"Trudy, this is amazing," Rachel gushed, peering around the ballroom. "I've never seen anything like it…or heard anything like it. It's hard for me to comprehend this is your home. Not in my wildest dreams…"

"Miss Trudy, could you make it fast and loud again like yesterday?"

"In just a second, sweetheart. Then we'll play it any way you want—that is, if you promise to dance with us."

Slowly twirling under Rachel's hand, Beth shyly nodded, accepting the bargain, then decided to wait by the piano with the boy, maybe show him the button that made the lid go up and down.

Once alone, Trudy looked to Rachel and frowned. "Earlier you told me you had reservations about coming. I hope that's changed."

Caught off guard, Rachel remained quiet, watching Trudy's stare move to Beth and then quickly return to her.

"Because up until twenty minutes ago, she was the only one who could make Chris smile like that."

Wanting to lie, claiming she didn't understand, Rachel instead stole her own glance at Beth. "No one will ever make him smile the way she can. It's a daughter's birthright—a special love like no other."

"I suppose," Trudy said. "But just the same…it's nice to see his face light up again."

Rachel scoffed with nervous laughter, "It was probably just the lighting or bad tuna for lunch."

She waited for Trudy's response, but none came. So without thinking, she added, "It's just we haven't seen each other in so long. That always stirs up old feelings." This time there was no waiting for Trudy's facial response. It was immediate, with Rachel responding just as quickly, "I don't mean to imply there were ever feelings between me and Chris—not those kind of feelings anyway. We were just really great friends."

"Uh huh," said Trudy, narrowing her eyes with a grin both warm and wicked, dripping with old-charm accusation.

"No, it was never like that. We hung out, but we were just friends."

Tilting her head to imply a margin of disbelief, she again replied, "Uh huh."

"No, really, that's it. It was a beautiful friendship, nothing more."

"Well! I'd like to thank you for bringing that friendship to my front porch this evening. It truly touched my heart, and apparently yours, too, because I could hear it beating all the way in the house."

Rachel blushed. "I admit we were pretty excited to see each other."

"Uh…that was obvious." Trudy beamed. "It would've taken a blind fool to miss that—"

"Here I am, Tru," exclaimed Jim, hurrying across the floor to take her in his arms, striking the only dance pose he knew. With much flair and pomp accompanied by his best British accent, he announced, "Dancing the paso doble, James Brooks and his partner, Trudy Trudeau."

Beth tugged on his pant leg. "Mr. B., this is my dance."

He scooped her up and struck his pose again. "Dancing the paso doble, James Brooks and his partner, Elizabeth Peterson."

Her high-pitched giggles brought Michael to stare at his mom and laugh out loud. Rachel, too, bubbled over.

"No, silly," Beth blurted, her giggles ending in a final gush. "We're all gonna dance. Show him, Miss Trudy."

In dramatic fashion, putting a finger to her lips, Trudy breathed, "Shh…listen."

The background music quickly faded into silence. The lights dimmed, faintly bringing a hush to fall over the room's guests. Trudy winked at the little girl and then spoke ever so softly. "Room...Beth wants to dance. She wants to dance...loudly."

Before anyone had a chance to react, the sound of electronic drums and layers of synthesized eighties pop filled the air with a high-energy pulsating drive even the finest discotheques would envy. Standing at the entry was Ann, Chris, and Lincoln. Though somewhat late to the party, they quickly danced their way into the mix. Beth's prediction of "We're all gonna dance" was spot on. Chris and Rachel promptly gravitated toward each other, and as the male vocal began, Rachel lip-synched each line to perfection, directing her complete attention toward Chris.

"We're no strangers to love. You know the rules, and so do I."

Chris answered back, "A full commitment's what I'm thinking of. You wouldn't get this from any other guy."

Taking one another's hands, they sang, "I just want to tell you how I'm feeling. I'm never going to give you up. Never gonna let you down. Never gonna run around and desert you."

Everyone joined in on the chorus, and fortunately the music was loud enough that even Lincoln got away with singing. Trudy was surprised that Chris and Rachel knew the song so well, since by her best estimation, both were only a year or two out of diapers when it had been popular. With the music beginning to fade, she asked them about the song.

Both laughed, but it was Chris who started the explanation. "For twenty years—no, longer—to this day, that's one of my mom's favorite songs. When I was growing up, she'd play it all the time, even waking me and Bailey up with it on Saturday mornings."

"I'd go to their house," blurted Rachel, "and she'd have all of us sing and dance in the living room. That would be the first song played every time, guaranteed. And when the Petersons had a party, she'd play it three or four times an hour—no kidding."

"Mom was hot for Rick Astley. Still is!"

"Pastor Chris..." Trudy asserted, overacting her shock, "that's your mother."

"I'm just being honest, Tru. Back me up here, Rache."

You Are My Love

Not wanting to be rude, Rachel shrugged demurely. Her voice was timid. "It's kind of true. She did like him a lot."

Chris scoffed. "What are you talking about? She had the hots for him, and you know it. Remember the T-shirt? Remember that?"

His voice became very soft, not in volume but tone. An ill-behaved glint turned up a corner of his mouth. "You remember the other song she always played, Rache?" Trudy was the only one in a position to see the momentary exchange.

"I do." She smiled, her eyes first flashing a steely glare before recapturing their ever-present twinkle. No cue was given, no two-measure count, yet Chris and Rachel came in together, their voices blending perfectly.

"Wake me up before you go-go…" Clasping hands, they began to dance their rendition of the jitterbug. "Don't leave me hanging on like a yo-yo."

Chris picked her up by the waist and spun around twice, to the glee and delight of both Michael and Beth. Applause rose from the adults, and Trudy noticed another little glint between the two, this time holding much longer, conveying something private and obviously intended to stay that way, its meaning hidden brilliantly in the laughter they now shared. Unnoticed, Trudy spoke quietly into the air, and the deep baritone voice of Bill Medley led soft strings through the instantly recognizable opening verse.

"Now I've had the time of my life…"

Glances of love, as if tugged by heartstrings, were exchanged between Lincoln and Trudy; this was also the case with Ann and Jim. Chris hadn't completely released Rachel to walk away, and now he stared into her eyes. Beth and Michael also stared at each other, but this was out of confusion. And by the time Jennifer Warren finished her vocal line to the slow-moving intro, everyone had paired up and was ready for some Dirty Dancing. There would be no lift—only laughter.

When the song ended, Trudy held up her hand and quietly announced, "Everyone to the Gathering Place. We have barbecue to enjoy."

There were no arguments, only sounds of scampering carnivores excited with anticipation. Ann raced Chris back to the kitchen. Mr. B. and both kids pretended to be airplanes, and Lincoln deferred to the wine cellar. Rachel and Trudy strolled casually to the opening of the beautiful entryway, where Rachel turned back around, taking in the ballroom one more time.

"I love this room. It's amazing," she said. "And the sound—the sound is incredible, but how do you control it? I mean, I could barely hear you, and I was standing right next to you. I don't understand."

Pulling a small ruby pendant from the neckline of her blouse, she said, "I call it my keeper, because it keeps track of me anywhere on the property. A friend of ours developed it as a medical monitor for his wife. Lincoln had the computer geeks turn it into my personal assistant. Beats hiring a full-time disc jockey to follow me around the house. If you're interested, he can tell you about the whole system, I'm lost as to how that stuff works; I just tell it what I want, and it does it. There's also a console that lets me program the voices of friends, their playlists, whatever, so they can use it without wearing this ball and chain around their neck. But if I'm in the same room, it gives me complete control to override any command, a feature Linc hasn't figured out how to wire around…at least not yet." She smiled, tucking it away.

Still in amazement, Rachel shook her head. "I just can't believe you operate all this just by talking…by whispering."

"Speaking of, we better get in there before they start whispering about us."

As Rachel turned to take a last look at the room, her stare fell to the piano. "Before I go back to Seattle, would you mind if I…"

Trudy's faint smile and surprised look hid well the loud cheering going on in her head. "I know you sing; I didn't know you played. Maybe after dinner, if you're up to it."

"Yeah, maybe an old-fashioned sing-along. I love it when everyone crowds around the piano. We'll get Jim to play too."

"I think that's a beautiful idea, Rachel. Make sure you bring it up." She grinned. "Now, let's have some dinner."

Walking across the floor, Rachel asked, "When everyone ran out of here, did I hear you say dinner mix?"

"I did! It's already playing in the other room."

At the Gathering Place, like the ballroom, the music was pristine. With no precise origin, the sound seemed to hang in the atmosphere, never overpowering conversation, simply drifting through it. Rachel walked in to see Chris and Ann dancing to Harry Connick Junior's "It Had to Be You." With their impressive precision, it was easy to see this was not their first dance together, and even though the space was small for such moves, they made it work with only minor revisions. Chris thanked Ann, saying, "Oh, look, there's my girlfriend. I should probably ask her to dance."

Ann and Trudy shared a grin behind Rachel's back. But acting surprised, Chris quickly retorted, "Oops, too late. Her husband's back."

The women giggled as Lincoln entered the room. "That's twice today people have laughed when I walked into a room. I'm starting to feel a little self-conscious."

Beth ran over and touched his leg. "Not to me you don't. You feel like the same ol' Mr. Trudy."

The girl grinned and scampered away to join Michael on the front deck, where they watched the many outdoor lights reflect off the darkened waters of Brennan's Cove. Lincoln opened a bottle of Cabernet and carefully poured it into a large decanter he carried to the table. Ann grabbed plates and silverware, placing a full roll of paper towels in the center. Jim laughed. "Do you really think we'll need all those?"

"Those are for you. We have ours," she remarked, holding up a small handful. "It's barbecue. We've seen you eat."

Over everything else, he heard the bubbling laughter of Trudy, but given she was feeling better and had Ann as reinforcements, he wisely chose not to comment. Rachel was told to take a seat while Ann and Trudy prepared two large platters with a variety of meats, a bowl of potato salad, and one very large bowl of Ann's favorite, Smokehouse Spicy Mac and Cheese. There were chips and vegetables for dipping, and some of Nels' Cottage Ice Cream for dessert.

Lincoln returned with five wineglasses, and as he began to pour, Rachel said shyly, "I'm sorry, Linc, I'm not much of a drinker, especially when it comes to red wine. I had a bad experience once."

A quiet chuckle came from Chris, and Lincoln was not about to let it pass. "You have something to add to that, Chris?"

"No, not at all. It's Rachel's story."

"There's no story. I just don't drink red wine."

"Chris seems to think there's a story here," Lincoln challenged, lifting an eyebrow while filling Ann's glass.

"No, really, there's no story!"

Turning his head, Chris covered his mouth to hide a guilty smirk, and again Rachel countered, this time with a gentle sternness, "There's no story!"

Trudy and Ann walked to the table. "I love red wine stories, don't you Ann?"

"They're some of my favorites—except they all end about the same," she shot back.

"Maybe Rachel's has a surprise ending?" Jim said, returning from watching the kids, who were now playing in the yard with Jass, "She's always been full of surprises."

Before Rachel could speak, Chris leaned close. "The sharks are gathering."

"Thanks to you," she sniped.

Having been in the Brooks/Trudeau aquarium many times himself, Chris knew there was little hope she'd escape at this point and said, "I'm sorry. I don't know what I was thinking. But really, it's your own fault. You're the one who brought it up. A simple no thank you would've ended it right there, so you might as well tell 'em the story now. Look at it this way: confession is good for the soul."

But his handsome smile only fueled the fire behind her eyes. There was a long silence as everyone watched the unspoken tête-à-tête between them. A series of rapid frowns, nods, and sneers ended with Rachel giving in.

"Fine. It's really no big deal."

One last time her eyes locked on his, hoping he would interrupt, say something, but instead he nodded for her to continue. His look seemed to dare her, even taunt and entice, stirring memories of playful challenges he'd so often presented her in their youth. A half smile crept along her lips. Her eyes no longer sparkled; they blazed. Turning sharply to face the others caused light to glisten fiery red through the loose curls draping her shoulders. Finally, almost casually, she said, "Bailey got me drunk."

"Bailey!" everyone gasped. Everyone except Chris; he was busy chuckling to himself, knowing there'd be a feeding frenzy of questions, probably starting with Ann, then Jim, and right on around the horn. Battling a twinge of regret, he almost felt sorry for Rachel, but not enough to stick his toes in the already-churning water. She looked to him for help, but his Cheshire grin made it clear she was on her own.

Not fazed in the least, she grinned, shrugged, and even allowed a soft giggle. "Yep, it was Bailey." And then Rachel looked directly at Ann as if to answer the obvious question before she could ask. "Doug was out of town. Her mom and dad were out of town. She felt this incredible freedom. Yeah, this was all Bailey, totally her idea. But I'll admit I was a more-than-willing participant once we got started, and I'm pretty sure I was the one who opened the second bottle."

As predicted, Ann was the first to comment. "Second bottle? How old were you two?"

Rachel's nonchalance remained unshaken. "My senior year, so seventeen. Bailey was sixteen, and you were still seventeen, weren't you, Chris?" Rachel asked with a tantalizing smile of her own.

Feeling the water rise and the sharks circling, he swallowed hard. "I should check on the kids. Where'd they run off to?"

Also as predicted, Jim spoke up next. "You were there, Chris?"

Rachel leaned close to Chris and with a great deal of poise muttered, "I've heard confession is good for the soul."

Shades of red flushed his cheeks, but after only a moment's thought he admitted almost defiantly, "Okay, yeah, I was there..."

"As a participant! He was there as a participant," Rachel emphasized.

To deprive Rachel the pleasure of seeing him squirm, he promptly confirmed. "Yeah, I was. I arrived shortly after the first cork was pulled, and like Rache, quickly became a willing participant. We went through that first bottle pretty fast and were starting to feel a little giddy and adventurous. Keep in mind, before that, none of us had ever drank anything stronger than a Mountain Dew. This was a whole new experience, one I personally was not ready for. Oh, don't get me wrong. After that first bottle, the drinking part came easy. It was the throwing up and the hangover I had problems with. At first I lay there praying I'd die, but then I pictured myself staggering up to the Pearly Gates begging Saint Peter for an Alka-Seltzer. So then I started praying I'd live…"

Rachel was not the first to burst into laughter, nor was she the loudest. Both honors went to Lincoln. But hers was just enough to seize the attention of Chris. "Go ahead and laugh, Rache, but I didn't throw up in the hot tub…"

Now bellowing with laughter, Lincoln wailed, "This just keeps getting better at every turn. So, we have you three kids drunk off your butts, sitting in a hot tub, and somebody throws up?" His great laughter filled the room. "Was there a chain reaction?"

It was during this moment of feverish laughter that Trudy, completing the prediction, leaned close to the couple and whispered, "Still think confession is good for the soul…Pastor?"

He and Rachel looked at each other, his attention resting on her tender smile. Desperately apologetic, he addressed Rachel softly, but loud enough that everyone could hear. "I know we promised never to discuss what really happened that night, but you don't know these people like I do. If we don't tell 'em, we may never see the kids again."

She smiled at his melodramatics but saw a glimmer in his eye that brought a slight frown to her brow.

Placing his folded hands on the table, he began. "Rache, we've carried this around long enough," he told her, then immediately shifted his attention across the table. "Jim, Ann, I'm sure you heard rumors around school…"

Everyone could see Rachel shift in her seat. What they didn't see was the gentle kick she gave Chris under the table. However, her delivery was too gentle, so he continued.

"I think Rachel and I have denied those rumors long enough."

Again Rachel shifted, this time just a little harder. Although it got his attention, he was determined to carry on.

"But know this: it was entirely my fault. I'm the one who talked her into it and then made her promise she'd never tell a soul. We even made

Bailey promise, but she may have already been passed out by then; I don't remember."

He put his arm around Rachel, and his eyes became soft and tender. His voice was calm and trusting. "I have to tell 'em, sweetheart. I know we promised, but it was so long ago. They understand we were just kids."

As she gazed on his charming face, the glimmer in his eye, now a blinding twinkle, tickled her heart just as it always had.

In return, her eyes sparkled with approval. Her lips formed an enticing grin, lifting him emotionally, just as it always had. Looking around the table, he started to speak, his tone heartfelt and regretful.

"Okay…here's the truth of the matter." He momentarily turned his attention back to Rachel and hugged her softly. Holding her hand, he returned his stare to the faces of his dearest friends, and it was with great remorse that he began to confess.

"Yes, that night I took advantage of Rachel. I'm not proud of it, but I did it. I apologized then, and I apologize now. To this day I don't know what came over me, what I was thinking, and if you hadn't begged me to stop… well I'm just not sure what…"

His voice fell silent. A sense of uneasiness moved about the Gathering Place. Somber looks of concern, disbelief, and confusion replaced the jubilant smiles. Chris remained solemn, his tone earnest, and in an attempt to shelter Rachel, he pulled her closer to him. He felt the eyes of his friends rest on him like hot coals.

"I never meant to hurt her. I was nervous and afraid. It was my first time, and I didn't know what I was doing, but there in the middle of the night in my parents' pool, I forced her into"—his eyes filled with shame; his voice softened—"being my baptism dummy."

For a split second, the room remained totally silent, and then it erupted with resounding laughter. But even that didn't stop him. He embraced Rachel, leaning her back and gently raising her up to hold her close by his side. "We practiced a long time. Over and over I'd dunk her and bring her up, dunk her and bring her up. After about ten or twenty times, she grabbed me around the neck and in short breathless gasps managed to say, 'Chris, stop. You're drowning me!'"

Again the table roared. Rachel had nothing to add to his story but continued quietly laughing and giggling in the gentleness of his embrace. There was a look between Trudy and Ann. As old friends they understood this look well, and as women they understood it even better. Trudy was the first to speak. "Since you half drowned her, did you at least carry her out of the pool and attempt to resuscitate her?"

"I did carry her out." He glanced at Rachel. "But no resuscitation was needed."

Ann smiled at Rachel. "But was it wanted?"

"Was it offered?" Lincoln barked flippantly at Chris.

Before he could answer, Rachel leaned forward. "What was offered was another glass of wine."

Chris laughed. "No, you insisted we have another glass, and I believe that's where the third bottle came into play."

❦

Pulling from a corner of the business district, the city bus bullied its way into the congested downtown traffic en route to the only park and ride in north Tacoma. Her attire was both fashionable and noticeably expensive, and like most young women making the bus commute, she carried a small, indiscreet backpack where she stored, among other things, a pair of Salvatore Ferragamo high heels. These same women brought sneakers to change into before walking to the bus stop. And it was one of those fashion-conscious women who found a seat on the crowded bus next to the old man.

There was nothing different about this evening. While boarding, she noticed a number of young men offering their attention with smiles and polite greetings before resuming their conversations, staring out windows, or reading the latest headlines. And like always, she'd smile and turn away, pretending to ignore them, all the while secretly knowing she would become the topic of conversation, stared at over the folded page of the *Seattle Times* and observed in the reflection of the windows, because everyone knows that's just what men do, and that's what they did everywhere she went. Some days it was hard being so attractive.

But the old man had been reading when she boarded and barely noticed her. Without looking up, he continued reading for the next two stops. This annoyed the woman; after all, she was young, single, noticeably successful, and by all standards very attractive and not used to, nor did she take well to, being ignored. It didn't faze her he was old enough to be her grandfather or somebody she'd never stop to give the time of day. Yet his intense reading and total disregard of her presents irritated her to no end.

Entering the freeway, the bus slowed to join the evening crawl. It would take twenty minutes to travel five miles before exiting at the park and ride. The old man turned another page and continued to read. She never wanted to seem rude, but boredom, having its limits, took over. Twitching her nose with a cute little snicker, she inquired, "That must be a really good book. You haven't looked up since I sat down. What's it about? Sex or vampires? All the good books are about sex or vampires lately. That's what made *Twilight* so great. It had everything—sex, vampires, violence, but after seeing the movies, I realized I was more of a wolf girl. You know, werewolves, running with the pack and all. Seriously, I'd rather sleep with a cuddly puppy dog than a cold, dead bloodsucker any day. Vampires give me the creeps. You ever been to Forks? the place is full of 'em. Luckily there's a lot more werewolves than vampires; at least I think there is."

The old man marked his page with a finger and then turned to the young lady and smiled. "Forks? Yes. Many times when my wife and I were young, but I don't recall seeing any werewolves. Although I do believe we saw Bigfoot walking the streets of Moclips one evening. But now that you've mentioned it, I suppose it could've been a werewolf."

The woman sat, nodding her head, allowing what the old man said to sink in.

And just as it did, he spoke again. "The thing was covered in long, matted hair, and big, covered in hair, and very, very big. Yes, that's how I'd describe it."

Her eyes narrowed slightly. Her lips pursed, drawing into a slim smile. "You don't believe in that kind of stuff, do you?"

Perhaps it was something in her tone or a reflection in her stare that caused him to pause. He wasn't sure, but there was something…something different about her from a second ago. Maybe his imagination, he thought.

Perhaps the strain of a long day. But whatever it was, it made him cast out the simple answer he was about to give. And so he began.

"I'm sure God has created many things I won't see in my lifetime and some that I will but won't understand. Of course, the other side of that story is, whatever God creates, Satan attempts to replicate, to counterfeit. Thus vampires, witches, and werewolves—or at least the people claiming to be such things—could most certainly exist. But it's not the occasional shadow on the wall or bump in the night that frightens me. As a matter of fact, I'm not afraid of things, but for things. I'm afraid for every man, woman, and child that will die without ever giving a thought to eternity. It's the largest step they'll ever take, one they know is inevitable, yet it's the one they least prepare for, research, or even give much thought to at all."

This was a lot more conversation than she had expected, about a subject she never wished to speak about, with a man who had never even given her a second look. She had heard about the Bible thumpers who often rode the bus lines, preaching fire and brimstone, the end is near, but not in her wildest imagination could she have envisioned herself sitting next to one. Was that why the seat was empty? Everyone else knew he was one of… those? Was everyone pointing and laughing, whispering behind her back? How frightening; how embarrassing. No, even worse, how humiliating.

But a very odd thing occurred. It started as a small, crumpled thought unfolding into an idea that lay before her, a smooth realization. It was not this soft-spoken old man she was afraid of, but the thunderous laughter that never came, the fingers that never pointed. And for the first time in her adult life, she understood no one had been paying any attention to her at all. Also for the first time in her adult life, she relaxed and smiled, introducing herself not as Deborah Maddox, finance consultant, but simply, warmly, as Debbie.

Traffic being heavier than usual almost doubled the time, but she hadn't noticed. And even if she had, she wouldn't have cared because this old man, this Bible thumper, never preached at her but simply talked to her. Speaking less to her mind and more to her heart than anyone she'd ever heard before. There was no mention of the wrath of God, only the love of Jesus. He said nothing about change your ways or go to hell, but follow Christ and go to heaven. He made her laugh by saying, "The real estate in eternity is quite simple. Either live in a mansion up the hill, or go snorkeling in the sea of fire. You choose."

She had a hundred questions but only asked one. His answer was swift, direct, and for the first time since she was twelve years old, caused her eyes to flood with tears. The old man produced a soft, pleasant-smelling handkerchief from the inside of his overcoat. Peculiar, she accepted it; even more peculiar, she felt no embarrassment; and plain out strange, she didn't care who was watching. Somehow she knew this man sitting next to her was the only person to truly care about her since she'd lost her mother three years ago. She had only vague memories of her father but had heard recently he was recuperating from heart surgery someplace in upstate New York. Her only thought at the time was *That's what drugs do, Daddy*.

The old man also had a hundred questions, but he chose to ask only two, the first being, "If God was to call you today, are you prepared to step into eternity?"

Her answer was not surprising, but it brought tears to her eyes once again. Not sobbing; that would come later. Just dampening her face with one or two tears every now and then. Without giving it a second thought, she rested her head on the old man's shoulder. His voice was so soothing, so comforting, and so filled with love that she never wanted the bus to stop. Gently she held his hand, feeling him give up his place in the book to hold hers. The young lady knew, even as he asked the second question, this would be the most important answer of her life.

Yes, in that instant she would think of many things. But the one that played over and over in her mind was the empty seat. The bus was crowded with men and women, many standing. Yet as if waiting for her, there was an empty seat next to this wonderful old man. *Peaceful*, she thought. That was how his words made her feel—peaceful. When was the last time she'd felt that? Truly felt at peace. She wondered. A scene began to form in her mind—a picnic, funny clothes, and both of her parents.

"The key to heaven is faith in Christ," the old man said, interrupting her thoughts. She squeezed his hand. "Would you like to accept Christ into your life?" On his shoulder he felt her nod yes. "Then let's whisper this little prayer together. Father, we come before you as sinners…"

The bus had almost completely emptied out before she moved from his shoulder. "My car's right there. Can I take you somewhere?"

He declined, of course, saying, "I'm almost home, but thank you."

Reaching into a side pocket of her purse, she presented him with her business card. "Promise you'll come see me right after New Year's. I want to take you to dinner or lunch or something. Promise me."

❦

A thin layer of ice had formed on the windshield. She would sit, allowing the heated leather seat to keep her warm until the defroster melted the ice and removed the chill of the trapped Northwest air. This gave her a few minutes to think about what had just happened, and, to her astonishment, how wonderful it made her feel. It was so unusual, so out of character for her. Oh, she talked to strangers on the bus all the time, but this was different. This was incredibly different. She giggled. She laughed, and finally through a windshield of melting ice, she looked into the crystal-clear heavens. Her eyes again filled with tears, and it was then she began to sob.

"It's been a long time coming, God, but thanks for never giving up on me. After Dad left, Mom and I never went back to church. But I promise you, that'll change. I want to be a part of your family again. I want to be in heaven when I die. And God, thanks for saving me that seat. And bless that old man over and over and over......"

❦

On the nightstand, housed in a paper frame, sat a picture faded with age. For the past sixteen years, it had been his most prized possession. There were times early on when, besides the clothes on his back, it was his only possession. A simple photo of the three of them picnicking on the lawn at Forest Park, dressed in turn-of-the-century costumes as part of a Meet Me in Saint Louis celebration. On that day his family meant more to him than anything, but that changed rapidly over the next year as he spiraled into a life of addiction. His wife, Susan, would have no part of the drugs and soon filed for divorce. Shortly thereafter she told him she was taking their daughter out of state to get away from him. And so she did. Seven moves in two years, finally landing permanently in San Diego. It wasn't long before she began her own battle with addictions. But there were many occasions when she would fall asleep thinking about the wonderful man she had once married. He too would lie in the darkness, envisioning the only woman he had ever loved and the child he longed to hold. But once it was over, they never spoke again.

His habits changed over the years but never vanished completely. Occasionally attending an AA meeting, engaging in counseling groups, or spending long periods of time in rehab centers from Saint Louis to New York, he always found himself drifting back to the point of a needle. He was never quite sure how it happened, but one Sunday morning, waking in the back pew of a small evangelical church, as the choir sang, he bowed his head and prayed. It was four days before he injected himself again. But that following Sunday, he stood one day sober in the front row of the church, then stood in the same spot the following Sunday three days sober. Frequently he would make it a whole week, and after a while, he almost made it a month. Over the years he prayed relentlessly, never turning from God or the drugs, yet he remained standing in the front row, an example of a broken life Jesus continued to work on. He would pray for members of the congregation and invite them to pray for him. Though it took some time, they came to accept the man behind the sickness, and this church became his family.

Years of abuse had taken their toll many times over, and that afternoon he laid down a remarkable sixty-six days sober. Before drifting off to sleep, his eyes focused on his most precious possession. Forty-five minutes later, he opened them once more. It took effort to focus on their faces, but once clearly in view, he was content to again close his eyes. The room was dark when he opened them for the last time, unable to focus at all. He could only make out the blurry outline of the old frame. Though he'd prayed the same prayer thousands of times over the years, he knew this would be the last time he would utter it to God. This gave it special importance, so, too, giving him the strength to speak aloud, his voice hoarse and raspy, barely carrying to the nightstand. But he knew it filled the throne room of heaven.

"Father, be with my little girl," he prayed, repeating the words out loud many times and even more times silently as he drifted away to the cool summer grass of Forest Park. It would be there that his addiction would end and he would meet his Lord.

Two thousand miles away, his daughter, remembering to pick up coffee, exited Highway 18 one ramp earlier than usual. She applied the brake, and the car slid to the left, skidding over a patch of black ice. Reacting swiftly, she regained control, coasting to a stop at the bottom of the grade, where she sighed a breath of relief while waiting for the light to change. There was very little cross traffic, and it seemed to be moving well above the posted thirty-five-mile-an-hour speed limit. She made a mental note to start taking this route home to avoid the downtown congestion, but she'd never have that opportunity. The noise behind her came suddenly. The impact, much less than it could've been, was still enough to push her small car over yet another patch of ice into the headlights of traffic.

For an instant all went dark, falling silent and still, and then came the sound of shoes on asphalt, people talking, crying, and the cold night air ignited in chaos. A man's gentle voice spoke to her calmly; the stroke of his hand brushing back her blood-soaked hair was unbelievably comforting. After a moment, her eyes opened slightly, revealing a face soft and young, gentle and kind. Not a face she recognized, not even slightly familiar, yet she knew she'd walk with him into eternity. In the distance the faint sound of sirens announced their urgency…but she never heard them.

CHAPTER FIFTEEN

"How was your friend? Did you get all caught up?" Rennie asked, placing a steaming bowl of vegetable beef soup on the counter where she knew he'd eventually sit.

The old man hung his overcoat on one of the brass hooks next to the front door and shuffled the last few steps to his usual spot. There he sat, more tired than hungry, but the soup's comforting aromas changed that quickly. Tonight grace would be just three nearly silent words, "Thank you, Lord," which he uttered even before answering Rennie's question.

"Yes, we're all caught up again. Well, for another few months anyway."

"Glad to hear that," she said, setting a cup of coffee in front of him. "It doesn't look like you got any rest since I saw you this morning. You doin' okay?"

"Long day!" he uttered softly.

Concern brought small lines to the forehead of the tired waitress.

Wrapping his hands around the cup to warm them, he added, "And by the way, my friend Helen said that was the best biscuit she's ever had and begged me for the recipe."

From the pass-through, Dutch peeked out. "See there? Didn't I tell you he was out chasing women? And using my biscuits to woo 'em at that."

Haley, the new waitress, hung an order on the wheel. "Believe me, Dutch," she purred, smiling affectionately toward Peter, "he doesn't need help from your old biscuits to woo anybody."

Childishly, Dutch mimicked her words in a whiney falsetto voice.

The old man grinned and continued. "I may have fibbed a little by telling her the recipe is an old family secret passed down from—"

"The grumpy monkey atop the family tree." Haley chortled.

Though not intentional, the old man joined her soft laughter. Dutch stuck his face deeper into the pass-through. "Did you hear that, Rennie? She flirts with my customer, insults my biscuits, and calls me a monkey!"

Rennie turned to the girl. "Way to go, Haley. You catch on quick. That's worth a bonus, that is."

"What!" Dutch yelped through the opening. "You keep that up, she'll be making more than me pretty soon."

Over her shoulder, Rennie smiled. "Relax. You have nothing to worry about, baby. She already does."

Their ponytails swayed in unison as they walked back to their customers. Dutch winked at the old man. "Those two sure hit it off. She makes Rennie smile, and that's nice, ya know?"

His attention snapped fully to the old man. "Hey, Pete, you've got me reading that book of John. But dang if I can figure out what he's talking about. I always heard it was, 'In the beginning God created heaven and earth,' and this John guy is talking about, in the beginning there was a word. Next thing you know, the word's turning into flesh, and I just can't make heads or tails out of what the boy's saying. Maybe if you're gonna be around tomorrow…hang on, Pete!"

Dutch ran to the oven, where he removed two single loaves of garlic bread and brushed each with a mixture of olive oil, minced garlic, and his own secret blend of Italian spices before returning them to the oven to brown another few minutes. A large pan of sautéed beef tips and Porcini mushrooms would be the last order of the day; that was unless Peter wanted something other than just a bowl of soup.

Returning to the pass-through, Dutch noticed the old man resting his forehead on both hands over his soup bowl as if in prayer. But after almost a full minute and calling his name twice, Dutch finally tapped the round silver call bell. "Order up," he said loudly, believing that would get Peter's attention. The old man remained undisturbed. Across the room Rennie glanced up from her notepad. Dutch hit the bell a second time, also getting Haley's attention.

"I'll be right back with your pie." Rennie smiled, hurrying away from the table. Her eyes focused solely on the window, where Dutch filled one side gesturing sharply toward the old man. But it was Haley who arrived first, lightly embracing the old man's shoulders as she stood by his side.

"Peter?" she whispered softly, and after repeating it twice, he responded sluggishly, lifting his head only enough to release the pressure from the back of his hands. His mind was slow to focus, as were his eyes, making the soup bowl appear unrecognizable for a number of very slow-moving seconds. As the world came into focus, he heard her voice again. "Hey, Sugar Bear…" she said affectionately.

Haley… He smiled to himself. *Sugar Bear*, he laughed inwardly. *Sweet, wonderful girl; so much like Rennie they could pass for sisters.*

And there was Rennie's voice. "You okay, Peter?"

Though his surroundings were now sharp and clear his thoughts were foggy, taking him an extra moment to answer. Even when he did, his voice seemed tired, allowing some of the words to become drawn out. He silenced himself and then began again. "I'm afraid the day has been rather exhausting."

Rennie's caring hands lightly gripped his arm. Her normally smiling face, now distressed, stared at him lovingly, as did that of Haley.

"I think I just need to go home and lie down for a while," he said, rising slowly on unstable legs. Both women steadied him, gently easing his large frame back onto the seat.

"You just sit here for a bit while I get a cold washcloth. You got him, Haley?"

The girl nodded her head rapidly, not taking her eyes off him. "Don't worry. I've got you, Sugar Bear. You want to try a sip of water?"

"Thank you…" he managed wearily.

The ice danced to the rhythm of his trembling hand as he raised it to his lips, making him suddenly aware of just how weak he'd become. The cool liquid failed to bring refreshment; instead, he remained deeply lethargic, believing if he were to rest his eyes even for a moment, they might never open again. *The angel of death speaks to me*, he thought. A smile helped to suppress his urge to laugh. *It's not death that speaks, you old fool*, he thought, *but the angel that watches over tired old men too dumb to know when to go home and get some rest.* The smile by this time had faded completely, not to return at all.

"You doing' okay, Sugar Bear?"

He answered with a slight nod.

"You're the first person I've seen get sick *before* eating Dutch's cooking," she teased, hoping to bring another smile.

And it did, not so much because of her remark but that she again referred to him as Sugar Bear. *Wherever did that come from?* he wondered.

She giggled quietly, as if able to read some minute change in his expression. "My grandpa. That's what I use to call him back when I was little—Sugar Bear. I don't remember why exactly. Maybe because he was so big and cuddly. I don't know."

The old man's lips drew back, fashioning into the warm smile that over the weeks had become so familiar to Haley. "Maybe it was because you were very small and simply loved being held," he surmised.

"Still am and still do," she admitted. "He had the best lap and the greatest stories."

Now the ice danced to a lesser rhythm as he slowly returned the glass to the counter. Sighing deeply, he closed his eyes, savoring the comforting aroma of the rich soup. He thought of Ruth Anne. Readily a scene formed in his mind of her removing fresh bread from the oven and ladling homemade soup from a large stock pot before joining him at the table, where he'd say grace and they'd spend the next half hour, forty-five minutes, or sometimes a good part of the evening sharing personal news and events that had made up their day. Sadly he imagined the cottage-style kitchen that had once sat at the rear of the home would no longer be recognizable, but that was fine because without Ruth Anne, it wouldn't be the same anyway. After all, that was why he had sold the place, and that nice couple who bought it were now making memories of their own, in a home all their own.

"Put this on the back of your neck," Rennie demanded softly, moving to stand by his side. "It's pretty cold. Maybe put it on your face. That might feel better."

Not wanting to give up the vision of Ruth Anne, he held his eyes closed, placing his face in the cool, refreshing towel and thanking God for dear friends. But something wasn't right. As he'd anticipated, the rigors of the day had brought some physical discomfort, but there was more to it than the aches and pains of a tired old man. From the moment he stepped from the bus, his thoughts had seemed chaotic and tangled, as though a bit of the day, the people, places, and even conversations had lost all chronological order. It wasn't until methodically glancing at the beautiful name Ruth Brothers on the transom that his mind graciously restored the day's history in what he believed was the proper order. Then again, at this very moment, he couldn't be sure. And for now, anyway, it didn't matter. In just moments he'd open his eyes, and there would be Rennie's smile, the humorous Dutch, and sweet little Haley. Oh, and that glorious soup—its heavenly aromas, hindered only slightly by the damp towel, still made his mouth water. *This is wonderful*, he thought. *This is home, where things are perfect even when they're not. Yes, home*...he smiled.

Inhaling deeply, filling his lungs with cool air through the moist cloth, his mind began to clear. He wouldn't rush to speak and was thankful Rennie hadn't rushed her inquiries. Haley returned to the customers, and Dutch placed the final orders on the pass-through. Reaching to tap the call bell, he stopped, not wanting to startle the old man. He waited to catch the eye of the young waitress. Afterward, his stare fell to his wife. "Rennie, everything okay? We need the paramedics?"

From under the towel came a muffled voice. "Though some people wish otherwise, I'm still quite capable of speaking for myself. Everything's fine, and there is no need to call for anyone." Breathing deeply, he removed the cloth, lifted the glass again with shaky hands, and repeated, "I'm fine—just a little tired. There's no need for all this fuss."

Rennie smiled. "No fuss."

"Oh, you ain't seen fussin'." Dutch grinned, coming around the end of the counter to freshen his coffee. "She's just gettin' warmed up. There's a lot more fuss yet to come. Ain't that right, baby?"

Rennie gave no acknowledgment, continuing to focus her attention on the old man. Dutch returned to close the kitchen, and Haley delivered the final entrées and then turned the Closed sign on before serving a second slice of deep dish apple crumble to the young couple sitting at a booth next to the front window. The old man and Rennie enjoyed light conversation. The soup, just as he thought, seemed to renew his strength, and soon Rennie, too, believed he was back to his old self, laughing and joking, even pulling Dutch and Haley into the conversation.

Thirty minutes later he found himself, fully clothed, lying crosswise on his bed, pondering three distinctly separate matters, each a pleasant diversion from the realities that had traveled with him throughout the day. So for now, he would lie quietly in his room and fill his mind with happier thoughts. Thoughts that would bubble inside and bring small burst of laughter to the otherwise bleak surroundings he called home.

Sugar Bear. What a silly thing, and for a time he imagined Haley as a child curled up in her grandfather's lap—the best lap—listening as he told great stories. Sugar Bear. How silly. And the old man smiled. Almost without warning, a burst of laughter shook him, filling the room. Envisioning a frustrated Dutch always brought a hearty laugh, but a frustrated Dutch attempting to read his Bible—now, that was hilarious. The language alone must've been priceless. Oh, how he'd have loved to be a fly on the wall. But as suddenly as the laughter began, it stopped. That also didn't last but a moment before his cheeks lifted another gentle smile.

"Vampires..." he said, breaking the hush that enveloped the room. A chuckle followed, quickly growing into a series of giggles. "Werewolves and Bigfoot...Moclips, Forks. Somebody call for help. The peninsula is being overrun with vampires and Sasquatch and werewolves, oh my..." His laughter filled the room, filtering onto the second-floor landing and down the stairwell.

Sitting up, he took his Bible from the top of the nightstand. Without opening it, he began to pray. Tonight the prayer would be one of thanks, starting with his salvation through Christ to the life he and Ruth Anne had shared in the Lord's service. The many blessings God had given him; friendships past and present; people who had touched his life; led his way; lent a hand, a shoulder, or a smile. He then acknowledged and gave thanks that God had used him to guide others to Christ. Immediately the young lady from the bus entered his mind, and for now his prayer would end.

Rising slowly, his shoulders burned, his back ached, and his legs were as unsteady as they had been earlier. Even so, he made his way across the room to the small kitchen sink covered with dents and scratches from years of abuse by the many tenants before him. He filled a glass with cold water, took two pills from a prescription bottle, ambled back to the bed, laid his head on the pillow and his Bible on his chest, and rested his eyes for the next few minutes.

"Werewolves!" he snickered, reaching to turn off the lamp sitting atop the nightstand. And then once more he rested his head. "Werewolves!"

Rennie had been standing at her window for some time when the old man's apartment went dark. Dutch put his arms around her, lightly kissing her cheek, tasting her tears. He asked, "You all right?"

Her reply was weak "No…" The light snapped back on. The old man sat up, letting the Bible fall to his lap. Tears burned his eyes, bringing pause before he spoke. "Lord, I'm so afraid," he choked, wiping a tear from his cheek.

"No, not of werewolves…" He laughed, though it was short lived. His eyes moved to a five-by-seven photo sitting on a small end table by the front door. Within the beautiful porcelain frame sat Ruth Anne dressed in her wedding gown, her eyes, her smile, everything about her promising, I'll love you forever. Usually the photo made his heart stir with warm, undying love, but not so this evening. A plethora of fear and anxiety carried the great weight of distress not only to his heart, but to his very core, causing his stomach to twist and spasm. Deep inside everything trembled much like his hands had earlier and as they were again even now. Had he ever known such fear before? Ever in his life? No, not that he could remember.

"Am I to wake one morning and find the woman in this photograph a complete stranger? All memory stolen by a thief hiding within my own body?" Minutes passed with the old man sitting in silence. When finally he did speak, it wasn't with ire or indignation but with calm resolve, entreating God, "With just her memory to lean on, it's been hard. Now that, too, will be taken from me—and not quickly, but ripped from me one page at a time."

Unable to stare at the photo any longer, he buried his face in his hands. "She's all I have to hang on to, Lord. Please don't allow this disease…" As he clutched the Bible with both hands, his words became unintelligible whiffs of air. He pressed the worn book to his chest and cleared his throat. His voice remained unable to muster little more than a loud whisper. "Lord, tell me it's not possible."

Though the words were muted, once released they seemed to explode in his ears, burning his eyes with unfallen tears, shaking his soul to rise and be heard, giving him the strength to say to God clearly and precisely, "I'm afraid of forgetting her." The Bible pressed harder into his chest, his voice again became breathless and hoarse, he gasped, "And you Lord."

✿

Dutch took Rennie into his arms and held her more tenderly than she could ever remember. His kiss weakened her knees, which should have caused her to smile, but her lips refused to give up their soft submission. His words, "I love you," were not only said, but delivered in such a way that she felt them lie upon her heart. Moments later he carried her into the other room, and it was because of this that Rennie had not seen the light in the old man's apartment come back on. Nor had she seen him leave the brownstone a short time later.

✿

"Did you forget drinks for the kids?" Trudy inquired with a soft glare.

"No, of course not. The cooler in my office is full. Come on, kids. Let's go pick something out."

Chris motioned for Linc to sit. "I got this. Can I bring something back for you, Rache?"

"Whatever you're having's fine; thanks."

As the kids followed Chris out of the room, Lincoln cleared his throat, getting Rachel's attention. "Coward," he coughed into his closed fist, nodding toward her empty wine glass. The intimidation made his face glow with childish delight, a mask that feebly hid the true mischief maker beneath. This, of course obvious to Rachel, brought a smile.

"You're terrible." She laughed in reply to his humorous dare.

Trudy agreed emphatically. "He is a terrible man. Look how he's corrupted all of us."

In a single motion, everyone at the table raised their glass. Lincoln raised the bottle. "Are you absolutely sure, my dear, there's only a sip left? And with Chris and the kids out of the room, well…"

From the doorway of Lincoln's office, a very excited Michael shouted, "Mom! Mom, come here. You've got to see this. You've got a see it." Then he disappeared back into the room.

Jim looked at Rachel. "Something's got him wound up."

With a frown steeped in curiosity, she stood. "What could he have possibly found exciting in this house?" she laughed sarcastically.

"Mom," the boy called again.

"If you'll excuse me…" Her eyes went directly to Lincoln, who still held the bottle. "You might want to save that last little sip. Something tells me I may need it when I get back."

Perhaps due to the vastness of the other rooms, the office seemed compact, giving a feeling of coziness yet with plenty of room to move about. The furnishings were modest—a small desk, a few chairs in a mishmash of colors and fabrics, and two corner tables, one holding a brass lamp and the other an out-of-place rain hat. A large bookshelf covered the wall behind the desk. On the opposite wall was the object of Michael's attention.

Stepping into the room, Rachel's eyes focused on her son. "What did you find so…" Her steps slowed almost to a stop. And like her son, she was fixated by a beautiful oil painting of a familiar yet personal scene. Michael tapped her on the hand, and without looking, she draped her arm over his shoulder and pulled him close.

"Isn't that the picture in the book we saw today?" he asked, studying it carefully.

Chris joined them in the center of the room. "I'm not sure what book you're talking about, but I did the original photo for your mom. I just never gave it to her." He caught himself and quickly looked at Rachel, his expression both confused and apologetic, unsure of what he should be saying in front of the boy.

"Did you paint this?" Rachel asked.

Beth rushed over and whispered something in Michael's ear, and the two headed toward the door. Chris called to Michael, "Would you mind taking these back to the table with you?"

"Sure!" he said, reaching for the two bottles of soda in Chris's outstretched hand. Michael placed them side by side. Looking up at his mom and Chris, he smiled. "Look. It's just like that other picture—Orange Crush and Dr. Pepper." There was an obvious twinkling in his eyes, and his smile broadened. Turning on his heel and moving toward the door, he began to sing quietly, "California dreaming...La da da da da," and then he too rushed back to the Gathering Place.

"We met Ann at the school this morning. She showed him a couple of Jim's photo albums, and now he's convinced I started a riot."

"Only one?"

"Very funny!" She sighed, looking toward the painting. "So you paint now?"

He grinned. "No! Most of the artwork in the house—paintings, sculptures, carvings—are by Linc. And if you were looking at Jim's *Labor of Love* albums today...I don't know if you noticed the covers or not, but..."

"Linc did those?" She gasped. "They're amazing. I mean, all of this is amazing," she said, indicating she meant the house.

"Linc's a pretty talented guy—retired physician, best-selling author, incredible artist. He loves to tell stories, so be prepared."

In her mind, large puzzle pieces slowly began to float into place. "Did you say he's a writer?"

"Yeah."

Stepping around the desk, Chris pointed to a number of books on a long shelf. "He's written all of these."

She instinctively followed him, though she could clearly see the familiar pink-and-orange striped borders of what was commonly referred to as the Iris collection. Chris continued to speak and point, but she didn't hear a word he said, nor did she avert her eyes from the series of books. She also was not conscious of her left hand searching for the desk chair somewhere behind her. Backing slowly, she leaned on the edge of the desk.

"Are you okay, Rache?" Chris asked, a bit alarmed.

Her eyes were only slightly wide, as if mildly surprised, but that changed rapidly with each word. And then, each sentence carried its own facial expression. "Linc? The man out there—that's Lincoln Trudeau? The... Lincoln Trudeau?"

Her hands began to tremble and perspire. A feeling of nausea lodged itself in the pit of her stomach, and the room suddenly felt very warm. She hadn't experienced such anxiety in years. *Fresh air*, she thought, but that would mean walking by everyone, and she couldn't do that.

Chris was smiling and saying something reassuring, she was sure, but nonetheless, it didn't stop her interruption. "I'm so embarrassed. Why didn't Ann or you or somebody tell me that was Lincoln Trudeau? I can only imagine what he must be thinking. Did you hear how I was talking to him? Laughing and joking around like we were old friends."

Like a frightened child, she covered her mouth with both hands and then placed them together looking as if she were in prayer. It took her a moment to speak, and when she did, it came as a whisper. "He hugged me!"

Chris raised his eyebrows slightly. "You may have encouraged that a little." He laughed.

"I can't believe I was laughing and dancing around like a fool. And…and you—telling him that stupid story about us. I feel like such an idiot."

"Hell, Chris feels like an idiot all the time," Lincoln said from the doorway. "I feel like one half of the time, more when Trudy's around."

"Mr. Trudeau, I…"

"Mr. Trudeau, is it?" he said softly. "I was hoping our friendship would last a little longer. At least through dinner, anyway."

He and Chris smiled, and Rachel blushed faintly. "I had no idea you were the author. No one mentioned it until just now, when Chris…"

Lincoln motioned for her to pause as he moved to lean against the desk beside her. Embarrassment left her unable to look him in the eye, so she stared at the floor as he spoke. "Rachel? You don't mind if I still call you Rachel, do you?"

Her head tilted just enough that she could see his smile, and he could see another warm blush delicately color her cheek. Still too embarrassed for words, she nodded, her gaze quickly falling back to the floor.

"Well, good then!" he said, placing his hand on top of hers. Again her head tilted, this time allowing him to see her smile, and she saw a gentle caring face of a man filled with true humility and kindness. His voice rested on her like a song, engulfing her senses, begging her to listen closely.

"Do you feel the least bit uncomfortable right now?" he asked, pausing just long enough to give her hand a slight squeeze. "Well, so do I, and I know for a fact so does Tru. You see, while you're sitting in here all full of admiration for who I am, we've admired you since your high school days. Twice we saw you perform, and both times you took our breath away."

At some point she had raised her head and was now staring at him blankly. His eyes were bright with honesty, his smile growing with affection. "That's right! I knew who you were the minute you stepped onto that porch. And hell, if Chris wouldn't have gotten in my way, I would have run up and hugged you. So listen. I believe you and I are standing under the same light with neither casting a longer shadow. So if we can simply replay those introductions and renew our friendship as equals, I trust it may last beyond dinner. What do you think?"

She stood, her eyes twinkling as she reached out her hand. "I'm Rachel. It's a pleasure to meet you, Link."

"The pleasures mutual." he smiled, rising to stand. "But I don't shake hands with friends."

The three of them briefly talked about the paintings and sculptures, with Lincoln assuring her there'd be a full tour tomorrow, but now, they were late for dinner. As she passed through the doorway, from behind she heard Lincoln say to Chris, "We should probably wait to tell her who Trudy is."

In midstep Rachel paused to look over her shoulder at the two men smiling innocently. Leading her by the hand, Chris whispered, "As a kid, did you ever read *Under the Bear's Umbrella?*"

Her eyes darted to Lincoln, whose warm smile and gentle nod of confirmation caused her knees to weaken. A split second later, halfway through a deep breath, she proceeded to walk toward the Gathering Place, her step quick, her smile light. She found it comforting to hear the laughter of her son and Beth playfully being amused by Trudy as she sat them at a small kid's table next to the fireplace. Jim and Ann were sharing their own set of giggles and celebrating a toast between themselves when Lincoln asked, "Is this a private affair, or may local riffraff join in? Not that it matters anyway; we're here, and we're taking over." Raising a new wine bottle, he offered, "May I freshen anyone's glass?"

With a smile, Rachel pushed hers across the table.

Once dinner was over, Ann and Trudy insisted everyone stay out of their way while they cleared the table. The men, with the help of two princesses and a small boy, unloaded the desk and placed it in Chris's garage. Lincoln and Jim went back inside while Beth insisted on taking Michael and Rachel on a tour of her house. Chris mildly objected, joking, "The maid's on Christmas break, so please ignore the dishes in the sink, Beth's bedroom, bathroom, closet, and anyplace else she's been this morning."

The home was beautiful, well kept, and tastefully decorated, and from the living room, it had a magnificent view of the sound. But it was the second floor—more precisely, the glass-enclosed deck off the master bedroom—that provided the more spectacular view. And that, coming at the end of the tour, permitted Beth and Michael to return to Miss Trudy's, where Mr. B. would be playing music soon, if he hadn't started already, Beth advised. She ran to the door and stopped. "Will you sing for me?"

"How about if we sing together?" Rachel replied.

Shyly, Beth moved from the door to join Michael at the bottom of the stairs, and excitedly they ran back to Miss Trudy's house. Inside, Mr. B. was tending to the fireplace in the Great Room, Mrs. B. and Miss Trudy were talking out on the deck, and Mr. Trudy had his head in the refrigerator. Both kids joined Mr. B. at the fireplace, and soon Michael moved to the piano; Beth quickly followed. Once comfortable on the bench, he began to play. Jim smiled approvingly at the boy's ability. Ann and Trudy shifted their attention, as did Lincoln, who made his way toward Jim. Beth stood next to Michael in awe.

❧

Lights from a small boat moved through the darkness of Hood Canal. Absorbed by its slow steady progress, Rachel's thoughts also began to drift. Chris too shared a thoughtful moment while watching the boat move leisurely over the water into the nightfall. Neither he nor Rachel spoke, though later both would lie awake thinking of the many things they wish they'd said. None had to do with the view, the boat, the lights, or Hood Canal, but how simultaneously they'd noticed their reflection in the large plate glass window they'd been staring through. It was their image each spent time recalling—standing behind her, his hands resting on her shoulders; Rachel had placed her right hand to her left shoulder, tilting her head fondly atop their intertwined fingers. It was an unconscious act for both, and when their eyes happened to focus on their ghostly reflections in the glass, it brought a startling moment of realization and surprise that caused them to step back and simply stare at each other. But what transpired was not the expected embarrassment each secretly harbored. There were no expressions of regret, no apologies—essentially not much conversation at all. And without the necessity of words, they left the room, not in complete silence but with a hushed chattering of giggles that often accompanies innocent guilt. At the bottom of the stairs, Rachel spotted a photograph of Beth and a woman she believed to be the girl's mother sitting on a motorcycle, with Brennan's Cove in the background.

Chris smiled. "The biker babes of Brennan's Cove."

Rachel picked up the photograph and examined it closer. "She's so pretty, Chris…" Her voice trailed only momentarily, so as not to dampen the mood. "But she's a blonde. You never went out with blondes; what's up with that?"

"The redhead was taken," he replied promptly.

Rachel pursed her lips to one side, forming what Chris recognized as her trademark "you're so full of it" smirk, something he'd seen many times back when. And like back when, he smiled and placed a kiss on her cheek before taking her hand to leave. For a brief moment he wasn't sure he wanted to leave, and in that same moment, neither was she. Jass, who'd been waiting on the front porch to play, hurried them along with his sudden whimpering. Rachel reluctantly stepped onto the porch and tossed a partially chewed stick back into the yard. Jass continued to wait on the porch. Chris took Rachel by the hand and turned her to face him closely.

Like his mother, Michael didn't allow the music to end, creating simple melodic arrangements and tempos to segue easily from one song to the next, raising the eyebrows and broadening the smiles of the adults, especially Jim, who understood the measure of theory one needed to accomplish such a feat so effortlessly, or—what he believed to be more likely—the boy had inherited great genetics from both his mother and father.

Entering the room, Rachel was not surprised to see everyone gathered around the piano, but she was stunned to see her son the center of attention, especially since it wasn't something he often enjoyed. Music had always been a part of his life, and she had begun teaching him piano at age three. Though not a prodigy, he was extremely talented and enjoyed learning and watching his mother share in his excitement when he finally got it right. And now he was about to do something he loved as much as anything. It began with four simple notes. He watched Rachel smile as she hurriedly made her way across the room to take her place on the bench next to him. She repeated the same four notes again and again. Lincoln spoke softly, not wanting to interrupt or disturb the piece, "'Carol of the Bells,' one of my favorites."

Michael added a descending bass line and chords. Rachel began the melodious melody and countermelodies, and soon the four hands of mother and son intermingled over the keys, producing not only a beautiful song, but a true spirit of love and enjoyment contagious to all. When the music ended, there came a round of applause. Rachel hugged the boy, and Mr. B. whispered something in Michael's ear, causing him to excitedly give up his spot on the bench. Rachel, too, started to move, but Jim held her in place. "Oh no you don't. You learned a lot more than musical theater at Irvine. I want a duet. 'Sleigh Ride,' key of G. And don't let it get boring."

With a short count and a nod, she began leading Jim through an amazing series of renditions, beginning with traditional and moving flawlessly into boogie, jazz, and pop, all while throwing in a key change or two just for a little extra spice, even incorporating mash-ups of "Mary, Did You Know," "Emanuel," "Hark the Herald Angle Sing," and, to everyone's delight, "You're a Mean One, Mr. Grinch."

Out in the yard, the night had become still and quiet, undisturbed by the gaiety trapped within the thick walls of the Trudeaus' home. Chris and Jass would play one quick round of fetch before Chris joined the others gathered around the piano, a scene he watched unfold through one of the large front windows. *It's like a Rockwell painting of the people I love*, he thought, feeling his heart melt. Taking two steps toward the window to get a better look, he stopped suddenly to recall and examine exactly what he was thinking. "The people I love!" he said softly, his eyes scanning the figures now laughing and singing. And like it had always been from the first day he met her, it was Rachel who captured his focus, his thoughts, and his...

Jass growled viciously and began backing away from the splintered shadows reaching out from the darkness beyond the footbridge at the edge of the yard. The dog, slowing only to sniff the air and watch the dark perimeter for movement, whined a mournful cry. From his memory leaped the face of the dying elk, eyes pleading, the air filling with its last gasps for life. The dog turned in fear but quickly spun back around, bearing his teeth and digging his claws deep into the cold ground. But no longer able to catch the scent and never actually seeing what manner of creature produced it, he continued to back slowly, growling deep, guttural tones, hoping to keep the invisible predator at bay once again.

Normally this would be where Chris teased the dog about squirrels, falling leaves, shadow monsters, or butterflies landing on his nose, but there was something in that growl, that posture, even the way Jass concentrated his stare on the brick walkway beyond the wooden footbridge, that signaled to Chris that this might be more than the dog's imagination. At that distance light from the compound dwindled quickly, painting a solid shade of darkness over everything beyond the little creek and the near edge of the footbridge. Though it hadn't been there a moment ago, a stiff breeze made its presence known, stirring the trees and Trudy's California state flag high atop the pole in the center of the yard. Again the dog growled. Chris smiled but had to wonder if it truly was just the wind upsetting Jass.

The dog sniffed the air. Chris again smiled, remembering this was a dog afraid of the dark. If there were a scent in the air, Jass would be frantically pawing at the front door to be let in, which was not a bad idea, considering a winter chill had caught a ride on the unexpected flurry now swaying the treetops.

"Let's get inside, Jass. But you have to be good, or Tru will put you back out in the cold."

The dog swiftly ran to the porch and waited by the door. Chris had only taken a few steps when from behind came a loud snap, followed by the rustling of bushes. He spun around quickly. There was something out there after all, something large. He attempted to peer into the forest to identify the source, but the darkness remained too dense. A second snap reached through the blackness, as if to poke the dog. Trembling, Jass curled his snout, baring his teeth, scanning the yard twice before looking to Chris and pawing the door. On Chris's left another sound commanded their attention. From within the branches of a tall evergreen next to his house, a small dead limb, broken in the last storm, fell to the ground. Jass whimpered and pawed the door again, causing Chris to smile. "You know, Jass old buddy, you almost had me believing…"

The front door swung open. An inviting glow spilled across the porch before being blotted out by Lincoln's large frame. Jass, not waiting for an invitation, ran to the Great Room and lay down next to the children, though his eyes focused on Trudy.

"I was getting worried about you." Lincoln laughed, stepping back to make room for Chris to come in. "You're missing the whole show. That girl's taking Jim to school. I mean to tell ya, she can play hell out of that piano, and so can her son. And, PS, daddy, I think Beth has a little crush going on."

Before Chris could say a word, applause rose from the other room. Ann's voice easily rose above it. "Chris, get in here. Rachel says you two have a surprise for us."

Chris looked stunned. Lincoln smiled and asked, "Another baptism story?"

When the two men entered the room, Jim remained seated at the piano. Rachel stood on the side, motioning with one finger and a wink for Chris to join her. Cautiously he did, and Rachel took his hand, addressing the room. "When we were sixteen, Chris lost a bet…"

Knowing what was coming next, Chris, blushing deeply, tried to pull away. More with her pursed smile than her grip, Rachel held him steadfast. Smugly he leaned on the piano. "Shall we tell them about the bet you lost, Rache?"

Before blushing herself, she nodded for Jim to begin playing and continued her story. "I'm sure you know how Chris hates to sing in public."

"There's a good reason for that." Lincoln blurted.

Trudy glared, her agitation lifting her voice above the music playing softly in the background. "There's the pot calling the kettle black."

Everyone giggled, and Rachel continued. "We performed this as part of a Christmas program our youth group did every year for Bethlehem Retirement Center. I always loved the song but never had anyone to sing it with."

Chris knew there was no getting out of it, so without squabbling, he took Rachel by the hand and escorted her to the center of the room, where they shared a smile, both immediately slipping into character. Rachel attempted to step around Chris, beginning to sing. "I really can't stay."

"But baby, it's cold outside," he retorted.

"I got to go away."

"Baby, its cold outside."

And outside the wind died as quickly as it had come up, but where the outstretched light fell between the shadowy fingers of the yard, branches snapped as thick bushes rocked to one side. And then the night fell silent once again.

※

With the chimes already signaling his unexpected arrival, the old man stood pondering what he'd say when his dear friend came to the door. He exhaled deeply, and visible plumes of breath hung stagnant in the crisp night air, creating their own ghostly shadows within the dim light of the narrow brick alcove harboring a single heavy wooden door. It opened slowly, and a welcoming glow fell upon the old man. Warmth moved over the threshold to touch his chilled face, and a familiar voice said, "Peter? Please come in out of the cold. Is everything all right?"

The man spoke not in tones of alarm, but with definite concern. The old man stepped inside. "I'm sorry to disturb you, Jon, especially this late in the evening, and I hope you'll forgive me. And yes, everything's fine. Or maybe it's not…" he added, shaking his head with an awkward grin. "I suppose I wouldn't be standing here at this time of night if it were."

Before Jon could comment, a gray-haired woman with a slight build made her way down the hall. "I thought that was your voice," she said, pleasantly surprised, and then, moving with natural elegance across the ornate rug lying atop the entry titles, she gently embrace her friend, saying, "I just got home myself and was about to make some hot chocolate. I use Ruth Ann's recipe, you know? I'll make enough for the three of us. Now, come in by the fire and get warm." And with that she headed into the kitchen.

"Jon, I don't wish to impose. Perhaps I should come back at a decent hour."

"Nonsense. You came for a reason. Now, if you've changed your mind and don't wish to discuss it tonight, well then, a cup of Ruth Ann's hot chocolate should be reason enough to stay and visit."

Understanding the beautiful friendship they shared, the old man forced his emotions to retreat and lowered his head humbly so as not to display further the despondence that had led him here in the first place. As he spoke, his voice seemed weak but full of joy, which made his friend smile with empathetic love. "I do miss the taste of her hot chocolate…"

※

It was shortly after nine when Rachel announced, "I hate to bring this to a close, but we have two babes that need to get to bed. I know one of them will wake up grumpy if he doesn't get his sleep."

"Mom…" Michael blushed.

When Chris immediately agreed, both babes protested with groans of displeasure, promising to wake in good spirits if allowed to stay up just a little while longer. But Rachel and Chris stood together and brought the subject to a close swiftly—that is, until Beth, who'd played this crowd many times before, suddenly and with little effort gave her depiction of the most dejected child on the planet. Her sad little eyes briefly met those of Mr. and Mrs. B. and then Miss Trudy, stopping fully on her most trusted and dearest pal, Mr. Trudy.

Lincoln moved to put his arm around Rachel's shoulder. "Now, I don't know this for a fact, not having kids of my own, but I've heard it said, if you wish your child a good night's sleep, one should sing them a lullaby before bed."

Rachel caught the slight wink he gave the children just before he added, "And as a physician, I always prescribed lullabies just before bedtime. Sometimes I'd recommend two, with a shower of kisses to help calm the giggles."

"I think you may have been overprescribing, doctor." Rachel smiled and then gave the children her own wink before once again sitting on the bench next to Jim. Chris took a seat on the floor between the two kids.

Jim whispered something in Rachel's ear. His hands moved slowly over the keys, producing a series of notes gracefully intertwining the melodies of two beloved children's lullabies, recognizable by even the youngest member of the group, her lips forming the words soundlessly. Though it was not the song Rachel had been asked to perform, she began singing softly to the little girl, "Twinkle, twinkle little star, how I wonder what you are. Up above…"

As the verse ended, Beth laid her head on her daddy's chest. Chris pulled her close, smiling warmly as he did. Jim still didn't begin the song he'd whispered to Rachel but continued to play without pause, incorporating the melody of the second lullaby. And though the structure of the song remained the same, he began adding lavish cords with subtle melodic overtones, hoping to create a stylish jazz-scape for Rachel to move about vocally. And move about she did, holding everyone spellbound from the very first line.

"When you wish upon a star…makes no difference who you are…" Her voice, strong and pure, caused the hair on Lincoln's arms to stand, something that hardly ever happened outside of the national anthem being sung during an occasional trip to San Francisco to watch a 49ers game. Anne snuggled deep into the oversized cushions of a large accent chair on the near side of the room, closing her eyes to capture every tone and nuance as they washed over her in soft relaxing waves.

Jim held the final chord as if suspending the notes in midair, creating a dreamlike space for Rachel to begin the song he'd originally whispered in her ear. Focusing her eyes on the children nestled in Chris's arms, she began to sing quietly.

"Somewhere over the rainbow…way up high…" Trudy also focused on the scene as Rachel continued to sing. "There's a land that I heard of once in a lullaby." Trudy took a deep breath, hoping to hold her emotions in check.

But even so, she needed to blot a runaway tear from the corner of her eye, and still Rachel's voice hung in the air, her gaze never leaving the children and Chris.

Trudy sipped from her glass, letting the dark-red liquid rest on her tongue momentarily, in doing so refusing to read anything more into the scene than she already had. Yet something cried to write this memory on her heart. She again studied the scene. Tender and loving were the children's faces, but of course they would be. And Rachel, with that beautiful voice, her face aglow and eyes twinkling with affection, could just possibly be a real princess. This thought made Trudy smile, and again she took a sip, and again it rested momentarily, serving to mount even deeper contemplation. But it was Beth who interrupted her thoughts, placing a finger on her soft little lips and shyly blowing a kiss to Rachel. This brought a smile to Trudy, and her eyes quickly focused on Chris. With his arms around the children and his gaze on Rachel, his eyes, too, twinkled with affection.

From behind and ever so gently, Lincoln wrapped his arms around his wife, causing her to melt lovingly into his embrace. His touch, always coming at just the right moment, held the ability to stroke her heart with love never imagined. And now, as if knowing her thoughts, his breath carried a single word to her ear. Deeper into his embrace she leaned, carefully blotting another tear from her eye. *Yes*, she thought, saying the word under her breath and etching it on her heart. "Family."

CHAPTER SIXTEEN

The hot chocolate was unmistakably Ruth Ann's—rich and creamy with just a hint of hazelnut. Peter, savoring more than the taste, closed his eyes, envisioning cherished moments from years ago. Jon, about to speak, chose to give whatever memory had brought warmth and softness to the visibly strained face of his old friend a few extra moments to "coddle the soul," as his wife, Audrey, would often say. And he too found that first sip sweet with memories, as if Ruth Ann's shy laughter and gentleness swirled within the soothing mixture, rising into the room on soft clouds of steam, which in itself seemed to convey aromas of the love, compassion, and wistfulness that were the very essence of the beautiful young girl he and Audrey had met at the Fourth of July picnic the summer before sophomore year.

It would be three weeks into the school year, while studying alone in the library, when Ruth Anne would be approached by a senior named Peter. He needed no introduction; his athletic achievements and outgoing personality made him one of the more popular boys on campus. Still, his introduction was courteous, asking permission to speak with her and apologizing for his somewhat rude interruption. It didn't take long for Miss. Hawkins, the elderly librarian, to swoop down and loudly shriek, "Quiet! There are people studying here," even though they were the only ones left in the building. Over the years the specifics of their first meeting grew vague and unimportant, but the gruff words of the Hawk remained and were often teasingly repeated with a gentle poke and a smile.

But this was not the memory the old man now brought to mind. There before him, as if guarded from reality by closed eyelids, he watched warm sunlight filter through willow trees not yet shading the small red brick patio in back of the church. On a white bench beneath an arbor of Japanese wisteria sat Ruth Anne, filled with happiness and hope, a tinge of embarrassment and the deep, beautiful love only a bride exhibits so openly. Her pose was not for the photographer but her husband alone. An image that not only lived in a frame at his apartment but for decade after decade had been displayed in his mind and treasured in his heart. He'd always prayed that come the time he took his final breath, it would be his last earthly vision. But now he feared his breath would linger far longer than his memory, and with that thought, he inhaled deeply.

It was Audrey who broke the silence. "Every time I make this, it's like she's right here with me."

"I was just thinking the same thing," Jon added.

Peter's smile never formed completely before he took a second sip, again closing his eyes. "I'm not sure where to begin..." he said, pausing momentarily to arrange his thoughts. Then, opening his eyes wide, he chuckled heartily. "Vampires! I guess that's the best place to start. You know they've already taken over Forks?"

Jon, almost choking on his chocolate, glanced at Audrey.

Peter smiled and continued. "Don't worry, my friend. The werewolves still remain in control of the peninsula. And I say there's never been much to Forks anyway, so let the vampires have the place." To punctuate the statement, he nodded his head with a short snap and calmly sipped from his cup before resting his eyes once again.

Jon's thoughts were jumbled, his words unable to form. A deep frown displayed visibly his concern for Peter's mental health. Audrey, on the other hand, raised her cup almost to her lips before asking, "You must be reading *Twilight?*"

Jon, shook his head, somewhat surprised his wife would bring up such nonsense. Peter however, was not surprised in the least. For as long as he could remember, Audrey had been fascinated with macabre folklore of all kinds. So with a soft smile he admitted he hadn't read the book, and then spoke briefly about his encounter with the young woman on the bus, saying he'd promised to have lunch with her sometime after the New Year. Perhaps even invite her to church. It was then he paused, his thoughts collecting over the next few moments until, as if seeing clearly for the first time, gathered pieces of a puzzle drifting into place. Slowly his thoughts became words whispered aloud. "It was an angel. An angel saved that seat for her."

From the heater vent, a quiet whoosh of warm air rushed to maintain the room's comfort. This sound, irrelevant any other time, now became the measure of silence within the room. Another sound that was normally trivial was the small creaking noise from Jon's chair as he leaned forward to emphasize disdain for Peter's ridiculous tale.

"I've heard a lot of nonsense from you over the years, but this beats all. Vampires, werewolves, and now angels saving a seat on a bus. Where do you-----"

"Jon…" Audrey chided, turning an apologetic look toward Peter. Her voice softened with concern. "Vampires aren't the reason you came here tonight. What's wrong, Peter?"

For an instant embarrassment warmed Jon's face, but it was the shame in his heart that burned hottest. The chair creaked once again as he repositioned his body, and his mind. Of course he'd apologize to Peter as well as Audrey; he'd loved them both for the past sixty years, and they'd all made their share of outbursts and apologies, so he knew forgiveness was there for the asking. But not wanting to be a further distraction, he'd wait for Peter's answer.

Peter hadn't made eye contact with either one but sat quietly staring into the sweet darkness that remained in his cup. Even with his eyes open, he could visualize Ruth sitting under the arbor. *But wait*, he thought. *Was it Wisteria or Bougainvillea…?*

Audrey studied Peter, his turn down stare, the gentle tapping of his index finger on the side of the cup, and then worn momentarily like a mask a soft scowl of confusion raised. With suddenness he looked at her. She stared back into his eyes, and as if knowing what he was about to say, inhaled deeply, holding her breath to still her heart.

"I'm dying," he whispered.

❦

With Ann's help Trudy sat the kids in large recliners, covered them with snuggly blankets, and dimmed the lights in the theater to start the movie.

The opening scene began without fanfare. An orchestra quietly played, a choir melodically setting the Disney tone as the camera drifted high above turn-of-the-century London as the narrator declared, "All this has happened before; and it will happen again…"

"Miss Trudy, I love *Peter Pan!*" Beth whispered.

"Me too! Thank you for talking Mom into this."

"Yeah, Daddy too!" Beth added in her quietest voice.

"I'll peek in on you pretty soon," Trudy whispered. "You need anything, we're right in the other room."

Jim sat at the piano quietly entertaining himself, Lincoln returned to the wine cellar, and Chris grabbed one of Trudy's heavy jackets off the rack for Rachel before donning his own and walking her onto the deck overlooking Brennan's Cove.

"Chris, this place is so beautiful."

"Yeah, they have a beautiful home."

"No, I mean this." And with her hand Rachel made a wide sweep of Brennan's Cove. "This entire place. The landscape, the homes, the sense of family between all of you. It all fits so perfectly, so beautifully. It's everything you used to talk about, all your dreams rolled into one beautiful package—church, children, home, the greatest neighbors in the world, and it all sits right where you dreamed of living, in the woods with a view of the sound."

Chris placed his hands against the rail and leaned into it slightly, taking in the cold waters of the cove. From the corner of his eye, he saw Rachel staring at him, her warm breathe moved in vapors mere inches from the front of his face before quickly dissipating, and though he wanted to look at her, he resisted. His breath, too, hung momentarily in the air, and for a second he enjoyed watching the two mingle in the dim light before vanishing into the darkness. A memory of long ago drew a smile and made him wonder if she ever thought of those times.

From behind and slightly above, a succession of clicks brought a soft orange-and-blue flicker to a large outdoor gas heater. The warmth was quickly welcomed by their smiles. Just on the other side of the great window stood Lincoln holding a remote control in one hand, with the other first gesturing to his eyes and then pointing to Chris as if to say, I'm watching you. Ann moved by him swiftly and closed the curtains. Chuckling, Chris and Rachel allowed their smiles and stares to lock on each other. Each turned slowly to face the cove, and though the laughter faded the smiles remained. As they stared out over the dark waters, little was said for the next few minutes, each lost in their own thoughts. So many things he wanted to ask her; so many things she wanted to tell him. But none were told, none were asked, and perhaps if not for a distant shooting star, nothing at all would have been said.

"Did you see it, Chris? You have to make a wish…remember." Rachel, holding onto the rail straightened her back and put her face to the heavens. With eyes closed she began to smile. Seconds later, she turned to face Chris, taking him by both hands, her eyes filled with excitement. "Did you make a wish?"

Now it was he who wanted to look to the heavens, but he found himself, as often happened, helpless in her gaze. Suddenly he had so many things he wanted to tell her. And she had so many things she wanted to ask. But neither spoke a word. Their eyes searched the other's heart until, in a voice as soft as the breeze that had begun to move loose strands of Rachel's hair, Chris said, "I made the same wish for such a long time; at one point it became a prayer. And then tonight, when I saw—"

"Hey," Jim hollered from the sliding glass door. "Lincoln's threatening to sing. I could use some help in here." They heard the door slide closed with a thud, followed shortly by the muffled sounds of Jim back on the piano.

Again their gaze searched the other's heart, and again there were so many things to ask and so many things to tell. But again, neither spoke. Rachel gripped his hand tightly. He placed it gently on her cheek, and from the cold waters of Brennan's Cove jumped a fish, causing both to laugh and fall into a gentle embrace, however only momentarily. But in that instant it was not simply their eyes that locked, but something deeper, stronger, something neither had experienced in quite some time. And he knew there were many things to be asked, and she knew there were many things to tell.

❦

It was nearly eleven o'clock when Chris carried a sleeping Beth to bed. A short prayer later, he turned off the little princess lamp and walked to the doorway, where he paused to look back, quietly thanking God for such a beautiful blessing. Entering his room, he chose not to turn on the light or turn down the bed, but walked directly into the glass-enclosed room overlooking the sound. His hand found the copper chain dangling from under the glass shade of a tall floor lamp. With a gentle tug came a soft glow, which was unable to fill the room with brightness but was sufficient to chase away the night from around the desk where he now sat. Removing a daily journal from the bottom drawer, he hesitated before opening it. This nightly ritual had begun in high school after he'd heard Mrs. Jordan speak on the subject.

"Often we forget how our walk with God took us from where we were to where we are," she told the class. "What issues we focused on along the way, and what was the true center of our life at a given time. Like medical records track our physical health, we can use a journal to record the changes in our spiritual condition. My dad gave me my first journal when I was nine. Now I have an entire bookshelf full. And yes, I do go back and read them from time to time, and some of the earlier ones are pretty humorous. And Mr. Huffman, if I hear you make one remark about my age, you'll spend a week in detention..."

Chris bought a journal that afternoon and began faithfully recording something every day, be it an event, observation, or simply a prayer. Naturally there were a few blank days, even an occasional week, but he was reasonably true to the task, at least until Linda's death. After that the entries became sporadic, some evolving into dark and spiteful confrontations with God, words and emotions Chris thought himself incapable of ever exhibiting toward anyone, especially God, yet his indignation spilled across the pages in his own hand. So on May 3, five months after the accident, he stopped writing altogether—that is, until November 7, when, from the back of the church, he and Trudy watched from the shadows his daughter's first rehearsal with the kids' choir. That evening he filled three pages thanking God for Trudy's love, patience, and determination.

Chris walked to the window and looked out over the sound, allowing his mind to regress to younger days and happier times. Fifteen minutes later, with eyes moist, he returned to the desk to again open the journal. He scribbled a single word, smiled, and placed the book back in the drawer. Soon he found himself on his knees again in prayer, reconfirming his love and trust for the Lord, asking for peace with the past and strength for the future, things he had asked for once upon a time, but not once since the accident.

This was a moment of healing for Chris, coming on so strong he could almost feel the hand of God lie upon his shoulder. That night, for the first time in almost a year, a dream brought joy to his heart and a long-forgotten song to his mind. Perhaps Bailey would perform it before she left for Tampa?

He'd filled other pages since that night in November, writing mostly of God's love, Beth's progress, and his sister's upcoming move. It was the latter he wrote about least and prayed about most. Bailey's absence was sure to have an enormous effect on Beth, a concern Trudy expressed privately as she and Chris sat by the fire pit watching her and Lincoln play in an early snow that had come a week before Thanksgiving. That evening Chris opened the drawer, removed the journal, and stared for some time at a new blank page before finally laying his pen down and walking to the window. The dark channel of water allowed his thoughts to drift on the nightscape without diversion, but this brought a gathering armada of fears, visions, worries, and doubts to quickly mount an assault on his already sinking heart.

He began to pray, and as he did, a lone vessel cut through the glassy waters of the channel, its small running light demanding his attention. For a moment his prayer became fragmented—rambling sentences of disjointed words, each hesitant in their fall from his lips. His eyes continued to focus on the light, as did his heart, mind, and soul. This small, seemingly insignificant beam, barely piercing the night's darkness, suddenly illuminated in Chris, the hope, trust, and faith he'd so desperately sought to regain for some time. As if relieved from a great burden, he gasped a deep cleansing breath and paused for a number of seconds before guardedly continuing to pray. But this was not merely a continuance of the prayer from a moment ago. It held no despondency, no voice of worry or cries of fear; instead, the words were as soft as gently falling snow, spoken with assurance, thankfulness, and praise for the One whose light Chris knew always shone through the darkness; just sometimes he needed to look through the window to see it.

He quickly moved to his desk, picked up the pen, and wrote two words. A memory of long ago touched him tenderly, and again he looked out the window and then back to the page. "I'd be there," he said, nodding his head. From the corner of the desk he picked up a framed photo of his sister and Beth. Staring at it for some time, he again nodded and said, "I'd be there."

Since making that entry, he'd opened the book only once, and that was on the anniversary of the accident. He'd spent most of the night writing just two pages, thinking out each sentence before putting it to paper. And once he felt it was complete, he read it over a half a dozen times before moving to stare out the window. His heart felt heavier than he could ever remember, and an ocean of tears sat waiting to be released as he began to read.

"My darling Linda…It's time to say goodbye…"

That night he dreamed she was sitting on a lawn overlooking the ocean. In the distance stood the lighthouse they'd stayed in shortly after their wedding and where she was sure Beth had been conceived. Their conversation was as brief as the fading trail of a shooting star, yet all was spoken that needed to be heard by the heart. Smiling, Linda stood and walked alone to the edge of the yard. As she turned to face him, the ocean breeze moved through her hair, placing her words softly in his ear. "Thank you for leading me, for showing me the way. I know I'll always have a place in your heart, but you're right…it's time to say goodbye."

The sea and the sky fell away, leaving an unimaginable volume of stars stretching over an expanse of space never ending. In the distance the lighthouse cast its beam through the heavens of eternity, and though her figure stood alone, Chris sensed there were multitudes there with her. The wind again moved her hair, bringing to him not only her voice but the very scent of her soul. And it spoke to him. "This is where we say goodbye."

Showing Rachel the view earlier this evening was the first time he'd returned to the room since making that entry. Now as he reread it, he recalled the dream and all Linda had spoken of. It was true; she'd always have a place in his heart. And that thought made him smile.

Deciding to add nothing, he placed the journal back in the drawer and turned off the tall floor lamp beside the desk, sending the room into darkness. His eyes adjusted quickly even as he proceeded to cross the room. From the window something caught his eye, stopping him in the center of the room. There were no vessels moving along the dark strip of water, no moonlight glistening off the surface. Only a landscape of silhouettes and shadows dressed in various shades of black and gray lay beyond the double-pane glass. However, his focus was not beyond the glass, but the glass itself—a ghostly figure staring in from the cold, the casting of his own reflection back into the room. But it wasn't him alone that occupied the window's opaque portrait. And at first he believed imagination had recalled their images. Then, oddly, even without truly seeing the soft features of her face, the details of her eyes, he felt helpless in her gaze, and he knew…it was not imagination but his heart which painted her likeness. So then, returning to his desk, he wrote, "My beautiful Lord, thank you for tonight. You allowed my daughter to meet a true princess, become infatuated with a young prince, and dance with more joy and happiness than I've witnessed in a very long time. And as for me?"

Unconsciously he twirled the pen through his fingers, contemplating the question. Over the next few minutes, there were two words that could've easily fallen onto the page, and over the next few minutes, they did.

❦

In the Brooks' downstairs guestroom, lying next to her son, waiting for sleep to find her, Rachel recalled small snippets of the day's events, lingering on the ones she wished to commit to memory and cherish in her heart for years to come. But quickly it dawned on her the day was not filled with simply cherished memories, but treasured blessings time and again, hour after hour. Unable to remember a time when she had felt so blessed, so loved, she was led to prayer. "Thank you, Father," she whispered aloud. Nothing further needed to be said, though she knew much could've been. But God knew what was on her mind and in her heart, and she knew He would still be listening when she came to Him again. She didn't realize just how soon that would be.

Snuggling deeply into the pillow, she thought about the reflection of her and Chris, its nostalgia, innocence, but most of all how incredibly wonderful it had made her feel inside. She'd not allow guilt to steal it from her, nor embarrassment to tarnish its virtue—an unforeseen moment orchestrated by chance, she thought...or was it?

Turning on her back, she stared at the ceiling, visualizing her first view of him from Trudy's porch—that lasting embrace, all the laughing, joking, singing, dancing, stories, wine, and on and on and on; unforeseen? The question brought a muffled giggle, and at the same time, the silence of the room was suddenly disturbed by a light tapping on the window. Startled, she listened quietly. It came again, and then once more. "Rache? Rachel?"

Cautiously making her way to the window, she pulled back the curtain and had to stifle a much louder snicker. There was Chris standing in the cold, barefoot, no shirt, with only his jeans on. "Be at my door tomorrow morning at six. There's someplace I want to take you and the kids. Wear your grubs. Oh, and Jass will insist on joining us. So bring him along." And with that he kissed his finger and placed it on the window.

Just before Rachel's heart melted completely, she too kissed her finger and placed it on her side of the glass directly on top of his. Their eyes embraced like years ago when he'd sneak to her house and tap on her bedroom window simply to say good night and share a finger kiss through the glass.

Rachel slid back into bed and stared at the ceiling. For the next few moments, her smile was secretly her own, but her thoughts were excitedly shared with the Lord. "Now, that was truly unforeseen," she whispered with yet another slight chuckle. For the next few minutes she found herself praying in a manner she hadn't for quite some time—joyfully. Afterward, turning on her side, snuggling deep into the pillow, she wondered where Chris was planning on taking them. Did it matter? she thought. No! It was time spent getting reacquainted with an old friend. Snuggling deeper into her pillow, she smiled and thought...friend?

You Are My Love

The hours had passed quickly, as they often did in this home, where the chiming of a clock dictated the evening's closure always sooner than those gathered around the table preferred. But tonight the chiming went unnoticed time and again by the intensity of love and compassion; sorrow and laughter were offered minute by minute, hour by hour, story by story, and left to Jon and Audrey, the night would've continued on as if time stood still altogether. How long had it been since they'd shared an evening like this? A time to reminisce with open hearts the years left behind them. Had the question been brought up, Audrey and Peter knew the answer: three months prior to Ruth Ann's passing, which now brought this evening silently into perspective for them both. Jon, never good at recalling such things, didn't allow it to cross his mind but simply embraced the time with the two people in life he loved most. Before the night was through, as he so often did, he'd led them in prayer.

Putting on his heavy coat, the old man shook his head. "I didn't mean to keep you two up this late..."

Just then the clock behind him chimed the hour as if demanding their attention.

"You should let me drive you home," Jon suggested for a third time. "Or at least call a cab."

"I'm fine," Peter replied.

Audrey adjusted his collar, placing an extra-thick woolen scarf around his neck, tucking it deep into his jacket. "Merry Christmas," she added, hugging him tightly. Her perfume had changed very little over the years, always faint, somewhat elegant. At one point he knew the name of her favorite, but that had slipped from memory long ago. He guessed there were other things he'd probably forgotten about her as well, small things, insignificant really, especially in view of the many beautiful memories they'd shared so easily throughout the evening. Memories steeped in nearly a lifetime of friendship, never more distant than a few miles apart—that is, with one exception.

At nineteen Peter was called to serve on the battlefields of Korea. Eighteen months later, he returned a military hero with two purple hearts and a Silver Star, which he seldom spoke about. His life, his focus, his love, and his passion remained his beautiful Ruth Anne, who shortly after his return, in front of God, family, and friends, vowed to love him until death do they part, a promise she gladly and most lovingly kept.

That August, somewhat reluctantly, Audrey married Jon. It wasn't that she didn't love him or thought she could do better, which she easily could have. The problem was she never pictured herself as a preacher's wife, a career path Jon had chosen only after visiting Pacific Lutheran University with Pastor Burroughs. But Audrey's problem wasn't Jon. Audrey's problem was Audrey, and she knew it. In high school she enjoyed being slightly rebellious, dragging Jon to parties where she would drink beer, smoke cigarettes, and occasionally add whiskey to the mix; all of which he found extremely disgusting yet somehow arousing at the same time. Well, until she'd throw up in his car, or, thankfully, more often than not, on someone's lawn. Shortly after their wedding, her tastes began to change. A six-pack of beer became a single glass of wine; whiskey grew into scotch but was only enjoyed once or twice a year, and for the most part she put smoking behind her. However, that slightly rebellious attitude, like her perfume, changed very little over the years, and though Jon didn't always appreciate it, he wouldn't have had it any other way.

There was one other thing that changed very little over the years, and that was her love for Jon. Even now her heart reminded her many times throughout the day she could've never done better. And as far as being a preacher's wife…she wouldn't have it any other way.

But there was another man in her life she'd loved since high school, and that man, of course, was Peter. It was never a secret love, no hush-hush talk behind anyone's back. Audrey made her feelings perfectly clear right from the start, yet she assured everyone her heart belonged to Jon. She loved Peter in another way, placing him in the role of the big brother she never had. This affected Jon to some extent, but as he got to know Peter and their relationship grew closer, he too looked to Peter as a brother and was thankful he was always there for him and Audrey.

Ruth was not as quick to accept Peter, responding slowly to the senior's charm and affections, cautiously guarding her feelings from the young man it seemed the whole school was in love with, which made her ask why he'd invited her to homecoming when he hardly even knew her name. After turning down his invitation twice, she eventually accepted, not because he was cute, popular, or persistent, nor because of his intriguing charisma that seemed to overwhelm certain friends of hers. No, it was none of that. She accepted for no other reason than to get Audrey to shut up about it and leave her alone. Much more frightened than excited, she believed Peter would quickly tire of her. After all, she wasn't terribly athletic, nor did she fit into the social group he ran with. But at the dance, his focus remained almost entirely on her. She was surprised to find they shared more interests than not, with the biggest surprise coming when he asked if she'd like to go to church with him that Sunday. She wasn't much of a churchgoer but agreed.

That Sunday morning in front of her house, she asked where he'd parked. Pointing to the church at the end of the street, he laughed. "It's such a beautiful morning, I thought we'd walk."

Suddenly, almost comically, Ruth Anne knew she must've passed that building hundreds of times without ever really noticing it was a church. This would be something she needn't mention to Peter, but later that afternoon, while watching Audrey practice blowing smoke rings, she shared it with her. Audrey's first response was, "There's a church by your house?"

The following Sunday Jon accompanied Peter and Ruth, even staying after responding to The Call, a program designed to welcome, counsel, and pray for those taking their first steps in faith. And though he didn't leave on fire for the Lord, he looked forward to reading the pamphlet and talking to Peter, who'd been raised in the church. As he walked from the building, Jon felt renewed, different somehow, eager for change. And then, stopping short at the top of the steps, he saw Audrey sitting on the hood of his old 1940 Chevy sedan. Her amorous glance seemed to heat the very air he breathed.

Blowing double smoke rings, she threw her cigarette to the ground and slid over the contours of the hood and high rounded fenders, resting one foot on the ground and the other on the face of the hubcap. To Jon, never had that car looked so sexy. As he crossed the parking lot, his stride increased, and his eyes focused sharply on her lustful smile. She waited for his approach and then took one step forward to meet him, her lips moist, beckoning to be kissed. He held her just shy of arm's length; in every rhythmic current of her breath, the noxious odor of tobacco was carried as much to his moral senses as to his nostrils. Her eyes, glistening wells of seduction, enticed him to take her into his arms, but he didn't. He knew he needed to speak quickly before his resistance could be crushed by her sensual allure, yet he really didn't know what to say. So he said exactly what he was thinking. "Audrey, if there is a hell, there's a pitchfork with your name on it!"

She affirmed his words with a soft yet beckoning smile, opened the driver side door, and slid across the blanket-draped seat to her spot in the center. Once inside he turned the key, and the engine came to life. And like always, putting her arm around his neck, she kissed him on the cheek and then relaxed her head onto his shoulder. "Are you coming back next week?" she asked timidly.

"Damn right I am. And the week after that, and the week after that, and the week after that."

The gruff tone in his voice carried away her smile. Audrey sat quiet for a second or two, reflecting on his answer and the seriousness with which it was delivered. She'd seen him angry before, just never at her, though time and again she'd given him plenty of reason. With noticeable sincerity, her voice wavering nervously, she asked, "Then, can I…come with you?"

There was hardly a pause, but to her it seemed time had stopped, waiting for him to speak. Jon sighed, feeling his wall of resistance crumble. "Of course you can." Turning in his seat just enough to embrace her with one arm, he breathed "I love you" and then pressed his lips to hers.

His face was warm, his touch soft. Feeling his words play in her heart, she backed away, taking in a shallow breath. "I love you too, Jon," she whispered, returning his kiss, but this time ever so softly.

The words were almost foreign to her lips. Abandoned at age two by her father, this was the first time she'd ever spoken them to anyone other than her mother, and if asked, she couldn't remember the last time that was. But they felt wonderful. She felt wonderful, and she'd speak them one more time just to hear their sound before allowing one final kiss. Afterward, giggling an apology for her behavior and then retrieving a stick of Juicy Fruit gum from her purse, she quickly removed the wrapper. Jon felt a tinge of disappointment as the thick, sweet smell filled her mouth.

That following Sunday was the first of many that they, along with Peter and Ruth, attended services together. Peter, with his knowledge of Scripture, quickly became Jon's mentor, and shortly before summer, Ruth Anne began to feel comfortable enough to teach third – and fourth-grade Sunday school. But Audrey ventured out on her own, first visiting seniors in nursing homes, where she'd sit and have conversations, assist with simple tasks, and, when the subject arose—and it often did—read to someone from the Bible. After doing this for several months, one afternoon she spoke to the pastor and obtained a list of shut-ins no longer able to attend services.

It wasn't long before she became overwhelmed by the needs of so many. Another trip to the pastor's office brought an unexpected announcement from the pulpit the following Sunday. He briefly spoke about what he called her "mission" and then with no warning at all invited her to the platform. This would be her first experience with public speaking. No preparation, no notes, just tell the people what you're doing.

She looked out over the congregation, and her heart raced. She felt weak and flustered. Jon sat forward, his nervousness evident, as it was with Ruth Anne. But then she saw Peter, relaxed, smiling, confident that she would do just fine, and though she couldn't tell for sure, she believed he winked his much-needed encouragement as well. She took a deep breath and then let the air rush from her body, carrying with it the poisonous anxiety that so often causes one to choke on their own words. She began. Her voice, confident and strong, held the attention of everyone, allowing her message to resonate in the hearts of many. She spoke for a little over three minutes, never once about herself but about the faces, the eyes of loneliness, and the smiles of immeasurable gratitude for showing the elderly and sick, some on their deathbeds, the simplest gesture of kindness she knew. "Talk to them. Read to them. Pray with them. They just wish to hear a tender voice," she said.

The pastor again surprised her by announcing the church would be supporting another new reach out ministry, A Tender Voice. And there would be a sign-up sheet in the foyer for anyone interested. In the end there were fourteen names, mostly those involved in youth group and choir, but also three elderly men and women. The following Sunday, in a small blue envelope, an anonymous gift of $500 was found on the altar with a note that read, simply, "May God bless A Tender Voice Ministry." No one ever stepped forward for recognition of the gift.

The following September, the beginning of her junior year, Peter left to begin his military service, and Jon took an after-school job as a mechanic. She and Ruth Anne began making plans to expand A Tender Voice Ministry. Their service would include grocery shopping, meal preparation, running local errands, and even housecleaning for shut-ins in the community. They would need to charge a nominal fee to cover expenses, but that could be waived for those unable to pay. So with minimal help from Ruth Ann's father, they drew up a three-year business plan and took it to the pastor and church board of directors. It was immediately turned down for one simple reason: "You're schoolgirls, not housemaids or errand boys. Young women and women in general know nothing about business and finance. Most can't balance a household budget, let alone take on this type of endeavor. You should be concentrating on finding good husbands."

Not waiting for the ripple of laughter to die down, Audrey stood up, clutching the proposal in her hand. "No, gentlemen, what we should be concentrating on is finding a good church, one that respects and values all of God's children equally—male and female."

❦

The task of finding a new church fell mainly on Ruth Anne, as it was during this time that Audrey's Saturday nights made Sunday mornings come too early, too loud, and too painful to be shared with choirs, sermons, or even God, as far as she was concerned. Then, by happenstance, Audrey found the church. It came as a result of her continuing to visit shut-ins and convalescent homes with whom she'd built close relationships. And it was through the elderly Mr. Avery that she heard of the church. The frail old gentleman, no longer capable of remembering many details, gave Audrey his old street address and said, "It's one block south of my house, down Allerton. Great big place about the middle of the block; you can't miss it. I'd be grateful if, when you get in the neighborhood you'd stop by and ask about that young pastor. He'd only been there a year or two when they brought me here, but his sermons were the best my old ears had ever heard, and my pop was a pretty good preacher back in the day."

That Sunday Audrey dragged herself to the church, where she sat in the back hoping to separate her headache from the strains of the choir. But as the pastor began to speak, she felt she was hearing God's word for the first time—a message packed with emotion, historic details, and practical application, giving her a clear understanding of the passage and topic they were studying. She was excited to tell Jon and Ruth about the experience, but first, she'd need to speak to the pastor regarding Mr. Avery. Their conversation was brief, with the pastor jotting down the information on the back of a bulletin and promising to stop by Thursday afternoon. He thanked her twice, saying he wished he could talk more, but he was late for a flight, and he hoped to see her again. Maybe Thursday?

On Thursday Audrey cut her afternoon classes, making sure she'd be there. But entering Mr. Avery's room, she found it was empty. At the front desk, she was directed to the multipurpose room at the end of the building. Peering through a small window in the door, she could see Mr. Avery in his wheelchair, the pastor, a good number of the choir, and more than a handful of faces from church. Her eyes flooded with tears as she watched Mr. Avery sing and smile, laughing joyously with his friends who believed that kind old man who sat in the front row every Sunday must've passed away. Audrey didn't go in but walked to the little chapel in the center of the building, and there, by herself, gave thanks.

Jon and Ruth loved everything about the church, and both loved its effect on Audrey. Though some Sundays were still rough for the girl, at least she was there, Bible in hand. When Peter came home on leave shortly before shipping out for Korea, he was excited to visit the new church and surprised to learn Reverend Burrows was the father of Stephanie Burrows, his old babysitter. There were a number of people in the congregation he knew, and he didn't hesitate to introduce Ruth, Jon, and Audrey to each one, introducing Ruth as his girlfriend. After church Ruth kidnapped him for some much-needed alone time. The next day at school, she told Audrey that Peter had proposed, showing off the small engagement ring he'd given her. Audrey couldn't have been happier but still teased, "If you hadn't said yes, I hope you know I would've married him!"

Ruth Anne giggled and then again admired her ring. "I did know that. Why do you think I said yes?"

Audrey's love for Peter, like her perfume, had changed very little over the years, and as she held him now in the warm foyer of her home, she felt her tears begin again. The evening had brought many tears after he announced the doctor's latest findings. The discussions that followed, for the most part, were simple, straightforward, and to the point. His life would go on the same as it had day after day since he had lost Ruth. He had no special needs and was quite efficient at taking care of himself and his affairs, at least for now. As he knew there would be, Audrey and Jon made gracious offers, each one kindly, lovingly denied by the person Audrey repeatedly called a stubborn old man. Of course that just made Peter's smile broader, his laughter louder, and his love deeper for the silly old woman and her wonderful husband.

"If you're going to cry, let's at least break out the photo albums and have a good one. I'll even join you," he said at one point. It took little coaxing for Audrey to bring them to the dining table, where all three shared heartfelt stories of what each one considered family. And there were tears.

In the foyer Peter felt Audrey tighten her hug. Her breath faltered as she fought off another round of tears, but then quickly she stepped back, readjusted his collar, and wiped her tears on his sleeve.

Peter chuckled. "At least it wasn't your nose…"

Audrey had no smile to give. "It was, but just a little," she shot back, stopping a tear from leaving her red, swollen eyes. "Now get out of here before we lock you in the closet and never let you leave, you stubborn old man."

Peter beamed. "I love you, too, silly old woman." He kissed her hand, turned to hug Jon, and then paused. "I wish you never would've retired, Jon. Your sermons were so beautiful, a gateway into the heart of Christ, as your lovely bride once put it. I miss 'em. Try to recall 'em once in a while, but…" Lingering on the thought, he finally smiled. "I love you, brother." And then he hugged his friend warmly.

Jon opened the door, and Peter stepped into the cold night air. He quickly turned around with eyes wide, saying, "Perhaps you could write a sermon about angels on the bus. Or maybe the saving of Sasquatch..."

With loving disgust, Jon chuckled in response. "Or maybe vampires and the kooks who believe in them?"

"God bless," Peter said, preparing to navigate the four steps down to the walkway.

Audrey ran onto the porch, threw her arms around him, and began to cry. She attempted to speak but then said nothing, content to silently be held one more time. It was another full minute before he moved along the walkway to stand and wave goodbye before crossing the street. Audrey held Jon's hand. Jon silently prayed for his friend, then stepped back inside and shut the door. In the small entry, the couple held each other for quite some time, stroking the other's heart with words of love and comfort before Jon retired to his office, closing the door behind him. And there, for the first time since Ruth Ann's death, his tears fell unchecked. Moments later Audrey sat by the fire permitting her own tears soft escape. In the flames her imagination wandered back over the decades, remembering how Peter and Ruth Anne held a spot in every major decision, event, and goal in her life. After a while Jon entered the room. Immediately his own memories danced in the flames. Holding Audrey's hand, he kissed her on the cheek, and for the first time since Ruth Anne's funeral, he became suddenly aware of the sweet, smoky flavor of scotch on her breath.

❧

Startled awake by her own voice, Rennie glance at the fluorescent face of the alarm clock, which now read 12:07 a.m. For the next few minutes, she sat on the side of the bed, her heart racing, her hands trembling. She blotted perspiration from her neck and face with the edge of her nightgown. Nightmares had been a common product of her childhood, even continuing into her teens and twenties, but none this bad. This would disturbed her sleep for many years; and though it quickly cleared from memory, a strong sense of foreboding remained.

Quietly making her way to the kitchen, where light from a nearby streetlamp filtered through the sheer curtains of the window just above the sink, she glanced out over the parking lot at the rear of the building. At this time of night, expecting the lot to be empty, she was surprised, but more concerned to see the familiar rust-covered '78 Chevy Impala belonging to the current boyfriend of Layla, the local street musician living in the apartment next to Peter. From inside the car, a small orange glow flickered momentarily. A plume of smoke rose from the driver's window into the still night air.

Rennie drew her hand back from the light switch, even stepping into the shadows while still maintaining a clear view of the entire lot. Something wasn't right. Why would he park in this lot instead of Layla's, where over the last month she'd noticed his car numerous times? A trend that left her troubled to some degree, mainly because there was something about the man she didn't like, didn't trust, and didn't want in her neighborhood. Though not a close friend, Layla was more than just a neighbor and acquaintance. She was one of a handful of people Rennie genuinely cared about and didn't want to see her used, hurt, or something even worse.

The answer as to why he was parked in her lot came quickly as a dark sedan pulled slowly into the parking lot. As he exited his car, the dome light showed clearly he was alone. There was no lingering conversation with the occupants of the sedan, just a quick exchange of what she recognized as cash for drugs before both vehicles disappeared from separate exits. Acting on intuition, Rennie moved to a vantage point by the living room window overlooking the narrow parking lot across the street. She watched the battered Impala pull to the far end, where a veil of darkness concealed its appearance. Walking quickly, the man disappeared into the old brownstone. Moments later, light filled Layla's apartment, casting shadows onto the pulled window shade.

For just a second Rennie wondered if Layla had started using drugs again, a habit the girl entered rehab for shortly after her twin sister's death a little over a year ago. She knew the girl still drank wine on occasion, but even those times were far and few between anymore. For the most part, Layla had cleaned herself up and worked hard at staying that way, taking classes at the community college and even volunteering to entertain at local drug awareness programs. But Rennie knew from watching her own father battle addiction, you're never more than one party away from dancing with your demons.

"Get away from that man, Layla," Rennie cautioned in a whisper. "He'll drag you down and leave you for dead, girl."

But then another thought occurred to her, one that seemed a little more plausible, considering the girl's highly visible pursuit of positive changes to her lifestyle. Maybe, just maybe, Layla knew nothing of this man's late-night endeavors, which just might be the key to getting him away from her and out of the neighborhood. It might be time for a girls' night out. Dinner and then a trip to check out that lovely little dessert shop over at Poet's Corner.

Grinning with hope, Rennie turned to retreat to the kitchen. She quickly turned back as something caught her attention. From below the window, a dark silhouette stepped onto the vacant street. It was Peter. Instantly recalling the episode at the counter, Rennie's heart stopped. Had he come for help and she not heard the buzzer? Hoping to get his attention, she lifted her hand to tap the window, but before striking the glass, she watched as Peter was washed in the headlights of an approaching police cruiser. Rennie's smile returned as Officer Redding stepped from the car. The two men stood talking and laughing for the next few minutes, and then, apparently seeing nothing unusual or alarming with Peter, the officer returned to his car to continue his rounds.

Rennie watched the old man enter the building, her eyes jumping to the second floor, where a large shadow swiftly filled Layla's shade before the room fell dark. A cold chill caused her to shiver. Her eyes drifted, anxiously awaiting the soft glow from the lamp just inside Peter's front door. She would remember it as one of the longest minutes she'd ever endured. Finally, when the light appeared, she sighed with relief, satisfied he was safe.

Rennie returned to the kitchen for the water she had never poured. But her thoughts remained on the building across the street. Not taking the time to raise the glass to her lips, she hurriedly returned to the shadows of the living room and was somewhat relieved to see darkness still occupied Layla's window. But for some unexplained reason, it was the light from

Peter's room that filled her with a disturbing uneasiness, recalling not the visions of her nearly forgotten nightmare but the deep sense of foreboding it had left as a greeting when she awoke. Once again becoming aware of her unquenched thirst, she took a sip. Her eyes wandered to the old Chevy still resting in the dark corner of the lot. One of the neighborhood's many feral cats lay warming itself on the hood.

"Pee on it, Garfield," she whispered aloud, raising her water glass as if to give the animal her permission. The effort brought on a twinge of guilt, yet it was hardly enough to subdue her quiet case of giggles. Before she could take a sip, Peter's light went out, plunging the building into complete darkness. It was then her eyes found the faint orange flicker of a cigarette lighter coming from Layla's window, the shade pulled back just enough that even in the darkness she could make out the man's image…his finger pointing directly at her.

Jolted with a sudden rush of adrenaline, she hurriedly spun out of view, placing her back tightly against the wall, covering her mouth to mute the scream rushing to escape. On the carpet lay the glass, its contents dampening the soles of her feet, but fear held her steadfast against the wall. Her mind raced, questioning the validity of what she had just seen—or had she seen anything at all? Sheer logic told her it was simply imagination, and after dwelling on it for a minute longer, she concluded it could be nothing else. It only made sense. Still on edge from the nightmare and seeing that little creep pushing drugs in her backyard was enough to get anyone's imagination working overtime. Besides, there was no street lamp on her side of the block, leaving the room completely dark. And what about the curtains? There was no way he could have seen in. She had to have imagined it—she had to have. But what if she hadn't?

For a moment Rennie was tempted to wake Dutch, but she knew how that would play out. Groggily he'd say it was a bad dream, just her imagination, and then he'd put his arm around her, making her feel as safe and protected as the day she ran away to marry him. Her heart began to slow. Her body relaxed. She knew that man would stand up to Satan to protect her. After all, he'd already stood up to her father. Feeling the corners of her mouth pull to a soft grin, she picked the glass off the slightly damp carpet she knew would dry by morning and set it on the end table directly in front of the window. More consciously than not, she didn't glance over to confirm her theory but moved quickly to the bedroom, crawled under the cover, and woke Dutch just enough for him to hear her say, "I had a nightmare."

Stretching his arm out, he felt her snuggle into his neck. "Ain't nothing gonna get my girl while I'm around," he mumbled, pulling her tight against him. "I'll keep you safe, baby. Don't you worry; I'll keep you safe."

Rennie lay awake for quite some time, letting her mind fill with thoughts, scenarios none of which included the druggie staying the night with Layla, but instead centering almost exclusively on Peter. This wasn't the first time she lay awake concerned for the old man. Over the last few months, there'd been more times than she dare count. And she didn't believe the episode at the counter this evening had been the first, noting he didn't wish to discuss the matter, nor did he seem bothered by it. And now that she was thinking about it, there'd been other times he'd seemed despondent, sluggish to a point of mild confusion. But of course when confronted, Peter had a way of sloughing things off with a chuckle and a smile that made the whole world seem positively beautiful.

Aggravation quickly rode the back of her concern, leaving her to conclude that tomorrow she and Dutch would have a heart-to-heart with Peter. And since he wasn't a man who spoke about personal issues easily, she knew it would be a difficult conversation. But it was one that needed to take place and needed to take place immediately. If nothing else she had to know what the old man was dealing with and the level of care he needed at this time and would need in the future. She and Dutch didn't have the financial means to pay caregivers and such. Neither would that be a consideration; family takes care of family, always, period. So he could stay in the small apartment next to theirs, and when the time came, Dutch could put a door connecting the two—easy peasy, she thought, her mind made up. Yes, something would be said, and something would be changed, and yes, Peter would have a tizzy, but she didn't care.

Rennie's smile reappeared, as she just bet Peter hadn't a clue what a southern girl's love for family could be like. But he would learn real quick.

As for the old man, the long walk home over quiet streets had brought the perfect ending to an exhausting day—a time of personal reflection and continued memories not left at the bottom of a cup of chocolate but recalled with such love he wished his journey home would never end. Life hadn't always been good; neither had it been all that bad—a wondrous blend distinct in its own creation, sweet and salty like Milk Duds and popcorn. That was how Ruth Anne had described life. Or was that her favorite movie snack; he wasn't sure. So after giving it great consideration, all of about three seconds, he came to the conclusion it was probably both.

Many times along the way he stopped, looking to the empty space around him, and for no other reason than to let his heart release its own emotion, he would say, "I love you, Ruthie, and we'll laugh again, dance again, and some would say love again. But that's not true. You can't resume something that has never ended."

But the frigid temperature wasn't much of a distraction. His step was brisk and sure; his wit, lighthearted and quick, left him disappointed that he had only himself and the lamppost to share it with on such a wonderful walk. But it was his heart, filled with the joy of a man in love, that kept him warm. Of course, that was nothing new for Peter. Never had there been a day something hadn't touched his heart, stirred his emotions, or given him cause to thank God for the experience, and this day had offered no exception. So he concluded the final twenty minutes of his walk in conversation with God, himself, and the lampposts.

"Sugar Bear," he uttered aloud, passing the old playground, lifting Haley's name to the Lord, as he did. Biscuits Helen, Dutch, and Rennie—again the names were lifted heavenward. "And my friend Jon, who I am most thankful you placed in my life, and his not-so-blushing bride, whose tender voice of graciousness changed all of our lives." He then included Officer Redding and the Boys in Blue Breakfast Club, bus drivers, doctors, street vendors, and more in his impromptu prayer. At the end of the block, he turned to look back onto the many walkways weaving in and out of the tall evergreens standing in the darkness. "If ever there's a place for werewolves, vampires, and a Sasquatch or two, that'd be the place, Lord." And then he crossed the street, his laughter echoing through the night.

Unconsciously, his walk slowed, giving him rest before he continued the next segment of prayer. It was always a special part of his walk, a time when he'd recall the many faces of children whose names he either didn't know or couldn't remember, those who had touched his heart and blessed his days. Sometimes he'd include their parents, siblings, or friends, and sometimes, like this night, he'd include individuals who were simply in need of some special attention, an extra word, or who just lay heavy on his heart.

"Lord, I lift up your sweet little songbird. Keep her safe from those who would do her harm," he prayed, offering Layla's name. And then he slowed almost to a stop. "I pray for her young man also, that he comes to know you and forgets Layla altogether. So I ask that you remove whatever's blocking his path and lead him on his way…far, far away. Perhaps he'd make a wonderful monk in Tibet? Just a thought, Lord." And then, coming to a complete stop, the old man peered into the clear night sky, but only a few stars peered back, most remained hidden by the glow of the city lights. "And lastly, Lord, I thank you for placing an angel on the bus."

Two minutes from home, his steps were now lumbersome. Cold air bit at his cheeks and nose, leaving them a deep red. Turning the corner at the far end of the block, he noticed a figure entering the front of his building. Moments later Layla's lights came on. Disappointment filled his eyes but quickly gave way to the brightness of renewed prayer. "Keep her safe from those who would do her harm," he whispered into the ear of the Lord. Crossing the street, he added, "Tibet! Just give it some thought."

Headlights washed over the street, bringing a smile to the old man's face. Officer Redding stepped from the vehicle, and like many times before opened the conversation with yet another scolding about late-night walks, the dangers of subfreezing temperatures, and, just for good measure, adding there'd been an armed robbery only a few miles away. Like many times before, the old man thanked the officer for his concern, and within seconds they were laughing and joking as if running into each other on a bright sunny afternoon, neither having a care in the world. As Officer Redding pulled away, he, too, would bend the Lord's ear. "Thanks for getting him home safe…again."

Even after stepping into the entryway, the old man's lungs ached from the cold. His legs, heavy and tired, made the stairway a bit of a challenge. The door squeaked its usual greeting, opening into a room, warm, silent, and peaceful. It had been a long time since he'd felt so tired. The day had robbed him of his energy but showered him with blessing after blessing. Hanging up his coat and scarf and removing his socks and shoes were as close to preparing for bed as he could manage. Even so, before turning off the light, he glanced across the room at the photo of Ruth Anne. Touching his fingers to his lips, he blew her a kiss. "I miss you so very much, my darling."

While his eyes adjusted to the darkness, lights, like small twinkling clusters, began to appear before him. Thinking it was merely brought on by exhaustion, he closed his eyes and took a deep breath and then another. For a few moments, his eyes were held closed by the sheer weight of fatigue, but then, slowly, they began to open. The lights, so tiny that at first he believed they were gone, but they were not. He continued to lie motionless, allowing his eyes to scan the room for a source that would cause such reflections, but there was none.

Though his eyes begged to close, he forced them to watch the subtle movements of what appeared to be thousands of colored beams dancing about on a space no bigger than the head of a pin. For a time he found them fascinating, incredibly calming, and then, as if carried away on a wisp of air, they vanished. But there in the darkness, the tired old man smiled, somehow knowing they hadn't left him at all. He didn't have, nor would he ever need, an explanation as to how he knew exactly where they were in the room— one or two by the front door, one by the bookshelf, and another at the foot of his bed. But he wondered, were there others? Perhaps, but sleep's lullaby sang to him fondly. His eyes were gently closed, and the old man inhaled deeply. A vision quickly formed in his mind—not a vague, dreamlike image, but a scene vivid in every detail, alive and vibrant, so true in appearance his other senses accepted it as reality. Sitting on the side of his bed, wearing a beautiful white gown, was the twenty-year-old Ruth Anne. He felt her loving touch brush the hair away from his forehead, where she then lightly placed her lips. When she leaned back, he could see the arbor in full bloom. "Japanese Wisteria." He smiled. She took his hand, and they walked deeper into his dream, deeper into his sleep.

The vivid colors suddenly became muted, as though a dense fog rolled over the world, creating a thick wall of separation. No longer could he see her face; no longer could he feel her hand. Air rushed into his lungs, and he called out her name. In his chest, his heart beat fiercely. His hands clenched the empty air where she had been by his side. Her name rose in the room, and his eyes shot open. There was darkness except for the luminous face of the clock on the nightstand. It was 2:12.

Uncomfortably warm, he sat up to remove the clothes he'd fallen asleep in but stopped before even unbuttoning his shirt. At first the noise seemed distant, possibly coming from outside. But then the man's voice, loud, vulgar, and belligerent, came through the thin walls separating his apartment from Layla's. The clatter of upended furniture came next, vibrating the floor. Peter reached for his shoes, and all got quiet. Layla was crying, pleading for the young man to leave, though muffled her words remained intelligible. Something heavy slammed up against the wall, causing the cross above his bed to fall. There was a soft cry, a moan, and then again a heavy thud against the wall. The old man got to his feet, hearing Layla's muffled cry for help followed by a moment of scuffling and yelling.

Rushing across the room, the old man heard Layla's door open violently. The narrow landing filled with obscenities in both male and female voices. Peter flung open his door. Layla screamed, her head swinging sharply around from the force of the young man's slap, splattering blood over the front of the old man's shirt.

"Go back to bed, Santa Claus, before I give you some of—"

The young man's head felt as if it exploded, his jaw shattering from the old man's fist, causing him to crumble to the floor like a rag doll. Peter put his arm around Layla, supporting the battered girl, ushering her toward his open door. Her scream was lost in the ear-piercing report of the first shot.

Two more followed in quick succession before the young man made it to his feet. An attempt to yell brought bolts of excruciating pain, spinning the room from under him. Lying on the floor, convulsions ran through his body attempting to stave off the pain. But the agony continued, as did the spinning leaving him barely able to find his balance. Unsteady he made his way down the steep stairway, coming to a long pause on the bottom landing. Staring at the blood on his hands, his mind raced. A guttural moan, more animal than human, rose to fill the small confines, and then, with murderous intent clear in his mind, he struggled to crawl his way back up the stairs. Three shots pierced the air with concussive force; acrid smoke rose undisturbed. There at the top of the stairs stood Layla; in her hand the gun he had dropped while making his escape.

Minutes later Dutch burst through the front door, his shotgun at the ready. Recognizing the crumpled body at the bottom of the stairs, he called out. "Peter, it's Dutch. I'm coming up." Cautiously he made his way up the creaky old stairway until his eyes were at floor level, and he could see Layla sitting on the floor by Peter's door. There were objects scattered about the floor he recognized as things that had sat on the end table just inside Peter's front door. And lying next to the overturned table was Peter.

Rennie, standing at the bottom of her own stairway, advised the 911 operator she could hear sirens in the distance, and at that moment, she also heard Layla yell to her from an upstairs window.

The old man was no longer aware of time or the commotion around him. At first there had been only the soft whimpers of Layla and then the pleading voice of Dutch. Peter could no longer keep his eyes open, and from just above him, the words of a beautiful prayer were being lifted to God. The old man listened intently, unable to believe it was the voice of his dear friend Dutch.

With the pain replaced by a numbing chill, his eyes remained heavy. And then came the southern drawl of Rennie, her voice so soft, so sweet, as if she'd come to wake him for breakfast. Her lips touched his forehead where a short time ago Ruth Anne had also placed hers. He never noticed Rennie's tears falling onto his soft white beard, but he felt them in her voice, in her breath, and in her gentle touch.

The old man suddenly felt the presence of others close by. Bob Redding had been the first officer up the stairs, followed by the little female officer the old man called Angel Eyes because she reminded him of the actress Mona Freeman. There were others, though not close by. He could hear their voices but didn't much care what they were saying; it was Rennie who held his full attention. "Peter, listen to me." Her voice calm but excited, she whispered in his ear, "She's here. She's here, Peter. Ruth Ann's right here." Again he felt the warmth of a kiss against his forehead, and his eyes opened slowly. In Rennie's hand was a badly chipped porcelain frame still protecting the beautiful photo of Ruth Anne. The old man's cheeks rose with a slight smile so faint only he knew it was there. His eyes closed but immediately opened again. There, around the frame, were the same small lights he had seen earlier.

"She's right here, Peter," Rennie assured him again. "I can feel her. Peter, she's here."

Carried to him on a gentle wave of air was the sweet scent of Japanese wisteria. The old man watched the photo come to life. Ruth Ann's head cocked slightly to the left, her smile drew gently to the right, the sparkle in her eyes confirming forever love, and then she stood, extending her hand.

Rennie lay beside him, unaware of what the old man was witnessing, but she truly believed he sensed the same presence she did. She caressed his head. "She loves you; we love you. You're in our hearts forever."

Dutch leaned down and whispered in his ear, "Peter, you led me to Christ. I'll be the man. I'll be the Christian you want me…"

His voice faded, and Peter could once again hear the beautiful prayer. Words and thoughts lifted with eloquence for the ears of a King, a Lord, and a God. Peter knew these were not the words being spoken by his friend but those that dwelt within his heart, carried to the throne by…angels? The Holy Spirit?

He then heard the gentle laughter and soft voice of Ruth Anne. Rennie's tears fell onto his beard. Her hand pushing back locks of his hair, she again kissed his forehead. Later she'd recall a sweet fragrance of summer, so delicate, so faint it would disappear within an instant, yet there'd be many times throughout her life she'd catch its scent move by her on a breeze, embrace her in the stillness of a room, or simply touch her in a time of need or prayer.

She needn't look around to know the sadness in the room, so many tears, so many prayers. Continuing to hold the frame steady, she watched as the old man closed his eyes for the last time.

CHAPTER SEVENTEEN

Audrey discovered the envelope Peter had placed under one of the photo albums still sitting on the dining table. Inside she found a scribbled note giving a brief account of his visit to the old neighborhood and the two stops he'd made afterward, first to his bank and second to the law office of Charlotte Goodman, the daughter of their late friend and attorney, Carl Bradford.

There were few details given about either visit other than anonymously he had made provisions for Layla, shortly after her sister's death, providing rehab, college tuition, and living expenses while she worked toward her degree, all which had been supervised and maintained by Charlotte's office under the guidelines set by Peter. He'd also set up a substantial trust for Rennie and Dutch, with Audrey as the administrator. The remainder of his estate was to go to her and Jon. At the very bottom of the note he'd written, "Audrey, for many years now I've been holding on to something that belongs to you. I don't know what's in it, but I was told I'd know the right time to give it to you. I believe the time is now. Go check your mailbox."

Hurriedly she walked to the entryway. When she opened the front door, the early-morning air, much colder than the night before, chilled her immediately. Next to the door on the side of the house hung the pretty white mailbox Ruth and Peter had given her and Jon as a housewarming present many years ago. Inside was a very thick manila envelope. On the outside was written, "Greater love I could never ask for than what your friendship has brought me." The handwriting was not Peter's but the elegant penmanship of Ruth Anne. Audrey's eyes teared up, yet her heart leaped with childish excitement, as if receiving a letter from a distant pen pal. Her exhilaration stole her breath until she was nearly back at the dining room table. She cut through the layers of yellowed tape that sealed the top closed and carefully slid the contents out onto the table as if it were priceless treasure. And to her it was.

For almost a minute she stood squeezing herself with folded arms while occasionally brushing away rivers of uncontrollable tears. Finally taking a seat, she allowed herself another moment to calm emotions. This would prove to be a futile effort because for the next few hours she would read letter after letter, a poem Ruth had written when she first became ill, laugh at long-forgotten photographs, and then read each letter a second time and a few even a third. Her tears never truly disappeared, sometimes gushing irrepressibly and other times simply blurring her vision, hiding the words or images, allowing her emotions a moment of rest and peace.

But even before she began to read, there was something that stood out more than anything else in this heaping pile of memories—a small blue envelope exactly like the one found on the church altar those many years ago, which was now housed in a beautiful frame in her office. Even the front of it had the words "May God Bless, A Tender Voice Ministry."

Inside was a letter from Ruth Anne. At the very top was a rudimental drawing of an eye, a secret code the girls had developed in high school and occasionally practiced long into their adult life. It was a simple code meaning "for your eyes only." In the event others were present, an excuse would be made, the contents put away to be read in private later. Without reading a word, Audrey broke down. She walked to the back porch for a breath of fresh air, where she zipped up her jacket, sipped her coffee, and began to read:

Hey, Sis,

I knew you would open this first, so let me start by saying I'm giving this big envelope to Peter on my deathbed. (Go get some Kleenex. Better grab the box—you've got a lot of reading to do.) I've asked that he hold on to it until such time as you, and only you, need a good laugh, a good cry, and a world of good memories. Can we trust him not to open it? We can. Peter's a man of honor. He loves me and you enough to place our friendship and privacy above his own curiosity, and just the fact that you're reading this is proof of that. He'd be so angry at me for what I am about to write, but I want to give you one more reason to love my husband as much as I do, not that you ever needed another reason.

So I'll get right to the point: It was Peter who put the five hundred dollars on the podium. I'd bet my life on it…oops, I guess it's too late for that now, but you get the point. I found a few of these old blue envelopes in his mom's rolltop desk. You know, in one of those hidden compartments everybody in the world knows about (except Peter, I guess, because they would've been long gone by now). Furthermore, and you and I have talked about this dozens of times, I know for a fact. Well, almost, anyway. Peter was the one who supplied the fifteen hundred dollars to start up our business. Charlotte, Carl's daughter, came to visit me a few weeks ago, and as we were telling stories, she remembered hearing her father talk about a time he and Peter put a smelly old alley cat in the trunk of your car. Ding, ding, ding. Ring any bells? But of course she didn't mention the bag of money the cat was tied to.

But Peter was in Korea at the time, so this is what I think happened. Peter somehow persuaded his mom to withdraw the money from his savings. She then got the money to Carl, who got your trunk open; that poor cat; so you'd hear it and find the bag of money and (voila). A Tender Voice is born, and nobody could possibly suspect Peter. Sound pretty far-fetched? Well someplace in the mess in front of you is a letter from Peter to his mom, thanking her for taking the money out of his account and giving it to Carl. No explanation why or anything else, but it was exactly what we found in your trunk—fifteen hundred dollars, minus the cat.

I haven't questioned Peter about it, nor will I. I believe the subject was put to bed long ago, so if the old boy is still around, don't say anything. (I know that'll kill ya, but please honor my wishes, as I'm writing this on my deathbed. Ha ha ha—made you cry.) But honestly, don't say anything, just give him one of those infamous snuggle-and-kiss thank-yous you so innocently got away with. At least I had the decency to kiss Jon behind your back. Just kidding. Okay, once at a party in high school, when they were playing two minutes in heaven, somebody pushed us in the closet and locked the door. Oh, wait a minute—that somebody was you. I think you did it so you could run outside and kiss that Miller boy. You were such a tramp. God, how I idolized you.

Over the past month I've written you a letter, sometimes two, every day. That's the pile you see in front of you. They contain my thoughts, stories, secrets—yes, secrets—and all that "Audrey, you're so wonderful" stuff I've never been able to finish without you telling me to shut up. Remember when the city gave you that award and you paid the sound guy fifty bucks to screw up my microphone? The speech I'd planed on giving is in the pile somewhere.

I think my meds are kicking in, so I'd better say what's truly in my heart. I'll save you a seat next to mine in heaven. Hug Jon at least once a day for me, and please, keep my secrets safe, all of them. And most importantly, take care of my big ol' boy.

Audrey, thank you for sharing your life, your dreams, and all the trouble you caused along the way. We sure had fun, didn't we?

Love, RA

It would be twenty minutes before Audrey was capable of opening another envelope. She chose to open the oldest one first, the one addressed to Peter's mother. The letter confirmed what she and Ruth Ann had suspected all along, but Ruth Anne was wrong about it being one more reason for her to love Peter. It was a million reasons, because thanks to Peter's anonymous contribution, the two young female entrepreneurs took their business plan and ran with it, which over the years grew into a nonprofit organization listing, among other things, tutors for children of homeless parents, food banks, home care, free medical transportation services, two sixteen-bed hospice centers, a staff of thirty-six full-time employees, and a legion of volunteers from numerous churches participating in home visitations throughout western Washington.

Audrey had remained president and CEO until her sixty-eighth birthday, when she made the announcement that Nicole Brookmeyer would be serving as the new CEO. Audrey stayed on as president another two years before stepping down to simply enjoy the benefits of coownership. Up until her death, Ruth Anne held 49 percent of the company and sat on the board of directors. When she passed, it went to Peter, but he wanted no part in the operation of the business, even offering Jon his seat on the board, an offer Jon steadfastly refused.

Audrey knew it'd always been difficult to keep secrets from Peter. Somehow he could sense the slightest little something in her expression, twinkle in her eye, or the touch of her hand. It was like he could read her soul from across the room. And he always had a cute little way of letting her know he knew she was concealing something. He whispered in her ear, "Are you going to share that secret or take it to the grave?" Of course she always denied having any secrets, and she now planned on continuing that tradition.

It was shortly after ten a.m. when Audrey heard the back door open. Not expecting Jon for another hour or two, she was surprised to hear his voice, followed by the soft voices of others. When they entered the kitchen, her eyes first went to Jon, his face clearly distraught. Behind him was the young pastor and his wife from church. Removing his hat was Officer Redding.

❧

Audrey read and reread the letters dozens of times over the next seven months, giving Charlotte Goodman a key and permission to burn the envelope and its contents, which she would find hidden in the antique rolltop desk in the spare bedroom. No one, including Charlotte and especially Jon, was ever to open the envelope. On the day of Audrey's funeral, the second-hottest day of the year, Charlotte sat on her patio enjoying a cigarette and a glass of scotch while she watched the envelope disappear in the roaring flames of her fire pit. Ruth Ann's secrets would be safe for all eternity.

❧

It was almost 7:30 before Ann finished with her shower and headed downstairs to make coffee. Noticing the door to the guest room ajar, she half expected Jass to wander out to follow her downstairs. Reaching the bottom and still no dog, she thought about quietly calling him but decided if he needed outside or wanted breakfast, he'd come down all on his own. Something else occurred to her. He had a boy to play with, and both might already be outside visiting with Lincoln, an early riser who loved to sit and read, retreat to his studio and paint, or simply walk the point and watch the sunrise. That was where she imagined the dog and his boy could be found. By this time she'd made her way into the kitchen and saw the tablet propped against the coffeepot, a note from Rachel explaining Chris had invited her and the kids to go on an early-morning adventure. Where to, she didn't know, but thought they'd be back around noon. The note ended with an apology and hoped Ann didn't think her rude for accepting the invite. There was also a PS: "the dog's with us."

Thirty seconds later, still in her robe, Ann knocked at Trudy's front door, barely waiting for Lincoln to get it open before rushing in. "Where's Trudy? She up yet?" Ann tittered, making her way to the kitchen to pour herself a cup of coffee. "Rachel left me a note. Seems Chris invited her and the kids on 'an adventure' this morning." Again she giggled, raising an eyebrow.

"Yes I know." Lincoln nodded, taking his usual seat at the Gathering Place. "Took the dog along too."

Ann smiled and walked to the end of the counter, where she grabbed a fistful of cookies before taking her place at the great table. "You saw 'em leave?"

Lincoln smiled, taking his turn raising an eyebrow. "I spoke with Chris while Rachel got the kids situated in the back seat." And then, offering no further information, he stole a cookie, sipped his coffee, and winked at Ann. Going up against the honed skills of Vice Principal Ann Brooks in a round of cat and mouse was a rare treat, one in which she took pleasure in as well but would never admit. But this morning's game would be cut short with the timely entrance of the still-sleepy-eyed Trudy. She didn't speak but waved good morning to both, poured a cup of coffee, grabbed a fistful of cookies, and gave Lincoln a good-morning peck on the cheek before sitting next to her friend, placing her head on Ann's shoulder as if to catch a quick nap.

Ann said, very calmly, "Chris took Rachel for an adventure."

Trudy perked up.

Lincoln retorted, "And the kids."

Curling her grin into a slightly crooked smirk, Ann continued. "They sneaked out before the sun came up. Rachel left me a note."

"And the dog. They took the dog," added Lincoln.

Flustered but touched by his goading, Ann spouted teasingly, "Okay, we get it. The whole damn family went." Her voice ended abruptly as she quickly realized what she had said.

Lincoln chuckled. "Family? Who said anything about family? I simply said they headed out together this morning; that's all. You two are the ones talking about family. And if you ask me…"

Trudy held up a single finger and quietly spoke. "No one asked you."

❖

Four cookies and half a cup of coffee later, Trudy was up to speed on the latest gossip from Brennan's Cove. By this time, on a quest for coffee and the subsequent whereabouts of his wife, Jim ambled into the gathering. At the counter he took those first needed sips and then made his way to the table with the open bag of cookies, of which only four remained, and one of those was broken. Offering to share, Jim watched as Lincoln took one and Ann pulled out two, handing one to Trudy, leaving only the broken pieces at the bottom of the bag. His doleful look brought laughter to the table, but still, no one gave up their cookie.

Struggling to get her voice above a whisper, assuring them there was no cause for alarm, Trudy offered up her quiet opinion.

"I gave it a lot of thought last night after we all went to bed. These two haven't seen each other in years, so of course they're going to be excited to get reacquainted. And there was a time last night I also caught a glimpse of family, desire, and love between them, but—"

The roar of an engine pulling into the compound cut off her words; it was Amy. The Camargue-red exterior of her SUV glistened in the bright morning sun, but according to her husband, Wes, even it paled next to his wife's radiant beauty. At 5'10", this thirty-four-year-old wearing a pair of ragged old Vans, faded Levis, and a paint-splattered sweatshirt with "Changes in Latitudes" on the front looked anything but radiant stepping from the driver's side.

Opening the door, Lincoln called, "Hey, baby girl, everybody's in here."

Quickly she made her way in, giving everyone hugs and hellos, commenting on her mom's and Trudy's bathrobe attire and how wonderful her father was looking, before moving to the coffeepot. "Who does that?" she asked, holding it up. "There's barely enough to cover the bottom of the pot. Really, who does that?"

Everyone pointed at Jim. Amy rolled her eyes and shook her head. Trudy pointed to the other end of the counter, and Lincoln spoke for her. "We got a Keurig or whatever it's called. One of those one-cup wonder machines. The cup things are in the drawer underneath. Try that Italian dark roast. It's pretty good. You don't have to drink a gallon of water to get a cup coffee."

Amy wasted no time fixing a cup, adding a splash of fresh cream Trudy always kept on hand and then took a seat next to her mom. Spotting the cookie bag still sitting in front of her dad, she reached in, her hand finding only half a cookie. "Who leaves a half a cookie?"

All fingers pointed to Jim.

"They ate the rest," he asserted strongly, hoping to shift the blame.

Everyone simply shrugged as if denying his claim while Ann began a new conversation.

"I didn't expect you here until this afternoon."

"Well, that was the plan, but…"

A second vehicle pulled into the compound. Amy smiled and ran to the door. "Wes, we're in here." she cried, continuing onto the porch and down the steps.

Wearing a dark-blue captain's uniform, the handsome pilot stepped out of the truck. They greeted each other with a kiss, and she led him back inside, where there was another round of hugs, hellos, chitchat, and small talk. Amy played barista, making an array of one-cup wonders, even managing to blend up a double-chocolate candy-cane grande with a dollop of Cool Whip for her daddy. Trudy, still struggling with her voice, was content to be a semisilent participant in this spontaneous little party. Sometimes, especially in settings like this, it proved very interesting to sit back quietly and people watch, even if the people you were watching were those closest to you in life: her husband, cheerfully entertaining and always attentive to their guests' needs and conversations; Ann, elegant, beautiful, with a wit as sharp as a knife; Jim and Wes, like peas in a pod, as they say, fishing, football, and music, but their true common interest was the incredible love for the woman who at this particular moment sat between them. And it was that beautiful woman who suddenly captivated Trudy's attention. Had she changed her hair, her makeup? something was...not different, just not the same.

Lincoln's voice suddenly rose louder. "So you drove past the airport to come all the way out here, just to turn around and go back to the airport?"

Wes blushed as the room fell quiet, and all eyes focused on him. "I did, but I'll be back tomorrow. They asked if I'd lay over until New Year, but I told them, I'm not about to miss my mother-in-law's dinner and Trudy's New Year's at the Cove."

He looked fondly to Ann, then to Trudy. "As a matter fact, there's a case of champagne in my truck I'd like to use for a special toast at the party, if that's okay. I also have sparkling cider for those who don't drink, can't drink, or may be experiencing a temporary medical condition."

Quiet talk and gentle shrugs worked their way around the room. Trudy's eyes again fell on Amy. *Radiant*, she thought.

Leaning on her husband, Amy blushed. "We have an announcement."

❖

Pulling into the parking lot brought a burst of clapping and high-pitched giggles from the back seat. "Doughnuts!" Beth cried, pointing at the old two-story brick building. It might have simply been her excitement that caused Jass to perk his ears and stand in the far back compartment of the ten-year-old Jeep Cherokee, but most likely it was the word "doughnuts," a word spoken often by Jim on Sunday mornings.

The place didn't look like any doughnut shop Michael had ever seen. There were no giant plastic doughnut signs out front or drawings of doughnuts on the building, and no windows tempting you to come inside. But from watching her reaction, Michael knew there must be really good doughnuts in this place, so he joined in her excitement. It was then that his mom, reading the faded white lettering scrawled across the age-worn bricks, said, "Delaney's Pastry? You brought me a cake from here."

Chris looked surprised. "Good memory."

"Good cake." Rachel smiled.

"I'm glad you enjoyed it."

"I still have the Valentine's card that came with it and the locket you gave me."

"You were my daddy's Valentine?" Beth cooed from the back.

Rachel's stare didn't drift from Chris. Her answer, refusing to be held back, came so softly, had she'd not have heard it she wouldn't have thought she spoke it at all. "I was."

Quickly Beth asked with a giggle. "Did he give you sprinkle kisses? That's what he gives me sometimes."

Rachel's eyes twinkled, her lips parted into a very faint smile visible only to Chris, and again her voice came softly; however, this time with a gentle coyness. "Did you give me sprinkle kisses, Chris? I don't recall."

Chris, on the verge of blushing, turned to the kids and eagerly asked, "Who's ready for doughnuts?"

❦

Thirty minutes later, they were walking along the shoreline of Deep Lake, at Millersylvania State Park. The air was chilled and invigorating, filled with the scent of old-growth cedar and fir. Overhead, a small flock of Canadian geese called to a boy and his father paddling their kayaks on the still waters. These were the lake's only other visitors except for the young red fox who sat watching intently from behind a storage shed quite some distance away.

Chris led the way, making it seem more of a medieval quest than a stroll through the forest. The great wooden buildings became abandoned enemy forts. "Be careful; their navy is hiding in yonder boathouse," he warned.

Jass, though not recognizing any of the words, sensed the peril in Chris's voice and decided to return to the safety of the pack, taking the tension off the long leash but feeling it begin to mount in his face and shoulders. New surroundings with unfamiliar smells had always made the dog tense and skittish anyway. Add the memories of yesterday with the quiet woman and the unknown threat lurking in the dark beyond the bridge that had made the man stop playing, and Jass was ready to go back to the car. After all, the little ones might have left a bite of doughnut in the back seat.

Chris led them to the bottom of a grassy mound, and he, the dog, and the kids crawled cautiously to the top to observe the Forest Bandits gathered in the meadow below. A plan was drawn up to chase the bandits into the icy waters of the lake, where the swamp rats would devour their flesh and use their bones to pick their teeth.

"Charrrrrge!" Chris yelled.

"Charrrrrge!" screamed the kids, launching their attack.

Rachel, still at the bottom, watched them disappear over the top.

Jass, suddenly realizing this was all just play, might not have led the way, but he had their back.

The battle was fierce, with yelling and laughter, jumping and barking, swashbuckling sword fights, and dazzling acrobatics performed mainly by Captain Chris and then tried by all.

But when the Forest Bandits saw the Flaming-Haired Princess standing at the top of the mound, many of them fell over dead right where they stood. The rest were driven into the lake for the swamp rats to gobble up.

From the safety of the storage shed, the young red fox watched the performance, tilting his head first to one side and then the other, looking to gain some insight as to why these humans were running and yelling, waving their arms, chasing the wind to the edge of the water. And of course there was the dog, arrogantly prancing about, obviously proud he hadn't continued his pursuit straight into the cold waters of the lake like so many other dogs the fox had witnessed. It was a well-known fact throughout the forest community that dogs were not very bright creatures, and this one seemed to typify that belief with his barking and jumping and spinning in circles for no apparent reason at all. Though you'd have hardly noticed, at that moment the fox grinned, thankful he was a fox.

Stepping cautiously from the shadows of the shed, he continued taking in their celebration, mesmerized by the activity, not fearful at all, knowing he could escape with ease at any time. Throwing stones from the shore, the humans disturbed the calm waters, causing a family of frogs to leap from their pads, though they were much too far away to ever be in danger. As too were the family of ducks that suddenly appeared from a wide stand of cattails to merely complain about the noise, but they complained much of the time anyway, so the fox paid little mind. It was the female left atop the mound that saw him wander from safety in his desire to keep the other humans in view. Forgotten by the fox, she'd moved surprisingly close, where now, standing very still, she observed his beauty and shy curiosity.

It took less than a minute for the young fox to become bored with the shoreline activities. Again thankful he was a fox, he turned with a sly grin to move back to the corner of the boathouse. And it was then he noticed her, and had it not been for the fright she caused, he would have surely been embarrassed. Yes, the little fox knew he had forgotten the lessons his parents had so lovingly taught him. He'd taken his eyes from the woman, and then, to his shame, failed to sense her approach. Frightened and humiliated, he disappeared into the thick brush that skirted the wetlands, making his escape to the far side of the lake, where alive but out of breath he would lie quietly, giving the encounter great thought over the next few hours.

Rachel said nothing of the fox, knowing it would bring needless disappointment to the morning, so instead she ran to the celebration in progress, picked Beth up in her arms, and declared, "Long live princess power. Come forth, mighty warriors, and let us christen you Knights of the Wooded Glen."

Chris bowed. "These knights are at your service, milady's."

He then smiled at the boy, who stood beside him smirking through a hint of embarrassment. "Oh, but these days..." he said with quiet suspense just before proclaiming loudly, "These days are off to battle the Pirates of the Playground." And off he and Michael ran waving their invisible swords as they went.

A short time later, the four walked beneath the towering trees of the campgrounds on their way to the trailhead. Chris wasn't surprised to see only three of the 120 tent sites occupied, two with travel trailers, the third a small dome tent with a large blue tarp stretched out above to direct any rain away from the camp. Most of the sites were large and designed for privacy, each with a table and fire ring, and were all within a short walk of the many showers and restrooms maintained daily by members of the National Forest Service.

Summertime filled the grounds to capacity, yet the bike trails and hiking paths that crisscrossed the 850 acres of forest and wetlands were never too overcrowded to enjoy. But during the winter months, few campers braved the harsh damp climate, which might change from a cold bleak day to one of intense downpours and icy winds rather quickly. Nevertheless, up until the birth of his daughter, Chris had always been one of the few. He'd choose the same site year after year, not out of habit or convenience, but desire. Set back from the main thoroughfare and hidden from the rest, it provided undisturbed solitude, a personal retreat encouraging times of reflection and prayer, which always seemed to renew his spirit.

Having shared it only once many years ago, he found it humorous, with all the people who used it during the summer, that he continued to think of it as his own—a spot so intensely private and personal he'd never even shared it with Linda or his dad, who loved the outdoors. There was a time when he and Bailey sat at the table after a day hike, but they didn't stay. Following graduation he and the boys came down, but they didn't stay either. And today, for the first time in years, he was excited to be back, to share its views and a memory or two, stories of playing guitar around the campfire, waking up to snow on the ground, or maybe the time lightning struck a tree twenty feet away. He was sure Michael would love the big storm story.

It wasn't far from the trailhead, so they'd stop there before venturing into the woods. That is, once everyone used the restroom. Beth tried to get a squirrel to come to her, Michael discovered the amphitheater, Jass discovered a squirrel of his own, and Rachel ran back to the truck to get the small backpack containing the three bottles of water and a variety of snacks Chris had left sitting on the front seat.

As promised, the view from the campsite was breathtaking. With snowcapped mountains as a backdrop and the lake shimmering in the bright sunlight, it was postcard perfect. Nestled between tall evergreens were the historic log shelters built by the Civilian Conservation Corps back in 1935, and a long wooden trail bridge wound through the wetlands, disappearing into a thick array of water plants and trees.

In the opposite direction was Miller's Glade, an area roughly the size of two football fields bordered by a narrow paved road separating the short-cropped grass from the dense forest before turning into miles and miles of unpaved bike trail. At the near end stood yet another log shelter. Though much smaller than those at the lake, it managed to house eight picnic tables and a serving area with a sink and running water. Restrooms were at either end of the building and could be accessed from within the open structure. A small playground sat just to the side of the building.

Chris accompanied Michael and Beth down to the swings. Jass, not a fan of swings, was content to watch from the sidelines and found a nice shaded bench to lie next to. After a quick check of the area, Chris, satisfied it was safe, looped the retractable leash through the bench slats, telling Jass he was in charge and to watch for approaching Forest Bandits. Then he left the kids with a push and returned to the site and Rachel. His approach was not quiet, yet it didn't disturb Rachel's gaze. A young couple unloading their kayaks would soon be joining the father and son on their almost-silent voyage around the lake, an activity she had enjoyed greatly as a teen but hadn't experienced since leaving the Northwest.

Turning to walk through the site, she said, "I didn't recognize it at first."

"Yeah," Chris replied, looking around. "A storm redecorated the place about five years ago. But it left me a view of the lake, so I didn't complain much."

Rachel's eyes scanned the area. "Must've been quite a storm. I don't remember that boulder in the middle of—"

"No, it wasn't there. The thing used to sit back in the brush a ways. Moving it was quite a job."

"You moved it?"

Chris laughed. "Well, not by myself I didn't. I had Doug and Scott and the Timmons twins help. Even so, it took us about five hours to move it twelve feet. Bobby never copped to it, but that's what caused his hernia. He told his dad he did it in the weight room. He almost lost his scholarship over it. Man, I felt bad."

"Wait a minute. What on earth possessed you to move it in the first place?" Rachel giggled, walking to stand next to the massive stone. "Were you guys bored one day and decided, gee, let's go move a rock?"

Stepping beside her, Chris grinned. "Not exactly. If you'll remember, it was kinda 'your' idea."

"My idea?" Again Rachel laughed. "I don't recall playing Wilma Flintstone and asking you to move the furniture."

He grabbed a bottle of water from the backpack, unscrewed the lid, and handed it to Rachel before sitting on top of the table, his devilish smile sparking an equally wicked gleam in his eye.

"Right before we left that morning, you and I spent twenty minutes moving this heavy ol' table over to where the rock is now."

Rachel started to take a drink but stopped mid-sip.

"So you do remember! And do you remember why?" Chris asked, almost teasingly.

She began to feel a blush warm its way over her face, down her chest and quite possibly even onto her arms. Putting her hand to her mouth to cover a smile, she asked timidly, "Is that the spot?"

His smile permanently fixed, Chris just nodded.

There was no hiding her embarrassment, nor did she try to. "Are you sure? I mean, someone could've moved it before you came back."

"No, no one moved it. Back then hardly anyone ever used this site. Even now, people think it's too small, too isolated, and those that do stay here don't spend much time hanging out in camp all weekend."

Rachel borrowed his devilish grin and countered, "We did!"

Chris watched her eyes sparkle in the sunlight and then move quickly to the kids, who continued to play on the swings. They held her gaze even as she began to speak. "I never told anyone. Not Peg—especially not Peg; could you imagine." They both chuckled. "Mike asked about us a couple times. Okay, a bunch of times," she admitted, taking a sip of water before handing the bottle back. "I just refused to talk about it, and he knew why." Her eyes again caught the sun, no longer exposing their sparkle but now revealing a glimpse into the beautiful woman behind them. "But I sure talked to God a lot about it—about us."

Another long stretch of silence passed. Chris leaned forward, preparing to stand, but instead relaxed, staying on the table's edge. "I know what you mean. I've had my share of talks with God about it…about us…once or twice over the years. Other than that, I've never spoken about it either. Bailey had her suspicions, and Linda asked her about you once—how serious was our relationship…"

He could tell that got Rachel's attention, so he added, "And why you had to leave town so quickly."

Her eyes narrowed slightly, waiting to hear more. Chris, not one to disappoint, explained, "Well, you know Bailey. Somebody throws her a slow pitch like that, she's going to hit it right out of the ballpark."

Rachel looked at him disdainfully. "This isn't going to be good, is it?"

Chris took a long sip of water and shook his head no, but he wasn't able to keep from releasing a very timid chuckle, prompting him to blurt out, "She told Linda I found out you were pregnant with Scott Curzio's kid."

"No she didn't!" Rachel snickered, rolling her eyes.

"Yeah, but that wasn't the worst of it. You had twins, and they looked just like Scott, all big and hairy, with that prepubescent mustache and sideburns he had back in seventh grade. Oh, and did I mention…the twins were girls."

Their explosive laughter erupted, capturing the attention of the kids, but only for a second. And then as the swing lifted Beth and the wind pulled through her hair, she thought, *I love to hear my daddy laugh.*

Michael also had thoughts as he watched the sky come closer and then drift back and grow closer again. Yes, his mother's laughter was beautiful, and it made him feel wonderful to hear it ring out like that. But it was the deep, resonating tones from Chris that brought him to smile. Any description of sound a five-year-old could explain would have fallen short as to why it made him feel warm and safe with a glow of happiness tickling his smile to surface. As the sky came closer and then drifted and grew closer again, Michael thought of another time, another man who had made him feel much the same way, and as the sky came closer again, he tried to picture the kindly old man from the bookstore.

❖

Chris took another drink. "You know, Rachel Callahan…huh, Donahue…sorry," he corrected ruefully.

Shrugging her understanding, she waited for him to continue.

"What I was going to say is, I wonder sometimes, what if things had been different back then? What if we—"

"Chris, wait!" she blurted excitedly, startling not only Chris but a small bird from its perch on a nearby tree. Retrieving her purse from the backpack, she produced the smudged envelope reclaimed from the back of the piano. "I wrote this the day I left, right after you gave me the plant and stuck the card in my pocket. Two hundred dollars—really, Chris? I tried calling you from Portland to tell you where I left your money. That way I knew you'd get my note. But of course you didn't answer, and it didn't even go to voice mail. I tried calling a half dozen times before I finally just gave up. I did talk to Peggy a week or so later. She said you'd already left for Biola, so I just gave up and forgot all about it until yesterday. Anyway, here it is. Sorry it's so late."

She handed him the envelope, grabbed two water bottles from the table, and ran to join the kids, looking back once on her way.

Before opening the envelope, Chris walked over to lean against the big rock, letting his own memories of that day fill his thoughts. This was the same envelope he'd slipped into her jacket pocket. One corner featured two little hearts, which were the same illustrations as the front of the card inside. Carefully opening the envelope, he saw the card missing, but he remembered exactly what he'd written in it, word for word:

My darling Rachel,

Today you shared with me your list of what-ifs, and after giving it some thought, I'm going to address them all as simply and honestly

as I can. Just fill in the blank. Answer applies to questions 1 through infinity and may be used anytime between now and forever.
Question: "What if_____?"
Answer: "I'd be there."
But of course, that leaves me with my own question, What if I _____?

Chris

Rachel had written her note on staff paper carelessly ripped from a music tablet found in one of the practice rooms, and Chris knew exactly which room. Opening it carefully, he began to read:

My beautiful Chris,

Love your note. I hope you really didn't expect to find your two hundred dollars. I'm taking it just in case. What if I break down and need to get a room or gas money to come back home? Thank you. I hope to get it back to you soon.

As recently as two days ago, you came to my window to leave me a good-night kiss. I was surprised, considering we weren't together any longer, but that's just the love inside you, and I know I'll never experience that kind of love again. You were my first kiss, my first dance, my first love, and I'll cherish that forever. When I think of you not being right around the corner, it scares me to death. But like I've heard you say plenty of times, we never know what God has in store for us until He lights our way, and I believe God may light our path again someday. In the meantime that'll be my prayer. I know that sounds strange considering the present circumstance, but like I said, you are my first love.

God bless and good luck at Biola

R.

He carefully folded the note, placed it back inside the envelope, and looked around the small camp, envisioning images of a weekend long ago. Funny—he once thought how every memory of that weekend centered around her. Her first attempt at building a fire, her playing guitar while he cooked breakfast, or hearing her sing as he waited outside the showers. Even after ten years, each memory held such a place in his heart, but none so much as when they awoke that April morning to the quiet beauty of a late-season snowfall, her face aglow like a child on Christmas morning filled with wonder and surprise, immersed deep in the magic of the moment. But that weekend held many other enchanted moments. And not all were restricted to the little hidden campsite they'd called home.

Looking to the playground, he felt new memories waiting to fill places in his heart she had never completely abandoned, places that, as a young man, he had felt her unlock by the mere sound of her voice—her laughter, song, kindness, compassion, and love. As he watched her play with the children, heard her laugh, saw her smile, he felt the gentle turn of a key in his heart. Yet there was something missing, something not quite complete. He stood in thought for only a few seconds and then, embraced by his own soft laughter, patted the big rock on the back like an old friend and said, very quietly, "I'll be right back."

❖

Listening over the years to Chris share memories and speak to God of Rachel oh so many times allowed the rock to know the man's heart very well. And had the stone the ability to smile, maybe even chuckle, it surely would have as Chris, walking in the direction of the playground, began to hum a song it had heard a younger version of the woman sing once upon a time.

"My mom caused a riot singing that song." Michael laughed as Chris entered the playground.

Chris smiled. "She sure did. I was there." Dancing to his own melody, his tall frame didn't come to rest in front of the lovely redhead in blue jeans. Instead he took her by the hand and twirled her under his arm. Rachel giggled, the kids laughed, and Jass sat quietly, enjoying the floor show. Three more steps and one last twirl, and Chris ended the song, taking bow.

Once the applause died out, he took two steps and then, placing his hands close to his face, he froze. In a cautionary voice filled with mystery and suspense, he asked quietly, "Did you hear that?"

Everyone stood silent, listening, but no one heard a sound.

"There. Did you hear it?" he said, just above a whisper.

And again everyone listened intently but still heard nothing at all.

Chris gathered everyone close and again whispered, "It's the enchanted forest calling. Its calling us to go"—he grinned dreadfully before blurting out, loud and gruff—"into the woods."

Beth jumped, her squeal turning to giggles to mask her fright. Rachel joined with giggles of her own, while Michael laughed heartily, taking a step back before proudly stating, "My mom was Cinderella."

Chris looked at Rachel, clearly needing an explanation. Beth crawled into Rachel's lap, and, still full of giggles, situated herself and said to her father, "I told you she was a princess!"

Rachel smiled, squeezing Beth. "I got to pretend I was Cinderella, in a play called *Into the Woods*."

Beth's eyes widened slightly. "I like to pretend I'm a princess too."

Michael stepped closer to his mom, addressing Beth. "Mom knows the real Cinderella. She goes to our church."

Rachel looked at Chris. "I worked at Disneyland."

Beth, too, looked at her father. "That's where all the princesses work." Her gaze fell back to Rachel. "Daddy's taking me there this summer. Do you guys want to go with us?" she asked, her attention moving to Michael.

The boy didn't wait for his mom to answer, quickly explaining, "We have to find a new house and move the rest of our stuff up here, so I don't think we can. But maybe next time. Do you think so, Mom?"

All eyes were on Rachel. Chris was as anxious to hear what she had to say as the kids were. "We'll have to see. But for now, we have an enchanted forest calling us, so let's get going...into the woods."

The center of excitement shifted rapidly from "the happiest place on earth" to the trail disappearing through the trees. However, even before leaving the playground, Rachel stopped and asked Chris, "Aren't you forgetting something?"

Looking around, he scratched his head, checked his pockets, and then pointed at everyone as though taking a headcount. "Girl, girl, boy, boy, dog. Nope, everything seems to be here."

Both kids giggled. Even Jass gave a whine. With a half smile, Rachel shook her head. "Backpack?"

❃

Soon they were deep into the forest, making their way on winding trails through dense foliage, sometimes having to step over or around branches lying across the path, remnants of a recent winter storm. The trees were tall and magnificent, but occasionally the little band of explorers would see where one of these towering giants had fallen, pulling up its massive root system and lying it on its side, where it would rest as tall as a house. There were also spaces where the forest became less dense, the narrow paths skirting large open areas lush with small streams that seemed to show up out of nowhere, only to vanish behind boulders, branches, and stumps. Places where old and new growth intertwined, moss not only lay like thick carpet over the ground but as blankets wrapped around the trunks and branches of trees, sometimes hanging in long matted strings from thin limbs. And though it hadn't rained in days, moisture could be found throughout the foliage. Even the air felt heavy and humid; sunlight cast a greenish hue over the visually captivating and truly enchanting place. At the third such area they came upon, Chris led the others from the trail into the large beautiful space, and in the center sat a long table crafted from a tree that had fallen many years earlier, the bark stripped away, its top level and smooth to the touch. A second log was used as a bench.

"That was quite a hike. You ready for a snack?" Chris asked, setting the backpack on the table.

"Yeah," the kids yelled in unison.

Opening the pack, he peered inside. "Well, let me see what we have. How about some pickled pigs' feet?"

"Ewww," the kids cried in unison once again.

"We have some swamp rat stew?"

There was squirming and laughter before another chorus of "Ewww" could be sung.

"Look what I found down at the bottom. PBJs for everyone." Chris smiled, pulling out a plastic container with four sandwiches inside.

There was a more encouraging chorus sung, and then Beth asked, "Does it have Miss Trudy's goo jam?"

Chris picked up a sandwich and took a bite. Nodding his head, he confirmed, "That's goo jam, all right." And then he sat it in front of the little girl.

She stared at the missing bite. "But Daddy, you took a bite out of it."

"I had to make sure it was goo jam."

The girl frowned, attempting to sort out the problem with her dad's actions. But then Rachel picked up the sandwich and also took a large bite, saying, "Yep, that's goo jam." And she placed it back in front of Beth.

The little girl's frown turned to a look of shock and confusion. And with that, Rachel and her father burst into laughter. "Oops!" her dad said, removing another sandwich from the container. "I'm sorry. This was yours. That one's Michael's."

With everyone except Rachel eventually getting a whole sandwich and Chris taking a moment to bless the meal, stories and laughter filled their time at the table. It wasn't long before Michael spotted something very, very peculiar nearly thirty feet away from where they sat. At first he thought it was just his imagination, because he knew he imagined things quite easily. But the longer he stared, the more it became clear it was not his imagination—but a very tiny door as real as any door he had ever seen, and this door was set at the base of a very tall tree.

"Look," he said, pointing in the tree's direction. "There's a little door on that tree."

Everyone looked. Chris quickly said, "That's a fairy door. They're everywhere up here—in the forest, gardens, backyards."

"Can we go look?" Michael asked.

"It's okay with me," Chris said, looking at Rachel who nodded the go-ahead. Michael helped Beth down from the bench, and Chris smiled. "There'll usually be others close by."

"Don't touch 'em," Rachel added.

The kids scurried to the base of the big tree, quickly discovering there were also two tiny windows and a fenced yard.

Looking at Chris, Rachel grinned. "We had an associate pastor who would've knocked it over. He gave a whole sermon on fairies, gnomes, and elves last summer because someone put a gnome in the church garden. He said they were evil spirits, and parents shouldn't even be reading fairy tales to their children."

Chris gave a little shrug. "I don't have a gnome in my garden, but I do on occasion use fairy tales to illustrate a message. Red Riding Hood, for instance, exemplifies what Jesus meant when he said, 'Beware of false prophets, which come to you in sheep's clothing.' There were a lot of things familiar to Miss Hood—grandma's house, her bed, even her night shirt, but thankfully, a closer inspection tipped Red off. A cry for help brought her savior, the woodsman, and everyone lived happily ever after—except Grandma and the wolf."

Rachel giggled softly. "You forgot the goodies in the basket were blessings." She giggled. "You told me that analogy in seventh grade. Oh yeah, I remember. You were pretty impressive back then."

"I like to think I've improved with age."

From the base of the tree, Beth called, "Daddy, come here quick. Lookie. There's a door on this tree too."

"We'll be right there."

Putting his attention back on Rachel, he pulled the envelope from his shirt pocket, holding it for both of them to see. There were many things he wanted to say, wanted to ask, wanted to tell, but instead he took her hand and said nothing at all. Rachel, too, had all the same thoughts, same feelings, and she too remained quiet, both allowing their sentiments to be spoken through their eyes, their smiles, and a gentle embrace of the other's hand.

"Daddy?"

Both smiled. "I have something at the house I want you to see," Chris said, finding his voice. "Do you remember the card that was in here? What it said?"

Rachel blushed lightly. "I'd read it so many times I had it memorized before

I reached Portland. Funny thing, though. I came across it a couple months ago, stuck in the pages of my Bible. I set it on my nightstand, it's still there."

"Mom!" Michael called, with just an inkling of aggravation.

Chris clasped her hand with both of his. "What if..." he said, and paused to watch her smile broaden, "you and I go for a walk when we get back. I don't think the gang would mind watching the kids for a little bit. That is, if it's okay with you."

"Just like old times, Chris. You lead, I'll follow."

"Just not to Biola..."

"That was your decision."

In unison each kid yelled for their respective parent.

Rachel almost laughed, saying, "They harmonize well." Then she placed her lips softly on the back of his hand, whispered something he couldn't quite make out, and said loudly, "What if, Chris Peterson—oh, sorry; Pastor Chris." And then she added sarcastically, "I guess that won't take much getting used to at all."

Her giggles interrupted their thoughts, changed the mood, and even got the attention of Jass, who'd spent most of his time sitting by Chris's feet, remembering yesterday's walk through the forest with the Quiet One. For the past five minutes, he'd not taken his eyes from the children but to look cautiously around the area and sniff the air for danger. *Safe...yes, I am a good boy*, he thought.

Rachel stood to join the kids, but before she could go, Chris again grabbed her hand. His thoughts rushed to return, but the mood sustained its reluctance, forcing his words to evaporate swiftly before being spoken, leaving him to simply touch the back of her hand to his lips, look into her eyes, and shout loudly, "Tag, you're it" before running toward the kids with Jass close behind.

It was his playfulness that touched her heart even more than the kiss to her hand. *Playfulness*, she thought, *his playfulness*. Realizing how much she had missed his lightheartedness, she ran to catch him, and he made sure she did. Their hands briefly touched but did not lock together.

Impatiently Michael motioning to his mom and Chris. "Look. Look what Beth found."

Beth, who would normally be standing with a little bit of pride in her discovery, was on her hands and knees beside a stump whose splintered neck exposed the rot and decay of its nearly hollow center. Thick, gnarled roots protruded up through the muddy ground to expose the twisted interwoven structure, no longer able to impede the ever-eroding soil, leaving holes and tunnels to run deep under the aged remnant of a once majestic tree. Arriving, Rachel and Chris stared with childlike wonder. There, within the tangled roots, stood a small house no more than four inches high. The walls, constructed of bark, supported what resembled a thatched roof made of moss. Twigs woven together with blades of grass made up the front door. On the side wall was a chimney made of pebbles. Scattered about the roots and holes were numerous ladders and walkways, ropes of twine, and stone fences made of small rocks and pea gravel.

The foursome marveled at the sight, playfully theorizing the nature of its inhabitants. Chris quickly reminded them that such things were only make-believe, little doll houses built by human hands, not the home of Tinkerbell, who only lived in storybooks and movies. "And Disneyland," Beth added. "She lives in Disneyland, Daddy."

They carefully explored the area and soon discovered other houses built into other stumps and trees and along some of the narrow branches. High in one of the trees, Michael spotted a bridge spanning almost ten feet from one tree to another. But most appropriately, it was Beth and Rachel who discovered a drawbridge. Once lowered, it revealed a secret castle hidden deep within the hollowed remains of a long-dead tree.

There were no man-made products to be found, no metals or plastics. Every structure was fashioned from what could be supplied by the forest. Some, like the castle, were engineered and constructed with meticulous detail, while others were simple frames of twigs and bark leaned against a stable object such as a rock or tree for support. Yet all were fascinating. In total they counted sixteen scattered about the area, but everyone agreed there were probably more that went undetected, as most blended into the surroundings so well.

At the far end of the area, where the forest closed in on itself, a deer trail cut narrowly along the upper edge of a shallow crevice populated by dense undergrowth and a shallow brook that could be heard but not seen.

"It's a beautiful walk. A little quicker than the path, and it'll dump us out on the near side of the wetlands. A little jaunt along the wooden walkway to the footbridge, and we'll be back at the lake. What do you think? Everybody up for it?"

"Sounds like a plan!" Michael beamed.

"Let's do it, then," Rachel said, looking back to see they hadn't left anything. "Chris..." she gasped suddenly.

"It's right here." He laughed, holding up the backpack. Then he, too, saw what had caused the woman to call out. On the side of a massive fir tree they had just passed stood a door eight feet high by three feet wide, built in the same manner, using the same materials as the little fairy doors. Chris wondered who would put in such time and effort building the thing and then choose to hide it behind a tree, where it could only be seen from the seldom-used deer path.

Michael very timidly asked, "Are there giant fairies?"

Beth grabbed her daddy's legs. Rachel, too, waited for an answer, and Chris was quick to give one.

Chris giggled. "Of course not. This door is altogether different than the rest; it was put there by the park rangers. They needed some place to store their gardening tools and didn't want to put up an old metal shed. Think how ugly that would look out here. So they keep everything inside that tree. Nobody notices because it blends right in. Pretty clever, don't you think?"

Both kids remained quiet, pondering what they'd just been told, with Beth finally asking, "But why's it so tall?" Even Michael was curious.

Looking very serious, Chris answered, "Well, they have to get their ladders in and out, don't they?"

Michael and Beth looked at each other, and after a moment, displaying satisfaction, nodded in agreement and were ready to continue their journey. Pleased with himself, Chris winked at Rachel, who smiled and said low enough only he could hear, "Toolshed? You haven't changed a bit."

It took nearly twenty minutes to reach the wetlands and another five to the footbridge. There a young couple stood looking into the plant-filled water, hoping to catch a glimpse of the aquatic life that called the wetlands home. Jass greeted them as though they were friends not seen for a long time. Michael and Beth said hello as they ran to another somewhat larger playground just the other side of the bridge. Chris and Rachel stopped and chatted, asking the young girl if she would mind taking their picture.

"Only if I can get you to take ours," she said.

And over the next few minutes, lasting memories were made for all. With a quick thank-you, the couple made their way onto the wooden path heading through the wetlands.

Leaning on the rail, the bright sunlight warming her face, Rachel sighed. "I've thought about this spot so many times. I still have the picture of us the ranger took. She was so sweet. She thought we were married."

"We thought we were married," he said, looking at her sheepishly.

"I don't recall being married by Doug as a lark, made us believe we were truly married."

Chris stared deep into the water. "I'm not so sure we didn't believe it. 'In God's eyes'; remember saying that?"

Her gaze joined his in the still, clear water.

Chris placed his hand on top of hers. "When I told Bailey that Linda and I were getting married, she promptly informed me I was already married to you…in God's eyes. We enjoyed a good laugh, but there was an undertone. I honestly thought that was why she and Linda never really connected the way I expected."

Rachel's face and tone became very serious. "Do you think Bailey knew? I mean, about us coming here and…"

"Setting up house? No. But what she did know was…"

"Daddy! I need to go."

"Me too," Michael said, getting off the swing.

Chris smiled at Rachel. "When nature calls, I'd better answer quick."

Rachel was left alone at the footbridge with Jass and the backpack while Chris escorted the kids to the restroom. The dog looked up at the woman, not wondering why they weren't running with the others but simply acknowledging their moment alone. Rachel seemed to understand the look and knelt down, accepting two kisses Jass had been waiting to give someone since leaving the forest, confiding in her, albeit silently, a thankfulness to be out of the woods, safely sitting in the warm sunshine. Rachel also had something to confide and felt comfortable Jass would go no further with it.

"What Bailey did know was how much I loved her big brother." Her hand ran gently over the dog's face and down his back. "And maybe…"

"Rache," Chris called, walking backward, his hands cupped around his mouth. "We'll meet you in the parking lot. You have the keys."

She confirmed with a wave and watched as he stumbled and almost fell. Her words to the dog were accompanied by soft giggling. "Like I was about to say, some things never change."

※

From the restrooms to the parking lot, the conversation between Beth and Michael had returned to the agreed-upon greatness of Disneyland, with Michael, being the true expert, taking the lead. "Honest. They have a parade at night, and it has a gazillion lights, and fireworks, and everybody singing and dancing and waving from on top of these things that drive by, and they have every princess in the world there. And after the parade, you can get your picture taken with them; and they even have stores where you can buy princess clothes and stuff. You'd make a pretty princess, Beth…ah…I mean…"

Before he had a chance to retract a word, she blushed. "Thank you, Michael."

Embarrassment lit his cheeks. Chris acted like he wasn't paying attention but later would enjoy sharing the story privately with Rachel.

※

The trip back to Brennan's Cove lulled Jass and the kids to sleep rather quickly, giving Chris and Rachel an opportunity to talk candidly, though not as in-depth as both knew would eventually come. Though certain topics weren't off limits, they were discussed cautiously, so as not to be overheard by little ears that might wake unnoticed. But before Rachel heard about how Chris and Linda met, Bailey's brief move to Nashville to be a country singer, and the physical struggles Beth had overcome, she'd asked about his church.

"It's five minutes out of the way. Besides, I left my toolbox there yesterday, and I'll need it to finish a couple things I've got going at the house."

"Anything I can help with? I'm pretty good with a hammer and paintbrush."

Chris remembered Rachel's efforts at set building. "No, no. I'm good. It's just a couple little things I'll probably put off anyway."

Quickly changing the subject, he inquired about her decision to return to Seattle. But as it turned out, she was still undecided where they would settle in the Northwest. After Southern California, she wanted nothing to do with city life ever again, so she had set her sights on Orting or maybe Yelm; just someplace in the country.

It was her aversion to the city that brought the conversation around to Linda. Chris said, "She was born and raised in Brooklyn, loved everything about it—the people, noise, congestion. And she hated the suburbs, hated the country even more. I kid you not; she didn't even like walking through Christmas tree lots."

"And yet you moved to the forest. That doesn't make sense to me."

"I lived there before we got married, and she thought she'd be able to adapt, but she didn't. Not really, anyway. And honestly, she would've left if"—his eyes darted to the mirror—"she hadn't gotten pregnant."

Rachel looked at her son. "They change the whole dynamic of marriage, don't they?" Her eyes found those of Chris, and more as an afterthought, added, "He did for us, anyway. Not saying Michael didn't love me before. He did, but I was always playing second fiddle to something—his music, school, ministry, and a few little whims that came up along the way. But when the baby came, his whole focus became the two of us, so I suppose parenthood helped our marriage too."

Chris laid his hand on top of hers, saying, "Mike and I had our disagreements. Every single one of them revolved around you. But even so, I liked the guy. I just expected, and believed, he'd love you like I did. And when—"

She didn't let him finish. "But he didn't. He couldn't. Just like it says in that note you have in your pocket, I knew I'd never experience that kind of love again, the kind of love you gave me, the kind of love we shared from our first kiss to..." She didn't allow herself to finish, though there'd been more she wanted to say. But for now, she would leave the words unspoken on the back of his hand with a gentle kiss.

He too had words that would remain unspoken, but they would not be placed on the back of her hand, spoken in a soft whisper carried over his lips; they would simply dance in his eyes, move along his smile and be felt by a gentle squeeze of his hand.

Rapidly the softness in his expression changed. "Well, there it is," he said, pulling into a long driveway winding its way through the parklike setting. At the far end, a rectangular brick building only recognizable as a church by the large wooden cross above the main doors stood majestically in among the trees. To the far right was a number of narrow single-story buildings. A sign announced, "Faith Elementary and Adult Learning Center parking and pickup stay right." Directly behind the church was a very deep parking lot stretching to the end of the property. To the left of the church was Beth's favorite place, the playground. As Rachel took in the complex, it became a challenge for her not to giggle. She remembered Chris telling her all through their high school years how someday he hoped to be the pastor of a little country church, maybe bigger than the school chapel yet small enough that it would still feel intimate. But this building could hold ten school chapels; maybe twenty.

Watching her carefully, Chris asked, "Why are you smiling?"

Her smile grew rapidly, but she managed to control the inevitable by biting her bottom lip. "Wait. That's more than just a smile. You're hiding a giggle or a laugh or something. I'm gonna be the butt of some joke, aren't I?"

The inevitable gush of laughter appeared in subdued bursts, their volume hushed with a hand, brought Chris to chuckle also, though he still didn't know the reason behind her laughter. The kids began to stir, waking up slowly. Uncovering her mouth, Rachel made a broad gesture, taking in the scope of the complex. "This doesn't look like the little country church you used to tell me about. Intimate—I think that's the word you used back then. Or maybe you said *infinite*, and I just misunderstood. No, I'm pretty sure it was intimate—you know, cozy, comfy, not too big."

Chris couldn't help but chuckle again. "The place sat abandoned for years, and then God decided he wanted to fill it with His people. I was just lucky enough to be looking for a new building at the time."

Stretching from her nap, her voice still filled with sleep, Beth asked. "Are we stopping? I need the bathroom."

"Just for a minute. I forgot my tools."

Suddenly rejuvenated, Beth sat up taller in her car seat. "This is our church. A lot of people are here sometimes. They like to hear Daddy pray, 'cause he's such a good screecher. And they like Aunt Bailey and the Norb too."

"Mr. Norby," Chris corrected, shooting her a look of disapproval by way of the mirror.

Rachel found herself once again biting her lip. "When your daddy and I were growing up, he used to screech all the time. So I'll just bet he's a really a good screecher now."

"He is. Aren't you, daddy?"

"I'm one of the best screechers in the church. Why, I can screech like nobody's business." He laughed as he pulled into an unmarked spot next to a small brick stairway behind the church. "Okay, everybody out. I'm going to hook Jass up under the tree, and we'll hit the restrooms and begin the five-cent tour."

Rachel held the door, and Michael slid off the seat onto the ground, where he frantically checked his pockets twice before asking his mom, "Do you have five cents?"

※

On the door at the top of the stairway, a large brass placard with raised lettering read Private. It opened into a short, narrow hallway offering two doors, each with its own brass sign, the first reading Pastor Chris, the other at the far end stating Everyone Else. He was quick to point out Elise, the church secretary, had installed them to prevent people from accidentally walking into his office. She also had a lock installed on his door, but Chris lost the key years ago.

"She's the Norb's wife," Beth said, before her jaw went slack as she felt her father's disapproving stare weigh heavily on her shoulders. Her head lowered in disgrace, she quietly corrected, "Mr. Norby's wife, I mean."

❦

The tour was interesting, Chris hitting all the major details, Beth giving each stop her own little backstory, careful to meet her father's approval. There was a lobby with a coffee shop reminiscent of Starbucks, a small bookstore, an extensive student library, information centers for numerous clubs and ministries, and even a small chapel where each morning at six thirty communion was offered by one of the associate pastors. Downstairs was the nursery, Sunday school classrooms, a number of offices and conference centers, and a very large multipurpose room typically used by the youth group. But it was the main sanctuary that was most impressive, capable of holding thousands. Its soft tones and use of wooden beams to support the slightly domed ceiling somehow made the whole thing feel more intimate than Rachel would've ever expected. The room was remarkably quiet, allowing very little sound to reverberate off its heavily textured walls and carpeted floor. The stage, deep and wide with its dimensions defined by long pastel curtains on three sides, helped bring focus to a beautiful Christmas mural of a night sky over the distant town of Bethlehem, a robed man standing with two others pointing to the bright star.

"Those are the wise men, and that's where Jesus was born," Beth said, knowing her dad would be proud she knew that. And of course, he was. "Can we go play?" she asked, looking up at him with pleading eyes.

Chris looked to get Rachel's approval and then told the kids, "There are still some puddles, so be careful. And stay out of the mud. We'll be out in a few minutes."

Beth turned to run but tripped, falling to her knees. Michael, right there to help, made sure she was okay, and then the two ran giggling from the room, leaving Chris to say, "The boy's a real gentleman."

"He has his moments."

"He's a good kid; you did well. Believe me; I know how hard it is raising one by yourself. If it weren't for Tru, I don't know what I would've done. And Lincoln too. He's always been right there; and Bailey…"

Pausing, he wrinkled his forehead. "Hmm, maybe I don't know how hard it is after all." He grinned. But then, pausing a second time, his grin quickly fading, he said, "It just feels like I'm always doing it alone."

"It feels that way, I know. Sometimes it's hard to separate being alone from being lonely. Suddenly you wake up one morning, and it's breakfast for one, an empty seat in the car, and more real estate in your bed. That's alone. Lonely is everything that follows…"

"You pick that up in counseling?" Chris asked, half joking.

Rachel didn't answer, leaving him to think perhaps he should apologize. But she didn't allow it, rushing to finish her thought.

"I went through the whole gamut—denial, anger, depression. You know, all the stuff they talk about in the support groups. You joined a support group, right. Oh wait, you're a pastor. I'll bet you lead the group. Oops, there I go making bets with you again. You'd think after last time, I'd learn."

Slowly, her smile appeared, and she thought perhaps she should apologize; but he didn't allow it, rushing to take her hand. "I don't know. I'm kinda glad you're a slow learner."

Outside, Beth stood at the edge of the playground, pointing to the thick forest thirty yards away. "Hey, Migel…"

"It's Michael, with a 'ka' sound." He laughed. "I know it's hard for you to say sometimes. And that's okay. A lot of words are hard for me to say." He chuckled again. "So why don't you just call me Mike. I've always liked that name, and it's a lot easier to say—that is, if you don't mind."

"Mike?" she stated, as if giving it some thought. "I like it too." She giggled and then pointed back to the forest. "Think there's fairies in there?"

Michael studied the terrain, noticing how different it was from where they had been earlier. There were no open areas; everything seemed to be squished together, bushes on top of bushes, trees on top of trees, creating almost a wall with no trails he could see. "I don't think so, Beth. There's no room for them to fly."

She looked up at the older boy and then back to the forest. "Yeah, they have to have room to fly," she said.

Michael, without looking away, nodded. The two stood quietly, taking in the dense woodlands, perhaps hoping they were wrong and a fairy would magically appear to point them to a secret path. But that wasn't the case. The only things they saw were what played out in their imaginations. So it was a simple game of pretend that lured them close to the forest's edge after they made their way across a narrow meadow that normally acted as a sufficient buffer between the playground and the dense thicket beyond. Their whispers and quiet giggles, careful not to travel far, were still quickly carried into the woods on a cool, light breeze. Just a few feet in front of the start of the underbrush, Beth motioned for him to bend down so she could whisper in his ear. Her words were puzzling, so at first he thought she was still pretending. But when he questioned her, she shook her head no and promised, "It's true." The girl whispered, still careful to be quiet.

Without saying as much, the boy seriously doubted the little girl's claim, but then again, he thought, her daddy owned this great big church, so Michael couldn't imagine Beth would ever tell a fib, especially one this big.

Sensing his disbelief, she took a single finger, saying in a voice somewhat above a whisper, "Cross my heart," and then she did so. This was good enough for Michael, dispelling his misgivings and tempering the suspicions that now left him feeling a little guilty for having in the first place. And for Beth, his smile was enough to show he believed her. But when he apologized out loud, she was filled with gratitude, which quickly gave way to embarrassment.

Standing silently, they looked into the woods for another minute or two before making their way back to the playground as quietly as they had come. Soon they were back to climbing, swinging, sliding, and finding the mud they had been asked to stay out of.

※

"How'd you do it?" Chris asked. "How'd you deal with having your world turned upside down, your life instantly changed?"

"For a long time, I didn't," she said. And for a second she considered making light of the subject. But then she remembered Ann repeatedly saying she didn't believe Chris had dealt with Linda's death at all. Rachel wondered if this could be his way of starting a dialogue.

At one time they could talk about everything, holding back secrets from the world but never from each other, spending hours on end touching topics, ideas, and beliefs shared only between each other. But that was a long time ago. Even so, something in her heart led her to believe time was irrelevant when it came to the two of them, and she was about to test that theory. "Are we talking, Chris? Seriously talking?"

He considered the question, remembering also the many intimate discussions they'd once shared. His faded smile reappeared but faded again quickly before he spoke. "I've needed to talk with someone for a long time," he admitted, pausing to give it just a little more thought. And with no change in expression or tone, he finished by saying, "And you finally showed up. So yeah, Rache. We're talking."

With half a smile and a shake of her head, she replied, "You want me to believe you've been waiting for me to arrive on your doorstep?"

Still displaying no change in his somber guise, he shrugged. "I think maybe I have."

Her smile broadened. "You're so full of it."

"You know this is a church, right?" He grinned.

"Oh, I'm pretty sure God will agree with me on this one."

Chris, not offering a rebuttal, reluctantly fell silent. However, a roll of his eyes and schoolboy smirk waggishly conveyed his sentiment. Rachel fought off a smirk of her own, adopting his more serious tone as she broke the silence. "Chris, if we're going to talk—I mean seriously talk—this is probably not the time or place for that to happen. Maybe we should—"

He stopped her. "You're right. Not that I'm full of it, but perhaps another time, another place would be—" His voice cut off abruptly, and then, through a half-hearted grin, remarked, "Those words seem very familiar. Have we said them before?"

"Maybe. Once upon a time." She sighed.

"That's right. The 'love' conversation you could never find the right time or place for us to have. That is, until we…"

"You know this is a church, right?" She giggled.

"Oh, I'm pretty sure God will agree with me on this one. Every time I'd bring it up, you'd claim it wasn't a good time, the right place, or any number of excuses you could pull from your 'not now' list. Well, I'm not gonna let you get away with it this time. I know a place, and we'll make the time."

"Are you inviting me camping?"

They stood looking at each other, Rachel folding her arms across her chest, cocking her head with an inquisitive smirk much like the one she had wanted to tease with earlier. Slowly, Chris smiled. "You know this is a church, right?"

Remaining lost in the depths of their gaze, neither fully smiled nor altered their expressions in the least. Stepping forward, Chris ran his hand along the contours of her face. Her arms slowly fell to her side, where he clasped her hand gently, intertwining their fingers, their thoughts, their memories...their emotions. The world seemed to rush in around her, leaving his unfaltering stare her only point of reference. Warmth surged through her entire body, increasing its intensity as it went, leaving her flushed and stealing her breath. Unable to maintain her composure much longer, she inhaled deeply, saying somewhat hurriedly, "Okay, Pastor Chris. We need to go find the kids."

Gently he held her. But without commenting further, she took a step back.

Chris declared, "So it's *pastor* now?"

"It is! And by the way," she said, taking in the Great Room, "you have a beautiful church, though I have to say it's just a little bigger than the country church you used to talk about."

"Seats around two thousand, but we support enough small ministries, home groups, youth, sports, music, and a ton of special interest stuff, on top of the school. But even so, people still think of it as a small church. No one gets lost in the shuffle. There's always someone they know and feel comfortable enough to sit with."

"Say what you want, but that's a huge ministry. Our congregation is half the size, with a handful of ministry groups, and Pastor Wilson, I think, prays it doesn't get any bigger."

Her words caused Chris to wrinkle his brow slightly. "When it comes to ministry, size doesn't matter. It's all about loving and serving the Lord according to His will and letting Him lead the church. Maybe you noticed next to each staff member's office there's a reference, such as Colossians 3:23, Titus 2:7–8, and the one Bailey insisted on having outside her office, Proverbs 16:3: 'Commit to the Lord whatever you do, and He will establish your plans.' Each refers to working for the Lord and is placed there to remind us daily the one reason we're all here."

Rachel's eyes brightened, her smile broadened, and when she spoke, her voice was like a soft melody. "I love listening to you. Your passion comes out in the simplest things. Even as kids, you always delivered God's message so clearly. And more than anyone, you taught me about..." Feeling the warmth returning, she took a deep breath but was unable to stop herself from taking a step toward him. It was then she realized he hadn't let go of her hand. Bringing them to her lips, gently kissing their entwined fingers, she said softly, "You taught me about love—God's love." Again she took a breath. "And about our—"

"Mom! Mom, quick! She fell," Michael yelled from the entrance door before turning to run back to the playground. From over his shoulder he called, "Over here. She's over here."

Rachel had only dropped a few steps behind Chris on their run to the playground, where Michael knelt beside the whimpering Beth. "It's my leg. My leg didn't work again, Daddy," she sniffled through tears that seemed to be drying quickly.

Her father also knelt beside her, brushing her hair back, asking, "What else hurts? Did you hit your head, knees, elbows?"

"No! My leg didn't work when I stood up..."

Michael hadn't moved from the girl's side and now looked at her father and pointed to the top of the slide. "She stood up and just tumbled down and then went over the edge. Lucky I was there to catch her. Well sort of. We both fell in the mud...I'm sorry Mr...."

"You tried to catch her?"

Beth set up suddenly excited, not waiting for the boy to answer. "He catched me, Daddy, so's I landed on him. I woulda fell in the mud, but Mike catched me. He didn't let me get hurt. He catched me. Really, Daddy."

Chris looked at Michael, but before he could say a word, the boy smiled at Beth. "That's just what big brothers do."

Rachel stood with her arms crossed, proud of her son but a little curious about his newfound relationship and the shortening of the name he'd always insisted upon. Chris, embracing the kids, glanced up to see the pride on Rachel's face.

"I guess we're family now." He nodded happily, squeezing the kids, who let go a loud cheer.

Chris beamed, getting hugs from them both. Rachel smiled, though somewhat cautiously, perhaps even a little strained. Quietly she watched this loving man attend to his daughter, moving her leg gently, much like a trainer checking for injuries. Satisfied she had been more frightened than injured, he turned his attention to the boy, showing equal concern. "Does anything hurt? Can you move your arms, legs? Your back feel okay?"

"I'm fine," Michael answered quickly.

Chris responded equally as quickly, "No cuts, bruises, bumps, or scrapes?"

"Nope, I'm good."

"Nothing strained, pulled, twisted, or torn?"

Michael, to the point of exaggerated frustration, exclaimed, "Watch. I can run and jump. Even do a cartwheel. See? I'm fine."

Chris, pretending to be unimpressed, shrugged. "Yes, but can you juggle?"

Perplexed and somewhat startled, Michael took a moment to process Chris's comment. Not because he didn't understand this form of humor—his mother demonstrated it all the time—it had just come so unexpectedly.

※

While locking the doors of the church and collecting Jass, Chris found a private moment to detail for Rachel the extent of Beth's injuries from the accident, her time in the hospital, and the loving care Trudy provided in restoring the girl's speech and motor skills.

Hardly stunned by anything when it came to the Trudeaus, Rachel shook her head and chortled. "They don't talk about themselves much, do they? I'm starting to think they're in the witness protection program or something."

Chris didn't answer, but he continued giving praise and credit to Trudy for the progress and success of his daughter's recovery. "Her speech is still rough at times, but without Trudy…" After taking a deep breath, he continued. "And her leg. This is the first time she's had a problem in a while. I think the hike may have been too much for her." Again he paused and took a deep breath. "She'll have to go through another surgery when she turns five. She's just been through so much…" His voice dropped off.

Rachel put her arms around his waist and laid her head on his chest, holding him tightly. From the back seat Michael and Beth watched intently, then looked at each other and smiled.

CHAPTER EIGHTEEN

The atmosphere around the Gathering Place went as Amy expected, with tears of delight from her mom and Trudy and hugs and kisses from Lincoln, while Wes became enjoyably caught up in the chaos of the moment. But there in her father's eyes was what she most expected—that doleful expression, resting for only an instant before being replaced by a glint of reflection, something she had witnessed at every birthday and graduation for as long as she could remember. But of course it wasn't limited to birthdays and graduations. There was her first date, the day she got her driver's license, her college acceptance letter, her engagement, her wedding, and now...well, she wasn't surprised to see that wonderful expression make its appearance today. No, she was thankful. It simply reinforced what she always knew: when it came to her, he wore his heart on his sleeve, and she would forever be...his little girl.

Following the others, he congratulated the couple and then whispered a string of words in his daughter's ear that he knew in no way expressed the love he felt in his heart. But to Amy, it conveyed everything. He noticed her hug seemed tighter and lingered longer than it had in years. Even so, it was accompanied by a second hug and whispered words of her own. He mouthed one of the words; a smile lit his face. "Papa," he repeated aloud while looking into her eyes. "Has a nice ring."

Later, by himself, he strolled to the end of the dock and stared into the dark waters of the cove, allowing distant memories to drift on the surface of the soft rippling tide. This was where he had taught her to swim, to fish, and to boat, and where she had taught him that it takes an extra measure of patience to be a daddy. After reflecting through years of summers, his glance moved to the compound, where scenes of his baby girl laughing and playing leaped from his mind to take their place around the yard. A two-year-old Amy toddled from the steps of the cabin to magically become a spirited six-year-old jumping rope by the garden, where suddenly she was a gangly young teen waving to him from the footbridge before showing up as a striking adult, making a surprise visit home from college. "College…" he muttered under his breath, not realizing he'd spoken the word aloud. Even so, it caused him to shake his head in disbelief that time had passed by so quickly.

Turning once again to face the cove, he leaned his forearms on the pier railing, clasping his hands together as if in prayer, and soon, he was. Inaudible words depicted his inward thoughts and brought times past into clear visions that gently moved from his heart to his lips.

"Thank you, God, for my family, my friends, and all that you have given me," he concluded, returning his attention to the dark waters of the cove.

Familiar footfalls along the wooden planks of the pier broke the serenity, chasing away his thoughts, though he knew they'd wait patiently on the surface of water to return another time. There was no need to turn around. He knew five more steps and she, too, would place her forearms on the railing and clasp her hands together as if in prayer, and she did. Neither said a word but allowed the peacefulness to return, bringing with it not only his beloved memories but hers as well. From just beyond the trees, the high-pitched cry of an eagle pierced the stillness of the morning air. Their eyes quickly found the soaring bird just before it disappeared behind a hedgerow of trees that stretched along the shoreline of the channel.

"Walk with me, Daddy?" she said, allowing an augmented pause to build between them before taking his hand. "It's been a long time since we've walked the shore in search of the perfect stone."

She had touched his heart, and he was now thankful the eagle chose that moment to cry out once more as it swooped into the cove, coming to perch on the bow of the anchored old rowboat.

"Is that the Old Fisherman?" Amy asked in hushed tones, not wanting to frighten the bird.

"He showed up yesterday to say hi to Linc, bug Trudy, and invite Jass for a swim."

Quizzically, she frowned. "Jass...what?"

As they made their way off the pier, Jim shared the Jass mishap, leaving Amy shaking her head. "We should've named him Dummy Dog, like I wanted."

Her dad nodded in agreement. Even the Old Fisherman, with a burst of short squeals, seemed to chuckle his approval before taking flight to disappear behind the hedgerow of tall trees lining the wide channel.

Bounding from the porch and making her way across the compound, Ann called for their attention. "Aim, I need you. We have a lot to do in Pauslbo. Jim, can you run out to Sara's and pick up some things? The creamery's open until noon today."

Although Ann's statement carried all the earmarks of a question, Jim knew better, leaving him to nod. "For you, the world, my sweets."

"And Jim, if you see a sign on the gate says Closed, just drive on back. She's there."

Stepping onto the porch, Lincoln called to Jim, "Mind if I ride along?"

And before anyone could say a word, Wes, too, walked onto the porch. "Ann, do you want the champagne and stuff at your place or Trudy's?"

Ann spun around midstride to look at Lincoln and Jim, saying with authority, "Will you two give him a hand. He needs to get to the airport, and Aim, my list is on the kitchen table. Look it over and add whatever you think we'll need. Okay, let's do this. Jim, you know what else I need."

❦

Standing in the shadows of the open doorway, Trudy grinned as she listened to her friend calmly delegate errands to be run, chores to be done, and time frames to be met. Glancing at the clock, she suddenly realized that in less than thirty minutes, the good people from Life of the Party Catering would arrive to begin decorating the ballroom. As in years past, she alone would meet with the designers to bring to life an imaginative New Year's theme. And as in years past, Ann would wait along with the other guests to be surprised.

Rushing upstairs, she threw on jeans and a loose blouse, pulled her hair into a ponytail, applied a token amount of makeup, and felt ready to begin the work ahead. Because her voice hadn't fully returned, she carried a pocket tablet and pen just in case she needed it. Of course, the ruby pendant she now fastened to her blouse could connect to the sound system, correcting her voice digitally and amplifying it into the room. But in truth it made her voice sound unnatural. Not robotic, but highly electronic. Therefore, she never used it. She'd even asked one of the programmers to eliminate the function altogether, but of course he didn't, knowing he'd have to answer to Lincoln if he were to ever find out.

After getting a kiss from Amy and a hug from Ann, Wes was the first to leave. A short time later, receiving kisses of their own, Jim and Lincoln began the hour-long drive to the Dungeness Valley Dairy, just the other side of Sequim. Waiting for her mother, Amy added very little to the list. Ann, much like Trudy, threw on jeans and a blouse, ran a brush through her hair, took a few extra minutes to do her makeup, and was out the door in what Jim would've claimed record time.

Trudy, still in her bedroom, whispered into the pendant, "Is there a note from Lincoln this morning?"

Quietly the room filled with music, bringing a smile to her face. The song followed her downstairs, and as she stood at the window overlooking the cove, the chorus began and filled her with warmth only love can bring. Though she didn't sing the words, her lips formed each one ("I've been waiting for a girl like you to come into my life"), melting her heart and lifting her spirits to soar even higher than that stupid eagle that was again circling above the trees.

When the trucks from Life of the Party Catering arrived, she directed them to the staging area toward the rear of the ballroom. There she met with Maura, the lead designer, and each of the eight gentlemen who would be doing the heavy work. She remembered most of the faces from times before and greeted them all with a soft-spoken "Welcome, and thanks for your help. There's soft drinks in the ice chest next to the fountain and beer in the cooler when we're done." Almost in unison the guys looked at Maura, who nodded her approval, albeit reluctantly.

"Let the work begin," called out a tall, brawny man, seemingly in charge.

Shortly after one o'clock, Trudy heard Chris pull into the compound. Through the back glass, Jass, expressed his joy to be home, his excitement rising with each step Trudy took toward the vehicle. There was no barking, only whimpers and cries and tapping of paws. When Chris opened the rear door, Jass was met with gentle strokes and pats of love from his friend the Quiet One. She smelled of strangers, causing the dog's hair to bristle, ears to perk, and eyes to scan the yard rapidly. Images of the dying elk flashed through his memory, as did the events of last night with Chris.

"Come on, boy. You're going to play with the kids and leave Trudy and her crew to their work," Chris said, scanning the yard. "I take it Anne has everyone running party errands?"

"From here to Sequim and a couple places in between. I don't expect any of them back till after three."

"Do we have dinner plans yet?" Chris asked.

"I have my spaghetti sauce simmering on the stove."

Chris smiled warmly. "We can bring garlic bread and a salad. That sound good, Tru?"

With the raise of an eyebrow and a glib little smirk that teasingly pulled to one side, she replied, "Yes, Christopher, that would be nice if the two of you brought a dish." There was no mistaking Trudy's inference, but Chris decided not to further encourage by offering a response.

Rachel gathered the kids and a number of bags from the back seat and left the picnic basket for Chris, who she had a feeling would forget it. And he would have, had she not reminded him when she passed him to greet Trudy.

"I don't know what you're doing over there, Trudy, but if you need help, I'd love to lend a hand," she offered sincerely.

Trudy frowned, holding her hand up and shaking her head. "No, but thanks anyway. They'll have it done in an hour or so, and then I want to hear all about this secret morning getaway of yours."

Chris stepped in between them. "Tru, you're getting as bad as your husband. It's not like we had a midnight rendezvous or sneaked out like a couple of kids."

Trudy tilted her head as if in thought. "A midnight rendezvous? Hmm…"

With her eyes squinting slightly and her smile thinning as it widened, she said timidly, "It was pretty brisk out last night. I would think cold enough for a parka, or at the least one of those pullovers you wear sometimes. Or a T-shirt. Wouldn't you agree, Christopher? At least a T-shirt?" And without saying more, she began walking toward her front porch. Chris and Rachel stared at each other. Trudy continued to cross the compound, giggling and whispering loud enough only to amuse herself.

※

The kids ran upstairs to Beth's playroom. Jass opted to curl up by the fireplace in hopes Chris would get the hint. Rachel, too, moved to the hearth, admiring a painting above the mantle. A blend of subtle earth tones seemed to caress the soft features of Beth's face staring with wonderment into a gentle breeze that left her hair slightly out of place.

"Did Lincoln do this?" she called to Chris, who was standing at the kitchen counter.

"He did. I came home one night about a month ago, and there it was. I'm not sure, but I think he burned the Walmart print that used to hang there. Can I get you something to drink?"

Giggling could be heard at the top of the stairs, and a moment later there was the muffled sound of running, a short pause, and then a burst of laughter, giggles, and squeals that even got the dog's attention. Rachel walked to the staircase and called up, "Michael, you be careful with her. No roughhousing."

There was no reply—only silence, and then the sound of a door closing. Beth appeared, making her way down the stairs to sit on the third step from the top. "He was laughing so hard he had to tinkle." She giggled. "That happens, you know!"

"It does, I know!" Rachel laughed.

"Is it okay if we play outside, Daddy? We won't bother Miss Trudy, and we won't go near the water, promise," Beth asked, her face glowing with excitement.

Chris looked to Rachel before saying, "Why don't you show Michael your castle. I bet he would like that. I'll get some old towels and dry off the slides."

"Yeah!" Beth squealed. "Mike, come on. Want to see the castle?" she called down the hallway. A second later the boy rushed from the bathroom still drying his hands on his pants.

Fifteen minutes later Chris and Rachel came back in, to the delight of Jass. As Rachel prepared two cups of coffee, Chris built a fire.

"What did we do before Keurig?" she asked, not expecting an answer.

"I kept a teakettle on the stove," he said, walking over to join her in the kitchen. "But now that I think about it, I didn't use it very often."

Handing him the warm cup, Rachel, for a moment anyway, quietly held his stare before shifting her eyes back toward the hearth.

"Nice fire."

"Good coffee," he countered.

She grinned and again met his stare. "Earlier you said you had something to show me. Is this—"

"Yes," he blurted before she could finish. "I did, didn't I? Come on. It's upstairs."

She watched that mischievous grin of his begin to form and for a moment hesitated to say anything. But she finally asked with a hint of sarcasm, "Upstairs?"

"Upstairs!" He winked.

Putting her acting skills to use, Rachel blushed with innocence. "You know people will talk, Pastor Chris?"

"I hope so, Miss Rachel." he answered flirtatiously.

The fire crackled, disturbing the dog's nap but not drawing the attention of the couple at all. Staring into his eyes, Rachel watched a look of solemnness come to his face. Chris led her up the wide staircase, neither speaking until they stood just outside Chris's bedroom door.

"Chris..." she breathed; the softness of her voice unveiling her apprehension.

Chris squeezed her hand twice in quick succession, triggering memories of codes used throughout their teens to convey messages wordlessly between them. Maybe it was because Chris had used this one more than any of the rest, she recalled its meaning so easily—*follow me*. And without letting go of his hand, she did.

"I can't imagine you ever get tired of the view. It's like walking into a tree house. I love how the windows frame the canal on one side and the intimacy of the cove on the other. It's a beautiful room, Chris. I could stay here forever."

"You're welcome anytime."

Though his voice remained calm as he offered her a seat at his desk, Rachel detected an underlying sense of eagerness in his movements and expressions. Chris opened a drawer and placed the journal before her.

"Last November, I wrote something I'd like you to see."

"Chris, wait a second!" Rachel drew back. "This doesn't feel right. You never let anyone read your journal, ever. I can't imagine you've had a change of heart."

The big man stood oddly silent for a moment. It was true; he'd never shared his journal with anyone other than God. But her statement, as incidental as it was, defined perfectly his emotional state on that November night and possibly even more so this very moment.

"You know, that's exactly what happened—a change of heart," he affirmed as much to himself as to her. "I hadn't thought of it quite that way. Not in those terms, anyway. But that's exactly what it was, what it is, what it's been. Yes, a change of heart!" He smiled.

Taking her hands in his, he leaned close. "Rache, back in the day there was nothing you and I couldn't talk about. We discussed everything; remember? Always sharing our innermost thoughts and feelings, visions, hopes, dreams."

She suddenly felt wary, but his eyes warmed her with their tenderness. "Love—our love," he added softly. "We could talk about anything without fear of judgment or remorse. You knew me better than anyone! Better than Bailey, my parents, my pastor. In reality, even Linda never came to know me as deeply as you. You were my..."

His eyes searched the air for the right words. "I don't know what you were, but whatever it was, you apparently still are because I have to share this with you. I need to share it with you. Please!"

Without giving her time to respond, he opened the book, allowing it to randomly fall to a page toward the front. January 14. The words were large and bold, only vaguely resembling the beautiful penmanship Rachel had once known so well. The lines, filled with bitterness, stung her like a vicious slap. He then arbitrarily turned to another, February 16, and again venomous words leaped from the page, tearing at her heart. Feverishly he rifled through several more pages until Rachel laid her hand on top of his.

"Stop," she insisted, turning away from the increasing hatred that filled entry after entry, date after date.

But when she again looked into his eyes, Chris didn't see the shock, anger, or disgust he feared would be starring back at him. Instead he found the loving gaze of true understanding, eyes that didn't judge but held empathy for his pain and anger. Eyes that saw clearly his cry for God's comfort and love. Just as they always had, her eyes carried to him the voice of her heart, making no immediate exchange of words necessary. Even so, she placed a finger on his lips, not in an attempt to keep him silent but merely to reassure him he didn't need say anything. As he had done earlier, she now cradled his large hands in hers, whispering a single word that stirred both their hearts.

"Grief."

The word itself seemed sinister to Chris. Always unwelcome, yet persistent in delivering its angst and sorrow to all it touched. However, it might have been the warmth of Rachel's hand gently caressing his own or perhaps the compassion that filled her voice, but grief would not make residence in his heart today—at least not to the point of making him a prisoner of depression once again.

"You know, Chris, you and I have always been a lot alike. My grief led me to some horrible places too, places where inwardly I screamed the same things you were writing, and God didn't get angry or leave me to find my own way, He continued to embrace me in every step of my journey. But of course I don't need to tell you that. You've been teaching that very thing for as long as I've known you."

Making no attempt to dilute the remnants of her own pain, she continued. "I heard it said, grief weighs heavy. But I didn't know what that meant exactly until one day I found it lying on my heart."

Intuitively Chris nodded, silently recalling his own encounter with grief and the weight it placed on him. Without dropping her gaze or letting go of his hands, Rachel sat back. "Maybe this isn't a good time, what with the kids and everybody—"

"No, please. Everyone's gone; the kids are playing; Trudy's busy. No one's going to bother us. It would mean a lot to me, please."

After talking with Ann and Jim in the bookstore, she had prayed God would send Chris someone he felt comfortable enough to talk with, but never did she imagine it would be her. She felt a smile pull against her cheeks as she thought, *Careful what you pray for next time, Rachel Donahue. Careful what you pray for.* And with that, something else came to mind, prompting her smile to fade, her eyes to squint as she recalled discussions from their past.

"I'll continue under one condition," she declared, her voice flat and pragmatic. "You don't make this conversation all about me. It's a dialogue, a time to share with each other. Agreed?"

"Of course!" he said with surprising earnestness. "I've wanted to talk to somebody, needed to talk to someone for quite a while, but it's not easy sharing something like this. I mean, it's deeper than sharing a piece of your heart. It's like—and I know this sounds cliché, but baring your soul. And honestly, Rache, you're the only one I've…ever…"

As he listened to his own words his voice tapered off. Watching his eyes, Rachel waited for him to continue, and then, from his heart, his voice tender and full of emotion, he said, "I've been waiting for you."

A frown raced over her brow, and afraid she would think him crazy, Chris quickly explained, "I'm not saying I expected you to show up at my doorstep, although I am very thankful you have. What I'm saying is, lately God's been showing me things are all right. I'm all right. It's time to close the door on the past and allow him to open a window to the future."

A smile deepened his dimples. "I just never expected to find you at that window."

Though many things crossed her mind, she wasn't to say a word for fear he'd not continue. Chris, realizing her silence was meant for him, began to share, with reservations, the critical emotions that had left him with doubt and despair, questioning not God, but the strength of his own faith, something he now believed was stronger than ever. And with Bailey the only ripple in the pond left to rock his boat, he believed that once her move was complete and things calmed down, life would begin to take a turn toward normalcy, or at least as close to normal as he had come to expect as a single parent.

And then he stared without focus, not at a nearby object but into a distant memory, leaving each breath to be drawn long and deep. His vision, filled with images both joyful and tragic, conveyed a grin disordered and tangled, resting somewhere between sorrow and gladness, bitterness and affection. With time passing nary a moment, still deep in thought, he said, "I think you would've liked Linda!"

Rachel offered a heartening look but continued to remain silent, hoping he would open up and share his feelings. And he did to a point, more so than he had with anyone over the past year and more so than he ever thought possible. And then without warning, he asked, "How did you do it? When Mike died, how did you hold it together—take care of your son and continue moving on through life?"

"I guess it's my turn now."

Chris realized the sudden change in direction and looked at her apologetically. "If you don't mind talking about it, I would love to just shut up and listen for a while."

So she made herself comfortable in the chair and moistened her lips, and as Chris held her hand, she began to speak.

"For a while—quite a while—I was numb. You know, couldn't think, couldn't function, and didn't seem to care about anything. Not to mention a week after Mike's funeral, I had a birthday party to throw. Invitations were already sent, the cake ordered, and the birthday room at a local pizza place reserved. On the afternoon of the party, I get a call from my friend Katrina, wondering where I was with the birthday boy. In the background I could hear twenty screaming kids and half as many frustrated moms vying to be heard. Michael and I arrived just in time to thank the four or five kids that stayed for cake, which only reminded me I had forgotten to pick it up from the bakery.

"Since all the kids were from church and I didn't want to face their mothers' ridicule, we didn't attend that Sunday, or any Sunday for the next six months. And you know, it's funny. I don't remember a lot about that time. It was like I just turned myself off. What I do remember is becoming so comfortably numb with my anger and depression that I blew off the other three stages of grief everyone talks about. I prayed to God constantly for the first couple of weeks and then swore at him for the next couple of months. I was a mess and dragged my kid down with me. Where were all of my good Christian friends, my support system, you ask? Calling my cell phone, leaving bags of groceries at the front door and notes in the mailbox. But like I said, I was comfortably numb. Oh, there were a few times I'd answer the phone, but I'd mostly listen, not saying much at all."

Her eyes fell to the journal. "There was this one night in particular, I found myself stomping around my bedroom praying out loud some pretty unthinkable things, and it wasn't the first time. But I looked up to see my son standing in the doorway, watching, listening, and then I prayed not only had he not heard me, but that God hadn't either."

Her gaze again found Chris, and she squeezed his hand. "Crazy, I know. After that I quit praying altogether, took a step back from God, walked away from the church, and just tried to breathe. That same night Peg called to tell me our dad died."

"I'm sorry, Rache." He sighed softly, his condolence acknowledged with only a smile.

"My first real breath came when I cleared the house of everything that reminded me of Mike. His keyboards went into storage, pictures into the closet, and his clothes to Goodwill—all except a few T-shirts he'd worn all the time. There was this one he'd worn to rehearsal the night before he died. For months I'd hold it to my face, and I could still smell him."

She inhaled deeply. "And then, one night it was gone. I looked everywhere but couldn't find it. By midnight I was frantic. I woke Michael and ask him if he'd seen it."

Her grin looked more painful than pleasant. "He told me it was a under the sink. Thinking he was helping, he'd used it as a dust rag. A dust rag!" she exclaimed, raising her voice slightly. "The last essence I had of my husband, and now it reeked of Pledge."

Tittering softly, her gaze drifted to their hands, which had become intertwined. As she spoke, her stare again went to him.

"I found myself holding Michael just to see if he smelled like his father, but of course he didn't. I was heartbroken, at least until the next morning when I realized—I mean consciously realized for the first time since Mike's death—the sun was coming up, God was on His throne, and it was a new day. I jumped out of bed and into the shower. Twenty minutes later, my hair still damp, my son at my side, we headed out the door to IHOP for breakfast. But before we could get to the car, my friend Cassie pulled up and asked if Michael could go to the cabin for the weekend. Her husband's family was having a big get-together, and there would be tons of kids and plenty for Michael to do. Reluctantly I gave in to their pleading. Thirty minutes later, for the first time in months, I was alone."

Observing a multitude of small changes in her expression, Chris knew the memory was being staged somewhere deep behind the eyes he had always found so beautiful. Her lips parted as if to speak, but instead she revisited the memory once again, this time for a second longer.

"I knew if I didn't leave the house right that minute, I wouldn't leave it at all. I'd be back in my pajamas, curled up on the couch eating week-old pizza for breakfast, and watching *Always*."

"*Always?*" Chris looked at her curiously.

"You really haven't seen it?" she inquired with disbelief.

Chris shook his head, causing her to place both hands on her heart and swoon in an overdramatic fashion. "It's such a beautiful movie. How could you not have seen it? They're in love—Dreyfus and Hunter. He's a pilot… and…you know what? Forget it! I'll bring a copy out with me, and we can watch it some night."

"So you're planning on coming back?" He grinned.

Though her look held no response, her hands moved unhurriedly to rejoin with his, all while picking up the conversation as if it had never strayed.

"Standing there alone, I knew it wouldn't take much for me to lapse back into my depression, so off I went. It'd been a few years since I'd had a day to myself, no one to answer to, no time restrictions, just go and enjoy some me time. So I ended up driving out to this place called Tom's Farm, down by Temecula. It's not really a farm, although I guess it may have been once. But now it's little craft shops and antiques, a huge produce stand, and a place to get an old-fashioned hamburger and sit by the pond feeding the ducks and listening to a musician or band playing in the background.

Anyway, for years I used it as a getaway, an escape, my alone place. I never told Mike about it, not that he would've cared. It wasn't his kind of place. Besides, it was where I went to think…"

Her eyes fell away but quickly returned, carrying a glint of despondence Chris felt more in his heart than saw in her gaze. Almost offhandedly, she continued. "And on a couple of occasions, made some pretty big decisions sitting by that little pond."

Again her stare fell away, this time not to readily return but focusing on the gentle way he held her hand. *Comforting,* she thought. *Don't let go.*

His eyes held her stare, and with great effort, her gaze slowly pulled away as she began to speak.

"That day there was a duo, a man and wife playing guitar and singing soft rock from the eighties. And at the end of their set, the girl began thanking the crowd for listening. But the guy said he'd like to play one more song. His wife was a little taken back but stepped away from the mic, turning the stage over to him.

"'We're not big country music fans,' he told us, 'and I haven't played this song in a couple of years, and I hope what I'm about to say doesn't offend anyone. But this song was put on my heart, and I feel like it needs to be played for somebody here today. Somebody needs to know, it's all right.' And with that he began to play that Brad Paisley song 'When I Get Where I am Going.'"

"Beautiful song…" Chris said.

Only a little surprised he was familiar with it, she tilted her head, raising an eyebrow, smiling softly. "It is! And at the time I'd never heard it. But every line spoke to my heart. To my soul, really. I didn't cry…well, there may have been a couple tears that got away, but I wasn't alone. There were other people dabbing tears from their own memories. And it wasn't like it left me sobbing. If anything it awakened my spirit and brought a level of peace to my heart I hadn't felt in quite some time. Afterward, the couple thanked the crowd again for coming, and I strolled over to the pond to take a few deep breaths and consider the song's message, but mostly to feed the ducks."

Chris had some doubt in his mind as to the importance of the ducks, believing they wouldn't be more than a small distraction at best. But he easily pictured her sitting by the pond casting thoughts onto the water while fighting back another round of tears. Yes, he knew Rachel's heart, her emotions and sentiment, making his version a bit more plausible than her fanciful depiction of self-appointed mother duck.

"I had been sitting there maybe fifteen minutes when I realized there was someplace else I needed to go. I made a dash for the parking lot, and as I was about to get in my car, the singer and his wife pulled up next to me. Leaning out his window, he said, 'Excuse me; I just want to tell ya, that song was put on my heart the minute you sat down. Somebody up there wanted you to hear it, so I hope it helps, and we're sorry for your loss, if that's what it pertains to.' And out of the parking lot he went, not allowing me a word.

"Once in the car, I started to laugh, thinking, there I was, sitting on a lawn with fifty or sixty other people, and God had used this guitar player to bring me a message so loud and clear even I couldn't mistake it for coincidence. But just to make sure I got it, He had the guy drive up and tell me in no uncertain terms, he'd played the song specifically for me."

Still harboring disbelief, Rachel grinned and shook her head. "God wanted my attention, and He wasn't just tapping me on the shoulder to get it. He was kicking me in the butt to make sure I got it. And I did. Mike was happy in heaven, and now it was time for me to move on with life and get back to being a mom. But like I said, there was still someplace else I needed to go.

"The drive back to Irvine was filled with daydreams and memories, some which made me laugh out loud, but most reminded me just how empty I felt. Sometime along the way, I found myself deep in prayer, and before long I was just having a conversation with the Lord, something I hadn't done in a while—not without getting angry, anyway. The next thing I knew, I was at my destination. My eyes were red and swollen, I looked and felt like a mess, but I didn't care. A few minutes later, I sat in an empty sanctuary playing the last piano my husband ever played. And even though I knew the pastor and his wife were in the building, no one came in. No one bothered me. It was simply me and the Lord wandering down the musical path that had led Mike to that church and ultimately…that piano."

She inhaled slowly. Her smile, soft and warm, reflected the tone of her voice. Her eyes danced to the music twinkling deep within the memories that lay behind them. "At first I was playing for me, trying to feel Mike's energy through the keys. But after a few minutes, I was playing for the Lord, thanking him for picking me up and praying I wouldn't fall again anytime soon. I didn't stay long—ten, fifteen minutes, maybe—but when I got back to the car, there was a note on the windshield. It said, 'That was beautiful. Please come back anytime.'

"Over the next few weeks, a number of things just kept telling me it was time to let go and let God. You remember that old saying, right?"

Of course he did. He said it all the time.

Not wanting him to interrupt, she continued. "But you know me. I had a brand-new list of what-ifs. So letting go, even while holding God's hand, was frightening, at times almost impossible. Yet I could feel Him leading me, giving me answers, and providing a means to overcome every what-if I threw His way."

Chris could only imagine the magnitude of her list and fought to keep from chuckling.

"I know it sounds strange, Chris, but I found myself feeling a bit overwhelmed by God's love and attention. At times it became smothering..."

Feeling an explanation was needed, she blurted, "I mean in a good way, though."

Chris grinned, reassuring her with a gentle squeeze of the hand as he spoke. "I've been there!" he said softly. "You ask God to show up in your life, and when He does…well, it can be a little overwhelming, I know. I've been somewhat overwhelmed myself lately!"

Rachel studied his facial expression, so kind and gentle, just as she remembered and treasured through the years. His large hands rubbed gently over hers, causing the beat of her heart to rush, her thoughts to slow, and her lips to part. She hoped he would speak before she acted impulsively, yet she prayed his silence would linger another moment, second, minute…

"Love's a funny thing, isn't it?" he inquired warily, chasing away his own hidden urges.

Rachel inhaled sharply, believing he'd somehow read her thoughts. And then, blushing, she realized how ridiculous that was and looked away. What she didn't realize, but Chris noticed immediately, was something she'd done many times back in the day. Back then it had been her way of secretly revealing to him her emotion: stroking the back of his hand ever so softly with her thumb before burying her hand deep within his gentle grasp, as if to hide shyly from the world.

Perhaps now it was just some odd muscle memory that made its way up his arm, but something caused the beat of his heart to rush, his thoughts to slow, and his lips to part. Quickly he moved the conversation forward.

"Did you have one of those defining moments?" he asked. "You know, where you knew the grieving was over, there were no more tears to cry, and it was time to get on with life?"

Not needing a moment to form her thoughts, she said almost instinctively, "I suppose I could give you a laundry list of things that helped me find closure, but closure for me has been inconsistent and a little deceiving at times. I think about him, miss him, and even wish he'd lived to be there for his son." Her eyes drifted from his, her head tilted to one side as if bemused. "But then I wouldn't..."

Abruptly her words cut off, seeming to evaporate into silence like words often do when they're more afterthought than dialogue. Ushering in a lingering disquiet that after a moment caused Chris to ask, "Wouldn't?"

She remained silent but smiled, thinking, *I wouldn't be here with you now.*

Keenly Chris raised an eyebrow.

However, before he could probe further, Rachel dodged his question by saying, "I suppose the one thing I've learned over the last few years is that life is still filled with what-ifs. But it's the I wills that matter most to God. You know—I will believe, I will trust, I will follow, and so on. But most of all, at least for me anyway, was coming to accept that I will move on."

Chris laughed. "God loves that I will stuff, doesn't He? And you remember, back in junior high, I made some I will promises to Him as well. I will have faith, I will believe, and I will trust. But it was Linda's death that made me realize—a realization that came only recently, I'm afraid, one you tried to teach me over and over—that God wants us to know life is also filled with what-ifs. What if one day it's just you and your daughter? What if, one day you question your faith? What if, one day..."

Chris stopped. It was now his turn to study her expressions, and like his own, hers were kind and gentle, yet interrupted briefly with lines of wonder and concern, which were still unable to distract from the intense affection she wore so beautifully.

"You know the problem with God?" Chris asked rhetorically. "He lets us talk too much and listen too little. Take my journal, for instance. God allowed me to vent my anger time and again, page after page, until one afternoon as the kids' choir rehearsed a song for their program, He spoke to me through the quiet voice of my daughter and even quieter voice of one Miss Trudy. That moment was a tipping point for me. Not a turning point, but the moment my heart began to change, to embrace whatever path God was to lead me and Beth down.

"For a while it remained uphill. Not that I continued struggling to make sense of Linda's death, but simply to overcome the loneliness I felt every day. And then, one night last November, I…well…I thought of you," he stammered before his voice trailed off in search of words to make sense out of what he was about to reveal. But none came, leaving plenty of time for Rachel to review his statement, which left her stunned with curiosity.

"Me? What are you talking about, Chris? What's this about November?" she asked, confused.

Laying his hands on the journal, he said, "You need to see for yourself."

With no desire to read more of his pain, she sharply turned away. But as Chris thumbed through the pages, her curiosity grew, and she found herself unable to shy away. His rifling became silent. At the top of the margin, she read "November 7."

Even at first glance, it was apparent by the aesthetics alone this entry was far different from those he'd previously shown her. His elegant penmanship had returned, capturing perfectly the passion within his heart. Reading the love for his Lord, his daughter, and Trudy stirred Rachel's emotions, bringing her to the brink of tears. But then, abruptly her sentiment changed to confusion when, at the bottom of the third page, obviously disconnected from the rest of the text, was scribbled a single word: *Rachel*. Before she could ask, Chris shrugged his own bewilderment.

"I don't know, Rache. At least at that moment I didn't know why I wrote it, other than I felt God whisper your name to my heart. It was so clear and so vivid I wanted to open the window and shout, hoping somehow my voice would find you." Shrugging again, he nodded toward the page. "But instead I quietly wrote it down."

And she again divided her attention between the fretful expression he now wore and her name on the page.

Pausing, Chris took a shallow breath. "But then, like I had so many times before, I prayed for you, for me, fo…"

The words trailed off, leaving his breath to hang silent in the air. Laying his hand against her cheek, he directed her gaze into that of his own. "For us," he resolved in a subsequent exhale not much louder than the last. Without another word he began turning pages, stopping on an entry dated December 12.

His eyes again met hers. "One night, a few weeks back, after talking with Trudy about Beth and what to expect once Bailey left for Tampa, I found myself up here staring out the window in search of answers to questions I hadn't brought myself to face until then. I guess in my heart I was hoping Bailey's move would somehow get postponed, or better yet, canceled altogether. But after talking with Trudy, I knew I had to pull my head out of the sand and deal with all these concerns that were beginning to pile up pretty darn quick. Did I mention Bailey had begun questioning their decision to move? Oh yeah! And naturally that angered Ted, who, it turns out, had a notepad filled with questions of his own he brought to me for answers. I told him I already had enough on my plate, what with having to deal with Beth, the church, the worship team, and my sister running off to Florida."

He glanced to the desk and back to Rachel. "Sorry! Her leaving still doesn't sit well, I'm afraid. Disturbs old wounds, I guess."

Rachel remembered the beautiful photo of Linda and Beth downstairs. However, before she could speak, Chris, with a gentle shake of his head and the slightest inkling of a smile, said softly, "I sometimes think about what might have been and wonder how I ever let you walk out of my life."

I've wondered that myself, she thought before realizing the wounds he spoke of were not caused by the loss of his wife, but those she herself inflicted years before. And again, before she could speak, Chris broadened his smile and said, "But the truth is, Rache, you've never really been out of my life. I've managed to keep you just a thought away, locked-up memories I've never been willing to part with—never will part with."

More out of instinct than impulse, Rachel stroked the back of his hand ever so softly with her thumb and then buried her hand deep within his gentle grasp as she, not wanting to interrupt, waited for him to continue.

"So that night, as I stood at the window, I wasn't surprised God put you on my heart a second time."

Feeling him squeeze her hand gently, Rachel watched his attention fall to the journal. Turning hesitantly to face the open page, she read the familiar inscription.

Question: "What if_____?"
Answer: "I'll be there."

In her eyes the many shades of green were suddenly awash with a shallow pool of tears, but a gentle smile lifted her cheeks just enough to keep them from spilling over. He raised her hands to his lips, not in a kiss, but simply a touch before moving her hand across his cheek to rest his head in her palm. He then kissed her wrist tenderly, allowing it to fall slowly back into her lap. Memories flooded her mind.

Chris stood, slowly raising her from the chair. "May I?" he asked, extending his arms to embrace her.

Without a word she stepped into him, her head pressing against his chest, her eyes tightly closed. Inhaling deeply the scent of her hair, he immediately restrained the words wishing to rush from his lips. Both stood quietly lost in their own thoughts.

When Chris again spoke, his voice was soft, the words powerful, full of affection she remembered all too well.

"I could hold you like this forever."

Suddenly her heart filled to where it easily could have taken her breath, but it was at that moment Chris leaned back just far enough to allow his hand to caress the contours of her face, so gentle, so lovingly, increasing in her a rush of memories and emotions all too familiar, all too missed, and all too desired. In that instant there was much her heart demanded she confess, not only to Chris, but inwardly to herself.

Staring into her eyes, he felt his heart proclaim everything his mind already knew and had known for as long as he could remember. In that instant there was much his heart confessed inwardly to himself, and he too felt a rush of emotion all too familiar, all too missed, and all too desired, and again, he held her in his arms. Closing his eyes, not in an attempt to shut out his surroundings or disarm unwelcomed guilt, but to simply give himself a moment of what he had needed for so very long. A moment that couldn't have been shared with anyone other than the woman he now held in his arms. The first woman he had ever held, ever kissed, ever danced with and ever loved. He supposed there were certain things a pastor shouldn't do, and being alone in this setting with this beautiful woman would probably top the list. Yet he found himself praying the moment would never end.

Chris was the first to speak but only relinquished his embrace enough to stare into her face. "I know it sounds crazy, but I believe with all my heart, God brought you to my door as an answer to prayer. I'm not talking about prayers just over these last few months, but ones that began the day you left and continued for—"

"Years?" she interrupted. "I used to pray you'd come and take me away. Bring me back with you to the Northwest and…and…"

"And live happily ever after. I think I promised you that, once upon a time." He grinned.

The silence that lingered between them held no feelings of awkwardness, but seemed to gather a peaceful moment of youthful reflection, causing each to blush shyly, before Rachel answered, "Yes, you did. You were to be my knight in shining armor. I was so in—"

Chris, placing a finger on her lips to silence her words, could not silence his own heart, and again he held her in his arms. Placing her head on his chest and her arms around his waist, she clutched him firmly, listening to her heart speak words her mouth once expressed freely. Again he inhaled the scent of her hair, and she felt his arms embrace her—not tightly, but just enough to merely squeeze the words from her lips even as he, too, spoke them.

CHAPTER NINETEEN

*I*n the short time he had known Beth, Michael had made a few incisive discoveries. Not only did she possess an outgoing personality and fearless quest for adventure, but her yard was like one gigantic park waiting to be explored. Beth assured him as long as they stayed away from the water, didn't venture too far down the driveway, avoided the path to Jupiter Falls, and never wandered beyond the footbridge, they were free to play anywhere. But they could never, ever, under any circumstance go where the angels came to picnic.

"Angels?" Michael inquired, thinking he misunderstood.

After listening to the girl describe this secluded woodland of magic and splendor, Michael's curiosity and imagination soared, much like the eagle she had brought to his attention flying high above the compound.

"Is it far?"

"Not too far! Just over the bridge and down that path, and then back and forth down the bricks and down another path. So I guess maybe it's kind of far, but it don't matter. I'm not supposed to go there by myself anyway."

"I'm with you."

Beth thought for a moment, but even then didn't answer right away. This gave Michael time to rethink his position, knowing his mother would hold him responsible if the girl got in trouble for taking him someplace she shouldn't go.

"Maybe later your dad will take us, and we can picnic with the angels. We'll take some of that goo jam. I'll bet angels would love goo jam. I know I sure do!"

Beth giggled in agreement and then remembered. "We don't go there now. It's too wet and stuff. Besides, it's too cold for the angels to picnic anyway, and that place is cold and dark even when the sun's out. And it's kind of spooky looking. But beautiful too."

Even though Michael wanted to see the place, he knew it was best to listen to the girl. Besides, there were other things to see, perhaps not as interesting, but they wouldn't get in trouble for doing so. And Beth was more than eager to show him around.

Opening a side gate, they entered the compound. A minute later, the two stood atop the old wooden footbridge, which easily spanned ten feet bank to bank. Narrow openings along the guardrail allowed a safe view of the water as it shadowed the sloped terrain down the far side of the Trudeau property to reach the bottom, where it widened and slowed to a crawl before disappearing into the wetlands, consuming about two acres of shoreline.

"My daddy goes down there sometimes." Beth fretted, pointing in the direction of the dense vegetation. "He takes pictures of birds and frogs and grass and stuff. He catches fishes there, too, with Mr. Trudy. But it's not a safe place to go," she warned, turning her attention to the boy. "I'm glad I can only go as far as the big tree and stay on this side of the sidewalk, away from the creek. Daddy says if I don't, I could get swept into the ocean and carried off to China."

Her mood had turned serious, and Michael supposed he felt the same but had no explanation as to why. That is, until she added, "He'd be terrible lonely if that happened, because Mommy died and Aunt Baily's going away..."

Michael thought her words seemed to hang over the stream and then fall like teardrops onto the water. He thought of his father, but only for an instant. His mother's loneliness swept through his mind and came to rest on his heart. Stepping to face the girl, he said, "Your dad loves you. He'd be terrible lonely all right." And with no other words spoken, Beth hugged him.

Leaning on the rail supports, each was lost in the view and their thoughts. Below, the creek, strewn with large rocks and branches, gave the shallow current a voice as soothing to the soul as to the mind. Even for the children, it spoke softly, calming the vigor of their youth, albeit only momentarily, for soon their voices rose again, accompanied by subtle bursts of laughter and tempered squeals.

"I wish I could take you to the angel place, but the forest is kind of off limits."

Looking around, Michael understood why. Everywhere the sound was not, the thick forest stretched out in all directions for as far as he could see—an easy place to get lost or have a mishap or worse, he thought with a chill.

Resigning herself to spend time on the bridge, Beth said, "Sometimes if you look real close, you can see fishes in there. Do you like to fish? I do! We go down there." She pointed to the dock. "I have to wear a life jacket in case I tumble in; but next summer Mr. B. promised to teach me how to swim. He taught Amy how, and she swims good. I don't think I'm going like it much, though, 'cause that water's cold, and I don't like cold water. So I might not learn."

Michael grinned. "But once you learn, you can swim wherever you want. Warm, cold, it won't matter. It'll just be fun. We can go swimming together. I love to swim."

Bursting with giggles, Beth swooned with joy, but it was not entirely due to having a swim partner. As wonderful as it was living where she did, it was also at times a very lonely place for a little girl—something she had only recently begun to realize.

"Are you moving close by? We can play every day."

Her excitement made him chuckle. "I wish. This place is great. Maybe after you learn to swim, your dad will get a boat or put a slide on the end of the dock, and we could swim there."

Her giggles grew into childish squeaks and coos, the clapping of hands and shuffling of feet. When she spoke, her words jumbled on top of one another, causing her laughter to die, her smile to fade, and her shoulders to slump. "Sorry. That happens sometimes. Makes me sound goofy, I know. But it's better than it was. Sorry Michael."

His stare was filled with compassion and understanding. "It's no big deal. My words get tangled up all the time, so I sound goofy too. But it happens to everybody. You don't have to say you're sorry."

Her smile slowly made its way back, bringing with it a slight blush, which seemed to be held in place by a sudden cool breeze. "Brr!" she emphasized with a shiver.

Michael immediately pulled a bright-red scarf from his jacket pocket. "It's Mom's. She left it on the bench this morning. I forgot to give it to her." Stepping closer, he wrapped it loosely around the girl's neck and pulled a flap up to cover her nose and mouth. "How's that? Better?"

Nodding her head, she could smell the scent of his mother, bringing to her comfort that seemed to warm her inside as well as out. "Thank you!" she responded, though slightly muffled by the scarf.

"If you're too cold, we can go in," he added.

She responded promptly. "No! Let's see if we can find more fairy doors. There has to be one somewhere in all these trees. Don't you think?"

Michael agreed. And so the search began.

❦

At the bottom of the stairs, Jass began to whine and bark softly. In the upstairs room, Rachel sighed. "You're being paged."

Jass again whined, but a second later, seeing them at the top of the stairs, he began his happy dance. As they approached the bottom steps, the dog bolted for the door just as the doorbell rang. Quickly glancing at each other, Chris and Rachel felt a twinge of guilt flush their faces. Opening the door, Chris invited Trudy in, but the offer was neither accepted nor denied. She simply stepped into the doorway clearly flustered, saying with a slight crack in her voice and a gasp of breath, "I fed Mildred's horses this morning, but I forgot to feed Binx, and I can't leave the house. They're redoing some of the decorations. Would you mind running over? She's been in Portland a couple days, and I'm getting so forgetful. Oh, that poor cat."

"That mangy old cat's fine." Chris grinned. "It probably ate the fish out of the aquarium."

"Oh no," Trudy gasped. "You don't think..."

Rachel shook her head in mock disgust, trying hard to hide her giggles. "Chris, that's not nice. Apologize. You used to like cats. What happened?"

"That thing's not a cat," he corrected. "He's a twenty-five-pound dust mop with eyes. Believe me, he's not going to miss a meal. Thing would eat its own tail first."

"Chris," both ladies flared in unison.

"I'm kidding!" He laughed, hiding a wink from Trudy. "She still keep a key under the milk can?"

"She does!"

"Okay, give me a second to round up the kids, and we'll head on over. Don't want Binx to shrivel up and blow away."

Trudy stepped to the porch. "I'll take care of the kids. You two get going. Oh, and you'll have to use the path. She forgot to leave me the gate opener. Hey, while you're down that way, why don't you show Rachel up to The Point?"

Detecting a gleam in Trudy's eye, Chris smiled but said nothing. Jass followed the Quiet One out the door. Trudy, catching a glimpse of the kids in front of a small stand of trees next to the bridge, made her way across the yard. Removing her cell phone from a jacket pocket, her fingers danced across the keypad, and a grin, oh so devilishly wicked, delivered an almost silent chuckle. "Hi, Mildred. Are you still at Nels? Oh, good. Don't hurry home, and don't feed Binx when you get there. No, everything's fine. I'll explain later."

※

After grabbing their jackets the two headed onto a path edged by trees and underbrush that for the most part ran parallel to the shore, exposing beautiful views up and down Hood Canal. Scattered tide pools of all sizes dotted the gravelly beach, signaling low tide. Oyster beds lay exposed and ready for harvest. Timbers deposited by great storms were stacked in heaps along the shoreline, and a family of seals argued fishing rights with a couple of boys in a rowboat. It had been a long time since Rachel had walked the shores of Puget Sound, taking in its beauty and tranquility, listening to the surf fashion a rhythm distinct to itself, by way of its surroundings. Chris took her by the hand and strolled closer to the water's edge. A little more than a quarter mile from the back gate of his yard was the rock bulkhead and stairway winding its way to Mildred's house atop a short but steep cliff. The home was Dutch colonial with a steep gambrel roof. Three dormers matched the one over the front entryway. The garage mimicked the style of the home, as did the stables, which sat on the far side of the property. Her garden was simple—a variety of ferns, perennials, and shrubs all native to the area grew dense and lush, disturbed only by wide gravel walkways outlined in river rock with small areas of colorful baskets hanging from thick wooden pergolas. It was under one of these pergolas next to the house the milk can stood, and under it, just as Chris knew it would be, was the key to Mildred's back door. Lying in the kitchen, sprawled on a rug, was Binx.

Rachel grinned. "He does look like a dust mop."

"I told you!" Chris boasted. "I see his tail, so maybe we should count the fish before we go."

❖

It was a fifteen-minute trek and slightly uphill to The Point. As they approached, the path narrowed to an end, and there appeared through the trees a small clearing notched out of the forest. In its center stood an immense marble rotunda with eight Corinthian columns.

Rachel's expression showed clearly her dismay. However, even before she could think to ask, Chris answered, "I don't know much about it other than it was brought here for a wedding sometime in the nineteen thirties, I believe from Greece or maybe Italy. Trudy knows. She has records of it from the old lodge, even a few photographs of the wedding."

He watched her move her hand over the cold surface and then commented, "It's solid marble. The columns alone must weigh about two tons. I don't know how they ever got 'em up here. And can you imagine what it cost. I mean, even back then it would have been a fortune."

Rachel glared. "You can't put a price tag on love, and obviously someone loved that bride a lot. Maybe her rich daddy. Oh, I know. It was that young American millionaire who swept her off her feet and brought her here from her humble fishing village on the coast of Greece."

With a smirk Chris rolled his eyes, snickering. "Always the romantic. You sound like Ann and Trudy."

"Then I'll fit right in," she piped glibly, then twirled and walked away.

"Uh huh…" Chris retorted, joining her on the dirty pine-needle-covered floor.

Defined in great detail was an eight-point compass covering a large portion of the circular floor. Inlaid were opposing shades of marble, creating a two-tone shadow effect, the same as on maps of antiquity. At each main point a severely tarnished brass letter depicted the corresponding compass direction.

Rachel smiled. "What a beautiful star or compass or whatever it is."

"It's a 'compass rose.' Not sure why it's called that though."

Rachel's smile broadened. "I'll bet Lincoln knows!"

Her playful jab gave Chris reason to broaden his smile. "I'll just bet he does. But I know something he doesn't."

Further displaying her playfulness by acting surprised, she asked, "And what would that be? After all, Lincoln's the most intelligent man I've ever met. A doctor, an author, a man brilliant enough to marry Trudy and settle next door to Mr. and Mrs. B. I mean, this guy's got to be the smartest man in the world. So what could you possibly know that he doesn't?"

The corner of Chris's mouth pursed somewhat as he watched Rachel fight off the urge to laugh. "I'll tell you what I know. I'm just not going to tell you here. Come on, there's some place I want you to see. I think you'll like it." Taking her by the hand, he began walking toward the forest. A narrow path twisted through the dense trees. After walking only a few minutes, Chris stopped and pointed to a large white metal sign proclaiming Beware, Poison Oak. Stepping from the path, he made his way through the thick underbrush to stand next to the sign. Rachel hadn't moved from the trail.

"Aren't you coming?"

Without a word she pointed to the sign.

"It's not real. I had it made to keep folks out," Chris said. "I don't like people using this path because it comes out close to our place, just up from the bridge, and you never know who's walking these trails. As you can see, it works better than a fence."

She stood studying the underbrush. Chris laughed. "It's safe, I promise." After she carefully made her way to him, Chris added, "Now, it does get a little tricky up ahead. It's pretty grown over and it's really steep, but once we reach the bottom, it dumps us out a little over hundred yards from the bridge, and it's just a little farther to where we want to go."

Rachel didn't question but followed, gripping his hand tightly, not only to maintain her stability through the thick underbrush, but to allow her heart the pleasure of his touch once again. He too held on, not only as a gentleman helping to guide and balance her, but to feel his own heart beat with great joy at every squeeze of her hand, song in her laugh, and step she took. Twenty minutes later, walking from the bushes onto a well-traveled footpath, they stopped to catch their breath. In their eyes, amazement glistened at what they beheld. And what they beheld was each other. After so many years of wandering different paths, they now shared the same trail.

Again he felt her grip his hand, and again she watched him lead their way. At the bottom Chris pointed in the direction of the bridge, but a bend in the trail, thick vegetation, and tall trees blocked the view. It was possible, though still not easy, to make out one of the towering rooftops of the Trudeau home. Smoke rose from the chimney and curled on the soft, cool breeze that had not reached the forest floor. Minutes later, they stood looking at the brick walkway of switchbacks down the side of the ravine.

At the bottom, Chris knew it opened onto the long-forgotten remains of a natural amphitheater at the base of a massive rock formation—an impressive place of beauty, enchantment, and isolation. This was where Chris went to escape, to regroup and start over, to let go of what was and embrace what is. A place where he had cried himself dry on more than one occasion, and for more than one reason. This was where in complete solitude he'd fall to his knees and pray. A physical place where he could truly let go and let God, as they say. A place where the presence of God welcomed him ever so deeply.

But the place wasn't his alone. Lincoln and Trudy walked the forest path many times, but due to the bricks being buried under years of undisturbed dirt and leaves, they had never noticed the walkway twisting down the steep ravine until one day when Trudy took Ann's grandmother for a morning stroll. The elderly woman stopped and began to use her heel to uncover a few of the bricks. With great reluctance Trudy joined in, and soon the two women descended the walkway to be richly rewarded by its beauty. After pointing it out to Lincoln and the Brooks', Trudy only returned a handful of times over the next few years. She then showed it to Chris shortly after he moved to the cove, and he fell in love with it. There was one other person who loved it every bit as much as Chris—his daughter Beth. Just last July she told him, "It's so beautiful, I bet angels picnic here." The following day Chris bought a picnic basket, and once or twice a week, right up until late September when the fall chill settled over the sound, he and Beth shared a meal with angels.

※

Only minutes into their search, Trudy joined the curious youngsters on the other side of the bridge, about ten yards down the path. "It's not a good idea for you to be over here without an adult," she chided, placing her hands on her hips.

After a quick glance at Michael, the little girl's smile rose beneath the fabric of the scarf. "But you're here with us, Miss Trudy! Will you help us look for doors?"

"Doors! What kind of doors?" the woman asked, perplexed by the question.

From the other side of the bridge Jass whined loudly before giving one sharp bark. Again he whined, spinning in a slow circle as he did. Coming to a stop, his nose in the air, he began to sniff.

"Fairy doors!" Michael replied.

"Fairy doors!" the woman scoffed. "Oh, yes. I haven't seen any lately, but of course I haven't been looking either."

Beth pulled her scarf down far enough to rest it on her chin. "I think we could find a lot where we go picnic at the angel spot. You want to go see?"

Trudy shook her head. "Not today. It's getting too cold. Besides, I need two brownie tasters and a piano player. Maybe you can help me find someone."

"We can do that, Miss Trudy," Beth squealed, her eyes bright with excitement. "You know I'm a good brownie taster, and Mike can play the piano. So, see, you don't have to find nobody. We can do it both. We can do it real good too."

She then took the boy's hand and started to walk quickly back over the bridge, saying to him, "You're gonna thank me. Her brownies are good, really good…I promise." Turning slightly, she called to Miss Trudy, "Are they warm brownies?"

"Just took them out of the oven. They'll need to cool a little more."

Quietly Beth said to Michael, "Teamwork. You play a song, and I'll blow on the brownies. It makes them cool faster, okay?"

"Yeah, teamwork." the boy agreed eagerly. "Just don't blow so much it makes you dizzy. That happened to me once."

Waiting at the edge of the bridge to greet the kids, Jass whined, this time clearly out of excitement. As the kids reached him, a series of whines and kisses followed; however, the dog quickly stopped and looked for the Quiet One. There she was, still on the other side of the bridge. Three loud barks shattered the peacefulness and were quickly followed by two more. Prancing, his front paws ventured onto the wooden slats of the bridge but quickly returned to the damp earth his hind feet had nervously dug into. His body quivered, and again he whined. The Quiet One spoke his name as she neared. Her voice soft, her touch assuring, brought another round of whines and kisses before they all retreated to the warmth of the home.

Michael rushed to the piano, Beth and Jass sniffed out the location of the brownies, and Miss Trudy said goodbye to the work crew and then disappeared into Mr. Trudy's office, returning a few moments later with a very large photo album.

"Your aunt Bailey put this together a few years ago and gave it to us. For safekeeping, I think. It's filled with pictures she took of fairy doors, houses, bridges, ladders, all that and so on. We'll look at them after we have brownies. Sound good?"

Beth nodded her head excitedly, Michael continued to play the piano, unaware of the conversation, and Jass made his way over to a rather large window in Lincoln's office, where he peered nervously at the wooden footbridge. For an instant he thought there was movement in the dense underbrush; but after standing perfectly still for quite some time and seeing nothing unusual, he chose to return to the main room and lay peacefully in front of the fire. The warmth was good, covering him like an unseen blanket.

Soon, lulled to sleep by sweet smells and soft music, the dog drifted into dreams of times past—a small puppy asleep under his master's piano, the melody wafting through the house on the aroma of turkey pot pie. And then, suddenly, he was in the front seat of Amy's car sharing french fries and ice cream. Snow…it was snowing, Amy loved the snow; they would run and roll and leap all morning long; the crisp air would be filled with her laughter and his playful bark. Yes, this was good. This was the best good. Bad was never present in any form, yet he felt it approach—big, fast, and silent. Its face a blur, he turned to run, but it was upon him. Jerking himself awake with a yip, he looked around. There was no snow, no Amy, and no french fries. And though he knew he was safe in the Quiet One's home, he let out a soft cry.

At the same moment came another cry, this one piercing the air from high above. Perhaps a cry of warning for the man and woman the great bird watched disappear under the shelter of the dense trees, or possibly a cautionary notice for the predator now watching them?

❖

Unlike the part of the forest they had just come from, this area was clearly different. The vegetation was larger than any Rachel had ever seen, giving the impression they had stumbled onto an abandoned set from a Jurassic movie. Even the air had changed, thick and dank, as if an afternoon shower had just passed. Yet there was no unpleasantness. On the contrary, a sense of serenity embraced them as they moved about the magnificent beauty. But it was the splendor of the great rock wall, establishing the backdrop of the natural amphitheater, that remained the cornerstone of the setting. The stage, level with the ground, was thick granite, cut and ground smooth to create a performance platform capable of accommodating a large array of productions. Clearly outlined was the seating area; however, it had been reclaimed by ninety years of reforestation. Now all that remained of the long wooden benches were the ornate iron tresses sticking up through the lush undergrowth and storm-toppled trees. But even this scene offered its own surreal beauty.

The sun had broken through a small opening in the dense organic canopy where, even on sunny days like this, there could be seen a steady dripping from the water-laden branches. Radiant beams of sunlight became spotlights of awe and wonder glistened like small rainbows from heaven falling through the trees to rest on the soft damp floor of the forest.

"Heavenly, isn't it?" Chris asked.

"It is!"

"Beth believes this is where angels come to picnic."

Rachel's eyes danced over the area. "I have to agree with her."

"Trudy showed me the place years ago. Said it would be a good place for me to practice my sermons, and you know, I still do that once in a while." Squeezing her, he added, "When it's warm, anyway."

Laying her head on his arm, she held him tight and listened as he continued. "Trudy also believes angels come here, but she hasn't given me an explanation as to why she thinks that. However, she did tell me as a child she believed her guardian angel was an old, worn-out teddy bear she kept hidden under her bed. She used to talk to that bear every night, share things with it she never shared with anyone. Maybe that's where her stories came from. But she was also quick to add she's never seen angels or teddy bears down here."

Rachel's giggle was soft, and she felt him squeeze her hand again. The air was motionless, allowing the flora-covered ground to temper all sound, much like the hush of freshly fallen snow. It was peaceful as both Chris and Rachel rested on the mossy trunk of a recently fallen tree. No words were spoken aloud, yet each heard in their own mind and heart inner whisperings that spoke louder than a thought yet softer than a sigh, filling the ears with silence and numbing the senses so as not to be disturbed, rushed, or averted. Minutes were not measured by the tick of seconds but simply by one's own heartbeat. And at precisely 147 beats later, Rachel asked, "Back at the house, did I hear you say…"

The treetops swayed slightly on a gust of cool wind, the air filled with a legion of displaced droplets, creating a unique rustling sound as they hit the thick foliage on their way down. This again filled the air with an array of rainbows dancing through spotlights of sunbeams. Rachel fell silent, content to gaze at the beautiful light. Chris was content to gaze at Rachel.

When finally she did speak, her voice echoed a nuance steeped in reflection and hesitancy. "Did I hear you say…I mean when you were holding me…did we say?"

"I think we did!" he answered, his voice filled with thought was soft and distant.

Again she looked to the lush canopy, watching the mist dissipate and the rainbows fade. Her next move was more reactionary than premeditated. Led by nostalgic recall, she stepped in front of him and gently leaned back against his chest, closing her eyes as though hiding her thoughts from the world. His movement was also reactionary, placing his arms around her, inhaling the scent of her hair, squeezing her gently, his eyes scanning this hidden place filled with God's beauty. His thoughts now spoke to him quietly, saying, *It's never been as beautiful as it is this very moment.* Gently taking her by the shoulders and turning her to face him, he began to speak, his voice gentle as a summer breeze, like that delivered after a cold winter brought a warmth that made her melt.

"It's not like I ever stopped loving you," he began. "I just fell in love with someone else after a while. But yesterday, the second I saw you, my heart was so filled I thought it would burst. When I held you, I never wanted to let you go again, never wanted to say another goodbye without knowing you'd return. Last night after I tucked Beth in, I lay in bed thinking about my life, the times I spent with you, and the times without you. Not making comparisons, but trying to understand my own heart. And then I went to your window, and when I came back, seems I brought a question back with me, one I haven't allowed myself to ask my heart in a very long, long time. Is it possible after all this time?"

Paralyzing fear stilled his voice, but her eyes drew out his words. "I'm still in love with you?" he said just above a whisper.

Silently she ask herself the same question, and in the span of a breath, had her answer.

"Yes…" they spoke in unison.

He leaned forward; she pulled him close. "I love you," they whispered, and as their lips came together, so, too, did their hearts.

The crew from Life of the Party Catering had just left when Amy and her mother arrived back at the compound. Amy, seeing Chris's vehicle, was excited to tell him the news of her pregnancy, a topic they had discussed privately on numerous occasions. She felt close to the young pastor, at times referring to him as, "the brother I never had." Six years his senior, she'd already left for college by the time he was making his presence known in high school. Although they had met on a few occasions through her mom and dad, it was only after he bought what was originally to be her house at Brennan's Cove that they became friends. Over the years their shared interests in all things outdoors helped build an even deeper friendship, a relationship Wes embraced and fit into immediately; not so, Linda. Ignoring the fact she disliked the forest and all that went with it, it was clear to Chris she also harbored a touch of jealousy toward Amy, insisting Chris miss a number of activities throughout the years, events he told Amy and Wes only recently he was now looking forward to being a part of again.

So before helping her mother unload the car, Amy rushed to Chris's front door, where she knocked, rang the bell, and called his name numerous times, but to no avail. This, however, did cause Trudy to open her door, enabling Jass to race across the compound, barking his greeting with loving exuberance. Trudy hurried to help Ann, who was gathering bags from the back of Amy's car.

"Have you seen Chris?" Amy called.

"They walked up to Mildred's a little over an hour ago, and then they were going up to The Point," Trudy said, directing her look more toward Ann, who understood by her friend's tone that she was attempting to raise Amy's curiosity, which it did, of course.

"They? Don't tell me he's making Beth walk all that way. She's not ready for that level of hike yet, is she?" Amy asked, more agitated than curious.

"Beth didn't go. She's at my house napping with a friend."

"I'm glad to hear that. It's quite a hike from here. So who's with Chris?"

"You're sure inquisitive about him all of a sudden," Ann said. "What's up with that?"

Grabbing a number of bags and pausing next to her mother, Amy replied, "I'm excited to tell him about the baby. I mean, you know, it's his doing, right!"

And without another word she made her way into the house, leaving Ann and Trudy to stare questioningly at each other before dashing through the door. Carelessly setting the bags on the kitchen counter, Ann turned to her daughter. "Not that I believe it for a second, but I would love to hear an explanation…"

With deliberate calmness Amy began to unpack a bag. "Oh, it's true! Even Wes will tell you it's true. Look how long we tried to have a baby and couldn't. We asked Chris to help us out, and the next thing you know, I'm pregnant. I have to give Wes some credit, though. The whole thing was his idea. Do you want these candles in the living room?"

Watching Trudy and her mother internalize the information made it impossible to contain her laughter. "We ask him to pray for us, and he did. He drove all the way out to the ranch just to pray with us. We couldn't even get him to stay for dinner. And my due date—it's exactly nine months from the day he came to the house. Oh yeah, this is his doing all right. But you two—you should be ashamed having those kinds of thoughts. I'm a married woman."

Three loud blasts from an unmistakable horn echoed through the trees just before the bright-yellow Volkswagen Bug with a license plate stating BUG OFF roared up the drive. Stepping from the driver's seat was Bailey, greeted excitedly by the three women and Jass.

Ann was the last to be hugged and the first to ask, "Where's Ted? I thought you two would be driving out together. Things are okay, I hope," she said with slight concern.

"Things are hectic, but it's all coming together. Elsie is interested in buying the car. Lord knows she needs it, but Norb doesn't want to spend that much, so Ted's trying to work out a deal for them."

"Not the Bug?" Amy shrieked.

"Heavens No!" Bailey gasped. "I'd get rid of Ted before I would my Bug." Everyone laughed but suspected there was more than a grain of truth behind her statement. "Where's the guys? Shouldn't they be out here lending a hand?"

Ann and Trudy turned to walk to the front door, Ann saying over her shoulder, "I saw ours parked at Nel's place."

"Mine's working today," Amy quietly added.

Bailey lifted a suitcase from the back seat. "And Chris! Is he wearing his invisible man costume today, thinking if he disappears he won't have to help?"

There was laughter and chatter as the women made their way through the house, though Chris's whereabouts was never truly explained, nor was it mentioned he was with anyone. Instead, Ann simply averted the topic by removing a wooden plaque from one of the bags. Holding it up to the wall, she asked, "What do you think? Is this a good spot?"

Bailey was the only one to speak, reading aloud, "Grandma's Kitchen. That's really cute. I love the little kids looking up at their—"

There was soft giggling from Amy and Trudy, which caused Bailey to stare questioningly their way. For a little longer than a moment, her thoughts were somewhat blank. Her attention shifting back to Ann, who, like a game show model, showcased the plaque with broad sweeps of her hand. Quickly Bailey snapped back around to face Amy; and the room erupted with joy, filling the house with childish giggles, coos, and squeals over the next few minutes.

"Does Chris know?"

"Not yet. He wasn't here this morning when we told everyone."

Outside, Jim's truck came to a stop alongside the Bug. The two men gathered up the treasures from their errands and made their way onto the porch as the women spilled out the front door. However, amid the cacophony of excitement, it was Trudy's quiet voice that almost magically directed everyone's attention to the footbridge.

"See, here they come," she repeated softly. Strolling hand in hand over the bridge were Rachel and Chris.

For Bailey, it was as if the world slowed to a stop. Sounds became muffled if heard at all, and images shrouded in disbelief blurred her vision like a dense fog obstructing her view. But reality cleared the air with a breath of certainty, bringing years of nearly forgotten memories to dance through her mind. At first unable to move, she abruptly felt herself walking forward, trotting quickly, and then running. Time and distance seemed to have no correlation as she and Rachel rushed toward each other, yet never seemed to get closer. Her eyes filled with tears, perhaps from seeing her dearest friend for the first time in ten years or maybe just knowing her brother's heart so well it shared the emotion; either way, they were joyous tears. And then, with startling abruptness, the women were wrapped in each other's arms, only letting go long enough to confirm the reality of the moment before embracing again. Later that evening she would tell Ted there were only three things she remembered about that instant: seeing happiness return to Chris's face, the joy in Rachel's hug, and the love shared in their eyes.

As the two old friends carried on, Amy slowly wondered over, giving them time to enjoy their reunion. Seeing her, they rushed to include her. Chris excused himself to help the others carry in the last of the bags. Amy put her arm around his in a quiet plea not to leave just yet, so without questioning, he stood listening as she spoke to Rachel. "My mom told me about Mike's death. I'm so sorry."

Bailey held Rachel's hands and then gently hugged her. "I'm sorry too, Rache. Chris told me just last week, but he didn't say anything about you being here, or I would've come sooner."

Her stare fell to her brother, who raised his hands in defense. "I had no idea. Ann sneaked her in yesterday while I was gone."

Like old times, Rachel diverted the siblings' attention away from each other by thanking both women for their thoughts and prayers and then assured them there would be no sadness to dampen the festivities, saying, "My life's good and getting better all the time."

It was impossible not to notice a smile pass between her and Chris. This gave Bailey the excuse to bubble over with excitement and hug her friend again. It gave Amy an opportunity also.

"Hey, Chris," Amy said, stepping close to him and placing a kiss on his cheek. "You really do have a knack for making babies. Doctor says I'm about six weeks along."

Without missing a step, Chris embraced Amy, saying, "Well then, my job is done. See, I told you all it takes is a lot of practice and a little prayer. Or vice versa!"

Rachel, enjoying their playful banter, rushed to hug Amy. "Congratulations. When do I get to meet the daddy?"

"He'll be here tomorrow," she replied before her attention was taken to Trudy's porch. "Well, who do we have here?" She smiled, her gaze falling back to Rachel. "Must be yours?"

Making his way down the steps, Michael waited at the bottom for Beth, who was just coming through the door. Rachel was about to answer when Chris said, "Yes, they are." And again a smile passed between the couple.

❖

The evening went much like the one before, filled with stories sprinkled with laughter, food, and antics egged on by Lincoln and Chris. However, there were a few significant differences, the greatest being the almost constant prattle regarding Amy's pregnancy, with Chris making unremitting reference to the baby bump as "little Christopher," while Bailey, took her turn in the crosshairs of the group, thanks to the stories told the night before. But this night it was Michael, not Trudy, who encouraged everyone to gather around the piano by straying off to sit at the instrument and quietly beginning to play. Beth was the first to join him, to stand by his side watching his fingers dance over the keys. Bailey followed, taking her place next to her niece. She was as beautiful in real life as in her photos, Michael thought. But his mom was right. She was old, Aunt Peg's age, and married to a really nice guy she said knew everything there was to know about Captain Jack Sparrow and the Pirates of the Caribbean.

When Rachel and Chris entered the room holding hands, Michael and Beth looked at each other and smiled. Soon everyone was there, and Michael started to move from the bench. But his mom, placing a hand on his shoulder, said, "Hang on." Then she looked at Bailey. "Do you remember 'When I Take His Hand'?"

"Of course!"

Utterly surprised, Michael set at full attention. "You, you know that song?" he stammered.

Bailey giggled. "Your dad wrote it for me and your mom to sing at a talent show."

Rachel huffed, "Not true. He wrote it for Bailey. She was just kind enough to let me perform it with her."

Bailey wrinkled her nose slightly and winked at Michael. "Your mom's voice is why we took first place."

"Also not true."

Michael smiled at Mrs. B. and then began to play the delicate intro as masterfully as his father ever had. Stunned, Bailey stepped back quietly expressing her astonishment to a beaming Rachel.

As the women began to sing, their voices blending beautifully, Chris retrieved his camera from the Gathering Place. Returning to stand at the end of the piano and bringing the trio into frame, he was suddenly struck by the memory and similarity of a shot he had taken long ago, a photo he was sure still hung somewhere in Jim's office back at school. But of course now there was one glaring difference, which for a moment saddened Chris. But as he often did, his mind presented his heart a beautiful illustration that warmed his soul. For Chris, this photo would forever show the work of the Son, leading others through the Father's word…and music. He smiled to himself. And with that he took half a dozen shots before retreating to sit beside Amy.

❃

Around seven thirty the entertainment was briefly interrupted by the arrival of David and Natalie Spencer, along with their fifteen-year-old daughter, Krista, neighbors from the bottom of The Point, just down the road from Mildred. David sat in the car as Natalie made her way to Trudy's front door. Krista hurried to ring the Petersons' doorbell as well as impatiently knock two or three times before hearing Lincoln greet her mother and call out, "We're all over here, sweetheart."

Of course Trudy insisted the whole family come in out of the cold, meet Rachel and Michael, and enjoy a cup of something to warm their spirits. Lincoln produced another bottle of wine while Amy filled cups with hot chocolate for herself and the youngsters. Chris retrieved two sodas from Lincoln's office.

The adults lingered at the Gathering Place while Krista and the kids chose to sit in front of the fire. The older girl gave Beth an elegant box of handmade chocolates from Schocolat, her favorite shop in the Bavarian styled town of Leavenworth, deep in the Cascades.

"I have another one at the house," she said apologetically to Michael. "I'll bring it tomorrow. As a matter of fact, I have a bunch of goodies I'll bring. You'll be here tomorrow, right?"

"Yeah, I think so."

Beth quickly blurted, "Oh yeah, I'm never gonna let 'im go. He's my big brother…sorta, kinda anyway. But his mom's a princess, real and true…a princess, ahu huh."

Michael quietly grinned and shook his head, but not so Beth would notice. Turning from the girl, Krista secretly winked at Michael and then, looking back, said, "I knew there was something special about her from the moment I walked in. She's very pretty, but how do you know she's a princess?"

The little girl's eyes widened, her face flushed. "If she looks like a princess and sings like a princess, then she must be a princess, even though she says she's not. But I know she is. Just look…don't cha think she's the fairest of them all. Don't cha?"

"Oh, brother. I need some water," Michael jeered, rising to go to the kitchen.

Beth moved very close to Krista's face, staring into her eyes and speaking with an unexpected sincerity. "She brought my daddy's smile back too. She would have to be a princess to do that, I think." Looking toward Michael, the little girl added, "And he's not like other boys. He doesn't laugh and make fun of me. He saved me from getting hurt today. Daddy agreed; he's like a big brother."

Again her eyes looked deep into those of Krista, and again the older girl could see sincerity far beyond the years of the child before her. When Beth spoke again, her voice was soft and quiet, conveying an uncertainty with short pauses between her words.

"I think God…you know, maybe…heard me pray and sent them here." Beth's stare softened even more as if pleading for assurance, and the older girl smiled.

"God hears our prayers, Beth. You know that. So if you've been praying for a princess…"

"No!" Distress filled the little girl's voice. "Not for a princess. For a—"

"Beth!" Rachel said, entering the room, making her way to sit on the hearth next to the girl. Leaning close, she whispered, "Your daddy and Michael took Jass outside to go potty, and…"

"I know…he wants me to go potty too." she complained, pursing her lips to one side as she jumped to her feet, placing her hands on her hips to show her displeasure. But slowly her expression began to change, as did her body language.

"I'll be right back." she squealed, hurriedly making her way out of the room.

Rachel smiled. "I hope she doesn't think she has to go outside with Jass."

Krista giggled. "Well, there was this time…"

They both laughed, but still watched to see exactly where Beth was headed.

"Your mom tells me you'll be working for the Youth Conservation Corps this summer. That's pretty exciting." The young girl smiled. "My mom works for the Forest Service, and Dad's a game warden, so it's kind of a tradition."

"Then you plan on following in their footsteps?"

"I love the forest and all, but probably not. I'm leaning more toward marine biology. Mom got me into scuba when I was ten, right out there in the sound. From day one I fell in love with it. And since then, almost every vacation has been diving somewhere in the tropics. I love it. The water's clear; you don't need a dry suit to keep warm, and the abundance of sea life is incredible. It's so much different than the sound. Not that it's bad here, it's just different."

Rachel smiled. "I tried it once in Southern California, and it was beautiful, but too scary for me. I can't imagine scuba diving in the sound. The water's freezing cold even in summer."

Sipping her chocolate, Krista grinned. "Yeah, up here the water's cold and murky and a little scary to some, but the back trails can be too, when you suddenly come face-to-face with a crazy hiker holding a joint in one hand and a gun in the other ready to shoot the first thing that moves. Or even less dangerous, predators like bears, cougars, or wolves."

Rachel chuckled. "Chris and I saw a couple bears once when we were ca…"

Realizing her near misstep she rushed to continue, "Kids! Well, in our teens. That was a long time ago, you know how time flies. And then suddenly they were just gone; it was over in a blink. Who knew they'd disappear so fast."

"Yeah, time really flies for sure. I'll be sixteen in August, and I wonder where...oh, wait. You're talking about the bears, not your teens disappearing aren't you?" The young girl smiled, her dimples deepening on both cheeks.

"Take your pick." Rachel laughed. "Bears, teens—they both give me chills thinking about 'em."

Bailey entered the room and plopped down next to Krista. "Hey, Rache, did she tell you she has a great voice, plays guitar, directs youth choir—not to mention is my go-to girl on the worship team."

Before either one could answer, Jim rushed in.

"Shhh..." he said, placing a finger to his lips. He gathered up the girls and ushered them to the piano.

"At one time or another, I've heard each of you sing this song," he said without revealing the title or playing a note. "Would you mind trying it as a trio?"

The girls looked at each other, waiting for him to continue, but he remained silent. Surely he didn't expect they'd agree without knowing what song he wanted them to sing. But remembering the trust she had always placed in him all through school, Rachel began to smile. "Of course!" she heard herself say before she could get lost in fond memories.

Sprightly, Krista giggled. "I'm in!"

After taking a sip of Rachel's Orange Crush, Bailey huffed reluctantly. "Of course I'm in. I'm not going to be a stick in the mud, but would you mind telling us the name of the song?"

Coming in from the cold were Michael and Chris, Jass scampering through the door first, trotting steadily to lie once again next to the fire. Beth ran from the restroom to rejoin the girls, but not before asking Michael to come with. Poking his head around the corner, Chris smiled at Rachel just as Jim started to play a familiar intro. The girls whispered among themselves for mere seconds, letting Jim continue to repeat the intro, summoning an exodus from the Gathering Place to take seats around the piano. And then, as Jim painted the silence with soft, delicate tones, Bailey began to sing.

"I can only imagine..."

Midway through the verse, Rachel and Krista layered harmonies around the melody, weaving a translucent richness of artful subtlety. Because the second verse had more of a rock feel, Krista took the lead, surprising Rachel with her strength and control. But when Rachel sang the final chorus, each word became powerful in its meaning, building with emotion, driving the song's message to the heart and imagination of all those present. As Jim slowed the tempo and brought the opening melody back into focus, it was Bailey who softly sang the reprise of the verse to end the song.

For the tick of a few seconds, as if the room itself had stopped to listen, there was silence. Bailey watched her brother, his focus on Rachel, and then she found Beth, who was also captivated by the woman. In the remaining millisecond, Bailey's heart filled with that wonderful hope only the recognition of undisguised emotion unveils. Her brother and niece were far beyond the sentiment of the song. Each saw something different, someone different in this woman, yet each envisioned the same desire—a vision of love.

The silence came to an end with a loud booming voice straining in an effort to hold back any tears that would give away his sentimentality. "Damn, you girls can sing," Lincoln blared. "I want to get a recording of that. I mean, you girls are great…absolutely great!"

The big man rose from his chair and made his way into the kitchen, quickly returning with a box of tissues he graciously made available to his wife and guests. Jim began to play again, sending notes through the buzz and accolades coming from his audience. The music resonated for another half hour, and then the adults adjourned back to the Gathering Place, and Krista and the kids joined Jass by the fire. Michael told the girls about his journey through the Ape Cave, and Beth talked about the fairy doors they had seen that morning at Millersylvania Park.

Fascinated, the older girl told them, "My mom has a couple photo albums filled with fairy doors she's come across over the years. Just last summer we found some down by the amphitheater where you and your dad go sometimes."

Beth looked surprised. "You did? There's fairies down there?"

Krista giggled. "Well, I can't promise, but we've seen their doors."

Wonderment slowly lit Beth's face, bringing a glowing smile to Krista, who continued. "One of these times we'll hike down and see how they held up over the winter."

The small girl squeaked with excitement, hurrying to stand in front of Michael, her tiny body jumping up and down without leaving the floor. As happened earlier, her words raced out in a jumbled sentence, making no sense at all. And for a moment the joy in her face faded. Gently Michael took her hand, saying, "Remember what we talked about? It's no big deal." The boy felt her lightly squeeze his hand, elation brightening her face once again.

Looking into his eyes, she took a deep breath. "That's the place I told you about—the place over the bridge where angels picnic."

Michael's imagination swirled with vibrant images bursting with Disney magic and wonder. Eagerly he inquired of Krista, "Do you really think we could find them? What about tomorrow? Could we go tomorrow? I don't know when we're leaving. And I'd love to see the angel place. And the fairy doors, and…and the am the theeter."

Krista's giggles returned, though repressed as not to offend the boy. "Amphitheater!" she corrected. "And I doubt your parents will let you go. The bricks can be pretty slippery this time of year, and it can be dangerous if you're not careful. Summertime would be—"

"We'll be careful. I promise," Michael insisted, unable to wait for the girl to finish. "Summertime! We're moving. I don't know where we'll be this summer. We'll be careful, Krista. I promise. We promise."

His pleas didn't fall on deaf ears. Many times Krista had pled her own case when her parents insisted something was unsafe due to her age, inexperience, or physical abilities. Like last year when she begged to join them on their climb of Mount Rainier. What began as a flat-out "no, and there will be no further discussion" eventually ended with a family photo taken on the summit, which now hung above their fireplace.

So with great understanding, Krista sighed. "Well, let's see what the next few days bring. Maybe we can sneak away for an hour or so. That is, if your parents say it's okay."

The girl knew Pastor Chris would never agree unless he was there to supervise, and that was unlikely with the New Year's party just two days away, and all they still had to do to prepare for it. Stealing a quick glance toward the Gathering Place, she could see Rachel whispering something in Chris's ear, causing him to touch his forehead to hers and smile before walking out of the room, only to return a moment later with a cup of hot chocolate the two shared, just as the girl had seen her parents do many times. And there was something else she noticed, something else her parents did, not every day, but enough their daughter recognized it when she saw it. It was there in a simple look, a touch, a smile, a shy push—the everyday things made special when two people in their playful affection show a deep and undeniable love for each other. It all seemed pretty clear to this teenage romantic, but then again, how could that be? Didn't they say they hadn't seen or spoken to each other since high school? Which left her surprised they even remembered each other. After all, that had been a long time ago. But they both look really happy; and after the year Pastor Chris had had, a little happiness was probably just what God ordered.

Just then, Beth interrupted Krista's thoughts by asking a question the teen only partially heard. This didn't matter much, because the little girl had barely taken a breath since beginning to tell Michael of her adventures at the place angels came to picnic and where fairies built their homes. Fortunately for Krista, Beth continued to ramble on, allowing her to put her attention once again on Pastor Chris and his princess. Wouldn't it be wonderful if…her thoughts were interrupted by a faint vibration in her hip pocket, bringing her quickly to her feet.

"Looks like it's my turn for the restroom," she told the kids, making her way out of the room.

Once alone Krista took the phone from her pocket and read the text: "Tomorrow 8:30 The Point."

Her fingers danced swiftly over the touchpad. "Can't wait to see you. 8:30 it is."

"43"

"432"

Catching a glimpse in the mirror, she saw the reflection not of the fifteen-year-old girl who preferred baseball caps and ponytails to skirts and curls, but of a woman, strong and self-confident, who knew her feelings and was more than capable of telling the difference between a childhood crush and love that would last a lifetime. Besides, her parents liked Jack. And why shouldn't they? He respected the outdoors, worked hard, was a good student, and put family above all else. When you got right down to it, he was a pretty wonderful guy.

Krista took another look at the woman staring back at her, and with less effort than she imagined, the woman's eyes became almost bewitching. It would take practice to perfect that seductive stare, but she knew Jack would love it. Love…the word itself made her feel warm inside. After all, that's how you know you're in love…right? When someone makes you feel warm inside? And Jack—could definitely make her feel warm inside.

At sixteen, Jack was the youngest of Nels' three sons, and like his father, he was tall, just over six foot, muscular, handsome, and wore his hair pulled back in a ponytail draped below his shoulder blades. He was reserved, quiet, polite, and a gentleman. He had the respect of most everyone in the community, especially the seasoned sportsmen. Like Krista, he enjoyed the forest, but unlike the girl, when it came to the ocean, he preferred being on the surface, not exploring its depths. A few months back, hoping to entice him to go diving, she invited him to watch GoPro footage of her recent dive off Cozumel. This sparked his interest—that is, until David put on a clip of sharks just a few feet away from the camera. Jack would need a lot more convincing after that.

"Love…" she whispered, turning from the mirror. Yet the word escaped louder than expected, prompting her to swiftly place a hand over her mouth. Hushed giggles followed as she thought about the thickness of the walls and how if she were being attacked by a bear, there was a good chance no one would hear her screams. So again she said the word, this time speaking it aloud.

Looking back to the mirror, she watched as the mature woman with the seductive smile faded unrecognizably into the familiar features of the high-spirited fifteen-year-old tomboy Jack could not get enough of since their unexpected meeting last May at the top of Jupiter Falls. That morning as her parents prepared to leave for a conference in Olympia, Krista reminded them she'd be going to the falls to photograph the three pools for her class project and might meet up with her friend Ashely and her mom for dinner. What she didn't tell them was Ashley's dad caught her smoking with a group of friends up at Hickory Lane Park, so dinner plans, along with any other plans, were now on a two-week hiatus while the smoke cleared. But for Krista, that just meant she'd have a full day to spend however she wanted. Not that there was ever anything exciting to do around Brennan's Cove. But an early-morning stroll to the pools would get her outside and make the pools an interesting photo subject. But arriving at the trailhead just after seven thirty, she decided to forgo the pools and hike a mile and a half up the fire trail to the first vista on the nine-mile loop. She'd been there a few times before with her mom and dad and knew the view would make for a spectacular shoot. She was not disappointed.

The sky was blue, the air crisp. Below, spotty patches of fog nestled between the tree-filled canyons blurred the contours of the mountainous terrain. After taking a series of inspiring shots and wishing she'd brought a larger bottle of water, she decided to continue up the steep grade to the next overlook another mile away. Though in good shape, she quickly grew tired, winded, and was now beginning to get hungry.

"Why didn't I bring an energy bar?" she asked herself, drinking all but the last few ounces of water. And again she moved up the trail, photographing anything that gave her reason to stop and rest.

The day warmed quickly, though passing under the shade of a tree brought a chill her windbreaker was unable to completely ward off. The terrain become steep; the trail, narrowing quickly, turned away from the edge of the mountain into the thickly wooded forest, where she estimated the temperature dropped ten degrees. Forcing herself to keep going, praying there would be sunshine and warmth soon, she gathered her determination and continued on. An hour later she found herself out of water, out of breath, and almost out of energy. However, this didn't seem to pose a great concern to the girl, as now midway up the hill, standing in the glorious sun light next to the gnarled stump of a once-giant western cedar, she knew the swift-moving water of Jupiter Creek was less than two hundred yards away.

Only four miles into the loop, she would return the same way she had come. But first she needed to rest. Hoisting herself up onto the smooth surface of the stump's smooth top, she was amazed at its twelve-foot radius. *How tall must this tree have been*, she thought. Lying on her back, her eyes closed and her body now warm by the unobstructed sun, she thought of all the beauty she'd seen on her morning journey.

"You a sacrifice?" a voice close to her asked.

Panic rushed through her, and like a coil the young girl twisted, leaping to her feet in one graceful move ready to meet her aggressor.

"Nice dismount," Jack said with a slight grin. "I didn't mean to startle you. Truth is, I didn't see you until—"

Angrily Krista shouted, "How could you not see me? I'm lying on top of the biggest stump in the world, and you couldn't see me? Really…really, Jack, you couldn't see me until what?"

His thin smile lingered. "Until I took my eyes off the three guys walking this way."

Slowly she turned to see the men approaching. The beat of her heart sped faster than it had all morning. Fear tingled her scalp and ran down her back and arms, stealing her breath. Jack placed a hand on her shoulder, his voice calm and assuring. "Just stay here. You'll be fine."

Approaching the men, he recognized Evan Hall, a local hiking enthusiast from the little town of Hoodsport, some thirty miles south of Brinnon. The four men spoke briefly before Jack returned to Krista, who watched the strangers disappear down the steep trail to Three Pools.

"It was Evan Hall and a couple of his buddies. No threat there."

"I want to apologize," Krista said, glancing into his eyes. "I thought I was the only one around. I mean, I didn't even hear you walk up, but I'm glad you were here. I don't know what I would've done…if they…they could have been anybody, you know…they could have…"

Her mind, of course, had already explored the worst possible outcomes, the darkest scenarios, and envisioned the tormented faces of her parents hearing the news of what had happened to their daughter. A daughter, from the time she could venture beyond the backyard fence, was taught "Never, ever walk the trails alone."

The young man watched her lip quiver while tears formed in her eyes. "You really scared me," she managed to say, her voice hoarse with emotion.

His apology came quick, though not as quick as her impulsive embrace. With her head on his chest, he felt her gentle sobbing, her warm breath and the breaking of his own heart. He had never meant to frighten her. This was the girl he had adored from afar for almost as long as he could remember. Gently, carefully he embraced her and again stated his apology. The moment turned to seconds, rolled into minutes, and still they held each other. Her tears had stopped, and her thoughts were now more from embarrassment than a vision of what could have been. Perhaps sensing her humiliation, Jack relaxed his gentle hold and was the first to speak. His stride slowed to move away, his tone light, assuring her things were going to be just fine.

"There's sandwiches in my backpack, an extra sweatshirt, a few cookies, couple energy drinks, water, face towel, tissues, mirror…help yourself to whatever you need. I've got to pee really bad, so I'm just gonna step behind that tree over there…"

Krista giggled, looking into the beauty of her surroundings, allowing reality to rush back into focus. Not realizing it at the time, this would be a moment she would cherish for years to come. A glimpse into the bravery of this wonderful man and a lesson learned by the naïve little girl she had been, coming here alone. Never again would she leave herself so vulnerable, and never again would she hike alone. No, she wanted this man by her side from that moment on, and yes, he would forever be her hero.

He invited her to join him. They said goodbye to the nine-mile loop and began a trek over unmarked paths and narrow deer trails that seemed to vanish behind them as though kept secret by the forest itself. The deeper they advanced, the more spectacular the sights became. However, Jack wouldn't allow her to photograph any of them, saying beauty is to be honored and respected, not looked upon as mere scenic landscapes on a cell phone. She admired his connection with the forest, his knowledge of all that surrounded them. Over the course of the day, she felt blessed listening to the stories of his great-grandmother's childhood, playing along the same paths they now walked, experiencing the same places they now stood, and for passing down the precious love this sixteen-year-old man boy held in his heart for the land. A love Krista was just beginning to understand and experience herself.

By midafternoon they reached the place his dad simply referred to as the Mystic—a lagoon at the bottom of a small basin hidden beneath old-growth conifers painted lush with green moss. Giant fern camouflage was the only pathway leading to the water's edge. The air along the narrow bank seemed heavy and dank, the water dark, almost black, and on occasion, an odd-colored fog could be seen, not merely lying on the water's surface but rising up in wisps, carried aloft on unseen currents of air. But on this day the air was clear and still, the sound of silence ushering the visitors into a state of serenity where the darkness of the pool offered a slate for the mind to reflect.

"As you can see, these places have remained mostly undisturbed since my grandmother came here. I've never showed it to anyone, but what I want to show you next is…well, sacred to my family. There's some things in the forest that can't run away from people, so I'll need you to promise never to reveal the location."

Krista studied the young man's face and wondered why, after so many years of barely having conversation, he suddenly trusted her with such information. But then she had to laugh. Not openly, but enough to coax forward a confession she didn't believe he would be surprised to hear.

"I'm so turned around…" She chuckled aloud. "I couldn't retrace our steps if you handed me a map. This is a textbook case of not being able to see the forest for the trees. What I see is everything blends together and closes up behind us. The trees and brush are so tall and thick, they block out the mountains or any landmarks. I haven't a clue where we are. I can only pray nothing happens to you, because I wouldn't know which way to run for help. We'd probably both die in here."

Again she studied his face, his thin smile making another appearance. Gazing beyond the pond, she added, "It's not my place to share. So yes Jack, you have my word. I'll never tell a soul."

The deal was closed with a handshake that Jack never released. Instead he led her twenty minutes to a small wooded glade, where standing under the pure white branches of an old dead tree, her promise was sealed with their first kiss.

"My family calls it Noni's tree. That was my great-grandma. It's an Oregon white oak, but that's not why it's white. It's a ghost tree. Story is, as a young girl, Noni would come here to play in its branches while her father fished the stream. Even as a teenager this was where she'd come to get away, think about life, and sometimes to just talk to the tree. Then one year, she brought her husband and introduced him to the tree. And the following year, shortly after giving birth to my grandma, she passed away suddenly. Her husband, knowing how much she loved the tree, decided that was where she would be buried. And so she was. A year later he found the tree had died, and a year after that, its bark began to turn white. The elders said this tree was not like the ghost trees of Rialto Beach, who died by the waters of the sea. Her tree died of sorrow and now allows her spirit to dwell within it forever. So you see, that's why this place is so special to my family—to me. My biggest fear is someone will find her tree and vandalize it...or worse."

"I'll never tell a soul. I swear," she said, placing his hand on her heart. Their second kiss followed.

The walk back took a little over ninety minutes, but Krista enjoyed every step of the way, begging to hear all the stories Jack knew about Noni. Over the summer they would visit the tree a half a dozen times, and it was there, for the first time, under the pure white branches of Nonie's tree, they secretly pledged their love. A gentle breeze kissed their skin, and both knew it was a blessing from Noni.

That day they began to whisper their desires, dreams, and plans to someday marry; but they knew even though their parents approved of their friendship, they wouldn't stand for how deep their feelings had become. Teenage love was not in the plan for either family. Five years ago, Jack overheard Nels telling Brett, his eldest brother, "There's plenty of time to be in love after college. But if you're just wanting more responsibility, it wouldn't bother me if you get a job and pay your own way. It'd give me a chance to get that new car your mom's been asking for." Brett was now a petroleum engineer living in Alaska with his new bride.

※

Once more Krista's phone vibrated. "432+=" brought her to giggle, and she quickly texted the code "1432+= gdnt," speaking as she did, "I love you too plus sum, good night!"

Returning to meet with the children, she was surprised to find Bailey had taken their place by the fire. "Rachel and Trudy are tucking them in under the guise of watching a movie." Bailey grinned. "I wanted to talk to you about doing a special at church. Just a song or two as a trio, like tonight. What do you think?"

"I'd love to sing with you guys. That was so awesome."

"Well, here she comes." And then, leaning closer and in a very hushed tone, she added, "You ask her. I'll be right back."

Two minutes later, all those at the Gathering Place made their way to the sitting area in front of the beautiful rock hearth. All eyes were on Rachel, making her feel as though she had done something wrong or was being judged for a transgression she knew nothing about. The room was silent. Finally Bailey asked, "Well, will you do it?"

CHAPTER TWENTY

When Wes called that evening, Amy had just slipped into bed. It was early even by Amy's standards, but nevertheless it'd been a long day, and she was exhausted, a detail Wes easily recognized by the tone of her voice.

"Baby, you sound tired," he said softly into the phone. "I won't keep you. Just wanted to say good night, and I love you."

"Mmm…we love you too…Daddy." she replied wearily.

Closing his eyes, he grinned. "Wish I were there to hug you both."

"Yeah, me too. I need one of your hugs…" Amy's voice trailed into the darkness but then returned. "I told Chris about the baby, and Mom broke the news to Bailey. Chris thinks we should name her after him."

"You mean him. We should name him after Chris," Wes corrected, chuckling into the phone.

"Whatever!" Amy sighed sarcastically, snuggling deep into the warmth of the heavy comforter. "I have the loves for you tonight."

"You do?"

"Mm hmm, I do. The evening's been filled with love and romance, and, and I wish you were here with me."

Puzzled by her comment, Wes questioned, "Love and romance? Am I missing something?"

"I spent the evening watching Chris fall in love with his high school sweetheart. Although I'm not sure they ever fell out of love. At least it doesn't appear that way. You'll see for yourself tomorrow. Speaking of tomorrow, Trudy wants you to make sourdough garlic bread in her pizza oven again. You good with that?"

"That's a clever ploy by Trudy to get me to stop at Boudin's for their sourdough loaves. Luckily, we went there tonight for pizza, and I grabbed a bunch for her. I know she loves that place."

"Oh, Good. You'll be her hero. Will you be back here by two?"

"I'll be back by noon. Now, what's all this about Chris?" he asked, more perplexed than ever.

"I'm so tired!" Amy yawned. "We'll catch up in the morning, okay? I love you…we love you."

Wes knew once the yawning started, it would only be a matter of minutes before she'd be asleep.

"I love you," he said, softly.

She smiled. "Is that for me or the baby?"

He too smiled and quietly replied, "Both!"

❦

Shortly after Amy left to go to bed the Spencer family also called it a night, Krista promising the kids she wouldn't forget the fairy albums or the treats.

Lincoln poured a nightcap for himself and Jim, and the two stepped outside onto the deck where Chris and Rachel had stood the night before. The overhead heater, sensing their presence, supplied a break from the evening chill, but they still found themselves talking about the weather as they gazed up into the clear night sky.

Their wives sat at the Gathering Place talking about them. And even though it was impossible for Trudy to hear what the men were saying, she giggled, getting Ann's attention. "Watch!"

Her soft voice requested a new song, and a moment later, while Randy Travis sang "As long as old men sit and talk about the weather," both Lincoln and Jim watched as the ladies raised their glasses in a mock toast, prompting the men to help Randy sing loudly the next few lines. "As long as old women sit and talk about old men."

At the end of the chorus, kisses were blown, carried on invisible currents impervious to worldly obstructions such as distance or bad aim. Soon after, the ladies resumed their discussion on romance, and the gentleman turned their gaze back to the night sky.

Bailey had received a text from Ted saying he had closed the deal with Norby and was going to stop by the house before heading to Chris's place, but that had been almost two hours ago. A little concerned, she left Rachel and Chris sitting by the fire and along with Jass went out front to give Ted a call.

"I was just getting ready to call you," he said, picking up the phone on the first ring. "That couple down in Mossy Rock called back. They want the boat but can't pick it up until tomorrow morning, so save me one of Trudy's biscuits. Is there anything you need from the house?"

For Bailey the news of the sale was bittersweet. When they met in Santa Barbara, that boat was his prized possession, costing him two summers of hard work as a hot tar roofer and whatever job he could muster after school during the wintertime. So yes, it made her sad to see it go. To trailer it across country would cost a fortune. Even so, she had been trying to figure out some way they could afford it.

"Don't worry Ted honey, when we get to Tampa, we'll get you a new boat. That'll be our first priority. Well, right after we get a house…with a pool…and a palm tree; we need a palm tree. It's like owning a blue tarp in the Northwest. It shows you're not just passing through, but a permanent resident."

His quiet laughter, like always, touched her heart and made her smile. And though she could tell he was sad, his sense of humor was still intact.

"As long as I have you, I don't need a boat. Or a house. Or a pool," he said, his voice building. "Dang it, Bailey, it's sunny Florida. We'll just set up camp on the beach, crank up some Jimmy Buffett, blend a frozen concoction, and chill under a big ol' palm tree. Who knows, we might even hold services right there on the beach. What do you think? We can do that, can't we? I mean, we could just be living the life, sweetheart, just living the life."

Her laughter now touched his heart. "It's a good thing we're moving, because you sound more and more like my brother every day. Oh, speaking of Chris, tomorrow you'll get to meet Rachel, the girl he married before Linda."

"What are you talking about? Hey, put Lincoln on the phone. I want to tell him to quit feeding you alcohol. It makes you crazier than normal, and I don't need that right now."

As if proving his point, her laughter became giddy, but only for a moment. "It's true!" she declared, proceeding to rattle off her matrimonial checklist. "They were seniors in high school. He proposed, she accepted, vows were said, I dos exchanged, man and wife, kissy face, kissy face, let the party begin. It was that simple, quick and to the point. A small ceremony, but it was beautiful. We even took pictures—like wedding pictures, you know. Cutting the cake, first dance, all that bride-and-groom stuff. I even downloaded a marriage license off the internet. Oh yeah, we did it right! Chris had his true love, and I had the sister-in-law I'd always wanted."

"What happened?"

For a moment Bailey became lost in her thoughts, remembering a time shortly before her and Ted's wedding, when she and Chris spent an afternoon hiking the hills above Millersylvania Park. He suddenly began talking about Rachel, confiding she would be in his heart always. It became almost a sermon on love, relationships, and trusting God with your heart. When she'd ask about their breakup, he simply said, "Sometimes the greatest act of love…requires you to say goodbye." Even then she could remember the heartbreak in his voice, on his face, and in the trembling of his hand as he sipped his water.

"I don't know," she replied. "He never really said, but tonight, you could tell there was something very special between them."

"Define special."

"You'll see when you get here tomorrow. They'll define it for me in the first five minutes. Speaking of love, let's talk about the boat. I don't want to see it go. We had some pretty special times on that boat."

Ted had to agree, and for the next few minutes, he spoke as though he were losing a family member. Had it not been for the insistence of Jass pawing and whining to go back inside, the fond memories could've gone on for quite some time. Each said I love you, sent phone kisses, and then Bailey quickly added, "Hey, if you think about it, grab my old photo albums. They're packed in a box by the bookshelf. I think Rachel would enjoy that. Thanks, babe. Love you."

After letting Jass in the house and not wanting to be inside just yet herself, she stood against the handrail sipping at the remainder of her wine and looking into the clear, star-filled sky. The air was cold, her heart warm, her thoughts drifting with romance. She considered a walk to the footbridge, where a better view of the moon and stars would be visible. In Santa Barbara she would sometimes spend an evening on the beach and there, alone, ask the moon about romance and love. But the moon doesn't know a thing about love, and stars may hear your wishes, but they have no power to grant them come true. So putting her memories aside, she leaned against the handrail whispering a prayer for God to hear.

"Thank you, Lord, for keeping them in your arms, your mind, and your heart, for hearing their pain, being their comfort, and knowing their love." For a split second she envisioned a myriad of youthful memories, bringing a whisper to her thoughts, her lips, her Lord.

"Their love…" she heard herself breathe softly into the cold air. And then, for the next few moments, she didn't speak at all, though she knew her heart was heard clearly in heaven.

"Their love…" she again whispered. "Thank you, Lord, for bringing them home to each other. Thank you so much…Amen."

The fire, beginning to die out, still warmed the backs of Chris and Rachel, who continued to sit on the hearth speaking in hushed conversation, an exchange of words that brought warmth unlike that of the fire, left her to blush and look toward the Gathering Place, reassuring their whispers had not been detected by the highly trained ears of Mrs. B. nor the enchantingly perceptive Belle Trudeau.

It was most likely coincidence the two women chose that moment to stand, Ann making her way toward Rachel, stopping just short of entering the Great Room.

"Would you two like to join us in the courtyard? Tru turned on the falls. I think you'll enjoy it. Oh and I'll show you a painting of my grandma."

Just then Trudy appeared, handing her friend a chilled glass of Chardonnay while producing a glass for herself and two more yet to be filled. Nodding for the couple to come along, she then disappeared down the passageway.

Lifting her glass to her lips and speaking over the rim, Ann smiled. "Come on. I'll introduce you to Grandma." And then she, too, made her way quickly to the beautiful gate like entry of the in-door courtyard. Just inside, she waited next to Theophilus and Kodiak for the couple to join her. Back at the fireplace, Rachel eagerly pulled Chris to his feet, and though he was more than willing to follow, Rachel pushed him to lead the way.

From the deck, Lincoln and Jim had watched their wives entice the young couple. Lincoln, of course, was the first to comment. "'Follow me,' said the spider to the fly."

"You'd think Chris would know better." Jim sighed.

After taking a sip of his drink, Lincoln revealed, "Just a bit ago, Tru told me she saw him at Rachel's window last night after we all went to bed. Said he was out there with just his jeans on."

"Crawling in or crawling out?" Jim laughed, certain neither would be the case.

"Just standing there talking, 'til he turned blue I guess. Hell, that's some powerful love. It was down in the twenties last night."

"How does that song go? 'No shoes, no shirt...got frostbite.'"

Both men chuckled and then quietly enjoyed their drinks. After a few moments, Lincoln said, "Reminds me of a quote from one of my favorite poets. 'You know you're in love when you can't fall asleep because reality is finally better than your dreams.'"

Jim nodded. "Very nice. Robert Frost?"

Grinning, Lincoln winked. "Dr. Seuss."

At the opposite end of the courtyard, in a small alcove hidden by a cluster of tall plants, the three women and Chris stared at the lovely portrait of Ann's grandma, wearing a classic Barbour jacket, blue-and-white checkered shirt, pearl stud earrings, ruby-red lipstick, and the same windblown, somewhat shaggy pixyish hairstyle she'd worn since the sixties. At first glance she seemed nothing like her well-kept granddaughter and definitely not the person Rachel had imagined. They shared a few physical characteristics, the high cheekbones and dimpled chin being the two most prominent. But more so, and just as evident, was the intrinsic self-confidence both could emit by way of appearance alone, a trait once feared by a timid young redhead student, now envied by the adult Rachel had become. As she studied the elderly woman on the canvas, she saw more of the stately woman standing beside her.

"Can you believe she was in her eighties?" Ann commented, without taking her eyes from the portrait. "Every morning, coffee and toast for breakfast, and out the door by seven. That was her routine, rain or shine. And if you weren't ready, she'd stand by the door and wait in a huff. It would drive me crazy. Isn't that right, Tru?"

Trudy nodded as Ann continued. "And that jacket! My mom hated that jacket. I think she burned it or threw it away or something. So then, Grandma went to Nordstrom's and bought another just like it and charged it to Mom's account. I remember my mom having a fit. It was expensive. Well then, Mom showed Grandma an advertisement in some newspaper flyer of these men out hunting wearing the same jacket. About a month later, my Mom got a letter from Grandma. In it was a photo she'd clipped from a magazine of Princess Di wearing pearl earrings sporting that same Barbour jacket. Grandma had written a note that said, 'Feel like a true Princess. Went hunting today, bagged a strand of pearls at Nordstrom's. Merry Christmas to me!'"

"She didn't." Rachel gasped.

Chris laughed. "I know her granddaughter. Bet she did."

Ann nodded her head. "I'm not sure how she convinced the salesgirl, but she was able to charge them to Mom's account. Of course she paid her for 'em in the end, and then some. The whole point was just to make Mom stew, and it worked. It always worked. Grandma knew when, where, and how to push my mom's buttons. Take a look at that grin. I imagine that's the look she had writing that note."

Trudy stepped closer to the couple. "Carrie had an ornery streak; that's for sure. But she could also be the sweetest person in the world. And oh, how she loved Lincoln. Thought he simply walked on water. It's because of her, Linc had these little waterfalls put in. She loved the sound, the soft tinkling, as she called it. Said it was like listing to nature's wind chimes. Almost every night she'd come to the courtyard, set the lights, and sit by the pond listening to music. Told me it reminded her of Hawaii. I found out a later she'd never been to Hawaii, so the four of us took her to Maui that

August. One night at the hotel, we were all sitting out on the patio next to a little waterfall when Doris Day came on the radio. After the song ended, she looked at Linc and said, 'I guess Doris sounds pretty much the same everywhere, but their fountain doesn't hold a candle to your tinkling.'"

The chuckling, led mostly by Chris, made Trudy's normally quiet giggles rise to meet the shy laughter of Rachel. Ann grinned, keeping her attention mainly on the painting.

"Here's to you, Grandma," she said, raising her glass. "I miss you."

As they left the alcove, the sound of the gentle waterfalls led them to a small pool at the base of the rock wall, where all but Ann took a seat. Trudy quietly directed the room, and in dramatic fashion, the ceiling and walls became awash in hues reminiscent of an island sunset. Distantly, the soothing voice of Doris Day drifted through the air, bringing a private moment between Ann and Trudy, placing a smile on both their faces.

Producing a second bottle of Chardonnay, Trudy filled two more glasses and set them in front of the couple before refreshing Ann's and returning to her seat. Staring into the rippling water, Ann began to speak even before turning around to join the others. Her mood was somber, though not depressed. Her eyes held no tears yet glistened with a sea of memories.

"Sometimes I have these melancholy nights," she began.

Trudy, knowing well the first line of Ann's story, smiled her encouragement.

"On those nights, I'll pour a little glass of wine and wander out on the deck just to sit all bundled up watching the moonlight glisten off the snow-covered mountain. And that's when I think of her."

Pausing briefly, she looked at Chris, who she knew loved hearing Grandma Carrie stories, but he definitely had never heard the one she was about to tell. Her gaze found Rachel, and remembering their conversation from the other day, she felt quite comfortable to proceed.

"Funny—I hardly ever used to think about her. Oh sure, once in a while she'd pop into my head, but..." Her eyes drifted back to the pond, but only for an instant. "Well, anyway...a few years ago, Jim spent every evening one summer working on the music to a new play. Amy was visiting friends in Italy, and I was feeling pretty lonely, to say the least. So one night I filled my glass and headed for the deck. It wasn't ten minutes before Jim stuck his head out just to tell me he loved me, and then he asked if I was wearing a new perfume. Before I could say no, a wisp of scented air moved through me. The sweet familiar fragrant was unmistakably Grandma. It caused me to almost drop my glass."

"Through you?" Rachel asked, thinking she misunderstood.

"Yes, for a split second it was like she stepped through me. Hugged me, maybe. I don't know. It wasn't so much physical or even spiritual really. Nothing like the movies. My hair didn't blow, she didn't appear as a ghost or anything like that, but I knew for just an instant we had shared the same space. Euphoria swept over me. I walked around the deck hoping somehow to bump into her, to inhale her fragrance one more time." She smiled. "My sudden romp chased Jim back to his piano, muttering something about hormonal craziness."

Again Ann's stare found Chris. "I spoke to her…and to God. I found myself sitting there thanking both for the time I got to spend with her. And then, about an hour later, I went in the house to say good night to Jim, and when I hugged him, he could still smell her perfume on me."

Retrospect brought Ann's gaze to fall to her hands; a sip of wine brought it back to the couple. "Listen to me rattling on."

Chris immediately spoke up. "Not at all. I wish I could have met her. Everything I've heard, she sounds like a great lady. Did she ever come back? I mean…"

"No, not like that…not…" Ann thought for a moment but turned her attention to the small pool.

Trudy placed an arm around her friend, and they all sat quietly listening to the tinkle of the falls in the background. A few minutes passed, but the sounds were so peaceful, the mood so relaxing, nothing needed to be said until Trudy took it upon herself to restart the conversation by discussing the only subject she believed worthy to interrupt everyone's thoughts.

"I never knew my grandparents, so it was nice to have Carrie around. Thankfully, we hit it off. Turned out we had a lot in common. I suppose it was her love for the rain and the outdoors and her…stories that brought us so close.

"We'd spend mornings walking the trails or exploring the shoreline, but whatever we did, eventually she'd get around to sharing one of her stories, her viewpoint on the world, or something that had found its way into an earlier conversation. And believe me, nothing was off limits with her.

"While up at The Point one morning, she asked how Linc and I met. I told her we met when he proposed to me in Golden Gate Park, but she didn't believe me."

"Is that true?" Rachel asked.

Trudy laughed. "Not exactly. He introduced himself first and then told me he was the man I was gonna spend the rest of my life with. I thought he was crazy, a prankster or something worse, so I tried to walk away. But he followed me. Wouldn't shut up. Just kept walking and talking, becoming less frightening and more annoying by the block."

Rachel giggled. "What did you do? How did you get rid of him?"

Looking around at her beautiful surroundings, Trudy quietly shrugged. "I haven't...yet!"

A smile passed between her and Rachel as she continued. "Carrie loved the Point, the bride, the romance, and…"

"No you don't. You have to tell me about you and Lincoln. He really proposed the day you met…and you said yes?" Rachel asked. "Come on, that happens in fairytales and romance novels, not in real life."

With a subtle smile, Trudy agreed. "You're right! From the moment we met, he's brought me love stories with fairytale endings, and he continues to overwhelm me with some new means of exhibiting love each and every day."

Taking a sip of wine, she spent the next few minutes painting a romantic picture of love at first sight and the lifelong romance that followed for her and Lincoln. The young couple listened intently while the storyteller strung words of emotion into passionate sentences, creating pages of beautiful visions illustrating her tale of love.

At some point Rachel, unmindful of her hosts and the questions that would surely follow, reclined into Chris's chest, intertwining her fingers with his while secretly envisioning or perhaps recalling the ecstasy of her own young love from years past. But Chris knew these two women well enough to know they had been making a mental list of questions from the moment he had held Rachel on the porch. So it was with that understanding and a kiss to Rachel's head that he let go of the attractive woman's hand and wrapped his arms around her shoulders, pulling her tightly to him.

Trudy's voice softened only slightly but slowed to a crawl as she processed their open display of affection. However, her lapse was brief and not worth mentioning by those watching. Besides, taking another sip from her glass seemed to justify the pause. When she spoke again, her voice, though still remarkably pleasant, was noticeably softer. Clearing her throat and soothing it with yet another small sip helped very little, so a second, somewhat longer sip was taken.

"Lincoln claims he falls in love with me all over again every morning, and I believe that's true. Not because of me, but because of him. That's just the way he is—a romantic. But more than that, he's just plain sappy, and I love that about him and hope he never changes."

Before she continued, she again cleared her throat, bringing a wrinkle of concern to Ann's forehead. Her voice remained soft, as peaceful as that of their surroundings and as comforting as the story she continued to share. After a while, she told of a time when Carrie joined her and Lincoln on the patio to watch an August sunset.

"That evening Linc presented her with a small bouquet of summer flowers, which touched her deeply, almost bringing her to tears. Offering no explanation at first, she sat quietly watching the sky as the sun brushed the clouds with color. Suddenly, she began to recall a time her husband brought her a little bouquet of wildflowers he'd collected from around the farm. She couldn't express enough how much she loved them. The next morning she found him up on the tractor plowing circles around their old gray barn. This went on for an hour, and then off to the fields he finally drove. The following morning he began painting the backside of the barn; the morning after that the front. It took him a week of mornings to complete both sides, and she didn't hesitate to express her displeasure with having a big yellow barn for the neighbors to laugh at. But in less than a month an acre of wildflowers encircled that old barn, swaying rhythmically in the gentle wind and warm sunshine. She had to admit it was a beautiful scene to sit and take in, one she never tired of. Over the years, to the consternation of their neighbors, many coats of bright-yellow paint were applied to the place. To this day it stands amid an acre of wildflowers that continue to spend their summer swaying to the rhythm of the wind."

With the timid look of a captivated child, Rachel sighed. "What a beautiful story. Please, tell me there's more. I could listen to you all night."

Softly, Trudy replied, "There is a little more to the story, something I've always found interesting."

After setting her wine down and with the same storytelling craftsmanship she had displayed previous, she continued. "The sunset was beautiful. Dark silhouettes of distant clouds splashed with dramatic color blazing up from the horizon to quickly fade into the night sky, leaving us all wrapped in twilight and the lingering warmth of mid-August. The next hour was spent laughing and talking, sharing stories and listening to the songs she loved, each one bringing its own spark to her eyes and lilt to her voice. There came a moment when she looked to the stars and whispered into the night words we couldn't make out. We made no intrusion, holding our own words and thoughts at bay, giving her the quiet privacy she silently requested. After a few moments, her gaze found us, and her expression revealed she was surprised we were no longer in conversation but focused solely on her. Most times when she was startled or surprised, she giggled quietly and waited for others to speak. However, this time, as if answering an unspoken question, she calmly said, 'True love…once it takes up residence in your heart, it never allows you to say goodbye. Unlike everything else in life, it's impervious to the passing of time. Our bodies, memories, dates, names—all fade in its wake, but not true love. Once you've experienced it, it's there for a lifetime. Even when the physical ties have become broken and are long gone, you can't shake it loose.'

"She then asked Linc to explain what happened that day in the park that made him believe he'd spend the rest of his life with someone he hadn't even met. It was a question he'd answered a hundred times before, and each time he simply claimed it was love at first sight.

"But she was having none of it, pointing out, 'First sight only provides opportunity for attraction, not love. Love is constructed over time, assembled in layers like the perfect tiramisu. I'm afraid I don't see love at first sight as a possibility at all.'

"Lincoln's response was immediate, so instantaneous it even took me by surprise. 'I spent most of my youth daydreaming about the woman I would marry. I knew exactly what she would look like, her mannerisms, the color of her hair, the sound of her voice. Even the type of clothes she would wear through the changing of the seasons. When I saw this woman sitting on the grass, she met none of my criteria, but it didn't matter. What mattered was trying to keep my heart in my chest as I sat down beside her. She was nothing like the woman in my imagination. She was far beyond what I ever could have imagined. But I was hers even before our eyes met. Had she taken me by the hand and marched me to city hall, I would've married her right then. I didn't need to know anything about her. My heart knew it all. At that instant I knew I would love her until I took my dying breath. No matter what life threw at me, she would give me the strength to be victorious.'

"And then he paused. A quizzical look pinched his brow and brightened his cheeks as if he'd stumbled across some enigmatic truth. Raising an eyebrow, he grinned. 'You know, Carrie, you may be right. First sight doesn't provide an opportunity for instant love unless—now stay with me on this—every minute detail about Tru was wrapped up and placed in my care like a present the day I was born, ready to be opened the very moment I laid eyes on her. I'm sure that's—'

"'Horse pickles,' Carrie barked, filling the air with laughter and holding up her hand, not allowing Linc to continue his nonsense. Lincoln, of course, tried to press on, but she would have none of it, insisting we change the subject. I disagreed and asked about her thoughts on the subject of love, something she had only mentioned in passing a few times. At first she shrugged me off, but after a moment, she surprised me by suddenly saying, 'I believe sunrise always brings a new day and sunset puts it to rest, that children daydream, the elderly reminisce, and both glance at love simply from opposite directions of life. So when the day greets you with love, fill it with childlike vision and store the memory in your heart like treasure, because in the end...as the sun sets, memories are all you'll have of this ol' world. So why not fill them with love?"

Trudy fell silent, the peaceful sound of the falls embracing them all. After a while she added, "The woman loved romance. Not romantic novels or that kind of nonsense, but honest love stories, true stories. She would've loved you two."

Chris breathed something into Rachel's ear and the two sat forward, but Ann was the next to speak.

"Grandma took things at face value, not how she imagined or wanted them to be. She'd never do that, especially when it came to things of the heart."

Ann's dark eyes met those of the couple, and her familiar matriarchal guise, even now, after so long, indicated she knew their secrets. And just as when they were of school age, both wondered if perhaps she did. But unlike their memories, her look faded, replaced with the assurance she knew very little.

"It's easy to see something's going on between you. I don't know what it is exactly, and I'm not going to say I'm not curious. But I imagine you're as curious as I am—as we are," she corrected, nodding toward Trudy. "All evening I've tried to remember something you said, Chris, something about love burning, but I can't seem..."

"Love's like a fire; it was part of a lesson I gave at Lake Surrender, during Couples Camp. I'm surprised you remember it, though. That was what? Three, maybe four years ago?"

"Two. I bought the tape. You remember the part I'm talking about then, right?"

"I think so. More or less, anyway."

Grouping his thoughts for only a second, he began. "I think of love as a fire. It starts as a small flame of desire, kindled by twigs of wonder and kindness, fanned through acceptance and curiosity, stoked with branches of trust and understanding, and continuing to build into a roaring blaze, which if tended with care will eventually bring warmth and light to all that come near. But sometimes these flames are left to die, leaving hot embers of neglect as remnants of its once glorious beauty. If abandoned completely, it becomes cold dry ash, scarring the landscape of life before being scattered to the winds and forgotten forever."

Wondering if she would feel the warmth of his heart, he took Rachel's hand and was not surprised to feel the warmth of her heart. When he began to speak again, she thought his voice was as tender as his touch, but her thoughts quickly disappeared, overtaken by his words.

"Sometimes a neglected, even abandoned fire can smolder quietly for a very, very long time, its light concealed, its warmth buried by those who once danced within its flame before parting to venture down life's road. But then, without warning, there comes a stirring, and with sudden voracity flames begin to rise in swirls of long-forgotten passion to dance with fiery brilliance, once never imagined.

"Not merely a rekindling, the fire is a testament. To what you ask: persistence, prayers, patience? I don't know. All three are credible, and assuredly there are more. But the reasons are unimportant. What's essential is the flame itself remains to burn, to glow, to warm, to give hope to true love."

His words hung in the air, where they were quickly drowned by the sound of the many waterfalls. Squeezing Rachel's hand, he looked upon her tenderly. The young woman, radiant from a passing blush, acknowledged him with her own loving stare, the twinkling in her eyes like stars in the night sky. And so, once again he found himself helpless in her gaze.

Her breath became shallow when she could breathe at all. There were no words said. None were needed. No guilt or shame or burdens of regret to quell the moment, because suddenly the moment was theirs and theirs alone. With the semblance of sunset aglow all around, the sound of the falls, the distant music—all became an extension of their very being, their emotion. The world appeared to vanish from view, leaving each with a single focus, unbroken and undisturbed, drifting without direction or intention. Time refused to pass in this fragile space. No conscious demand of urgency beckoned from the horizon as each shared a single thought. No, this moment, like so many before, would endure a lifetime.

With hushed breath, Ann whispered discreetly, "That's not on my tape!"

Chris made no attempt to comment. His thoughts, like his gaze, remained held by Rachel, who now slyly caressed his hand and hid her own thoughts deep within a muted sigh. Trudy's thoughts were playfully entertaining atop a freshly filled glass, and Ann chose to share hers by asking, "Did you add that recently? That last part, I mean?"

Without averting his eyes, Chris replied, "Recent?" A smile touched the couple's lips. "No, I can't say it was recent." Shifting his attention to the other two women, he admitted, "We know you have questions, and honestly, we can't blame you. But thing is, we have questions ourselves. Sure, we still harbor some old feelings for each other…"

"That's obvious, Skippy," Lincoln boomed, making his way through the room. "These two old busybodies get you to set a date yet?"

Chris laughed, thankful for the big man's levity, but even more so his timing. "Not yet." He grinned, looking at Rachel.

"That's good. You don't want to rush romance. It needs time to develop depth and character, like a fine wine."

"Said the man who proposes before saying hello." Rachel chuckled under her breath, just loud enough for Chris and Trudy to hear.

Greeting her husband with a roll of her eyes, Trudy stated, "Oh I get it. Kind of like, no wine before its time sort of thing." Though faint, there was a flash in her eyes only Lincoln observed, and before he could react, she asked, "So, Studley, I guess that makes you the Annie Green Springs of romance?"

Erupting with laughter, Chris shouted, "Studley?" Glowing with delight, he repeated it again, again howling loudly, his guffaw echoing throughout the room. "Studley."

Timid by comparison, the women joined in his amusement. Of course, Lincoln, being a fun-loving sport, played the dupe, puffing out his chest, challenging, "I suppose you think there's someone here more studley than I."

"I'm right here," Jim called out, making his way into the spacious room, to be met with a reverberating discord of boisterous laughter.

A few seconds later, Bailey entered the room to stand beside him. "What did you do, Jim?" she asked, dumfounded by the laughter.

"I was answering you. Did you get lost?"

"I was checking on the kids. Makes me want to stay and have one of my own. I feel like I'm giving up more than I—"

The music, though still distant, seemed to rise in volume around them with the distinctive voice of Jimmy Durante advising, "Fairy tales can come true…It can happen to you…If you're young at heart…"

Bailey's smile, like her words were tenuous. "Dance with me," she whispered, more as a thought than a request.

Without a word Jim gently moved her across the open floor with precision and grace. Every twirl, every spin brought applause from the group, and soon her smile, like her words, were filled with laughter once again.

For the next hour stories were shared, tales were told, moments remembered, each person bringing something to the conversation, whether by individual account or joint venture. This was a time for fun, closeness, and most of all, family. No secrets were hidden; neither were they revealed, although Lincoln mentioned skinny dipping in Lake Shasta before Trudy put the kibosh on the story and promptly announced they were going to bed. Ann and Jim made their way home, with Jass leading the way.

Now it was just like old times; the three of them together again, the way it was supposed to be all along; at least as far as Bailey was concerned. A multitude of questions played in her mind, questions she'd wanted to ask for many years, and now with the opportunity at hand, she instead announced she, too, was going to bed. Hugging them both, she turned to walk away, but after taking only one step turned back, she threw her arms around Rachel. Her voice was soft, quiet, just above a whisper. "I love you so much; he loves you so much." And for a moment Bailey held Rachel tightly, and then just as quietly as before, said, "Marry him before I leave for Florida. Last time my boyfriend married you. This time my husband will. Although I look at it as just renewing your vows."

Both women chuckled, their tones harmonious in the air. Bailey placed a good-night kiss on Rachel's cheek, smiled, and then rushed to leave the room before the first emotional tear ran from her cheek.

Chris, holding Rachel's glass, asked, "What was that about?"

Taking her wine from his hand and placing it just under her lips, allowing its spark of seduction to twinkle in her eye, she asked, "Your mom still have her garden?"

CHAPTER TWENTY ONE

Amy was the first to wake up, first to shower, and first out the door. She didn't go far, just to the end of the wraparound porch, where she sat at the long wooden table enjoying a hot cup of coffee. Nothing special, no flavored syrup or designer foam. This morning she felt like a Folgers-in-your-cup kind of girl—blue jeans, flannel shirt, baseball cap, and tennis shoes. Not bothering to tuck her shirt in was a rare fashion statement even when working with the horses on her ranch, but this morning it helped to hide the fact she could no longer buckle her belt. Later she'd use an icepick to make an extra hole, but for now, leaving it off felt good. Everything about the morning felt good. The ocean fragrance adrift on the cool, refreshing breeze woke the forest to share its scent, leaving the mother-to-be believing it was the perfect marriage of aromas. But of course that reminded her of Wes, the perfect man for her, the perfect father for their child. This made her think of her own childhood, her parents, and how lucky she was to have been raised in a home filled with love, kindness, and laughter.

A half cup into her thoughts, the soft creak of the front door drew her attention. It was Michael and Jass, both hurrying to the table to wish her good morning—the dog with kisses, the boy with smiles and giggles.

"My mom will be out in a minute," the boy said. "She's getting coffee. Have you seen Beth this morning?"

"Not yet. I think we're the first ones up. How's your time at the cove going? Beth showing you around?"

"I love it! She's so lucky; it's awesome here. I never knew there was such a place. I mean, in the middle of the forest. I thought only bears and lumberjacks lived in the woods. Well, and animals and stuff. You know what I mean?"

Amy's smile assured the boy she understood. "I grew up here. Every summer, anyway, and weekends and most holidays. And, of course, any chance I got to stay with Aunt Tru, I jumped at it. Where Beth lives—that used to be my house."

"Wow. Have you ever been…" Michael thought for a moment, trying to remember how to say the word correctly, and then slowly he asked, "to that ampletheeder?" Once said, he knew it was wrong, so he pointed in the direction of the bridge. "The place where the fairies live? You ever go there?"

"You mean the amphitheater? Sure. I love that place. Very mysterious, though. As a kid I'd run up and down these trails all the time looking for new things to explore, but I never found that place, which is weird considering how big it is and how much I played on the old trails. I probably passed it a thousand times growing up but never saw it. It was like it was invisible, just waiting for my great-grandma and her Gifts to find the path."

"Gifts?" Michael inquired, cocking his head in a curious stare.

"That's a story for another time. If you want, we can walk down this morning. I take it you haven't been?"

"I haven't!" the boy replied with a degree of eagerness.

"I have to warn you, sometimes it can be really beautiful, and other times it can be a little spooky. And you never know which you're going to get. Are you okay with spooky?"

Michael's eyes grew as big as his smile. "I'm okay with spooky. I touched the very back wall at the Ape Caves. We turned off our flashlights and everything. Even sat and played a game in the pitch dark. Now, that was spooky. So see, spooky doesn't bother me a bit."

"What's this about spooky?" Rachel asked, pushing open the squeaky screen door to step onto the porch. "Good morning, Aim."

"She used to live here and has been down to the fairy place bunches," Michael exclaimed hastily. "She said she'd take me to see it this morning. Remember those little doors and houses we saw? Those fairy doors? That girl Krista has pictures of them at this place. And Amy said sometimes it's spooky, so I told her about the Ape Cave. That place is really spooky, huh, Mom?"

Rachel glanced at Amy. "Did he have an abundance of coffee, sugar… drugs, all of the above this morning?"

Amy grinned, shrugging her shoulders and shaking her head. Michael looked confused but said nothing as Rachel took a seat at the table, raised her cup to her lips, and then, pausing, added, "Your mom will be out in a minute. She has Trudy on the phone. I guess she and Linc went for an early-morning walk and should be back soon to host breakfast at their place."

Wrinkling her nose, Amy sighed. "Breakfast hasn't been my favorite thing lately. You hear stories about morning sickness, but you never imagine…"

"I know what you mean. It was brutal, but mine didn't last long. Maybe a month at best!"

"I hope mine doesn't. I found if I eat some gingersnaps first thing and some fruit an hour or so later, I'm good to go the rest of the day. No problems. Of course, that's subject to change daily."

Jass nuzzled the boys hand before running to the steps and into the yard.

"I think he wants to play," Amy said.

Michael hurried along the porch, stopping for only a moment to grab a well-chewed tennis ball from its resting place next to the front door. At the bottom of the steps, he threw the ball and watched excitedly as the dog retrieved it and placed it at his feet. Again the boy threw the ball, and again the dog brought it back. After the third time, Michael ran to the other side of the yard, where Jass joined him for the game to continue. And continue it did, from one end of the compound to the other.

Rachel's attention quietly shifted from her son to the beauty of the morning. The faint sound of a fish jumping in the cove exemplified the peacefulness surrounding her. The chill of the air, more refreshing than harsh, made her next sip of coffee even more enjoyable. As Rachel spoke, Amy detected a noticeable softness to her voice, something as a young girl, Lincoln explained, was a person's forest voice; a quality as natural as the temperate sounds of water moving over stone, the whisper of leaves in a gentle wind.

"I've been in the city so long, I forget places like this exist," Rachel said. Her voice, quickly disappearing into the silence, gave the flutelike call of a distant thrush time to welcome the morning with its beautiful yet haunting melody—so beautiful, in fact, the bird repeated it a second time.

Amy's face reflected her own content, and it was with her forest voice she revealed, "I've spent my whole life in the country. Couldn't wait to go off to college, and then couldn't wait to get back." Quickly scanning the compound before resting her sight on the screen door, she said quietly, "But it didn't take long for me to realize…I needed a little more personal space."

The spark in Rachel's eye and a slow creeping smile confirmed her understanding. "Your mom was saying you have a ranch up in Cle Elum. That's up by Leavenworth, isn't it?"

"Yeah. We're about twenty to forty minutes away, depending on who's driving. Wes may fly jets, but he drives like an old lady. You like horses?"

"If you're asking have I ever ridden one, the answer is no. But I think they're gorgeous animals."

"You and Chris need to come spend a few days with us. He loves to ride, but I don't think he's been in years. It would do you both some good."

The thrush echoed its song once again, causing Rachel to pause momentarily before muttering faintly, "I think people are talking already. Could you imagine if we stayed the night at your place?"

Embarrassed, Amy shook her head. "I mean, the whole family—you two and the kids. We have five bedrooms and a bunkhouse we can stick Chris in if you'd like."

"What do you mean? I'm thinking the guys can stay out in the bunkhouse with the kids, and you and I can have a moms' night in."

Both women giggled and began sharing pregnancy stories while Michael and the dog continued to play in the yard. Ann, slightly more vivacious than usual, arrived at the table with a warm plate of sweet rolls and a large carafe of fresh coffee. Her greeting seemed a little too bubbly for Amy, leaving the young woman guardedly suspicious.

"Mom, you're awfully giddy this morning. What's up? You're even blushing." She smirked, not hiding her cynicism.

Ann, reclining in her chair, cup in hand, cheeks flush, gushed. "It was your dad…"

"Eww." Amy squirmed. "Don't tell me that. Nobody wants to hear that stuff. Yuck!"

Rachel bit her lip to keep from laughing. Ann sat unfazed, continuing to smile, holding her cup with chic elegance, finally adding, "Your dad called me Grandma this morning is all I was saying. Grandma!" She giggled, triggering yet another flush of her cheeks. "I'm going to be a grandma!"

For an instant Amy felt the desire to tease her mom about shawls, gray hair, and the increasing need for Depends, but instead leaned close and with a hug said lovingly, "You're going to be the best grandma ever. By the way, where's the future Grandpa this morning? He owes me a walk."

With her eyes she gestured upstairs. "Still in bed. Said he was jumping in the shower, but I haven't heard the music yet." Looking at Rachel, she explained, "He's showered to music as long as I've known him. Loud music, but as far as I'm concerned, the louder the better. Helps drown out his morning singing voice, which is like a mash-up of Bob Dylan and that funny guy with the gravelly voice. Played in *Independence Day*. What's his name?"

"Harvey Fierstein. Love him," Rachel said.

"Yeah, that's him. Sounds just like him."

From high above the compound, the eagle watched as the dog and boy frolicked about the yard, and once again, he was thankful he was not a dog. After a while the bird's cry cut through the crisp morning air, causing the young boy to stop and look up, mimicking the sound with a high-pitched squeal—more like the piglets of fall, thought the mighty bird, thankful, too, he was not a young boy.

Over the next ten minutes, Ann shared a series of anecdotes depicting her own maternal bliss, an experience she never wanted to repeat but of course was thankful to have experienced once in life. Each story was delivered with the rhythm and timing of a well-rehearsed comedic monologue, though as far as Amy knew, these stories had never been shared before, at least not with her. Yet her mother provided details as clear and fresh as if they had happened yesterday, bringing Amy to understand a level of her mother's love that had been stored away, waiting patiently to be given at a precise moment in time. This was not simply just another mother-daughter dialogue but a mother-to-mother bond, making it a special moment that neither minded sharing in the presence of Rachel. It didn't take long before Amy felt tears roll over her cheeks, and with choked laughter, she blamed it on hormones.

With sincere understanding, Rachel produced a small packet of tissues from her jacket pocket. "Keep 'em. You'll need them the rest your life, what with your tears, the baby's runny nose…or worse."

"Oh, let me tell you about a box of Kleenex," Ann said. "Amy had just started crawling…"

The stories flowed another few minutes before the mom-to-be called a timeout, hurrying into the house to use the downstairs bathroom. Minutes later, she stood just inside the screen door listening to her mother entertain Rachel with yet another baby story. Both women laughed, and then Rachel began her own narrative, bringing yet another understanding to Amy: parenthood is a collection of day-to-day events, snapshots sealed in time capsules deep within the loving heart of a woman who will peek inside from time to time to relive her most precious memories of motherhood. But as Amy swung the screen door open and saw the loving look on Ann's face, she also understood it is not simply memories relived…but those continuing to unfold.

Without moving toward the table, she pointed to the plate of sweet rolls. "You two enjoy. I'm going to go get some fresh air. The smell is getting to me, if you know what I mean."

Ann sipped her coffee and smiled. "I once had a bout of morning sickness while teaching a sex education class using some week-old fruit…talk about nausea."

This was not something the mother-to-be found interesting in the least, and she quickly exited the porch. Jogging past Michael, she shouted a challenge. "Race you to the bridge?" And without a word, the boy bolted, quickly overtaking the woman. She made no effort to catch him but lagged just close enough to cause him to worry. Reaching the base of the bridge, he tagged the heavy wooden structure, lifting his arms in triumph.

"The winner and always champion," he crowed, performing a victory dance reminiscent of Rocky Balboa.

Nonetheless, it was short lived, as Amy sped past, chuckling. "The center post at top of the bridge, silly goose."

Her victory dance was much the same as the boy's, but when he protested, she placed his hand in hers, raised it as high as it would go, and began singing, "We are the champions…my friend…" The boy was good with that and even joined in. The bird, now thankful he was not a young woman, disappeared down the sound in search of his own breakfast.

Michael called for Jass to come, but the dog would not approach the bridge, deciding instead to join the women on the porch, hoping a bite of sweet roll would fall unnoticed to the floor. He sat at their feet, looking as pitiful as could be with ears drooped and head tilted, and it took less than a minute for the warm, buttery treat to make its way onto the floor, where quickly it was devoured and the pathetic dog look repeated.

With a squeal Beth emerged from her house and onto the porch, the screen door slamming behind her. The dog's attention turned away from Ann, who had just dropped a second nibble onto the porch inches from his paw. He knew it was there but chose to greet the little girl as she ran through the yard. An exchange of sweet giggles for dog kisses put a slight prance in his step as he returned to continue breakfast with Ann. Beth followed, giving Ann and Rachel morning hugs before running to greet Amy and Michael on the bridge. The conversation moved quickly from good morning to Michael saying Amy had volunteered to be their tour guide to the amphitheater. Of course, Beth would need to get permission from her dad, who, as it happened, was making his way to join Rachel and Ann at that very moment. Bailey, only a minute behind, like her niece, slowed to exchange sweet giggles for dog kisses before bringing her enthusiasm to the table with greetings and hugs and bubbly laughter.

Standing at the corner of the porch next to Ann's flower bed, Beth called to her dad, "Amy wants me to take her to the fairy place. That's okay, yeah? And Mike's never been. He wants to go too, okay?"

With a mouthful of sweet roll, Bailey mumbled loudly, "Me too. I want to go." Grabbing another sweet roll, she scampered to meet the child, and the two ran hand in hand to the bridge. Offering the extra sweet roll to the others brought smiles to the kids and a polite decline from Amy—at least until the overpowering smell of the sugary cinnamon roll reached her nose, prompting her to dash off the bridge in the direction of the forest. There the fragrance of morning wilderness embraced her with a gentle waft of refreshing air, chasing away the unsettling sensation churning in her stomach.

Turning, she watched Bailey and the kids make their way off the bridge. "Stop!" she cried, pointing to her startled friends. "Don't bring those things over here. Eat 'em, give 'em to the birds, the fish, the ants. I don't care; just don't bring 'em any closer."

Bailey took one more bite before tossing hers into the bushes. "I'm donating mine to the forest creatures," she said to the kids before hurrying toward Amy. "You guys can stay behind if you want," she then called over her shoulder.

Beth and Michael looked at each other without expression and simultaneously donated their treats to the creatures of the forest as well before running down the trail to catch the ladies. Five minutes later, at the top of the brick walkway that would take them down to the amphitheater, Amy paused, suddenly overcome by another wave of nausea. It took a minute to subside but passed without incident. However, once they reached the bottom, her luck ran out.

Being a gentleman, Michael led the others away, giving Amy her privacy. And after putting a comfortable distance between them, he stopped to look around. No one spoke; no one moved. The sheer beauty before them was paralyzing. The place was just as enchanting as Beth had described yet as spooky as Amy had warned. Beneath the thick canopy of evergreens, the early-morning light cast an eerily green tint over the moss-covered landscape. Shadows loomed, and imagination could and sometimes did bring them to life. Silence, like an invisible wall, seemed to mute the sounds of the outside world and even hush those from within, leaving its enigmatic beauty as quiet as a tomb. This was not merely something the boy imagined but was knowledge he somehow understood, as though given to him in whispers passing on a breeze. However like the sound, there was no breeze, no stirring of leaves, or swaying of branches—no movement at all. The air, like the shadows, hung over the abundant undergrowth of the once-magnificent amphitheater motionless. Yet shafts of light from the morning sun made their way through the crowd of trees, bringing to his face warmth as soothing as a mother's touch, as comforting as her voice, laying any fears or reservations he might have to rest. His eyes followed the gentle slope of the land to the old stage still some distance away. The towering rock wall with its ledges and outcrops, breathtaking even to a young boy, seemed to beckon its guest to examine it closely and stand in awe at its magnificence. Before realizing, Michael found himself leading the others around fallen branches and giant ferns that littered the ruins of the once-beautiful tiered sections of seats dotting the grounds of the amphitheater.

Gazing on the wall seemed to make the world around him fade away, but Amy's voice quickly brought it back.

"Beautiful, isn't it?" she said, now standing a short distance away from the three of them. "And to think, for fifty years the forest closed in around it, no one remembering it ever existed. If my great-grandma hadn't found those bricks, who knows if it would have ever been found."

"You know she didn't find it," Lincoln's deep baritone voice boomed from the bottom of the ramp, startling the group, turning their focus quickly in his direction.

"Mr. Trudy," Beth squealed with a gasp of giggles. "You scared me."

"You scared me too!" Bailey echoed, though not sharing Beth's amusement.

The big man apologized, making his way around the fallen trees and through the once-beautiful venue. Beth greeted him with a hug, as did Amy, who asked, "Where's Trudy? I heard you two went for a walk this morning."

The big man pointed to the final switchback of the ramp. There Trudy stopped and waved to everyone before drinking from her water bottle and continuing down. This excited Beth, but she knew it would take Trudy a few minutes to get down to them, so she join Michael sitting on a freshly fallen tree.

With a curious gleam and a glint of attitude, her voice tempered with the heat of challenge, Amy asked, "What's this nonsense? Grandma didn't find the walkway?"

Lincoln smiled, cocking his head. "It's true. She told me herself one of her Gifts led her to the bricks. Although she did admit she never saw the Gift there. She was just drawn by"—he paused as if thinking, and then, scratching the side of his head, concluded in an unobtrusive voice—"'an invisible presence that warmed her spirit.' Her words, not mine." He grinned.

A smile spread slowly across the young lady's face. She stepped closer, and her arm found its way around his thick waist. "You do know that was Grandma's way of describing angels, not gifts. Nevertheless, the discovery was hers."

Draping a big arm over her shoulder, Lincoln grunted. "I suppose!"

❧

After Trudy's arrival and after a minute or two of warm greetings, they all walked to the stage, where Trudy pondered, not for the first time, if it had ever been used, or had the resort closed before it was ready? Was that why no one remembered it? It didn't appear in any of the lodge records, and the county survey maps showed it as undeveloped land.

Her thoughts were interrupted as Amy began to speak again, pointing out to Michael that the sculpted animal faces on the wall were much like the ones on the stones of the great fireplace in the Trudeaus' ballroom. She also pointed out the hidden cave to the far side of the stage, big enough to park two semitrucks inside, yet almost impossible to detect from the seating area.

Bailey and Beth made their way to the table where Chris had staged his daughter's picnics last August, the young girl saying next time she wanted to set a place for her guardian angel to join her.

"We'll bring chicken legs and root beer popsicles. Angels like root beer popsicles, you know."

Still on the stage, Michael continued admiring the wall. Placing her hands on the boy's shoulder, Amy slowly turned him around, kneeling, using her forest voice, and cautiously pointing a finger, she said, "Watch the base of that tree. There he goes, see…nope, he stopped to get a look at you. See him?"

The boy wrinkled his nose. "That's a weird-looking squirrel."

Nodding in agreement, Amy continued to speak softly. "Yes, that would be a weird-looking squirrel, if it were a squirrel at all, but it's a long-tailed weasel. Cute little guy, but vicious. Ruin your day quick. Best to…" But before Amy could finish, the weasel was gone.

"Stay out of his way?" Michael asked.

"Yep. Stay out of his way."

Moments later Amy was leading them through a maze of downed trees and thick undergrowth through the remains of a stone archway.

"At the base of those boulders," she began, "is a stream my Girl Scout troop called Fairy Brook. If you look close, you'll see it follows along the hillside and disappears into the bushes at the bottom of the slope. There are four little caves we used to believe led to the fairy world, but we'll save that hike and story for next time.

"Oh," she cried, pausing to point to a small stand of trees just to the side of the boulders. "Look, there's a fairy door…and another. There's a bunch of 'em. See 'em?"

The group made their way over to examine the find, counting seven doors, a bridge, and what appeared to be a tiny church steeple atop a hollowed-out branch lodged between two large roots running over the damp soil. Inside the hollow were five rows of pews and a silver thimble embossed with a smiley face for a podium. Exploring only a few minutes, Beth tugged at Amy's jeans with a request.

"Will you tell us a story? A forest story? Please…"

The woman smiled and sat on a large flat stone. The young girl sat on a smaller stone a few feet in front of her. Amy had great stories and shared them with Beth the same way Miss Trudy sometimes did. They were easy to follow and understand, and most took place right here in the forest. Michael joined Beth, and Bailey leaned against the rough bark of a thick evergreen, Lincoln and Trudy next to her. With everyone comfortable, Amy began to speak in her storyteller voice.

"One evening many summers ago, I was walking on that trail right up there, when suddenly I heard the sound of music; like fiddles and flutes and things like that. So I started down the ramp to see where it was coming from, and as I drew near to the bottom, all across the forest floor, dozens of little tiny lights began to glow from the bases of the trees and rocks and along the edge of this stream. They were so beautiful, and the way they twinkled, I knew they had to be the lights of a fairy city. Carefully I made my way to the bottom of the ramp, where I stood perfectly still, not wanting to scare the fairies. For some time I didn't move and kept ever so quiet, hardly even taking a breath. But I was a young girl and filled with curiosity. I'd heard stories of the fairy dance and wanted more than anything to see it. So I tiptoed farther down the ramp, careful not to make a sound. But when I stepped off the final brick and onto the ground, the lights instantly went dark, the music stopped, and from a distant tree branch, I heard an owl ask who I was. I told him my name, yet he asked again. So again I said, 'My name's Amy.' But he still must not have heard me, because he asked for a third time. 'Who? Who?' he demanded to know. "

Michael laughed. "He wasn't asking your name. That's what owls say. They say, who…who…" the boy mimicked and again burst into laughter.

Though Beth didn't totally understand, she laughed also and then asked, "What happed next? Did he ask again?"

With complete understanding and compassion for the girl, Amy continued.

"No. He flew home to get new batteries for his hearing aids, I think. But his home was a long, long ways away, so he decided to stay and play with his little baby owls, right up until bedtime."

Beth smiled warmly, her imagination working to see every detail of the scene. But even so, her smile faded along with the images of her imagination. "Did the fairies dance some more? Did you ever see them dance?"

Amy stood. "No, and I'm too old to see them now. But every once in a while, I still hear their music in the early hours of a summer's eve."

The little girl's eyes grew wide, questions filling her imagination once again, causing her own excitement to steel her voice. Leaping to her feet, her small hands resting at her side balled into tight fists, she began to quiver with anticipation. This frightened Michael, but seeing the expressions of hidden laughter on everyone's faces assured him the young girl was okay. He watched as her excitement dissipated almost as quickly as it had come on, but when her voice returned, her words were jumbled like before. Looking to Michael she took a breath, and stepping closer, she whispered to the boy, "It's okay. It happens to everyone sometimes, huh?"

Michael nodded.

The girl turned to face Amy. "Can we come down and listen sometime?

We'd like to hear the music. And we're not old; maybe we can see the fairies. And if not, maybe the angels will be here. They play music, too, I think."

"Angels! I believe this is where we came in!" Lincoln said, taking Trudy's hand to leave.

But from the top of the boulder behind them, a low growl could be heard, bringing to them all a chill as primal as the growl itself. A shiver passed through each one, standing their senses on edge, snapping their vision to the top of the boulder, where glaring back was a massive cougar. His growl increased in volume and pitch; his snout curled to display long, terrifying teeth. As the big cat shifted its weight, he growled again, more ferocious than before, causing them to cower, believing the beast was about to attack.

"Stay behind me!" Lincoln said instinctively, pushing the children toward Trudy and Bailey. "All of ya, stay behind me."

His gaze never left the animal. "Get out...get out of here," he yelled powerfully, raising his body, extending his arms out to his sides and above his head in an attempt to make himself look much larger than he was.

But the cat, undeterred, simply answered with a high-pitched cry, snarling viciously at the man. Again Lincoln bellowed demands in deep, rasping tones the animal understood clearly. But it, too, understood the frightened cries of the children. Its mouth widened in a heart-numbing hiss. Lincoln pushed back at the fear coursing through his body and mind, continuing his verbal assault. "Go...get back."

The animal moved gracefully, as if to emphasize the strength and power of its long, muscular form. Again it growled, baring its teeth. However, this time, it shifted its stare to the children huddled within the shelter of the women. Sharply spinning back to the man, rage filled the beast's face. Anger laid its ears flat and dilated its yellowish-green eyes in a penetrating stare. And still again, another violent cry pierced the forest and the hearts of the group.

Envisioning the outcome of their battle, the man stood fast, distancing himself from the icy voice of panic. There was not a person here the man would not willfully give his life to defend, but he knew that would not be enough to save even one. Listening for those behind him, he heard no sound at all. And the cat, as if to purposely fill the man's ears with distraction, gave a low, soft, drawn-out growl, which then burst forth in a provoking predatory scream.

"God, save us," he heard himself plead breathlessly, after which he, too, displayed his extended frame, shouting words somehow even more thunderous than before. But this only proved to further enrage the ferocious beast.

Lunging toward the edge of the rock, the great cat, demonstrating his fearless aggression, presented its own threat in a high-pitched cry shadowed by another loud hiss. It knew that it would be through the man it would acquire the young prey. The man would be an easy kill, almost no effort at all. And the females, like the elk at the water hole, would be mere sport, leaving the small ones for the taking.

As it prepared to attack, its yellowish eyes glistened, muscles tensed, claws extended, announcing its murderous desires sharply in one last lurid cry. Its weight shifted suddenly, propelling its great mass forward. With a prayer on his breath, the man refused to retreat, but the animal's gaze suddenly turned. In that moment a shrill, ear-piercing sound cut the heavy damp air, bursting through the dense canopy above to reach far beyond the expanse of the amphitheater. Without taking his eyes from the animal, Lincoln knew, behind him stood Trudy with a silver whistle removed from a pocket, clenched between her teeth.

As clear as if she had been standing on the bridge, the sound blared across the compound to reach Ann's porch. She looked at Chris, who wasted no time leaping the railing and running at full speed in the direction of the trail. But it was Jass that sped over the bridge first and disappeared down the trail even before Chris reached the bridge.

With the noise of the whistle still in his ears, the big cat dropped unexpectedly, to lie flat on the stone, his gaze coming to rest not on the woman but on the magnificent rock wall above the stage. The air seemed to gently vibrate as a single ray of light reflected off its surface, casting a golden glow about the animal's face, slowly spreading to engulf the entire boulder where the cat now rested peacefully. Its focus remained on the wall even as Lincoln hurriedly yet cautiously ushered everyone through the clutter of downed trees, back toward the brick walkway. The cat stood and began to pace.

Chris, though in good shape, felt the pain brought on by a long sprint, but it couldn't slow him down. Jass, feeling lost on the trail, paused to listen for his people, and in an instant was scampering down the walkway.

A second sound thundered past the dog, echoing through the forest, stopping him momentarily. Distantly he could hear Chris getting closer and the voices of Lincoln and the children somewhere below. Barking twice, louder than he ever had before, signaled he was on his way. And again he swiftly started down the walkway.

Upon reaching the bricks, Chris was now close to panic, but he continued down without breaking his stride. Adrenaline surged through his body, leaving every part of him to tremble uncontrollably, weakening his effort. He could see the group gathered at the bottom of the walk, most crying, Lincoln staring back toward the boulders. Jass was poised between them and the overgrown terrain they had just passed through, ready to attack and defend against any predator making a challenge.

They greeted Chris with hugs, sighs, squeals, and tears. Lincoln pointed to the base of the boulder, where the cougar lay motionless in a pool of blood. He then pointed to the top of the rock wall. Standing with a high-powered rifle was Nels' son, Jack. Above, riding on a current of air, was the eagle. Catching only a glimpse of the scene below through the dense canopy of trees, he thought, you are a brave dog after all.

Minutes later, out of breath, Ann and Rachel arrived, Ann carrying her pink camo Springfield .30-06. Jim was another minute behind, dripping wet, wearing a shower cap, robe, and slippers, toting a rifle of his own.

❧

At the Gathering Place, as could be expected, calls were made, stories shared, and nerves calmed. Chris, with Rachel's help, prepared refreshments while Lincoln, suddenly overcome with the reality of the event, adjourned to his office to down two double shots of his treasured Macallan twenty-five-year-old scotch. Trudy, Amy, and Ann were still trying to calm one another with humor and love. Bailey and the kids sat by the hearth, talking in soft whispers and were soon to be joined by Rachel and Chris.

Remarkably, neither Beth nor Michael had shown even the slightest sign of being traumatized. On the contrary, both simply wanted to sit by the fire with a mug of Trudy's hot chocolate and get warm. Their conversation was quiet, interrupted only by an occasional giggle and once when Beth initiated a group hug. But the conversation was much different from that of the adults gathered at the table. There was no mention of being frightened or attacked by the animal. No, they spoke in agreement, with composure and poise well beyond their years.

"I think you guys might want to hear this," Bailey said as Chris and Rachel sat down. "Go ahead. Tell your dad what you told me."

Beth looked to Michael, silently inviting him to take the lead. The boy smiled his acceptance but held his thoughts, hoping to find the perfect way to convey them without sounding foolish. Seconds later, concluding it didn't truly matter what anyone believed or not, he and Beth both knew and agreed on what they had seen.

"There was an angel on the side of the wall," he said sincerely, remaining calm. For the next few seconds he studied the looks on the faces of his mom and Chris. Showing her support, the little girl gently leaned against his side, nodding her head in agreement. Michael continued to recount what he and Beth had seen while the girl, remaining as tranquil and subdued as the boy, interjected only to support his statements.

"There was a light!" Bailey said matter-of-factly. "It focused on the cougar. That was when he laid down."

Entering the room, Lincoln held up a single sheet of paper. "It looked just like this."

Beth instantly recognized the color page she had given Mr. Trudy just days ago to hang on the refrigerator.

"My guarding angel," the little girl squealed, bringing an end to the peacefulness in the room. "It's him. Look…it's him; he guarded us. Remember, Daddy? Remember my verse, Mr. Trudy? 'The angel of the Lord camps around those who love him.' Remember? Uh huh!" Her eyes widened with self-gratification, and she paused only a fraction of a second before going on.

"And all of us love angels, and Jesus, and God, so my angel guarded us, didn't he? Mr. Trudy protected us like Miss Trudy's bear, and the angel guarded us like my verse said. Just look at my color page."

As she stopped to catch her breath and size up the reaction of her audience, the room fell almost silent, except for the distant chime from the mantel clock in Lincoln's office. With a sudden gasp, as though she had found Waldo, Beth began again.

"Maybe that place is the angels' campground. That's why they picnic there! I bet that's it. That's why they picnic there. Yep!"

Uncertain as to what to make of his daughter's claim, Chris simply nodded while thinking of an appropriate response.

Michael, examining the page, looked to his mother. "It was him. Look!" The boy's voice remained as calm as before, but it was his timbre that conveyed the child's adamancy. "He's standing on a wall in that same yellow light…see…and the light shines on those lions' faces, keeping them still. It was him, Mom, honest. Look, it was Michael, the angel the old man at the bookstore told me about. It was him!"

She didn't need to examine the page. Her facial expression, not one of disbelief or ridicule, was that of an empathetic mother loving her son's naïveté while admiring his belief.

However, before she could display any reaction, Lincoln somberly spoke up. "I saw it too."

His stare moved from Rachel to the boy to Chris. "I didn't see the figure of a man or an angel, but I did see a light. Gold in color, warm, somehow comforting, coming from the wall. The cat saw it too. It lay there like a little kitten, mesmerized, unable to take his eyes off it."

"I saw the light," Bailey said. "It was like a glow, but I didn't look to see where it was coming from. I was too focused on you and getting out of there. But I was so afraid I didn't even remember where the walkway was."

The women made their way in from the Gathering Place, led by Amy. "We were just discussing that. I thought the glow was a reflection from the sun, but the direction's all wrong. And what with all the trees…"

Taking a seat between Michael and Beth, Trudy asked, "Did I hear someone say they saw an angel?"

Both kids looked to their parent for guidance, but Trudy didn't wait for answers. As if telling the kids a story, she began.

"I used to walk with a woman that saw many things in our forest, some that spoke to her and others that she spoke to, and some that would walk beside her in silence. There were mornings we went to the old ruins of the amphitheater, and on many occasion she would see the place filled with a warm glow that I was unable to see, and speak to her Gifts—or maybe angels; I don't know. But I never doubted her or the truth of what she claimed to see. To her the ruins were a special place she enjoyed visiting again and again, and I believe she would be the first to agree with you. There was an angel looking over us, giving a big brave man the strength and love to lead us to safety under the protection of his umbrella."

Her eyes moved to her husband, who looked to Chris, saying, "Will you lead us in a little prayer, Preacher?"

※

Twenty minutes later Krista arrived alone, explaining that Jack had called his dad to come examine the cougar, thinking it might be the one killing pets and livestock throughout the peninsula. She notified her parents, who arrived shortly after Nels pulled into the compound. A few minutes later, Jack's suspicions were confirmed. At approximately two hundred pounds and just under eight feet long, this unusually large and aggressive cougar was almost certainly the one that had killed two heifers down in Matlock last week and the elk at Jupiter Falls, just days ago.

※

It was just after ten when Ted pulled in, the Beach Boys' "Kokomo" blaring from the cab of his truck. He recognized Nels' Ford Lariat but wondered why there was a Washington Fish and Game truck parked in his usual spot. "What's Bailey done now?" he said under his breath.

In a flash the woman in question was there to greet him with hugs even before he could step from the truck. Even more exuberant than usual, Bailey rattled off, "Check out the cougar Jack shot. It almost ate us. Lincoln got us under the angel's umbrella and led us the hell out of there. I've never been so afraid in all my life."

For a moment the ramblings of his high-spirited wife brought a smile to the young pastor, as he doubted what he believed had to be an over-the-top exaggeration of facts. Continuing to listen, he scanned the compound for logical explanations to Bailey's wild claims, but what he found only broadened his smile into a weak chuckle. A hunter, a butcher, and a game warden—it sounded like the opening line of one of Lincoln's jokes, yet here they stood waving him over. And then from the far side of the compound, Chris emerged hand in hand with an incredibly attractive redhead.

"Ted, I'd like you to meet Rachel. I believe she is going to be our new music director."

Bailey snickered. "She'll be a lot more than that!"

"I don't know about music director, but I've been looking forward to meeting you," Rachel said, extending her hand. "Anyone that can put up with this one has to be a pretty good guy."

"She's easy. It's all the voices in her head that keep me awake at night."

"I meant putting up with Chris!" she said with a wink.

Almost instantly he understood Bailey's fascination with her childhood friend, their closeness apparent in so many ways. The other thing apparent was the noticeable change in Chris. Clearly there was a connection between him and Rachel that exhibited their feelings, their adoration for each other, or as Bailey put it, "something very special between them." He seemed refreshed, ready to embrace life again. Yes, clearly, Rachel was an answer to prayer.

❀

Amy might not have shown the enthusiasm Bailey had when her husband arrived, but she was just as excited. Spending twenty minutes on the phone telling Wes about the cougar incident made further explanation almost unnecessary, although he wanted to hear everyone's story and thank Lincoln and Jack for saving the lives of his wife and unborn child. He would give Trudy special attention and declare her Brennan's Cove's Official Whistleblower.

Wes had not bothered to change out of his uniform at the airport, leaving Michael extremely thrilled to shake the hand of a real pilot. The boy had a million questions but only made it to number four before his mother sent him outside to play with Krista and Beth—just not very far from the house. When Amy introduced Rachel, Wes paused for a moment, obviously confused, and then he gasped excitedly. "Wait—you're the singer. The portrait in Linc's office. I know you; at least I've heard people talk about you. Some of it was even good, if I remember right."

"I've heard those same folks speak about you," Rachel, shot back with a rueful grin "They love you. Said you're the greatest per...oh, wait. That wasn't you at all. Sorry, my mistake."

Wes was pleasantly caught off guard by the woman's humor, but more so by the genuine warmth she offered. There was an instant connection between the two, bringing them to laugh and tease more like old friends than new acquaintances, each leaving an arm around the other long after their hug had ended. Rachel could not have known how much her seemingly insignificant banter meant to Wes and Amy, a sign, perhaps, of a budding friendship between the four of them.

"Congratulations," Chris said, giving Wes a hug slightly stronger than usual. "Didn't I tell ya, a little practice, a little prayer, and now, look—a little Chris is on the way. Glad I could be of assistance."

"Well, Uncle Chris"—Wes smiled, stepping back—"I'm sure little Wes will grow to appreciate your contribution. And if I may say so—"

"You may certainly not!" Amy said, gently pushing her husband aside.

"You don't even know what I was going to say," he protested.

"We've all heard enough from you two. Besides it's time eat. Trudy put stuff out for sandwiches."

Throughout the meal and for some time afterward, the photo albums Bailey had asked Ted to bring made their way around the table, prompting stories and laughter. As always, they were mostly led by Lincoln and Chris. Bailey set on one side of her brother, Rachel on the other, and each had a piece of their story to tell. Rachel's reaction to every page was taken in lovingly by Chris, who knew that other than yearly school pictures and a few snapshots he had given her, she had no photo record of her youth whatsoever. Cameras were one more thing her father disapproved of, though no one knew why.

After looking through three of the albums, Chris whispered something in Rachel's ear, not sure what her reaction would be. Glowing with excitement, her eyes still held some reservation.

"It's okay," he whispered softly in her ear, accompanied by a kiss only she could hear. She smiled timidly, and again he breathed words meant for just her. However, this time they were followed by a kiss to her cheek witnessed by all. Standing, he took her by the hand and guided her from the chair. "We'll be back in two minutes."

Tipping his head, glaring over the dark frames of his reading glasses, Lincoln pretended to give caution. "Two minutes, preacher. I'm watchin' you. Two minutes."

Up in his office, Chris sat Rachel at his desk for a second time in as many days. From his pocket he produced a crowded key ring, a bright-red key instantly catching Rachel's eye. He used it to unlock the drawer at the bottom of an oak gun cabinet and removed an ivory-colored memory book. Embossed over the hard cover in the same pale lettering was the word "Forever." The book's landscape platform gave elegance to the silk-finish pages inside, each bringing a glimpse into an extraordinary night of love.

Rachel turned to the first page, revealing a collage of various snapshots of her and Chris throughout their teens. An introduction across the top of the page, looking as though Bailey had scrawled it in her own dramatic hand, read, "It was their world; their time, their story...the dawn of their love and the beginning of their forever."

"Bailey put this together after you left. I think she was hoping it would make me go after you." He kissed the top of her head, and then she heard him add, "And it almost worked."

Rachel looked up, and he kissed her forehead, making her smile.

"It's been a long time since we looked at these pictures together, remember?"

"I do. You and me sitting in the parking lot outside Walgreens. Seems like there were a hundred pictures."

"Bailey used almost every roll I had in my camera bag that night. A hundred and eight frames."

"I knew there were a lot. She didn't put them all in here, did she?"

"No, she was pretty selective. I think she only used maybe fifty, sixty. Okay, seventy-five at tops. Take a look."

"You told everyone we'd be right back. I don't want Linc to—"

"This will only take a few minutes."

The second page was an out-of-focus view of the lighted tree and gazebo in the Petersons' backyard. Below, written in the same dramatic hand, were the words "Some Enchanted Evening." This brought the first shimmer of tears to Rachel's eyes.

The two spent the next fifteen minutes quickly scanning through the book, promising to sometime soon spend a leisurely afternoon enjoying the memories page by page, laugh by laugh, kiss by overdue kiss.

Smiling with concern, Chris asked, "Are you sure you're okay letting everyone see it?"

Taking a moment, she finally answered, "I have concerns about the kids seeing it."

"They're playing with Krista and Jack. I don't think we could pull them away if we bribed them with chocolate cake."

Rachel stood and put her arms around his neck, allowing him to gaze deep into her eyes and see the truth in her heart. "I love you, Chris Peterson. I'm not ashamed to let the world know I've always loved you, and—"

"Rache." He stopped her, allowing her to gaze beyond his eyes to the desires that filled his heart. Unable to speak, his words lost in his thoughts, Chris passionately took her in his arms and placed his lips gently to hers. When they spoke, the words rode on toneless breaths as soft as their kisses. Breathing in each other's words filled their senses with feelings they had always known lay waiting deep in their hearts. It wasn't long until the words drifted about them in purrs easily heard by the small figurine on a nearby shelf. But like most loyal figurines, he would keep them to himself.

When they returned to the Gathering Place, there was a time of simple confession as to their past relationship. Bailey became excited when Chris asked her to guide them through the book she had so lovingly made. Rachel added, "It never would have happened if not for you."

With a little pride and a lot of love, the young woman opened the album for the first time since giving it to her brother all those years ago. On occasion her eyes flooded from joyful memories as page after page captured the beautiful makeshift wedding staged by her and Doug.

The affair, far from elegant, still managed some romantic magic. An apple crate podium dressed in lace held two silver wedding rings beautifully fashioned by Chris in metal shop. Behind them lay a new family Bible Bailey had purchased with money saved for a special occasion. Mason jars sheltering tea light candles glistened, suspended by thick white ribbons from the branches of the old poplar tree. Guests were limited to Piddles, the new kitten Bailey had rescued from the shelter, and Blue, her four-year-old Siberian husky, named for his magnificent icy-blue eyes.

Most of the photos were typical wedding poses—bride coming down the aisle, exchanging vows, kiss the bride; the wedding party, the guests, portraits, candid moments, laughter, cutting of the cake, a toast with champagne, and a heart-shaped pizza courtesy of Doug and Armando's.

"You two had a beautiful wedding, if I do say so myself." Bailey giggled girlishly.

Chris smiled at his sister and then turned his attention to Rachel. "I still have that ring. It's a little snug nowadays, but I still have it stashed in..." His face flushed. "I mean, I keep it in my backpack. That way—"

"That way"—Bailey giggled—"no one could ever stumble across it. Like the Bible you had me stash—oh, I mean keep at my place for 'safekeeping.'" She mocked with air quotes and an exaggerated wink.

For the next half hour, there was much discussion around the old Gathering Place, mostly about the photos and almost all bringing about some much-needed, good-natured teasing and laughter. Trudy did, however, reprimand Lincoln for inquiring about the honeymoon and if the marriage had been consummated.

But to everyone's astonishment, Rachel immediately spoke up. "Well, Linc, he wasn't a preacher at the time. And look at this picture of him, ladies. Put yourself in my shoes."

Like everyone else, for a moment Lincoln sat stunned. And then, with a glib smile, he acknowledged her cunning aversion.

"Clever girl." He chuckled. "That's one way of not giving a definitive answer."

Trudy's smile playfully bore all the signs of an adolescent girl lost deep in a rapturous glow of desire. And while persistent in her blissful character, the woman swooned. "Oh, my darling husband, she answered the question! She answered it perfectly."

Laughter echoed throughout the room. And it was then that Bailey remembered another book she had made but decided at the time to never share with anyone. It now lay at the bottom of the box. A small book, with only fourteen photos no one would ever give a second thought. That is, with the exception of two people sitting right there at the table. Oh yes, they would have thoughts, memories like the book itself, never to be shared with anyone, and she was sure that was how they would want to keep it. But of course, that was about to change.

For now there were still odds and ends the ladies needed to complete before Ann's dinner that evening, and the men had chores to finish, errands to run, outdoor lights to check, and a fire pit to ready. Trudy nominated Rachel to help Chris make his six-layer Frito pie, giving Bailey an opportunity to join them while Wes helped outside.

Chris carried the box of albums to his house and set it on the kitchen table, planning to look through them again, just he and Rachel. Bailey had other plans. She retrieved the book and strutted slowly across the room to stand on the other side of the kitchen counter from the couple. Smiling smugly, she said with an air of impudence, "You know how you two always said I couldn't keep a secret? Well, I've been sitting on this one for ten years, and I haven't thought of telling a soul, not even Wes. Especially not Wes! "

Allowing her smile to fade, she shrugged, focusing her eyes on her brother.

"At first I couldn't understand why you had pictures of a campsite mixed in with the wedding photos. But then I noticed this one."

She placed the book on the desk for them to examine. It showed a weathered picnic table sitting in a snow-covered campsite. A large plate of bacon and sausage, scrambled eggs on one side, two over easy on the other. In the background was the Petersons' old family tent, the entry flap partially open, exposing little more than shadows inside.

Bailey, seeing clearly a noticeable change on the faces of the couple as they recognized the scene, began to grin that wonderfully awful grin everyone always dreaded. Oh, how she would love to play this up for a while, to hear any and all fabricated explanations her trapped-like-a-rat brother could muster. But instead, in a voice as warm and sweet as melted honey, she noted, "I could be mistaken, but if you look very close, I believe that's the neck of your guitar lying on that sleeping bag Rache'. And well, considering these came from the same roll of film as the wedding, I can only assume you'll want your next honeymoon to be someplace warm, like Florida?"

Over the next few minutes, there would be much conversation, all culminating in laughter and love. Even though she had already vowed to forever keep their secret, Rachel nevertheless made her pinky swear. And her brother, just like back when they were kids, insisted on a spit swear to seal the deal. This, of course, brought up an entirely new conversation, which also culminated in more laughter and an abundance of love and hugs.

The dinner, like always, was everything everyone expected and then some. Michael and Rachel were genuinely welcomed by all, and Mildred secretly told Trudy she thought Chris was smitten with the pretty little redhead. Trudy acted shocked and gasped her disbelief while concealing a smile. To Beth's delight, her daddy said a most beautiful grace, which left everyone joyful. A picture was taken of the whole group gathered round Dix's king cake; Ann would see the young woman got a copy. Michael found the Baby Jesus in his piece and promised his mom would buy the cake next year. And of course, there was music. Those who could play instruments played, and those who could sing sang. Even Lincoln joined in on a chorus or two. There were stories set to music and toasts throughout the night, and Ann recited a poem about friendship, which brought tears to some and laughter to all.

After goodbyes and good nights were all said and done and the sounds of clouds drifting past the moon faded in the dark, there was a tapping, almost so quiet it went unheard. But it was answered in secret with whispers of love and silent window kisses that would link their hearts and dreams until they held each other once again.

"I love you," they vowed, each placing a hand on the cool glass between them. "I love you."

CHAPTER TWENTY TWO

6:54 a.m. brought beautiful morning twilight to the cloudless sky over Puget Sound. Trudy, dressed in gray sweats, sat on the side of the bed slipping on pink sneakers over thick green socks, anxious to go for a quick walk before the gang came to the Gathering Place for breakfast. But Trudy, along with the rest of Brennan's Cove, was unaware of the tall man tying a small inflatable raft to the end of her dock, his female companion waiting for his signal. And it would come just as Trudy was about to kiss her sleeping husband on the cheek.

The tall man waved, signaling the woman, and both grinned. A large black dial held within her grasp turned smoothly to the right, stopping only once as she examined the setting. Smiling, she bumped it up another few notches—three…four…and one extra for good measure. As she removed her hand, the word *Volume* became clearly visible. There were two switches just above the black dial. She flipped one that read All Speakers. Her hand paused over the second, labeled CD Player. Her smile grew; the man waved his approval.

Taking a deep breath, she paused and exhaled completely before flipping the switch. And then the air erupted with the rhythmic sounds of drums, percussion, and piano, followed by the unmistakable voice of Joe Cocker, "Feelin' Alright?"

Trudy ran to the window and threw open the heavy blackout curtains, exposing a view of the cove and what she already knew awaited. There, in the early-morning shadows, sat the tug. In the wheelhouse, her sister-in-law Kellie waved and pointed to the end of the dock, where Eric stood leaning against the lamppost doing his best James Dean.

"Eric!" Trudy squealed, jumping and waving before letting the curtain fall closed. "It's Eric and Kellie!" she again managed to squeal, running past a still-startled, half-asleep Lincoln.

She spoke his name in strained whispers from the bedroom staircase to the deck at the end of the Great Room. Scurrying down the steps to the dock, her love, her joy, her shock, all overwhelming, pushed her forward into Eric's arms. When he lifted her off the ground, young girl memories brought a rush of tears down her cheeks and just like long ago her brother wiped them away and blew their trails dry. Looking deep into the others eyes triggered a second embrace and then a third. Two short blasts from the tugboat's whistle and laughter from the wheelhouse brought their focus to an overly excited Kellie.

"I want hugs too. Come get me," she yelled.

❀

It wasn't long before the space around the Gathering Place filled with conversation and chaos. Amy and Ann, with the help of Rachel and Bailey, put breakfast on the table while Eric and Kellie shared their retirement plans of returning to San Francisco for a short spell before cruising south. For how long and how far they didn't know exactly, but they'd heard Costa Rica was nice. Trudy was hoping they were kidding but feared they were not. After breakfast, Eric took everyone on a guided tour of the boat. It was big and beautiful, and according to Michael and Beth, all the rooms had funny names like cabins, wheelhouse, galley, and, the one both found most amusing, the head. Soon Eric had everyone back on shore and ready for the day's activities. To the kids' grumblings, baths were first on the list.

Amy and Bailey volunteered to take the kids to the Children's Music Theater in Olympia for the final performance of *Gretchen and the Seven-Foot Santa*.

The guys helped light the compound and prepare the lower parking area. From there, the Shuttle People would provide transportation to and from the event, with the Trudeaus offering rooms to those who had the need to stay.

The catering staff arrived at six, the band at eight, and the guests shortly thereafter. The ballroom had been outlined with tall evergreens, decorated with crystal ornaments, stars, figurines, and twinkling white lights. A stage was set at one side of the room so as not to obstruct the terrace view or the beautiful fireplace. Three long tables held a vast variety of hors d'oeuvres, pastries, and party bags filled with hats and noise makers. Ice sculptures adorned each table, and crystal glasses held drinks of all kinds. As always, the night was unforgettable for all who attended. But for Trudy it was a night she would cherish and recall often over the next few years, bringing a time of change that seemed to engulf her life and the lives of those loved ones around her. Eric and Kellie stayed at the cove for nearly a month before heading to San Francisco and beginning what Eric referred to as "Cruisin' through the Golden Years."

Trudy spoke to him often in phone conversations and listened to his outrageous stories of pirates and treasures designed to make her laugh and worry just a bit. And though she had made herself a promise never to write again, she completed a series of children's books about a ship named *Changes* and its adventurous Captain Eric. But it was that following December a new book was placed on her special shelf, a story Michael insisted needed to be told, *An Angel in the Forest*, a collaboration by Amy Brooks and Belle Trudeau that won the hearts of children and adults over the world. And Trudy was honored to participate in interviews and awards ceremonies with Amy and Lincoln by her side.

※

Peg heard from her sister only twice after arriving on Maui, and both conversations were brief, somewhat cryptic, and left her wondering if Rache was doing all right and why had she agreed to stay with the Brooks over New Year's, in a cabin of all things. And how did Michael meet a new friend if they were out in the woods? Who were these people her sister couldn't wait to introduce her to, and what was this other big surprise she was bursting at the seams to share? Yes, something wasn't right, and Peggy didn't like that big sis was evading her questions. But on the other hand, she was glad to hear some honest joy in Rachel's voice for a change. She even sounded almost back to her normal giddy self.

Just two days after returning to Seattle, she joined Rachel on a trip to Brennan's Cove to pick up Michael, who had begged to stay a few extra days with Beth and Chris. Of course, Rachel told Peg he was with the Brooks and never once mentioned seeing Chris at all. As a matter of fact, she gave up few details as to her and Michael's visit with the Brooks'.

As they pulled into the compound, Ann and Jim rushed to greet them. Chris and Michael ran up from the dock, the handsome pastor quickly giving Peg a big hug and kiss on the cheek, leaving the woman envisioning girlish whims from long ago that for a moment left her feeling giddy and weak kneed. She then watched as he passionately embraced her sister, gently kissing her twice, whispering, "I've missed you, sweetheart."

Seconds later Beth ran from Trudy's front door to leap into Rachel arms, smothering her with giggles and kisses before hugging Michael and being introduced to Aunt Peg. Suddenly Peg understood the reason why Rachel had spent New Year's with the Brooks', and of course, she couldn't blame her.

In a soft voice only her sister could hear, Peggy breathed, "Great surprise, Rache."

Squeezing her gently, Rachel replied, "Oh, there's more." Her eyes twinkled like diamonds in sunlight, making Peggy somewhat nervous as to what might be coming next.

Trudy, stepping onto the porch, was introduced by Chris, though it was Beth who drew everyone's attention. "Look, Miss Trudy. We have two princesses, just like Anna and Elsa." The little girl then added quietly, "But prettier, don't you think, Miss Trudy?"

Nodding, Trudy ushered everyone inside, her famous homemade pizza almost ready to serve. Lincoln walked up from the cellar.

"I'm Lincoln," he said, reaching to shake the attractive young lady's hand. "But my friends and Rachel here call me Linc."

"I'm Peggy, Rachel's sister, but I prefer to hug my friends, Linc."

The big man happily obliged and then asked, holding up a bottle of wine, "I know Rachel is, but is everyone else fine with a Barbera D'Alba? Oh, wait—the kids need some pop. Rache, you know where it is."

She had Peggy accompany her into Lincoln's office, where Peg was met with confusion seeing her sister's portrait. And then, when Rachel pointed

You Are My Love

out the Iris collection and the awards scattered about the room, Peggy almost wet her herself. Back at the Gathering Place, she was left starstruck, able to speak only in short sentences, while her knee bounced to the accelerated beat of her heart—this, to the absolute pleasure of Lincoln, who was tipped off by a wink and a nod from Rachel.

A short time later, Beth insisted they move to the ballroom, where again Peg found herself lost for words by the sheer scope of the room. As music filled the air, Lincoln with his country-boy charm took Peg's hand and twirled her gracefully while leading her around the floor in an awkward cross between a two-step and bunny hop known to all as the Lincoln Misstep. Amazingly, Peg had no problem following, even adding her own hokey-pokey twirl to the mix. Out of breath and laughing hysterically, both celebrated the fact that neither had any dancing skills whatsoever, which bolstered their friendship all the more.

At times during her visit, she studied her sister and Chris, Michael and Beth, and found herself caught up in the natural contentment of their love and how quickly they all had come to be like family. She felt no need to watch out for her big sister. This man showed his love in every action, every word, and clearly their hearts belonged to each other. She felt it was all meant to be, meant to work out just this way—God's way, she thought with a sigh and a prayer of thanks.

※

Three days later Peg met with Kevin for lunch at St. Joseph Medical Center. Entering the spacious atrium, she spotted an old man she believed was the man from the bookstore. Quickly approaching him, she snapped, "I want to talk to you about that expensive Bible you gave my nephew. That was—"

"A gift for his mother. Yes, of course," he said with a nod. "But first, a gift for you, my dear."

The air began to dance with light, producing a comforting glow from gathering figures appearing at once about the room, some standing, some walking, others sitting with an arm around a visibly distraught person in need of consoling. Though none spoke, Peg heard what she recognized as prayers carried on unfelt currents of air, drifting and swirling, rising through the confines of the building to a throne just beyond the last star to the east.

She watched in amazement. "Gifts!" she breathed almost silently before turning quickly back toward the old man. "But how do you know about…" she said into the air, franticly looking around, for the old man had disappeared.

On a small iron bench in the center of the room, she sat for some time watching her Gifts, hearing their hearts, their prayers, feeling their love. After that day she only saw them every so often and seldom spoke of them to anyone other than Kevin and her sister, and once on a walk with Trudy.

❧

That July Fourth, Wes and Amy welcomed a baby girl to the world. Amy kept the child's name secret from everyone, including Wes, until the following day. With her mother by her side and her baby in her arms, she christened the girl Annie, after her mom. Neither Chris nor Wes seemed too disappointed with the choice as they watched Ann cry and Jim shed a lone tear as he whispered to himself, "Dear Princess Annie. That has a nice ring…"

❧

Tampa had greeted Ted and Bailey with open arms; his laid-back style and scholarly application was the insight the church had been hoping for, and of course Bailey quickly brought her own energy and flair to the worship team. Within months the couple felt this was truly where God had called them. That first year they planted three palm trees in their new backyard. Bailey even managed to buy a couple of used paddleboards from a girlfriend down the street. The following year they acquired a somewhat smaller boat than their last but still enjoyed overnight excursions to the islands up and down the coastline. Bailey believed it was while on a week-long jaunt to the Tortugas that she became pregnant, eventually celebrating the birth of a girl they named Saylor.

❧

That August brought another celebration, one Beth and Michael prayed for every day since making an agreement to do so the day after the New Year's party. At the altar, standing with their parents, both children vowed to be the best brother and sister they could be. And to all who know them, it's a vow they've keep nestled deep in their hearts to this day. Of course, there were some who thought the pastor had moved a little too quickly with the new worship director, no matter how long they had known each other. But they saw the love between the two, and it didn't hurt that Rachel had stepped into Bailey's role with grace and humility, earning her the respect of the entire church.

After returning from their Florida honeymoon, Rachel was surprised to find an old friend had taken up residence in their living room. A gift from Jim—the Wurlitzer from room G would fill the home with music and Rachel's heart with love for many, many years. Soon there was yet another sound that filled the home and hearts of the family, an answer to one more prayer repeated more times than anyone cared to count. Yet when she arrived it was still a surprise, one that left the kids overjoyed. Beth and Michael settled on the name Maddie, and their new puppy seemed happy with the choice. But the pup was not the last addition to the family. On Beth's fifth birthday, Rachel gave birth to Dylan, a little girl with sparkling eyes and glowing red hair, and according to Beth, "She was the best birthday present ever." And Michael agreed.

Epilogue

The trade winds stroked the woman's long dark hair as she sat on the beach watching the tide jostle the water-swollen palms lying in the shallows of Balayan Bay, remnants of last year's typhoon that ravaged the Philippine island of Luzon. A quiet knocking caught her ear; her eyes searched for the source and came to rest between two small palms moving with the flow of the tide. At first the green glass melded into the surf and shadows, hiding its details, but the glistening sunlight fought to expose the rare find. Carefully the woman made her way through the decaying fronds of the tree to inspect her discovery. Again the sunlight danced over the thick glass. Carefully she plucked it from placid motion of the water. As she held it up, its contents remained unclear through its deep green tint. But suddenly her excitement rose.

"Come here. Look what I found," she called to her companion, who was still some distance from shore. The rugged young research diver from Southern California quickly swam to her side. The decision was made to wait until they were back at the bungalow with the moon overhead and a fire on the beach before they'd take a closer look. After all, there was something romantic about receiving a gift from the sea.

When the island breeze faded and the sky filled with stars, the young man built a small fire and held the woman's hand while they listened in silence to the waves serenade the moon. Soon their faces glowed from the embers, and the woman handed him the bottle. With great skill he removed the cork and retrieved the aged piece of scrap paper from inside. The note consisted of only two sentences, powerful enough to be thought provoking and at the same time tender enough to join the couple in a long and loving embrace neither wanted to end. In the lower right corner was written, "Tru, SF Bay" and a date forty-two years earlier, all within the outline of an open umbrella.

The End

Made in the USA
Coppell, TX
10 November 2021